LORDS OF THE AIR

Other books by the same author include:

RICH
RAILROAD
LADY OF FORTUNE
FAMINE
SOLITAIRE
MAIDEN VOYAGE
HEADLINES

LORDS OF THE AIR

Graham Masterton

St. Martin's Press
New York

Library of Congress Cataloging-in-Publication Data

Masterton, Graham.
    Lords of the air / by Graham Masterton.
        p.   cm.
    ISBN 0-312-04572-7
    I. Title.
    PR6063.A834L6   1990
    823'.914—dc20   90-37326
                                                           CIP

First published in Great Britain by Hamish Hamilton Limited

First U.S. Edition: November 1990
10 9 8 7 6 5 4 3 2 1

Contents

Lindau, 1923	1
London, 1930	22
Isle of Wight, 1931	32
London, 1931	49
Cambridge, 1931	58
Chichester, 1931	68
London, 1931	86
Chichester, 1931	101
Lisbon to Florida, 1932	120
Chichester, 1932	137
Florida, 1932	153
London, 1932	169
Chichester, 1932	182
Calshot, 1932	205
Darwin, 1932	222
Miami, 1932	244
Chichester, 1933	270
Barrow Creek, 1932	300
England, 1936	328
Darwin, 1937	356
London, 1939	370
Darwin, 1939	374
Miami, 1941	376

LORDS OF THE AIR

London, 1943	409
Darwin, 1943	419
Chichester, 1946	424
Miami, 1948	442
London, 1948	460
Darwin, 1948	472

LORDS OF THE AIR

Lindau, 1923

Gerhard was unaware of their eyes meeting across the table. Ceremoniously, he lifted one of the frog's legs out of the tureen on the end of his fork, and held it up, steaming. 'You and I, Herbert, we are nothing more than frogs who have taught ourselves to leap further,' he proclaimed, and then laughed.

Herbert held Mathilde's gaze for just one moment longer, and then turned his head smoothly back to Gerhard. 'You are wrong, my dear old friend,' he told him. 'We are frogs who fly.'

'Then obviously, among frogs, we are a superior variety.'

Mathilde peered into the tureen, and frowned. 'I have always wondered what they do with the rest of the poor frogs.'

Herbert said, 'They do just what they would do to us, if we were to lose the part of us that makes us the most desirable. They throw them away.'

Mathilde looked at him with quirky boldness. The steam rising from the open tureen veiled her expression for a moment, almost as if she were a bride, or a ghost, or a memory. 'But what is the part that makes you the most desirable? Surely not your legs. I have heard reports about Englishmen's legs.'

Gerhard chortled, and forked two or three more frog's legs on to his plate. 'Now then, Mathi, none of your bold conversation. Poor Herbert will be embarrassed.' He started to worry the frog's flesh off its toothpick bone. 'Mathi does love to tease, you know, Herbert. She won't be satisfied until she makes you blush.'

'Well, she won't find that difficult,' said Herbert. 'I have that sort of complexion that blushes very easily. At school, my English teacher used to call me Proper Hugh. I thought he was mocking me for being a prig. It was only when I was studying *Paradise Lost* in the sixth form that I understood it. "A smile that glowed celestial rosy red, love's proper hue."'

'You see,' said Gerhard. 'In England, they teach you to be devious from the moment you are born.'

Herbert raised his tall glass of chilled white wine. 'Perhaps we ought to drink a toast,' he suggested.

'*Jaha!*' Gerhard boisterously wiped his mouth with his napkin. 'We should drink to the flying frogs,' he said.

Mathilde shook her head. 'We should drink to our love, the three of us.'

They clinked the rims of their glasses. 'To love, then,' said Gerhard. And Herbert looked across at Mathilde, and said, 'To love.'

'And to the flying frogs,' smiled Mathilde.

The silver band played *Mädchen mit dem Rothen Mündchen*. The tall crop-headed waiters weaved to and fro between the potted palms as swiftly and as intently as men carrying buckets to a fire which they knew could never be quenched. Balanced above their heads they bore gargantuan trays loaded with pork-knuckles and breadcrumbed schnitzels and freshly-grilled fish, as well as sauerkraut and Teltow turnips and potato *Knödel*. And there were trays of beer, too, crowded tankards of Bäck'bier from Bayreuth, and jugs of local wheat beer with raspberry syrup.

The noise in the hotel dining-room was tremendous. Roars of laughter, shouts of delight, banging of cutlery, slapping of thighs and tabletops, and toast after deafening toast. Outside, beyond the glass-enclosed verandah, the pleasure-boats circled around the lake, glittering with lights, their smoke hanging like the veils of war-widows in a sky the colour of dying roses.

Herbert neatly cut up his roasted goose-breast. 'You would think, you know, that this was the happiest country on earth,' he remarked.

'It is holiday time,' Gerhard enthused. 'Not even a Depression can deter a German from enjoying his holiday.'

'Will we fly tomorrow?' asked Herbert.

'Oh, yes, I think so. Six o'clock, if the mist clears early.'

Herbert couldn't help smiling. 'Otto said that you were getting well over four hundred and sixty horsepower.'

Gerhard tried to look modest. 'I'm pleased with it, yes. But we still have some way to go. We haven't solved the problem of overheating.'

Herbert laughed. 'He's a genius!' he told Mathilde. 'The man's a genius and he won't admit it!'

Mathilde shrugged slightly, and looked away. 'Sometimes I wish that he would.'

There was a small, uncomfortable moment. Not seriously uncomfortable. After all, Mathilde hadn't actually said anything unpleasant. But she had left Herbert in little doubt that she didn't consider her marriage to be as romantic and bright as it ought to be. She suddenly smiled, however, and said to Gerhard, 'You haven't eaten your *zwiebelkuchen*, darling.'

Herbert watched them both a little warily as he continued to eat. The band played *Glückliche Fahrt*, with an ear-shattering excess of cymbal-clashing and strident cornet-choruses. Mathilde cut small pieces off her veal schnitzel and then cut them even smaller. Gerhard began to chew his way through his onion-cake and tell a story at the same time about the Germany flyer Wolfram Eisenlohr, with onion and potato and story all becoming inextricably mixed up.

Gerhard and Mathilde should have been brother and sister, instead of man and wife. At least Herbert always thought so. It was not that they looked particularly alike. Gerhard was blonde, thin-faced, with a long Aryan head and a prominent nose that seemed to have been chiselled out in several stages. His eyes were pale and his smile was small and his hands were long and intelligent and slender. He had always been magnetically attractive to women who liked sensitive men. Although he was now in his thirties he had a student's innocence about him which was emphasized by the little sprig of hair which stuck up from the crown of his head and the old-fashioned style of his evening clothes. Not that he *was* innocent. He had been brought up the son of a Tübingen landowner who had given him fortified Kulmbach beer at the age of two and taken him to a brothel at the age of twelve. When he was an engineering student, he had lived in Münich with a red-headed stage actress nearly twice his age and he had once fought a real duel with real sabres (but no blood). But he was always prepared to believe the best of everybody he met. He was always prepared to forgive. He was completely lacking in what the English called 'side'.

Mathilde was far more complicated, or liked to think that she was. She was dark-haired, with a simple fashionable bob, although

3

when Herbert had first met her in 1921 she had still been wearing Wagnerian braids. She was stunningly pretty. Every man who met her was infatuated with her at once, and wrote poems about her, some of them very bad indeed. She had dark, wide-set eyes whose lids had just the slightest of seductive droops. Her nose was short and classic. Her lips looked as if they had just finished a long and utterly abandoned kiss. Moist, and reddened, and somehow *crushed*. She was a small girl, only five-feet-three, but her breasts were full and her stomach was flat, and even in the pink-and-silver Madeleine Vionnet dancing dress which she wore this evening, with its straight bodice and its low waist, she looked voluptuous enough to have most of the gentlemen diners readjusting their chairs and focusing their monocles so that they could see her better.

Mathilde was the sole issue of the very late and very unlamented three-year marriage between the eccentric and temperamental Klaus Spritz, the German automobile millionaire, inventor of the rear-engined Spritzwagen, and the doubly eccentric and temperamental Hungarian opera-singer Ireni Csorba (now Mrs Perry T. Huntington III). Mathilde had met Gerhard at a trade fair in Berlin in 1920, which she had attended in order to please her father. Bored with engineering exhibits, bored with champagne, she had wandered around the stands until she had found Gerhard lying on a sofa behind his new water-cooled aero-engine, fast asleep, with his mouth wide open. She had kissed him, out of fun, out of perversity, and shouted in his ear, '*Deutschland erwache!* Germany, awake!'

Five months later, in the teeth of her father's furious opposition, Gerhard and Mathilde had married. Seven-and-a-half months later, Mathilde had slept with the wavy-haired racing driver Theodor Goetze. Only twice, but twice had been twice too much. If Gerhard had found out about it he had certainly never mentioned it. Yet their marriage had changed. It had been frivolous and empty from the start, a way of cocking a snook at Mathilde's father. Now it was simply empty. But Mathilde refused absolutely to consider divorce. She adored Gerhard. How could anybody fail to adore Gerhard? Besides, if she sought a divorce, she would be admitting defeat. Worse than that – *very* much worse than that, she would be admitting that she was no cleverer than her father.

Now she and Gerhard lived a life of great politeness; of mutually shared (or at least mutually suffered) interests; of extremely occasional acts of intercourse; of jazz records and weekend parties; and (of course) flying, with everything that flying entailed, which was

4

mostly long tedious days of tinkering with misbehaving engines and waiting for the weather to get better.

'We should go for a walk, after dinner,' said Mathilde. 'It's too warm for sleeping.'

Herbert put down his knife and fork. 'I'm sure I didn't mention sleeping.'

'Did you stay very long in Berlin?' Mathilde asked him.

'Two nights only.'

Mathilde smiled and shook her head. 'I love Berlin.'

Gerhard finished his meal and sat back. 'On the other hand,' he said, 'I dislike Berlin very much.'

Mathilde laughed. 'He didn't like the Resi. He thought the girls didn't wear enough clothes. And they were only the customers!'

Gerhard waved his hand dismissively. 'That's what you don't understand. That's the problem with the whole world. The men strive, and the girls don't wear enough clothes.'

'Such a philosopher!' Mathilde teased him. 'Do you know, when we were married, he thought that a vagina was a kind of musical instrument?'

'Mathi!' snapped Gerhard.

Mathilde was about to say something sharp in reply, but Herbert made a tiny suppressive gesture with his hand. Enough is enough, don't spoil it. Besides, Gerhard has drunk quite enough wine to sleep like a darling baby brother. Let's drink some coffee, and walk by the lake. Even the most impulsive of lovers can wait until daybreak.

It was nearly midnight but it was bright and boisterous enough to have been mid-afternoon. There were lights strung in the lime-trees all the way along the promenade, and the open-air cafés were still noisy with singing and laughter. At the entrance to Lindau harbour, a stone lion and a lighthouse kept watch over the dipping darkness of the Bodensee, waiting for the return of the steamers which circled the lake with lights and beer and dancing couples. *Dürfen Sie nicht Charleston tanzen?*

They linked arms, the three of them, Mathilde in the middle, and walked by the water's edge. The water gurgled and slapped against the stone embankment, shattering the lights into sparkling atoms. Gerhard was being philosophical again. 'I'm not a prude, you know, Herbert. It's good to see that we have learned to enjoy ourselves once more. There is nothing wrong in a little abandon. But, there is more to life than dancing and drinking and sitting half-naked in the Residenz-Kasino.'

Herbert was smoking a cigar. He blew the smoke out of the side of his mouth, away from Mathilde, and it ran out into the darkness like a small frightened ghost.

'My pater was in London on Armistice Day,' he remarked. 'He was walking down St Martin's Lane and he came across a man and a woman, copulating in a doorway, right out in the open, where everybody could see. They both looked at him, and all he could do was raise his hat.'

Mathilde laughed. 'Herbert, there is no point to that story whatsoever!'

'Well, perhaps not,' Herbert agreed, 'but if you had ever met my father, you would know how funny it was. He was a sidesman at Chichester Cathedral, and yet he took off his hat to a woman with her knickers around her ankles. I don't think he's ever been able to live it down.'

But Gerhard insisted, 'There *is* a point in what you say, whether you recognize it or not. Your father recognized that as soon as the human urge for killing has been satisfied, we are gripped by the urge to copulate. Killing and copulation, those two urges form the sum total of our pathetic lives! Create, and destroy! Everything else is secondary. Who can say whether it is more exciting to fornicate, than to commit murder?'

Herbert threw back his head and laughed up at the night sky. The stars jiggled in front of his eyes. They were all quite drunk. 'You're baiting me, Gerhard!'

'Why should I bait you? Don't tell me that I have a reason.'

It was then that Herbert felt truly guilty about what he was going to do. At the same time, however, he knew that he was going to do it, regardless of the consequences. There are some scenarios between men and women that have to be acted out for the sake of self-discovery, if nothing else. Perhaps the only risk, thought Herbert, is that one of us might fall in love.

They turned into one of the narrow alleyways that led toward the centre of the town. They were jostled by crowds of revellers coming out of the *bierstüben* on either side. There was hilarious laughter and accordion-music and the clattering of ladies' shoes on cobblestones. A man in a huntsman's hat and hitched-up lederhosen was urinating noisily against a wall and singing. '*Sah' ein Knab ein Röselein steh'n . . . Röselein auf der Heide . . .!*'

'Traditional German song,' Gerhard explained. 'The actions don't really relate to the words.'

Herbert glanced at his watch. 'Perhaps we should call it a night.'

'You're not afraid of a little rowdiness!' Gerhard protested. 'Come on, let's have another drink! The best nightcap I know! Some good Bavarian beer, and some schnapps to give it some flavour!'

He led the way down a small flight of steps into a bar called Zum Pumpernickel. It was fiercely noisy and hot and smoky, but Gerhard caught Herbert by the arm and led him across to a table in the corner. Several of the drunker customers stood up and whistled and applauded as Mathilde crossed the floor, but she retaliated by nodding and smiling and giving them queenly waves of acknowledgement. A sweating girl with chubby arms brought them pots of beer and glasses of schnapps, and they proceeded to toast each other and everybody sitting around them, and love, and the flying frogs, and love. They had to shout because of the singing and the roaring of voices and the accordion music.

'*Prost!*' cried Gerhard.

Herbert leaned forward and yelled, 'We have to fly at six o'clock tomorrow morning! It's almost one o'clock now!'

'To love!' Gerhard persisted.

Herbert glanced at Mathilde and the look in his eyes was serious and straight and level. Manoeuvring Gerhard into bed was reaching the point where it was more trouble than it was worth. With every toast, with every song, the evening was becoming less romantic and more contrived. They were all much drunker now and morning was nearer; and what had seemed at nine o'clock the previous evening to be alluring at any price still seemed arousing, yes, but also tawdry.

Gerhard reached across the table and clasped Herbert's hand, squeezing it and squeezing it. 'My dear friend, if all the world were just like you and me! If all the world could hold hands!'

Herbert, who had never admitted anything of the kind to any man in the whole of his life, said, 'Gerhard, never fear, whatever happens, I shall love you forever.'

Gerhard peered at him with reddened eyes. 'You mean that, don't you?'

'Yes, Gerhard, I do.'

'Perhaps you are not quite English, after all.'

'English? Who said anything about English? I am a frog!'

They brayed with laughter. A group of middle-aged Austrians who were sitting close by joined in their laughter and ordered them three more drinks. Together, they toasted the King of England. They toasted President Ebert of the Weimar Republic. They toasted the memory of the Habsburg empire. Then they sang

7

sentimental songs, and some of the Austrians had tears in their eyes.

At half-past four, a voice repeated, 'We'd better go. We're flying at six.' Herbert lifted his head and looked around and realized that the voice was his own.

He stood in front of the cheval-glass in his hotel bedroom and undressed very methodically. This was necessary because he hadn't been so drunk since his first evening at the Royal Aero Club. He tugged off his black silk necktie and laid it carefully on top of the bureau, smoothing it out with the side of his hand. Then he unfastened his collar-stud, and dropped it somewhere on the carpet. He went down on his hands and knees, but then the logical part of his mind told him that it would be more dignified to look for it tomorrow, and so he heaved himself back on to his feet again.

It's odd, he thought, as he unbuttoned his shirt. You don't *look* drunk. You look remarkably sober and ordinary. You look quite like yourself.

The only trouble is, how can you ever be *sure* that you look quite like yourself, even when you're sober? Does my face really suit my character? Or is it a mask, a bluff and handsome mask, concealing a devious and deceitful soul?

He managed after three toppling attempts to climb out of his trousers. He folded them with elaborate care, and hung them over the back of the chair. Eventually, naked, he went to the bathroom to brush his teeth. The same face examined him from the bathroom mirror, the same accusing eyes, only this time his mouth was filled with foaming pink dentifrice, like a hydrophobic bulldog.

He said to himself, as he dropped his toothbrush back into the glass, 'You have a wife at home. You have three devoted sons. Go to sleep. In ninety minutes' time, you're supposed to be flying.'

Herbert had never felt like someone who ought to be called Herbert. He felt more like a Reggie, or a Richard. Even Proper Hugh was better than Herbert. Proper Hugh, Improper Herbert. His face was square, with thick fairish eyebrows that betrayed the Scottish in him, and light brown animated eyes. His jaw was wide and strong, with a slight cleft in the chin. His father had always told him that the Lords had once been attacked by the Campbells during the '45 Rebellion, and that Herbert's great-great-great-great grandfather had been cut in the chin with a claymore – sustaining a wound that had been passed down against all the natural laws of heredity from one Lord to the next.

Herbert was broad-shouldered, heavily-built for a man not quite forty, with a triangular shield of fair brown hair on his chest, and thick shaggy thighs, like a Highland bull. His father had looked almost the same, at his age. In photographs, placed side by side, they could have been the same man. But their temperaments were wildly opposed. John Lord, Herbert's father, had always been single-minded, caustic, parsimonious, exacting – conventional to the core. He had been sentimental on occasions, but never sympathetic. Herbert, on the other hand, while he was equally determined, had inherited his mother's thoughtfulness, and much of her grace. He could flatter, and flirt, and talk diplomatically. He was capable of apologizing, when it was necessary. He was capable of falling in love.

Perhaps the only serious question that remained unanswered in Herbert's life was whether he had fallen in love with the right woman; or, indeed, if he had actually fallen in love at all.

He lifted the thick duck's-down quilt and climbed into bed. The mattress was uncompromisingly hard. It had probably been designed for Prussian officers, who kept their backs rigid as a way of life. On the wall overlooking the bed there was a lithograph of Jesus with a cheap dish on his head, looking sad. Herbert frowned at his wristwatch on the bedside cabinet. Four-forty-nine. He wished he had remembered to fill himself a glass of water.

His sinuses felt as if they had been packed with wet cotton, soaked in wine.

Outside his window, on the balcony which overlooked Lindau harbour, the sun was already shining. A thrush perched on the green-painted railing, and looked at Herbert through the window. The lake sparkled like smashed mirrors, and the morning air was wonderfully clear for flying. Herbert didn't know whether he was grateful or not. His forehead felt as if it were slowly being tightened in a tourniquet.

A stray drunk was still singing in the street below. *'Ihre Schönheit, ihre Schönheit, ist eine Herausforderung!'* Herbert buried his head in the pillow and squeezed his eyes tight shut and tried to think about nothing but aero engines. His favourite trick for getting himself to sleep was to imagine that he was dismantling one, piece by piece, and then putting it all back together again. By the time he had disconnected the push-rods he was usually deeply unconscious.

The drunk went into a coughing spasm and then was quiet. The morning wind lifted the net-curtains in slow, semi-transparent billows. Herbert lifted off the valve-springs and sank darkly into sleep. Jesus looked down at him sadly.

Minutes passed. Not much more than minutes. Then he felt fingernails stroking his shoulders, sharp but delicate, tracing pattern after pattern. He smelled perfume and warmth, and there was a momentary rush of cool air as the quilt was lifted and somebody climbed into the bed beside him.

Then lips were kissing his neck and hands were running down his sides, and Mathilde was breathily whispering to him, 'Herbert, Herbert, are you awake my darling?'

He felt her breasts soft against his bare back. He felt the crispness of her pubic hair against his bare buttocks. A hint of wetness amidst the hair.

He stiffened immediately. There was still time, even then. But he turned over and there she was with her mouth open and her arms reaching out for him and he was lost.

The first time, they attacked each other with almost hysterical urgency. They kissed and clawed and struggled and gasped. Herbert's passion for Mathilde boiled through him like a medieval madness, and he lifted her right up on to his hairy thighs as if he were lifting her up on to a cross, and thrust himself into her so fiercely that she buried her fingernails into the flesh of his shoulders and cried out, 'Oh God! You'll kill me!'

Afterwards, he lay back on the pillow and smoked a single Churchman's cigarette. Mathilde rose from the bed naked and went to the window, to look out over the lake. Her breasts were too large for her narrow back, white and heavy and marbled with veins. The cool breeze made her nipples crinkle.

After a while she turned to smile at him, one hand holding back the curtains. He smiled back. He thought that he had probably never seen a girl so utterly feminine and so entrancing. The sun illuminated the idly-curling smoke from his cigarette and the shiny curls of her pubic hair, so that he could see the pale plump skin beneath.

'Come away from the window,' he said. 'Somebody might see you.'

'Then they would be in luck,' she replied. But all the same, she let the curtain fall back, and walked around the end of the bed, until she came to the dressing-table. She picked up Herbert's toilet-water, Floris Special No 127, uncapped it, and sniffed it. Then she looked at the label. 'Ah!' she said. 'Your smell! I shall buy a bottle of this, when you have gone back to England. I shall soak my handkerchief in it, so that I can smell it while I am making love in bed with Gerhard, and think of you.'

She picked up the brass hand-mirror and scrutinized her face.
'Come back to bed,' said Herbert, but she gave her head a little
shake.

'I wonder if it shows, when you make love to a man who is not
your husband. I wonder if you look any different.'

She came across to the bed still holding the mirror. 'Do you
think I look different?'

Herbert said nothing, but watched her as she peered at herself.
A curve of reflected sunshine trembled on her slightly-parted lips.
'I think I have an ineffable glow,' she decided.

She lowered the mirror and examined her breasts. 'My breasts
look the same; except that now they are your breasts, as well as
Gerhard's.' She knelt on the bed, and laid the mirror down between her legs. Herbert watched her in fascination and alarm as
she opened herself with both hands and frowned down at what
she could see in the mirror. It was like an exquisitely-detailed
picture of a crimson rose, with glistening petals. Constance would
have died rather then expose herself like that. In fact, so would
every other girl that Herbert had ever known; girls from decent
families, anyway. His cigarette burned unsmoked between his
fingers. He stared at her face, wishing she would stop.

'Come to bed,' he said, hoarsely.

Herbert reached out and gripped her wrist, more hastily and
more awkwardly than he had meant to. She looked at him and
her expression was mesmerizing. He felt almost angry with her for
being so desirable.

'You think I'm terrible, don't you?' she told him. 'I scandalize
you.'

'You startle me, a little,' said Herbert. It was the second emo-
tional confession he had made that night.

Mathilde lifted up the hand-mirror again and stared at her face.
'I think I startle myself.'

'You're quite beautiful,' he told her.

She looked sideways at him without lowering the mirror.
'You're not my first lover, you know.'

Herbert remained silent for a moment. Then he said, 'You don't
have to confess anything to me, Mathilde. I'm not your husband.'

They made love a second time. It was almost half-past five.
Mathilde sat astride Herbert and rose gently and rhythmically up
and down, never taking her eyes away from him once. He watched
her breasts rise and fall. He wondered if it were possible ever to
own a woman like this. Gerhard certainly didn't.

She bent forward, locking her mouth against his, her nipples brushing the hair on his chest. She let out a muffled mewling noise, and quaked in his arms. Then she opened her eyes again and stared at him from very close to.

'I love you,' she said, although Herbert wasn't at all sure what that meant.

Neither of them realized that the shiny mahogany door had silently opened during their lovemaking, only an inch, and that for almost five minutes Gerhard had been standing in the corridor outside in his green Paisley bathrobe, watching them. His face was expressionless. Not until Mathilde bent forward and made her little mewling noise did he silently close the door again, and return to his room.

He stood in the middle of the room for a very long time, breathing deeply. Then he went to the bathroom, and stared at himself in the mirror. What is a man supposed to look like when his wife is fornicating with one of his best friends? What is a man supposed to say to himself? Gerhard thought: for some reason, I feel no pain.

There was a pair of nail-scissors on the bathroom shelf. Gerhard picked them up, and snipped them in the air a few times. Then he lowered the lavatory seat-lid, and sat down, and loosened his bathrobe so that his legs were exposed.

Very slowly, using tight control and a great deal of effort, he pushed the points of the nail-scissors into his right thigh. He heard the muscle crunch a little as the scissors went in deep. Blood welled up, startlingly bright, and ran down on either side of his leg. Soon he pushed the scissors in right up to the circular finger-grips.

He looked at the scissors dispassionately. He felt pain; *now* he felt pain, but somehow it didn't seem to matter. Perhaps I have no emotions whatsoever, Gerhard reflected. Perhaps I am nothing but an automaton, a machine made like a human out of flesh and blood and bone, but without character or personality. No nerves, no feeling, no immortal soul.

Perhaps she has already hurt me so much that I am incapable of being hurt any more.

He tugged the scissors out. Blood welled up and dripped off his bathrobe. There was blood smeared everywhere. He held one of the bath-towels under the cold water tap until it was sodden, and attempted to wipe up. It was only when he was on his hands and knees, attempting to clean the blood off the white floor-tiles, that he began to sob.

Three sobs, and then he stopped himself. His father had always told him that weeping was for women without beauty and for men with no hope.

They bounced out over the lake in Gerhard's smart little motor-boat. Away from the shore, it was surprisingly chilly. The sky was clear, except for a high swirl of cirrus clouds over the Allgäuer Alps off to the east, but there was a stiff and steady north-west wind blowing. Herbert had to hold on to his yachting cap, and the Bavarian Yacht Club pennant cracked and flurried on the highly-varnished stern counter.

Gerhard's seaplane was moored to a tender, sixty yards out from the shoreline. It shone silvery and sleek in the brightness of the morning, a two-seater monoplane, with two separate cockpits, each with its own tiny windshield. The seaplane's nose was long and streamlined, with two bulging torpedo-shaped exhaust manifolds over the engine. Its tail was painted with a two-headed eagle, in red; and on its fuselage was painted its name, *Lorelei II*. It danced on its pontoons like a nervous dragonfly.

'She's beautiful!' Herbert shouted, swallowing a mouthful of wind.

Gerhard nodded, without looking at him.

'Beautiful!' Herbert repeated, not sure that Gerhard had heard him. Gerhard seemed unusually cheerless this morning. Perhaps he was suffering from a hangover even worse than Herbert's, if that were conceivable. A muscle kept twitching in his cheek as if he were continuously grinding his front teeth together, and he hadn't said more than five words to Herbert since they had left the hotel. Mathilde had stayed behind, promising to watch the flying from the verandah. She had waved goodbye to them on the quayside with a tiny handkerchief. Gerhard had not waved back.

Gerhard's two mechanics Heinz Grüber and Uwe Schmidt were already out on the raft, making adjustments to the twelve-cylinder engine. They had already started it up several times that morning. Herbert had heard the dull droning roar while he was sitting alone in the hotel restaurant, eating his breakfast.

Gerhard and Mathilde had taken breakfast in their room. When they had appeared in the hotel lobby, Herbert had been given the uncomfortable impression that they had been arguing. Mathilde had been wearing a severely-cut summer suit, and one of those triumphant smiles which women always wear after arguments, either because they have won, and are feeling pleased with them-selves, or because they have lost, and that just goes to show what contemptible creatures husbands are.

Heinz was bald-headed and big-bellied, a walking testimonial to roasted pork-knuckles and Bavarian beer. He gave Herbert a strong hand to help him climb out of the motor-boat and up on to the tender's tilting deck. Gerhard tied up the motor-boat and climbed up on to the tender by himself, waving aside Heinz's offer of assistance.

Heinz shouted, 'I am still not so happy about the timing! And the overheating, also! We're losing too much coolant through the block.'

Gerhard looked up at the *Lorelei* with a tight, thoughtful expression. His cheek-muscle kept on twitching.

'It's not so bad as it was yesterday,' Heinz added. He obviously didn't want Gerhard to think that he was incompetent, or that he had been wasting his time. 'But, you know, I would rather have two or three more hours on it, before you take her up.'

Gerhard reached up and held the trailing edge of the *Lorelei*'s thin shapely wing, to balance himself. He thought for a little longer, and then he said, 'Run it. Let's hear it.'

Heinz hesitated for a moment. Then he said, '*Also*. You can see for yourself.'

He heaved himself up to the pilot's cockpit, while Uwe balanced like a tightrope-walker on to the front of the seaplane's pontoons. '*Kontakt!*' shouted Heinz, and Uwe swung the propeller. The propeller turned stiffly two or three times, and stopped. 'Again!' Heinz barked. Uwe swung it once more, and immediately the engine opened up with a deafening, rasping roar, blowing blue smoke out of the exhausts. Uwe hopped back on to the raft, holding on to his cap.

Herbert stayed where he was, his hands pressed over his ears; but Gerhard approached the seaplane with his hands by his sides and stood close to the engine housing, listening in deep concentration to the beating of the pistons. The fierce draft from the propeller made his brown coat balloon out, so that he looked as if he were inflated, like one of the Katzenjammer Kids in the funny papers.

Uwe stood close to him, concave-chested, his cap tugged down low on his forehead, his big greasy hands perched on his hips like two black crows. 'You can hear it, *ja*? It's still running rough. *Frukketi-frukketi-frukketi*. It's no good for the bearings.'

'Herbert!' said Gerhard. His eyes were bright, and he spoke with unexpected sharpness. 'Let's take her up,' he declared.

Heinz let the engine die down to a steady chug. 'Please, Herr Brunner! One more hour!'

'To do what?' Gerhard demanded. 'To tinker here, and to tinker there? You mechanics are never happy unless you're tinkering! The timing is a little off, yes. But you shouldn't pamper an engine like this. You should run it and run it and run it, until it learns to behave itself.' He paused, and looked around. 'It's like a woman,' he said, so quietly that Herbert only just caught what he said.

'Well,' said Heinz unhappily. 'I don't think so. If anything, it's going to get worse.'

Gerhard didn't reply, but took out his brown leather flying-gloves, and tugged them on, one finger at a time. 'Help Mr Lord into his place,' he told Uwe.

Herbert said, 'Really, old man, I don't mind waiting till later. You don't want to damage your engine-block. We could motor into Austria for lunch. You know – and think about flying after-wards. There's quite a reasonable restaurant in Bezau.'

Gerhard gave him a challenging slap on the back. 'We're flying, Herbert. That's what you came for, isn't it? You're not funking it, I hope?'

Herbert shrugged, and gave Heinz an uncomfortable smile. He was beginning to wonder if Gerhard had somehow found out what had happened between him and Mathilde. It gave him an un-pleasant sickness in the pit of his stomach, the same sensation as flying through bumpy cloud.

'Gerhard –' he began.

'We're flying, yes?' said Gerhard. 'You came here to fly.'

'Of course. But I don't want you to damage the *Lorelei* just for the sake of impressing me.'

'My dear Herbert, have I ever done *anything* for the sake of impressing you?' Uwe came forward with his hands clasped to-gether ready for Herbert to step into them. Herbert hesitated for a moment, and then placed his brown two-tone Oxford into Uwe's blackened palms. Uwe bunked him up the side of the seaplane, until he found the lowest rung of the ladder that was hooked into the cockpit. 'Thank you,' he said, and lowered himself into his seat. The cockpit was extremely narrow. Herbert could hardly fit his shoulders into it, and to keep his head below the level of the windshield, he had to crouch down in the awkward basketwork seat like a large boy who has outgrown his perambulator. He felt desperately uncomfortable, and somehow humiliated, as if Gerhard had put him into this position on purpose.

The seaplane's engine sawed and droned, and Herbert felt the aircraft swaying on its pontoons. Then it dipped and swayed even more, as Gerhard climbed into the cockpit in front of him.

Gerhard had already fitted his goggles over his eyes. He glanced at Herbert but behind his goggles it was impossible for Herbert to guess what he was thinking. He certainly wasn't smiling.

Herbert gave him a thumb's-up. Gerhard nodded, and settled himself into his seat.

They stayed by the tender for a minute or two, while Gerhard gunned the engine and satisfied himself that it was running smoothly enough to take them up. It was now twenty-past six. Herbert thought about all the guests at the Lindauer Hotel who must be muffling their ears with their pillows and cursing them to hell. He thought of Mathilde, sitting on the hotel verandah in her severe suit, watching two men who had made love to her, both in the same plane, their distant heads no more than specks. *Alle Menschen werden Brüder*, Schiller had written: all men become brothers. He thought of what he had seen in the hand-mirror, the glistening flower.

The *Lorelei*'s engine screamed furiously, and the whole fuselage juddered and vibrated. Herbert's teeth rattled together. God, he thought, I could do with a brandy. A brandy with a raw egg broken into it. No better cure for hangover and romantic complications. Herbert was happiest when he was flying; or when he was playing rugby or cricket or hard games of tennis. What had happened with Mathilde was quite out of character, or at least he thought it ought to be. He had never betrayed Constance before.

If only he could stop thinking about Mathilde. Her eyes, watching him. Her eyes, watching herself. Her smile, both obvious and enigmatic.

Gerhard waved, and Heinz and Uwe released the *Lorelei*'s mooring-lines. Immediately, Gerhard revved up the engine again, and the seaplane turned toward the north-west wind, the sun shining in its propeller in a gleaming scimitar.

'I'm going to take the longest run I can, and lift off over Langenargen,' Gerhard shouted. 'Have you fastened your harness? Mathilde would never forgive me if you dropped out.'

Herbert nodded that he was ready. Gerhard opened up the engine to its full 450 horsepower capacity, and the seaplane surged forward across the surface of the lake.

To Herbert, there had never been any sensation to compare with flying in a high-performance seaplane. In spite of his cramped position in the rear cockpit, with the slipstream buffeting and roaring across his ears – in spite of his uncertainty about Gerhard and Mathilde – he began to feel that exuberant thrill of speed and risk and thunderous noise, all mingled with the smell of oil and aviation fuel and raw polished metal, and the shattering of water against the twin pontoons. Unlike land planes, which were obliged to roll tediously over the grass before they became 'unstuck', as pilots called it, the *Lorelei* skipped toward her take-off speed like a flying-fish, sending up sheets of spray.

Herbert saw three men in a motor-launch waving to them, and he gave them an awkward left-handed wave in return. They were shouting something but he couldn't hear what it was. Good luck, perhaps; or bravo; or a hundred Bavarian curses for frightening the fish. He was actually beginning to feel a little anxious, because they had already covered well over 600 yards, and the *Lorelei* was still planing across the surface, jostling and bumping against every wave. Gerhard was heading directly for the Langenargen promontory, in order to take the best advantage of the wind, but if he didn't lift the *Lorelei* up into the air reasonably promptly, they would run the risk of water-skiing straight into the shore, at a hundred miles an hour.

What was even more alarming, the propeller torque at this speed was making the *Lorelei* lean further and further to the right, until her starboard pontoon was running under water.

Herbert sat tight-lipped and said nothing. It was bad form to start shouting instructions to an experienced pilot like Gerhard, no matter how much you might have the wind up. All the same, Herbert began to wonder if it was a terribly good idea to go flying with a man who might well suspect you of having an affair with his wife. Can such a man be trusted with one of the most powerful flying-machines in the world, and your life, too?

The *Lorelei* skated faster and faster across the surface of the lake, trailing behind her a high plume of golden-shining spray. She leaned even more disconcertingly to the right, until she ran into a diagonal swell and her wingtip actually glanced the water. Herbert screwed up his eyes against the hot smoky slipstream and peered up ahead of them, to the bright shoreline of Langenargen. He could see houses, trees, and several motor-cars. Still Gerhard kept the seaplane running in the water.

Herbert glanced behind him. Although he wouldn't have admitted it to anyone at all, he was quickly sizing up his chances of jumping out. They didn't look at all good. It would take no more than one unlucky blow from the tailplane, followed by a collision with the surface of the lake, and he would have been crippled, drowned, or both. In comparison, a high-speed collision with the shoreline would seem almost merciful.

'Gerhard!' he appealed. But at that moment Gerhard pointed

one finger to the sky, and shouted 'Upstairs!', and lifted up the *Lorelei*'s nose.

With a high-pitched bellow, the seaplane rose up out of the water, spray trailing like a bridal train from its pontoons, and flashed over the Langenargen shoreline at a height of only fifty feet. Herbert saw upturned faces, and people waving. Then Gerhard was climbing steeply and banking to port, so that they were curving out over the lake again. Above the leather-trimmed edge of the cockpit, his eyes watering, Herbert could see the misty outline of Friedrichshafen; and, as they turned, the sun was reflected on the water, transforming acres of lake into dazzling gold.

'Now, I'll show you something!' Gerhard shouted. He lifted the *Lorelei's* nose yet again, so that they gained even more height, nearly a thousand feet, and then he pivoted the seaplane on its port wing, and the sun and the sky revolved around them like a carousel. Herbert was exhilarated; but deeply envious, too. To be able to design and build the *Lorelei* had taken a combination of genius and wealth; and to be able to fly it like this took courage and imagination and immaculate skill. Gerhard had all of these things, and Mathilde, too, and the worst of it all was that he probably deserved them.

The *Lorelei* fell from one thousand feet to one hundred feet in a near-vertical dive. Herbert saw the lake rushing toward them head-on. Then Gerhard had pulled them up and they were flying level at over 150 mph, which was faster then Herbert had ever flown in his life. 'One hundred fifty!' shouted Gerhard. 'Last month, she managed one-sixty-six!'

They flew past the entrance to Lindau harbour flat out, and already there were crowds of spectators out on the quaysides, cheering. Gerhard waggled the *Lorelei*'s wings as they passed the Lindauer Hotel, although Herbert couldn't see Mathilde anywhere.

They turned again, around the eastern end of the lake, passing low over the tender where Heinz and Uwe were waiting for them. Gerhard waggled his wings again, to tell them that he was going to go for one last high-speed run, and then bring the *Lorelei* down.

As they began to gain height, however, Herbert could hear that the engine was running badly off-tune. There was a new sound, too – an ominous juddering screech, like a loosely-fitting fanbelt. If this had been Herbert's own plane, he would have taken it down straight away – not so much out of fear, but to save the engine from being seriously damaged. 'Gerhard!' he called, and stretched around his windshield to tap Gerhard on the shoulder.

Gerhard turned, and Herbert pointed first toward the engine-cowling and then toward his ear. 'You're off-tune! Sounds like you're running too hot!'

Gerhard shook his head, as if he couldn't hear, or refused to understand.

'*Zu heiss!*' Herbert bawled at him. But again, Gerhard shook his head.

They were now more than twelve hundred feet above the lake. The *Lorelei*'s engine was still roaring at full power, but its underlying off-key drone was becoming more and more notice-able. The exhaust that blew out of its manifolds began to thicken, and Herbert could smell oil and steam and overheated alloy.

'What is all this worth?' Gerhard shouted.

'What do you mean? What is all *what* worth?'

'All this! The world! The lake! The sunshine!'

Herbert looked baffled. 'Still don't know what you mean!'

'No? You don't know the value of anything? Herbert, my friend, what a man you are! I shall have to show you!'

With that, Gerhard steeply angled the *Lorelei* off to starboard, and downward, around and around in a corkscrew that grew faster and more sickening with every descending turn. They left a curl of black smoke behind them in the sky, and the *Lorelei*'s engine screeched in protest.

Herbert was pressed further and further down into his un-comfortable basketwork seat. His face was drizzled on one second with lubricating oil, and scalded the next with escaping steam. The lake rotated in front of his eyes as Gerhard took the *Lorelei* down and down into a spiral that steepened so dramatically that it became a spin – wings, pontoons, fuselage, tail – flickering around and around in the early-morning sunshine – and everybody on shore shielded their eyes and looked up at this silvery sycamore-leaf falling out of a golden sky and held their breath.

Mathilde, on the hotel verandah, abruptly rose to her feet. Her coffee spilled across the emboidered linen tablecloth, in the shape of an old woman's face.

The seaplane spun and spun and its engine moaned an extraordin-ary lament.

Crouched in the *Lorelei*'s rear cockpit, Herbert understood with complete clarity that Gerhard had found him out, and that this was his punishment – terror, death, possibly both. A duel of honour, fought not with swords but with bravado, and with fierce masculine possessiveness, and with the overwhelming possibility of being killed.

19

A fat man on the hotel balcony whispered, '*Heilige Mutter.* They're going to crash.'

While Herbert – not for his own sake, because Herbert had been brought up to believe that a punishment is a punishment and duels of all kinds have to be fought with a stiff upper lip, but for Mathilde's sake, and for Constance's sake, and for the sake of his boys – screamed out, 'Gerhard! Gerhard! For God's sake, man, she doesn't love me!'

Gerhard remained hunched in his seat. The *Lorelei* continued to drop.

'Gerhard!' Herbert roared at him, even though it was probably too late. 'Gerhard, for the love of God, she doesn't love me!'

Still Gerhard refused to reply. Smoke blurted past Herbert's windshield, and he closed his eyes and clasped his hands together and said, 'Oh God, protect Constance. Look after my boys.'

And then the *Lorelei* swooped out of its spiral, so close to the surface of the lake that its pontoons kissed the water and sent up a fountain of rainbow spray, out of which the silver seaplane emerged roaring triumphantly.

Herbert reached down into the cockpit and tugged out a handkerchief to wipe his face. He saw the harbour and the hotel; and as Gerhard turned back toward the tender, he glimpsed Mathilde, standing on the verandah.

She looked so tiny from here, one tiny pale face.

Gerhard brought the *Lorelei* back down on to the water, and circled the tender with intermittent bursts of aggressive power. Eventually, Heinz threw Herbert a line, and they drew the seaplane back to its mooring.

Herbert stiffly climbed out of the cockpit, and Uwe helped him down. Uwe said nothing but regarded Herbert with a fixed and philosophical stare. Gerhard climbed down on his own, and stood on the tender pulling off his flying gloves and smiling.

'Well!' he said to Herbert. 'Now you know something of comparative values. What this is worth, what that is worth. They didn't teach us such things at Harrow, did they?'

Herbert didn't answer, but went straight to the motor-boat, and climbed in. Gerhard said to Heinz, 'I won't be flying again this week. Take her back to the sheds for me, will you, and strip down the engine. I'll come down on Saturday afternoon to look it over.'

Heinz nodded, but he didn't look at all happy. 'Let's get that cowling off,' he said to Uwe, in German. 'I want to check the wings, too. They weren't built for aerobatics.'

Herbert sat in the stern of the motor-boat while Gerhard steered them back toward the quay. The first pleasure-boats of the day were beginning to emerge. A Bavarian breakfast on board the *Lohengrin*, complete with Egg beer and bratwurst. They could hear the laughter bouncing off the water like china saucers.

'This shall not happen again,' said Gerhard, in pedantic English.

Herbert took a cigarette out of its dark green tin, and cupped his hands to light it. He felt shaken and angry that Gerhard had frightened him into a confession. Gerhard said, 'I would consider it a favour if you were to leave the hotel immediately. I will arrange for a motor-car to take you to München.'

Herbert said, 'How did you find out?'

'About what?'

'You know what I'm talking about.'

Gerhard steered the boat into the harbour entrance, and headed for the steps. 'I saw you,' he said. 'You didn't even have the discretion to lock your bedroom door. What man, who finds his wife missing in the early hours of the morning, will not go looking for her?'

'That's a great pity,' said Herbert. 'What I said to you up in the air was true. She doesn't love me, and I don't suppose she ever could.'

Gerhard cut the engine and tied up the boat. Mathilde was waiting for them at the top of the steps. She stood with her arms by her sides and it was apparent from her silence that she had guessed what had happened between them.

Herbert held out his hand. 'It's a sad way to end a friendship,' he said, and meant it. He had known Gerhard since he was at Harrow. 'What I said last night . . . that I loved you . . . that wasn't just the wine talking.'

Gerhard held him close, and hugged him. 'There is no other solution, my friend. You may have my money, you may have my house. But there are two things which I will never let you take from me, ever. One of those is my wife. The other is my *Lorelei*. You understand me? They are mine, otherwise my life is not worth living.'

'I understand,' said Herbert. He would have done anything at that moment to be able to turn back the clock – back to the frog's legs; back to their walk along the quay; back to this morning. Back to the moment before Mathilde had wrapped her arms around him and breathed warmly on the back of his neck.

'*You see what you have done?*' Mathilde had asked him, opening her vulva like a full-blooming rose. '*You have possessed me.*'

21

Herbert climbed the steps. He hesitated for a moment, looking into Mathilde's face for some clue why this should have happened. Had Gerhard really seen them, or had she told him? But her face was inscrutable. Faces never betray reasons. The wind furled and unfurled the flags on top of the Lindauer Hotel, and he knew that he might never see her again, this strange scandalous woman.

'There is no need for farewells,' said Gerhard, climbing up the steps after him. There was a patch of brown blood on the leg of his trousers, and he was limping slightly. 'No,' said Herbert, 'I suppose not.' He acknowledged Mathilde with a nod and then he walked across the cobbled promenade towards the hotel.

Gerhard laid his arm around Mathilde's shoulders and kissed her hair. Mathilde remained where she was, her arms by her sides, while silent tears ran steadily down her face.

'He is gone now, Mathi,' said Gerhard. 'You will never have to concern yourself with him again.'

London, 1930

But Herbert and Mathilde did meet again, when neither of them was prepared for it, at Kempinski's restaurant at 99 Regent Street, on the evening of August 15, which was hot – one of the hottest evenings of the year.

Herbert didn't particularly like Kempinski's, but they specialized in German food, and he was meeting his old friend Claude Dornier, the celebrated German aircraft designer, and Dornier's chief test-pilot, the wartime seaplane hero Friedrich Christiansen. On the telephone from Brown's Hotel, Dornier had said, 'Herbert, I am so bereft for a German sausage. Is there anywhere in London that serves a German sausage?' Bartholdi's had no tables free, so the next best was Kempinski's.

Kempinski's style was solid and *gemütlich* like the lounge of a

Norddeutscher Lloyd ocean-liner. In the middle of the restaurant, on a brown-carpeted podium, a five-piece jazz ensemble with tight wing collars played *If You Knew Susie* in goose-step time. Above the crowded tables, the fans in the ceiling whirred like aeroplane propellers, and the aspidistras dipped and curtseyed in the constant draft. The conversation was brash and mostly German. Looking around, Herbert felt that he could easily have been in Hamburg, rather than London. Not Berlin, however. Kempinski's was authentic, but it wasn't Berlin.

Claude Dornier had craved sausage, and that was what they had ordered: bratwurst, and apples, and red cabbage boiled with onions and vinegar and drenched in sausage-fat. While they ate, Dornier talked endlessly about the Do-X, his immense inter-continental flying boat, which was being fitted out at Lake Constance for its gala flight to America in November. With twelve engines and a wingspan of a hundred and fifty-seven feet, the Do-X was by far the largest heavier-than-air flying-machine that the world had ever seen. It looked like nothing less than a ship with wings.

Dornier insisted, 'Herbert, you must come with us across the Atlantic – at least for part of the way. You could join us at Lisbon and fly maybe to Tenerife. All the way to Brazil, if you wish. It will be wonderful! We have already furnished the main saloon with Irish linen and French crystal and the finest Turkish carpets.'

Herbert smiled. 'You should have been an hotelier, Claude, not an aircraft designer.'

Friedrich Christiansen was straight-backed, crop-headed, with a face as tanned as a pigskin briefcase. 'She is like an hotel, yes!' he agreed. 'But she flies like a gull! When I first tested her, she jumped out of the water even before I was ready.'

'Please believe me, Claude, I'm keeping an open mind,' Herbert replied. 'But I must be frank with you. I'm not at all sure that you're going in the right direction. Do you really believe that the future of public air travel lies in such luxurious monsters? The rich will always be able to travel; but this Depression won't last for ever, and very soon your fellow in the street will be demanding the right to fly quickly from place to place. Your businessman, your holidaymaker, your family man visiting his relatives. What does it cost to fly from London to Paris these days? Just four guineas – compared with the first-class boat-train fare of £3 12s 11d. Soon the aeroplane will be cheaper than the train! And then we still have to think about the soldier and the sailor, too. We sell scores of aeroplanes to the War Office. Well – I don't believe that we have yet seen the last of war, and selling aeroplanes to the

23

government is my bread-and-butter. Without that, of course, I could never afford to race.'

'Herbert,' enthused Dornier, reaching across the table and pouring Herbert another glass of chilled Austrian wine. 'If you were to come in with me – if you were to help me to finance the Do-X and to build it in England under licence – in five years' time you and I could be the royalty of aeronautics! The kings of the air!'

'You do tempt me, Claude,' Herbert replied, 'but I'm quite happy being a Lord.'

They were all laughing at that when Mathilde walked into the restaurant, on the arm of a jowly dark-eyed middle-aged man. Herbert stopped laughing at once. He lowered his knife and fork and stared at Mathilde with such intensity that his two supper guests frowned at him in surprise, and then turned around to see what had caught his attention so dramatically.

'Isn't that Gerhard Brunner's wife?' asked Dornier.

Herbert slowly nodded, without taking his eyes off her. She, too, stared at him, even while her companion was drawing out her chair for her. She had changed. She had grown older; perhaps a little tireder, too. But her eyes were just as captivating and just as mysterious, and her mouth still looked sensual and crushed. She was wearing an elegant peach-coloured evening dress of close-fitting silk, decorated with a large flower made out of the same material. She wore the kind of little hat that Constance would have called 'too saucy by half'.

Dornier said, 'I haven't seen Gerhard for years, you know. He used to fly from Lake Constance all the time. Willy Messerschmitt said that he'd seen him at Bamberg once, and that he didn't look good. Drinking, perhaps. He always was a drinker.'

'He's entered his *Lorelei* for next year's Seraphim Trophy,' put in Herbert. 'So there can't be very much seriously wrong with him.'

'Do you know the man with her?' asked Dornier. 'I'm sure I've seen him somewhere before. In Berlin, possibly.'

Herbert stood up, and dropped his napkin on to his plate. 'Forgive me, Claude,' he said. 'I'll find out for you.'

Without another word he crossed the restaurant and approached Mathilde's table. Her companion could see that he was coming to introduce himself, and he sat up straighter and watched Herbert with an oddly prissy smile.

'Mathi,' said Herbert, taking hold of her hand and kissing it. Then, to her companion, 'Please excuse me. Mrs Brunner and I are old friends.'

'She has just told me that you were,' her companion acknowledged. His English inflections were exact, but he was obviously
German. 'She was expecting you to come over and make yourself
known.'

'Herbert Lord,' said Herbert, extending his hand.

The German stood, and bowed his head, and audibly clicked
his heels under the table. 'Joachim von Ribbentrop. I am
delighted.'

'Herr von Ribbentrop is the German agent for Johnnie Walker
whisky,' Mathilde explained. Herbert looked down at her, and the
expression on her face had nothing whatever to do with what she
had said. It was gentle, luminous, wounded, and infinitely
alluring.

'The von Ribbentrops, I regret, are a very boozy crowd,' the
German smiled. 'My wife is heiress to the German champagne-
makers Henkel.'

Herbert stared at Mathilde, and said, 'It's been so long.' His
voice came out as a whisper, although he hadn't meant it to.

Mathilde gave a fleeting, embarrassed smile, and then lowered
her eyes.

'Are you well?' asked Herbert. 'I never expected to see you in
London.' The real question was: *do you still think of me, after
seven years of enforced separation?*

'I'm blooming,' Mathilde answered. 'Just like the little rose on
the heath.'

'And Gerhard? I'm having supper with Claude Dornier. Claude
says Gerhard hasn't been frightfully well.'

'Life hasn't been easy for him,' nodded Mathilde. 'His parents
died; and then, only a month later —'

Herbert waited for Mathilde to finish her sentence, but she
didn't. Instead, she laid her hand on top of von Ribbentrop's
hand, her index finger just touching his gold wedding-band, and
said, 'Gerhard is a man in a million, you know that as well as I
do. Sometimes he finds things difficult, that's all.'

'Gerhard is a true knight,' smiled von Ribbentrop. He rubbed
his hands together so tightly that his knuckles cracked. 'Will you
join us for a glass of champagne, Herr Lord? I would consider it
an honour.'

'Thank you, no, I have to get back to my guests,' said Herbert.
'But perhaps another time.'

'If you're ever in Germany, you must visit us at Dahlem,' von
Ribbentrop suggested. 'Do you like to swim, and play tennis?'

'That sounds splendid,' said Herbert. He was watching Mathilde and the very sight of her was like a physical pain. He hadn't realized how much he had missed her; how much his conscious mind must have been suppressing his longing for her.

Mathilde touched Herbert's sleeve. 'It's good to see you looking so well, Herbert.'

'I'm not really well, you know,' he told her, so quietly that von Ribbentrop couldn't quite catch what he said.

'Not well?' Mathilde frowned.

'Are you staying in London for long?' he asked her.

'Only until Tuesday. Then we're taking the boat-train to the Hook of Holland.'

'May I see you? Just for an hour?'

'Here,' she opened her peach silk purse and took out a small gold propelling-pencil and a tiny notepad. 'I'm staying with some friends in Kensington. This is the telephone number. You can call me almost every day about four o'clock – well, between four and five.'

Herbert took the note and folded it. 'Herr von Ribbentrop,' he said. 'It's been a pleasure.'

Joachim von Ribbentrop stood up again, and shook hands. 'Any time you want champagne, Mr Lord, I can obtain it for you at very advantageous prices. None of your eighty-nine shillings a dozen.'

Herbert rejoined Claude Dornier and Friedrich Christiansen. 'I'm sorry,' he said, sitting down and placing his knife and fork together.

'You've finished?' asked Dornier, in surprise. 'Don't you care for sausage?'

'I'm not hungry, that's all. You'll have to forgive me.'

'Very well, I forgive you. You won't mind if I spear your sausage?'

'Please do.'

Dornier helped himself to Herbert's bratwurst. He still had his mouth full when he said, 'Von Ribbentrop. That's his name.'

'Yes,' said Herbert. 'Apparently he works for Johnnie Walker whisky.'

'I met him in Essen,' Dornier recalled. 'He's a great supporter of the Nazis. In fact, the reason he was in Essen when *I* was in Essen was to persuade some steel company to put money into Hitler's election campaign.'

'Ah,' said Herbert. He turned around in his chair, ostensibly to look at von Ribbentrop, but he couldn't take his eyes away from Mathilde. She was laughing, and lifting her glass of champagne. She caught him looking at her, but didn't smile, and quickly turned

26

her head away. Von Ribbentrop was bulging his eyes and blowing out his cheeks as he told her some funny story. '*Du hast den Bleistift vergessen!*' he cried, and slapped the table.

Dornier asked, 'Gerhard's well?'

'I'm not sure,' said Herbert.

'And what about the Do-X? Will you consider it?' Dornier found it almost impossible to attract Herbert's attention.

'What?' said Herbert.

'The Do-X, will you consider coming in with me?'

'Well, I don't know,' said Herbert. 'We'll have to see.'

On Sunday afternoon in Kensington Gardens it was thundery and dark. The grass was unnaturally green, as if it had been poisoned, and dogs and children ran through the trees like escaping memories of Herbert's own childhood.

They met on the steps of the Albert Memorial. Mathilde wore a long putty-coloured summer raincoat, and a feathered hat. Herbert took her white-gloved hand and pressed it against his lips. He wore no raincoat, only his light grey suit, but he carried a large black umbrella.

'Do you want to walk?' he asked her.

She took his arm, and they walked across the grass towards the Round Pond. He felt the warmth of her, and smelled her perfume. He could almost wish that Constance could appear now, and catch them both together.

'What are you doing in London?' he inquired.

'I was invited, that's all; the von Ribbentrops invited me. We went down to Sussex yesterday. Hildegard von Ostenau was having a birthday party for the twins. You must remember Hildegard.'

Herbert nodded. 'I remember. But I'm surprised to see you with von Ribbentrop. Did you know he's a Nazi? Not quite the clean potato, I would have thought.'

'He's marvellous at tennis.'

They walked in silence for a while, and then Mathilde said, 'There's something you have to know.' Herbert was surprised how German she sounded. 'Gerhard and I are going to be divorced.'

Herbert stopped and stared at her. 'I'm sorry,' he said. 'I haven't heard anything from Gerhard since that time at Lindau.'

'I think he has forgiven you for that,' smiled Mathilde. 'He was more angry with me than he was with you. He knew that I didn't really love him, and that I would always be unfaithful – with my mind, if not with my body.'

27

'What are you going to do?' Herbert asked her.

'I am going to marry someone else. His name's Theodor Keitel, he's an artist. Quite a famous artist, in his way. He has a beautiful house in Koblenz, on the Rhine, we're going to live there.'

'Koblenz is hardly Berlin.'

Mathilde smiled with a touch of regret. 'I think my Berlin days are over. It's time for me to start living respectably.'

Lightning flickered over the rooftops of Kensington Palace. A gust of warm, damp wind blew across the park. Hats and hoops fled away from it as if they were frightened. Herbert said, 'I never forgot that morning, you know.'

'Neither did I, my dear,' said Mathilde, and squeezed his arm.

'Have you ever thought of me since?' he asked her.

They stood on the brink of the Round Pond, watching the boats. Mathilde said, 'I thought of you more often than I can ever explain.'

'You could have written, you know.'

'No,' she said.

When it started to rain, she took him to her friend's second-floor flat in Queen's Gate. Her friend had gone to Dorking for the weekend. The flat was high-ceilinged, dark, furnished with expensive but worn-out sofas and chairs. There was an oil-painting over the fireplace of two serious children. Herbert stood by the window and watched the rain speckling the glass, and the black taxis with their wet roofs chugging up and down the street outside.

Mathilde poured gins for both of them. Thunder collapsed over their heads, and the room was so gloomy they could scarcely see each other.

'*Prost!*' said Herbert, as they clinked glasses.

'Here's to love, and to flying frogs,' Mathilde replied.

'I love you,' he said.

She nodded. 'In another lifetime, perhaps. The Buddhists believe in that, don't they?'

'I'm not sure that I have the patience to wait for another lifetime.'

'But you love Constance, don't you?'

Herbert stared out of the window. 'In my way, yes. Constance is a good mother, and a fine companion.'

'You love your boys, too.'

'Yes,' said Herbert.

The clock on the chimney-piece chimed five. Mathilde said, 'I'm having dinner with some friends this evening. I shall have to get ready soon.'

Herbert swallowed gin. 'In that case, I'd better go. I promised Constance I'd get back down to Chichester tonight.'

She touched his hand. 'Don't go yet. Stay and talk to me while I get ready. It's always lonely, getting ready on your own. The flat is so silent!'

'Mathilde . . .'

'Ssh,' she said, and pressed her fingertip against his lips. 'Come into the bedroom while I draw my bath.'

The bedroom was as large as the living-room, with huge sombre wardrobes and a wide bed covered with a faded pink satin quilt. All that Herbert could see from the windows was the soot-blackened wall of the next block of flats, dripping with rainwater. He sat in a creaking basketwork chair painted the colour of pink medicine and sipped his gin.

Mathilde stood in front of the dressing-table and unfastened her plain brown dress. Underneath it she wore a simple silk slip, silk stockings and garters and nothing else. Herbert watched her as she unclipped her garters. Her breasts swayed beneath the thin silk.

'Do you have a cigarette?' she asked him.

He took out his gold cigarette case and lit two Churchmans. She came over and took one of them from him. 'I was in America last year, you know. New York first, then Florida. It was quite an eye-opener. The Americans must have the worst taste in strolling-about get-ups that you've ever seen. And, you know, I'm a woman of the world, but I never knew that men's shorts came in such astronomical waistband sizes.'

'How's Gerhard taking it?' asked Herbert.

Mathilde blew out smoke and looked away. 'Badly. He keeps calling me on the telephone, and sending me letters. He doesn't understand that I've had enough.'

Herbert could have professed his love again; but he decided to hold his peace. He knew very little about Mathilde. She might never have loved him enough to cause him anything but pain.

She went through to the bathroom and turned off the geyser. 'There,' she called, 'it's ready. Come and talk to me. You can soap my back. And bring my drink, too.'

Herbert hesitated, but Mathilde came back into the bedroom and stood in front of him with her arms raised above her head. 'Here,' she said softly. 'You can help me out of my underslip.'

Herbert stood up. Without a word he took hold of the soft

shiny material of her slip and lifted it slowly upward. It made barely a whisper. Her breasts were so full that they were caught for a moment, but then they slipped free, heavy and warm and stiff-nippled. Herbert let the slip drop to the floor, and held Mathilde's breast in his open hand, and bent forward to kiss her. She turned her face away, so that he was able to kiss only her cheek.

She led him through to the bathroom by the hand. He sat on the cork-topped stool smoking his cigarette while she sat in the big old enamelled bath and washed herself. She told him all about her lover's art, about the scenes he had painted of German history, of Barbarossa and the Teutonic Knights, and how the von Ribbentrops had sponsored him and made him one of the most popular artists in German high society.

'And you love him?' asked Herbert, feeling a cad for having had to put it into words.

'Dearly,' said Mathilde. 'Now – you can soap my back.'

She stood up in the bath. Herbert picked up the cake of camellia-scented soap and lathered his hands. Then, in his formal Sunday suit, he began to massage Mathilde's naked body all over, her shoulders, her back, her breasts, her thighs. She stood with her eyes wide open watching him while he did so. His hands slipped down between her legs, and for a moment she reached out and balanced herself by holding on to his shoulder.

'If only you knew how much I have missed you, and why,' she murmured.

His fingertip was touching the taut crease between her thighs. 'You missed me for a reason?' he asked her.

She smiled, and kissed him. 'A secret reason. You will never know what it is. Now, I must rinse off this soap.'

He went through to the living-room and poured them both another drink. 'Have you met this fellow Hitler?' he called.

Mathilde came out of the bathroom in a blue Chinese robe. 'I met him in München. He was rather glum about something, I don't know what it was.'

Herbert watched her combing out her hair. 'You have a terrible effect on me, my love,' he told her.

'Any woman worth her salt should have a terrible effect on all men,' she said. She sipped her drink, and then she said, 'Do you know, in China, the characters which represent the male member are the same characters for Imploring Corpse?'

Herbert couldn't help smiling. 'No,' he said. 'I didn't know that.'

Outside the window, the rain was beginning to clear. This

morning's forecast on the wireless had said that the evening would be bright.

At half-past six Herbert had to start thinking about catching his train back to Chichester. Mathilde was sitting at her dressing-table painting her face. Herbert was oddly glad because he didn't like her with make-up on. He stood behind her, with one hand resting on her back, and then he said, 'I have to go now. We may not meet again. I do wish you all the very best of luck.'

'Herbert, you have always been the best.'

He poked with his finger and thumb into his waistcoat pocket, and produced what looked like a silver coin. 'Here,' he told her. 'I want you to have this. It means a very great deal to me. Ever since I've had it, it's always brought me luck.'

Mathilde took it, and turned it this way and that. 'What is it?' she wanted to know.

'It's German. It's a medal that was struck in 1916 to com-memorate the death of the air ace Oswald Boelcke in a mid-air collision.'

Herbert paused, and then added, 'My oldest son James gave it to me. He bought it out of his pocket-money when he was eleven.'

'A strange gift for a son to give his father.'

'Not really. Very apt, in fact. My older brother Francis was shot down by Oswald Boelcke in 1915, over Cappy. I always like to think that this medal is a reminder of the unavoidability of justice, an eye for an eye, especially in the air.'

Mathilde examined the profile of Oswald Boelcke on the medal. Then she said, 'Herbert, I can't take this. It's yours. Your son gave it to you.'

'We should have had a son, you and I.'

She gave him a small, odd smile. 'And what do you suppose our son would have been like?'

'A brilliant aviator. The best ever. I would have taught him myself, from birth.'

Mathilde hesitated, and then closed her hand over the medal, accepting it. 'I will treasure it for all of my life, Herbert, and when we meet again in the next life, I will give it back to you, so that no matter what I look like, you will know that it is truly me.'

They said goodbye on the landing, while they waited for the lift. They clung very close to each other. Herbert said, 'Be careful, you're squashing my Imploring Corpse.'

Mathilde would have laughed, but her eyes were filled with tears, and she was too grief-stricken even to speak.

31

Isle of Wight, 1931

Constance said, 'There's been some kind of an accident, darling. I'm sorry. Gerhard Brunner's dead. I had a telephone call from Dickie Morrison less than an hour ago.'

'Oh God,' whispered Herbert. He lowered the telephone earpiece for a moment and held it against his chest. He suddenly felt suffocated, as if somebody were pressing a pillow over his face.

'Are you all right, dear?' said Constance's voice, muffled by his tweed tie.

He lifted the earpiece again. 'Yes. Yes, I'm quite all right. It was a bit of a shock, that's all.'

'Dickie said he was frightfully sorry. You were all in Headmaster's together, weren't you?'

'Yes,' said Herbert. He was standing in the public call-box in the foyer of the Seaview Hotel. Outside the window he could see the seaplane tethered by the pier, rising and dipping in the unseasonable August swell. The sky was the colour of bell-metal, resonant and dark. At any moment, it was going to rain, and rain heavily.

Herbert asked, 'Does anybody know what happened?'

'I don't know whether I ought to tell you on the telephone.'

'Tell me.'

Constance hesitated. Then she said, 'Very well. It appears that he took his own life.'

'He committed suicide?' said Herbert. 'There must be some

32

mistake. Gerhard was very dramatic, but he wasn't the type to commit suicide.'

'Dickie doesn't know much about it, I'm afraid. He had a telegram from Rudi Klinger saying that Gerhard had killed himself. Apparently he was frightfully upset over the loss of *Lorelei IV*. Well, after his divorce from Mathilde, and everything.'

Herbert kept staring at the seaplane. From here, it looked like a tiny silver model. 'Mathilde, yes,' he said, but only because he could sense that Constance was becoming impatient with his continuing silence. A small boy in baggy shorts ran across the promenade outside, carrying a red tin spade and a bucket with printed pictures of seashells on it. What was it that Gerhard had said, all those years ago? *'We are nothing more than frogs who have taught ourselves to leap further.'*

'Do you want me to come down?' Constance asked him.

'Come down?' said Herbert. 'I don't think there's any need for that.'

'I shall if you want me.'

'Don't worry, Connie, it's quite all right. I've got an awful lot of flying to do. I shall only bark.'

'Well, if you're *sure* . . .'

'My darling, I'm quite sure.' He was talking now for the sake of talking. He didn't really want to talk at all. 'It's been a long time since I last saw Gerhard. We weren't exactly bosom chums, you know. Well, not for quite a few years.'

'All right, darling. I must go over to Worthing this afternoon anyway. Janice Blakely is having one of her lifeboat afternoons.'

'That sounds like rather a punishment,' said Herbert, trying to be jocular.

Constance gave a high, throaty laugh. 'Punishments, at least, are usually deserved. I shall probably be relegated to the count-the-lentil stall.'

Herbert said, 'Goodbye, darling. Thank you for calling,' and hung up the receiver before Constance could say anything else. He stood in the phone box with his hand clasped over his mouth until an elderly woman opened the door, and demanded, 'Are you quite finished, young man? I have to call my nephew.'

'Yes,' said Herbert. 'I'm sorry.' He left the phone box and walked across the hotel lobby between yellowing cheese-plants and sullen gangs of ugly leather chairs. On the wall hung a huge oil-painting of the pyramids of Egypt. Herbert had flown over the real pyramids only two years ago in an Imperial Airways Argosy. They had looked nothing like the pyramids in the painting. They had appeared worn-down and broken and ancient to the point of being frightening.

The receptionist looked up as Herbert reached the doorway, and called out shrilly, 'Will you be in for luncheon, Mr Lord? It's mackerel.'

Herbert said, 'What? Yes, probably,' and then hesitated with his hand on the revolving-door.

'We have faggots for those who don't care for fish,' the receptionist enunciated, as if she were practising it for an elocution exam.

'Thank you,' said Herbert, and went outside.

He hesitated for a moment under the hotel awning. The rain blew into his face and he tugged up the collar of his gaberdine raincoat. He felt extraordinary, as if his body had broken up into a jumble of pieces like a broken jug and only his raincoat was holding him together. He crossed the road with his arms held tightly against his chest and his head lowered. A passing Austin made a regurgitating sound with its horn.

He walked along the wet boards of the pier, towards the seaplane. There was hardly anybody on the beach, even though it was still the holiday season. The sand was grey and shiny. A man and a woman huddled with the primitive optimism of Ancient Britons under an arrangement of wet mackintoshes, and a young woman was walking her hysterical Labrador along the shoreline. The sea churned irritably, like an allegory of indigestion, but very rarely broke into spray.

At the end of the pier there was a small red fuel bowser parked, as well as an olive-green van and Herbert's own fawn-coloured Humber Pullman. Richard was standing in the lee of the bowser with his hands in his pockets, chatting to Bryan King-Moreton, who had managed the racing side of things at Lord Aeronautics for almost twenty years; and Wally Field, their chief mechanic. Richard was Herbert's second son, the son who by family consensus didn't look like Herbert one bit. 'Constance's boy,' they always called him, as if somehow Constance had managed to conceive him unaided. He was slightly-built, curly-haired, with protruding ears and delicately-drawn features. He had nothing of Herbert's Saxon solidity. But Herbert often looked at Richard and saw his own expressions looking back at him out of Constance's face, as if Richard were teasing him by wearing a mask.

Two weeks ago, Richard had been twenty-three and Herbert had bought him a second-hand Scott motorbike – partly because he deserved it, after passing his third-year exams in aero-engineering, and partly because he could accompany Herbert whenever he went flying.

As Herbert approached, Richard tugged his hand through his curls and made a sympathetic but discouraging face. 'It doesn't look as if we're going to get any flying in today, Father. Not unless this rainstorm eases off.'

'Afraid Richard's right, old man,' said Bryan King-Moreton. 'We can get her up, of course; but we don't have much hope of setting any records.'

'Bloody wonderful, innit?' Wally Field grinned, with an unlit cigarette end waggling between his lips. He was short, bow-legged, with a topknot of brilliantined hair and skin that had the soft congested texture of a week-old beetroot. 'Yesterday your wevver was perfect, but your engine was running like a tart wiv a metal leg. Now your *engine's* running perfect, and what 'appens? God turns on 'is bleeding 'osepipe and waters the bleeding garden, that's what 'appens. You'd think 'E done it on purpose, wooncha?'

Herbert said, 'Maybe He did. Who are we to question why?'

'Only the poor buggers what's gettin' watered, that's all. I reckon if you put me through the mangle, I'd give you two buckets of blood and six buckets of rain.'

Richard glanced at his father over the raised collar of his raincoat. He had quite deep-set eyes, like his mother, but they were livelier than Constance's; and much more mischievous. For a moment, however, he looked concerned.

'Father? Is everything all right?'

Herbert turned towards the wind. 'What's that? All right, yes, of course. Any reason why they shouldn't be?'

'I don't know,' said Richard. 'It's just that you looked rather down in the mouth, coming up the pier.'

Herbert said, 'Down in the mouth?' as if he had no idea what the words meant. Then he added, almost off-handedly, 'Your mother called. She said that Gerhard Brunner's dead.' Without waiting to hear what any of them thought about that, he turned to Wally and asked, 'Have you finished fuelling yet?'

Richard was astonished. 'That's terrible. You were at school together, weren't you?'

Bryan King-Moreton took his pipe out of his mouth. 'I say, Herbert, what rotten news. But if Brunner's dead, that leaves only the French.'

'That's right,' said Herbert, conclusively. 'That leaves only the French.'

'Did Mother tell you what happened?' asked Richard. He couldn't understand why his father was being so abrupt.

'He took his own life,' Herbert told him. For the first time, he looked them directly in the eye. 'He was divorced from his wife last winter. She went to live with some painter wallah. Yesterday there was a fire at his workshops, and the *Lorelei* was destroyed. He once told me himself that without his wife and his aeroplane, his life wasn't worth living.'

Herbert paused, and then he said, 'Apparently he meant it.'

'That's tragic,' said Richard.

'Yes, but it can't be helped. Wally, what about the fuel?'

Wally shook his head. 'Wasn't sure it was worth it, Mr L. Not until this wevver makes up its bleedin' mind.'

'I told you to fill the aircraft up,' Herbert snapped at him.

'Well, yes,' Wally agreed. 'But there ain't no point in filling 'er up if you ain't gonna fly, is there?'

'Wally,' said Herbert. 'The decision on whether I fly or not is mine and mine alone. It isn't yours. It isn't Mr King-Moreton's. It isn't even Richard's. So when I tell you to fill the aircraft up, I mean fill the bloody aircraft up. Now, get on with it!'

Bryan King-Moreton stood facing the sea with his hands on his hips and his pipe clenched rigidly between his teeth. 'I think the wind's going to give you some trouble, old man,' he remarked, as if he were talking to himself.

'Not more than thirty knots, is it?' Herbert replied.

'Well, no,' Bryan agreed. 'But it is gusting rather nastily, thirty to thirty-five knots. It might give you some difficulties on the turns, especially with a full load of fuel.'

Bryan King-Moreton was an aero-engineer from the pioneer days. Before the war, he had helped Alliott Roe to build the Avro Type F, the world's first totally enclosed aeroplane, and later he had worked with Wilfred Parke and Geoffrey de Havilland at His Majesty's Balloon Factory at Farnborough (soon to become the Royal Aircraft Establishment). He had helped to saw Parke's body out of his wrecked Handley Page at Hendon aerodrome, and when Geoffrey de Havilland had crashed his BS1 scout-plane, Bryan King-Moreton had thoughtfully collected up de Havilland's teeth and sent them to him in an envelope.

He was straight-backed, with bristly white hair and a bristly white moustache. He habitually wore a hacking-jacket and plus-twos and his shoes shone like horse-chestnuts. He was unmarried. His only loves were horses and high-speed aeroplanes.

Richard put in, 'If Brunner's not flying, we hardly need to push ourselves, do we? I mean, the chances are that the French are going to chuck in the towel, too.'

Herbert said, 'It doesn't matter a damn if we're the only plane flying. We're going to make sure that we stretch ourselves to the absolute limit. It's a matter of pride, national and personal pride.'

'Well, one can't argue with that, old man,' said Bryan King-Moreton. 'But it's probably worth waiting on the weather.'

'We can always try again tomorrow, Father,' Richard added.

'We're going up today,' Herbert replied, with deeply-suppressed passion. 'For Gerhard's sake, Richard, if nobody else's.'

Richard held his father's hazel-eyed gaze for a long time. He knew that Herbert wasn't going to be persuaded to call off today's flying, no matter what. In a flat voice, he called to Wally, 'Top her up, would you, Wally? I think we're going to be doing some flying.'

They waited on the drizzle-swept pier while Wally swung the boom which carried the fuel-hose out over the seaplane's fuselage. There were four twenty-five-gallon fuel tanks in front of the cockpit, and they would take at least another quarter of an hour to fill up. Herbert paced up and down with his hands clasped tightly behind his back, occasionally clearing his throat as if he were about to say something. Bryan King-Moreton placidly sucked on his unlit pipe. Richard leaned over the pier railings and watched their motor-boat rise and fall in the tide.

Above them, the clouds gradually began to unravel, and a gleam of washed-out sunlight illuminated the Solent like a painting by Turner, all mist and smoke and extraordinary yellows. The light also touched the silver wings of the seaplane, and ran along its polished fuselage. This was Herbert's fourth racing seaplane, and by far his fastest. He had christened it the *Chichester Special* because it had been built at his new factory just outside Chichester, bringing production of his twin-engined Lord Aquarius to a standstill for almost three months (to the distress of his eldest son James, who was in charge of Aquarius production, and to the tight-lipped horror of his company accountants).

It was the Seraphim Cup he was after – the *Coupe d'Aviation Maritime Jacques Seraphim*, the most prestigious flying trophy in the world. It had been won two years in succession by Britain, and if they won it this year it would remain permanently on its shelf at the Royal Aero Club. The two previous wins had been largely financed by public money, but under Ramsay Mac-Donald's Labour administration, the Air Ministry had refused to provide a single shilling for such élitist activities as air-racing, especially in the middle of a Depression. However – out of an extraordinary combination of patriotism, hardheadedness and vanity, Herbert had designed and built the *Chichester Special* out of his own pocket – or, at least, out of his company's own pocket.

The *Daily Telegraph* had quoted him as saying that 'I am proud to inherit the spirit of my forefathers, who considered one Englishman equal to any three given foreigners.' He would not tolerate 'MacDonald's poisonous doctrine that we are a third-rate power'.

The *Chichester Special* was a single-seat monoplane, its streamlined body made entirely out of thin strips of spruce which had been glued and shaped over a concrete mould – three layers of them altogether – creating a body that was rigid and strong, yet no more than a quarter of an inch thick. The seaplane's final high finish had been created by sandpapering the spruce by hand, then covering it with muslin and lacquering it until it gleamed pearly-silver. It was so smooth that none of the women who had visited Herbert's workshops had been able to resist sliding their hands along it.

The seaplane was powered by a monstrous 2,250-horsepower V-12 engine which grew so hot that Richard had designed a special cooling-system for it – five water-pipes which ran the entire length of the fuselage on either side. All the same, the engine started to overheat after twenty minutes, and in ground tests they had never run it for longer than half an hour, for fear that it would quite literally melt.

Herbert had been confident from the outset, however, that he could complete the required seven laps around the Seraphim course in less than fifty minutes. The course was a triangle, with each side measuring eleven miles, two hundred and thirty-one miles in all. That meant that he would have to fly the *Chichester Special* at an average speed of over three hundred and forty miles an hour, twenty miles an hour faster than the existing world seaplane record.

Wally finished filling the seaplane's fuel tanks, and swung the hose-boom back over the bowser. He climbed back up on to the pier, and announced, 'All yours, Mr L. All topped up and sweet as a nut.'

'Thank you,' said Herbert. A sudden gust of wind blew his hair up on one side, but the rain had blown away now. He took off his raincoat, and handed it to Richard, and then opened up the trunk of his Humber and took out his sheepskin flying-jacket and his goggles. He always wore his thick red woolly hat when he flew.

His mother had knitted it for him when he first took flying lessons, and, ever since he had given his Boelcke medal to Mathilde, it was something of a good-luck charm.

Bryan King-Moreton said, 'You'll watch the temperature, won't you, old man? We don't want to burn out the engine with only two weeks left until race day.'

'Good luck, Father,' said Richard.

'Yes,' said Herbert. He took off his right glove, and shook hands with Bryan, then with Wally, and lastly with Richard. He had never bothered with such formalities before, and they were all slightly embarrassed.

'Richard,' said Herbert. 'I'm relying on you, my boy.'

'Father?' asked Richard, not at all sure what Herbert meant.

'You *can* be relied on, can't you?'

'Well, sir, yes – of course.'

'Good,' Herbert nodded. But he was about to climb down the ladder to the seaplane when a small Austin Tourer drew up with a squeal of brakes at the far end of the pier, and a young man in a trilby hat and a billowing raincoat came running towards them. 'Mr Lord! Mr Lord! Before you go!'

The young man reached the end of the pier out of breath. 'Tommy Thompson, sir. *Daily Herald.* Could you spare a minute, before you take off?'

Herbert scarcely looked at him. 'I'm sorry, I don't talk to the Socialist press.'

'Well, sir, I've driven all the way from London. Hired the ferry specially, just for myself.'

'Am I supposed to be grateful? Or impressed?'

The young man took off his hat and wiped his forehead with the back of his hand. 'It's just that I wanted to ask you one or two questions, sir, about Gerhard Brunner.'

Herbert kept both hands on the ladder. 'I have nothing whatsoever to say about Gerhard Brunner, either to you or to anybody else, but especially not to you.'

'You *do* know what happened?' the young man asked him.

'Yes, I know what happened.' Herbert's voice was completely flat.

'Well, sir, it seems as if the German police are taking quite an interest in it.'

Herbert said, 'I was given to understand that Herr Brunner took his own life.'

'Yes, sir, he did. There's no question about that. But the police are going to investigate what happened to his aeroplane.'

Herbert looked at the young man in silence. Then he said, 'His aeroplane was accidentally set on fire, wasn't it?'

'Set on fire, sir, yes. But the suggestion seems to be that it wasn't an accident.'

'Somebody set fire to it on purpose?' asked Bryan King-Moreton.

'Well *that* don't surprise me one bit,' Wally remarked, with a sniff. 'Bloody Eyeties, I'll bet. Just because their chap Monti got killed, they don't want nobody else to win, neither. Next thing you know, they'll be sniffin' around 'ere, spergetty in one 'and, box o' matches in the uvver.'

Tommy Thompson dug into his sagging raincoat pocket and produced his notebook. 'It wasn't the Italians. The Dutch police arrested some chap in Amsterdam for trying to palm off some diamonds of what you might call doubtful provenance. When they searched his luggage, it turned out that he had maps of Lake Constance and details of how to get to the Brunner seaplane sheds. The chap's in prison now, in The Hague, and the German police are going to send some of their fellows to talk to him.'

Herbert said, 'Well? What is all this to do with me?'

'Well, we were hoping that you could tell *us* that, sir. The fact of the matter is that the chap they arrested was English, with an English passport. He left England two weeks ago, sailing from Harwich to Antwerp on a small ship called the *Dewsbury*. He travelled by train to München and then by car to Lindau. He had a return ticket to sail on the *Dewsbury* back to Dover on the twenty-ninth of the month. He had something else too, sir. A railway ticket to Chichester.'

Herbert gave a furious jerky gesture with his left arm. He was so angry that he had waved his arm three or four times before he was able to speak. 'Clear off!' he shouted. 'You just clear off! I know your sort, I know what you're trying to suggest! You just clear off and – hire your damned ferry back to where you came from!'

'Mr Lord –' Tommy Thompson interrupted, but Herbert stormed across the pier and snatched his notebook and tossed it into the wind. It fell and fluttered and swooped like a wounded seagull, and then dropped into the sea.

'Now you look here!' Tommy Thompson protested. 'The *Herald*'s going to have something to say about this!'

'The *Herald* is a rag that isn't even fit for lighting fires.'

Tommy Thompson tugged down the brim of his hat and looked

at Herbert defiantly. 'You should know all about that, shouldn't you, Mr Lord? What did *you* use? *The Times?*'

Richard grasped Tommy Thompson's arm. 'Come on, you, out of here! One more remark like that and I'll call a policeman! There's such a thing as slander, you know!'

Tommy Thompson shook him off. 'Maybe there is, but there's no law against asking pertinent questions, is there? Or even impertinent questions. *You* ask your Dad a question or two, perhaps he'll answer you, instead of blowing his top. Such as which comes first, his country, his friends, or that shiny cup he wants for his mantelpiece.'

'Come on now, clear off!' Bryan King-Moreton told him.

'I'll clear off when I want, and not before.'

'Wally,' said Herbert, in a voice that made him sound as if he had steel teeth. 'Get this man out of here, before I do him a serious injury.'

Wally advanced on Tommy Thompson with a long hexagonal spanner in his hand and Tommy Thompson immediately retreated. 'You hit me,' he warned, 'and that's assault!' But all the same he backed off along the pier, until he had reached his car. He climbed in, started the engine, and turned around. Before he drove off, however, he poked his head out of the sunroof, and cupped his hands around his mouth so that they could hear him better.

'Richard!' he yelled. 'Don't forget to ask your father what happened to Giovanni Monti!'

Then his little tourer rattled off up the road, and disappeared.

The four of them stood on the pier in the wind. Tommy Thompson's notebook was swirled by the sea and gradually washed up on to the sand. The man who had previously been huddled under his raincoat with his wife walked across and picked it up and turned it this way and that. Then he stood staring up at the pier, as if he were wondering whether he ought to give it back.

Herbert cleared his throat, and said, 'I don't have to tell you what poisonous nonsense that all was. Now, the weather's improving, let's do some flying.'

Bobbing inelegantly up and down on the incoming tide, the *Chichester Special* turned towards the Solent with her engine bellowing and screaming like a dozen competing sawmills. Wally immediately released the mooring-lines: there was no time to be wasted on unnecessary revving-up or chummy waves of farewell. With his hands pressed over his ears, Richard watched the seaplane ski friskily out across the waves, leaving two trails of foam behind her that swirled and turned and then fragmented. Bryan looked down at his stopwatch and said, 'He should be starting his take-off now.'

Almost as if Herbert had been able to hear him, the *Chichester Special*'s engine roared even louder. They could see Herbert's red woolly hat in the cockpit. Herbert raised one hand, signalling that he was ready, and then the seaplane began to speed away from them, kicking up intermittent bursts of spray with its pontoons.

The *Chichester Special* lifted itself out of the water four seconds ahead of time, its wings catching the sudden sun. It rose swiftly up to five hundred feet, angling itself slightly towards the north-east, in the direction of Hayling Island and West Wittering, the sound of its engine swelling and fading in the gusty breeze, swelling and fading, until the seaplane was nothing more than a needle-bright speck against a glaring grey sky.

Richard stood with his hands in his pockets. Wally sniffed. Down below them on the beach, the man had dropped Tommy Thompson's notebook back on to the sand. The weather must have been looking up, because the donkey man appeared, leading two moth-eaten donkeys behind him.

'Sounded sweet,' Richard remarked, meaning the *Chichester Special*'s engine.

'Sweet as a nut,' Wally repeated. 'Only 'ope he don't overrun it, that's all. It's a sod to strip down.'

Bryan was keeping an attentive eye on his stopwatch. 'Five point two-five minutes,' he said. 'We should be hearing him coming back in a moment.' Almost immediately they heard a distant droning over towards the mainland. Bryan let out sharp, high-pitched 'Ha! Ha!' and added, 'Marvellous! Marvellous! He's an ace, your pater, do you know that?'

They waited as the *Chichester Special* droned nearer.

Richard said, 'He had a damned cheek, that *Herald* chap. The way he was talking, anybody would have thought that it was Father's fault the *Lorelei* was destroyed. I mean, almost as if he set light to it personally.'

Wally took his wet, unlit cigarette out of his mouth. 'Trade union paper that, never believed in 'em, me. Not your unions. If a man's worth his salt, then he don't never need no union.'

Bryan was watching Richard keenly. 'You don't think that the pater might have had something to do with it?'

Richard said, 'Of course not, for heaven's sake. Not directly, anyway. But the trouble is, Father's quite a hero. Everybody wants him to win the cup, and this chap they caught in Amsterdam might have thought that he was doing him a favour.'

'The pater believes in fair play,' Bryan commented. 'Well, he does, doesn't he? You can't say he isn't fair, whatever else you want to say about him.'

Richard felt inexplicably unhappy. 'Yes, well of course you're quite right.'

They lifted their heads as the *Chichester Special* came flashing in towards them, its propeller keening, its wings briefly waggling in salute. The seaplane ripped over the beach at well over three hundred miles an hour, then turned and banked over the roof of the Seaview Hotel. Richard could see the red woolly hat, and he waved, even though he knew that his father was unable to wave back. The seaplane's shadow rippled at breakneck speed across the sand and into the sea, like an unhesitating bather. Then Herbert turned away on his second lap, out towards the Channel, leaving nothing behind him but a fading drone, a slight smell of kerosene, and a mounting feeling of real magic.

'Average so far, three hundred and thirty-nine point oh-seven,' Bryan announced. 'That's an unofficial world record.'

'We should of brought champagne,' Wally declared.

'It's a bit premature for that,' said Richard. 'Counting your chickens, and all that.'

'He'll do it,' said Wally, defiantly. 'That engine's running sweet as a nut.'

'Hazel or coco?' Richard teased him.

'Say wotcha like, I'm proud of it,' Wally retorted.

'Come along, we're *all* proud of it,' Richard told him, clapping him on the shoulder. '*Jolly* proud of it. Listen, we've got a few minutes to spare. Why don't you nip down to the end of the pier and have a smoke?'

Wally took the damp cigarette butt out of his mouth and examined it philosophically. Without a word, Richard reached into his pocket and offered him a packet of 10 Kenilworth. Wally looked at the cigarettes as if Richard had performed the Miracle of the Much-Needed Snouts.

'Well, thank *you*, Mr Richard. Don't mind if I do.'

'Take the whole packet, you deserve it. Don't look for the cards, though. I've already taken them out.'

'Not making the cardboard fairground, are we, Mr Richard?'

Bryan said, 'Cut along now, there's a good chap. You haven't got long.'

Wally went down to the beach to smoke, and to talk to the

donkey-man about the spinelessness of Ramsay MacDonald and the price of fags and the fickleness of girls wot you met at the seaside, while Richard and Bryan watched the *Chichester Special* roaring from one corner of the triangular race-course to the other. A small crowd had already gathered on the beach, and every time Herbert came banking over the Seaview Hotel they let out a cheer, and waved their bathing-towels.

Richard didn't find it particularly easy to express his feelings, but after the third lap he managed to say to Bryan, 'I'm pretty worried about Father, to tell you the truth. That news about Gerhard Brunner really seemed to hit him for six.'

Bryan was carefully packing his pipe. It was a ritual. It wouldn't be lit until they were well away from aviation fuel. 'They were chums,' said Bryan, briskly. 'They went to school together; and just after the war they were thick as thieves. The pater's bound to feel cut up, when you think about it.'

'I suppose so,' said Richard. 'But – I don't know. Something seems to be wrong.'

'Wrong?' Bryan frowned. 'Wouldn't have thought so. Don't think the pater's doing much more than behaving like a normal chap for once. And after all, he's entitled to. Just because Herbert Lord is a national hero; just because Harry Harper wrote that book about him, and you can't pick up a single copy of the *Illustrated London News* without seeing something about the *Chichester Special*; that doesn't make him what-d'you-call-it, super-human.'

'I know,' Richard agreed. 'But all the same.'

They heard the *Chichester Special* returning on its last lap. Bryan timed it over the hotel roof. 'Quite a lot slower that time. Three hundred and twenty-eight.'

Richard cupped his hands around his forehead so that he could see against the glare of the sky. The *Chichester Special* was circling around to the south-west, its windshield catching the sun in a sharp heliographic flash. Its engine sounded smooth, but there were twin trails of brown smoke pouring out of its exhausts.

'Overheating,' said Richard. 'He'd better bring her down.'

Wally came hurrying bow-legged along the pier to join them. 'He'd better not bollox up my crankshaft,' he said, blowing out a last nostrilful of smoke.

'Don't worry, he'll bring her down,' said Richard. And he lifted both arms in the pre-arranged signal to 'come on in'.

The *Chichester Special* turned and dipped; but then to Richard's surprise it abruptly angled away from them, and began to climb.

'What the bloody 'ell's 'e up to?' Wally demanded. 'Woss 'e tryin' to do, bugger it up good and proper?'

Richard said nothing, but watched with an inexplicable feeling of dread as the *Chichester Special* rose higher and higher, trailing sepia-coloured smoke behind it, until it was well over a thousand feet above the sea.

Herbert lifted his goggles and looked out over the tilted edge of the cockpit with his eyes slitted against the buffeting slipstream. From here, he could see the cloud-dappled stretches of the Solent, and the hills and the fields and the twisting white roads of the Isle of Wight, more like an illustration in a child's picture-book than a real island. If it hadn't been so hazy, he might even have been able to see his own house, a few miles north-west of Chichester, where Constance was now preparing herself for her 'lifeboat afternoon'. Poor Connie.

Herbert glanced at himself in the cockpit mirror. His face was grey with oil from the seaplane's exhausts, although his eyes were circled white because they had been protected by his goggles. A pierrot's mask, he thought. Highly appropriate for my last performance.

The *Chichester*'s engine was surging unhealthily, but Herbert continued to climb. He could tell by the smoke that was blowing past him that the bearings were burning out, and that it was only a matter of a minute or two before the engine would pack up completely, and (at this rate of climb) the seaplane would stall dead. From nearly a thousand feet in the air, the surface of the ocean would be as unyielding as concrete.

He had decided to 'end it all' while he was walking along the pier. It hadn't been a difficult decision to make. Nor, to Herbert, had it been new or unexpected. In many ways, he felt that suicide, or at least self-sacrifice, had been the inevitable conclusion to his life ever since he was born. His mother had been crippled giving birth to him. She had been in labour for twenty-eight hours, and she had never walked again. Something to do with the spinal column. His father had never spoken the accusation out loud, but he had always treated Herbert with frigid exactness, and would never allow him to push his mother's wheelchair.

Francis, his older brother, had always been the favourite, 'our adorable Francis', and in his adolescent years Herbert had sometimes believed that the only way in which he could redeem himself was to die. Then, at last, his father would be sorry.

Instead of cutting his throat, however, Herbert had courted

Constance Holland, the daughter of a local Justice of the Peace, and escaped from home at the age of twenty-one. Dear, sweet, honourable Constance. A wife without fault, a mother without peer, and a woman whom Herbert could never truly love. For the rest of his life, Herbert had found himself catching the eyes of pretty young girls, and wishing that he had married them, *any* of them, instead of Constance.

During the war, Francis had volunteered to go to France with the Royal Flying Corps, while Herbert had stayed in England, working on S. E.5s at the Royal Aircraft Factory. One day in 1915 he had taken the boys down to Chichester for the weekend and found the house in mourning. Francis had been shot down and killed. Herbert's father had stood in the hallway and whispered, 'Why *him*, dear God, and not you?'

And then Herbert had fallen in love with Mathilde. An impossible, ridiculous love; a fantasy that could never be fulfilled; an adolescent love of nuance and perfume and erotic dreams. And now Mathilde was gone, too, living with her Teutonic painter in Koblenz. *Ich habe mein Herz in Koblenz verloren* . . .

But, more than anything, it was the burning of *Lorelei IV* that had finally brought Herbert face to face with his failure. He had sent James to Lindau late in April to watch the *Lorelei* being tested. James, with binoculars and a stop-watch, had reported by telegram that Gerhard was daily flying at speeds in excess of three hundred and seventy-five knots. Last month, after hurried refitting, Herbert had realized for certain that the *Chichester Special* was incapable of more than three hundred and sixty knots, flat-out.

The day after, Captain O. P. Jones of Imperial Airways had met Herbert in the foyer of the Royal Aero Club, right beside the Seraphim Cup. He had clapped Herbert on the back, and said, 'We're all counting on you, Lord old boy. If we have to send the Seraphim back to Germany, where are we going to hang our hats?'

It was for Empire, Herbert had persuaded himself. *It was for England.* But instead of being temporarily disabled, the *Lorelei* had been gutted completely, and Gerhard had killed himself, so that even if nobody found out what Herbert had done, and he won the Seraphim Cup unchallenged, it would always be tarnished with the blood of his friend. Gerhard at last had got his revenge.

As far as Herbert was concerned, there was only one way in which his cowardice and his dishonour could be wiped from the slate. To take his own life – and to destroy the *Chichester Special* at the same time, so that Britain would be unable to enter for the Seraphim Cup.

The *Chichester*'s engine began to blurt out more smoke. The bulkhead in front of him was so hot that Herbert felt as if he had his feet in the fireplace. He climbed and turned and climbed and turned and the sunlight dazzled and died with every turn.

Herbert could picture Mathilde, staring at herself with fascination in his hand-mirror. She had given him that moment as a poignant memento; a picture that would remain in his mind as long as he lived; un-photographed, but as vivid today as the instant it had happened. He could see it now: the morning sunlight on her hair, the twin moles on the side of her neck, the curve of her shoulders. And, in the mirror, the glistening pink petals of her private flower, a gift that he had never been able to forget.

For no reason at all, Herbert began to recite Kipling.

'I've taken my fun where I've found it,
And now I must pay for my fun.'

At a little under thirteen hundred feet, when it was silhouetted against the altocumulus like a crucifix, the seaplane's engine cut out.

Richard was standing at the very end of the pier. His hands were raised in a curious gesture as if he were about to swallow-dive off. The sea slapped against the pilings, and burst into handfuls of brightly-polished florins. Bryan King-Moreton stood two or three feet behind him, with his cap off, his face stiff with disbelief.

Wally had sidled away, as if he already knew what was about to happen, and didn't want to be standing too close to Richard when his father was killed in front of his eyes.

There was a moment when the whole seaside world seemed empty and silent, as if fate couldn't decide what to do next.

Then the *Chichester Special* exploded, in a burst of pale fire. Its wings circled away, spinning like sycamore seeds. Its fuselage and its pontoons tumbled end-over-end, blazing fiercely. And amidst all of its pieces, there was a darker shape, dropping, mercifully not burning, and that was Herbert Lord, the lord of the air, Constance's husband, father of James, Richard, and Michael, one-time lover of Mathilde, friend of Gerhard, falling one thousand three hundred feet to the shining surface of the sea.

'Cheese and crust,' whispered Wally, although neither of the other two could hear him. The sound of the explosion reached them like a distant slap.

Richard watched the fragments of the *Chichester Special* drop one by one into the Solent. He was already thinking to himself: *why me, I'm the middle son, why does this have to happen to me?* Because in some obscure way he knew that his mother would blame him for it. *You were there. You were* there. *Why didn't you take better care of him?*

On the beach, the crowds who had been cheering Herbert as he flew overhead now stood hushed. The seaplane's wings were the last to fall. Then there was nothing but oil and wreckage on the waves, and the breeze fitfully blowing from the south-west. Bryan turned to Richard and he was white. 'We'd better get the boat out,' he said.

Richard couldn't take his eyes away from the sea.

'Wally, get the boat out,' said Bryan, and when Wally hesitated, 'there's a good man.'

Richard slowly shook his head. 'He did that on purpose,' he said, in a papery voice.

Bryan King-Moreton was trying very hard to stay rational. 'You can't say that, Richard. You can't know for sure. He climbed for a reason. You know the pater, he wouldn't have climbed without a reason.'

But Richard kept on shaking his head. 'He did it in on purpose. He knew the engine was overheating. He knew it would stall. He should have brought her in straight away.'

'Richard –' said Bryan.

'What?' said Richard. He was barely coherent. All he could think of was the dark shape of his father's body, dropping amidst the burning debris of the *Chichester Special*, not yet dead then, but far beyond any kind of saving.

Bryan grasped Richard's arm. 'Richard, listen to me. It was an accident.'

'No, it couldn't have been,' Richard protested. 'Bryan, it couldn't have been.'

Bryan said, 'Richard. Listen. It was an accident. Think of the publicity, for goodness' sake. The *Herald* will make an absolute meal out of it.'

Richard suddenly understood what Bryan was saying. He took off his motorcycling cap and stood bare-headed in the wind. Below the pier, Wally was bringing the motor-boat around to the steps. A policeman was hurrying towards them, his helmet couched under his arm. The crowd on the beach milled around helplessly. Some of them were crying.

'I'd better go and telephone Mother,' said Richard.

'Let me,' Bryan suggested.

'No, no, it's perfectly all right. Please. I'm perfectly all right.'

Neither of them moved. It was almost as if they were reluctant to carry on with their lives, after what had happened; as if Herbert's death should have been more spectacular and more prolonged – as if there should have been dramatic music of the kind they would have heard in the cinema. It had all been over so quickly. The sea was still churning, the clouds were still serenely disassembling themselves in preparation for a sunny teatime. Everything was as exactly as it had been five minutes before, when Herbert Lord had still been alive.

'You'd better ring James and Michael, too,' said Bryan.

Richard clasped his hand over his mouth and couldn't reply.

London, 1931

James had taken Lady Sheffield for the 3s 6d lunch at the Café Royal. Now they were lying side by side in a room at Brown's, with the curtains drawn, smoking cigarettes and talking teasingly about the difference in their ages.

The room was stuffy with the smell of dust and sex. James's shirt-collar curved up from the back of the chair like a beckoning lobster-claw. He hoped he hadn't lost his front collar-stud.

Susan Sheffield said, in her clear, unmodulated voice, 'You don't even remember the day they opened Selfridge's, now do you?'

James blew out a long stream of smoke. 'I don't suppose you do, either.' He knew she did, or she wouldn't have mentioned it; but it must have been sometime in 1907 or 1908 – well before the war, anyway.

'I was eleven, as a matter of fact,' Susan retorted. 'Mummy took me to see it the very first day. It was a great thing because there was a soda fountain, and the girls who operated the lifts used to wear this extraordinary uniform like a riding-habit.'

James rolled over and crushed out his cigarette. Then he rolled back again and propped his chin on his hand and stared at Susan in close-up. So close, in fact, that she shifted herself two or three inches away, because she was long-sighted, and couldn't focus on his face.

'What do you want for a wedding-present?' she asked him, trying to put him off-guard.

'A hot water-bottle,' he smiled.

'Pff,' she said, blowing out smoke; and then quickly stubbing out her cigarette, too. 'You'll have Henrietta to keep you snug.'

James watched her in amusement. He didn't love her. He wasn't even infatuated with her. But he liked her very much. He had always liked her, ever since the inauguration of Croydon Aerodrome in 1921, when *he* was sixteen and she was just two months married to Lieutenant Colonel Rodney Sheffield, OBE, AFC.

Rodney was now *Sir* Rodney; and Director of Civil Aviation. This meant that James's occasional affair with 'the Director's missus', as he liked to call her, afforded him very much more than sophisticated company and ardent sexual pleasure. He could also enjoy the small smugness of being able to think whenever he lunched with Sir Rodney that his detailed knowledge of Sir Rodney's wife was far greater than Sir Rodney's detailed knowledge of civil aviation; and he could get to hear about any new Air Ministry research before any of his competitors.

In James's view, social superiority was measured not in knighthoods, but in Having An Edge. Sir Rodney had been honoured by the King; but James knew that his wife had a pattern of moles on the inside curve of her left buttock which (when he joined them together with the trembling nib of an Owl, with her pubic hair tickling his knuckles) formed a perfect hexagon.

James was twenty-six, Herbert Lord's oldest son, and he looked so much like Herbert that people had frequently mistaken them for brothers, and even for each other. Like Herbert, James was solid, broadly-built, with a square Celtic forehead and a firm cleft jaw; and he had inherited from Herbert that thick light-brown hair whose waves defied even Vaseline Hair Tonic.

Like Herbert, James was susceptible to devastatingly strong feelings. Anger, jealousy, self-righteousness. Heroism, sometimes, of the story-book kind. But unlike his father, he was able to contain his feelings, quite tightly. He had a habit of keeping his eyes lowered when he spoke, which women found intriguing, but which often gave the impression to his business partners that he was lacking in conviction, or that he wasn't listening. In fact, he lowered his eyes to keep his emotions to himself.

Susan said, 'You're thinking again.'

'Perhaps,' James said, guardedly.

'There's no *perhaps* about it. You're *always* thinking. I've never known a man think so much. You should think a lot less. You should go to more parties. You should come to the Kit Kat with me; or the Embassy. I'll tell you what – we'll go to the Four Hundred tomorrow night. I'll drag Rodney along, and you bring Henrietta, and then we'll swap partners and dance together in the dark. Wouldn't *that* be exciting?'

James said nothing, but kissed her, and smiled.

She lay back on the pillow. She was very thin, but very striking, rather Grecian – or at least an Art Deco version of Grecian. Her hair was dark and wavy, her nose was straight, her lips were perfect bows. Although she was thirty-four, she was still considered by the daily newspapers to be one of the Bright Young Things. Roedean, Lausanne, Madame Vacani's, and then a coming-out that the *Daily Mail* had described as 'Extravagant with a capital X'.

She was pale-skinned, very nearly breastless, with dark sloping nipples. Her pelvic bones were so prominent that they sometimes felt like the jawbones of prehistoric creatures. But she had such sexual intensity that James had once told her that she could make the mattress-springs glow as brightly as the elements of huge Osram light-bulbs; and she let out extraordinary operatic shrieks whenever she made love; *Alfredo, Alfredo, di questo cuore . . . !* After an hour with Lady Susan Sheffield any man could walk with a self-confident strut, and preen his buttonhole, and smile at everybody he met.

'I'm thirsty,' she said.

'Gin?' he asked her. He was teasing her about her recent appearance in a Gordon's Gin advertisement. 'Lady Susan Sheffield says "A good cocktail *must* be made with Gordon's Gin."' It was all the rage for young society ladies to endorse products in the newspapers. This was despite the fact that Susan never touched gin.

'Champagne, of course. And then let's drive down to Cuckoo Weir and have a swim.'

James kissed her smooth, ivory-coloured forehead. 'Father's expecting me home tonight. He's been testing his new seaplane today, at the Isle of Wight. He's bound to have cracked at least one record. You know what he's like. The Malcolm Campbell of aviation. He always likes to have everybody around him, to tell him how marvellously well he's done.'

Susan hesitated for a moment. Then – when it became clear that James wasn't going to get out of bed to pour her a glass of champagne – she climbed out of bed herself and walked like a modern naked gazelle to the sitting-room, skinny, stilt-legged, where she lifted the bottle of Bollinger out of the ice-bucket and filled up their recently-abandoned glasses.

James rolled over to watch her. She wasn't his type, physically, but she was always marvellous to look at. With every tiptoeing step she looked as if she were about to launch into a Diaghilev ballet.

'He won't miss you, will he, if you don't turn up?' Susan asked him.

'Of course he'll miss me!' James retorted. Then, when Susan held his glass of champagne just out of reach. 'He'll miss me, I assure you. If it hadn't been for me, he wouldn't have stood a chance of winning the Seraphim Trophy.'

'He *is* going to win it?'

James took his champagne, and then kissed her. 'Of course he's going to win it. Pater wins everything, by hook or by crook.'

'And you?'

He touched her bare neck. 'I win everything, too. It's just that I don't feel the same urgent need as he does to tell the world about it. He's ten per cent hero and ninety per cent advertisement.'

'But you love him?'

James spilled champagne on his chest, and wiped it with a corner of the sheet.

'That's an extraordinary question.'

Susan slid her hands through his hair, and kissed him bow-lipped. 'I am an extraordinary woman.'

'Talking of you being extraordinary,' James said, as they climbed into her shiny cream-and-chocolate AC coupé, 'I was wondering if you'd been extraordinary enough to overhear the Director talking about night navigation.'

'James! What an odd thing to ask me! Night navigation? With what? Or why? Or whom?'

'With anyone. With the boffins at the Air Ministry, most of all.'

She opened her brown crocodile handbag and fished out her ignition keys. 'I'm beginning to think that you only make love to me so that you can pick Gordon's brains.'

James took the keys, kissed her on the cheek, and started up the engine. 'Great West Road, here we come!' he announced, sticking his hand out to indicate that he was pulling away from the curb. He glanced at the newsboy standing on the corner of Dover Street, but his mind was so preoccupied with talking to Susan that he completely failed to grasp the significance of the placard reading SEAPLANE DAREDEVIL KILLED.

'The thing is,' he said, 'the ability to fly accurately at night is the absolute key to the future of commercial aviation. Airlines can't even think of breaking even unless they can keep their aeroplanes flying all around the clock. They're competing with night-sleepers on the railways, don't you see, not just for passengers but for mail and freight.'

Susan knotted her scarf under her perfect chin. 'Why do you *always* have to talk about work? It makes me suspect that you don't really love me at all.'

'Did I ever say that I *did*?'

'You're a beast.'

He laid his hand high on her thigh, steering the sixteen-horse-power coupé with one hand. Her skin was warm through her thin silk dress and her thin silk slip. He could feel the rubbery protuberance of a suspender-button.

'I hope you're not forgetting that I'm betrothed,' he told her.

'You never let me.'

They drove around Hyde Park Corner under a sky that had grown unnaturally black. It was one of those evenings when you felt that God was feeling bitter and out-of-sorts, and that He was searching through His store-cupboard for a suitable calamity. They were trapped in Knightsbridge for a while by a herd of shining, shuddering taxis, but once they had passed Brompton Oratory the traffic thinned out, and James could put his foot down.

'I did hear Rodney having a chinwag about night flying with Norris Phelps,' Susan volunteered.

'Oh, yes?'

Susan lit two Craven-As at once, and passed one over to James so that he wouldn't have to take his hands off the wheel. 'Rodney was saying he preferred something called a Leda cable, but I'm not at all sure what that is. It sounds like a telegram warning young women to stay away from swans.'

James smiled, and nodded. 'I thought as much. Leader cables, "-er" not "-a". They're pretty hush-hush at the moment, but I've been hearing one or two interesting things about them.'

'They didn't sound at *all* interesting. Not from what Rodney was saying.'

'Well, of course they didn't to *you*. All you're interested in is nightclubs and fast company and how to mix American cocktails.'

'Brute.'

James glanced at her sideways and winked at her. 'A leader cable is a wire that's buried in the ground all the way around an aerodrome. It sends a current upward into the air, and that current is picked up by instruments in the aeroplane's cockpit, so that even in the dark, or thick fog, a pilot knows that he's close to his destination. He follows the cable round and round, flying lower all the time, until he can see the aerodrome with his own eyes.'

'And why is it so frightfully important that you know what Rodney thinks about them?'

'Because I've been trying to develop something similar for the aeroplanes that *we've* been building. And if Rodney thinks they're a jolly good idea, then our chances of winning more orders from Imperial Airways is going to be greatly improved. There's no chance, I suppose, that Rodney might have some kind of report on them knocking around his study?'

'I suppose he might. You're not seriously suggesting I steal it for you? That would be theft.'

'Oh, come on, Mrs Director; it would only be borrowing. Can you think of anything more romantic?'

'Yes, as a matter of fact I darn well can.'

They blared down the Great West Road at nearly ninety. The wind whistled past the windscreen and buffeted their ears. Speed limits had been lifted completely last year, and the roads out of town had become a racetrack for any Bright Young Thing with an urge for danger and the fast car with which to satisfy it. A friend of Lady Marguerite Strickland had been killed last month, deliberately driving on the wrong side of the road as he negotiated the curving road around Godalming.

James drove well but never allowed his foot up off the floor. They zipped around curves on squealing tyres and catapulted over humpback hills regardless of what they might meet on the other side.

It began to rain a little, only a few warm spots but enough to make the concrete road surface slippery. As they approached Windsor, and turned off towards Cuckoo Weir, James took the AC into a long sideways slide, and only just managed to straighten it out with a sharp snaking twist of the wheels.

Susan gasped; and as soon as James had parked the coupé under the overhanging elms close to the weir and tugged up the hand-brake, she reached out for him and kissed him ferociously as a cannibal. She was breathless and trembling with fear and excitement. To think that they might have rolled right over and been killed, and the coroner would have discovered from her body that only two hours before she had had sexual intercourse with a man not her husband! James kissed her back, but she was too excited to let him take control of her, and she bit his lips and his tongue until he could taste blood.

They took off their clothes and swam naked. Susan kept on her heavy silver bracelets and her silver Egyptian necklace and her long pendant earrings. Although it was only half-past ten in the evening the weir was deserted. Their pale bodies gleamed under the greenish water. Occasionally their hands splashed on the still surface.

Susan swam close to James and touched his shoulder. 'I'm cold, let's go in.'

James caught hold of her and kissed her. 'If the Director could see his missus now.'

'He would probably sigh, that's all, and tell me that my side-stroke needs improving.'

They waded on to the bank. 'He can't be *completely* sexless,' James remarked

'He isn't, but he thinks about sex only about as much as he thinks about buying new socks. He's one of these men who believes that as soon as you're married, that's *that* all over with. I tried to suggest something a little different to him once – "Perhaps, Rodney, if I were to turn my back, and you were to – ?" And do you know he stared at me like the dog with eyes as big as cart-wheels for what seemed like ten whole minutes, and then he said, "Susan, are you quite mad?"'

'What did you do?'

'I cried. Then I laughed.'

James took two borrowed hotel towels out of the dicky, and quickly rubbed Susan dry. She was shivering and goose-bumpy; her hair hung in rat's-tails. but he kissed her chilly lips and felt her knurled-up nipples against his chest and thought to himself that he would probably never meet another woman quite like this; and not simply because there *wasn't* another woman quite like this.

They dressed. Their clothes felt sticky and awkward because their skin was still wet. It was only when they were folding their towels and climbing back into the car that a boy appeared, quite suddenly, out of the darkness. He was wearing a floppy cap and enormous flannel shorts that looked as if he had only recently inherited them from an older brother.

'Well, hullo,' said Susan.

The boy stared back at her with hostility. 'Hullo yourself,' he retorted. Then he added, 'Flat bum.'

James and Susan watched him walk off into the evening, open-mouthed. It had never occurred to them while they were swimming that they might have been watched. Susan said, 'Well! Of all the nerve!' Then she clambered up on to her seat and shouted shrilly after him, 'My bum is jolly well *not* flat!'

When she received no reply, she screamed even more ferociously, 'Droopy drawers!'

James laughed so much that he couldn't find the ignition. He leaned forward on the steering-wheel with his face covered in his hands, and laughed until he gave himself a stitch. 'Oh, God!' he gasped. 'Oh, God, you mustn't! The doyenne of café repartee! The woman with an answer to everything! The lady who called Bernard Shaw "the male muffin" to his face!'

Susan slapped his shoulder crossly. 'What else do you say to a rude young urchin like that? And he was *looking*!' She sat down in her seat, and folded her arms, and said, 'I suppose you *agree* with him.'

'About what?'

'About my flatness,' Susan snapped.

James wiped his eyes and started up the engine. 'Let's get back to London before you get it into any more arguments. I don't think my heart can stand the strain.'

It was shortly after midnight when he arrived by taxi back at Iverna Court, the large block of red-brick Edwardian flats just off Kensington High Street which was the Lords' *pied à terre* whenever they were in town. As soon as he rattled open the lift-gate, he could hear the telephone ringing inside the flat. He unlocked the door and switched on the light. It was probably Susan calling him to let him know that she had got home safely. He walked across the hall and picked the telephone up, inspecting himself in the mirror as he did so. His hair had dried in the wind on the way back along the Great West Road, and was fluffed-up like a dancing-master's wig. He didn't know how Susan had managed to keep a straight face when she kissed him goodnight.

'Hello, my little mermaid,' he said, warmly. 'Everything tickety-boo?'

'James?' replied a distant, strained voice.

'Richard?' frowned James. 'What's up? Don't you know what time it is?'

'Of course I know what time it is, I've been trying to call you all evening.'

'What's wrong?'

'Haven't you heard? It's in all the newspapers; and they've had it on the wireless, too.'

James knew then what Richard was going to say. He remembered with sudden clarity the news placard in Dover Street, even though he had passed it by without even reading it. SEAPLANE. KILLED.

Richard said, 'There was an accident: the *Chichester Special* broke up. Father was killed straight away.'

James watched himself in the mirror. It was quite surprising to see the tears shine brightly in his eyes. 'I'll come down at once,' he said. 'How did Mother take it?'

'Well, how do you think? Dr Hallett's been round, he's given her something to calm her down.'

'And how are you?' James asked him.

'Me? I'm all right. Still shocked. I called Michael; he's coming down tomorrow.'

'Have you any idea what happened?'

'I don't know. We haven't been able to salvage very much. It blew up, that's all. Wally thinks it could have been a faulty fuelline.'

They talked a little longer and then James hung up. He stood for a moment in the hallway, with his hands by his sides. Then he went through to the sitting-room, switched on the light, and went across to the drinks table to pour himself a large whisky.

He had never imagined what life would be like without his father. Herbert Lord had always been such a dominant presence in the lives of his family and friends that it seemed almost absurd that he should suddenly not be there any more. It was almost like driving through Hyde Park and finding that Apsley House had disappeared overnight.

James went across to the bureau, where there was a small collection of family photographs in silver frames. At the back stood a small oval snapshot of his father, taken with a Kodak Brownie, laughing. James remembered the day when that photograph had been taken, a windy afternoon on the beach at Ryde.

He picked up the photograph and stared at it for a long time, sipping his whisky.

'You silly bugger,' he whispered. 'You silly, selfish bugger.'

But Herbert Lord carried on laughing; the beach continued to be bright; a small yacht leaned against the wind, and always would. The telephone rang again. James put down the photograph and walked stiffly out to the hallway. It was Susan.

'You're home safe?' he asked her.

'Yes, my darling, but Bunty Kennard called. She told me what had happened to your father. You do know, don't you?'

'Yes,' said James, flatly.

'Oh, my sweetness, I'm so sorry. Is there anything at all I can do?'

'I don't think so,' said James. 'Thank you for offering. I'll call you next week, if I may. I expect I'll be quite busy for the next week or so.'

'You're all right, though?' Susan asked him.

'Yes,' said James. 'I'm all right.'

Cambridge, 1931

Michael had never drunk so much gin in his life with such little apparent effect. At five o'clock, he was still sitting in his digs with a half-empty bottle of Gordon's on the table in front of him, his wind-up gramophone playing Debussy's *Pavane pour une enfante défunte* over and over again, and yet he felt utterly sober, his grief as raw and as fresh as a furious toothache.

The record came to a crackling finish, and he stood up to put it on yet again, lurching slightly, and tipped his bentwood chair over backwards. As he did so, there was a brisk postman's knock at the door, and a curly ginger head appeared. 'Michael? It's Dennis. Are you all right, old boy?'

Michael flapped both arms in a gesture of frustration and uselessness. 'Right as rain, Dennis. Right as rain.'

Dennis wrinkled up his nose and peered myopically across the room at the bottle of gin. 'I heard about your pater,' he remarked. 'I just wanted to make sure that you weren't moping.'

Michael wound up the gramophone, and settled the steel needle into the groove. Dennis, still leaning half-in and half-out of the door, listened for a while, and then remarked, 'That's a jolly miserable tune, if you don't mind my saying so.'

'Dance for a defunct infant,' said Michael. 'It's the only miserable tune I've got. You can't play the Hokey-Cokey when your father's just been killed, can you?'

Dennis thought for a moment, and then said, 'D'you mind if I . . .?' and nodded towards the gin, making a jiggling drinking gesture with his fingers.

'Come on in,' Michael invited him. 'I'm tired of being an orphan all on my own.' Only when he heard himself saying that did he realize how squiffy he was. 'Pull up a – piano stool.'

Dennis closed the door behind him and came across the room briskly rubbing his hands. 'I suppose you're going straight back to Chichester.'

'Well, I would have gone straight away. I *should* have gone straight away. But I couldn't actually face the thought of sitting in a train – you know, well, feeling so depressed.' He swallowed, and then he added, 'I just wanted to sit here for a while and think about it on my own.'

'I suppose your mater's been hit for a boundary.'

'Yes, I suppose she has.'

Dennis poured himself a generous gin in a pale blue teacup, and swallowed almost half of it straight down. 'I remember when our dog died. When was that? Last year sometime. The whole family went around in mourning for weeks. Well, he was a jolly good dog. He could fetch eggs in his mouth without breaking them. Most of the time, anyway.'

'Yes,' said Michael solemnly. 'My father could do that, too.'

It took a moment for Dennis to work out what Michael had said. Then he stared at him in a mixture of horror and surprise.

Micahel laughed, and then just as abruptly stopped laughing. 'No, it's not funny, is it? It's just that nobody tells you how you ought to behave when your father dies. Come to that, nobody tells you how you ought to behave when he's alive. He was quite a hero, you know, but I can't say that we knew each other terribly well. We weren't – comrades, if that's the word for it.'

Dennis finished his gin, and wiped his mouth with his handkerchief. 'I shouldn't have drunk that. I've got a tutorial in twenty minutes.'

'Who with?'

'Old Dukey, and I've run out of peppermints.'

Michael shook his head. 'Don't go, that's the answer. Stand him up! Any tutor who can't stand a bit of gin on a chap's breath isn't fit for the job. Come flying with me.'

'Flying? I hope you're pulling my leg. You're drunk as a lord.'

'Ha, ha!' said Michael. 'I *am* a Lord. And the Lords were born to fly. Drunk or sober, in sickness or in health. The Aero Club bought a new Moth last month. Well, not brand new, of course, but it's in first-rate order. Let's take it up! I can show you the sun going down over Wandlebury Ring.'

'Well, I don't think so,' said Dennis. But Michael slapped him on the back, and grasped his shoulder, and shook him with affectionate enthusiasm, as if he were shaking a puppy.

'Enough misery!' he declared. 'The best way to get over all this is to commune with the sky!' He reached over and took off the Debussy record, with a loud scratching noise.

Dennis looked distinctly unhappy. 'You really are a bit pi-eyed, old boy. Don't you think it would be better if we just communed with the ground?'

'Rot,' Michael retorted, dragging his scarf from the hook on the back of the door. 'And don't forget to bring the gin.'

The afternoon was fresh and sunny as they puttered out to the Cambridge Aero Club in Dennis's 8½ hp Gwynne cyclecar. Michael was sitting with his arms tightly crossed, puffing his pipe. He felt wonderfully light-headed, full of that buoyancy that gin can bring before the sun disappears behind the clouds and the balloons sink to the floor and the dance-music goes off-key.

'You're certain you're not too squiffy?' asked Dennis, for the fifth time.

'Squiffy?' Michael exclaimed. 'Don't know the meaning of the word! Turn left here, it's quicker.'

Michael was twenty-and-a-half, a slightly skinnier version of James, with darker eyes and gangling wrists and ankles. Last half, he had taken to brushing his hair straight back from his forehead in the style of Robert Donat, and he had also grown himself a small thin moustache. He always carried his meerschaum pipe around with him these days and annoyed almost everybody he knew by sprinkling spent matches all over their lawns and their cars and their carpets, and gouging out dottle into their potted plants. After he had taken to wearing a brown corduroy waistcoat,

Herbert had been quite worried in case his son was turning into a Socialist.

'Father, I'm *not* a Socialist.'

'And I'm not a Bombay lascar, but at least I don't go about dressed like one.'

Like most younger brothers, Michael was considered by James and Richard to be utterly irresponsible and exasperating, and most of the time he was; but at the same time he had managed not to lose that impertinent appeal that comes from being Mummy's last and favourite boy. He was still reading mechanical science at Cambridge, but he loved parties, and sports, and whenever he wasn't flying with the Cambridge Aero Club or the University Air Squadron he went home to Chichester to sail his dinghy and play tennis.

He had been closer to his mother than his father, but when Richard had telephoned him just after lunch to tell him that Herbert was dead he had felt as if his whole life had cracked in half.

They arrived at the aerodrome shortly after six. The wind-stocking wagged an admonishing red finger towards the north-east. Dennis drove the cyclecar over the tufty grass, and drew up outside the hangar. A Bristol biplane was circling over the trees above the far end of the field, making a lonely droning noise. Michael knocked his pipe on the running-board of Dennis's car, and climbed out. 'Bring the gin, but keep it under your coat,' he instructed.

Dennis reluctantly followed him into the hangar.

It was gloomy inside, and smelled of dope and aviation spirit and musty old sheds. The club's latest acquisition, the De Havilland Moth, was parked right in the front, its nose shining with fresh pale-blue paint. Michael patted it with satisfaction, and then walked across to the office, where a white-haired man with a beaky nose and oil-stained overalls was staring intently at nothing at all and drinking a mug of scalding-hot tea.

'Hullo, Ben!' said Michael. 'Haven't booked or any of that rot, but what about taking the Moth up for a spin?'

Ben kept staring at nothing at all, but slowly shook his head. 'Sorry, Mr Lord. Mr Jennings has booked her for har-pass six.'

Michael lifted his wristwatch and frowned at it. 'It's only just gone six now. I could take her up and bring her down again and he wouldn't even know the difference. Warm her up for him. He'd probably be pleased.'

Ben continued to shake his head and stare. 'He'd be hoppen

mad, that's what he'd be. It 'ud take me another quarter of an hour to top her up again, wooden it? And Mr Jennings always likes to fly punctual. Har-pass six to har-pass seven, then home to Church End in time for his supper.'

Just then, the biplane that had been circling the far end of the airfield floated down to land, its engine burping, its propeller shining in the late afternoon sunshine.

'You'll have to excuse me now, Mr Lord,' said Ben. He set down his mug of tea on top of a table that had already been circled by hundreds of mugs of tea, and pushed past Michael and Dennis with that same stare in his eyes. 'Sounds like Mr Borrowman's having trouble again.'

They watched him walk out across the grass. 'Well,' said Dennis with undisguised relief, 'that rather puts paid to that, doesn't it?'

Michael slapped him on the back. 'Nothing of the kind! The Moth's all ready for Jenners to take her up, all fuelled up! All we have to do is hop in and away we go.'

'You're mad! That's stealing!'

'Don't be such a weed, it's not stealing at all. It's borrowing. Stealing something is to take it away with the intention of permanently depriving the owner of its use. We'll be back in twenty minutes. Just a quick flip over the Gog Magogs, and back to base.'

'It's out of the question,' Dennis protested.

'Dennis,' said Michael, 'I've had a bad knock today. I want to fly.'

'Well, yes, I know, but –'

'But what? Are you my friend or aren't you?'

'Of course I'm your friend,' Dennis declared. 'And don't try to prove me otherwise!'

'I won't,' said Michael. 'All you have to do is climb into the cockpit, and when I swing the propeller, you turn on the ignition switch. What could be easier than that?'

Dennis said, 'I can't do it. Michael, I simply can't do it.'

Michael grasped hold of Dennis's arms, and looked at him as reprovingly as Lord Kitchener's recruiting poster. 'Dennis, you can, and you will. If you're such a jolly fine friend of mine, then prove it.'

Dennis licked his lips and looked anxiously up at the Moth's cockpit. 'All right,' he said at last. 'But no aerobatics. No flying upside-down, or any of that kind of thing.'

Michael glanced quickly out at the airfield. 'Come on, we'd better get our skates on, before Ben starts coming back.'

'Just promise me no aerobatics,' Dennis insisted.

'For pity's sake, Dennis, get in the cockpit!' Michael told him. Dennis climbed on the wing and swung himself awkwardly into the rear cockpit. Michael leaned over and said, 'That's the ignition switch there. Don't touch anything else. Once I've got the engine started, I'll take her over straight away.'

Dennis gave him a glum nod, and crouched in the cockpit like a man waiting to have his wisdom teeth extracted. Michael jumped down, walked around to the front of the aeroplane, and took hold of the polished mahogany propeller.

'Are you ready?' he called. Then, 'Contact!' and he gave the propeller a full-chested swing downwards. There was a sucking sound of pistons sliding in and out of cylinders, but the engine didn't start.

'Are you switching on that bloody switch?' Michael demanded.

Dennis, pale, gave him a thumb's-up.

'All right, then, contact!' shouted Michael, and swung, and this time the biplane's engine burst into ear-splitting life. Michael immediately kicked away the wooden chocks from under the Moth's wheels, and ran around to the side of the plane and hopped up on to the wing. He climbed into the front cockpit, fastened his straps, and without hesitation rolled the aeroplane out of the hangar and into the sunlight.

In the distance, he could see Ben waving at him. He cheerily waved back. 'Oh God!' shouted Dennis. 'We're going to be sent to prison for this, or rusticated at least! That's if we don't die first!'

'Courage!' Michael shouted back. '*When I can read my title clear, To mansions in the skies, I bid farewell to every fear, And wipe my weeping eyes.*'

'Bollocks!' screamed Dennis, in sheer terror, as the Moth gathered speed and jolted across the grass.

The engine was so loud that they couldn't hear Ben as he came cantering after them, windmilling his arms wildly as if he were trying to take off, too. Michael steered the Moth into the wind, revved her up, and let her dance right up into the evening air as if she weighed nothing at all. Almost at once, he angled her off to the south-east, towards the hazy shadows of the Gog Magog Hills. The airfield tilted beneath them like a billiard-table turned on its side by two over-enthusiastic removal-men.

'No aerobatics!' panicked Dennis, clutching on to the rim of the cockpit.

Michael gradually gained height, and all around them spread the winding roads and hedge-lined lanes of Teversham and Church

End and Cherry Hinton, gilded by the sun, a peaceful England at peace with itself. Michael, as he flew, felt both grief and exhilaration; and the tears streamed down his cheeks. Dennis, of course, was unable to see them, or he would have been even more terrified than he was already.

They climbed higher and higher, with the sun behind them, until they seemed to have left the world of humans altogether. The air was so thin that Dennis started to pant like a dog, and the Moth's engine began to struggle and blip. 'Can't – breathe!' shouted Dennis.

'It's all right!' Michael shouted back. 'Don't worry! We're going down now!'

He tilted the Moth's nose upward, and the biplane began to climb almost vertically.

'I thought you said we were going down!' Dennis screamed.

'We are!' Michael told him. 'But a special way! You'll never forget this as long as you live!'

'What are you going to do? No aerobatics, I told you!'

'Very simple!' Michael shouted. 'My own invention! The Michael Lord triple loop!'

'What?' shrieked Dennis.

'Triple loop!' Michael repeated. 'Hold on tight!'

'*No!*' Dennis shrilled at him. If they hadn't been five thousand feet up in the air, he probably would have climbed out. '*For God's sake, Michael, no!*'

Michael raised the biplane's nose even more steeply, pulling the stick right back into his lap. He ignored Dennis's screeching, because he knew with certainty and some regret that they were in very little danger. He would never have admitted this to anybody – perhaps not even to himself – but one of the reasons that he had asked Dennis to come up with him had been to safeguard himself from doing anything stupid. His father had always complained that Michael had a natural tendency to jump first and think later, and it certainly didn't help that he was grief-stricken and drunk. On his own, he might have been tempted to commune with the sky to the point of killing himself. But he had Dennis to take care of, and for Dennis's sake he would fly like an angel.

He lifted the Moth into a loop. Dennis saw Cambridgeshire over his head and nothing but the sky below him, and let out a howl of total fear. Then they were plunging down again, the engine blaring, the wind whistling in the wires, until they reached the bottom of the loop.

It was now – just when Dennis thought his ordeal was over –

that Michael flipped the Moth over, and dived into another loop, just below the first. This time, Michael could hear Dennis moaning; even though Dennis's lips were tightly closed. The Moth dropped, and then swooped up again, looping over and diving yet again. Michael described a third loop, just below the second, and now they were only two thousand feet above the ground. They had lost three thousand feet of altitude in less than three minutes.

Michael twisted around in the cockpit. Dennis's face was as white as paraffin wax, and his eyes were red-rimmed and staring. This was partly because of the centrifugal force of three loops, one after the other, which had exerted 450 pounds of pressure on his body and had forced his blood down into his feet.

'Are you all right?' he shouted.

'Never felt better!' Dennis called back, grimly.

'We'll take her back now,' Michael suggested.

'Just do whatever you bloody well like!' said Dennis.

Michael turned the Moth into the sun, and brought her gradually back towards Cambridge Aero Club. Dennis said nothing more, but sat crouched in the rear cockpit like a man who has come to understand the highest priority of human life and realizes it amounts to nothing more than keeping one's feet solidly on the ground at all times.

'I didn't mean to frighten you!' Michael shouted.

'You didn't!' Dennis told him. 'I know what it's like to be frightened! That wasn't anything like it at all!'

He took a deep breath, and then he shouted, 'That was sheer bloody terror!'

Michael coasted the Moth over the fields and the trees, dropping into dusk. The sky was alive with gilded insects, and swallows circled all around them as they slowly lost altitude. Dennis sat up a little, and began to look better.

They were less than a mile from the airfield when the engine suddenly cut out. There was no warning at all; no sputtering or coughing. It simply stopped.

'What's wrong?' Dennis called out.

'Don't know, could be a blocked fuel-line!' Michael answered him, over his shoulders.

'Well, can you start it up again?'

'Not without getting out and swinging the prop! But we should be able to glide back from here!'

Silently, the Moth drifted through the air, its own shadow following it eagerly across the farms and lanes and mustard fields, anxious to meet it. Michael peered ahead towards the airfield, and felt fairly sure that he had enough height to be able to glide in safely. He hoped very much that the muttering noise he could hear behind him wasn't the sound of Dennis praying. He held the stick between his knees, unscrewed the cap of his gin-bottle, and took a long, mouth-burning swig.

'Fancy a nip?' he asked Dennis.

'Just fly!' screamed Dennis. 'For God's sake, just fly!'

They were gliding lower than the treetops now, between a stately natural avenue of elms. The airfield was straight ahead of them, beyond a field where horses grazed and a narrow roadway and one more field of barley. Michael trimmed the Moth's wings so that she sailed silently and swiftly towards the airfield boundary. He could see that Ben and five or six Aero Club members were standing by the hangar, and that they had spotted him. They were all frantically waving at him to come down. There were two cars parked by the gate, too – a Bentley tourer and an Austin police-car.

'Looks as if we've got a reception committee!' Michael told Dennis, jabbing his finger in the direction of the airfield.

But Dennis didn't reply. His head was lowered and he was wringing his hands between his knees and praying to the Lord to deliver him safely back to *terra firma*.

Michael was almost sure that they were going to make it when he saw lights approaching from the north-east. A large cream-painted pantechnicon was coming down the road from the direction of Fen Ditton. It was so close that Michael could read the writing painted on the side of it, Willard's Removals.

There was nothing at all that Michael could do. The Moth's undercart was almost scraping the tops of the hedges, and he had no power at all left to manoeuvre. He could only watch in fascination as the pantechnicon trundled closer and closer, and pray (like Dennis) that they would miss it.

There was an inevitability about their collision that was almost wonderful. Michael saw the driver's face staring at him in horrified fascination. He saw the driver's mate open the door and leap straight out of the cab, into the ditch. He was just about to turn around and say something to Dennis – something like, 'keep your bonce down, old chap,' when his whole world was filled up with furniture van.

The Moth banged straight through the pantechnicon's plywood sides, into one and out of the other, tearing its wings and its undercart off as it did so. The wingless fuselage dropped on its belly in the barley field, followed by a tumbling collection of armchairs and pouffettes and magazine-racks and standard-lamps with fringed shades and tea-chests packed with crunching china. After what seemed like quite a long time, Michael opened his eyes. Everything was silent. Then he heard small voices, made tiny by distance, as the reception committee came wading through the barley from the direction of the airfield. 'Dennis?' he said, turning around. 'Dennis, are you all right?'

Dennis looked around him. 'I must be. This isn't heaven. This *can't* be heaven if you're here.'

Michael eased himself out of the cockpit. His knees were badly bruised, and the side of his jaw felt as if it were bulging out like a cartoon drawing of Tired Tim with the toothache. Dennis was dabbing at a nosebleed.

The pantechnicon driver came walking towards them white-faced. 'Gor blimey,' he said. 'I fought you was dead, for certain.'

For no reason at all, Michael clasped the driver's hand and shook it, as if they had both survived a famous naval battle or climbed the Matterhorn together. He felt extraordinarily exhilarated, and even when Ben and the Aero Club members approached him, and stood around the devastated Moth, rueful and perplexed, he couldn't resist smiling at all of them, and walking excitedly around with his hands in his pockets.

Gerald Johnson, the Aero Club secretary, finally came up and laid a broad, comforting hand on Michael's shoulder. He must have had lunch at The Cardinal's Arms, because his eyes were bloodshot, like fertilized chickens' eggs, and his huge grey moustache looked as if someone had been furiously wrenching at it all afternoon. 'Michael?' he said. 'Michael, old man?'

'I'm afraid I'm going to have to plead insanity,' said Michael.

'Well,' said Gerald, embarrassed. 'I've only just heard about Herbert. It was in the evening paper. The police have come along; Ben called them, you see, and you really can't blame him, can you? But there's no need for any kind of prosecution.'

He gently shook Michael to and fro, and Michael let him. Shock, perhaps; or the need to have somebody to tell him what to do.

'Under the circumstances –,' said Gerald, '– as long as you can pay – well, we're willing to forget it. I mean, we're all jolly glad that you're safe.'

Michael nodded. He felt in the pocket of his sports coat pocket for his pipe, but it wasn't there, and he couldn't remember where he might have left it. The sun had sunk down behind the elm trees now, and it was growing chilly. The stars were coming out. To

Gerald's embarrassment, he eased himself down on to his knees on the prickly stubble, and covered his face with his hand, and it was only then that he understood how lonely a son can be when he has to live on the Earth without his father.

Everybody else stood around and waited for him, except the pantechnicon driver, who lit up the cigarette end that he had retrieved from behind his ear, and began to gather up pieces of furniture.

Later, on the last train from Victoria Station to Chichester, Michael fell asleep; but woke up to see his own colourless face in the window, and nothing at all outside but the blackness of Sussex in the middle of the night. It was like opening his eyes to discover that he had been buried alive.

There was nobody else in the first-class compartment, but even if there had been, that wouldn't have stopped him from sobbing out loud.

Chichester, 1931

Under a sky the colour of writing-ink, the kind of sky that Herbert would have called 'pilot's delight', Herbert was laid to rest at Chichester Cathedral in the grassy triangular graveyard called Paradise, in a red-marble tomb surmounted by an angel with luxuriantly-spreading wings. Constance laid a spray of pink and red gaudetia at the angel's feet, and dropped two tears beside them. The polished stone reflected the slowly-moving clouds like a mirror.

'O God our help in ages past,' sang the choir. Only a few feet away rested the tombs of Herbert's mother and father, and his older brother Francis, the twenty-seventh victim of Germany's ace pilot Oswald Boelcke. The cathedral bells tolled dolefully; there were glossy black Daimlers parked all the way along West Street. In the crowd that waited in silence for the funeral party to emerge from the cathedral, small boys outnumbered grown-ups almost two-to-one.

Herbert Lord had been a small boy's hero; a handsome daredevil who had risked his life to make sure that English aviation led the world. The *Daily Express* called him 'The Empire's Icarus', and only last month Herbert had lent his name to an article in the *Boys' Own Paper* entitled 'Pluck In The Face of Daunting Odds: The Birthright of Every British Boy'.

In his requiem, Bishop George Kennedy Bell said that 'Herbert Lord was a man whose life ennobled everybody who knew him, a man dedicated to the twin faiths of Church and Country.'

Constance left the cathedral protectively escorted by James, Richard, and Michael. She wore a black silk calf-length dress by Schiaparelli, with a wide black hat and a black veil. Most of the newspaper photographers were courteous enough to stay well back, although a young photographer from the *Daily Mirror* knelt down in front of her and took a quick flash picture. 'I say! Play the game!' somebody shouted.

Constance was quickly ushered into her Daimler, and the cortège pulled away from the curb. There was spontaneous applause on all sides, and the crowds tossed white chrysanthemums, hundreds of them. The flowers pattered on the windscreen like locusts, and the road was thick with broken white blossoms. Some people waved Union Jacks; others wept. Four or five small boys came tearing after Constance's car until they were too puffed to continue, and gave up, with shouts of 'Sorry, Mum! Sorry!'

James took off his gloves and laid them over his knee. 'That's over, then,' he said, although not without sadness.

Richard said, 'It's all so jolly strange. I feel almost as if we're going to get home and find Father in the library, still alive, and shouting at cook for not having his lunch ready.'

James looked away. 'He's gone,' he replied. 'It's all up to us now.'

'I know what Richard means, though,' said Michael. 'It's terribly hard to believe that he's not here any more. I know it sounds crass – but wouldn't all this fuss have tickled him pink?' By now the family had overcome the shock of Herbert's death. Nobody picked Michael up for being flippant.

'So many dear friends,' said Constance. Behind her veil, her face was as pale as ivory. There were diamonds glittering around her throat, and tears glittering on her cheeks.

Michael said, 'Funny thing, though. Father always used to tell me he didn't want to die of old age.' He made it sound as if 'He Didn't Want to Die of Old Age' was a bedtime story that Herbert used to read for him.

Richard – 'Constance's boy' – said nothing, but stared out of the window as the Daimler drove them out of town towards the Lord estate at East Ashling. His collar was too tight for him, and chafed his neck. On either side of the road, the countryside was dense and hot and silent, West Sussex in midsummer. Fields of glistening honey-coloured barley nodded under the sun, ready to be harvested. Cabbage-white butterflies flickered in the hedges. The road was unmetalled, and the Daimler was soon covered in a fine film of white chalk, a vehicle fit for ghosts.

Constance reached over and squeezed Richard's hand. She knew why he was silent: it was their shared secret. They hadn't yet told James and Michael that their father had probably taken his own life. Eventually, of course, it would have to come out. But Constance had explained to Richard, 'I don't want to cause them any more pain than we have to, my dear. And besides, we don't yet know for *sure*, do we?'

Richard thought privately that his mother was deluding herself; but he would have done anything rather than hurt her. Consequently he had stayed silent while Bryan King-Moreton had given his brothers some technical apple-sauce about a ruptured fuel-line, and an accidental fire. James's godfather 'Teddy' Busk had been killed the same way, when he was testing a BE 2C for Geoffrey de Havilland, so perhaps to James and Michael there might appear to be some terrible poetry about it. In common with almost everybody connected with flying, the Lord family were deeply superstitious.

All the same, Richard found it impossible to forget the image of his father, falling a thousand feet into the sea like an angel cast out of paradise. He couldn't help wondering what his father had been thinking, as he fell. Regret? Elation? Terror? Or relief?

It was almost noon when the cortège reached the brick-pillared gates of Goodwood Lodge, which had been the Lord family home ever since Herbert's father had made a fortune out of copper in South Africa. They drove through the south park, along an immaculately-raked shingle drive, in between rows of goldenrod trees. Off to the west, on the hill that sloped up towards the village of Woodend, there were black-faced sheep grazing in the sunlight, part of Herbert's hundred-strong flock.

And is there Southdown mutton in the hereafter? Herbert had once asked, over dinner. *If there isn't, I don't want to go.* The house itself was a late Tudor mansion of soft red brick, with a heavy roof of Horsham slate. An ancient Rackhamesque wisteria had entwined itself around the porch, and trailed over the diamond-leaded windows. The rear of the house had been modernized, with garages, tennis-courts, and a heated swimming-pool inside a steamed-up glasshouse which they called the Crystal Palace, but the Lords had kept the nineteenth century ornamental gardens and *parterres*, and a man called Tennyson came every Wednesday to do nothing else but trim the dark-green yew-bushes that had been cut into the shape of chess-pieces.

When they were small, the three brothers had been terrified of those chess-pieces, especially at night.

They helped Constance out of the car. She stood in silence staring at the house. 'He loved the Lodge,' she whispered to herself.

James took her elbow and said, 'Come along, Mother.'

The funeral breakfast was to be held in the Long Hall, beneath large diamond-leaded windows with straw-coloured glass and gloomy seventeenth-century paintings of the Ashton family, who used to own Goodwood Lodge before the Lords. The Long Hall was cool and dim and smelled of three-hundred-year-old oak. In front of the fireplace, the banqueting table had been covered with a white linen tablecloth, and set out with huge oval dishes of smoked salmon brought freshly by rail from Scotland, cold boiled Sussex ham, beef and lobster and venison in aspic; all to be served and supervised by the Lord's butler, Dennis Minchin, and his three black-uniformed maids. Fifty bottles of Perrier-Jouët champagne were chilling in a huge galvanized jardinière filled with crushed ice from J. S. Nubbs fishmonger.

Constance went directly upstairs to her bedroom. She closed the door behind her and stood with her back to it, her eyes tight shut. She had appeared to be tall at the funeral service. The BBC commentator had called her 'gravely elegant'. But in her own room, in the proportions of her own house, she could be seen as quite a small woman, with delicate features, a heart-shaped English face and reddish-brown hair, streaked with silver, unfashionably long, although she had braided it for the funeral. 'Your rusty crown,' Herbert had called it.

'Herbert,' she whispered, if only to make sure that there would be no reply. 'Herbert, how could you *leave* me like this?'

What grieved her so much was the fact that he had *chosen* to leave her. She opened her eyes. What else in the world could have meant so much to him that, when he lost it, he had been so anguished that he didn't care if he lost her too? What else, or *who* else?

In front of her stood the four-poster marriage bed, with its carved-oak pillars and its heavy tapestry hangings, the wide Antarctic bed in which she now had to sleep alone. The French windows had been left open, because it was such a warm day. She stepped out on to the small oak balcony and looked out over the gardens. From the front of the house, she could hear shingle crunching and car doors slamming as the guests began to arrive.

A peacock whooped, out beyond the swimming-pool. It sounded like the cry of a dying child.

'No note, no clue, nothing,' she said. 'You could at least have told me what was wrong. You could have confided in me, my dear, instead of –'

She pressed her hands against her face. She made one single noise that was more like a disdainful laugh than a sob.

There was a knock at the bedroom door. Constance didn't reply. There was another knock, a little sharper, and James came in, holding the hand of his fiancée Henrietta Beesley. Henrietta had been Deb of the Year in 1928, and for fear of becoming a 'bag' had immediately become engaged to the Earl of Warwick. At last year's Henley regatta, however, the Earl of Warwick had shown a lot more interest in the new Deb of the Year, Margaret Whigham, and Henrietta had retaliated by showing a lot more interest in James Lord.

Henrietta was skinny and tall and very pretty, with short boyish hair which she had lacquered into Peter Pan side-curls. She wore a simple black day-dress with a black bow at the bust. Cecil Beaton had said she was 'photogenic', which for a 'rave deb' like Henrietta was the very latest compliment.

'Mother?' said James. 'Most of the guests are here now.'

Henrietta came out on to the balcony. 'Mrs Lord?' she asked, in her sweet little sugared-almond voice. 'Is there anything I can do to help?'

Constance smiled a sad smile. 'Henrietta, my dear, and James. You've been so thoughtful. How are the little ones coping downstairs?' When she was talking to James, she still referred to Richard and Michael as 'the little ones' – just as she still called James and Richard 'the big ones' when she was talking to Michael.

James said, 'They're doing pretty well, as a matter of fact. Michael is bullying everybody into gulping down two glasses of champagne within the first five minutes, and then he's taking them around and introducing them to all the people they're bound to hate the most – that's if they don't hate them already.'

'Well – Michael always *was* a partygoing sort of person, wasn't he?' said Constance. 'Not like his father. Herbert hated parties. He hated *juggling with his victuals*, that's what he always used to say. But he was shy, you know. Well, not so much *shy* perhaps as *inward-looking*. Michael, though – Michael has always loved a crowd around him. Herbert used to get quite worried that he was going to be an actor.'

'May I help you to change?' asked Henrietta. 'You must be feeling frightfully low.'

'No, no, don't you worry,' Constance told her. 'I shall be down in a moment. Elsie will help me.'

Henrietta shaded her eyes and looked out over the gardens.

'I love your roses,' she said. 'Can't you just smell them, even from right up here?'

Constance nodded. 'It's such a pity to think that Herbert will never see them again.'

'I suppose they must have gardens in heaven,' Henrietta suggested.

Constance thought: *when you take your own life, are you accepted in heaven? Or are you condemned to purgatory for ever and ever? Oh Herbert, Herbert, why didn't you tell me what was wrong?*

James came up and laid his hand on Henrietta's shoulder, and kissed the back of her neck. 'I say, Hen, why don't you pop downstairs and make yourself known to Amy Johnson? You haven't met her yet, have you? She's a terrific sport, for a girl.'

Henrietta nodded and smiled. She gave Constance a sympathetic daughter-in-law hug, and kissed the air on either side of her veil, *smick, smick,* and then she walked back across the room as glamorously as a young deer.

'She's *quite* charming, isn't she?' said Constance, once Henrietta had closed the door behind her. 'You could do very much worse, you know, than marry Henrietta. I hear that the Beesleys have been doing rather well lately. Duncan Beesley is awfully good chums with the Aga Khan.'

James tugged at the starched white cuffs of his shirt. There was perspiration on his upper lip. 'She's been a brick all week,' he said. 'Not the sort to flap.'

Constance became aware that James wanted to say something else. She didn't look at him straight away, but said, quietly, 'You're not worried, are you, dear?'

James shrugged. 'Well, not worried exactly. But there's something I want ask you. I could have picked a more tactful moment, I suppose, but I hope you'll forgive me. It really is fearfully important. Important to me, anyway. Important to the family, too.'

It took Constance a moment to focus her eyes on James through her veil. 'Are you going to tell me what it is?'

James was embarrassed. 'I could bring it up later, you know, if you'd prefer it.'

'No, if it's really important, we must talk about it now.'

James knew that he was tying a noose around his own neck. 'I was discussing Father's will this morning with John Tremlett.'

Constance looked wary. 'Yes?' she said. 'You know very well that your father left everything to me, to be held in trust for you and your brothers. When I die, the house and the business and all the investments will be divided *equally* between you.'

James took out his handkerchief and dabbed at his face. 'Do you mind if we go inside? It's rather hot out here.'

They went back into the bedroom. Constance sat in a small blue-upholstered crinoline chair, while James perched himself on the end of the four-poster bed. 'I don't know whether I've got hold of the wrong end of the stick,' he said. 'But the way John explained it to me, Father made a promise to Bryan King-Moreton – a *written* promise – that Bryan could run all the racing and experimental side of things, and not just as a sideshow, either. Apparently he's going to be given complete control of the seaplane sheds at Ryde and the workshops at Hayward's Heath, *and* the back building here at Chichester, too.'

'That's correct,' said Constance, with equanimity. 'Is there anything wrong with Bryan taking charge of the racing? He won't be interfering with *your* side of things.'

'Mother,' James protested, 'the days of racing aeroplanes are over. At least, the days of *our* racing aeroplanes are over. I think Father understood that four or five years ago. He was always talking about practical airliners for the ordinary fellow in the street. He couldn't resist one last heroic gesture, that was *his* trouble.'

'So what are you suggesting?' asked Constance.

'Some pretty drastic economies, for a start,' said James. 'One of the very first things I want to do is sell off the seaplane sheds, close down that mad-scientists' workshop at Hayward's Heath, and start concentrating all our efforts and all our investment capital into designing and building the kind of aeroplanes that can actually secure our future.'

There was a cold and lengthy silence.

Eventually, Constance said, 'James, my dear, you seem to be forgetting that your name is Lord; and that those racing aeroplanes of which you disapprove so much brought glory not only to your father but to the whole country.'

'Mother,' James replied, 'nobody can diminish Father's achievements. Father was a hero. But I have absolutely no interest in being a hero. I'm not cut out for it. I'm interested in being successful, that's all. I want Lord Aeronautics to be the most profitable aeroplane company in the world.'

Constance looked at James warily, and said, '*Profitable?*' as if profitability were something not quite nice to discuss at mealtimes. Like Socialism.

James persisted. 'The Aquarius is doing marvellously well; we've sold twenty-three already. But the Aquarius is only the beginning. We should already be working on the passenger planes of tomorrow – planes that we can sell by the dozen. There's such a ready market – Imperial Airways and TWA and Royal Dutch Airlines, as well as the Air Ministry.'

'James –' began Constance, but James was not to be stopped.

'Did Father tell you what happened with TWA?' he interrupted her. 'Goodness knows, we missed a golden opportunity there! You remember that disaster in March, when one of their Fokkers crashed, and killed that famous football coach Knute Rockne? Well, nobody wanted to fly by TWA after that, so they were shopping around for a complete new fleet - a whole new airline, right from scratch! They wanted to scrap all their Fokkers and replace them with a new all-metal twin-engined airliner. And all the time, we had just what they were looking for, here at Chichester – the Capricorn – Father's vision of the airliner of tomorrow! He had it on the drawing-board for two years. Two years! We could have had it flying by now! But we kept putting it off and putting it off because Bryan King-Moreton thought a new airliner was too mundane to bother with. Unexciting that's what he called it. So we never got around to working out any of the specifications for it, or thinking about what engines it was going to need. So when Charles Lindbergh at TWA asked us if we cared to submit a proposal, Bryan had to wire back and tell him, very sorry old man, we're just not ready.'

Constance lifted her chin. It was a gesture that James recognized from a lifetime of experience. It meant that she was deeply annoyed, and that she didn't want to hear any more. But James was committed to finishing what he had to say . . .

75

'We've squandered too much time and too much money and too much talent on the *Chichester Specials*. We simply can't afford to build that kind of one-off aeroplane any longer. The Yanks and the Italians do it far better than us; we should stick to what we're good at. This is the modern world, Mother, the days of the lone speed king and the glorious gesture are over for ever, no matter what you read in the *Illustrated London News*.'

Constance was silent for almost half a minute. It seemed more like half an hour. At last she said, 'Do you really think this is the right day for you to criticize your father? Not only your father, but the country he loved? The country he died for? Do you really think that this is the right day to suggest that we go back on a solemn written promise he made to one of his dearest friends? Bryan King-Moreton has worked with your father for twenty years.'

'Exactly,' said James. 'And his whole notion of aviation is twenty years out of date. Mother – I'm desperately sorry that I brought this up today. But Bryan King-Moreton is downstairs now, and he's already talking about designing and building another *Chichester Special* as a kind of tribute to Father, and before I know it all our best draftsmen and all our best engineers are going to be pottering around at Hayward's Heath. We have to tell him now, *today*, that it can't be done.'

Constance stood up. She saw her face reflected in the oval mirror on top of the chest-of-drawers. It looked like a mysterious portrait, a white face behind a smoky veil. 'I always knew that it was a mistake, letting you go to Oxford,' she said. 'You should have gone to Cambridge, like the little ones. You're too dogmatic by half.'

'Mother, please –'

Constance raised her black-gloved hand. 'James, that is more than enough. The subject is closed. I'm disappointed in you – disappointed and hurt. Today is the day of your father's funeral, and all that you can think about is commerce. The very least you can do is show your father some respect.'

'The same respect that he showed for us, when he killed himself?' James retorted.

Constance stared at him, too shocked to speak.

James lowered his eyes. 'I apologize. That was unforgivable.'

'Who told you that?' Constance demanded. 'Who told you that?'

James wouldn't answer. Constance came across the room and seized hold of his sleeve and shook it furiously. '*Who told you that?*' she screamed.

James kept his eyes averted. 'Nobody told me. It was the way he flew. His engine was overheating, Wally Field said so. He wouldn't have gained height deliberately, not unless he was thinking of – well, not unless he *wanted* to put his life at risk.'

Constance released her grip on James's sleeve. 'We'll talk about this later,' she whispered.

'I'm right, then, aren't I?'

Constance nodded.

James took hold of her and held her close. She wept silent tears, and they clung to her veil. 'I'm sorry, Mother,' James told her. 'I'm really so sorry.'

After a while, Constance managed to recover herself. She lifted her veil and wiped her eyes. 'I must go downstairs. All those guests, what are they going to think of me? Would you send Elsie up? I'll change as quickly as I can.'

James hesitated, but Constance said, 'Go along, now. We can talk later. But don't think that I've changed my mind about Bryan King-Moreton, because I haven't.' She paused, and then she added, 'I haven't changed my mind about your father, either.'

Henrietta was waiting for James at the foot of the stairs. 'You didn't upset her, did you?' she asked, handing him a glass of champagne that she had been keeping warm for him.

James swallowed more champagne than he ought to have done, and was obliged in mid-swallow to smile an effervescent good morning to the Honourable Mrs Richard Norton, who was every schoolboy's fantasy of a mature beauty (and James's too) as she crossed the hall.

'I can't say that Mother's exactly tickled,' he told Henrietta. 'Now, can you hold on a sec? I've got to find Elsie.'

'James –' Henrietta protested. 'You're always *off* somewhere.'

James discovered Elsie in the kitchen, folding aprons. Elsie was Constance's upstairs maid, a diminutive fussy red-cheeked Sussex girl who had been brought up in a single cottage near Woodend with five brothers and six sisters. Elsie believed in ghosts, the healing-power of St John's wort, the Second Coming, and the pulling-power of beauty-spots (she studiously painted one of her own on her left cheekbone, as a counterbalance to her maid's cap, which was fashionably tilted over her right eye). 'Poor, poor, poor Mrs Lord,' she fretted to herself, as she went upstairs.

James watched her go. He could have done with a cigarette. 'We'd better circulate,' he told Henrietta.

Almost everybody had arrived now, with the notable exception of Sir Clive Wigram, the King's private secretary, who had been a close friend of Herbert's, and Lady Astor, who had sent a man on a motorcycle all the way from Cliveden with an incomprehensible note of apology. The hall clattered with knives and forks and reverberated with solemn, deep-pitched conversation, as if Herbert's old friends thought that the more *profundo* their *basso*, the more sincere their tribute would sound. 'Frightful loss to flying, you know.' 'Frightful loss to the whole nation, if you ask me.' 'We'll never see his like again, that's the trouble.'

On the far side of the hall, James saw Sir Rodney and Lady Sheffield. Sir Rodney was standing with one arm behind his back, his fleshy nose lifted to the ceiling, as if he could smell some distant and reminiscent scent, saying nothing at all. Susan was wearing a black sheathlike dress and a black veiled hat, through which her crimson lipstick glowered at everybody around her. James gave Susan an interrogative look across the hall; Susan made a point of turning her head to one side.

'You will never know what hell I have to suffer,' she had told him once, her fingers dug deep in his wavy hair, her breath coming in short, irregular, high-pitched gasps. 'Don't ever, *ever*, tell me that you understand.'

'When a woman says that nobody understands her, that generally means that there is nothing to understand,' James had retorted.

'You can be such a bastard,' Susan had panted.

James had neither agreed nor disagreed; their affair had always thrived on hostility and ambiguities. And here she was, after all, drinking champagne as if it were concentrated sulphuric acid, tightness itself, tetchy, frustrated probably, and publicly grieving for her lover's father.

Susan could recite all of John Keats's *Ode To Apollo* by heart. *'Tis morn, and the flowers with dew are yet drooping.* She could play the violin-cello, thighs thrust apart, bow crying with passion. James looked at her and felt like shaking her in front of everybody; but of course he didn't.

The guest who was attracting the most attention was Amy Johnson, the slim twenty-eight-year-old girl who had been awarded a CBE last August after flying from Croydon aerodrome to Darwin, Australia, in nineteen and a half days. Amy's fair hair was newly marcelled and she was wearing a very stylish black coat-and-skirt and three rows of pearls. She was talking to Michael about the time she had become delirious while flying over the shark-infested Timor Sea.

'I kept reciting poetry. I even made some up. It was so tremendously bad that it kept me awake. Then I saw a cloud in front of me, and the cloud turned out to be Australia.'

'Well, I've always had a hankering to go to Australia,' said Michael. 'Is it true what they say about Aborgines dropping dead just because somebody points a magic bone at them? They had something about that on the wireless the other day.'

Lord Wakefield of Castrol was there, too, with his plate heaped embarrassingly high with salmon and lobster, and almost as much already churning around in his mouth. It was Lord Wakefield who had stumped up half of the cost of Amy Johnson's second-hand aeroplane, three hundred pounds, and he didn't stop reminding anybody who would listen.

At the far end of the room, on a Jacobean chair, sat Lady Houston, reliably reported to be the richest woman in England. She looked hot and vexed, and kept fanning herself with one black glove. Lady Houston had shelled out a hundred thousand pounds of her own money so that Britain could enter this year's Schneider Trophy, a rival to the Jacques Seraphim Cup. Today she wore an extraordinary black hat that resembled a raven settling on a wheelbarrow full of coal.

Malcolm Campbell had taken command of the geographical centre of the hall, his formal black funeral coat tightly buttoned, his hair shining and brushed. He was prodding Douglas Jardine the English cricket captain and telling him how disgusted he had been on a recent visit to London to have turned the corner into Portland Place and to have suddenly encountered 'slap-bang' in front of the new BBC building a huge male nude statue of Ariel 'with everything in abundance, except common decency'. Jardine looked even more 'backs-to-the-wall' than usual. Henry Royce, now sixty-eight years old, stirred his champagne with his little finger and stared out of the window. He was probably thinking about his lettuce bed at West Wittering. Anthony Eden in his thin moustache looked gravely sartorial and marvellously bored. In a small corner behind the door, Britain's two most celebrated aircraft designers, Reginald Mitchell and Sidney Camm, were arguing *sotto voce* about the problems of retractable undercarriages – while ignoring Lady Bridget Poullet, one of the year's most alluring debutantes, who was standing only inches away from them trying to explain to an amused and mystified Geoffrey de Havilland how to dance the rumba.

'It's an awful lot like flying' she said, 'only one never quite leaves the ground.'

'I see,' smiled Geoffrey de Havilland. 'Lots of rolling and yawing, but not much in the way of pitch.'

Michael had left Amy Johnson and was enjoying a prickly confrontation between Mr Quintin Hogg and a young undergraduate friend of his, Frank Hardie. Quintin Hogg was saying, 'If you refuse to fight for your country . . . if your enemy *knows* that you will refuse to fight . . . then you will actually *cause* war.'

But Frank Hardie shook his handsome young head, and said, 'If one side refuses to fight, there can be no war.'

Michael was wondering whether it would be too objectionable for him to try lighting his pipe when he noticed a young girl sitting in the sunlit window-seat all alone, looking out at the garden. She must have been about eighteen years old, but she seemed to possess great poise. She had bobbed blonde hair, pinned back on either side of a high, narrow, very English-looking forehead. Her nose was short and straight, and her eyes were the palest of blues, like rain-washed cornflowers. She was wearing a black calf-length daydress, and black gloves.

Michael excused himself from Quintin Hogg and Frank Hardie (the conversation had now turned heatedly to mustard-gas and poison bombs and the imminent German elections) and carried a glass of champagne over to the window-seat.

'Hello, I'm Michael Lord,' he said to the girl. 'You're all alone. I thought you might like a spot of bubbly to cheer you up.'

The girl smiled. She had a fetching dimple in her left cheek. 'I'm sorry. I'm not very good at funerals.'

'Well, I don't think any of us are. I want to be thrown out of an aeroplane into the Irish Sea when I die. I can't bear the idea of being shut up in a box and buried. It's bad enough dying without having your remains treated like Maris Piper.'

'Who's Maris Piper?'

'Not who, what. Maris Piper are early potatoes.'

'I think you've managed to shock me,' the girl told him. She had a slight lisp, which Michael found unexpectedly attractive.

'Oh, because of Father, you mean? You mustn't be shocked. Father was never very serious about dying. You can't be, if you're a flyer. If you psycho-analyzed everybody who loves to fly, I think you'd find that none of them takes dying very seriously.'

'You miss him, though, don't you?'

'Yes,' said Michael. 'I do miss him. It's very difficult to tell you how much.'

'And what about you? Do you take dying seriously?'

Michael shrugged. 'I think I'm rather more worried about life than I am about death. But then I'm young.'

The girl said, 'Well, I like your moustache. It's very natty.'

'I'm pleased to say that I can't return the compliment,' said Michael. 'And I don't even know your name.'

'Patricia Burne-Stanley,' the girl told him, and held out her hand.

Michael cried, 'Patricia Burne-Stanley! I don't believe it!' The last time he had seen Patricia Burne-Stanley had been at a children's birthday-party in Chelsea, when she was ten and he was thirteen. She had been skinny and awkward then, all knees and elbows, with wire braces on all of her front teeth, and ankle-socks.

'Kenneth Bloise's ghastly birthday-party!' said Michael. 'Don't you remember? They dropped all that red jelly on the carpet and Penelope Talbot wet her knickers!'

Patricia laughed. 'How could I ever forget it? It's engraved on my memory for all time!'

Michael took hold of her hand and vigorously shook it. James, catching sight of him across the room, thought *kiss it, you twerp, don't jack it up and down, she's a girl, not a petrol pump*. But then he turned his attention back to Lady Bridget Poullet, who was telling him very prettily about her holiday in Italy, and how her mother had furiously laid about their guide with her parasol for showing them the ribald friezes at Pompeii. James tried not to laugh too much, however. This *was* his father's funeral; and Henrietta was watching him from the opposite side of the room with the unblinking intentness of a peregrine falcon.

Richard was out in the garden talking to Bryan King-Moreton. They were sitting on deckchairs on the smooth lawn that backed on to the library, under the gently dipping shade of Herbert's favourite magnolia tree. Bryan was leaning back with his eyes half-closed, smoking his pipe. Richard sat hunched forward, dangling his champagne glass between his knees.

Bryan said, 'It's up to us, you know, to keep up the good work. I know that James is dead set against it. Always has been. But if Lord Aeronautics stops racing . . . well, we'll be nothing more distinguished than any other factory. We might be making aeroplanes, but then again we might equally be turning out boiled sweets or sausages or lawnmowers. We'll have chucked away twenty years of prestige, just for the sake of the balance-sheet. It's short-sighted, you know. Prestige doesn't appear in the credit columns, but it counts for very much more than your brother obviously understands.'

'James has always been the practical one, I'm afraid,' said Richard. 'He used to make kites at school, really wonderful kites, but he didn't fly them. He sold them to his friends.'

'You might have a word with him,' suggested Bryan. 'I mean, we don't want any bad feeling, don't you know, but he ought to understand that he's pretty much out on a limb, wanting to close down the racing side of things. I know the mater's keen to see us build a new *Chichester Special*, and I imagine that you're just as keen to fly it.'

'Well, I think we ought to,' said Richard. 'We can always try for the Seraphim next year.'

Bryan steadily puffed at his pipe. 'He was a great man, the pater. Odd, in his way. But then great men often are. I used to be chums with Robert Baden-Powell, you know, soon after he came back from South Africa, and he used to play practical jokes on everybody. Apple-pie beds, salt in the sugar-shaker. Great sense of fun.'

'I don't really think that Father was like that,' said Richard.

'No!' agreed Bryan, turning around in his deckchair and squinting at Richard one-eyed against the glare of the sun. 'But he was a visionary, nonetheless! And what we have to do is to make sure that his vision comes to pass!'

Constance appeared on the lawn, on the arm of the family solicitor John Tremlett. Both Richard and Bryan got to their feet. 'A very gratifying turn-out,' said Bryan, taking Constance's hand. 'Herbert would have been touched.'

Constance gave him a small tired smile. 'I've been talking to Mr Tremlett about the company,' she said. 'I didn't really want to discuss it today of all days – but, well, James insisted on bringing up the matter of the *Chichester Special*, and I wanted to clear things up as soon as possible.'

She paused, and then she added, 'You might as well know that James has guessed that what happened at Seaview was – not entirely an accident.'

John Tremlett patted Constance's arm. He had shiny hair parted in the middle, gold bifocals, and a nose that was a forest of broken capillaries. 'I have reassured Mrs Lord that the administrative structure of Lord Aeronautics is under her control, and that if she so wishes, it will remain substantially as it is today. We are all aware that James has certain views on aeroplane production, but it is Mrs Lord's wish that work on racing aeroplanes should continue, and continue it shall.'

'Well – I'm delighted to hear it,' Bryan replied. 'Herbert's memory deserves nothing less.'

Richard asked, 'Is James upset?'

'Don't you worry about that,' said John Tremlett. 'This sort of family conflict often occurs immediately after a bereavement. It's partly an expression of sorrow and anger, you know; and partly the Darwinian order of things, like foxes in the wild. James feels aggrieved that his father has so suddenly left him with the heavy mantle of family responsibility, and so he has set his face against everything his father held dear. But time healeth even the worst of wounds, you know, and James will come around. You'll see.'

'I must say that I want that Seraphim Cup more than anything else in the world,' said Richard.

Constance laid her black-gloved hand on his sleeve. 'My dear Richard, you shall have it.'

The Right Honourable Gordon Burne-Stanley, MP, anxious to return to London, found his daughter Patricia in the plum-orchard with Michael Lord, walking hand-in-hand through the long un-scythed grass, where limestone-blue butterflies flickered.

'Patricia!' he called. The afternoon was very hot. 'We have to get back to town!'

Michael released Patricia's hand, but Patricia caught hold of him again. 'You remember Michael, don't you, Daddy? I haven't seen him since I was ten!'

Gordon Burne-Stanley shook Michael's hand; an MP's shake, powerful but disinterested. He was one of the new breed of Conservative members, with very severe views on the idleness of the unemployed. 'We met at the cathedral, of course,' he said. 'Very sad occasion. But, well, life goes on.'

'Michael will be back in London next week,' said Patricia.

'Splendid, you must call,' replied Gordon Burne-Stanley. 'Now, Patricia, we really have to make a move. Your mother's gathering up her doodads; Parkeston's warming up the car.'

'Actually,' said Michael, 'I was wondering if I could take Patricia out for a spin next week. There's a whole crowd of us going, mostly from Cambridge.'

Gordon Burne-Stanley furrowed his bushy eyebrows. 'Is it . . . *appropriate*, d'you think, quite so soon?'

'It's nothing frivolous, sir. We're only going out to the country.'

'Well, then, I don't see the harm. Ask your mother, Patricia. Good to see you, young Michael. Must dash. What with the whole country tottering, you know.'

Patricia gave Michael the quickest of kisses, and went off with her father, leaving Michael standing in the orchard feeling as if he could do cartwheels. As he stood there, James approached, smoking a cigarette.

'That's a pretty young lady,' James remarked, with one hand in his pocket.

Michael nodded. 'I'm taking her out next week.'

'What, to Box Hill, with all that crowd from Trinity? That'll put her off you for ever. For goodness' sake do something sophisticated. Take her for dinner. Take her dancing. Take her to see *The First Mrs Fraser.*'

'Well, I will, when it's decent,' said Michael. 'I can't very well go painting the town red with Father just buried.'

James smoked and said nothing.

Michael said, 'You've had a bit of a set-to with Mother, I hear.'

James shrugged. 'I don't really want to talk about it.'

'I know what you were arguing about,' Michael told him, undeterred, 'and if you really want to know, I agree with you. We *should* think about economizing. The whole country's pulling in its belt these days. Patricia said that Philip Snowden's going to cut the dole by ten per cent, and put up taxes by £80 million. Unless we do, the Yanks won't lend us any more money. So Lord Aeronautics should be doing the same, not spending thousands and thousands of pounds on air-races.'

'You've changed your tune,' James remarked. 'I thought you were an incurable racing addict.'

'I am,' said Michael. 'But, you know, talking to Patricia . . .'

'Ah, Patricia,' said James. 'She's *very* well-produced. But I should spend your time looking at her, rather than listening to her, if I were you. Girls have a way of getting themselves into a tangle, when it comes to politics. Especially the daughters of Conservative MPs.'

Michael said, 'Henrietta's looking for you. She's over there, by the library windows.'

James glanced around. 'Ah, yes.' He sucked at his cigarette. 'Very steady girl, Henrietta. She should have been a nurse, or a tightrope-walker. The kind of girl you can trust not to keel over at the sight of blood.'

'I thought you liked her.'

James smiled. 'Of course I like her. Mother wants me to marry her. But you know, "a woman is only a woman, but a good cigar is a smoke".'

'Father used to say that.'

'Kipling said it first.'

James and Michael stood side by side in the orchard for a while, listening to the breeze rustling through the leaves, and watching the distant sheep grazing on the hillside. There was an unspoken appreciation between them that Goodwood Lodge was home, but that they couldn't stay here for very much longer. They were young, and they had their own lives to live. Herbert's suicide had left them both with an urgent and unwelcome challenge.

And Richard? 'Don't say anything to Richard,' cautioned James. 'He was there when it happened, remember. I think he still feels as if it was all his fault. The trouble is, I think Mother feels that, too. It's a pity they don't lay the blame where it all belongs.'

Michael swept back his hair with his hand. 'I'm not sure that I know *where* it belongs.'

James finished his cigarette, and nipped it out between finger and thumb. 'It's history now. But in Germany, in the twenties, there was a very glamorous couple called Gerhard and Mathilde Brunner, and what they were is what Father and Mother ought to have been, but weren't.'

'Well, I know the Brunners,' Michael protested.

James shook his head. 'You were *acquainted* with the Brunners, my young sprout. But you didn't know them, and it's probably just as well. Only Father knew them, and they killed him, in the end.'

James was walking around the side of the house when Susan approached him. She was walking as quickly as her tight black dress permitted, and fussily waving a large manila folder.

'James! Where on earth have you been?'

He took hold of her gloved hand, and blew a kiss through the veil of her hat. 'I thought that you and the Director had already left.'

'We're *supposed* to have left, but I made an excuse about powdering my nose: Rodney's sitting in the Daimler, waiting for me. Sighing a lot, I shouldn't wonder.'

She pressed the folder against James's chest. 'It's all that information you wanted, you know, on night navigation, and leader cables. It was frightfully difficult to get hold of it, and I must have it back by next Thursday. Rodney has to go to Ireland this evening, and he won't be looking for it until then. But I know that he's got a meeting about it at Farnborough on Friday morning.'

James lifted her veil, and kissed her properly. Her crimson lipstick smudged his cheek. She said, '*James*,' and tried to pull herself away, but he wouldn't let her.

'Let me walk you out to your car,' he said; and took hold of her elbow, and steered her around the house to the driveway. Sir Rodney was sitting in the back of his grey Daimler frowning at his watch.

'Lady Sheffield lost her way,' James smiled, as he helped her into the car.

'Ah, many thanks,' Sir Rodney replied. 'I have to get to Fishguard by seven.'

'Thank you for coming,' said James, and waved goodbye with the manila folder.

He stood in the driveway and watched as the Daimler drove away. Susan didn't look around, but her hand was lying on the back shelf, and she played her fingers in the subtlest of waves.

When the car had gone, James turned and went back in the house.

London, 1931

J ames had just poured himself a Scotch when the doorbell rang. He glanced across at the modern bronze clock on the bookcase. Michael, he thought. He's back early. He must have forgotten his key. He walked through to the hallway and opened the front door with a flourish. 'Enter, o lost soul!' he commanded.

But to his surprise, it wasn't Michael at all. It was Patricia Burne-Stanley, wearing a fur coat with a huge collar and a brown turban hat, and carrying a small crocodile suitcase.

'*Mon Dieu!*' he said. 'Miss Burne-Stanley! Come in, do!'

She stepped hesitantly inside. 'I'm early,' she said. 'Michael said to meet him here at four.'

'Unchaperoned?' James inquired. He had taken off his jacket and his waistcoat, and he plucked his braces with his left thumb, just to show Patricia how nonchalant he was, half-dressed in front of a young lady.

Patricia looked around the flat as if she almost expected to see Michael hiding behind the sofa. 'I told my people I was going out with Leslie and Alison Parry; do you know the Parrys? But they've got tickets for *Cavalcade*, and they weren't going to miss it for anything.'

James nodded, and smiled. 'In other words, you managed to wangle a date with Michael without anybody breathing down your neck?'

'You could say,' Patricia replied.

'Well, you're getting bold in your old age,' said James. 'Would you like a drink?'

Patricia blushed. 'You don't have a Moussec?'

'No, I don't have a Moussec; but I have some champagne.'

James went through to the kitchen, and opened up the gas refrigerator. 'Perrier-Jouët all right?' he asked her.

'What else do you have in there?'

'A month-old kipper and something that looks suspiciously like stuck-together chocolate profiteroles.'

James returned to the sitting-room with two flute glasses and the cold bottle of Perrier-Jouët. Patricia had taken off her fur coat and was sitting close to the gas fire. The flats at Iverna Court were centrally-heated, but it was bitterly cold and foggy outside, one of those dead frigid November days in the middle of London when even the trees seem to be holding their breath.

'What time did Michael say?' asked James, unwinding the wire around the champagne bottle.

'Half-past four. We were going to go for tea.'

'Oh, tea,' said James. He eased out the cork, no pop, no fizz, and filled Patricia's glass.

'I thought champagne was supposed to make a noise,' said Patricia.

James shook his head. 'Not if you open it properly. Gently twist the base of the bottle, not the cork. This cost 17s 6d a bottle. It has to be treated with respect.'

He lifted his glass, and said, 'Cheers. Here's to beautiful young ladies, and to you in particular.'

'I'm not beautiful,' said Patricia. 'Anyway, I don't care about beauty.'

James sat on the arm of the sofa and sipped his champagne. 'You didn't come out, did you?'

'I didn't want to. Mummy tried to make me, but I wouldn't.'

She was *furious*. She said that I'd spoiled her life for ever. "What's the point of having a daughter, if she doesn't come out," that's what she said. She spent three days in bed and wouldn't speak to me for two months. Actually, it was bliss.'

'You're quite the revolutionary, then?' smiled James.

'I'm independently-minded, that's all,' said Patricia, prettily crossing her legs. 'Besides, the season's such a cattle-market these days. No offence to Henrietta, she's lovely.'

'Well, yes, she is,' James agreed. 'But it's refreshing to meet a girl who hasn't fallen for all the ballyhoo.'

They chatted for almost three quarters of an hour. Then Patricia looked at her watch. 'I hope Michael's all right. He's never been late before.'

'He's probably getting blasé. He's like that, you know. Once he's got a girl around his little finger, he loses interest. You haven't let him kiss you, have you?'

Patricia went pink. James laughed and poured her some more champagne. 'I'm only joking. Michael's terrifyingly loyal, as a matter of fact.'

The telephone rang, and James went to answer it. 'Kensington 2442. Hullo?'

He clipped his hand over the receiver. 'Call-box. Probably Michael.' Then, 'Hullo? Michael? Yes, it's James. Where the dickens are you? Your delectable chum Patricia is here. Yes, she's been waiting for you for nearly an hour.'

He turned to Patricia again. 'He borrowed Freddie Carroll's Invicta, and the clutch went when he was driving through Dorking. He wants to talk to you.'

Patricia took the phone. 'Michael? This is awful! I even managed to shake off the Parrys. Well, no, of course not! But can't you find a garage? Well, can't you leave it where it is? Oh, Michael, this is *awful*. I can't go home until the Parrys meet me after the theatre. What am I going to do until then?'

She was silent for a while, and then she handed the phone back to James. 'He says he wants to talk to you.'

Michael sounded very far away. 'Listen, James, I'm in a terrible fix. Freddie made me swear that I'd bring the car back absolutely *virgo*. I'm waiting for a chap to tow it back to Chichester for me. I can't leave it here, somebody's bound to make off with the wheels or something.'

'Well?' asked James, with his eyes on Patricia.

'Well, could you be a chum and take Patricia out to eat? You know, just feed her and chat to her and keep her happy.'

'Hm,' said James. 'I'm not at all sure about that. I was supposed to be meeting Jimmy McLaughlin at Ciro's.' He winked at Patricia and Patricia smiled back.

'Oh, come on, James, do a chap a favour. If her people find out that she's been spending the evening alone, I'm going to be hung, drawn, castrated, impaled, and sentenced to everlasting doom.'

'Well . . .' said James. 'All right. But it's going to cost you a bottle of Moët.'

The operator interrupted to ask if Michael wanted to put any more money in, but Michael said no, and they were cut off. James cradled the phone, and spread out his hands in a gesture of resignation. 'You're stuck with me, I'm afraid, *ma chérie*. That's if you don't mind dinner with an older man.'

'Oh, Michael's so *disorganized*,' Patricia complained.

'Give the lad a chance, he almost made it.'

'But *Dorking*.'

'I know. He could have had the taste to break down in Reigate. Never mind. I presume that bag of yours contains an evening-dress? Let's see off this bottle of champagne, shall we, and then we can dress for dinner, and then we'll toddle off to Quaglino's and make pigs of ourselves. Do you dance, at all?'

'You're looking at the champion jitterbugger of 1931.'

'Well, then, that's marvellous; we can go on to the Café de Paris.'

'I mustn't be too late,' said Patricia cautiously. 'I've arranged to meet the Parrys at eleven.'

'Cinderella, you shall not only go to the ball, you shall make it back to Kensington High Street before you turn into Christabel Pankhurst.'

Patricia giggled, and lifted her empty glass. 'What about another one, then?'

At half-past seven, they took a taxi-cab up Piccadilly to Bury Street. It was a foggy November night, and the West End was thick with traffic from Hyde Park Corner to Leicester Square, mostly taxis and buses, but a fair number of Rolls-Royces and Armstrong Siddeleys, as well as more modest family cars like Morris 12s and Hillman Wizards. The fog was so thick that the streetlights had soft auroras around them, like illuminated dandelion-puffs; and in Piccadilly Circus the traffic-lights and the electric Sandeman's Port sign were as dim as if they were seen through veils of dirty lace.

Like most of the young people walking out in the West End, off to theatre or dinner or dancing, James and Patricia were both in full rig: James in white tie and tails, Patricia wearing a sleeveless silk evening-dress in palest eau-de-Nil, so clinging that she had decided (blushing hotly as she did so) to leave off her French knickers. Her mother had allowed her to buy this dress only after a long and tiresome argument. She wore it with the pearl necklace that her people had given her for her sixteenth birthday.

'Michael was going to take me to the London Casino,' said Patricia.

'That was gravely unimaginative of him,' James remarked. 'I really must give him some lessons in how to give a lady a good time.'

'But we *always* have a good time. He's a sweetie.'

James gave her an exaggerated older-brother frown. 'Just make sure you don't get too fond of him, that's all. If you give your heart to Michael, he'll crush it into miniscule pieces. They don't call him Mike the Mangler for nothing, you know.'

The taxi dropped them at Quaglino's and James tipped the cabbie threepence. He took Patricia's arm as they entered the restaurant; into the warmth and the laughter and the soothing tinkle of Leslie Hutchinson's piano-music, and Patricia glanced up at him and thought that there was nothing quite so exciting as walking into one of London's most expensive and fashionable nightspots with a handsome, mature man – a man who was old enough to make her feel like a grown-up, and yet very slightly fast, too. I mean, he was quite old enough to be some other woman's husband.

And James thought: this is a very pretty and personable young lady indeed.

'Keep us away from Mr Hutchinson, please,' James told the *maitre-d' hôtel.* 'I love his playing but tonight I want to talk.'

'Whatever you wish, Mr Lord.'

As she was seated, Patricia whispered, 'They know your name. Do you come here very often?'

'On business, as a rule. Never with beautiful girls. Well, not until tonight.'

'You're flattering me,' said Patricia.

'Yes,' said James, 'and you deserve it.'

He watched her as they ate. She was very excited and she talked a lot. Most of the time he wasn't even listening, just watching her. It was mostly about her holiday in Venice and going to State functions with Daddy and didn't Mr Herbert Morrison have the oddest ideas, at least Daddy thought so.

James deliberately chose the most lavish dinner he could. They started with *oeufs pochés Piemontaise* at 2s 6d, for which they could have bought the entire *table d'hôte* at Bertorelli's. They followed with *darne de saumon grillé* for 4s 0d; and then *carré d'agneau boulangère* for 3s 6d and an assortment of vegetables for 4s 10d. They ended the meal with a chocolate *bombe* for 2s 0d.

They drank Dom Perignon champagne with the fish, £1 the bottle; and a 1925 Château Lafitte with the lamb, 17s 0d. James could see Patricia glancing at the bill out of the corner of her eye. He took £3 out of his wallet and told the waiter to keep the change.

'That was perfect,' she told him. Her eyes were bright and she was just a little tipsy from the wine.

'The company made it perfect,' James told her. He laid his hand on top of hers and she didn't take it away. 'If you'll allow me to say so, there are certain people with whom you can feel an affinity right from the first moment you meet them. I don't know why it happens; but then who knows why lightning strikes where it does, why it hits some people and misses others. To me, Patricia, you're one of those people. I feel as if I've been waiting for you to come round the corner for all of my life, as if our meeting this afternoon wasn't accidental at all, but planned by fate.'

'You're engaged,' said Patricia, pretending to be doubtful.

'Who told you that?'

'Michael. He said you were engaged to Henrietta Beesley.'

'I've been walking out with Henrietta from time to time, yes, you're quite right. After all, a fellow can't go out dancing on his own, can he, for fear of being arrested! We went to Ascot together. We may even have *danced* together. But as for being engaged, certainly not! The only wedding-plans between us exist exclusively in my mother's imagination, and that's where they're going to stay, as far as I'm concerned. Why, I haven't seen Henrietta in a fortnight; and tonight I'm not at all sure that I want to, ever again.'

'You're very wicked,' smiled Patricia.

'I don't think it's wicked to be honest. And, if you want me to be honest, I think I'm beginning to take a considerable shine to you, Miss Patricia Burne-Stanley.'

Patricia looked at him seriously. 'You're not playing with me, are you?'

James smiled. 'I'm not James Cagney, you know. And I didn't approve of *Springtime for Henry* one bit. All that infidelity. Let's go dancing.'

'Don't forget that the Parrys are supposed to be picking me up at eleven.'

James said, 'You needn't worry about that. I'll call the *concierge* at Iverna Court and make sure that he tells them you were unavoidably detained, and not to fret. Then I'll call your people, and tell them that everything's fine, we met at the theatre, and that I had the impudence to ask you to dinner. They can blame me then, instead of you.'

Patricia giggled. 'You *are* wicked. I said you were.'

James picked up her hand and kissed it. 'To be *truly* wicked,' he said, 'a man has to indulge his most selfish desires without counting the cost either to himself or to those around him.'

Patricia withdrew her hand. Her breathing was suddenly shallow and quick; out of time with Leslie Hutchinson's languid piano. 'Would you ever do that, do you think?' she asked James.

'Would I ever do what?' asked James, and raised one eyebrow. He could tell that he managed to arouse her. Beneath the table she had crossed her thighs, and under the thin silk of her evening-gown she was unconsciously but rhythmically squeezing them together. Her lips were slightly parted. He could see the gleam of her front teeth.

'Would you ever be truly wicked?' whispered Patricia.

James thought for a moment, without taking his eyes away from her. 'Let's *not* go dancing,' he suggested, at last. 'I'm sure there's another bottle of Perrier-Jouët in the fridge.'

'But what about Michael?'

'Michael can find his own Perrier-Jouët.'

Michael was sitting in the saloon bar of a smoky pub just outside Dorking drinking warm bottled India ale and waiting for the local garage mechanic to arrive, so that Freddie Carroll's wounded Invicta could be towed back to Chichester. He had eaten two cheese-and-tomato sandwiches and smoked three cigarettes. Now there was nothing else to do but wait. The garage mechanic had refused to come out until he had finished his dinner.

Michael drained his glass; not quite to the bottom, because export ale always had a little fine sediment in it. He reached into his pocket for change and debated with himself whether he ought to buy another. A woman with a very red mouth and a ladder in her stockings was laughing loudly right next to his ear. Her companion was a bald-headed man with a green tweed suit and a large Bakelite hearing-aid. He was shouting out off-colour jokes as if he wanted to be heard two miles away. 'And *he* said, "I've got two words for you, my darling – let go!"'

Michael went up to the mock-Tudor bar. 'Have another?' the

barmaid asked him. 'Don't you worry – George'll be along in a minute. But he won't miss his dinner, won't George. He says it's sacred. Once he's washed his hands, anyhow, he doesn't want to get them dirty till he's eaten. Takes him half an hour.'

'Well, I'll have another,' said Michael. 'I was hoping to get back to Chichester by ten.'

'Going out, were you?' the barmaid asked him, nodding at his white tie. Michael was fully dressed for his evening with Patricia.

'Too late now, I'm sorry to say,' Michael told her, and he *was* sorry to say it. He hoped that James was taking care of things; and that he wasn't being off-hand with her. James could be extremely off-hand when he wanted to be. They had dated the Swiggert sisters once, when they were younger, and James had reduced Natalie Swiggert to tears, simply by looking at his watch every four or five minutes, and looking as if he wanted to be somewhere else.

Michael had just taken out his money to pay for his beer when a hand was laid on his arm. 'Here,' said the young man standing next to him. 'I'll get this one.'

'Well, no, that's all right,' Michael protested. 'I have to shoot off in a minute.'

'Won't hear of it,' the young man told him. 'Mavis, give me another barley wine, and whatever this gentleman's having.'

Mavis made a face but did as she was told. The young man gave her half-a-crown. He was tall, with brown curly hair that marked him as a Bohemian of some kind, a hawk-like nose, and bright near-together eyes. He wore a maroon corduroy jacket with pockets crammed full of notebooks and folded-up newspapers, and a grubby scarf of yellow wool.

'Dorking is not what you might call the hospitality capital of the south,' the young man explained. 'In fact, there are more surly so-and-sos per capita than in any other town in the south-east of England, and that's saying something. I try to be the exception to the rule.'

'Well, cheers,' said Michael, lifting his glass. From the way everybody else in the pub was looking at them, he felt rather embarrassed. Even the woman with the red lips had stopped laughing, and was staring at him through the smoke.

'You mustn't allow yourself to be abashed,' the young man said. He grasped Michael's elbow and steered him to a window-seat with flat damp cushions that were about as welcoming as sitting on night-cooled elephant droppings. A sharp draft blew through the badly-fitting window, directly on to Michael's neck.

The young man took out a packet of Capstan and shook it. There was only one cigarette left, and that was a half-smoked nip-end. Michael took out his silver cigarette-case and said, 'Here.'

'Passing Clouds, eh?' the young man said, in appreciation, taking one of the oval Turkish cigarettes. 'Don't get offered many of these. Little too posh for the *petit-bourgeois* of Dorking.' He leaned forward and fed from Michael's gold cigarette-lighter, his eyes half-closed. 'If Philistinism were a place, instead of a word, Dorking would be it. They sacrificed real trees to make artifical half-timbering. By the way, my name's Paul Heath. I'm the local Socialist; that's why everybody's staring. They think that the greatest achievement in life is to own an eight-guinea wireless and a heated tank for their tropical fish.'

'Michael Lord,' said Michael, and cautiously shook Paul Heath's hand.

'That must be your car outside,' Paul suggested.

'Well, it's a friend's, actually. The clutch went, just as I was coming up the hill from South Holmwood.'

'Is this the worst thing that's ever happened in your life? Breaking down, and having to wait here to be rescued?'

Michael put down his drink. 'Why, no, of course not. What on earth do you mean?'

'I don't know,' Paul replied, lifting his aquiline nose as if he were sniffing at Michael to decide what kind of an animal he was. 'You just look like the kind of young man to whom only *nice* things have happened. Privileged, good-looking, well-exercised, well-fed. The kind of young man who would never have *dreamed* of coming in here on purpose.'

Michael smoked for a while but Paul remained silent, smiling, waiting for him to answer. At last Michael looked at him and said, 'You're jumping to conclusions, that's your trouble. You don't even know me, but just because I'm dressed for dinner, you assume that I'm rich and spoiled and pampered.'

'Well, aren't you?'

'I'm comfortable, as far as money goes. But I'm not pampered, and I'm not the kind of chap you think I am. I was brought up to be independent, and to take care of myself, and not to whinge. If I ever get down on my luck, you won't find me begging, and you won't hear me complaining about the injustice of capitalist society, either. It seems to me that Socialists do nothing else. I'm all in favour of fair play, the same as you are, but I do think your average working-class fellow ought to show a bit of spunk.'

Paul laughed. 'I ought to take you up North with me. I ought

to take you around to talk to some unemployed miners. I ought
to take you into the home of somebody who's been living for nine
months on 14s 0d a week partial compensation, and sixpence of
that has to be spent in bus-fares going to collect it. Then you can
talk to me all you like about showing spunk.'

'I'm sorry,' said Michael, 'but however terrible the plight of
unemployed miners happens to be, it's absolutely nothing to do
with me.' This Paul was making him feel not only overdressed,
but seriously aggrieved. 'My family does whatever it can to keep
its own people working, nearly a hundred of them, and we pay
them jolly handsomely, too. We can't be expected to support the
whole of Britain.'

'What does your family do, then?' asked Paul. 'Financiers, are
they? Furriers? Manufacturers of footballs?'

'We build aeroplanes. Lord Aeronautics, at Chichester.'

Paul swallowed beer, and then nodded. 'Michael Lord, I suppose I should have guessed. Perhaps I owe you an apology; or
at least *half* an apology. You lost your father, didn't you, only
a couple of months ago? I read all about it in the *Daily Worker*.
So you *have* experienced something worse than being stranded
here.'

Michael said, 'You really don't have to apologize. I'm not
ashamed of what I am, and I'm not ashamed of anything I've
done. I believe in King and Country, and capitalism, and I believe
in every man standing up for himself.'

Paul finished his beer and looked up at the clock on the pub
wall. 'Let's have another one,' he suggested. 'George won't be
here for twenty minutes at least. I think I'm going to enjoy this
conversation. You don't mind paying, do you? That last round
cost me my last half-crown.'

Michael hesitated. He was beginning to feel nauseous from all
those hurriedly-chewed cheese-and-tomato sandwiches, drenched
in lukewarm India ale. The cigarette-smoke in the pub was
as dense as the fog outside, and he felt that he could scarcely
breathe.

Paul laid a hand on the sleeve of Michael's coat. 'Never let it be
said even in the cold-shouldering fastnesses of Dorking that a
member of the illustrious Lord family failed to stand his shout.'

'Very well, then,' said Michael. 'But this is really going to have
to be the last.'

'You must tell me what you think of Fascism,' said Paul. 'We
must talk about Mussolini, and Hitler. I'm fascinated to know
what a privileged young man like you thinks about the world

95

today. But let's get the drinks in first, shall we? Mine's a barley wine.'

Michael took out his folded handkerchief and pressed it against his forehead.

'Are you all right?' Paul asked him.

'I just feel a little bit dicky, to tell you the truth.'

'It's this smoke. It's quite enough to make anybody feel icky-pah-booh. What you need is some fresh air. Let's wait for George outside. We can take our drinks and sit in your car. Perhaps you could put the top down. That would be a lark.'

So they sat in their overcoats in the back seat of Freddie Carroll's Invicta, in the dark and foggy car-park of the Dog & Bacon, waiting for George the mechanic and drinking beer, and talking about everything from Socialism to contraception.

Paul thought that it was high time that the young of all classes declared their solidarity with the workers, and struggled for a new world of equality and compassion. He had been up North lately, visiting friends in Durham and Newcastle and other Distressed Areas. 'You have no conception of what life is like in the North. They are like a race of starving, staring-eyed semi-humans; more animals than humans. You talk about spunk. Spunk! They can't even talk about hope.'

He seemed to be contemptuous of almost everything and anybody. He was particularly scathing about Beverley Nichols, 'that chatty, fussy, country-cottage Fascist'. He didn't think much of Aldous Huxley, either; but he was quite in favour of football pools and the League of Nations. 'Between them, they represent a way out of a poverty, no matter how slim, and a way of averting war, no matter how ludicrous.' He was very much in favour of barley wine, and had three more.

When at last a breakdown-lorry with a catastrophic crash gearbox and one blinded headlight arrived out of the darkness, and noisily parked beside them, Michael felt that for all of Paul's leftist conversation, and for all of his general seediness, he had become a friend.

George was bundled up in a huge brown overcoat that smelled strongly of kippers. His hair shone with bay-rum. He chained the Invicta to the back of his lorry, burping systematically as he did so. Paul said, 'We must rendezvous in London, you know, next time I'm up. I think you'd make an excellent Socialist, and I'd quite like to have the honour of converting you. Besides, I'm very fond of oysters, and can't usually afford them, so perhaps you could treat me.'

Michael told him his telephone number, and Paul wrote it in the margin of his *Daily Worker* with a leaky pen. They shook hands. Paul said, 'You're an exceptional young man, Michael, take my word for it.'

'I've enjoyed it,' Michael replied. 'I don't know whether you'll ever manage to make a Red out of me. I wasn't brought up that way. But I've enjoyed it – and I must make a point of not quoting you to Mother.'

'Mother I suppose is a Tartaress in a tea-gown.'

Michael laughed, and clapped Paul on the shoulder. 'I must make a *particular* point of not quoting that.'

George started up his lorry and Michael climbed in beside him. George had spread the *Daily Express* on the passenger-seat, because of the grease. Michael waved to Paul and then they were grinding off into the fog, heading southwards for Chichester. George burped three or four times. Michael offered him a cigarette in the hope that it might settle his stomach. It was freezing cold in the lorry's cab, and the smell of kippers was even stronger than before.

George took the cigarette without a word of thanks and Michael lit it for him. 'Friend of yours is he?' George asked, jerking his head backward to indicate that he was talking about Paul.

'Well, no. I've never met him before.'

'Not your type, then?'

'I'm not at all sure what you mean.'

George burped and breathed smoke both at once. 'Didn't you look at his shoes?'

Michael frowned. 'His *shoes?* What about his shoes?'

'Suède,' said George, looking at Michael for the first time. 'That's what about them. Suède.'

A passer-by standing on the pavement outside Iverna Court that evening, if he had raised his eyes to one of the fourth-floor windows of this great soot-blackened block of Edwardian flats, would have seen a shadow flicker momentarily across the ceiling like a huge exotic moth, and then flicker again.

It was the shadow of Patricia, taking off her dress, and swirling it around her head, laughing. Then her thin silk underslip. Eyes bright, cheeks flushed, hair already tangled; as slim and innocent as a flower fairy.

James was pouring champagne. He came across the bedroom holding up two frosted flute glasses, and handed one of them to Patricia. The Columbia gramophone in the sitting-room was fluffily playing Beethoven's *Moonlight Sonata*. James hadn't had time to change the needle.

'I never knew what champagne could do to you,' said Patricia.

James sat on the edge of the bed next to her, in his shirtsleeves. The room was high-ceilinged, and papered in dusty pink, with paintings of skyscapes on the walls, clouds and sunsets and thunderheads. 'Champagne opens your eyes,' James told Patricia. 'And if your eyes are as pretty as yours, all you can see is prettiness.'

He thought she looked irresistible. But he had treated her all evening with restraint; holding her hand but never trying to force her to sit too close to him, or dance too close to him, or kiss him. As it had turned out, intoxicated with Dom Perignon and the daring of it all, it had been *she* who had first kissed him, in the back of the taxi that was taking them to Kensington High Street.

They had diverted the Parrys by leaving a message for them at the Drury Lane Theatre; then Patricia had telephoned her parents and said that she had met an old schoolfriend from Roedean, Bunty Hollister. With her eyes on James, she had said clearly, 'I'm staying the night, yes. Bunty will lend me some pyjamas.'

James had looked up at her, and she had smiled. It was then that he had known for certain that they were going to be lovers. Patricia had made up her mind.

Now she sat on the bed, challenging him with her eyes, wearing nothing but her brassière, slim, pale-skinned, pale as ivory, her thighs clasped tightly together but not too tight to prevent a tiny blonde wisp of pubic hair from escaping.

'Do you know something?' said James. 'If I were an artist, instead of a manufacturer of aeroplanes, I would consider you the ideal model.' He paused, and raised his glass to her. 'I would immortalize you in oils!'

She knelt up on the quilt, and kissed him. First his forehead, then his lips. He suspected that she had seen somebody kissing like this in a film. He kissed her back, still trying to hold himself back. She was very young, for all of her provocative behaviour. He didn't want to frighten her.

She loosened his necktie, and tugged it off. Then she twisted out his collar-studs, and unbuttoned his shirt. She kissed the bare half-moon of his chest, just above his undershirt.

'I'm not very good with men's clothes,' she told him. 'There always seem to be so many layers, and so many peculiar buttons.'

James kissed her ear. It tasted of Chamade. 'Let me help you,' he murmured. 'I'm quite an expert myself.'

He stripped off his shirt, his undershirt, his socks, his sock-suspenders, his trousers and his shorts. He tried not to do it too hastily. He was making love, after all, not rescuing somebody who was drowning. But Patricia stayed kneeling beside him kissing his shoulder and his neck, and ruffling his hair with her fingers.

Soon he was naked. She ran her hand down his chest, tugging gently at the crucifix of curly hair between his nipples. She kissed him, but she kept her eyes open. James realized that this was her first time, and that she wanted to see everything that went on. Her fingers at last slid into the forest of hair between his thighs. She was trembling. He reached for her shoulder, but she resisted him, and whispered, 'Let me do it. Let *me* do it.'

James said, 'The music's finished.'

The gramophone in the sitting-room was playing *splitch-hsssssss-splitch-hssssss* over and over again.

'No,' smiled Patricia. 'The music hasn't finished. It's just that you can't hear it any more.'

She sat astride his lap. Her bare legs were cool and smooth. She held his face in both hands and said, 'You're precious, James. You're so precious.'

He reached behind her back and unfastened her brassière, thick-fingered, more clumsily than he had meant to. Her breasts were small and high and very round, and her nipples were the palest pink, as if she had tinted them by leaning forward and dipping each breast in rose-water, nothing more.

'Do you know something,' James told her, 'I do believe you've seduced me.'

Patricia shook her head. 'You seduced me, my dear, the very moment I walked in here this evening. I've been yours, ever since then.'

James took her in his arms and gently laid her on the quilt. He reached over towards the bedside lamp, but Patricia held his arm and said, 'No. Don't turn off the light.'

They kissed as if they had all the time in the world to kiss. Languid explorations with teeth and lips and tongues. 'Patricia,' said James. Then, 'Pat-*riss*-ee-ah,' as if it were a strange foreign name that he had never heard before. Tenderly, he bowed his head to suck and lick at her nipples, until he could feel them tighten against the roof of his mouth. Patricia stared up at the ceiling like Ophelia floating in the weeds, her eyes open but unfocused, one hand stroking the crown of James's hair. At last James parted her thighs, and lifted himself up, and pushed himself slowly into her, inside her, as far as he could go.

Patricia let out the tiniest of gasps. She stared at James and for a moment he couldn't interpret her expression at all. He thought: *I've hurt her, that's the last thing I wanted to do*. But then she held him as tightly as she could, tighter and tighter, and kissed him and kissed him until he could hardly breathe.

Their lovemaking was arrythmic, the lovemaking of two people who are not yet used to the movement of each other's bodies. But their feelings swelled so fiercely that all they wanted to do was possess each other, to be part of each other, welded flesh, and towards the end of their coupling Patricia started to cry out, a high keening cry that sent goosebumps all the way up James's spine, and she shook and shuddered and threw her head from side to side, until her hair lashed at James's face.

They lay for a long time in silence. They could hear the traffic outside in Wright's Lane; taxis and cars and occasionally a horse-drawn hansom. James looked at Patricia across the hilly countryside of the quilt. He was reminded of that childhood poem about the Land of Counterpane. Patricia smiled back at him, dewy-eyed. She reached across and touched his shoulder. 'James Herbert Lord,' she whispered.

He kissed her, and then sat up. 'More music,' he said. 'And more champagne.'

'And what about Henrietta?' she asked.

He gave her a slight non-committal shrug. 'I always believe in crossing bridges when I come to them.'

He took Michael's robe down from its hook on the back of the bedroom door. He went through to the sitting-room and spent a few minutes changing the gramophone needle. Then he put on Schubert's *Moment Musical in C Major*. He returned to the bedroom with more champagne.

Patricia was still lying where he had left her, naked in the lamplight. Her eyes were now closed but he could tell that she wasn't asleep. Her lips were slightly parted; a single pearl-white droplet slid like a glutinous tear across her thigh. There is no beauty like spoiled beauty, thought James. He held both champagne glasses in one hand, and filled them until the foam ran down the stems, and dripped on to the floor.

Chichester, 1931

Elsie came into the dining-room carrying the roast turkey on a huge Worcester carving-dish, surrounded by roasted potatoes and decorated with water-cress, and everybody at the table applauded. 'What a wonderful monster!' cried Bryan King-Moreton. 'And cooked to a T, by the look of it!'

Constance smiled at her Christmas dinner-guests like an empress, acknowledging their compliments. 'Christmas dinner at Goodwood Lodge has always been unrivalled,' she said. 'Do you know something, even Mr Baldwin was trying to wangle himself an invitation. "Constance, my pet" – that's what he said, he always calls me "pet" – "Constance, my pet, I always feel out of sorts at Christmas. If I could only get away to Aix-les-Bains; or, better still, to somewhere in the country." Then, do you know, he looked at me so pointedly that I had to change the subject altogether.'

The table was set in the family dining-room. There were twenty of them altogether, including James and Richard and Michael, Bryan King-Moreton and Henrietta Beesley. Michael had invited Paul Heath, whom he had met in London five or six times since their first encounter in the Dog & Bacon at Dorking, for theatre, drinks, and supper. Michael had warned Paul not to be too political: and, obediently, Paul talked about art and ballet and why he hated Henry Moore.

Their guest of honour this Christmas was Herbert's old friend and mentor Hugh Trenchard, who had retired two years ago as Chief of the Air Staff and was now Commissioner of the Metropoli-

101

tan Police. Trenchard was in loud and excellent spirits, and was living up to his old Air Force nickname of 'Boom'. Richard, for want of anyone better, had asked a rather silly friend of Henrietta's called Alison Whitley, who henna'd her hair and painted her fingernails blue and knew every fashionable joke and every fashionable dance-step and kept singing, 'Today I feel so happy, so happy; I don't know why I'm happy, I only know I am!'

Outside the day was battleship-grey, and the clouds hung threateningly low over the bare bone-white backs of the Sussex Downs. It hadn't snowed yet, but it must have been cold enough. Half of the pipes at Goodwood Lodge had frozen, and last week they had lost seven sheep to exposure. It was the family's first Christmas without Herbert, and Constance hadn't realized how sharply she would miss him.

She was still dressed in black, although she had done her best to make the Lodge seem welcoming and merry. There were holly wreaths and crimson ribbons everywhere, and the ceiling-beams were decorated with tinsel and shining glass balls. The dining-table was heaped with flowers, and the silverware winked and sparkled in the light from the huge log-fire. But all those fatherly duties of Christmas, like opening the claret and carving the ham, had now fallen to James, and for all of the laughter and all of the warmth, Constance was always close to tears.

James stood up, and sharpened the poultry-knife. 'Bring the monster here!' he told Elsie. 'I've always wanted to do battle with a really big bird like this.'

'As long as you don't *hack* at it, dear,' said Constance.

'She used to say that to Father, too,' James replied.

'Well, this is one of those occasions when we miss the pater rather sorely,' put in Bryan.

'It looks like an *ostrich*, don't you think?' asked Alison. 'I mean, that's what I imagine an ostrich would look like, if you roasted it. Or a kiwi perhaps. They wouldn't be difficult to catch, would they, being flightless? Although, what would one *stuff* them with?'

'I beg your pardon?' Hugh Trenchard asked her, completely baffled.

'How's your police college idea going?' James asked him. He was anxious that Trenchard didn't think that he was being played for a fool. He was, after all, a peer of the realm and the father of the modern Air Force, and his opinion was still revered when it came to selling new designs to the Air Ministry.

'Oh, the college? It's coming along, coming along,' said Trenchard. 'We shall soon be seeing a far better police force in London.

Better educated, and far more up-to-date. Heaven knows we need it, in these days of unrest. Riots, Reds, hunger-marchers. The capital is on the brink of a Communist revolution, you know, for all that you can still get a bottle of Château Suduiraut 1900, if you know where to look for it. Only the thinnest of blue lines is preventing us from waking up tomorrow and finding that Trafalgar Square has been renamed Lenin Square, and that Nelson has been toppled from his perch and replaced by a likeness of Karl Marx, cast in spelter.'

'I wouldn't worry too much about that,' said Paul Heath. 'I expect the workers would concern themselves with feeding their families before they started toppling statues. What's a bottle of that wine you mentioned? Fifteen shillings? You could feed a family of four for a week on fifteen shillings.'

Michael kicked at Paul's shin under the table. Paul smiled at Trenchard and added, 'You could, of course, choose to spend your money on something else. It's your money.'

James detached the turkey's legs and began to slice the breast, watched in high tension by Constance; but not by Henrietta, who was sulking. Michael had shaved off his Robert Donat moustache only two days ago, at Paul Heath's suggestion, and nobody could quite get used to him. He looked five years younger, almost adolescent, and rather naked. Apart from Paul, he had also invited Geraint Arnold, a friend from the University Aero Club, who was amiable but slightly deaf, the result of having flown a Sopwith Pup into a tree.

'Did somebody say this was *ostrich*?' Geraint asked, in amused disbelief, as James passed him his plate.

'That's right,' said James. 'Elsie will help you to the coconut casserole and the giraffe-hoof delight.'

'Thank you,' nodded Geraint.

'Extraordinary,' said Trenchard.

Richard picked up his wine glass. 'I thought this might be an appropriate moment to make an announcement. May I, Mother?'

Constance already knew what Richard was going to say. 'Of course,' she told him. Now she took her eyes away from James's carving and concentrated on his face instead.

Richard said, 'Most of you know that – since father died – Bryan King-Moreton and I have been working very hard on a new version of the *Chichester Special*. We thought it appropriate that Father's death should be commemorated in some way; and the best way we could come up with was to design a new racing seaplane, a faster *Chichester Special*, and build it in time to enter for next year's Seraphim Trophy. And win it, of course.'

There was a little light table-banging, and discordant cries of 'Hear! Hear!'

Richard blushed. 'The announcement we have to make is that the designs of the new *Chichester Special* were completed late last week, nearly a whole month ahead of schedule, and that we shall start construction work on Monday, January 4.

'As you know, Flight-Lieutenant Stainforth took the world airspeed record up to 406 mph at the Isle of Wight in September. We plan to take the *Chichester Special* up to 420 mph or even faster. We want not only the Seraphim Trophy but the speed record, too.'

There was more applause, and cries of 'Bravo!' from Hugh Trenchard, whose wife at last said 'Shush, Hugh, this isn't a hockey match.'

James finished carving the turkey without saying a word, his face tight. He had been powerless to prevent Bryan King-Moreton from continuing his experimental work at Hayward's Heath, despite the fact that Bryan had requisitioned four of his best draftsmen and had already spent over seventeen thousand pounds on constructing a two-hundred-foot water-tank for pontoon tests, and rebuilding the *Chichester Special*'s sixteen-cylinder engine from scratch. James very rarely talked about the *Chichester Special*; it made him too angry to think of the time and the money and the waste of production facilities. They had already lost an order for six specially-converted Aquarius passenger-aeroplanes from the French line Air Orient. If there were any more losses, James was seriously thinking of taking Lord Aeronautics to the High Court, to challenge the wisdom of his father's will.

As the Lord family and their guests ate their Christmas dinner, the conversation burbled from aeroplanes to marriages to the latest films and back to aeroplanes. Bryan said loudly, 'Have you seen Geoffrey de Havilland's new bird? Splendid thing, he flew it for the first time in October. Steady as a rock, wonderful little plane. Based on the Moth, of course. He calls it the Tiger Moth.'

Michael said, 'Moths and I don't really get on.'

'Oh, you should see it,' said Bryan, enthusiastically, washing roast potato down with wine. 'Sure to make him a fortune.'

'Better than some aeroplanes I could mention,' James remarked, under his breath. But his mother caught what he was saying, right from the very far end of the table, and she gave him the hardest of looks, to shut him up.

James hadn't believed that Richard and Bryan King-Moreton could draw up their designs for the new *Chichester Special* so quickly. Originally, they had talked about starting work on the airframe in February or March, even later. Now it seemed that even more resources were going to be diverted to Hayward's Heath, and even sooner than James had anticipated. And this was just when James was test-flying his all-metal rival to the Douglas DC3, the Lord Capricorn.

'Absolutely hilarious,' said Jennifer Unwin, one of their neighbours. 'I said to my cook's daughter, what are these orange things? She said "Carrots". I said what are these green things, and she said "Cabbages". Then I said what are these *white* things, and she said "Parsnips". Well, that's very clever of you, I told her – now can you give me a word which covers all three things? And do you know what she said? "Yes, Mum, gravy."'

James was cutting up his turkey when Elsie came into the dining-room, walked all the way up to his chair, and bent forward to breathe in his ear. 'There's a telephone-call for you, Mr James. Urgent and personal.'

'Now? In the middle of Christmas dinner? Who on earth is it? Tell him to ring me back later.'

'I'm sorry, Mr James, he did say urgent and personal.'

'Well, who is it, Elsie, for goodness' sake?'

'Mr Burne-Stanley, sir. All he said was, urgent and personal.'

James hesitated, and then dragged his napkin out of his collar and put it down on the table. 'Very well, Elsie, thank you. Mother – everybody – will you please excuse me. I have to answer a telephone call, which is apparently urgent.'

'Shouldn't have been invented, the telephone,' Hugh Trenchard said, loudly. 'I hardly ever needed one, myself. One good bellow is worth twenty telephone calls. A telephone call can be kept secret. A good bellow always gets out beyond the door.'

James went into the library and picked up the candlestick telephone. 'Mr Burne-Stanley?' he asked. 'This is James Lord speaking. This is rather an awkward time to call. I've just sat down to my Christmas dinner.'

'You, at least, can eat your Christmas dinner,' said Gordon Burne-Stanley.

'I beg your pardon, sir, I don't follow.'

'You, at least, can keep your Christmas dinner down,' Gordon Burne-Stanley went on. 'My only daughter Patricia cannot, because she is suffering from sickness. In fact, her sickness was so severe this morning that I took her to see our local doctor. Yes, I interrupted *his* Christmas Day, too. I thought at first that she was suffering from food-poisoning, but the doctor's opinion was quite different. Patricia is *fzzz-crickle-scritch.*'

James could see his face in the magnifying mirror beside the telephone. He was sweaty and white. 'I'm sorry, Mr Burne-Stanley, there was a fault on the line. Patricia is what, did you say?'

'Patricia is to become a mother, James. The doctor has diagnosed that she is pregnant.'

There was an extremely long silence. But at last Gordon Burne-Stanley managed to say, 'She names you, James, as the father. Under much duress, I might add. She is loyal, I suppose, if nothing else.'

James said, 'I'd better talk to my solicitor, don't you think?'

'Well, it goes further than that, I'm afraid to say. This is completely confidential, but under the circumstances you had better know about it. You're quite aware, I'm sure, of my interest in the matter of unemployment? You remember the speeches I made in Glasgow, exhorting the unemployed to have no more children, and suggesting that the dole should be *reduced* on the birth of any additional child to a family whose principal breadwinner had been unemployed for longer than one year? Well, yes, those remarks attracted a great deal of attention, didn't they? The Weans Test, that's what the *Daily Herald* called it.'

'I'm not at all sure what this has to do with Patricia being pregnant,' James put in.

'My dear man, it has everything in the world to do with it. Last October Philip Metcalfe began to indicate that he was thinking of resigning from the Ministry of Labour. On Saturday night, he called the Prime Minister and told him that he would not be returning to his post after the Christmas holidays. The Prime Minister rang me and asked me if I would be prepared to take the job. My first Cabinet appointment, James; the single most important advance in my political career.'

Gordon Burne-Stanley was breathing hard. 'I cannot possibly in all conscience accept this post when my own daughter is pregnant out of wedlock. You have not only compromised my daughter, young man, you have gravely compromised my entire political life.'

James ran his hand through his wavy hair. He could hear the family at the dinner-table, laughing loudly. 'I really don't know what to say, sir. Are you absolutely sure that the child is mine? I've only seen Patricia once, when I took her out to dinner in November. She's Michael's girlfriend, not mine.'

It was obvious from the huffing on the phone that Gordon Burne-Stanley was having a great deal of difficulty controlling himself. But in a strangled-sounding voice, he managed to say, 'She's been talking to her mother. Her mother's got it all out of her. Apparently there's no possible doubt about it. You were the only one who – well, you were the only one.'

James was silent. Gordon Burne-Stanley said, 'There's no question of getting rid of it. Her mother's a Catholic; and quite apart from that the doctor doesn't advise it. If she gets rid of this one, she may never be able to have children again, and, good God, it's difficult enough marrying your daughters off in any case, with all their necessaries intact.'

'So what do you suggest?' asked James. He was feeling very chilled, all of a sudden, and he shuddered as if somebody were walking over his grave.

'Don't be too long, James, darling!' Constance called. 'Your turkey's getting cold!'

Gordon Burne-Stanley said, 'It's up to your conscience, old boy. I'll give you forty-eight hours to think it over, then I want you or your solicitor to call me back and tell me what you've decided. I have to talk to the PM on Monday, and give him a definite answer.'

'Very well,' said James. He hesitated, and then he said, 'A very merry Christmas, sir. And give my best wishes to Patricia.'

He hung up before Gordon Burne-Stanley could answer. He returned to the dining-room and sat down. Richard asked, 'Is everything all right, James? You look as if you had lost a pound and found sixpence.'

James picked up his fork, and prodded a potato from one side of his plate to the other. 'I couldn't have put it better myself.'

'It's not bad news, is it?' asked Constance, focusing on him sharply over the curling steam of the vegetable tureens.

James kept his eyes lowered, his feelings masked. 'No, Mother. It's not bad news. You might even say that I've just been given notice of a happy event.'

But, there was worse to come. When the family were gathered in the sitting-room after their meal, to take coffee and liqueurs and pick their favourites out of an enormous box of Belgian fondants, Michael stood in front of the fire and asked if he could have everybody's attention. His cheeks were flushed with wine and his eyes were very bright.

'Are you going to sing for us, Michael?' asked Henrietta.

'Oh God, I hope not,' said Richard. 'Michael used to be excused from singing in the school choir, because his voice upset the housemaster's cats.'

Paul Heath seemed to know what Michael was going to say, because he sat at the opposite side of the room, ignoring the noisy circle around the hearth and devouring Charbonnel et Walker chocolate mints as if he hadn't eaten for two days. James, glancing at him, thought that he seemed not only to know what Michael was going to say, but to disapprove of it; or at the very least to find it displeasing.

Michael briskly rubbed his hands together. 'You probably know that I've been seeing quite a lot of Patricia Burne-Stanley lately.'

James immediately turned his back and stared at his younger brother in growing alarm.

'I know this is probably premature,' said Michael – and James thought *premature*, what an ironic word to pick! – 'but Patricia and I have been getting along together like a house on fire. And, well, I've decided to ask her to marry me. Mother knows all about it, and has given her blessing. I shall be calling Patricia in Oxfordshire at five o'clock; she's expecting me to call. And that's when I'm going to pop the question!'

Everybody clapped; everybody except James, who lowered his head and shaded his eyes with his hand, and Paul Heath, who continued to devour chocolate mints as if his life depended on them. Constance stood up, and smacked her hands together like a pair of pale kid gloves. 'Michael, I'm *so* pleased! What a surprise! And she's such a lovely young girl! Really, James, your brother is putting you to shame! It's about time you popped the question to Henrietta!'

Michael said, 'I told you it was premature, but I have to confess that I'm absolutely smitten, and if she doesn't say yes – well, I think I shall have to shoot myself, or go to live in Australia.'

James raised his eyes and, as he did so, he found himself looking at Paul Heath. There was the oddest expression on Paul Heath's face. It was almost petulant. Paul held his gaze for a moment and then returned his attention to the mint chocolates. James felt disturbed and reached towards the side-table for a cigarette.

'Well, you really can't beat Young Love,' proclaimed Hugh Trenchard, as emphatically as if it were a cheap but honest Portuguese wine.

'Oh, she's bound to say yes,' put in Jennifer Unwin, their neighbour. 'When I saw you two together last month, Michael, I said to myself, those two are *made* for each other. Simply *made* for each other.'

Richard came forward and took hold of his younger brother's

hand. 'Well, then, young Romeo! Premature congrats for a premature announcement. And if she doesn't say yes, James and I will jolly well rag her until she does, won't we, James?'

James said nothing but sat back in his chair with his eyes lowered, smoking.

While Richard opened a fresh bottle of champagne and asked for glasses all around so that they could drink a toast to Michael's success, Henrietta came and sat next to James and laid her hand on his sleeve. She was wearing a calf-length day dress of bottle-green silk, with a square neckline and a wide floppy bow of white silk at the bust. She looked particularly petite and pretty.

'James?' she said. 'Is anything wrong? You look upset.'

James blew out smoke. 'No, no, Hennie, I'm perfectly fine, thank you. Top hole.'

Henrietta was silent for a little while, her fingernail drawing invisible patterns on James's sleeve. Then she said, 'It's queer, isn't it? I always thought that *we* would be the first.'

James looked at her. She gave him a quick, funny little smile.

'I don't know,' said James. 'Ever since Father died . . . I've had an absolute ton of responsibility. There just don't seem to be the hours in the day to think about getting married.'

'Then I'm wasting my time, waiting for you?'

'Hennie, sweetest, I didn't say that. It's just that there's so much more to *do*.'

'And you don't think that I could help you do it? I'm a bright, intelligent woman, James. I can ride and cook and sew and arrange flowers and organize dinner-parties. Haven't you any idea of how much of an asset I could be? And here I am, almost begging you to marry me, and I didn't mean to do that at all. The fact is that I love you, you rotter, and I do believe that you love me, too. But what have you done? You've allowed your youngest brother to beat you to the altar!'

James crushed out his cigarette half-smoked. He took hold of Henrietta's hands and squeezed them. 'Henrietta, the truth is I'm in a bit of a tight corner at the moment, one way or another.'

'Then it's off?' she said, loudly.

James shushed her. 'The truth is, Hennie, it isn't really on yet. Well, I mean, not officially. We have to give it time.'

Tears settled on Henrietta's cheeks. From the other side of the sitting-room, Constance had noticed that they were arguing and she was gradually lifting her neck in that chilling gesture of utter disapproval, her eyes as cold as a pelican's.

'Hennie, believe me, I love you,' James reassured her. 'But I have some rather complicated business to settle first, before I can ask you to marry me. Let's talk about it later.'

He gave Henrietta his handkerchief and she dabbed at her eyes. 'Oh, damn, look, my mascara's running.'

'Go upstairs and sort it out,' James told her. 'We can talk properly when everybody's gone home.'

Henrietta went up to her guest bedroom. James took another cigarette out of the silver cigarette box engraved with the words *To Herbert Lord, A Token of Appreciation from the Cambridge University Air Squadron, 1928.* He was about to light it when Constance came across and stood over him. 'Mother?' he acknowledged, and stood up.

'What's the matter with Henrietta?' she demanded.

'Cigarette smoke, that's all,' said James, trying to sound offhand. 'It irritates her eyes. She's allergic to certain brands. Craven-A, I think.'

'Don't you lie to me, James,' Constance warned him. 'She was crying, and she looked upset.'

'Well . . .' James admitted, 'there was a little of that. You know what girls are. Michael made his announcement and she came over all sentimental.'

'She wanted to know why *you've* never proposed?'

'I told her. I'm too busy. It wouldn't be fair to get married now. She would scarcely ever see me.'

'There's something else.'

'I beg your pardon?'

'There's something else, James, I can tell. I'm not stupid, you know, even though you always try to treat me as if I am.'

James stood with his lips pursed, thinking. Then he said, 'Can we talk in private?'

'Now?' Constance queried.

'I think we ought to.'

'Very well, then, I'll get my coat. Let's take a turn in the garden.'

Outside, there was a raw grey wind blowing through the orchard. The bare apple-trees lashed and dipped like hysterical women, and up above their heads the clouds ran madly. Constance wore an ankle-length sable with a huge collar and a fur Cossack hat to match; James had put on his sombre black wool City coat, with the astrakhan lapels, and his borsalino hat.

'I still like to get out, you know,' said Constance. 'I don't care how wild it is. Your father used to adore days like these.'

James looked around him. It was only ten to four, but the light had almost been swallowed up already. It didn't seem like Christmas Day. The world seemed strange and inhospitable, as if it had changed for ever, and nothing lay ahead but unfamiliarity and darkness. You could look at the landscape this afternoon and almost believe that England was at war.

'You're still angry with Richard, aren't you?' asked Constance. 'You're still angry with me, too.'

'I didn't come out here to talk about that,' said James.

'But it's true, isn't it? You were always jealous, because Richard and your father were so very close. And you're still jealous, because Richard is going to bring the same honour to the family name that your father did, *and* honour your father, too.'

'Mother,' James insisted, 'that was not what I wanted to talk about. The *Chichester Special* is another question altogether.'

'James, why don't you *help* Richard with the *Chichester Special*, instead of constantly making things difficult for him? You heard what he said today, the plans are all completed, they can start building next month. Why can't we make it a family effort? Why can't we all work together to give your father's name one final shining coat of gold?'

James turned his back to the wind. 'Mother – I'm not jealous of Richard and right at this particular moment the *Chichester Special* is not the most pressing of my problems.'

Constance held her collar close up to her face, so that James could see only her eyes. The wind ruffled the fur.

James said, 'Patricia Burne-Stanley is going to have a baby.'

'I *beg* your pardon?' Constance quavered.

'Patricia Burne-Stanley is pregnant. I found out today, during lunch. That's what that telephone call was all about.'

'You mean that Michael *has* to get married?'

James lowered his eyes. 'No, Mother. Michael doesn't know.'

'He doesn't *know*?' Constance queried. 'You mean she hasn't told him? Why on earth not? And why has she decided to tell you?'

'She didn't. That was her father on the phone, Gordon Burne-Stanley. Patricia's been sick, apparently, so sick that they took her to the doctor this morning. The doctor confirmed that she was pregnant.'

Constance knew what James was going to say. She stared at him like the poker-spined matriarch out of a Russian tragedy, gloriously hurt, spectacularly offended, her fury so complete that she was unable to take in the breath that would have enabled her to speak.

'The baby, apparently, is mine,' said James. He didn't look his mother in the eye. 'Although Michael has been seeing so much of Patricia, it seems that – well, they haven't been to bed together. I saw Patricia only once, that evening when Michael's car broke down; and, well, it appears that one evening was sufficient to make a mother of her.'

'How *could* you!' Constance breathed. Behind her, the trees lashed even more furiously. 'James – how *could* you!'

James shrugged. 'Well, I don't know. I suppose I was careless. Well, I *was* careless. But it's all rather too late now. Stable doors, and all that. The problem is that the Burne-Stanleys aren't too keen on getting rid of it, even though the Right Honourable Gordon Burne-Stanley MP has just been offered Philip Metcalfe's job at the Ministry of Labour. You can imagine what would happen if the Socialist papers find out that Patricia has a bun in the oven. They'd make absolute mincemeat out of him.'

'Dear God,' said Constance. 'I don't know what to say. If your father were alive, James, he'd have forty fits. I really don't know what to say.'

James laid his hand on her shoulder. 'I'm sorry, Mother. It's all rather a mess.'

'What did Gordon have to say about it?' asked Constance.

'I think he expects me to do the honourable thing, as quickly as possible.'

'But what about Michael? Oh, your poor brother!'

'I don't know. I suppose it rather depends on what he feels about bringing up James the Second. And it rather depends on Patricia, too, don't you think?'

'Did Gordon tell you what Patricia feels about it? Did you talk to her?'

James shook his head.

'My dear God, this is quite terrible,' said Constance. 'I'm glad that *you* can take it so lightly.'

'I'm not taking it lightly at all,' said James. 'I'm just trying to think what to do for the best.'

'She's a *very* nice gel,' Constance remarked, as if she were talking to the Worcester Pearmain right beside her. 'At least, I always used to *believe* that she was a very nice gel.'

'Mother, I don't want to marry her. To tell you the truth, I don't want to marry anybody just yet.'

'Well, I saw you arguing with Henrietta,' said Constance, stiffly.

James shook his head. 'I seem to have caused a great deal of trouble, don't I?'

'*Trouble?* That's an understatement. I don't expect you to marry anybody if you really don't want to. That would be folly. But I'm very unhappy about upsetting Gordon. He's our best ally in the House. We never would have managed to sell so many Aquariuses to the Air Ministry if it hadn't been for Gordon. And, quite apart from that, he was a *very* dear friend of your father's.'

'I suppose Michael would be the ideal answer,' James suggested. 'I mean, he's absolutely *dying* to marry her.'

Constance lifted her head in determination. 'I'll have to telephone Sara Burne-Stanley straight away. I'm hurt, James, I can't pretend that I'm not. But I'm glad you decided to talk to me straight away. It's the first sensible thing that you've done since your father died.'

She began immediately to make her way back towards the house, at a fast bustling clip. James stood alone in the bleakness of the apple-orchard for a while, and then followed her.

Constance said, 'Come in, Michael. I have something to tell you.'

Michael hesitated at his mother's bedroom door. He had realized half an hour ago that something was up, because of the way in which James and his mother had disappeared together into the orchard, and then, on their return, immediately hurried upstairs. He had heard the telephone in the hall *ping* just once, the way it always did when Mother was using her upstairs extension.

It hadn't occurred to him, however, that their comings-and-goings had anything to do with him. There were always intrigues being hatched at Goodwood Lodge: business tussles between James and Richard; social skulduggery between Constance and the friends she invited to afternoon tea; and all the urgent and secret family conferences that took place whenever the possibility of a major contract came up. He usually ignored them. He didn't work for Lord Aeronautics just yet, and sometimes he questioned whether he ever would. With James in charge of airliners, and Richard handling all the racing, there didn't seem to be very much for him to do.

'Sit down,' said Constance. 'Close the door.'

Michael sat down, smoothing his upper lip with his fingers. He was still unused to having no moustache. The space between his nose and his mouth felt as white and as noticeable as an unpasted billboard, and he was already wondering whether he ought to let his moustache grow back.

'James not here?' he asked, looking around the bedroom.

'I asked James to rejoin our guests. What I have to tell you, I wished to tell you in private.'

'It's not about Paul, is it?'

'Paul? Paul who?'

'My friend, the one I brought home. The one with the brown corduroy jacket. You can't really tell anything by people's shoes, you know. He's not like that at all. He just thinks they're comfortable.'

'Michael, what on earth are you talking about?' Constance queried. 'I wanted to talk to you about Patricia.'

Michael sat back, and thrust his hands into his pockets. 'I wondered what you and James were having such a furtive chinwag about. I see, it's Patricia. You think that I made a clot of myself, don't you, announcing to everybody that I'm going to ask her to marry me. Well, perhaps I did. But I did it in front of everybody because I didn't want you to have the chance to put me off. I know I'm the youngest. I know James doesn't think that a chap ought to get married until he's been out with half of the girls in the known world. But the fact is that I love Patricia very much, and I can't imagine ever meeting any girl better.'

'I know that, Michael,' said Constance, with unexpected gentleness.

Michael looked up. 'Then what?' he said. 'What's the objection? If I ask her, you know, the very worst she can do is turn me down. It won't be any skin off your nose.'

'You don't expect her to turn you down, though, do you?'

Michael frowned at his mother suspiciously. 'No, as a matter of fact I don't. But what exactly are you getting at? You haven't been calling her people, have you?'

Constance nodded. 'I'm afraid it was necessary. You see, Patricia might well have said yes to your proposal of marriage. But I'm afraid, my dear, that events have taken rather a – how shall I put it? – rather a *complicated* turn.'

Michael was silent. He gripped the arms of his chair as rigidly as if he were being hurtled involuntarily through the air.

Constance said, in that strangely high, distracted voice of hers, 'Patricia is *dearly* fond of you, Michael. So her mother tells me. But you probably weren't aware that during the course of your friendship she met and fell in love with another man.'

'Another man?' asked Michael, shocked. 'What other man? Who? She never mentioned another man.'

Constance paused, and then returned to what sounded to

Michael like a prepared speech. 'Patricia was ready at first to accept that her love for this other man was hopeless. He showed no continuing interest in her, and besides, he was already committed to another gel, or seemed to be. Because of that, Patricia would have been content to marry you.'

'Oh, I see,' said Michael, growing annoyed. 'First reserve, is that it?'

'Of course not, my darling, you could never be second-best. But romantic feelings are always madly unpredictable, especially when one is so young. It's the hormones, you now. You may *want* to be in love with somebody; you may *want* until you're quite black in the face. But wanting to be in love is not enough. Your father used to say that falling in love is like being stabbed in the back. You never know when it's going to happen; but, once stabbed, you can never be unstabbed.'

'So what . . . *complicated* turn do events seem to have taken?' asked Michael.

Constance stood up, and walked around Michael's chair, and laid her hands on his shoulders. 'My dear,' she said. 'Patricia is expecting this other man's child.'

Michael twisted his head around and stared at her. She gave him the gentlest of sympathetic nods, *it's true*, and he turned around again without a word and sat with his hands steepled over his nose and his mouth and his eyes watering with tears.

'She would have married you, my dear,' Constance whispered, 'but she says that she cannot expect you to bring up this child, and that every time she looked at it, it would always remind her of the man with whom she had fallen in love.'

Michael sat silent for a very long time, and the tears ran between his fingers and dropped on to the carpet. He was, after all, only twenty; and he had loved Patricia quite desperately. He had always felt that there was a mystical rightness about their meeting, love blossoming on the very day that he had buried his father. Bury the dead, and make a new beginning. He wasn't yet old enough to understand that he could fall in love as deeply as this twenty times over, before he was too old to fall in love at all.

'So, I did make a clot of myself,' he said, sniffing. His mother tugged her handkerchief out of her sleeve and gave it to him. It smelled of lily-of-the-valley. 'Why did you clap, when I made my ridiculous announcement? Why did you let everybody congratulate me? Why didn't you tell me straight away?'

'I didn't tell you because I didn't know. Not then, anyway.'

'Then when did you find out?'

Constance crossed the room and stood with her back to him. 'You must promise me not to be angry.'

'How can I make you a promise like that?'

She turned around, and lifted one warning finger. 'You must *promise* me, Michael, not to be angry.'

Michael shrugged, and wiped his nose. 'All right,' he said, in a coldy voice.

'James told me,' said Constance.

'*James* told you? But how di –'

Michael sat with his mouth open, scarlet-eyed, dumbstruck.

'James is fearfully sorry about it,' said Constance. 'He wanted to tell you himself, but I thought it better if I did.'

Michael was trembling all over. 'James is fearfully sorry about it, is he?' he repeated. Then, 'James is fearfully sorry about it?'

He stood up, almost overbalancing. He chopped one hand in the air again and again, as if he were beating away an hysterical bird-of-prey. 'It was James! Good God, Mother, it was James! Patricia fell in love with James! And he let her! He knew I loved her, and he *let* her! And he made her pregnant, too! He bloody well made her pregnant! And I never even took her to bed!'

Constance snapped, 'Don't! And don't blaspheme! It's happened! Nobody wanted it to happen, but it has! There's nothing you can do!'

'I can knock James's bloody block off!'

'You won't do anything of the kind and you won't speak that way in front of your mother! We're all sorry. James is particularly sorry. I think that his behaviour was despicable, but all I can say is that perhaps he's saved you from marrying somebody who could never truly love you.'

'Why shouldn't I marry somebody who would never truly love me? It seems to be the style in this rotten family.'

'How dare you!' Constance retorted. 'I suggest you go to your room and stay there until you can learn to behave in a civilized manner.'

'Like James, you mean? Taking advantage of his own brother's girlfriend, and making her pregnant? Is that what you call civilized?'

Michael wrenched open the door, and stood staring at his mother in apoplectic rage. 'You're an absolute witch, do you know that? You're a complete and utter witch!'

'Michael!' cried Constance. But Michael went out and slammed her bedroom door so violently that he cracked the plaster around the frame.

'James!' he bellowed, jumping down three stairs at a time. *'James!'*

Constance came out of her room, and called out after him. 'Michael! Michael! If you make a scene in front of our guests, I shall never forgive you as long as I live!'

But Michael couldn't hear, or didn't want to. He banged open the drawing-room door, so that it knocked over a small wine-table and sent liqueur-glasses and sugared almonds scattering across the carpet. The assembled guests, relaxing beside the Christmas tree in their chairs and sofas in a warm and comfortable atmosphere of cigar-smoke and brandy, looked up startled as Michael stalked across the floor with his fists raised.

Constance was already at the door. 'Michael!' she snapped. Hugh Trenchard turned this way and that and humphed, 'What? What? What's going on?'

James had been sitting with one leg crossed over the other, smoking a Player's Perfectos No 1 and talking idly to Alison Bradley about the theatre. He tried to look nonchalant as Michael came storming towards him; but then Michael seized the lapels of his jacket and tried to heave him out of his chair.

'You bastard!' Michael shouted at him. 'You absolute bastard!'

James said, 'Michael! What the thump! For God's sake, Michael, what *are* you doing?' and even attempted to look round at Alison and give her a grin of pretended perplexity. But then Michael twisted him sideways out of his chair, and the two of them overbalanced and sprawled across the floor. Lady Trenchard withdrew her feet and tucked her dress tight around her calves, just in case either of the brothers should accidentally glance upward.

For a moment or two, James and Michael grunted and wrestled on the floor. Constance shouted, 'Get up! Get up!' and then Richard tried to pull them apart. Michael pushed him away, scrambled up on to his knees, and punched James awkwardly on the left cheek.

'Michael!' cried Paul Heath. 'Michael, for goodness' sake, stop it!'

But Michael tried to punch James a second time; and this time James dragged him on to his feet, and punched him back, an uncompromising Oxford University straight left which hit the bridge of Michael's nose so hard that everybody in the room heard the bone crack. Michael staggered back, and then tumbled over the arm of Alison's chair, his arms and legs flailing, and down came the huge family Christmas tree right on top of him, tinsel, baubles, crackers, stars, branches, lights, presents, fairy and all.

Michael sat up, his shoulders draped in tinsel, blood splattering from both nostrils on to his shirt. He dabbed at the blood with his fingers, and then looked up at James, still stunned. James held out his hand and said, 'Michael, really . . . I'm terribly sorry.'

Constance stood with her hands raised as if she had been caught by a still photographer. Richard had a look on his face that was half disbelief and half amusement. Hugh Trenchard was frowning around for his brandy.

It was Paul Heath who knelt down beside Michael and gave him his handkerchief, and put his arm around him. 'Michael? Are you all right, Michael? Your nose is broken. Here, put your head back.'

Paul turned to James and said, with unexpected ferocity, 'We have to get him to the hospital, to have his nose set straight. You didn't have to hit him as hard as that. He's your brother, isn't he? You might have ruined his face for life.'

James rubbed his knuckles. He could have said something to Paul in reply, but he decided that it would be wiser not to. His father had once warned him against getting into screaming matches with women and nancies. 'I'll bring the car round,' he said. 'There's bound to be somebody on duty at the cottage hospital.'

'Dear God,' said Constance. 'This was supposed to be Christmas.'

'It's still Christmas,' James told her. 'It just seems that some of us are lacking the Christmas spirit.'

'Well,' said Trenchard, 'don't know what to say, quite.'

'Don't say anything, dear,' his wife advised him.

Richard knelt down beside Michael. 'Paul's right, you know, Michael. Better get that nose looked at.'

Michael nodded, with Paul's bloody handkerchief pressed to his nose. Some of the Christmas guests gathered up the sugared almonds, bobbing and genuflecting as they did so. Others worthily attempted to raise the tree, showering tinsel and pine-needles all over Constance's Axminster. Everybody was deeply embarrassed, whether they had been fighting or not.

James returned, flushed and over-anxious, to announce that the car was waiting by the porch. Michael was ushered away by Paul Heath, one arm around his shoulder. After this sorry little procession had passed him by, Bryan King-Moreton beckoned Richard to the hall outside.

'I can't say that I thought an awful lot of that,' said Bryan.

Richard said, 'No,' even though he was still watching Michael being helped into the Humber Snipe outside. There was a sharp smell of woodsmoke and petrol in the hall, outdoor smells.

Bryan said, 'I'm not too keen on family upsets at the moment, Richard, particularly if James starts to win your mother over. We're going to need a lot more cash from the company coffers very shortly; twenty thousand at least; and we need to have equilibrium. I don't want James riled. He's managed to swallow the *Chichester* up until now, but this kind of nonsense may be just the thing to turn him off.'

Richard took out a Kenilworth cigarette and lit it. 'It's up to Mother, in the long run. She's the majority shareholder, by far.'

'Yes, well, you're right,' Bryan acknowledged. 'But it sometimes baffles me, what the pater was thinking about when he made his will. The mater's a wonderful woman. A fine woman, don't get me wrong. But you can count the women who know anything about aeronautics on one hand; and the mater isn't one of them, sorry to say. She's swayed by sentiment, don't you see, rather than practicalities.'

Richard looked at Bryan through the drifting smoke of his cigarette and thought, reluctantly, that he really didn't like him as much as he had before. Richard had always felt that the family should keep together, no matter what. He hated arguments. Even when he was convinced that he was right, Richard was often prepared to concede that he might be wrong, rather than start an argument. He had loved his father; his father had bound his family together, and that was one of the strongest reasons for him wanting to build another *Chichester Special*: to bring his father's influence back into the family, to recreate those days when the Lords had been working together towards the same glorious end – the Seraphim Trophy, speed, glamour, and fame. Even James had admitted that he had loved those days.

What Bryan had patently failed to understand was that Richard wanted the Seraphim Trophy not to divide the Lord family, not to spite James, but to bring them all tightly together again, the way it had seemed to be when Herbert was alive.

Richard said, 'I'll have a word with Mother.'

'Would you?' said Bryan. 'Good man.'

Constance came in from the porch looking shaken. Richard held open his arms for her, and held her tight. Her fur coat was chilly, and there were tears in her eyes. 'Those brothers of yours, I don't know,' she told Richard's lapel. Bryan King-Moreton stepped back a little, clearing his throat briskly so that Constance was aware of how dutiful he felt.

Richard said nothing, but embraced his mother and shushed her and wished that his father were here. He could picture his father vividly, the way he had turned and smiled at Richard one bright afternoon when they had first flown the *Chichester Special*.

His father, however, was still falling from the sky, almost every night in Richard's dreams.

Lisbon to Florida, 1932

Claude Dornier waved from the open door of the giant flying-boat as James's launch circled around the hull and nudged cautiously up to the streamlined fairing which served as a boarding-platform. 'James!' Claude shouted out. 'I was worried you could not come!'

James stood up in the waist of the launch. He was wearing a blue blazer, white ducks, and small black sunglasses. Although it was only the second day of March, the temperature in Lisbon was seventy-two degrees, and the sheer silver sides of the Dornier Do-X were dazzling in the early-afternoon sun.

The Do-X had been moored in the River Tagus for two days now, in preparation for a special privately-financed flight across the Atlantic. She had been surrounded for most of that time by yachts and pleasure-dinghies and the clustering boats of local fruit-sellers, fishermen, and souvenir-hawkers. She had remained aloof; a hugh dignified whale, with a dozen shining propellers and wings that could have sheltered twenty families from the Alfama.

James had flown from Paris the previous day by Aéropostale, and stayed the night at the luxurious Hotel Vasco da Gama. He had lunched on lobster and pissenlit salad and Dom Perignon, and then come out from the Terreiro do Paco by private launch.

Claude Dornier seized his hand as he came aboard. 'It's so good to see you. I wanted to come to England, you know, for your father's memorial service. I wish it had been possible.'

James took off his sunglasses. 'I've been looking at this beauty all morning, from my hotel balcony. I really had no idea how enormous she was.'

'Come inside to the lounge,' Claude invited him. 'Everybody is here now, except for Miss Treat and her party.'

'Miss Treat?' asked James, following Claude into the cabin. 'You mean Chloe Treat, the film actress?'

'She's been touring Europe, spending money,' Claude smiled.

They entered the flying-boat's main saloon. Six or seven passengers were already there, drinking cocktails and smoking. James recognized most of them. Fräulein Leni Riefenstahl, the German film director, famous for her silent picture *The White Hell of Pitz Palu*; George Money, the American hotelier, accompanied by his tall svelte fashion-model wife Letitia Money; Paul Chamois, the fashion-designer, in an extraordinary silk smoking-jacket of hallucinatory reds and yellows and purples, with wide Chinese sleeves; and the bandleader Harry Roy, in a tight white suit, looking tired and overweight and liverish.

'Mr James Lord has joined us,' Claude announced, and James went around and shook those hands which required shaking and kissed those hands which required kissing.

'I'm so glad we have somebody on board who knows all about aeroplanes,' said Letitia Money, blinking at James with hooded, green-painted eyelids. 'You know, just in case the crew goes down with food-poisoning.'

'Oh, I'm very handy with a spanner,' James replied. George Money coughed, not knowing quite what to make of that remark.

'Have a drink,' Claude suggested. 'Why not champagne? I understand from Friedrich that congratulations are in order.'

'You should have brought your bride with you,' said Fräulein Reifenstahl. She was blonde and pale-eyed and disturbingly perfect. In her pale-grey suit and white silk stockings she exhibited the kind of Nordic severity that could make Englishmen bite their handkerchiefs.

'Herr Dornier tells me that this will be the very last flight.' She bent over and lifted an Eastman movie camera out of her bag. 'I shall be making my own diary, you see, on film.'

James raised an eyebrow. Claude shrugged, and said, 'It's true, I'm afraid. We had so many minor mishaps on last year's trip; and we were so badly delayed by all the visitors who wanted to look us over – well, most of our financial backers decided to withdraw. Your father was right, you know, when he declined to take part in this venture. Its time has not yet come. So everybody keeps telling me, anyway.'

James looked around the twenty-three-foot saloon, with its patterned carpets and plushly-upholstered chairs, and its curtained windows with picture-postcard views of Lisbon and the bright blue river. The walls were decorated with pale chinoiserie wallpaper, with flowers and leaves and little lantern-carriers, and the tables were laid with crisp white linen and silver cutlery and engraved crystal glassware. 'You must feel very sad, Claude, to say goodbye to all this.'

'To tell you the truth, I can hardly bear to think about it,' Claude told him. 'It is like dreaming about a great age of luxury and style, just for a moment, almost having it within your grasp, and then waking up, and losing it for ever. I am already making arrangements for the Do-X to go to a museum in Berlin.'

A white-jacketed steward came into the saloon, and Claude asked him to bring champagne. 'You don't mind Henkel? I was given a gift of twenty cases by the von Ribbentrops. I first met them, you know, in London, when I was having dinner with your father. Great socializers, both of them. Joachim von Ribbentrop told me I ought to be designing bombers. Bombers!'

They took their glasses of champagne up to the flight deck, which was curved like the bridge of an ocean-liner. Through the rectangular windows, they had a brilliant view of the terraced hills of Lisbon, jumbled tawny and white against a sky that was practically black. James could make out the Castel de São Jorge, the Moorish citadel which overlooks the Alfama, the old town; and the unfinished church of Santa Engracia.

Claude sat down in the leather-covered pilot's seat, and James sat in the co-pilot's seat beside him.

'It's a great pity that you couldn't have brought your Patricia,' said Claude. 'This flight would have made quite a honeymoon for you.'

James made a dismissive face. 'She hasn't been too well, as a matter of fact. Tired after the wedding, I shouldn't wonder. She's staying with Mother in Chichester.'

'Well, I wish I could say "perhaps next time",' said Claude.

'I shouldn't worry, if I were you. I don't think Patricia's frightfully keen on flying in any case. I'll take her on a cruise.'

Even though he was German, Claude had caught the flatness in James's tone of voice. He was quiet for a moment, and then he said, 'How is the *Chichester Special*? Richard has been working very hard on that, I hear.'

'I leave that to Richard,' said James. 'Richard is the one who believes that the future of air travel is in the hands of the speed kings and the daredevils. The fêted hero in the record-breaking aeroplane.'

'Your father was a speed king and a daredevil,' Claude reminded him.

James smiled. 'I see things rather differently from the rest of the family. I suppose I always have. Michael agrees with me. Politically, anyway. But he's the only one who does. Personally, I have never quite seen the point of glory, not glory for its own sake.'

'You sound like a lone voice, crying in the wilderness,' Claude remarked.

'Not really,' said James. He kept his face turned away so that Claude couldn't see the bitterness that he still felt at his family's hypocrisy. His mother in particular, with all her talk of it being 'folly' to marry the wrong woman. 'All the same, James, you *did* make her pregnant. And life is going to be very awkward for all of us if you don't make an honest woman of her.' Added to that, the gentle and poisonous reminder that *she* was the majority shareholder of Lord Aeronautics, and that things could be very much less pleasant if they didn't all pull together.

James had married Patricia for all kinds of reasons, all of them excellent. She was pretty, she was carrying his child, she loved him with a constant desperation that never let up from breakfast to bedtime. Even more important, there was a serious risk of him losing control at Lord Aeronautics if he didn't. He had stood in front of his bathroom mirror on the morning of their wedding at Chichester Cathedral and said to himself, 'Well, James, you could do very much worse.' He could have married Henrietta Beesley, of course. That might have been worse. On the other hand, it might have been better. Henrietta had sent him a crumpled handkerchief that had obviously been meant to be tear-stained, but had dried out in the post.

Michael, the other offended party, had sent James a very formal letter of apology on the morning of the wedding, claiming that he couldn't attend because he had the 'flu. Michael wouldn't have dared to refuse the invitation outright. He had given James and Patricia an Ekco wireless with a huge moving-coil loudspeaker and a low-tension battery in case their first house only had gas. He had wished them 'all the joy that ever was'.

Constance had bought them a twenty-four-foot yacht. It was moored at Bosham and it would probably stay at Bosham until it rotted and sank. James disliked sailing almost as much as he disliked tennis.

James and Patricia had been married for just five weeks now, but James was already beginning to ask himself how much longer he could put up with it. He had been tense and unhappy ever since Christmas, mainly because of the money that Richard was wasting on the construction of the new *Chichester Special*. But now Patricia had industriously started nest-building – telephoning estate-agents to find them a house 'not too grand, not too pokey' either in Chichester or Petersfield, or do you mind Midhurst, or we *could* go as far as Fareham, couldn't we, darling? And *must* you smoke, the smell of it makes me feel quite ill? And you *know* what Doctor Harris said, darling, we mustn't sleep together until baby's born – *then* it'll be all right, I promise. I'll be as naughty as you like.

James had come to understand that it was all a mistake; not too frightful, but a mistake all the same. You couldn't marry simply for the sake of business, or to save your family from social embarrassment. At least, *he* couldn't. He knew plenty of chaps who had. James could hardly bear to think about it; about the pain that he had inflicted on himself, not yet much greater than a toothache, but just as persistent; and about the much greater pain that, in time, he would have to inflict on Patricia. When the president of Atlantic and Pacific Airways had wired him from Florida with an enquiry about buying three Aquariuses, and he had heard that Claude Dornier was about to fly to Miami with the Do-X, he had told Elsie to pack him a single suitcase and left Chichester at two hours' notice.

Claude watched him, and sipped champagne. 'Why is it that I receive the impression that you are not as happy as you might be?' he asked.

'*Ich weiß nicht, was soll es bedeuten, dass ich so traurig bin,*' James quoted. 'I don't know what it means, my being so sad.' He turned to Claude and gave him a wry smile. 'Overworked, perhaps. Too much Henkel.'

'You can't be unhappy about your business. That new night navigation system of yours is streets ahead of the competition. You must be making a fortune out of it, Air Ministry contracts and all that!'

'We're turning a penny,' James admitted. 'But sometimes turning a penny is not quite enough.'

They were still sitting side by side in silence when one of the crew called out, 'Herr Dornier! The last of our passengers!'

'Ah,' said Claude. 'It sounds as if Miss Treat has finally arrived!'

James followed him down to the main doorway. Two motor-launches had already tied up beside the Do-X's boarding platform. A fellow in a flappy white suit and an enormous white hat had disembarked, and was turning around to help his lady companion up on to the corrugated aluminium fairing. James stood in the doorway, his eyes shielded from the bright sunlight, and watched in curiosity and amusement.

He had seen Chloe Treat only once, in a James Cagney picture, and all that he could remember was that she was a bleached-blonde wisecracking girl with far too much mascara and a line in flashy evening-gowns. As she approached the doorway, however, assisted by two of the Dornier's uniformed crew members, James found himself face to face with a very pretty girl in a peach-coloured day-dress, Worth of Poiret probably, a straw cloche hat by Agnès, and sandals by H. & M. Rayne. He stepped out of the doorway and held on to the diagonal strut in order to let her pass.

She lifted her face out of the shadow of her hat and smiled at him. He saw big grey eyes, a snub nose with a smattering of freckles, and lips that said 'kiss me' without even moving. She was so pretty that James forgot for a second where he was; or what he was doing.

'Are you the captain?' Chloe Treat asked him, with a giggle.

'The captain? Me? No, no. I'm just a passenger, like you. I couldn't fly this thing if you paid me.'

'What *would* you do if I paid you?'

'Come on, Ann, for Chrissakes,' complained the man in the flappy white suit. 'Let's just get on board.'

'James Lord,' James announced himself. 'And it's all right – I *do* know who you are. I saw you in *65 Shadowy Avenue*, didn't I?'

'You mean *79 Shadow Street*,' Chloe Treat corrected him. 'Wasn't I terrible? Do you remember the bit where I screamed, because I thought there was a mouse under the table? Wasn't I awful? Ee-ee-ee! I sounded like my brassière had snapped.'

'Ann, for Chrissakes,' the man repeated.

Chloe turned. 'Oh, you must meet Marty. This is Marty Rosen, my agent-stroke-manager-stroke-personal-confydong. But that's all the strokes he's allowed, aren't you, Marty? He's such a dear person!'

The long-suffering Marty Rosen had a tired, friendly face with purple circles under the eyes and a California tan that was begin-ning to turn yellow after a European winter. He was wearing the worst tie that James had ever seen in his life, emerald green with orange zigzags. He juggled with his luggage to shake James by the hand. 'Very good to know you, Mr Lord. Now, are we crossing the Atlantic clinging to the wing, or do we go inside?'

They climbed inside the Do-X, and James followed. Claude Dornier came up behind him. 'What do you think, then, James? Quite a cutie.'

'Yes,' James acknowledged. 'Quite a cutie.'

Claude checked his wristwatch. 'Three o'clock. Almost time we were off.'

'What?' asked James. He was watching Chloe Treat making her way through the saloon, towards the sleeping-cabins, the provocative boomps-a-daisy sway of her hips. Her sexuality was anything but subtle.

Claude made a propeller gesture with his finger. 'Almost time we were off. We're planning to reach the Azores by five o'clock tomorrow morning.'

James said, 'Good, good. Do you have a gramophone on board?'

'A gramophone? Yes, why?'

'I don't know. I feel like dancing.'

'First you are *traurig*, then you feel like dancing?'

James laid a hand on his shoulder. 'Oh, you know what we aviators are. Two personalities in one, Icarus and Daedalus. One part of us wants to fly steady and low, while the other part of us wants to fly so high that we set fire to our wings.'

Claude looked at James sharply for a moment, and then nodded. 'We have only foxtrots. Maybe some Strauss.'

James looked back at him and smiled, and began to sing *The Blue Danube*. 'Da-da-da-da-da-dah!-dah!-dah!-dah!'

Claude grinned widely, and took James's hand, and together they waltzed the length of the passenger-cabin, accompanied by the applause of their fellow-passengers.

One by one, the flying-boat's engines sputtered and growled into life. There were twelve of them, 525-horsepower Bristol Jupiters, coupled together so that six of them were facing forward and six were facing aft, supported on stanchions that rose from the top of the Dornier's wing. The flying-boat turned around on the river, the draft from its propellers ruffling the water into herringbone patterns, and then slowly began its take-off run, leaving behind it a wide wake of white foam, and a gaggle of small boats bobbing up and down.

The Dornier passed the western suburbs of Lisbon, the shining royal palace of Necessidades, and the convent and palace of São Bento. Sunlight flooded through the windows and danced on the ceiling of the passenger-cabin. In London, it was raining. James was sitting next to Fräulein Riefenstahl, although most of the Dornier's wickerwork seats were empty. The flying-boat had been designed to carry seventy passengers more than a thousand miles without refuelling. Once it had taken 169 passengers, with plenty of power to spare.

With a great droning roar, the Do-X lifted itself out of the waters of the River Tagus, and headed towards the Atlantic. Its twelve propellers shone like knives as it flew steadily westward; and fishermen looked up from their boats and madly waved their caps. James peered out of the window and remarked, 'They'll probably tell their grandchildren all about this.' He paused, and then he said, 'I'll probably tell mine.'

'Why do you think I wanted to come?' said Leni Riefenstahl. 'I have to go to America anyway, but nobody will ever fly like this again.'

James took out his cigarette case, and offered her one. 'You never know. This is just the beginning.'

He glanced around to see if Chloe Treat had reappeared from her cabin. Letitia Money gave him a friendly little wave, and George Money pretended to be looking at something on the opposite side of the cabin. Paul Chamois was sitting with his legs crossed, running his hands through his wavy grey hair again and again and reading a book called *Les Licornes Roses*. Two German stewards came around and asked what everybody would like for tea. Egg sandwiches? Sardine sandwiches, made with fresh Portuguese sardines? Toasted tea-cakes, muffins, crumpets?

'Claude told me you were just married,' said Leni Riefenstahl.

James said, 'It overtakes us all, in the end.'

'You don't sound so happy about it.'

'It's a change, that's all. It takes a little time to adapt. I'm used to being my own man.'

'But you must love her?'

James smoked, and sat back in his seat so that the basketwork creaked. 'Yes, to be perfectly truthful, I do. I love her very much indeed. But, I don't know. There are so many things that are crying out to be done.'

'So many pies, waiting for you to stick your finger into them?' smiled Leni Reifenstahl.

At that moment, Chloe Treat came bustling and flustering into the passenger-cabin, wearing a silky white afternoon dress with a white feather boa. She was followed by Marty Rosen, in a blue-and-cream striped blazer, very Cannes Yacht Club. Marty Rosen looked as if he didn't mind where he was, and with whom, just so long as he wasn't here, on this flying-boat, with Chloe Treat.

'Well, goodness!' Chloe exclaimed, as she came past James's seat. 'It's the captain, I do believe! Aren't you supposed to be up at the front, playing with your joystick or something?'

She clapped her hand over her mouth. 'Oh, I'm so *sorry*! You're not the captain, are you? You told me! Me and my impetuosity! Marty's always telling me off for my impetuosity, aren't you, Marty?'

'Beaned it in one, dearie,' replied Marty, with high disinterest.

'We're having tea,' said James, rising from his seat. 'Won't you and Mr Rosen join us?'

'Tea?' Chloe exclaimed. 'Don't they serve champagne exclooseevamong?'

'My dear,' put in Leni Riefenstahl, 'I think that if you drank nothing but champagne for six days, your head would begin to suffer a little, don't you?'

Chloe sat down opposite James, fluffing up her boa. 'The way I look at it, it's *my* head.'

'Don't tell that to Mr Zukor,' said Marty Rosen. 'The w: *j he* looks at it, your head belongs exclusively and in perpetuity to Paramount.'

Chloe reached forward and squeezed James's knee. 'Isn't that awful? Can you imagine your head belonging to somebody else, while you're still alive? It makes you feel like you're living through the French Revolution. You know, the guillotine and all that?'

James said, quietly, 'The only people who lost their heads in the French Revolution were aristocrats, you know. Ladies of the upper classes.'

Chloe's grey eyes widened. She looked quickly at Marty, but Marty was peering out of the window. Then she looked back at James and said, in a fluttery little voice, 'That's the sweetest compliment. That really is.'

Out the corner of his eye, James could see that Leni Riefenstahl was hiding her amusement by cupping her hands over her face. But he wasn't ashamed to persist.

'Some of the aristocratic ladies tried to escape from Paris by dressing as peasants. But, you know, the Revolutionaries could always tell. It didn't matter if the ladies deliberately broke their fingernails and filled them with dirt. It didn't matter if they blackened their teeth. A lady is always a lady, and she can never disguise it, no matter what she tries to do.'

Chloe primped her hair. 'Do you know something, James – it *is* James, isn't it? – do you know something, James, you're right. I've been touring in Europe for four months and I never once met anyone with perspicacity like yours. What a waste! I've been up to my duff in *schloßen* and *châteaux* and art galleries, four months of dances and soirées and Christ alone knows what, pardonnay mon Fransay, James I can't *tell* you. And here you are, waiting for me, like Nemesis, on the flying-boat back home. Or, who is it, Nemo?'

'*Gott in Himmel*,' murmured Leni Riefenstahl, under her breath.

Chloe leaned forward, and took hold of James's hand. 'You have to tell me one thing, you know, before – you know.'

'Yes?' said James; although he understood, like St Peter, in a vinegary, early-Christianity kind of way, that his moment of truth had at last arrived.

'You're not attachemong?' said Chloe, with a face as bright and provocative and unashamedly rampant as any face that James had ever seen.

'It depends what you mean by "attachemong",' James smiled.

'It's French,' Chloe explained. '"Attache" meaning attached. "Mong" meaning – you know – "mong". Whatever that is. I mean, half the words in French end in *mong*. It must mean something. There's even a *place* called Le Mong.'

James sat back. 'Why don't you take some tea?' he suggested.

'Marty,' said Chloe, 'did you bring that cover of *Screenland*? Show Mr Lord that cover of *Screenland*.'

'Miss Treat,' said James, 'I know *who* you are. What I really want to know is *what* you are.'

Marty said, 'Jesus. Here we go again.'

But Chloe beamed like a satisfied angel, and pouted her lips, so that James had no alternative at all but to kiss them. They tasted of milk and tangerines. Leni Riefenstahl looked out of the window with great concentration, as if she were thinking about her next picture. Anything was better than thinking about what was going to happen next between James Lord and Chloe Treat. *Ach du lieber Gott*, hadn't we seen it so many times before?

The gramophone played *Indiana* and *Get 'Em Again*, while the Dornier flying-boat droned out across the moonlit Atlantic. James and Chloe foxtrotted with the soles of their shoes two thousand feet above the ocean, and everybody sat back in their chairs and

drank von Ribbentrop's champagne and enjoyed the spectacle of
two young people newly in love. It was all madness, but these
were days of madness, and the Do-X was madness, and here they
were with the moonlight pouring in through the windows, and the
gramophone wavering and the waves wrinkled far below them like
silver skin, and all they could care about was love and scandal.

'Do you know how improper this all is?' asked Chloe, as they
returned to their seats, and the steward poured them more
sparkling Henkel.

James offered her a cigarette. 'Is it improper to dance?'

'It depends where the dance takes you, nestpah?'

James sat back and watched her for a while saying nothing at
all. He remembered the way she had looked in *79 Shadow Street*;
her innocence; her vulnerability. He wouldn't have believed that
anyone so sweet on the screen could be so tough and forthright in
the flesh. But, in the flesh, she was very much prettier. She was
wearing an evening dress of sheer white organza, so fine that her
skin glowed through it. It had a low neckline embroidered in
silvery thread, and flowing sleeves as thin and as gauzy as a fairy's
wings. Her nipples would have showed through the fabric if they
hadn't been covered by artfully-embroidered silver butterflies,
three butterflies feeding at the pink tinge of each breast, very *Vie
Parisienne*. Between her thighs she was discreetly covered by a
twining silver flower motif which gave the impression that you
could *almost* see something, not quite, and in any case you
shouldn't be so prurient as to look. An overskirt of the same sheer
organza came from her hips on either side of this flower motif and
whispered all the way down to the floor.

She gave off some perfume which James hadn't encountered
before. It had been specially blended for her by Isabey at 26
Faubourg St Honoré in Paris. It had no name, only her personal
number.

'Fräulein Riefenstahl tells me you're a newlywed,' said Chloe.

James shrugged. 'I've been married for five weeks, two days,
nine hours, and eleven minutes.'

'Separated from wifeykins so soon? You surprise me. The first
time I got married, I didn't leave the budwah for five weeks, and I
certainly wouldn't have let Farris go off without me. Poor Farris,
wreck we yes sat in patchy.'

'I'm sorry?'

'Wreck we yes sat in patchy,' Chloe repeated, irritably. '*You*
know. Rest in peace.'

The flying-boat passengers dined that evening on thin slices of smoked quail, decorated with endive; then baked flounder stuffed with shrimp; followed by prime steaks from the Pentland Hills in Scotland, matured and served with wild rowan jelly from Moniack Castle. Chloe drank champagne thoughout the meal, and told James all about her first husband Farris and how he died (frustration, cocaine, and a Hollywood swimming-pool). 'He was floating around and around, staring at me with his eyes open, I mean not accusingly or anything, just as if he wanted to say something like, you won't forget to cancel my shirt-service, will you? I cried *pails*, of course.'

At one o'clock in the morning, the cabin lights were dimmed, and the stewards put away the backgammon sets and cleared the coffee-cups and asked if any of the passengers would care for chocolate. Marty Rosen came up to the club chairs where James and Chloe were talking, and stood beside them buttoning his tuxedo.

'Come on, Ann, dearie, time to flog the feathers.'

Chloe reached behind her and took hold of Marty's hand. 'Marty's my human alarm-clock,' she told James. 'He tells me when to get up and when to go to bed. He tells me when to eat, when to drink, when to talk, and when to shut up. He gets me to the studio on time and he gets me back home again, right on the button. He's so God-damned efficient I feel like wringing his stringy little neck. But what would I do without him?'

'Come on, princess,' said Marty. 'Say goodnight to Mr Lord and don't forget your wrap.'

James stood up and helped Chloe to drape her wrap around her shoulders. She stared at him from very close up. So close, that he could only see her in soft focus, like the movies. The flying-boat's engines reverberated through the cabin, making the kingwood trim vibrate, so that when she whispered something to him, he couldn't quite catch it. But he was sure he heard the word '*cabin*'.

'Goodnight, then, Chloe,' he told her, kissing her hand. 'It's been unique.'

'Unique?' she smiled. 'There's never been a night like it, ever.'

After Chloe had retired to her stateroom, James sat by himself for a while in the darkened lounge and drank a small glass of German brandy. He switched on the reading-light beside his seat, and took out the letter that was folded in his inside pocket. It had arrived this morning, forwarded from Paris, although it had originally been franked in Oxfordshire. Pale blue writing paper, with deckled edges, no printed address.

'*You will forgive me my darling for not having written sooner. Your marriage to Miss Burne-Stanley was so unexpected. And you could have discussed it with me, I would have understood, even though it would have been painful. It's doubly painful as it is, I feel as if you couldn't trust me to be brave.*

'*What will happen to us now? I hear from Bunty that Miss B-S is podding. Did you marry her because of that? Or is it Real Love? Here I am, high and dry, with no way of talking to you. Do you think we could meet? You know that I never expected to marry you my darling but a woman like me needs somebody like you for the sake of her pride and her femininity and above all to stop her from going completely ga-ga.*

'*Buy me dinner when you get back, I promise not to weep or anything silly. It's the least you can do for me, in return for pinching all those papers on night-flying. All my love for ever and ever.*'

James refolded the letter and put it away. There were times in his life when he wished that he knew no women at all, that he was a hermit who lived on an island in the Outer Hebrides, subsisting on prayer and herring. He drained his brandy-glass, said goodnight to the stewards, and turned in.

As the eastern sky began to pale, James eased himself out of his high-sided mahogany bed, and lifted his maroon lambswool dressing-gown down from the back of the door. He picked up his wristwatch from the bedside table. Three-fifteen. It would take them almost two hours to reach Ponta Delgada, in the Azores. Everybody would be asleep now, except the crew.

He looked out into the passageway. It was deserted. He closed his door gently behind him, and made his way forward, tightening up the cord of his dressing-gown as he went. Chloe Treat's cabin was off to the left. Claude Dornier had christened it the 'bridal suite'.

James could feel the huge flying-boat dip and yaw beneath his feet, while the engines droned on and on, out across the ocean. It was an extraordinary sensation, to be able to walk about an aeroplane in flight, dressed as if you were walking around a luxury hotel or a country house. He could almost have been convinced that the Do-X was the vision of tomorrow's aviation.

He turned the corner in the corridor, and there to his complete surprise was Marty Rosen, wearing a white silk bathrobe, and smoking a cigarette. Marty had been staring out of the flying-boat's porthole at the grey mist which blanketed the ocean below them. His legs were bare and hairy and lumpy with varicose veins.

He turned to James without any signs of astonishment whatsoever, and flicked his cigarette ash on to the Chinese-blue carpet.

'Well, well,' he remarked, in a voice dry from smoking and tiredness. 'The dawn patrol.'

This turn in the corridor led nowhere but to Chloe's room. James could do nothing but lift his hands in mock-surrender. '*Kamerad*,' he said.

'Oh, don't worry,' said Marty. 'I'm her alarm-clock, not her keeper.'

He reached into the pocket of his bathrobe and took out a dented silver flask. 'How about a belt?'

'Too early for me, I'm afraid,' James told him.

'Hmhm,' said Marty, and flipped back the top of the flask and swallowed bourbon. He shuddered and sniffled, and then he fastened the top and dropped it back in his pocket. '*Chacun à son goût*, as the lady would say. With the emphasis on *goût*.'

James stood with his hands in the pockets of his dressing-gown, a little unsure of what he ought to do next. 'Is she asleep?' he asked Marty.

'Ann?' said Marty. 'Who knows? She's probably waiting for you.'

'Why do you call her Ann?'

'Why the two-toned tonkert do you think? It's her name. Ann Robinson. You don't think anybody gets themselves baptized Chloe Treat, do you?'

James watched Marty for a moment, as Marty sucked at the butt of his cigarette and then squeezed it out between finger and thumb. Smoke drifted out through the hairs in his nostrils. 'You can go in if you want to,' Marty told him. 'Go on, go ahead. But take some horseradish. She'll probably eat you alive.'

'That's rather a cynical remark,' said James.

Marty grunted and smiled. 'Not if you know her, it isn't. She's a what-do-you-call-it, an egotist, an overpowering egotist. She'd be no God-damned good at what she does, if she wasn't. Do you have any idea what it takes, to be a movie star? It's worse than giving blood. When you're a movie star, you have to give everything. Your blood, your skin, your teeth, your eyes, your privacy, your religion, your whole God-damned soul.'

He took out his flask again, and unstoppered it. 'I was telling you lies. *She* was telling you lies. I'm not her alarm-clock. I'm more like her priest.'

He swallowed more whiskey, and then shrugged, and burped, and said, 'My mother should be happy, wherever she is. She always wanted me to be a rabbi.'

James attempted a smile. Then he nodded his head towards Chloe's door, and suggested, 'Perhaps I'd better let her sleep.'

'You can do what you like, it's your life. It isn't very often you get the chance to get laid in mid-air.'

James wasn't sure whether Marty was mocking him or not. But he knew that it would be impossible for him to go into Chloe's cabin and attempt to make love to her with Marty hanging around outside, eavesdropping. The Do-X began to turn, and James could detect a slightly different note in the engines. It was probably too late anyway. They were making their approach towards the archipelago of the Azores, and the stewards would be serving breakfast soon.

'You make an excellent watchdog, Mr Rosen,' James told him. 'Perhaps I'll see you at breakfast.'

Marty made a dismissive face. 'It's no skin off my *tochis*. Guys like you come and go, come and go. You ought to form a union. The Brotherhood of Poor Schlimazels Who Have Fallen Irrevocably In Love with Chloe Treat. Go ahead, knock at the door. Be the next on the list. Rapunzel, Rapunzel, let down your teddy. It's your life. Just so long as you remember that it's hers, too. All I'm doing is protecting my living.'

James stood for a while with his tongue in his cheek feeling very English. Then he said, 'I can't quite believe that you're as cynical as you try to make out, Mr Rosen.'

Marty forked a cigarette out of his pocket between two fingers. 'Don't ask me. I don't even know what cynical means. What is it, some kind of poison? Or a bicycle with no saddle?'

He suddenly turned his dark near-together eyes on James and said, 'A man could get hurt, you know, trying to ride a bicycle with no saddle.'

James hesitated for a moment, then dropped his gaze to the floor. 'Yes, well,' he said. 'That's all rather by the by, don't you think.'

'Rah-ther,' Marty replied.

James returned to his cabin, took off his dressing-gown, and filled his washbasin with hot water. He lathered his badger shaving-brush and began to shave. The face in the mirror was a white soapy mask, but he knew what that face was thinking. He had lain awake for most of the night, twisting between his hand-embroidered sheets, tyrannized by the drumming of the engines, wondering whether he ought to knock on Chloe's door. Being deflected by Marty Rosen hadn't changed the fact that he had actually made the decision to betray Patricia. And the decision, having been made, could never be revoked; even if he never touched another woman in his life.

He had discovered something, that adultery is committed with the heart, and not the body. The body is simply the instrument of the heart's intent.

He dressed, in a cream wool blazer, and a dark red shirt with a white collar. For the first time in months he thought: *I look like my father. I could almost be him.*

There was a note waiting for him on his breakfast table, propped up against the silver flower-vase in which a single fresh orchid quivered. A small pale-pink envelope, with his name, *James*, written in lilac ink. He picked the envelope up, and he was conscious that Chloe was watching him from the other side of the sunlit saloon.

'Coffee, Herr Lord?' the steward asked him. 'Mocha, or arabica?'

James said, 'Thank you, arabica,' and tore open the envelope. Inside was a small folded note on airmail paper as thin as a butterfly's wing. It said simply, *'Gentlemen are très rare. Thank you for respecting me. You are invited to a private champagne party at 1119 Stone Canyon Drive, Bel Air, Hollywood whenever the mood takes you. C.'*

James studied the note for a while; then folded it and tucked it into his handkerchief pocket. Chloe caught his eye and smiled. This morning she was wearing a simple Chanel suit of pale blue cotton, and a matching hat. Marty Rosen was sitting with his back to James, smoking and filling his coffee-cup with bourbon, but when he saw Chloe smiling he turned around and gave James an extraordinary look: not hostile; not even contemptuous; but resigned and dry and almost admiring.

James ate *prosciutto* and chilled Portuguese melon and looked out of the flying-boat's window with absurd self-satisfaction. He realized now what game Marty had been playing, or he was fairly sure that he did. Marty liked him. In fact, Marty adored him. Marty considered that a man like him would be perfect for Chloe's career. English, well-connected, wealthy, but already married – ideal fodder for the Hollywood gossip columns, wonderful publicity with months of mileage in it. There had already been stories in the American papers about the noticeable friendship between the Prince of Wales and Mr and Mrs Ernest Simpson (not, God forbid, in the British press); and affairs with well-appointed Englishmen were all the thing.

However, things couldn't be rushed. Marty was obviously alert to the fact that, these days, Chloe was seriously attracted only to men who were moral, and aloof, and veddy veddy correct. Men of class; men she couldn't usually get. Her life with Farris had been appalling. She didn't want an encore. Marty must have been waiting outside Chloe's door all night, smoking and drinking and hoping that he wouldn't fall asleep before James put in his expected appearance. James was slightly ashamed that he had. But he was quite pleased that Marty approved of him. The thought of having a well-publicized affair with a world-famous Hollywood film actress seemed dangerous but immensely appealing.

The Do-X began to lose altitude. Leni Riefenstahl appeared, dressed in a sensible square-shouldered linen suit. She sat down opposite James and asked for lemon tea.

'*Guten morgen, gnädige Fräulein*,' James greeted her.

'And the top of the morning to you, sir,' smiled Leni.

'Did you sleep well?' asked James.

'Oh yes, I always sleep well when I travel. I sleep on trains. I sleep on ships. There is no reason to stay awake on a flying-boat. Mind you, there was one moment during the night when I woke up and thought of all that empty air between the bottom of my bed and the sea below, and I felt as if I were falling.'

James stirred his coffee. 'Yes,' he said. 'I felt as if I were falling, too.'

'And you fell?' Leni asked him, with sudden and extraordinary understanding of what he was saying.

James looked at her with great care. 'Perhaps I was on the brink of falling,' he told her.

Leni smiled. 'To be on the brink of falling is not to fall,' she said. 'But, sometimes it is very difficult to draw back from the brink, *ja*?'

Chloe gave James a finger-wave across the saloon. James, slightly embarrassed in front of Leni Reifenstahl, gave her a quick open-handed wave back. 'She likes you,' said Leni, and laughed.

James picked up his coffee-cup. The reflected sunlight from the cup danced in a curve on his forehead. 'I like her, too.'

'Oh-ho,' Leni laughed. 'You *like* her? You think she's the cat's pyjamas!'

Chichester, 1932

It started to rain as they wheeled the *Chichester Special* out of the sheds on its trolley, and so Richard had to sling his trenchcoat over the open cockpit. There was a small smattering of applause, and Wally Field let out two or three piercing football-field whistles without even taking his cigarette out of his mouth.

The rain drummed on the roof of the corrugated iron sheds, and filled the concrete yard with puddles. Amidst these tatty surroundings, the *Chichester Special* looked unreal, a shining dream in polished aluminium and silvery fabric.

She was two feet longer than the aeroplane in which Herbert had died, with a specially tuned sprint engine capable of 2,750 horsepower. Her wings were smaller and thinner, but Bryan King-Moreton had redesigned her pontoons to compensate for the loss in lift. She was the ultimate in sleekness and power, and everything about her shone.

Bryan King-Moreton stood with his hands clasped behind his back, inspecting her with undisguised pride. 'If only Herbert could have seen this,' he said. The shoulders of his fawn raincoat were dark with damp, and there were drops of rain on his white moustache, but he stood bare-headed, as if he were attending a memorial service.

In a way, he was. The rolling-out of the new *Chichester Special* was a ceremony to show that the spirit of Herbert Lord still lived.

Richard said, 'Wally's finished his bits and pieces on the carburettors. We can run her down to Bosham tomorrow, for her buoyancy tests.'

'Well, there's no hurry,' Bryan told him. 'We can wait until Monday, if you want to. You look all in.'

Richard shook his head. 'I'm all right. I want to make sure that she's tested and ready before James gets back. If we can show Mother exactly what she can do – if we're absolutely certain that we can take the Seraphim Trophy – then James won't have a leg to stand on.'

'Well, I quite agree,' said Bryan. 'I must say that I've been worried for a couple of weeks now that the mater's been wavering somewhat, especially after that last audit. I kept telling her, you can't put a cash value on the *Chichester Special*, you know, not in pounds, shillings and pence. What it costs us in capital, it will more than make up for in prestige. Buy your aeroplanes from the firm that won the Seraphim Trophy, that kind of thing. Lord Aeronautics, keeping Britain great. But James, well . . . James is a very persistent chap.'

'It sometimes beats me why he's so dead set against it,' said Richard. The rain was running from the brim of his trilby down the back of his neck, so he turned the collar of his jacket up. 'He seems actually to *hate* it. I mean, not just because of the cost, but to *hate* it.'

'He's not a natural airman, that's why,' Bryan replied. 'Not like your father. Your father was born with invisible wings, same as you. Just because a chap builds aeroplanes, that doesn't make him a natural airman.'

Richard shrugged. 'I suppose not. Listen – we'd better get back to the house. Mother's expecting us for lunch at one.'

'Good gracious, is it as late as that? What time are the press supposed to be here?'

'Three. They're sending a photographer down from the *Illustrated London News*.'

'We'd better get a move on, in that case.'

They left the yard and walked through the main factory building. It was lunchbreak: most of the men were sitting in the corner eating sandwiches and drinking tea. The half-built carcasses of six Lord Aquarius passenger-planes stood supported on jigs, waiting like hopeful amputees for their wings to be fitted. There was a heady aroma of glue and aircraft dope in the air; underlaid by the heavier odours of oil and spruce. On the factory walls there were rainbows of coloured paint, and pinups of girls in bathing-costumes from *Pictorial Weekly* and *London Life*.

'Good luck, Mr Richard!' one of the men called out. 'She's a beauty, that one!'

138

Richard smiled, and gave the men a wave which he hoped didn't look too regal. 'Thanks, Dan! I don't think we're going to let you down!'

They drove to Goodwood Lodge in Richard's new Whitlock Sportsman's coupé, which was bright yellow, with a black weatherproof top. Constance had bought it for him after an accident in mid-January on the Scott, in which he had been somersaulted over a stone wall at Houghton village. He would have been killed if he hadn't landed in a snowdrift.

As they drove around Chichester Market Cross, Bryan said, in an unusually diffident growl, 'We've been friends, don't y'know, for a good many years, the mater and I.'

Richard said nothing, but leaned forward and wiped the windscreen with his handkerchief.

Bryan turned to him, his collar so tight that it gave him three double-chins. 'When it comes down to it, you know, cards on the table, you'd be perfectly within your rights to ask me, what would a lady like the mater be expected to see in a chap like me? Bit of an airborne vagabond, I suppose, when all's said and done. But, we have one or two things in common, the mater and I. Well, apart from the fact that we both knew the pater so well. We're both interested in aeroplanes, and farming, and we both play bridge quite tolerably. We're both patriots, Britain's continuing glory, that kind of thing. Good liaisons have been founded on very much less.'

Richard turned and frowned at him, and Bryan suddenly realized that he didn't have the faintest idea what he was talking about. Bryan cleared his throat, and tugged at the skirts of his raincoat, and pretended to be staring out of the window, even though it was completely obscured with condensation.

Richard said, 'She's still trying to get over him, you know. She still can't understand why he killed himself.' He paused, and then he added, 'I can't say that I can understand it, either.'

'Well, it's a mystery,' said Bryan, trying to be patient. 'But I dare say that the Lord God knows what happened, and I suppose that's all that matters. The pater wasn't the type to enter into anything lightly, not without consulting his Maker, so to speak.'

'I suppose not.'

As they drove up to the house, they were surprised to see Michael's sports car parked outside the front door, a white Standard Avon nine-horsepower special. Michael hadn't been back to Chichester since James's wedding in mid-March, although he had talked to Richard on the telephone a couple of times.

Apparently he had spent most of his free weekends in London, going to the theatre with Paul Heath. He had been going to political meetings, too, and he had listened to Walter Greenwood talking to three dozen young middle-class Socialists about how he had written *Love On The Dole* on his trouser-press, because his table had been taken away under the means test.

Richard was pleased to see another car parked outside, too: a maroon Bentley tourer. That meant that his actress friend Elisabeth Bergner had interrupted rehearsals to come down to Sussex for the public unveiling of the *Chichester Special*. Elisabeth was the current darling of London's theatrical society. She was a refugee from Germany, a Jewess, and Richard had met her at a party given at Wilton's restaurant by Leslie Henson and Robertson Hare. Richard and Elisabeth had been seated by chance at the same table, and as more and more guests had arrived, some invited and others uninvited, they had gradually been wedged closer and closer together until Elisabeth had almost been sitting on Richard's lap.

The party had been a riot; and for the first time since his father's funeral, Richard had been on really cracking form. He had told the story about the man who thought that he was a turnip, and everybody had roared. He and Elisabeth had shared a pheasant and a bottle of champagne, and by midnight Richard had fallen irrevocably in love. He had taken Elisabeth home and kissed her on her doorstep.

Elisabeth had touched his lips with her fingertip, and said, 'I cannot love anybody just at the moment, Richard. I am thinking only of my acting. But let us always be friends.'

Richard still harboured the romantic fantasy that Elisabeth would wake up one morning and realize that she couldn't live without him, but he knew in his heart that he wasn't really her type of chap – any more, really, than she was his type of girl. She was Jewish, to begin with; and an actress; and what Richard needed was a steady dedicated Anglo-Saxon girl who would help him tirelessly with his business and uncomplainingly with his social duties, and give him an acceptable number of chubby Anglo-Saxon heirs.

He lived in hope, however; and he adored Elisabeth's company. In fact he was so pleased at the thought of seeing her that he failed to notice just how agitated Bryan had become. Bryan, however, took hold of Richard's arm as they approached the house, and made an extraordinary noise like a dog that wants to be taken for a walk. The rain dripped from the wisteria leaves around the porch. Inside the house they could hear laughter and somebody trying to play *With A Song In My Heart* on the piano.

Richard looked at Bryan in bewilderment. Bryan said, in a series of short scrappy barks, 'Thing is – what I want to ask is – well, I want to pay the mater my respects. Wanted to know what you thought about it, don't y'see.'

Richard now realized what Bryan had been trying to ask him in the car. He hadn't actually been listening. Now he suddenly understood all this business about 'good liaisons' and 'having things in common'.

He didn't have the chance to answer. The front door opened and Constance appeared, in a tailored grey coat and skirt, looking a little flushed from her first glass of sherry. 'I'd given you up!' she exclaimed. 'Lunch is almost ready; why don't you wash your hands straight away!'

Bryan took off his hat, and stiffly inclined his head. 'Constance,' he greeted her. Then he glanced at Richard, and it was clear from the expression on his face that he was daring Richard to mention even one word of what he had just said.

They went inside. It was Elisabeth who was playing the piano. She was large-eyed, elfin, an elegant waif with a perfectly-cut bob. She wore a pink-and-white day dress with wide sleeves, and her hair was pinned back with pink-and-white slides. She had been driven down by Norman Jorritt, the owner of the New Century theatre in the Strand, who was leaning against the piano with one eye closed against his dangling cigarette and a large glass of Scotch in his hand.

Norman was stocky, red-faced, but was always fastidiously dressed. James had described him as looking like a homosexual Army officer on his weekend off, although nobody had any evidence that Norman's love life (if he had one) was anything but pukka.

'Enter the birdman, stage left!' he cried, as Richard came in. 'Come and listen to Europe's loveliest lady making an utter hash of *Life Is Just A Bowl Of Cherries.*'

Richard came over and kissed Elisabeth's forehead. She smiled at him and kissed him back. He hesitated for a moment, but turned around then and clasped Norman Jorritt by the hand. 'You've made my day. I'm frightfully pleased that you could come. I'm sorry about the weather.'

'I thought it always rained in the country,' said Norman. 'I'd have been jolly disappointed if it hadn't. I went to Swan & Edgar 'specially, and bought some Wellingtons. I'd hate to take them back *wellie intacta.*'

'How are you, my dear?' Richard asked Elisabeth.

She stopped playing, and smiled. 'I'm really very well. I'm dying to see your aeroplane.'

'Do you know Bryan King-Moreton? You probably don't. He's our chief wallah, in charge of racing. Elisabeth Bergner, Bryan King-Moreton. Bryan, this is Elisabeth Bergner.'

Bryan took Elisabeth's hand, and bowed as creakily as if he were wearing a corset. 'I'm charmed, my dear. Richard has been speaking very admiringly of you.'

Richard blushed, and said, 'Yes, well.'

Bryan said, 'You won't mind excusing me, just for a moment? I'd like to see the mater before lunch.'

Richard dragged a chair up close to the piano. 'How's your new play?' he asked Elisabeth. 'Poppy saw you in rehearsal. She said you were fearfully good.'

Elisabeth tinkled a few high notes, and then said, 'Oh, well, I don't know. They all expect me to act like a waif. I'm not so sure that I am.'

'You haven't got a drink, old man,' put in Norman. 'Whisky-and-splash?'

'Just a small one,' said Richard. Then he turned back to Elisabeth, and said, 'I'll take you straight back to the factory after lunch. The seaplane's really first-rate. You'll love her. All we have to do now is test the pontoons – the floats, don't you know – just to make sure that they're watertight, and that she sits in the water the way she's supposed to. Then we can take her up.'

'That's so exciting for you,' said Elisabeth, touching the back of his hand.

Richard was suddenly embarrassed. He lowered his eyes. 'It may not seem like it to you. But for Bryan and me – well, it's something of a dream come true.'

Elisabeth smiled warmly. 'You know something, Richard, sometimes I think that you will never grow up. You're just like a boy, playing with his new toy. And, do you know, it's so charming. Everybody pretends to be so bored these days. I think I like you more than I can say.'

Richard gave her hand a squeeze. 'Elisabeth,' was all he could manage to say.

Norman brought over a large crystal goblet brimming with whisky and soda. 'Here you are, old chum. Just the ticket for facing the Press. If you can't out-talk them, at least you'll be able to out-breathe them. Chin-chin.'

He leaned against the piano again, and took out another cigarette. 'I must tell you, I was auditioning for our Christmas show last night. I saw fifty girls in sixty minutes, enough to make a sheik weep. Most of them pretty as hell, but talented? I think I've seen llamas that could dance better than most of them. But then there was one who came tripping on to the stage wearing a sort of a bathing-costume. She started this truly furious tap-dance, *rap-a-tap-a-tip-a-tap-a*, and do you know while she was dancing, legs kicking, arms swinging, her bathing-costume gradually crept downwards. Everybody was absolutely riveted, myself included I'm ashamed to say. Because inch by inch, her left breast appeared in view, and then her right breast, and she still kept dancing, *rap-a-tap-a-tip-a-tap-a*, with her bare breasts jiggling up and down, and then she stopped, and went down on to one knee, and flung her arms wide, and I have to say that everybody in the auditorium gave her a standing ovation.'

'Norman, you tell such terrible stories,' said Elisabeth. 'I suppose you gave her a part?'

'Of course I gave her a part. You think I have no soul? She confessed that she had made the costume herself, and that she had deliberately designed it so that it loosened as she danced. Now *here*, I thought to myself, is a girl with initiative!'

Just then, Patricia appeared, in a blue silk tea-gown with a ruffled collar. 'Tea-gown' was what dress-designers euphemistically called maternity dresses; but there was no doubt now that Patricia was pregnant. Her face had become rounded and her hair shining and flat on her scalp; and even though her stomach wasn't yet particularly prominent, she walked into the room as if she were carrying a small anvil in front of her.

'Hullo, Patricia!' said Richard. 'Is Michael about?'

'Is Michael here? I haven't seen him, I've just woken up from my morning nap. I didn't realize he was coming down.'

'You've met Elisabeth, haven't you, and Norman? Do come in. What would you like to drink?'

'Oh, not for me, thank you. I mustn't.'

Norman said, 'You're blooming, my dear. Producing more Lords seems to suit you. What did Coleridge say? "So for the mother's sake the child was dear, And dearer was the mother for the child."'

'Whatever that means,' put in Elisabeth.

'Well, precisely,' Norman agreed. 'Never could stand Coleridge anyway.'

Patricia sat down on the sofa and spread out her dress. Her cheeks were flushed and her hair was wispy at the back of her neck. 'We had a telegraph from James this morning; he's reached the Azores already.'

'You must miss him, so soon after your wedding,' said Elisabeth.

'Well, I have plenty to do,' said Patricia. 'I'm going out tomorrow to look at a house for us, in Halnaker. Four bedrooms, and a stable.'

'I hope it has a manger, too, for when baby's born,' Norman teased her.

'Norman, that is *not* funny,' Elisabeth protested. 'Please excuse him, Patricia, he has an appalling sense of humour. If he is not obscening, he is blaspheming.'

'I thought Jews enjoyed jokes about Jesus,' said Norman, pretending to be stung. 'You know, nervous guilty laughter and all that.'

At that moment, Michael walked into the room. Richard turned around on the sofa and said, 'Michael! This *is* a surprise!'

Michael looked thinner than before. His face was pasty, and he had grown another moustache, a small toothbrush moustache this time, which gave him a down-at-heel appearance, like a teacher at a boys' primary school. He wore a sleeveless pullover which had unravelled at the bottom, and baggy unpressed flannels. There were plummy-coloured circles under his eyes as if he hadn't been sleeping.

He shook Norman and Elisabeth by the hand, but he kept his eyes on Patricia. Patricia stared at the vase of dried honesty in the fireplace and didn't say anything, not even hullo.

'Name your poison,' said Norman. 'I've appointed myself barman for the day, on account of the excessive lentitude with which the libations have been distributed.'

Michael frowned at him as if he had been speaking in Russian. 'I beg your pardon?'

'A drink, dear boy. I'm offering you a drink.'

'Oh, nothing, thanks. These days I only drink stout.'

'Stout? You're not thinking of becoming a midwife, are you? They always drink stout. My younger brother still flinches at the smell of Guinness on anybody's breath. He says he can remember being blasted by it, the moment he came out of the womb. Another victim of post-parturitional halitosis.'

Michael went over to Patricia and stood beside her. Norman was about to say something else, but Richard raised a finger to his lips, warning him that the situation was sensitive, and to keep quiet. Elisabeth said, 'Would you like another melody? A good old German melody. What about *Sah' ein Knab ein Röslein steh'n . . . Röslein auf der Heide!*'

'Only if you let me accompany you on comb and Izal,' said Norman.

Michael said to Patricia, 'How are you feeling? You do look awfully well.'

Patricia quickly glanced up. 'I'm still sick sometimes. Not very often, thank goodness. It was frightful at the beginning. Well, you know, don't you? I have an awful craving for chocolate pudding. I'm sure I'm going to end up enormous.'

'You, er . . . James isn't here.'

'No, it's a terrible shame, him having to go off to America like that. But he was quite excited about flying in the Do-X. He had a business meeting. It was something to do with selling some more Aquariuses. But he should be back in a fortnight.'

Michael took a deep breath. He glanced quickly at Richard, and then he said, 'I'd like to talk, if we may.'

'We *can*,' said Patricia. Her voice was a little too high. 'We can always talk.'

'I mean, privately. Just you and I.'

'It's almost lunchtime.'

'Well, after lunch, perhaps. You see, the thing is, it was all rather unfinished, wasn't it, you and me?'

'I was sorry you couldn't come to the wedding,' said Patricia.

'Couldn't bear to, actually.' There was an odd muffled sound in Michael's voice, as if his mouth were full of sponge cake.

Patricia picked distractedly at her gown. 'I know you were hurt. I'm very sorry about it. It wasn't easy for me, either.'

Richard came up and laid his arm around Michael's shoulder. He thought that Michael smelled rather musty, like somebody who only takes a bath once a month, and never takes their corduroys to the cleaners. To be painfully frank, he smelled like a Socialist.

'Are you coming over to the works this afternoon?' he wanted to know. 'We're having the grand unveiling. Champagne, everything. We were up most of the night, finishing her off.'

Michael nodded, 'Yes, all right. Paul Heath might be coming down later. Do you think he could come along, too?'

Richard shrugged. 'The more the merrier. I didn't think that rolling-out new racers would be quite his cup of tea.'

'Well,' said Michael, rather fiercely, 'there's more to almost everybody than meets the eye. Wouldn't you say so, Patricia?'

Lunch was boiled ham, and tense. Constance sat at the head of

145

the table looking tired. She wore a grey frock with a floppy collar which didn't suit her. She kept turning her fork over and over, which irritated Richard no end. Patricia and Michael sat together and scarcely spoke. Bryan King-Moreton had elected to carve the ham and was making a scrappy job of it because it was over-cooked. Richard ended up with not much more than a plateful of rags.

Fortunately, Norman Jorritt had drunk enough whisky before lunch to have reached maximum volubility, and while everybody else picked at their lunch and chafed in their seats and glanced at each other in varying conditions of anxiety or regret, Norman planted his elbows on the table and ignored his ham and parsleyed potatoes and unravelled one silly remark after another like a stage magician tugging flags out of his sleeve.

'Of course one has to be invited to the Royal Academy for the private viewing; it's socially essential; but it's equally essential to sneer at all the pictures. If the sky is painted blue and the grass is painted green, you must loudly accuse the artist of being the bourgeois slave of an outworn representational aesthetic. If the sky is painted green and the grass is painted blue, you must just as loudly accuse the artist of being a mental deficient who should be sterilized in case he passes on his affliction to future generations.'

Outside, the rain began to clear, but the day remained un-seasonably cold and misty. Constance asked Michael, 'How long do you think you might be staying, dear? The Sandells are coming on Saturday. I'm sure Victoria would love to see you.'

Michael kept his eyes on his plate. 'You don't have to matchmake, Mother. I'm quite capable of finding my own part-ners.'

'You're not still going around with that ghastly Paul Frith?'

'Yes, Mother, and his name's Heath. He's quite a brilliant chap, in his own way.'

'He's a Socialist.'

Norman drank half a glass of Châteauneuf-du-Pape without breathing. For a moment, his eyes popped. But then he swallowed hard, and said, 'It's quite all right to be a Socialist, Mrs Lord; and quite all right to be a Fascist. What you must never, *never* be is a Liberal. This is the startling new age when the wishy-washy go to the wall.'

Constance said, 'Paul Frith gives me goosepimples, I'm sorry to say. He's always creeping up behind one, and smelling of onions.'

'How many political struggles have been won or lost on a smell?' Norman demanded. 'Perhaps if Alexander the Great hadn't reeked so strongly of garlic and *feta* cheese, the civilized world wouldn't have fallen so readily before him.'

'Norman, you are tiddly,' said Elisabeth. 'Eat your lunch before you begin to upset everybody.'

'Well, you're quite right,' Norman agreed. 'And such a splendid lunch! Do you know something, I have no patience at all with this modern habit of having one's meat carved in secrecy, in the kitchen, or by a butler with his back turned. It is the task of the host to do the carving, to make an exhibition of it, and to apportion the meat according to whichever of his guests and family he favours most. Outside bits to the favourite lady, gristle to the misbehaving son! I am like the immortal Shepherd who liked to see his food in its integrity.'

'Norman,' insisted Elisabeth, '*tais-toi.*'

After lunch, Richard and Norman smoked cigars in the library, and Elisabeth went upstairs to make a long telephone call to London. Bryan King-Moreton cornered Constance in the sewing-room, where she had gone to find her spectacles. It was a small room, wallpapered in pale pink Regency stripes. There was a framed photograph of Herbert on the wall, tinted by hand so that he looked as if he were advertising a particularly bracing seaside resort.

'Ah, Constance!' said Bryan, with an abruptness which startled her.

'Bryan? Is everything all right?'

'Of course, yes! I didn't mean to – well, I didn't mean to give you the impression that everything *wasn't* all right. Everything's –' he clapped his hands together. Constance stared at him, waiting for him to continue. 'All right,' he finished.

'I'm sorry the ham was overdone. Cook's been having trouble with the Aga.'

'No, no, that's perfectly –' he hesitated to say 'all right' yet again.

'We'll have to leave soon, won't we?' asked Constance. 'Did Richard say that Bernard was coming over?' Bernard was the Duke of Norfolk: he and Herbert had been gruffly friendly. They expected him to motor over from Arundel and make a little speech. 'This symbol of Empire,' that kind of thing.

Bryan stepped back and almost knocked over Constance's needlework frame. 'Constance, I – difficult, but – Constance, I really must talk to you.'

'Now?' Constance asked, peering over Bryan's left shoulder towards the door.

Bryan nodded. 'Yes, Constance, now. Today being such a special day. What I mean is, today, somehow, we've managed somehow to redeem Herbert's reputation. Not publicly, of course, he's never lost his reputation publicly. But within the family, between ourselves. When we rolled out the *Chichester Special* this morning, do you know, I really felt that we'd managed to bring Herbert back to life. And I wondered whether you might consider bringing something else back to life.'

He was standing stiffly upright, his hands clasped together, his eyes a little wild from stress. Constance said, with undisguised suspicion, '*What*, Bryan? What do you want to bring back to life?' Although she thought: *My God, I know!*

Bryan said, 'I thought – well, some years ago now – back at the beginning – long before we were building anything like the Aquarius or any of that – well, I always liked to think that you and I had a special sort of *rapport*. Quite within the bounds of propriety, of course. Ha! Ha! you know what I mean, I'm sorry, nothing to be – well – *ashamed* of. Everything in its proper place, don't you know? And, well, *that*. That is what I thought you might consider reviving. That rather special sort of – what-you-might-call-it. That *rapport*.'

Constance touched Bryan's shoulder with great kindness. 'Bryan . . . it's been so many years.'

To Constance's embarrassment, Bryan dropped down on to one knee, and clasped both of her hands between his. 'Constance, Connie, please. It was altogether different when Herbert was alive. I was quite prepared to take the navigator's seat, you know what I mean. I admired Herbert so much; I was always happy for you. But now that Herbert's gone . . .'

He pressed his white bristly moustache against the back of Constance's hand. 'Constance, I am quite devoted to you. Do you think there is any chance for me at all?'

'Chance, Bryan?'

'Constance, I think of you with quite extraordinary affection.'

Disconcerted, Constance tugged her hand away. 'For goodness' sake, Bryan, this is beginning to sound like a bad West End play.'

'Constance, I mean it. I love you. I want you to marry me.'

Constance slowly looked down at him as if she had never seen him before. 'Bryan?' she asked.

Bryan was incapable of speaking. His eyes watered, and he had to take an immense swallow to prevent himself from bursting into tears.

'*Bryan*,' Constance repeated. 'I had absolutely no idea.'

Bryan climbed stiffly back on to his feet. He held Constance in his arms and stared into her face with such intentness that she found herself smiling. 'Bryan,' she said, 'you're a dear, dear friend, but really.'

'I don't expect to be any kind of substitute for Herbert,' Bryan admitted. 'Herbert was a hero, a man in a million. But I can protect you, and take care of you. I can play a jolly good hand of bridge. I can carve. And I'm really not that much of an ogre to look at, am I?'

Constance looked at him for a long time. Then she said, 'It's quite a notion, Bryan, I have to admit that.'

'I can only tell you, Connie dear, that I love you so awfully much.'

Constance said nothing, but patted his arm just once and then turned away. Bryan stayed where he was, watching her, breathing deeply, as if he had been running. Her profile against the brownish afternoon light of the sewing-room window was like the old Queen's profile on a penny. Bryan took out his handkerchief and discreetly wiped his eyes.

At last, Constance turned back and said, in a matter-of-fact tone, as if she were discussing a jam recipe, 'Do you know, since Herbert went, it has never occurred to me, not once, that I might one day marry again?'

'I very much wish that you *would* consider it,' said Bryan. 'Perhaps it's too soon, I really don't know. If it is, you must accept my apologies. I'd rather walk over broken glass than do anything to hurt you.'

'That's awfully dramatic of you,' said Constance.

'You make me feel dramatic.'

'Dear Bryan,' said Constance. 'Bryan the Navigator. I hope you haven't been suffering *too* much, all these years. I'd hate to think that you suffered.'

'Well – love, suffering, they're almost the same thing, aren't they?' Bryan replied.

'I don't know,' Constance frowned. 'I've loved – or, at least, I *think* I've loved – but I've never suffered.'

'You *will* consider my proposal, though?' asked Bryan, a little desperately.

Constance took his hand again, and smiled. 'Yes, Bryan, I *will* consider it.'

Patricia meanwhile was in the garden, picking nasturtium leaves for a salad she was planning to make that evening. Raindrops glittered on the leaves like beads of mercury.

Michael was standing a little way away, trying to get his pipe to go. The afternoon silence was punctuated by his sucking and puffing and the tinkle of spent matches falling on to the crazy paving.

Patricia gathered up the nasturtium leaves in her apron. She looked at Michael with her head tilted to one side. 'You do forgive me, don't you?'

Michael sucked, and puffed, and shrugged. 'There's nothing to forgive, is there? You know what Tennyson said, *thy fate and mine are sealed, I strove against the stream and all in vain.*'

'I didn't think Tennyson was quite the thing for Socialists,' said Patricia. She felt guilty enough about what had happened without Michael rubbing it in.

Michael concentrated on his pipe for a moment. It wouldn't go. At last, he lowered it, and said, 'I would have married you, you know. Even with James's child.'

Patricia smiled in that secretive self-satisfied way that pregnant women do. 'You never would, Michael. James's child is James's, and you can't alter that. Besides, I'm his wife.'

'So where is he now?' Michael challenged. 'You've only been married for a month and a bit. Where is he now?'

'It was important. He thinks he can sell four Aquariuses in America. He would have stayed behind if he could.'

Michael let out an ersatz schoolboyish laugh. 'That's priceless, isn't it? All I can say is, you obviously don't know him as well as I do.'

'Michael,' said Patricia, looking at him gently, 'don't be jealous, please.'

'Jealous? I'm not jealous. It's nothing at all to do with being jealous. James is James. You can't change him, whatever you do.'

'I'm sorry,' Patricia repeated.

Michael said nothing, but shrugged, and looked away, focusing on the far end of the flower-garden.

'It would have meant lying, for the rest of my life,' Patricia insisted. 'It would have meant pretending, every single day, for year after year, that *you* were its daddy – when all the time it was James.'

'You seemed to find it jolly easy to lie before,' said Michael.

'No,' said Patricia. 'I never lied to you, not once.'

'You didn't think it was lying when you conveniently forgot to tell me that you'd jumped into bed with my brother? Omitting to tell the truth is just as deceitful as lying, don't you know.' The words came out of his mouth like ashes, ashes that clung to his tongue and his lips. 'You could have told me, you know. You could have spared me from making such a bally ass of myself.'

'I'm sorry, Michael. But it really wasn't any of your business.'

'Of course it was my business. You were my girlfriend. He was my brother.'

Patricia said nothing, but dipped down to pick another nasturtium. She was plainly trying to avoid an argument. The skies were clearing fast. Over towards the west, God was opening his windows.

'Patricia,' Michael fretted, 'you'll never be happy with James, you know.'

Patricia looked up. 'Of course I will. I love him. I fell in love with him the very first moment I saw him. Now I'm his wife, Michael. I'm carrying his baby.'

'Nonetheless.'

Patricia stood up, suddenly bold. 'What do you suggest, then? Do you suggest that I sue for divorce, on the grounds that my husband's younger brother doesn't consider my husband quite suitable? Do you suggest that I leave him, and go to a clinic in Switzerland, and give birth in private? Do you suggest that I carry on some kind of affair with you, whenever James is away on business?'

'You suggested it, not me,' said Michael.

Patricia stared at him in fury. 'How *could* you suggest such a thing? How *could* you? Don't you have any consideration at all? My goodness, Michael, whatever you say about James, he always puts my feelings first, always. Why do you think that I went to bed with him? He treated me like a woman, instead of a child. He treated me like a mistress, instead of a chum. Michael, I liked you. I always liked you. I like you still. But liking is a hundred miles away from loving.'

'I see,' said Michael. 'Could you have *ever* loved me, if James hadn't taken you away from me?'

'I don't know,' said Patricia. 'Perhaps.'

Michael looked down at his scuffed suède shoes; then at the western horizon, where the sun was beginning to brighten the Downs. 'It was only one evening, you know,' he remarked. 'To stay faithful to me, just for one evening, that wasn't very much to ask, was it?'

Patricia stood up. The sun caught her hair and made it glow. She looked very beautiful, almost saintly. 'Michael – you can't blame me for falling in love.'

Michael turned, as if he were about to go. Then he swung his

151

arm and slapped Patricia on the right cheek, so hard and so unexpectedly that she stumbled, and almost dropped her apronful of nasturtium leaves.

She stared at him, her cheek blazing, her eyes wide. She didn't speak. She didn't protest. Like most incidents of real violence, this one took place in complete silence, without dialogue, except for the sound of the blows. Michael slapped her again, harder this time. His face was white, expressionless. Patricia begged, 'Michael —' but then he hit her again, and this time he caught her off-balance, and suddenly she stumbled back, snatching the air in panicky handfuls, and tumbled down the stone steps into the sunken lavender garden, her arms and legs flailing.

Michael ran down the steps after her. She lay in a curiously stylized position on the crazy paving, her wrists and ankles cocked like a figure in an Ancient Egyptian frieze, her face pressed resolutely against the well-trimmed grass. 'Patricia! *Patricia!* For God's sake!'

She neither moved nor spoke. Michael lifted her eyelid with his thumb and her pupil was tiny and shrunken. He shook her, but she felt like nothing more than a jumble of sacks. 'Patricia, it's Michael, please!' She was still clutching her apronful of nasturtiums. 'Patricia, please! Patricia!'

He shook her again, but she remained floppy and unresponsive. He stood up, and looked around, but there was nobody in sight; only Eaves, the gardener, and he was well out of earshot, tying up the bean-tunnel.

'Oh, God,' Michael prayed. 'Oh God, please help me.'

But Patricia stayed where she was, concussed on the path, her face as grey as newspaper. A thin line of blood had already slid down the top of her stocking, and started to explore the pattern of the crazy paving.

Florida, 1932

James and Chloe were toasting each other in fruit juice cocktails on the patio of the Palms Hotel when the deputy manager came hurrying out, his hair shiny, his face bright, clutching a telegram. 'Mr Lord? Miss Treat – I'm really sorry to bother you –'

He handed the telegram to James and stood less than ten inches away from him, staring at him unblinkingly, his lips silently mouthing the words which he already knew by heart. James unfolded the telegram and read it very slowly. Then – to the manager's disappointment – he folded it up again and tucked it into the breast pocket of his blazer. 'Thank you,' he said.

'Nothing serious?' asked Chloe. She was flirtatious and theatrical; but she had lived through enough pain of her own to be able to recognize that odd defensive flicker of the eye when somebody has been hurt – almost as if a burning match has been thrust at their face.

'Just – a note from my mother,' said James. He turned to the manager, who was still hovering, and repeated, 'Thank you.'

'Well, don't mention it,' replied the deputy manager. 'We try to be of service. And, you know, if there's anything that I can do . . .?'

'No thank you,' James told him. 'I don't really think that there's anything that anybody can do.'

The deputy manager walked off, his white ducks flapping. James reached beneath the table for the bottle of champagne which wallowed in a bucket of iced water between his feet, and filled up their fruit-juice cocktails to the brim. 'Here's to the anti-Prohibitionists,' he said, wryly. Beyond the railings, the Atlantic breakers roared and horsetailed in the morning wind, and above their heads the palm trees furiously rattled. Chloe reached across the table and touched James's hand.

'It's bad news, isn't it? Something terrible's happened.'

James shrugged, and turned away, out towards the ocean. It looked today the way that Winslow Homer used to paint it, deep and slabby, full of turquoise sunlight and dark green shadows. James's eyes were watering, because of the wind, because of the sand, because of his disloyalty.

'My wife was expecting a baby. I've just heard that she's lost it.'

Chloe squeezed his hand. 'Oh, James, I'm so sorry. I'm really so sorry.'

'Well, as I said, there's nothing that anybody can do.'

'Will you fly back to England? Claude's going straight back to Portugal tomorrow, isn't he?'

James took out the telegram and unfolded it again. 'Mother says that she's well, all things considered.'

Chloe said, 'When was the baby due?'

'July. A midsummer baby.'

'That's truly awful. Your poor wife.'

James sat silent for a while, and then said, 'Come on, let's take a walk on the beach. I think my brain needs clearing.'

Chloe took off her strappy gilt sandals and left them on the table. They went down the concrete steps to the beach, and began to walk northward, a little way apart from each other, with the wind rippling their clothes and the ocean thundering and fuming so loudly that they could scarcely hear each other speak.

They hadn't walked further than two hundred yards when James turned and took Chloe in his arms, holding her tightly. She looked up at him, puzzled, thinking at first that he needed comfort, that he wanted her to shush him and baby him and tell him that everything was going to be all right. But he kissed her forehead, and then her cheeks, and then her lips, and she knew then that he wasn't grieving; and that although the telegram from his mother had upset him, it had also come as a profound relief.

'You don't love her, do you?' she asked, her lips glistening from his kiss.

He shook his head. 'I thought that getting married was the right thing to do. It was an absolute disaster, right from the word go. And it was all my fault, too. I can't blame anybody else.'

'What are you going to do?'

'I don't know. What *can* I do? I can't divorce her, unless she divorces me. There are no grounds.'

Chloe kissed him and smiled. 'You're not as rock-hard as you try to pretend, are you?'

'I've never tried to pretend that I'm anything but utterly soft.'

Chloe took his arm and they continued to walk along the shoreline. The pale grey sand sizzled against their ankles. 'Do you believe in Fate?' asked Chloe. 'Do you ever read your horoscopes or anything?'

James shook his head.

'I believe in Fate,' Chloe told him. She stopped, and turned towards the wind. It blew her blonde hair away from her forehead, and made her light pink cotton dress cling to her body, her breasts, her thighs, the soft curve of her stomach. 'I believe that Fate arranged for you and me to fly on that airplane together; and I believe that Fate arranged for your poor little baby to die.' She closed her eyes for a moment, enjoying the feel of the wind, but then she opened them again and said, 'Was it a boy or a girl?'

'Mother – didn't say.'

'Do you know, how about that, isn't that a *tragedy*, to live and to die and your father doesn't even know what sex you are?'

'It never really lived, did it?'

'I don't know. I like to think that babies are alive from the moment their parents first kiss.'

James stood next to Chloe watching her, watching the way the wind threw up her hair for the sunlight to catch. 'Do you have to take that flight this afternoon?' he asked her. She and Marty were booked on South-Eastern Airways' three o'clock plane to Atlanta; and thence by train and plane to California.

She smiled. 'If I'm not back on Wednesday morning at seven a.m. *exactemong*, Mr Zukor is going to have my garters for guts. We're starting principal photography on *It's Hot In Heaven*. Even *les étoiles* like me have to do what they're told.'

'You can't even stay for another day?'

'*Ne t'attong kwatwa serl*,' said Chloe. 'Do you know what that means?'

'I'm afraid that I don't.'

'It means look after your own fanny because nobody else will. Loosely translated.'

James smiled. 'I accept your advice. But I'm still going to miss you.'

'You don't think I'm going to miss you, too? Why don't you come out to California, when your business is all finished?'

'I don't think so. Not this time, anyway. As soon as I've tidied things up here in Miami, I'm going to have to go straight back home. Patricia deserves that much.'

'Well, you're a swine, but you're a swine of gold,' said Chloe. She lifted her face and kissed him directly on the lips. That milk-and-tangerine taste, with a little added sea-salt. He held her close, and they stood together for a long time, with the sun flashing signals through the palm-trees, and the sea eternally grumbling, and what passed between them was a silent promise that the infatuation which had whirled them off their feet on the dance-floor of the Dornier flying-boat would not die here; and perhaps not ever.

They returned to the hotel. Marty was sitting on the patio wall in his shirtsleeves, smoking a cigarette and looking out to sea. 'Did you hear the news?' he asked, as they approached.

'What news?' asked Chloe.

'Amelia Earhart landed in Ireland. First woman to fly the Atlantic.'

'Well,' said Chloe, 'that just goes to prove what I've always said, anything a man can do, a woman can do better.'

Marty took off his sunglasses and rubbed his eyes. 'Ann,' he said, 'do you know what you are? You're a platitude with tits. It's a good thing for you that I love you.'

'Are you ever the rudest person in the entire universe?' Chloe retorted; but quite unoffended. She turned to James, and said, 'Isn't he ever the rudest person in the universe?'

But James couldn't reply. He was standing in the pale grey Florida sand with his hands helplessly down by his sides, and his eyes streaming with tears.

The Essex taxi jerked to a stop outside the corrugated-iron shed and James climbed out. The sweaty-faced driver held out his hand and said, 'Dollar-fifty,' without taking the stogie out from between his teeth. James gave him two dollars, and told him to keep the change. 'How the rich live, hunh?' remarked the taxi-driver, and reversed his whinnying hack all the way to the perimeter fence in a cloud of buff coloured dust.

James drew back the tails of his white linen jacket and stood with his hands on his hips, looking around this so-called airfield. The sky was almost completely cloudless, except for a few frazzled cumulonimbus. The temperature must have been wavering over a hundred. A freshly-painted sign outside the corrugated-iron shed announced *Ticketing Office, Atlantic and Pacific Airways*, but the only indication that James had arrived at the headquarters of the second-largest airline in Florida were two Stinson Tri-motors parked side by side on the scrubby grass, both painted bright yellow and emblazoned with the blue letters APA. The airfield had been cleared out of flat swampland on the west side of Carol City, to the north of Miami: the far perimeter was bordered with scrub and swamp bay and Florida hickory, and there was a strong musty smell of stagnant water and sub-tropical mould.

James pushed open the juddering shed door and called, 'I say! Anybody there?'

There was no reply, so he ventured inside. The shed was dim, with a pungent creosoted floor. It was furnished with two wooden church pews, presumably for passengers to sit on while they were waiting for their flight; a desk made out of an old door supported on orange-boxes; and a huge electric fan with a fraying flex. There were maps on the wall of Florida, New York, and Washington; as well as timetables, a railroad clock, and scores of curled-up testimonials from satisfied APA customers. James read one or two of them, and was delighted with a pencilled letter that said: '*Fuss time I eva flewd and neva saw evathin look so tinie b4 housses autos peepl treas.*'

'Anybody there?' he called again. But there was no reply. He opened another door, but it turned out to be a closet, filled with brochures and boxes of blank tickets and old newspapers. The shed appeared to be deserted. James walked out of the door, and around to the back, where a brindled mutt was sleeping in the sun with flies in its nostrils. 'Halloo?' he shouted, and the mutt snuffled, but didn't bother to open its eyes. James hesitated, and then walked over to the aeroplanes parked on the grass. In the nearer of the two aeroplanes stretched out on a convertible sleeping-berth, a big-bellied man slept like a child, his thumb tucked under his upper lip.

James hesitated for a moment. The man continued to sleep. There was silence, apart from the endless chirruping of insects, and the man's contented breathing, and the ticking of James's watch. At length, James took a deep breath and shouted, '*Halloo! Is anybody there?*'

The man's tiny little blue eyes blinked open, and he stared, stunned, at the bulkhead in front of his face. Then he heaved himself up into a sitting position. 'Jesus! You scared the hell out of me!'

'I'm looking for Eddie Feinbacker,' James told him. 'I have an appointment.'

The man wiped his mouth with the back of his hand, sniffed, and thrust out his hand in greeting. 'You're James Lord! I'm Eddie Feinbacker. Pleased you could make it. I was just catching up on some zees. First time I've had the opportunity in months.'

James knew Eddie Feinbacker by reputation, because he had been one of the most famous of America's wartime fighter-pilots. He was a crop-duster's son who had fitted awkwardly amongst the college-educated pilot officers of the American Expeditionary Force. He had sworn a lot, spat a lot, and hardly ever joined his fellow pilots at the bar of the Hôtel du Crillon. But he had taught himself to fly his Nieuport fighter like a demon, and had shot down fifteen German aeroplanes and eleven observation balloons. 'Out of the sun, one burst of bullets, and he's gone.'

He had a big round leathery head, like a basketball, with small protruding ears and a small pouting mouth that looked as if it was the tight leather sphincter where you would pump the basketball up.

'I wasn't sure you would come,' he told James, hauling his suspenders on to his rounded shoulders, and then foraging around for his shoes. 'You know, seeing the way things are.'

'Don't you have any flights today?' asked James.

'Not today, not tomorrow, neither. Things are kind of unsettled right now.'

James said, 'Mr Feinbacker, I've just flown all the way from Europe at your request to sell you some aeroplanes.'

'Yes, you have, and I appreciate it.' Eddie Feinbacker stood up, and negotiated his way out of the plane. 'You don't have to call me Mr Feinbacker. Eddie'll do. Even President Wilson called me Eddie.'

'Well, I'm sure that what was good enough for President Wilson is good enough for me.'

'Come on over to the office,' said Eddie. 'One advantage of being in the international flying business is the ease of acquiring good liquor.'

'It's a little early in the day for me.'

'You shouldn't think of it that way. Today hasn't properly started yet. This is one last drink from yesterday.'

They climbed out of the Stinson into the shadowless sunlight. Eddie whistled to his mutt as they walked across the airfield towards the makeshift office. 'Hey, Flamerino, how you doing, boy?' He turned to James and said, 'That's what we used to say during the war, whenever we set a German airplane on fire. Flamerino.'

'Yes,' said James. 'My uncle was on the Somme.'

'I was at Toul and Rembercourt with the Old Ninety-Fourth. A fully-qualified Guimper.'

They went into the office, and Eddie dragged a chair across so that James could sit down. He reached into one of the orange-boxes that supported his desk and took out a bottle of Haig. After further rummaging, he discovered two cloudy-looking glasses, and filled them both. 'Here's mud in your eye,' he declared, and heaved himself into the Western-style chair behind the desk.

James lifted his glass but didn't drink. 'When do you think you might start flying again?' he asked, trying not to sound too insistent.

'Well, that depends,' said Eddie. 'Could be never, the way things look. You've heard all about Mr Walter Folger Brown, the Postmaster General? He's in charge of awarding all the airmail-carrying contracts. Two days ago we had the official news that Brown just turned down our bid to fly the mail between Miami and Atlanta. The letter's here someplace. "Dear Mr Feinbacker, the Postmaster General regrets." That pretty much spells doom, as far as we're concerned.'

'That doesn't exactly tally with what I've been hearing,' said James. 'I thought you were making a profit without any assistance from the government at all.'

'Checked our credentials, hunh?' asked Eddie, taking a mouthful of whisky and straining it between his teeth before swallowing it. 'Well, you're absolutely right. My brother Nick and I started this airline five years ago, right after Nick sold out his tuna-cannery business down at Key West. And we made it pay. By cracky we made it pay. We cut costs right down to the bone. Those Stinsons are just about the most economical airplanes flying. We always taxi them on the ground on one engine, to save gas, and we only use high-test fuel during take-off. Once we're up in the air, we switch to regular automobile fuel, which is a whole lot cheaper. We don't serve coffee and sandwiches, we don't provide maps or antimacassars or salt-water taffy or fancy literature. All we do is get you there.' He hesitated, and looked across at James with those bright tiny eyes. 'I'm not saying it was *easy*, but, yes, certainly, we made it pay.'

'Can't you continue to make it pay?' James asked him. 'If you didn't fly the mail before, why do you need it now?'

Eddie said, 'Listen – Walter Brown awarded the contract to South-Eastern Air Travel. This was in spite of the fact that their bid was more than three times higher than ours.'

'He's allowed to do that?'

'Sure he's allowed to do that, because of what it says in the Watres Act, which incidentally he drafted himself. Well, being in the business, you probably know what it says in the Watres Act – that the Postmaster General is permitted to bypass lower bids and to give the mail contract to the "lowest *responsible* bidder". Where it gets tricky is with Brown's definition of "responsible". In *his* view, a responsible airline is an airline that flies a daily scheduled service over a route in excess of two hundred fifty miles, *both day and night*. That cuts out just about everybody except the really big boys – and I guess you heard about the way that Transcontinental and Western Air Express were forced to merge into TWA, just so they could qualify to carry the mail. Pop Hanshue of Western told Walter Brown that he was crazy as hell, those were his actual words, you're as crazy as hell, but in the end he didn't have a choice.'

Eddie stood up, and walked across to the maps on the office wall. 'Walter Brown is one of those men with a dream, do you know what I mean? He thinks that America's air traffic should all be handled by three or four big competing airlines, with big airplanes carrying dozens of passengers. He has the idea that, in the end, they'll be carrying so many passengers that the government won't have to subsidize the air-mail any more. He thinks that if the airlines are bigger, the people who make airplanes will be encouraged to design bigger and faster transports, which can carry more mail, and which incidentally can also be used by the military.

'A dream, that's what Walter Brown has. The trouble is, Walter Brown's dream is our nightmare. He's pushing all of us smaller independent operators out of business. Now that South-Eastern have the US mail contract over the same route as us, they can offer their passengers luxury flying at only a few dollars more than us. They don't even have to be carrying any mail – they get their subsidy just by having space *available* for mail.

'Ask yourself – who's going to want to fly in a cane-backed bucket when they could be flying in an armchair? Who's going to sit in a drafty Stinson eating out of their own lunchpail when they could be relaxing in a Ford or a Junkers and nibbling sandwiches with the crusts cut off?'

He paused, and shrugged, and said, 'I'm real sorry, James. I dragged you all the way here on an expectation. I believed with all my heart I was going to win that mail contract, then I would have needed three of your Aquariuses at least, maybe four. And I could've afforded to buy them, too. Now what, I've been kalsomined.'

James sipped a little whisky. 'Who's running South-Eastern these days? Is it still Erle Pepper?'

'Good old Erle,' Eddie grinned. 'Fieriest bastard in the business.'

'Well, if you're not in the market for any of my aeroplanes, I suppose I'd better go and speak to him. At least my trip won't have been a complete waste of time.'

'Wouldn't trouble yourself,' said Eddie, equably. 'He's already taken out an option on thirty of those new DC-1s.'

'Oh,' said James. 'I see.' He thought with a wave of particular bitterness of the ill-fated Lord Capricorn airliner, delayed and delayed by Bryan King-Moreton's vaingloriousness, stillborn on the drawing-board while Herbert and he flew one-man racers. Out here in America, where business was business, the gilded heroics of the British Empire seemed to James to be even more shrunken and amateurish than ever. He already knew that TWA had taken an option on sixty of Donald Douglas's new all-metal airliner; he hadn't realized that South-Eastern had shown so much interest as well.

'How about something to eat?' asked Eddie. 'There's a good old-fashioned diner in Carol City, serves excellent conch chowder and blackened ribs.'

James nodded. 'Yes, that sounds an excellent idea,' but his expression had suddenly become thoughtful.

'How about a drink now?' asked Eddie, filling up his own glass.

James shook his head.

'Something on your mind?'

'Yes,' said James, 'I think there is. I was wondering if there might be a way of winning this airmail contract after all.'

'I don't follow you,' frowned Eddie. 'It's been awarded, plain and simple, signed, sealed, and delivered. Walter Brown isn't the kind of man who changes his mind.'

'But what if South-Eastern proved to be unreliable?'

'Well *that* sure isn't likely. Erle Pepper runs the tightest ship going. They fly Ford Tri-motors four times a day to Atlanta and back, dead on schedule, and two Condor sleepers at night. Best time-keeping record in the south-east, best safety record in the south-east.'

'Supposing that were to change?'

'It sure isn't likely.'

'No, I suppose it isn't, but you can't always be sure, can you? Running an airline's a funny sort of business. Very unpredictable. Look what happend to TWA after that crash that killed Knute Rockne.'

Eddie pouted out his lower lip. 'I guess. But that was an act of –' he pointed his finger up to the ceiling.

James said nothing more, but sat upright in his chair looking at Eddie in apparent expectation.

'What do you want me to say?' asked Eddie, letting out a sudden laugh. 'Airplanes crash by accident, not because you want them to. And I'm not saying that I want them to.'

'I'm not talking about crashes,' said James, 'I'm talking about delays. Late flights, cancelled flights. If South-Eastern suffered three or four months of consistently bad time-keeping, wouldn't that give Mr Walter Folger Brown sufficient reason to reconsider his decision? The mail must get through, you know. Through dark of night, through desert heat, whatever it is they say.'

Eddie Feinbacker eased himself upright in his chair. 'Are you trying to say what I think you're trying to say?'

James shrugged. 'You can interpret it in any way you wish. You weren't ever under the impression that running a successful independent airline had anything to do with moral spotlessness, were you?'

Eddie looked unhappily down at his empty whisky-glass. 'I'm not so sure that this is my kind of game.'

'For goodness' sake,' snapped James. 'What are you going to do? You're not going to sit back and drink whisky while Walter Brown buggers up everything you and your brother have been slaving like blacks for, are you? Eddie, you're a war hero! Fight back!'

'Well . . . I sure don't mind fighting back if it's a fair fight,' said Eddie. 'But what you're suggesting . . .'

James smacked the top of the makeshift desk. 'Were you fair to the Germans, when you came diving on them out of the sun? Is Brown being fair to you? What about Erle Pepper? Don't tell me that *he* didn't grease a few palms at the Post Office. Listen, Eddie, I'm suggesting nothing more than minor tinkering. Missing spare parts. Sand in the bearings. Water in the fuel. Nothing rash, nothing dangerous. Just an endless series of irritating delays – while *you* continue to run an economic and punctual airline.'

Eddie thought for a moment, and then slowly shook his head. 'I'm sorry, James. This isn't my kind of game. Besides, I don't have the money to keep on running a service, just in the hope that Walter Brown's going to change his mind. We're down to the bottom of the barrel as it is.'

James held out his glass. 'Pour me another drink.' Then, 'How much do you want for the whole airline?'

'I'm sorry?'

'I said, how much do you want for the whole airline? I'll take it off your hands. If you can't make a go of it, then I certainly can.'

'You want to buy me out?'

'You can still work here, you and your brother, that's if your scruples will allow you. In fact, I'd be very glad if you did.'

Eddie pointed at him. 'Tell me I'm dreaming,' he demanded. 'Tell me I'm back in the plane, asleep.'

'I'm serious,' James insisted. 'How much do you want?'

Eddie let out a loud sharp shout of disbelief. 'You came all the way from England to sell me some airplanes, now you're offering to buy my whole damned airline. You sure know how to throw a man a mackerel.'

'Do you want to discuss it with your brother?'

'No need, there's nothing to discuss. We've talked it over already. You can have it for two hundred seventy, all in, which is what Erle Pepper's been offering.'

'Make it two hundred and fifty and you have a deal. It's worth twenty thousand just to stay independent.'

'All righty, so long as I can okay it with Nick,' said Eddie. 'Two hundred fifty it is.'

James stood up, and held out his hand. 'Agreed then, in principle. I'll have to send a wire to London. We can go and see your lawyers tomorrow morning.'

'I feel like somebody hit me with a baseball bat,' said Eddie, shaking James by the hand to settle the sale. 'I just sold five years of my life in five seconds flat.'

'I don't think you should look at it that way,' James told him. 'I think you should start preparing yourself for the next five years, which are going to be ten times more profitable.'

'If you can keep APA flying, that's all I care about,' said Eddie.

James put on his hat, and straightened it. 'Not only am I going to keep APA flying, I'm going to make it the biggest and most successful airline in the southern United States.'

'Well,' said Eddie. He looked around him, and then he raised his glass. 'Goodbye to all of this, and hallo to whatever's coming next!'

'Let's go and get something to eat,' James suggested. 'Dramatic business deals always make me feel hungry. What did you say, blackened ribs?'

They met at the Blue Moon Club, in the Cuban district. The club was smoky, hot, and crushingly noisy, with fans circling the ceiling and a thatched bar that was supposed to look like a beach cottage at Cárdenas. The bartender's face was so black that all James could make out were his eyes, his teeth, and the glistening red reflections on his cheeks and forehead of the lamps around the bar. At the opposite end of the club, on a stage not much larger than a wine-table, a bosomy young Cuban woman in a red handkerchief top and a swirling red skirt was dancing a furious rumba. Her thick black hair was swept up in combs, and there was a huge beauty-spot on the side of her nose. Every time she stamped her feet, her breasts jiggled tumultuously in their handkerchiefs, and her devoted audience screamed and whistled and shouted out, '*Hrrrrrr! Bravo, Maria! Pummel me, Maria! Suffocate me! Give me no mercy!*'

Eddie Feinbacker was already there, wearing a loud yellow-and-blue shirt and a Panama hat that looked as if it had been fished out of the Panama Canal. He was leaning one elbow against the bar and clapping his hand against his thigh in time to the music.

'Hey, James!' he called, as James edged his way past the damp naked back of a black girl who had just been dancing. 'Come and take a look at this! Maria Estovez, eighteen years old. They call her something in Spanish which means "Catastrophe to Men".'

James took off his hat and wiped the sweat from his face. 'I thought you said we were going to meet somewhere quiet.'

'This is quieter than the Cócinos Club. What'll you have to drink?'

'They can serve liquor here?'

Eddie made a show of looking slowly around the club. 'Do you see anybody here who looks even remotely sober?'

'All right, then,' said James. 'I'll have whatever you're having.'

Eddie turned around to the bartender, and whistled sharply between his teeth. 'Toussaint, bring this gentleman a Suffering Bastard. And bring another one for me.'

James replaced his hat. Everybody else in the Blue Moon Club was wearing a hat.

Eddie said, 'You've never had a Suffering Bastard until you've had one of Toussaint's Suffering Bastards.'

James said, 'I've never had anybody's Suffering Bastard. The name's enough to give me a hangover.'

Eddie let out a lopsided laugh. 'Light rum, dark rum, lime-juice, curaçao, and orgeat syrup. After two glasses, you can fight any man in the room. After three glasses, you can make love to any woman in the room. After four glasses, you can do both at the same time.'

'After five?'

'After five, you can't do either.'

Toussaint the barman set their drinks down in front of them. 'Enriquez just call from the airfield, Mr Feinbacker. Says he got himself a take-a-nickel problem. Says ten minute.'

'Thanks, Toussaint, you're a white man,' said Eddie, and passed him over a sharply-folded dollar-bill.

James sipped his drink and leaned back against the bar and watched 'Catastrophe to Men' shaking her skirt as hysterically as if she were trying to dislodge an earwig. Beside her, a five-piece Cuban band in sparkling blue gaucho costumes were playing guitars and maracas and trumpets with furious abandon. They sounded as if they were each playing a different rumba, and racing each other to see who could finish his rumba first. Somebody shouted, *'Ow! ow! ow! Maria! Kill me, Maria! Jump on top of me, Maria!'*

Eddie said, 'I talked to Nick. Explained your offer.'

'How did he take it?'

'He says it sounds okay. He doesn't want to have any more part in running it, though. He's going to take his share of the money and go back to Key West to catch tuna. He always was a fisherman, rather than a flyer.'

'So we can visit your lawyers tomorrow and draw up the deed of sale?'

'I guess so.'

'You don't seem frightfully enthusiastic about it. You haven't changed your mind?'

Eddie swallowed rum, and shook his head. 'I'm just leery about messing with Erle Pepper's airplanes, that's all.'

'Can you think of another way of winning that airmail contract?' James asked him.

Eddie said, 'No, I can't. But it isn't exactly legal, is it?'

'Neither is liquor, but you're drinking it.'

Eddie scrutinized James with his piercing little eyes. 'You know something, James, to look at you, I wouldn't have given you credit for this kind of operation,' he remarked. 'You look like too much of a gentleman. Too English. Mind you, I met plenty of English flyers during the war. Mick Mannock, I met him. Albert Ball, Andy Beauchamp-Proctor. I met all of those guys. All of them dead now, all killed. But to talk to them, you know, you wouldn't have thought they were anything more than jawly decent young cheps. They'd talk about cricket, and girls, and motorcycles. But then they'd start to tell you how many Huns they'd killed, how

165

many enemy pilots they'd burned to death, flamerinos, you know? Sizzle-sizzle wonk! And then you'd understand that you weren't talking to jawly decent young cheps at all, you were talking to killers. Real killers, who killed for the joy of it.'

James was silent for a moment. Then he smiled, and shrugged, and said, 'I do rather think that you're misjudging me, you know. Giving South-Eastern Airways one or two timetable problems isn't quite like sending Huns down in flames. We're not going to kill anybody. We're simply going to make sure that the contract for carrying the mail is taken away from the *wrong* airline and awarded to the *right* airline, which as far as you're concerned is *yours*.

'You mean *yours*,' Eddie reminded him.

James lifted his glass. 'I suppose we ought to drink to that.'

He took a large mouthful of Suffering Bastard and almost choked. 'God Almighty! What brand of rum do they use? BP Ethyl?'

After about a quarter of an hour, during which the blue cigar-smoke grew measurably denser and the merengue dancers grew visibly sweatier and Eddie downed two more Suffering Bastards, a short stocky Cuban in an orange-and-white striped blazer came up to the bar and shook Eddie by the hand. His cheeks were pitted with acne scars and he smelled strongly of lavender hair-cream.

'*Cómo está usted*. Eddie, how are you?'

Eddie slapped him on the back. 'Enriquez, *hombre*. Glad you could come. Here – meet Mr James Lord, of Lord Aeronautics in England.'

Enriquez bowed his head to James, and shook his hand. 'I am very honoured. I have worked once on a Lord Aquarius. That was a beautiful airplane, beautifully made. Very good finish, beautiful airframe, beautiful engines.'

'Thank you, that's a compliment,' said James, 'May I buy you a cocktail? We seem to be drinking Suffering Bastards.'

Enriquez tugged up the waistband of his pants. 'A beer for me,' he said. 'I went to Key Biscayne once and saw how they make that rum. Everything goes in, sugar, cockroaches, seagull shit. They make gasoline better than they make that rum.'

'I was thinking of ordering gasoline next time round,' James remarked.

They drank a toast of greeting, and then James said, 'Shall we get right down to brass tacks? Eddie tells me you're the chief mechanic at South-Eastern Airways.'

'Deputy chief mechanic. Chief mechanic is Willy Mulligan. Top-notch guy, Willy. He used to work for Alfred Lawson, way back.'

'Oh yes – I remember Lawson,' put in Eddie, his voice slightly dragging, like the feet of the merengue dancers. 'He was the first guy ever to build an airliner – I mean a proper airliner that wasn't converted from a mail-plane or a bomber. It was like a damn great box-kite, that plane. Good plane, though, never did hear what happened to it. Lawson gave it all up, and started some nutty religion called Lawsonomy.'

Enriquez hadn't taken his eyes away from James. 'Eddie told me maybe you had some business to talk about.'

'Well, that's quite right,' said James, 'I understand that you and Eddie have known each other for quite a number of years.'

Enriquez nodded.

'I also understand that Eddie has done you one or two favours, now and again.'

'Eddie's helped out,' Enriquez agreed, cautiously. 'But, you know, Eddie's a good man, he don't ask for nothing.'

'He's not really asking for anything now. But the thing is, it looks very much as if his airline is going to have to close down. Now that South-Eastern have won the air-mail contract, APA won't be able to compete.'

Enriquez squeezed Eddie's arm. 'Eddie – that's bad news. I didn't know. I'm sure sorry to hear that. But what can *I* do?'

'Quite a lot, actually,' said James. 'You can make quite sure that South-Eastern *loses* the air-mail contract.'

'Hey, how can I do that? I'm only the deputy chief mechanic. Anyway, what are you talking about. I'd be cutting my own throat. Mr Pepper says that everybody gets a big pay hike next month, because of carrying the air-mail. And, believe me, I need that money. My daughter Alicia is sick in the hospital, tuberculosis.'

James said, 'Whatever Mr Pepper pays you, I'll pay you half as much again. What's more, if Southern-Eastern loses the air-mail contract, you can come to APA as chief mechanic.'

Enriquez glanced at Eddie in bewilderment, but Eddie gave him a resigned, blurry smile. 'He bought the airline,' he explained. 'From tomorrow, it all belongs to him. I'm going to go on running it, but it all belongs to him.'

'It's all yours, APA?' asked Enriquez, as if he were suspicious that he was being taken for a sucker in some devious practical joke. 'I guess that's good. But what do you want *me* to do?'

James put down his drink. 'It would be easy enough, wouldn't it, to make sure that, say, one out of every three South-Eastern air-mail flights is delayed by mechanical failure. Not for too long – but long enough in each case for the plane to miss its connecting flights in Atlanta.'

Enriquez appealed to Eddie again. 'This is on the level?'

James said, 'Remember, you'll get one-and-a-half times as much as Mr Pepper's going to pay you, and a guaranteed job as chief mechanic.'

Enriquez asked, 'Just for making the flights late?'

'Just for making the flights late.'

'This was your idea?' Enriquez asked Eddie. But Eddie shook his head and turned a thumb toward James.

'You may thank this devious limey,' he remarked.

'Well . . . I don't know,' said Enriquez. 'I could use the money, sure. I need a new automobile. I want Joey to go to college. But, Mr Pepper's always been straight. He's always taken care of me. I wouldn't want to do anything to hurt him.'

'Perhaps he *is* straight,' said James. 'Perhaps he *has* taken care of you. But he's made quite certain that Eddie goes out of business,' James put in.

'It's pretty tough, running an airline,' said Enriquez. 'Some people win, some people lose.'

'You're quite right,' James agreed. 'But I'm going to make sure that APA is going to win.' He paused and then he said, 'What kind of automobile do you have your eye on?'

Enriquez looked at James through narrowed eyes. 'What kind of a question is that?'

'Tell me, what kind?' James repeated.

'Dodge,' said Enriquez, suspiciously. 'Dodge Standard Six.'

'How much is it?' James asked him.

'Seven hundred thirty-five dollars.'

'You know where to buy one?'

'Sure. I pass the showroom every morning. It's standing in the window. It's red, you know. Cherry-red.'

James reached into his inside pocket and took out his gold propelling-pencil and a visiting-card. 'Here,' he said, 'write down the address of the showroom on the back of this. I'll go there tomorrow and buy the car for you. You can pick it up on your way back from work.'

Enriquez took the pencil and the card. His hand remained poised above the card for nearly half a minute. Finally he looked up, and whispered, 'You are bribing me, hunh?'

'That's right,' said James, without smiling. 'I'm bribing you.'

London, 1932

The rain began just as the train pulled out of Three Bridges station and joined the main London to Brighton line. It pattered on to the windows and streaked the soot. Michael sat opposite Paul, pale-faced. Both of them were joggled from side to side as the train's wheels negotiated the complicated criss-cross points.

'Have they set another date?' asked Paul, shouting above the banging of metal wheels on metal rails. He was wearing a large home-knitted cardigan in a livid shade of diarrhoea brown, and he had tried cutting his own hair.

Michael said, 'Next week, I think. The Press were furious. The chap from the *Illustrated London News* said that he wouldn't come down again, even if they flew him down.'

'So Richard's none too pleased, either.'

'No,' said Michael.

The engine began to chuff sturdily, and the train picked up speed. Paul looked at his watch and said, 'We should get to Victoria by eight. We can go for a drink at the Bag O'Nails. What you need to do is to get completely plastered.'

'I'm plastered enough already. I think I'd rather go home.'

Paul leaned forward in his seat and grasped Michael's hand. 'Mike – you can't blame yourself for what happened. You heard what the doctor said, she was quite likely to have lost it anyway.'

'She wouldn't have lost it if I hadn't bloody well hit her. Paul, I hit her! How could I have possibly *hit* her?'

Paul shrugged. 'Quite honestly, a court of law would have said you were provoked. She was a silly, disloyal, upper-class bitch. I don't think you were right to hit her, but I can quite understand why you did.'

The train clattered through Horley station without stopping. Dim lights, Victorian ironwork, Nestlés chocolate machines. Michael wiped the condensation from the window with his hand and peered out into the darkness. There was a thin curve of yellow light far in the distance, over towards Guildford, like a lonely albatross with outstretched wings, but otherwise the evening was monstrously black. Michael felt trapped, as if this overpowering sky had been clamped down over Surrey specifically to prevent him from escaping, no matter how quickly he hurried towards London.

He could hardly bear to think about what had happened this afternoon. From the moment Patricia had fallen into the garden, everything had become a jagged jumble of fright and anger and hurrying people. A navy-blue St John's Ambulance had arrived at Goodwood Lodge with its bell ringing. Patricia, conscious, white-faced, and already in premature labour, had been stretchered away wailing. She had sounded like Violetta in *La Traviata*. Richard had stood close to Michael, calm and grave and unusually pro-tective in his heather-mixture sports jacket, but Constance had stared at Michael as if she could happily have seen his heart stop on the spot. Norman Jorritt and Elisabeth Bergner had remained in the drawing-room, shocked and embarrassed. They had made an excuse and left early. Of course the rolling-out of the new *Chichester Special* had been postponed, at least for a week. At half-past three, to make things worse, Paul Heath had arrived with a bottle of Guinness in each sagging pocket, smelling strongly of onions after a ploughman's lunch, and Constance had gone to her room and closed the door, and the balcony windows, too, so that nobody could call up to her from the garden, the way that Herbert sometimes used to, after an argument.

Michael had drunk three large Scotches, one after the other; and by five o'clock he had been far too squiffy to drive back to London. Richard had given him and Paul a lift to Chichester station. They had driven the whole way in silence.

Turning away from the train window, Michael said, 'I wish to God I'd never gone down there.'

'Why *did* you go down there?' asked Paul. 'You swore absolutely blind that you wouldn't.'

Michael shrugged. 'God knows. But when it comes down to it, they're still my family, aren't they, whether I like them or not?

And I was beginning to feel as if I didn't belong to them any more.' He paused, while Paul watched him. 'I think I just wanted to join in.'

'You were beginning to feel starved of self-importance,' said Paul. 'You were feeling deprived of the glory of the Lords.'

'For God's sake, do you really think that I'm as small-minded as that?'

'Come on, Mike,' Paul reassured him. 'I was only joking.' He reached forward and took hold of both of Michael's hands, between his. 'I know why you went. You went because of Patricia. Patricia did the dirty on you, but you've never had the chance to ask her *why*, have you? One can't leave love affairs unfinished, hanging in the air, any more than one can leave anything unfinished. For goodness' sake, it's like walking out of the pictures halfway through, and never finding out what happened in the end. You have to know *why* she wanted to marry James, instead of you. Particularly since he's your brother.'

Michael said, with a wretchedness that sounded like a squeezed-out face-flannel, 'I killed their child.'

'Accident,' said Paul.

'No, Paul, it wasn't an accident. I did it on purpose. At least I *hit* her on purpose.'

'Mike, for goodness' sake be sensible! You didn't hit her on purpose. You were tormented beyond all measure. Patricia Burne-Stanley is nothing but the spoiled she-whelp of one of Britain's most appalling families! She's a Fascist, and a plutocrat, not just by birth but by inclination. She betrayed you with your own brother. She taunted you! She taunted you beyond any reasonable endurance! Lots of honest working-class men woud have killed not just her baby but *her*, too! Listen to me, Mike – Mike! Listen! – you were *justified* in hitting her! You were justified in hitting her because of her class, and you were also justified in hitting her because of the pain she caused you. You struck a blow for Socialism and you struck a blow for decency, and most of all you struck a blow for yourself, and your own emotions, which Patricia Burne-bloody-Stanley had treated with *complete* contempt!'

Paul gripped Michael's hands tight. 'Mike, can't you understand! If you think about what happened in the context of international Socialism, it wasn't your fault!'

Michael took one deep breath after another, his jaw juddering with misery. 'Oh God, Paul. It doesn't matter whether it was my fault or not. And sod your international Socialism. I killed their child, Paul. Out of jealousy, and anger, and God knows what.

171

Paul – I took that baby's life. Because of my temper, somebody's whole life isn't going to be lived. A life like mine! A life like yours!'

They were approaching Redhill, and the train was slowing down. The rain was lashing fiercely against the carriage windows. Michael begain to sob, deep painful sobs, his agony so abrasive that he couldn't even squeeze out any tears. The train racketed over four sets of points; the brakes began to squeal. Michael sat with his back upright, his eyes tight shut, crying out loud like a sealion.

'Mike,' Paul soothed him. 'Mike, it's all right. I'm sorry, Mike, I didn't mean to upset you. Please, Mike, listen.'

Paul sat next to Michael and took him in his arms and rocked him and kissed him. 'It wasn't your fault, Mike, it wasn't. I know it was terrible, I *know*, but it wasn't your fault.'

Michael's ribs ached. He felt that he couldn't catch his breath. He clung on to Paul's cardigan as if it were his only anchor on the real world. Paul kissed his forehead, and then his cheeks. His kisses smelled of Guinness and onions. 'It wasn't your fault, Michael,' he whispered, over and over and over again. 'It wasn't your fault.'

The train was jostling and squealing into platform 3 when their compartment door slid open, and somebody stepped in from the corridor. Michael realized that something was wrong only when Paul suddenly took his hands away, and sat rigidly upright. He opened his eyes, and frowned at Paul, and said, 'What . . .?' But Paul was sitting with his arms folded and his face taut, and there was a look on his face which Michael had never seen before.

Michael turned around. A railway policeman with a thick hearthbrush moustache and a raincape was standing in the doorway, staring at them. Just behind him, a woman in a pea-green hat was trying to look over his shoulder.

'Is there anything wrong?' said Paul, in a high, challenging voice.

The policeman looked from Paul to Michael, and back again. 'I'd say so, Madame Butterfly, wouldn't you?'

'What the devil is that supposed to mean?' Paul demanded.

With exaggerated weariness, the policeman reached under his raincape and took out his leather-backed notebook. The train was just coming into the station, and the compartment flickered with yellow light. 'Redhill,' said the policeman, ducking his head a little so that he could see the station signs out of the window. Then, producing his pencil, 'You're both of you under arrest. This lady made a complaint.'

'Complaint?' said Paul. 'Complaint about what?'

The woman appeared to be frightened, but the policeman was enjoying himself. 'Un-Godly acts, that's what they call it. Two men of the same sex, kissing and canoodling like man and wife. Not to put too fine a point on it, nancy behaviour in a public place.'

'We weren't doing anything at all,' said Michael, his face as white as flour.

'Sorry, Alice,' said the policeman. '*I* saw you; and this lady saw you; and that's a police allegation corroborated by an independent witness.'

The train ground to a shuddering halt, and the locomotive let out a thunderous barrage of steam. 'Get your coats, girlies,' said the policeman. 'We're going to have to report this little lot. Take some statements, and such like.'

'This is completely ridiculous,' Michael protested. 'We weren't doing anything at all. I have to get back to London.'

'Redhill police station first, Alice,' said the policeman. 'You're both of you under arrest.'

Paul stood up. 'This is an outrage. I'll have you reported to your Chief Constable for this. My friend has just suffered an appalling family tragedy today; and I was trying to comfort him. Nothing more passed between us than normal human sympathy.'

The policeman wrote this down, in round childish letters. Then he looked up, smiling, and said, 'This lady says you was kissing.'

'Well, perhaps this lady needs her eyes tested,' Paul retorted.

'I myself saw you in what I can safely describe as a position of unnatural intimacy, seeing as how both of you were of the male sex.'

'I was holding him, you stupid man. He was crying. You can't arrest us for that.'

The policeman put away his notebook. 'Oh, I can, Madame Butterfly, and I will. Now, shall we collect our coats, and get off the train?'

'Michael,' said Paul, desperate now. 'Mike – tell him. Tell him who you are!'

'I'm Michael Lord,' said Michael, not at all sure that he wasn't making matters worse. 'That's Lord as in Lord Aeronautics. My father was Herbert Lord.'

The policeman was unmoved. 'You should be thankful your father's dead, you should, Alice. A chap like Herbert Lord wouldn't have taken too kindly to finding out that his son was a nancy, now would he?'

173

'I find your language and your insinuations extremely offensive,' Michael replied, in a trembling voice.

'Not half so offensive as I find you, Alice,' the policeman told him. 'Now, let's get cracking.'

Richard arrived at seven o'clock the following morning to collect him. He came down the steps of the redbrick Victorian police-station, his raincoat over his arm, his face so pale that it almost dissolved in the bright amber sunlight. Richard held his arms open to embrace him, but Michael said, 'Not here. They'll probably arrest me a second time.'

'Where's Paul?' asked Richard, opening up the car door so that Michael could climb in.

'They're keeping him here for further enquiries. Apparently he's been caught for doing this sort of thing before.'

'You mean he really is a queer?'

Michael nodded. 'I never really doubted it. I was warned, you know, the very first night I met him. The driver of the breakdown truck told me to watch out for his suède shoes.' He grunted without humour at the memory of it.

'Isn't there anything we can do to help him?' Richard asked.

Michael shook his head. 'Even if there were, I wouldn't do it.'

Richard slammed his door shut, and looked at his younger brother questioningly. But it was obvious that Michael didn't want to talk about Paul Heath any more.

Richard started up the engine, and steered the little yellow tourer out into the road. 'John Tremlett said that things could be difficult. The police are insisting on pressing charges.'

'They shoved me around quite a bit,' said Michael. 'They kept calling me Alice.'

'Michael, I really don't know what to say.'

Michael shrugged, and stared red-eyed at the road ahead. They were driving up the hill to Merstham now, and northwards be-tween an avenue of flaky-trunked plane trees. This part of Surrey was all fields and farms and green rounded hills, and little blue-and yellow-painted wayside cafés offering country cream teas, 1s 6d.

'I really can't think what they arrested you for,' said Richard, against the buffeting of the wind.

'They arrested me for outraging public decency.'

'Well, yes, I know that, but –'

'But what?' Michael demanded. 'What were we actually doing?

174

Is that what you want to know? What the hell do you *think* we were doing – buggering one another in the luggage rack?'

Richard yanked the crash gearbox into third. 'You know jolly well I don't mean that. And you don't have to be offensive, either. As if you haven't caused everybody enough distress already, with Patricia. Good God, Michael, we're trying to be understanding, but Mother thinks you've gone completely off your trolley, and I'm beginning to agree with her.'

Michael said defiantly, 'If you want to believe that I'm a queer, Richard, then you may. I'm not, as a matter of fact, but it's a free country, you can believe what you like.'

'I don't believe you're a queer for one moment,' Richard replied. 'I *do* believe you're a thumping idiot.'

They drove through the dormitory village of Purley and eventually into the suburbs of Croydon, crowded with cheap small Victorian houses and shopping-parades. Richard had to negotiate his way between the delivery-vans and the horse-drawn milk-floats and the grinding, swaying trams. The sun began to die behind the clouds.

Suddenly, in a voice that was constricted with considerable pain, Michael said, 'I'm sorry, Richard. I can't tell you how sorry I am. I can't even begin to think how I got myself into this mess.'

They were approaching Croydon's North End. Richard slowed down for a brewer's dray, pulled by four massive shire horses with braided manes. 'I just want you to promise that you'll lie low for the while, until we can sort things out. And stay away from Paul. He's a nice enough chap, I know that, but he's trouble with a capital T.'

'He told the police he loved me,' said Michael, his voice muffled.

'He did *what*?'

'He told the police he loved me. That was why he was kissing me.'

'Oh God. But why did you *let* him?'

'I didn't let him. You don't honestly think that I'd *let* him, do you? I was upset about Patricia, that was all. I was having a howl. He put his arm around me, just like anybody would. I didn't even *realize* he was kissing me.' Michael bit his lip, and then added, 'You won't let them print anything about it in the papers, will you? I'll never be able to show my face at Cambridge again.'

Richard blew out his cheeks. 'I'm not sure that there's anything I can do. They've been on the phone already. The *Daily Mail*, anyway, and the *Daily Express*. Somebody from the *Surrey*

175

Mirror must have called them last night. What do they call them, a stringer.'

'You didn't tell them anything?'

'I didn't really have to. They knew most of it already.'

Michael covered his face with his hands. 'I can't bear it,' he said. 'I really can't bear it.'

Richard reached over and affectionately shook his shoulder. 'Come on, Michael, you'll get over it, I promise. Mother's a bit put out at the moment, but we're all behind you. It's just going to take a little time, that's all. John Tremlett knows the Chief Constable pretty well, and he's going to try to pull a few strings. You won't go to court.'

'Well, that's all very well, but what about Patricia? What's James going to say? He's going to kill me.'

'That's one bridge we'll have to cross when we come to it,' said Richard. 'We sent him a telegram yesterday, after you'd left. Bryan thinks that he may be able to fly back on the Dornier.'

'And the *Chichester Special*, I've ruined all that, too.'

Richard shook his head. 'It's no use crying over spilt milk. The *Chichester Special* won't fly any the worse for a week's delay. We may even have time to finish all the buoyancy tests before we roll her out.'

Michael swallowed, and nodded.

'Come on, buck up,' said Richard. 'I'm going to stay in town with you until John Tremlett's got this business all sorted out; then perhaps you can come back down to Chichester.'

They drove through the suburbs of Thornton Heath and Balham; acres of red-and-yellowish London Stock brick; and into the slums that surrounded Clapham Junction, hills that had once been lavender-fields covered with undulating rows of slate-roofed terraces. Michael said nothing more until they reached South Kensington; but Richard glanced at him from time to time to make sure that he wasn't looking too depressed. For all of her anger at what Michael had done, Constance had charged Richard with making sure that he didn't do anything 'silly', like throwing himself off the Albert Bridge, or sticking his head in the gas oven.

Richard hadn't needed telling twice. His father's suicide was still as vivid in his mind as the moment it had happend. Not even the winning of the Seraphim Trophy could redeem Michael, if he were to die, too.

Patricia was sitting in the conservatory with a quilt over her knees reading a book when her mother came in with both hands raised like a performing poodle (she had been stuffing a chicken, and they were shiny with grease). 'Patricia, Dr Hallett's here.'

Patricia lowered her book. Her eyes looked suspicious and dull. There were mauve circles under her eyes. Her hair needed washing, and it was held back with two pink barrettes. Her mother hadn't liked to nag her too much. Patricia was, after all, 'recovering'.

'Can't he come tomorrow?' asked Patricia. 'I don't really feel up to it yet.'

Dr Hallett appeared behind her mother and waved his arm like a railway signal. 'Good morning, young lady! Don't worry, I haven't come to examine you, or anything tiresome like that. I just want a few minutes' chat.'

'All right,' said Patricia, in a tired voice. She closed her book and put it on the cast-iron side-table next to her glass of Sanatogen Tonic Wine. Dr Hallett laid a reassuring hand on Mrs Burne-Stanley's shoulder, and murmured, 'I'll pop into the kitchen, shall I, as soon as I've finished?'

Patricia had never liked Dr Hallett. There always seemed to be something menacing about his joviality. He had dry hair like a helmet of breakfast-cereal, and deep crimson veins in his nose. He noisily dragged a cast-iron chair over the tiled conservatory floor and sat down and crossed his legs so that she could see his maroon sock-suspenders.

'Well, how do we feel today?' he asked her.

'*I* feel quite well,' she replied. 'How do *you* feel?'

'You're – ah – reading! What's that you're reading?'

'*Our Mutual Friend.*'

Dr Hallett took out his gold half-glasses and inspected the book's spine. 'Well, well. *Our Mutual Friend.* Quite a few years since I read *that!* "Do other men, for they would do you," eh?'

'That's from *Martin Chuzzlewit,*' said Patricia.

'Aha! Is it? Well, Dickens is Dickens is Dickens.'

Patricia said nothing, but sat up straight and expressionless, in order to underline the absurdity of what Dr Hallett had said.

Dr Hallett took off his glasses again and cleared his throat. 'The thing is, m'dear, I've had a talk with Mr Mentmore, your gynaecologist.'

'Yes?'

'He made quite a thorough examination of – how shall I put it? – all the relevant parts.'

He took a deep breath that whistled slightly in one nostril, and then he said, 'What happened to you . . . well, there was always a risk that you would lose the child anyway. You are not one of those women for whom childbearing would ever have been particularly easy. Given your internal constitution, it was a small miracle that you did happen to fall – and that you carried the baby for so long. In a normal pregnancy, a fall of that kind would not have been nearly so likely to induce a miscarriage.'

Still Patricia said nothing. The smell of lunch began to penetrate the conservatory; the smell of overwatered palm trees and lunch.

Dr Hallett said, 'In Mr Mentmore's opinion – and I'm very, very sorry to have to tell you this – you will be unable to bear any more children without an unacceptable risk to your own life.'

Patricia stared at him in silence for a very long time. Dr Hallett coughed uncomfortably. 'We did our very best,' he said. 'But we must always think of the existing patient rather than the patient not yet dreamed of.'

'Not yet dreamed of,' Patricia repeated. There were no tears in her eyes.

Dr Hallett reached over and took her hand. 'I'll have a word with your mother. You have your tablets, don't you, to help you rest? But please believe me . . . if there's anything at all that I can do –'

'No,' said Patricia. Then, 'Thank you.'

Dr Hallett stood up. 'I'll come tomorrow.'

Patricia didn't reply.

She stood upstairs at her bedroom window watching Dr Hallett's dark-green Humber disappear between the cedars. She heard her mother calling, 'Patricia! Where are you, darling? It's almost lunchtime!'

She looked around at her single brass bed, her bookshelf crammed with pony books, most of them tattered now, the rosettes she had won at the Haslemere gymkhana. She looked at the flowery wallpaper which had always seemed to have grotesque faces in it whenever she was feverish or couldn't sleep.

She looked at the row of dolls, all propped up on top of the bureau in their frocks and their hats and their baby-suits.

She picked up the largest of the dolls and tilted it backwards so that its eyes closed. 'Miranda,' she whispered. 'My dear Miranda.'

For a moment she held the doll close. It was as hard and uncomfortable as always. Hard china head; hard china fingers.

'How can you love me, Miranda?' she asked. 'I'm such a bad mother. I lost your sister. Your only, only sister.'

She grasped the doll's ankles, and smashed its head on to the brass rail of her bed. Unnervingly, the doll bleated out, *'Mammaa!'*

She smashed its head down again and again. Her skull broke open; the wire that tilted her eyes came loose. Patricia beat her and beat her until her arms were hanging loose and her stuffing was flying in the air.

Then she dropped on to her knees on the carpet, clutching the shattered remains of the doll tightly against her breasts, and sobbed in agonized silence.

On the following Monday morning, John Tremlett came up to London by train and Richard and Michael met him for lunch at Overton's, in Victoria Buildings, opposite the station. Overton's was crowded and old-fashioned, with thick linen napkins and heavy cutlery, like an Edwardian *wagon-lit*. They all chose the fried plaice, with broccoli and new potatoes. Michael asked for Guinness but then changed his mind and joined Richard and John Tremlett in a bottle of Muscadet.

John Tremlett looked exactly what he was: a smooth well-off country solicitor. His nails were perfectly pared and there was dandruff on his black business coat. He kept pulling out his pocket watch to check the time, because he had arranged to catch the ten-past-three back to Chichester.

'Michael – I won't make any bones about it,' he said, ironically picking a fishbone out from between his pursed lips. 'Your position is one of extreme jeopardy. A possible jail sentence.'

'Jail?' asked Richard, in horror. Michael stayed silent.

John Tremlett nodded. 'The evidence, I regret, is rather damning. What's more, the Chief Constable is something of a zealot when it comes to sexual offences; particularly homosexual offences. He seems to believe that God has given him a personal mandate to purge Surrey of what he calls "catamites and assorted nellies".'

Michael kept his eyes fixed on his plate. His cheeks felt almost feverish. The agony and the humiliation of what had happened last week hadn't abated even slightly: if anything, it became worse with each passing day.

John Tremlett reached over to the chair beside him and opened his briefcase. 'We have, however, had a stroke of luck. Your mother was talking on the telephone yesterday with Mr Gordon Burne-Stanley. About Patricia, of course. But she brought up the matter of your arrest.

'You may be aware that Mr Gordon Burne-Stanley is a close friend of the Home Secretary, and on his behalf the Home Secretary immediately contacted the Chief Constable at Guildford and did what he could to sort matters out.'

'I'm surprised he bothered,' said Michael. 'After all, I assaulted his daughter, didn't I, and successfully managed to murder his first grandchild.'

John Tremlett was not amused by this remark. 'You will be relieved to hear that the charges against you and Mr Heath are going to be dropped. But it was necessary for the Home Secretary to give the Chief Constable certain assurances on your behalf.'

Michael lifted his eyes. 'You mean, I have to promise that I won't ever again be caught embracing men in trains?'

'Rather more than that, I'm afraid,' said John Tremlett. 'Mr Burne-Stanley's motives for intervening in this matter were not at all charitable. Quite the reverse. He had already been discussing with his solicitors the possibility of taking out a summons against you for common assault against Patricia. To be quite frank, as far as Mr Gordon Burne-Stanley is concerned, hanging would be far too kind a punishment for you.'

'If that's how he feels, why on earth did he help to get me off?' asked Michael.

'Because, my dear Michael, he was advised by his own solicitors that in your defence, you would probably be pleading provocation. So, quite apart from the fact that the court might possibly take pity on you, and be relatively lenient, the whole sorry history of Patricia's affair with James would have to come out in open court. *Not* a prospect that Mr Burne-Stanley happens to relish.'

John Tremlett fastidiously wiped his narrow mouth with his narrowly-folded napkin. 'Therefore, in return for dropping the charges against you, he authorized the Home Secretary to give the Chief Constable the absolute assurance that you will immediately leave the country, and not return for a period of five years.'

'Leave the country?' Michael demanded, in astonishment. 'You can't possibly be serious! What do you mean, leave the country? I'm still halfway through university!'

'That, I regret, is the stipulation,' John Tremlett insisted. 'I regret, too, that the conditions of your father's will mean that you will forfeit your share in Lord Aeronautics until you return to England as a working director. But my opinion is that you have very little choice in the matter. And I am bound to say that your education would suffer far worse if you were to be imprisoned for a sexual offence than it would be if you were to emigrate and seek to continue your studies elsewhere.'

Richard said, 'It's a bit strong, don't you think, expecting Michael to emigrate?'

'I'm sorry, it's the very best that your mother and I could do.'

Michael, who had at first been flushed, had now turned quite white. 'Five years?' he said. 'And forfeit all my inheritance? My God.'

'Well, it needn't be *too* bad,' said Richard. 'You could find a place in Paris, or maybe in Brussels, and we could pop over to see you whenever we felt like it. At least the family's airborne.'

John Tremlett was checking his pocket-watch again. 'I'm afraid that *won't* be possible,' he said, without looking up.

'Why not?' Michael demanded. 'Burne-Stanley may be able to force me to leave the country, but he can't stop my people from coming to see me.'

'No, he can't,' John Tremlett agreed. 'But he has made a special condition that might make visiting rather tricky. He requires you to go to Australia.'

'*What?*' shouted Michael. 'Australia! He must be mad!'

'Michael – come on, Michael,' said Richard, taking hold of his brother's sleeve. 'Calm down, or they'll turf us out.'

'You're worried about being thrown out of a restaurant, when I'm being thrown out of the entire continent!'

'Michael, please – I do beg of you,' said John Tremlett.

'Australia? Of all the bloody nerve! Australia! That's archaic! That's eighteenth-century! That's just like transportation!'

John Tremlett furrowed his forehead. 'Well, yes, it is rather, I have to agree. But I do understand that parts of Australia can be really very pleasant at this time of year.'

'I can't believe this,' said Michael. 'I *can't* go to Australia!'

'I'm sorry,' John Tremlett interrupted, although he patently wasn't sorry at all. He lifted his hand to the waiter for the bill. 'I really must be shooting back now. Mr Burne-Stanley is expecting me to call him with an answer before six.'

'My God,' said Michael. 'My God.' He was shaking.

'May I take it that you accept his offer?' John Tremlett asked; but didn't bother to wait for an answer. 'Perhaps you'd both like another brandy. Bit of a shock, and all that.'

Chichester, 1932

As the *Chichester Special* was towed out into the sunshine, the crowds cheered and clapped and enthusiastically waved their Union Jacks. At least five hundred people had turned up to see the seaplane rolled out, and in spite of their disgruntlement at last week's abrupt postponement, the national newspapers had all arrived in Chichester, too – even the imperious bowler-hatted photographer from the *Illustrated London News*, who stood on the roof of his Morris van with a huge antiquated wet-plate camera and insisted on absolute silence while he was taking his pictures.

'Three cheers for Mrs Lord!' called out Wally Field, as Constance stepped out of her car. She was wearing a long-sleeved calf-length dress with splotchy red-and-pink flowers on it, and a droopy red-and-pink hat, all rather Ascot. She read out a short speech which she had written on lavender notepaper, but because of the breeze and the shuffling of feet very few people could hear it, although everybody clapped when it was over. Constance was attentively escorted by Bryan King-Moreton, whose white hair was gleamingly brilliantined, and who (like Richard and Wally Field and all the rest of the Lord mechanics) was kitted out in new white overalls, of the racing-driver style worn by Captain Eyston Cables.

Michael was there, too, but he was wearing a flat golf cap and a red-and-green striped blazer that looked as if it had been kept all winter in a damp cricket-bag. He kept himself to himself, at the back of the crowd. He had only four days left at home. He was booked to leave from Southampton early next week on the *Alexandria*, bound for Darwin. He had decided on the spur of the moment on Darwin because one of his school friends had emigrated there; a nervous stuttering boy called Watling, who had farted a lot in maths.

The family had heard nothing more from the wrathful Gordon Burne-Stanley, except a curt message that Patricia was still 'jolly poorly'. The Burne-Stanleys had conceded that what had happened had not directly been Constance's fault, but relations between the families were decidedly chilly. In private, Gordon Burne-Stanley had referred to the Lord brothers as 'Constance's pack of wild mongrels'.

Richard stood up in the cockpit of the *Chichester Special* and waved for quiet.

'We apologize for last week's postponement, which as you know was caused by a very sad family accident. However, we hope very much that we can make up for it today. Mr King-Moreton has been able since last week to take the *Special* down to Bosham for her buoyancy tests, and I am delighted to be able to tell you that she passed with flying colours. This afternoon, therefore, we propose to take her up on her maiden flight from the Air Ministry seaplane station at Calshot. It's rather a long drive, but we're laying on a bus, and Mr King-Moreton informs me that the bus is extremely well-stocked with champagne.'

There was laughter and jeering and more applause. Then the Mayor of Chichester suggested, first of all, a minute's silence in memory of Herbert Lord, followed by a prayer for the safety and success of the new *Chichester Special*. He spoke in a deep vibrato about 'this winged steed, which bears the name of our historic and beloved city'. Finally he called for three rousing cheers for Lord Aeronautics.

A bottle of champagne was smashed against the seaplane's propeller-boss by Lady Plunket, whom Herbert had always disliked, especially her dancing exhibitions. 'I name this ship the *Chichester Special*!' she cried, then – when corrected in a stage whisper by Bryan King-Moreton – 'oh, have it your own way, aeroplane then!' Afterwards, a hundred invited guests were taken by cars to the Dolphin Hotel, where a champagne buffet had been laid on, with cold lobster salad and chicken vol-au-vents.

Michael came up to Richard with one hand in his pocket and remarked casually, 'Bryan's sniffing up to Mother rather a lot, isn't he? He hasn't been further than three inches away from her all day.'

'Oh – yes, well, I didn't tell you about that,' said Richard.

Michael stared at Richard in annoyance. 'Didn't tell me about *what*? Not another grisly secret! Why does this family insist on keeping everything hidden under its hat?'

'To tell you the truth, it slipped my mind,' said Richard. 'What with all your problems, don't you know.'

'No, I don't know. Tell me.'

Richard offered his brother a cigarette. 'The fact is, Bryan's asked Mother to marry him.'

Michael was astonished. 'You're pulling my leg! Bryan's asked for the mater's hand in holy wedlock? God Almighty!' He paused, shaking his head, and then he said, 'I say – she hasn't said *yes*, has she? That would mean B.K-M for a stepfather! Or step-pater, should I say. Richard, I simply couldn't stand it!'

'Well, she's talked about it,' said Richard. 'She quite likes him, you know. They used to walk out together when they were younger, before she and Father really fell for each other. Apparently he's had a torch or something burning in his heart for her ever since. I think she finds it terribly flattering. I mean you can see why. And she *has* been frightfully lonely lately.'

Michael lit his cigarette and blew out smoke. 'You sound as if you actually *approve*.'

'It's up to her, isn't it? She's perfectly capable of making up her own mind about it. But it would make her happy, I think. And it would take a load off *my* shoulders. She's expected me to take care of her ever since Father died. I mean, I *love* her and all that rot, but I'm not her husband, after all.'

'I'm totally discombobulated,' said Michael. 'I think I need another drink.'

Richard said, 'You won't say anything, will you? Mother hasn't made up her mind yet, by any means. I don't want her to think that any of us disapprove. It's *her* life, don't you know.'

'Mum's the word,' Michael promised. 'Or, rather, Dad.'

Michael went off to find himself a fresh glass of champagne. As he did so, Constance came up and took hold of Richard's arm. 'Dear Richard,' she said. 'You've done so well. Your father would have been *so* proud of you.'

'Wait till you see her fly,' said Richard, kissing his mother's forehead. He thought that she looked a little tired. It was probably the strain of Patricia's miscarriage, and all of Michael's shenanigans.

Constance gave him a tight smile. 'We've just had a telegram from James. He couldn't get back on the Dornier. He's going to fly to New York tomorrow, and come back on the *Ile de France*.'

'Did he mention anything about Patricia?'

'He sent her his love. But there was something else, my dear. He's asked the company to put up a quarter of a million dollars.'

'What? What on earth for? A quarter of a million dollars! That's – what – sixty-three thousand pounds, almost!'

'He says he wants to buy an airline, the same airline he went out to visit, Atlantic and Pacific Airways.'

'Well, he can't! It's completely preposterous! I mean – what on earth does he want an airline for? We're overstretched as it is. I thought he went to Florida to sell aeroplanes, not to buy them. I mean – what does James know about running an airline? Absolutely nothing! I hope you told him no.'

'I thought we ought to discuss it first. But I'm going to wait until James gets back.'

'Oh, Mother,' said Richard, 'there's absolutely nothing to discuss. We just haven't *got* sixty-three thousand pounds, not as available capital, anyway.'

Constance squeezed his arm. 'I thought I ought to warn you that James dropped some hints about the forty-eight thousand pounds which we earmarked for winning the Seraphim Trophy.'

'But you can't possibly approve of that! We've already decided – winning the Seraphim Trophy is absolutely vital, especially if we're going to compete on anything like an equal footing against de Havilland's and Vickers and Handley Page. Winning the Seraphim Trophy is going to be worth a thousand times more than all the advertising and all the lobbying and all the sales exhibitions you can think of!'

'Well, you know that I agree with you on the whole,' said Constance. 'But James works very hard for the company, and I respect *his* opinion, too.'

'Mother –' said Richard, 'if I can prove to you this afternoon that we can win the Seraphim race outright, will you please tell James that he can't have his money? Please? He's only doing this because he's annoyed that we've managed to build another *Chichester Special*.'

Constance kissed his cheek. 'You two, always squabbling.'

'Mother –'

'You don't have to worry,' Constance reassured him. 'This is for your father's memory, and for Bryan, as much as it is for you.'

Although it was a warm day inland, there was a stiff south-westerly breeze blowing off the Solent on to Calshot Seaplane Station, which most of the newspaper reporters found unacceptably trying. They stayed for a while, to watch the *Chichester Special* being winched off its tender and down the concrete ramp to the water. But then – with the exception of Alex Earnshaw, who was writing a special report for the *Daily Mail*, and Harry Harper, who had been commissioned by Sampson Low to write another book about aeroplanes for their 6/- *Romance of Flight* series – they hurried back to the bus, knees bent, *ventre à terre* like Groucho Marx, to take serious advantage of four cases of Perrier-Jouët champagne and six bottles of Glenmorangie malt, and to discuss the future of British flying in loud, confident, and incomprehensible voices.

'What a bloody awful racket, is he off?' one of them said, when the *Chichester Special*'s engine was started up, and Bryan King-Moreton turned it out towards Stansore Point.

Bryan King-Moreton gave a regal *Boy's Own Paper* wave as he powered the seaplane out into the Solent, although he knocked his funny-bone on the edge of the windscreen. Space was even tighter in this latest version of the *Chichester Special*, but he and Richard had deliberately done everything they could to streamline it, and to save weight. Bryan's bottom was wedged into a small bucket seat, lined with tan leather. He wore no parachute: there simply wasn't the room for it, and apart from that he would usually be flying at lower than two hundred feet – so low that he would never have the time to bale out, if anything went wrong.

As Bryan steered the *Chichester Special* further away from the shore, the waves began to grow choppier, and the seaplane began to dip and bob like a duck. He revved up the *Chichester*'s engine and the seaplane let out a low, throaty roar. Its pontoons skated over the water, leaving behind them a distinctive arrowhead pattern. Bryan twisted his head around once and saw Constance standing on the hard, waving, and he lifted one brown-gloved hand and saluted her back.

Then he drew back the throttle as far as it would go, and adjusted the propeller to fine pitch, and the *Chichester Special* filled the afternoon with thunder. It surged forward across the waves, dipped, sprayed, dipped again, and at last lifted itself out of the water in a last cascade of sun-glittering droplets.

Bryan banked it over Stansore Point, the greeny-fawn fields tilting on his left, the misty grey sea wheeling on his right, and then dived right down to two hundred feet, which was the optimum height for high-speed flying.

He ducked his head to one side and saw the sea flashing under his wings. His altimeter read a hundred and sixty feet. The slightest mistake at this height, and he would dive nose-first into the Solent, and be flying thirty feet under the water before he knew it. He eased the throttle back, and the *Chichester Special*'s engine blared more harmoniously, a symphony orchestra rather than a chorus of demons.

Bryan was singing, a song he had learned in the nursery. '*England! Where the sacred flame, burns before the inmost shrine! Where the lips that love thy name, consecrate their hopes and mine!*'

Gradually, as the tower of Calshot Castle came back into view, with its flags and its windsock flying, he opened the throttle up again, and the seaplane screamed along the shoreline, its shadow flying wildly ahead of it. The airspeed indicator quivered its way towards three hundred and seventy-five knots – three hundred and eighty knots – then touched four hundred.

As he streaked past the seaplane station, the *Chichester Special* was touching four hundred and ten knots, and Bryan could see by the rev-counter that the engine still had plenty of power in reserve. He began gradually to climb as the seaplane crossed the inlet to Southampton harbour and approached Warsash and Titchfield on the opposite beach. '*England!*' he sang, as he wheeled over the mudflats. '*Where the sacred flame!*'

He climbed higher and higher, banking as he did so, almost up to eight hundred feet. The sun, which had been behind him, now turned around him to shine on his propeller. '*Burns before the inmost shry-hine!*'

His joy was complete.

Bryan was a practical man: not particularly ambitious, but practical. When the last *Chichester Special* had exploded over the Isle of Wight, and Herbert Lord had come tumbling down from the heavens, Bryan's first instantaneous thought had been: *that's it, it's over, the whole thing's over, and I'm out of a job.*

Instantly, he had felt deeply ashamed of himself, but the fact remained that he was fifty-eight years old, and that his only skill was designing and flying high-speed experimental aeroplanes. If Lord Aeronautics stopped building racers, as James intended them to do, and concentrated instead on commercial aircraft, the chances were that Bryan would very quickly find himself retired.

Bryan was haunted by the memory of what had happened to his father. The late Clive King-Moreton had been one of the best railway architects in western India. He had built termini like palaces, and signal-boxes like castles, and twice been congratulated by the Queen. But the Empire had declined, and so had

Clive King-Moreton. He had died of lung-cancer as the owner of a shabby petshop in Lewisham, in south-east London. Even today, the smell of hamsters made Bryan feel physically ill; and it was because he never wanted to smell hamsters again that he had poured everything he knew into this latest *Chichester Special*: every scrap of knowledge, every wrinkle of experience.

With its new supercharged engine, the *Chichester Special* was absolutely the fastest and most advanced aeroplane ever built. In a shallow dive, it was probably capable of 500 mph, although Bryan doubted that its propeller could stand up to the stress.

Bryan wasn't interested in speed records, however. His sole preoccupation was the Seraphim Trophy, and in winning for himself the place that Herbert had once held in Constance's esteem. If he could win the Seraphim Trophy, his chances of winning Constance would rise like a hymn; and if he could win Constance, his future with Lord Aeronautics would be assured. The spectre of the Lewisham petshop would be exorcised for ever. '*No hamsters, ever!!*' he had written in his diary, in copperplate, in purple ink.

He turned the *Chichester Special* southwards, over the wider reaches of the Solent, still climbing. The sun was now directly in his eyes, and he had to hold his gloved hand against his forehead to keep out the glare. He carried on singing bursts of patriotic song. The 2,750-horsepower V-16 engine accompanied him with regular throbs of pure power.

He was almost at the top of his climb, and ready to dive back towards Calshot, when the seaplane began to judder a little. Bryan immediately adjusted the propeller pitch, but the juddering grew steadily worse. The engine began to drone off-pitch, and the fuselage shook furiously from nose to tail. Bryan's teeth rattled together and his vision was so blurred that he was unable to read any of his instruments.

He glanced back over his shoulders at the wings and the tail-plane, but there was no sign of anything flapping loose. He dipped the *Chichester*'s right wing, and eased the stick forward, and gradually the vibration began to fade away. By the time he was diving back towards the Seaplane Station, for one more four-hundred-knot fly-past, the seaplane was steady again, and the juddering had completely disappeared. He whistled a couple of bars of *Land Of Hope And Glory* between his teeth.

Richard and Constance were standing next to the concrete ramp when the *Chichester Special* came screaming past them at over four hundred and twenty knots, less than a hundred feet from the sea. Somebody with a stopwatch called out, 'For hundred and twenty-one point three!' Richard hugged his mother tight, and kissed her on both cheeks. 'We've done it! Bless you, Mother, we've done it!' and then the *Chichester Special* was turning and climbing yet again, ready for its descent to the water.

On this turn – although they couldn't see it from the shore – the juddering was even worse, and Bryan was sure that he could hear a stringer crack, somewhere in the fuselage behind him. The seaplane felt as if it were dipping and skidding, both at the same time, and trying to keep it steady was as difficult as driving a horse-and-carriage diagonally down the steps of St Paul's. Bryan turned to port, and dived, and eased off the throttle mixture, and the juddering died away again, but inside his leather flying-jacket he was soaked in sweat. He swallowed, his throat dry with fear and disappointment. There was no question about it: this new *Chichester Special* was a powerful and temperamental bitch, particularly on climbing turns, and it would probably take months of redesigning to tame her. The Seraphim Trophy race was due to be flown from Ryde on the last Saturday of September. Even if Bryan were lucky, and the *Chichester*'s problems turned out to be far less serious than he felt them to be, they would be unlikely to have her ready in time.

The triangular course that had to be flown for the Seraphim Trophy involved three violent hairpin turns, at speeds which often caused the competing pilots to black out for a second or two, as their blood was drained down to their feet. If the *Chichester Special* was going to start shaking and skittering every time its pilot took a corner, then it would be far too dangerous to fly.

Bryan throttled right back, and let the seaplane sink growling towards the sea. Those two steep turns had introduced a light tremble into its performance, like a nervous and unpredictable animal. The pontoons slapped on to the water; slapped again; and then settled; in a cloud of sparkling spray he revved it up towards the ramp.

Constance was waiting for him as he climbed out of the cockpit and on to the tender. She held her arms by her sides, a simple pose, her hat whipped by the wind, but her eyes were bright. He came up the ramp, unfastening his flying-helmet, tugging off his gloves.

'You were marvellous,' said Constance. 'Four hundred and twenty knots! I'm so proud of you!'

She took hold of both of his hands and kissed him. 'This is a great day for me, Bryan; you don't have any idea. I feel that the windows have been opened up again.'

Richard came up and shook Bryan's hand. 'That was absolutely wizard! How did she handle? She looked wizard from here.'

'She, er –' Bryan began, and even lifted his hand to demonstrate what had happened on the turns. But then Constance took hold of his other hand, and squeezed it, and said, 'Something quite marvellous has happened today, Richard. I've rediscovered something I think I always knew.'

She smiled, with tears glistening on her eyelashes, she said, 'I've rediscovered how fond I am of Bryan. He and Herbert were so much alike. So much daring; so much courage. And always such *style*.'

She kissed Bryan on the cheek. 'We're going to win the Seraphim Trophy! And, Bryan, the day after we bring it back to Goodwood Lodge, and set it in the hall, we're going to announce our engagement!'

For one clipped complicated second, Bryan's eyes met Richard's; but Richard wasn't at all sure whether Bryan was anxious about Constance's implied condition that he *had* to win the Seraphim Trophy before she would marry him; or whether he was trying to tell him something else altogether. In any case the Press arrived at that moment, to take pictures of 'the human bullet' as they would inevitably call him, and to ask him what it felt like to travel at more than four hundred miles per hour.

Bryan allowed himself to forget his distress at the seaplane's misbehaviour, and wallow in the glory of being a popular hero. 'Of course, one is jolly well aware second by second that if one so much as pops one's head out of the cockpit, the slipstream will more than likely tear one's head right off one's shoulders.'

'Do you ever feel windy before a flight like this?' asked a spotty young man from the *Daily Sketch*.

Bryan lifted his head as if he were already posing for his commemorative statue. 'A test pilot has to have nerves of braided wire; otherwise he can't be a test pilot.'

'So you never think about anything going wrong?' the boy persisted.

'Of course I do. Death sits on one's shoulder like Long John Silver's parrot. Don't *you* ever think about death? My only anxiety is that I shouldn't die as anything but a man, while serving my country.'

Constance listened to this with her arm linked possessively through Bryan's arm, her face glowing. 'Yes, Bryan and I have been friends for very many years,' she told Margaret Applewhite, from the *Tatler*. 'He's a wonderful man. He and Herbert were the greatest of chums. And of course Herbert would have approved of my marrying him. Well, we will, as soon as he's brought the Seraphim Trophy home.'

'That sounds rather like one of those fairytale challenges,' Margaret Applewhite remarked. 'Fetch me the dragon's head, and you shall have my hand in marriage.'

'My life has *always* been a fairytale,' Constance replied. Bryan laughed, but Margaret Applewhite thought that he looked rather grim.

A young reporter with a cigarette in his mouth and his hat tilted back in approved Fleet Street style said, 'Is Jacko Gibbons still working for you?'

Bryan ignored him at first, and posed, with a fixed grin, for a hero-and-widow picture for the *Daily Mirror*. He recognized the young reporter from Seaview; and the very last thing he wanted to do was talk about Jacko Gibbons.

'Tommy Thompson, *Daily Herald*,' the young reporter persisted. 'Is Jacko Gibbons still working for you?'

Constance looked up at Bryan and frowned. 'What on earth is that chap talking about? Who's Jacko Gibbons?'

'I really don't have any idea,' said Bryan. 'Shall we break this up now? I could do with a cup of tea.'

Tommy Thompson came after them, and walked close beside them as they returned to their car, surrounded by applauding mechanics and spectators. 'You must remember Jacko Gibbons! He was the fellow who was supposed to have sabotaged Gerhard Brunner's seaplane, the *Lorelei*. He served three months in prison in Amsterdam for trying to sell diamonds that didn't belong to him.'

'I really don't know what concern that is of ours,' said Constance.

'Oh, didn't you know? He's here in Chichester,' said Tommy Thompson. 'He was spotted two days ago, having lunch at the Old Oak Café in East Street. Egg and chips, actually.'

'I still don't know what concern that is of ours.'

'P'raps it's coincidence,' Tommy Thompson suggested, as Constance climbed into her Daimler. 'But you'll be going in for the Seraphim Trophy soon, won't you? And it always helps if the opposition is having trouble with their machines. Such as fires, and such.'

Bryan turned on Tommy Thompson, bristling. 'You listen to me, you guttersnipe. We chased you away once, at Seaview. Any more insinuations like that, and I shall have you dealt with.'

'So you can categorically deny that Jacko Gibbons is working for you, or ever has worked for you?'

Bryan, with one foot in the car, tried to keep his temper. 'As far as I recall, Mr Thompson, Jacko Gibbons *was* employed by Lord Aeronautics at one time. He did some assembly work in the engine-shop at Burgess Hill, about two years ago. Then he left, I really can't remember why. That was the last that any of us saw of him.'

'Lord Aeronautics didn't by any chance help to pay for his advocate when he was up before the magistrates in Amsterdam?'

'Why on earth should we have done?'

'Don't tell me that Lord Aeronautics didn't take care of one of their own?' Tommy Thompson asked, one eye squinting against the sunlight.

'Jacko Gibbons was not "one of our own", as you put it. And I very much resent your line of questioning.'

'So you weren't aware that he was in Chichester?'

'Certainly not.'

'And he doesn't work for you, in any capacity?'

'No.'

Tommy Thompson touched the brim of his hat, smiled, and put his notebook away. 'Thank you for your help, Mr King-Moreton.' He leaned into the doorway of the Daimler and added, 'Mrs Lord.'

On the way back to Chichester, Constance said coldly, 'What was all that about?'

'M'dear?' asked Bryan.

'That obnoxious young man from the *Daily Herald.*'

'Oh, him,' said Bryan. 'Nothing, nothing at all. You know what the Socialist papers are like. Always trying to create some scandal or other. Always trying to drag dear old Britain down into the dirt.'

Constance thought for a while, her cream-gloved hand holding the silk strap of the side of the car. 'We didn't, did we?' she asked.

'We didn't *what*, m'dear?'

'We didn't pay for that chap to be defended? When he was had up in Amsterdam?'

'Of course not,' said Bryan. 'Not to my knowledge, anyway.'

'Nor to mine, either,' Constance replied. 'But I'm beginning to wonder how much I know about the company I own.'

'I'm not sure what you're driving at.'

Constance gave him a fleeting smile. 'I mean that I have the feeling that Herbert didn't always tell me the truth, the whole truth, and nothing but the truth, so help him God.'

*

That night, shortly before eleven o'clock, Bryan King-Moreton appeared at the gates of the Lord aeroplane works wearing his crumpled off-white raincoat, tightly-belted, and his large brown trilby. Willy the night-watchman came forward with his old Alsatian gasping on its leash, and shone his bull's-eye lantern through the wire fencing into Bryan's eyes.

'Willy? It's me.'

'Mr King-Moreton? So it is! Begging your pardon, never seen you come back so late.'

Bryan took off his hat and ran his hand across his hair. 'Damn silly of me, left my watch in the kite this afternoon.'

'Well, that's all right, sir, hold hard, I'll open the gates for you.'

Willy unfastened the padlock and admitted Bryan to the factory yard. 'Will you be long, sir?' he inquired.

'That rather depends. Thought I'd give her a once-over, seeing that I'm here.'

'That's all right, sir, you take your time. Right marvellous flight this afternoon, sir, from what I gather. I was sorry I couldn't get to see it.' He sniffed loudly and tugged at his half-strangulated dog. 'If you fancy a mug of tea, sir, I'll be brewing up at har-past. Nora brought me down some condensed milk.'

'Right-ho, Willy,' said Bryan. Willy unlocked the door to the drawing-office for him, and switched on the lights. Then he opened the inner door to the main factory floor.

It was deserted and ghostly in there. Bryan's footsteps echoed on the concrete floor. Most of the five unfinished Aquarius airliners were shrouded in sheets, to protect them from dust. In the far corner, silver and silent, was the *Chichester Special*, on the trolley that was used to tow her to the sea.

Bryan approached the seaplane slowly, walking around to the nose. He laid a hand on her pontoon. This morning, when she had been officially rolled-out, he had loved her. An airborne mermaid; a seaplane so beautiful that she was almost erotic. But when he had flown her this afternoon he had fallen out of love; quickly and badly. She was a misbehaving bitch, not a mermaid. There was something terribly wrong with her and he didn't know what.

Even worse, he didn't dare to admit it to anyone else. Not now; perhaps not ever.

He circled slowly around her, scrutinizing her sleek shining body. On that second turn, he had heard something crack, but there was no external sign of any damage. He climbed up on to the trolley and trailed his fingertips along the whole smooth length of her canvas-covered tail-section. Not a dip, not a bump, not a single flaw. He could see his own distorted face mirrored in the hand-glazed surface.

'Bitch,' he said, out loud. There was only one thing for it. He would have to remove the pilot's seat and the bulkhead behind it and inspect the inside of the fuselage with a torch. If anything had broken, it was quite possible that the whole rear fuselage section would have to be stripped and rebuilt.

'Bitch,' he repeated.

He climbed up the access ladder to the cockpit with a canvas roll of hexagonal spanners and a torch. Bending over, grunting, he unbolted the small leather-covered seat, and pushed it forward to give himself access to the bulkhead. It was impossible to take the seat right out of the aircraft without removing the windscreen first, and that would have taken him another twenty minutes. As it was, it took him a quarter of an hour to loosen all the bolts holding the bulkhead into place, and push that forward, too, so that he could see inside the fuselage.

Leaning right over the edge of the cockpit, he played the beam of his torch all the way along the rear spars. At first, he saw nothing; but on a second, slower inspection, he saw what appeared to be a splintered stringer close to the root of the tailplane. From twenty feet away, it was very difficult to see exactly how serious the damage was; and inspecting it in close-up would have meant removing a large section of body-skin. More problems, more delay, more difficulty. Bryan could feel the Seraphim Trophy shrinking further and further away from him; and Constance, too.

He stood up straight, and wiped the sweat from his face with his handkerchief. The tail had held firm during landing; nothing else had broken. Maybe it was nothing more than a superficial split in the surface of the wood. In fact, the chances were that it was completely harmless. The *Chichester Special* was a bitch, yes; but any bitch could be managed by a man with enough strength and enough determination.

'My lady,' Bryan whispered, 'you're not going to beat me.'

He bolted back the bulkhead and the seat, polished the windscreen with his handkerchief, and climbed back down the ladder.

Willy was just coming out of the drawing office. 'Find your watch, Mr King-Moreton?'

Bryan reached into his raincoat pocket and produced the watch which had been there all the time. 'Damn stupid of me, fell down under the seat.'

'Tea's up, if you'd like some,' said Willy.

Bryan realized that his hands were shaking from the strain. 'Yes,' he said. 'I'd like that.' He remembered Herbert ribbing him for believing that hot, sweet tea was the cure for almost anything. He wondered if it worked for sheer blind funk.

His ship had docked six hours early, and so James arrived home from Southampton just before lunch. He looked tanned but tired. He refused Constance's offer of cold chicken-and-ham pie and pickles. 'I've been eating massively for four days – I feel like Billy Bunter.' Instead, he asked Richard to drive him over straight away to Haslemere to see Patricia.

'Michael left for Australia yesterday,' said Richard, as they drove. 'He's written you a letter.'

James lit a cigarette. 'I would have preferred to talk to him man to man.'

'He didn't have an awful lot of choice. If he'd stayed to see you, he would have missed his ship.'

'There are always other ships.'

'Yes,' Richard agreed. 'I suppose there are. But he was fearfully cut up about Patricia. He wasn't really ready to face you.'

James funnelled smoke out of his nostrils. 'What did he think I was going to do? Kill him?'

'Something like that.'

They arrived in Haslemere at two o'clock, and parked outside the Burne-Stanley's large new house with its pillared porch and its garages built to look like stables. The maid saw them into the sitting-room.

Mrs Burne-Stanley appeared, in a square-cut lime-green suit, looking anxious. She stared at both of them as if she couldn't think who they were.

'Mrs Burne-Stanley?' said James. 'I've only just this minute got back. Is Patricia here?'

'Patricia? Hasn't anybody told you?' asked Mrs Burne-Stanley.

James shook his head. 'What's happened? She's all right, isn't she?'

Mrs Burne-Stanley's lips puckered with unhappiness. 'She's had a sort of a breakdown, that's what Dr Hallett called it. They've taken her to Ivy Lodge.'

'Breakdown? What kind of a breakdown?'

'They're not terribly sure. They've given her something to calm her down. She's been acting in a very peculiar way ever since Dr Hallett told her that she wouldn't be able to have any more

195

children. Last week she went up to her room and smashed her favourite doll, her beloved Miranda. This morning she started screaming and she wouldn't stop.'

James said, 'Where's Ivy Lodge? What is it, a nursing-home?'

'It's just outside Shottermill, you can't miss it.'

'She *is* all right, though?'

Mrs Burne-Stanley waved her hands distractedly. 'She isn't the same, you know. She doesn't seem like my Patty any more.'

James laid his arm around Mrs Burne-Stanley's shoulders. 'Really, Mrs Burne-Stanley, don't worry too much. I'm sure that Patricia's going to be all right, now that I'm back.'

Mrs Burne-Stanley shook her head. 'That's just the trouble. It's *you* she's worried about. She can't give you any more children, you see, and she's quite convinced that you're going to leave her.'

'Well, now, that's nonsense,' said James. 'I love her, she's my wife. Why should I leave her?'

Mrs Burne-Stanley produced a handkerchief and carefully wiped her eyes. 'All men want heirs, don't they?'

Patricia had been sedated with quinalbarbitone. She lay in bed with the curtains drawn, so that the room was suffused with muted primrose sunlight. There was a vase of yellow roses on her bedside table: above her head was a reproductiion of *The Hay Wain*.

Her hair had been brushed and washed and tied with white ribbon. Her arms lay outside the blankets. Her face looked strange; and James immediately knew what Mrs Burne-Stanley had meant when she had said that 'she doesn't seem like my Patty any more'.

He sat down on the edge of the bed and took hold of her hands. Her eyelids flickered and she looked up at him and vaguely smiled. Her lips opened with the faintest of clicks. 'James? Is it really you?'

He leaned forward and kissed her forehead. Her skin tasted of antiseptic. 'I'm back,' he told her. 'My ship docked at ten o'clock this morning.'

'Oh, James . . . I'm so pleased to see you.'

'I'm pleased to see you, too. But what's all this? Throwing tantrums and ending up here?'

'Did they tell you?' she asked him. Her pupils were so wide she looked as if she were staring at him madly. 'They didn't tell you, did they?'

James glanced back towards the doorway, where Richard was waiting, half-in and half-out. 'Didn't tell me what, darling?' he asked Patricia.

'They didn't tell you anything about children – about me and children?'

James squeezed her hand, and gave her another kiss. 'Should they have done?'

Patricia shivered. 'James –' she said '– James, you must promise me, no matter what they say, you won't believe them, will you?'

'Of course not, my darling. Why should I believe anybody but you?'

'They'll say things!' Patricia whispered. 'James, they'll say things! Such awful things! Please don't believe them, they're all telling lies!'

James smiled, and stroked her hair. 'It's all right, you don't have to worry. I promise I won't believe them.'

Patricia slept. James sat beside her for a while, still stroking her hair. Then he left her, and rejoined Richard outside in the corridor. Dr Hallett was there, wiping his nose on a handkerchief the size of a bedsheet. 'Ah, Mr Lord,' he said, still wiping with his left hand while he extended his right.

'Good afternoon, doctor. My wife appears to be tremendously upset.'

'Well, it's the baby, you know,' said Dr Hallett. 'Her mind and her body were fully prepared for giving birth; every emotion and every ounce of body chemistry was running at full throttle. It's a bit like fuelling up one of your aeroplanes, Mr Lord, then roaring off down the length of the runway at full rip, only to find at the very last second that you can't take off.'

He looked in through the window at Patricia sleeping. 'I think it's what in flying terms you might call a prang.'

'Will she get over it?' asked James.

'Oh, no doubt about it. Give her a couple of weeks for her body to adjust, and she should be as right as rain.'

'What about . . .'

'Well, that's up to you,' said Dr Hallett. 'There's no medical reason why you shouldn't resume normal relations as soon as Patricia comes home. There's nothing wrong with *that* part of her interior.'

James interrupted. 'What I was going to say was, what about children? Is there any chance at all that she can ever have any more children? Some sort of operation, perhaps?'

Dr Hallett ran his hand through his hair. 'Do you want me to be frank?'

'Of course I want you to be frank.'

'Then, if it's children you want, you must start thinking about adoption.'

Dinner that evening was supposed to have been a celebration for James's return; but with Patricia under sedation at Ivy Lodge and Michael crossing the Bay of Biscay on the *Alexandria*, there was very little for any of them to celebrate. It was pork, with apricot stuffing. Bryan carved and got into a mess. Some of the apricot stuffing dropped on to his shoe, and all through dinner the dog was after it. Afterwards, James asked Richard if he wanted to go to the Feathers, for a drink.

'Don't you want to rest, dear?' asked Constance. 'I thought you might tell us all about what you did in America.'

'Not now, Mother. What I really want is a large whisky-and-soda and a game of darts.'

Peeved, Constance retorted, 'You'd be better off with a mug of Ovaltine and a good night's sleep.'

Richard drove them down to the Feathers on the outskirts of Chichester. The sky was still light, an odd Chinese mauve, even though it was well past nine o'clock. It was the night before payday, and the pub was almost empty. They went into the public bar and James practised tossing a few darts at the dart-board while Richard bought the drinks.

'Now,' said Richard, as he rejoined his brother. 'What's all this about Atlantic and Pacific Airways?'

'I've bought it,' said James. 'At least, I've signed the papers.'

'You don't have the authority.'

'I signed them on my own behalf; not on behalf of Lord Aeronautics.'

'Oh, I see,' said Richard. 'You've been and gone and bought yourself an airline, and now you expect us to give you the money to do it with?'

'You don't have to get shirty about it,' James replied. 'The opportunity came up, and I took it. This could be our greatest commercial breakthrough in years. Not only to *build* the airliners, but to operate them, too. We can get in right at the beginning. I can promise you, Richard, there are millions to be made. Millions!'

'You asked Mother for a quarter of a million dollars.'

James nodded, and threw two double-tops and a twenty. Richard stood watching him as he chalked up his score.

'You suggested we use the Seraphim Trophy fund.'

'That's right.'

'I hope you realize that you will only be able to do that over my dead body.'

James sipped whisky and then set his glass down. 'You shouldn't joke about things like that.'

'Oh, I'm serious, James. Winning the Seraphim Trophy comes first, second, and last, as far as I'm concerned.'

James made a face. 'Supposing you spend all that money and we still don't win it?'

'We'll win it, I can promise you that. Four hundred and twenty miles an hour on its very first outing, James! We'll knock spots off the Eyeties!'

James wearily rubbed his eyes. 'Richard,' he said, 'we can't build the future of this company on glory alone.'

'Perhaps not, but without glory it's not worth building at all.'

James tried to be gentle. 'It won't bring back Father, you know, if you win. He's dead now, for good and all. And it won't change the fact that he committed suicide.'

Richard turned his face away. James waited, and watched him. 'You weren't to blame, you know, for what happened. There's no earthly reason to suppose that it had anything to do with you at all.'

Richard said, 'I saw him falling, that's all.'

'And you can still see him falling?'

'Yes.'

James came across and held his brother's arm. 'I think you're just going to have to reconcile yourself to the fact that you will *always* see him falling, until the day you die.'

Richard turned back and looked at him with determination. 'No. Not if we win. I loved him, James. All I have to do is finish the job that he started.'

James sighed in exasperation; but Richard persisted. 'Listen,' he said, 'come over to Calshot on Saturday afternoon, and we'll take her up again. I'll fly her this time; and then you'll see what she can do.'

'Richard,' said James, 'I still need a quarter of a million dollars. I have until the thirtieth of April to pay up; no later. Otherwise I lose the airline.'

'Come down to Calshot on Saturday,' Richard told him, 'and you won't care about losing it. I promise you.'

The following day, Richard went up to London by train to have lunch with Elisabeth Bergner, who had just started rehearsals at the Criterion Theatre for *Spring Fever*. James spent most of the morning in Chichester going over the company books, and checking up on how much progress had been made in completing their order for three Aquarius transports for the Belgian airline Sabena. Wally Field told him that three of their best mechanics had been taken off the production-line to make last-minute alterations to the *Chichester Special,* and because of that they were almost a week behind. He called Bryan King-Moreton to his office.

'Well?' said Bryan, defensively. He had just been going off to lunch, and he was wearing a green thornproof jacket and a very white shirt.

'You've been borrowing my fitters again,' said James, without raising his eyes.

'Wally was quite happy.'

'Wally is not responsible for delivering three finished transports to Antwerp on the fifteenth of June.'

Bryan coughed briskly into his hand. 'Is that all? I'm supposed to be having lunch with the editor of *Flight.* Some article he's writing, on the Kings of Speed.'

James leafed through the progress reports on his desk. 'No, Bryan, that's not all. The *Chichester Special* has taken enough out of this company, as far as I'm concerned, and I'm warning you here and now that I'm going to do everything within my power to stop it. We've been suffering from something else, too, and that's your unremitting self-interest. Not only in the factory, either. Mother tells me that you've proposed marriage. Well, let me tell you this, Mr Bryan King-Moreton, I don't know what your reasons are, but I'm perfectly sure that they aren't romantic. You damn well keep your hands off my mother and you damn well keep your hands off my mechanics.'

Bryan puffed out his upper lip in annoyance, like an enraged frog. 'You've got your bloody nerve, James, talking to me like that. I knew the mater before you were born. I knew the pater before you were born. I flew with the pater on the first flight he ever made.'

'That's history, Bryan. I'm not talking about history. I'm talking about the future. This company has reached a point of make or break; and I'm going to make damn sure that you don't ruin it.'

'We're going to go for the Seraphim Trophy whether you like it or not,' Bryan blustered.

James closed the reports on his desk and shuffled them straight. 'We'll have to see about that, won't we? At the moment, both Mother and Richard are dead set on winning it and that means that I'm outnumbered. But you never know. The Lord moves in mysterious ways, his wonders to perform. Richard's going to take the *Chichester Special* up for me on Saturday, so that I can see her for myself.'

'What? He didn't tell me anything about it!'

At that moment, Wally Field knocked on the office window. 'Sorry to interrupt you, Mr James. We've been having trouble with those hydraulics again.'

'Wally –' Bryan protested, 'did Mr Richard say anything to you about taking the *Chichester* up on Saturday?'

Wally sniffed. 'He mentioned it in passing, first thing this morning, just before you came in. He said he was going to talk to you later.'

'Well, it's out of the question, the only person who can get the best out of her is me.'

James looked up at him in surprise. 'Richard's a perfectly well-qualified pilot. Father used to let him fly the old *Chichester*.'

'This is utterly different!'

'Well,' said James, 'it's immaterial to me who sits in the cockpit. I'd rather that neither of you did. In my view, the best place for that seaplane is in the Natural History Museum, alongside the pleisiosaurs and the whatchamacallumsaurs and all the other extinct amphibians.'

Bryan managed to control his temper. 'I'm late,' he snapped. 'I'll talk to Richard later.'

When Bryan had gone, James followed Wally out on to the shop floor, where four mechanics were standing around a jammed undercarriage strut, their hands on their hips.

'What seems to be the trouble?' asked James.

'Stuck,' said one of the mechanics, taking a roll-up cigarette from behind his ear, and pinching it back into shape.

James knelt down and examined it. 'Did any of you think to lubricate it before you tested the action?'

The mechanic with the roll-up shook his head. 'That's not my job, guv'nor.'

James stood up, 'What on earth do you mean, it's not your job? Your job is *every* job! Your job is to do whatever is required to get these aeroplanes built and flying! That includes everything from making the tea to looping the bloody loop!'

The mechanic looked at him sheepishly. James looked at his watch. 'No lunch-break today. Not for any of you. Get that bloody strut dismantled, check for damage, lubricate it properly and put it all back together again.'

He turned and marched back to the office. He didn't see the V-signs that were waved behind his back, but then he didn't need to. Even in small private companies like Lord Aeronautics, there was a growing feeling on the shopfloor of 'them and us', particularly since the Depression. There had been no pay rises at Lord for three years now, and James had even been considering a three per cent cut in wages, to keep up the company's profit margin.

He opened his office door, and to his surprise somebody was sitting on the edge of his desk. A thin man with chestnut-coloured hair, well-greased, and an aquiline nose, and eyes as sharp as the Pied Piper of Hamelin. He looked amused but guarded. He was smoking a cork-tipped cigarette, his right elbow couched in his left hand.

James hesitated for a moment, then entered the office and closed the glass-panelled door behind him. He walked around his desk and sat down.

'Well, well,' he said. 'Jacko Gibbons. I was told that you were somewhere around. Eating egg and chips, so my informant told me, in the Old Oak Café. What can I do for you?'

Jacko reached over and crushed out his cigarette in James's Imperial Airways ashtray. 'I don't think that's the right question, Mr Lord. The question is, what can *I* do for *you*?'

Richard took Elisabeth to Le Perroquet, in Leicester Square, because it was small and intimate and the waiters didn't hurry you. She was looking not just elfin today but exceptional; in a cream-coloured dress with wide sleeves that seemed to flow around her like a speeded-up film of summer clouds. He realized as he took her arm and guided her towards their table that he was in love with her.

'I'm in love with you,' he said, as soon as they had sat down, even before the waiter had taken their order for cocktails. 'I suppose you already know that.'

Elisabeth laughed. 'I'll have a glass of white wine; very dry.'

'A whisky for me,' said Richard.

Elisabeth reached her hand across the table and ran her fingertips over Richard's knuckles. 'Ever since I came here, I have never met anybody sweeter than you. You know that, my brave bold aviator!'

'You're making fun of me,' said Richard.

She blew him a little kiss. Those huge eyes of hers were dancing with amusement. 'Of course I'm making fun of you. We shall be friends for ever and ever!'

Richard looked at her closely. She smiled back at him. He picked up his menu and opened it. 'The five-and-six lunch,' he announced. 'I can recommend the prawn cocktail.'

'And what about the *suprême de volaille sous la cloche*?'

Richard nodded. 'It's a speciality. Father always used to call it "the superb thief under the clock". I'm in love with you; I mean it.'

Elisabeth's smile slowly faded, like breath from a window. 'Richard, you mustn't be.'

'It's not a question of must or mustn't. I am.'

'But, if you are in love with me, how can we remain friends?'

'People in love can be friends, can't they?'

Elisabeth with some sadness lowered her head and pretended that she was studying the menu. The lunchtime sunshine illuminated the fine blonde hairs on the back of her neck; and Richard would have given five years of his life to reach out and touch them.

'The prawn cocktail, then?' he asked her, artificially bright.

She smiled. 'You've forgotten already that I'm Jewish?'

'Oh, no – of course not. I mean – I apologize.'

'You don't have to apologize for anything, Richard. You have been kind and generous and attentive. You have listened to all of my problems and all of my silly tempers. I didn't mean for you to fall in love.'

There were tears in her eyes. She was an actress, after all. Tears could be produced whenever necessary. Richard produced a large clean handkerchief out of his breast pocket but Elisabeth had her own, tiny and lacy. 'I'm sorry,' she said, dabbing her eyes. 'Perhaps we'd better forget about lunch.'

'No,' Richard insisted. Then, 'No, let's have lunch together. Life isn't always what you expect it to be.'

'I've hurt you,' said Elisabeth. 'I didn't mean to hurt you.'

'I know you didn't. I know. I've been, what, hoist with my own what's-it's-name. Petard.'

Elisabeth took hold of his hand. She was all tears and smiles. 'Do you know what that means, petard? Norman Jorritt told me, only last week.'

'I have no idea. I thought it was a kind of spear. You know, stuck up in the air on your own spear.'

She giggled. 'No, no, petard is French for a little bit of breaking wind, you understand? So it means that you are blown up into the air – you know, like a little ball at the fairground – blown up high on your own –'

She covered her mouth with her hand to stifle her laughter. Richard, in spite of himself, in spite of his pain, began to laugh too. He looked at her shoulders, shaking with mirth, and he couldn't stop. All of the relief of telling her he loved her; all of the disappointment; all of the pain; all of it came out at once. He laughed and laughed so much that his stomach ached, and he had to lean back in his chair. Elisabeth openly wept, and let out such high theatrical giggles that Richard started laughing even harder.

They found themselves out on Leicester Square, amidst the golden dust and the honking traffic, the 5s 6d lunch abandoned. They said very little. The warmth and the friendship between them was complete.

Richard walked her hand-in-hand back to the Criterion. 'I love you,' he told her. 'I always will.'

She kissed his cheek; then his lips. Several passers-by turned to look at them. After all, Elisabeth was already famous.

'I love you, too, Richard Lord,' she said. 'Whenever you go flying, think of me; and take good care.'

She pushed her way through the doors of the theatre, and Richard stood on the pavement with his hands in his pockets, left with nothing but a large black-and-white photograph of her, on the placards outside. Opening June 1, Elisabeth Bergner in *Spring Fever*.

The theatre door swung shut, and he saw himself reflected in the glass. Curly-haired, well-dressed, but slightly-built, just like his mother. Constance's boy.

He was still standing looking at himself when a man with red-rimmed eyes and a greasy cap came up to him with his hand out. 'Spare twopence for a cup of tea, sir?' he asked, hoarsely.

Richard reached into his pocket. As the man watched in avaricious fascination, he counted out two half-crowns and two threepenny bits. 'There,' said Richard. 'That's for the five and sixpenny lunch I didn't have.'

The man was trembling as Richard pressed half a week's wages into his hand. He stayed where he was, still trembling, as Richard walked off, and, dry-eyed, hailed a taxi to take him back to Victoria Station.

Calshot, 1932

During the night, the winds had been up to mischief, blowing first from the south-east and then veering wildly to the south-west, so that by ten o'clock that Saturday morning they were warm but blustery, and the Solent was tossing with springtime squalls.

They had wanted to start flying straight away, but first of all Wally had had trouble adjusting the supercharger, and then the fuel-pump had developed a leak. By ten o'clock, James was growing hungry and impatient, and seriously starting to think about going off for bacon and eggs.

Richard came across the concrete ramp in his flying-suit, his helmet-strap flapping in the wind.

'We should be ready to go in five or ten minutes. There's a devil of a crosswind, but we should be able to top four hundred knots.'

Bryan took out his watch. 'Do you really think this is a good idea, Richard? We don't want to overheat the engine.'

'Oh, it's worth it, all right,' said Richard, cheerfully. 'It's worth it just to show James how bloody good she is. And, believe me, she's *bloody* good!'

James put his arm around Constance's shoulders and squeezed her. 'Do you think I ought to tell the vicar to call, and lecture your second-oldest son on the sins of vanity and profanity?'

Constance reached up to grasp James's fingers and smiled. 'Wait until you see her fly, then you'll understand why Richard's so proud.'

'Mother,' said James, 'I came here today with an open mind; in the spirit of fair-play. If she tops four hundred and twenty, then I may very possibly be converted. I'm not making any guarantees, mind you; but I have occasionally been known to change my mind.'

'Well, I hope so,' said Constance. 'We could do with some pride and some glory. Not only us; but England.'

'You're beginning to sound more like Bryan every day.'

'I'd rather sound like Bryan than any of your doubting Thomases.'

'Well, hear, hear, Mother. Here's for King and Empire; and for an atlas awash with crimson.'

Constance fussily extricated herself from James's embrace. 'I never know about you, James. Sometimes I think you're too sarcastic for your own good. At least, with the little ones, I always know where I am.'

The *Chichester Special* was bobbing in the water only thirty feet from the landing-ramp. Wally was trying to get her engine started with a bulky portable battery, unsuccessfully so far. Another Lord mechanic was making final adjustments to the instruments in the cockpit. There had been trouble with the air-pressure gauge and the altimeter. James said, 'I hope this isn't going to take all morning. If I don't have breakfast very soon, I'm going to pass out, and if I pass out, I shall be *quite* unable to make any objective judgements.'

'Don't poke fun, James,' said Constance. 'Richard and Bryan have been nursing this project like their very own baby. All the way through from conception to –'

James raised his eyes and looked at his mother darkly. 'Not a very tactful analogy, Mother.'

Constance said, 'If only I could believe that you were so sensitive.'

Richard, to change the subject, said, 'I wonder how Michael's getting on? At least he didn't have to go through the Bay of Biscay in all this wind.'

Nobody answered him. James took out his handkerchief and loudly blew his nose. Constance reached into her handbag for her sunglasses, which always made her look as if she were blind. At last Wally Field came over and announced, 'She's ready to fly, Mr Richard. Sweet as a nut.'

Richard tugged his white silk scarf a little looser. 'That's it, then. Let's see what she can do.'

'Good luck, Richard,' said James, clapping him on the back.

But it was then that Bryan lifted his hat, and simultaneously a telegraph boy came cycling down the hard, calling, 'Mr Rich-ard Lord! Mr Rich-ard Lord!'

Richard, surprised, said, 'That's me,' and the telegraph boy clattered down his bicycle with its wheels still ticking around, and produced a telegram from the leather wallet attached to his belt. 'Message from London, sir. They didn't ask for an answer.'

Richard tore open the telegram and read it quickly.

'Nothing terrible, I hope?' asked James.

Richard handed him the telegram. It said, ELISABETH CRUCIALLY ILL STOP ASKING FOR YOU STOP SIGNED JORRITT.

James handed the telegram back. 'Oh, Richard, that's frightful. What are you going to do?'

'I don't know.' Richard rubbed his forehead with the heel of his hand. 'I'm sorry. I think I'm going to have to call this a day. You don't mind, do you? We can do it again next week.'

Bryan came up, his hands clasped behind his back. 'Is everything all right? That wasn't bad news?'

'Elisabeth Bergner's ill,' said James. 'She's asking for Richard to go to see her.'

The telegraph boy was still waiting, his polished toecaps finely coated in dust. James stared at him for a moment, and then tipped him a shilling. 'Biff off now, there's a good lad.'

Richard took off his flying helmet, and handed it to James. 'I'm really sorry.'

'Well, that's all right,' said James. 'As a matter of fact, I'm rather relieved. Now I can go and have some breakfast with a clear conscience.'

'Couldn't *Bryan* fly?' asked Constance. 'You could fly, couldn't you, Bryan?'

Bryan shrugged. 'I suppose so. It depends what Richard feels about it. I don't want to steal his thunder.'

'No, no, don't worry about it,' said Richard. 'Bryan will probably fly her better than me in any case. James – Mother – I'll call you as soon as I get to London.'

They watched him drive away in his bright yellow Whitlock, his tyres squittering. He looked like a toy driver, in a clockwork car. James shrugged, and tossed his flying-helmet to Bryan. 'There you are then, Bryan. She's all yours.'

Bryan caught the helmet, and looked around, as if flying the *Chichester Special* were the very last thing he wanted to do.

'Go on, Bryan, you know her,' Constance coaxed him.

With a great show of mimed reluctance, shrugs, head-ducking, throwing-up of his hands, Bryan at last fitted Richard's flying-helmet on his head, and buttoned up his overalls.

'Four hundred and twenty?' asked James.

Bryan tugged on his gloves. 'I'll do my best.'

'Well, four hundred and twenty is what it's going to take to convince me.'

'*James —*' Constance protested. But Bryan said, 'That's all right, Connie. Four hundred and twenty it is.'

Wally helped him out to the seaplane's ladder. The sunlight was strangely foggy; and when Bryan stood up on the cockpit and waved to everybody on the shore, James had the unsettling impression that he was watching a dream; soft-focus, like a Hollywood version of a Norse legend, longships and men in white. Bryan waved and waved, long after the bystanders had finished taking pictures with their Brownie cameras. At last, Wally Field turned to James, and said, 'Get her away, then, Mr James?'

'That's it, Wally.'

Wally waved to the mechanic down by the battery-trolley; and the mechanic gave Bryan the thumb's up. With a ripping, ear-splitting roar, the *Chichester Special*'s engine opened up, and almost immediately Bryan turned her away from the seaplane station and headed out towards the Solent. A fine veil of golden spray hung over her; so that at times she was invisible. They knew she was there only because of the screaming of her sixteen cylinders, and the arrowhead wake which she had left behind her, and which now lapped against the concrete ramp.

Constance said, 'She's so beautiful, James. She's so glorious.'

'Well,' James replied, 'you remember Gray's *Elegy*. "All that beauty ever gave, awaits alike th'inevitable hour . . . the paths of glory lead but to the grave."'

'James, that's very morbid.'

'It's not morbid at all. I learnt it in the fourth form.'

'You accuse *me* of being tactless.'

'Mother,' said James. 'I accuse you of nothing.'

The screaming of the seaplane's engine grew even harsher, and she suddenly lifted herself out of the spray and up into the air, flying at an angle against the wind. Bryan took her up to five hundred feet, still flying west, and then turned her southward, towards Cowes.

James said, 'Darn it, I left my binoculars in the car.'

For the first few minutes, Bryan began to believe that his desperate prayers had been answered, and that the *Chichester Special* had miraculously sorted herself out. She dipped and ducktailed a little as she taxied along the water, but she lifted herself clean-limbed into the air, and in spite of the gusty crosswinds, she behaved herself immaculately on his first climbing turn.

Bryan checked his gyro compass, and tilted the seaplane a few degrees further towards the south-east, with the wind roaring and buffeting past his open cockpit. He looked towards Calshot and he could see the castle and the shoreline and the sea glittering like hammered glass. He lifted the seaplane's nose a little, and began to turn.

He didn't sing this time. He was far too anxious to think about singing. It was bad enough that he had kept the secret of the *Chichester*'s waywardness to himself; but he had gravely compounded his sins by tricking Richard into going up to London, simply so that Richard wouldn't discover for himself how badly the seaplane handled. At least, he wouldn't discover it yet. He was bound to fly her sooner or later. But as far as Bryan was concerned, it was better to postpone that moment as long as possible.

'Now, my lovely,' he told the *Chichester*, trying to be stern and seductive, both at the same time. 'I want you to behave yourself.'

He began to climb and turn yet again, so that he could soar down towards Calshot at maximum speed. But as soon as he lifted the seaplane's nose, the juddering started again, completely without warning, and far worse than it had been before. Bryan attempted to dip the *Chichester*'s port-side wing, and bring her nose back down again, but she slid and jumped through the air as awkwardly as if she didn't have a tail.

He began to dive. If he messed around at the top of this climb, trying to keep the *Chichester* steady, James would immediately realize that there was something wrong. The seaplane was vibrating so furiously that all of Bryan's instruments were a blur. He felt as if his bare skull was being pressed against the side of a road-drill. The engine began to scream off-key, and the wind banged against his ears.

James, on the shore, said, 'Give me those binoculars,' and the way he said it was so calm and terrible that Wally handed them over without a word.

James focused on the approaching seaplane just in time to see pieces beginning to fall from the tail. The rudder first, then the elevators; then the tailfin itself.

'My God, it's breaking up,' he said; although he wasn't sure if he had said it out loud.

Suddenly, the *Chichester Special* dropped from a shallow dive into a steep plummeting spiral. More pieces fell off; debris floated through the morning air like flocks of starlings. The engines started that terrible hopeless droning which James had heard over and over again, just before air crashes. Constance covered her face with her hands, but then took them away again, and stared at the falling seaplane with waxen intensity. 'Herbert,' she whispered. '*Herbert*.'

James took hold of her hand. It felt as bony as a cold roast quail. 'Mother, it's Bryan.'

Constance turned to stare at him. 'He hasn't got a parachute.'

James didn't answer, couldn't.

'James, he hasn't got a parachute!'

The *Chichester Special* somersaulted around and around, back-flipping now. One instant it seemed to be high above the sea. The next it had crashed nose-first into the water, sending up a huge plume of spray.

'Wally! The boat!' James shouted; and was already running down the ramp.

The Lord Aeronautics launch was moored by the steps. George Ruddock, their boatman, had started up the engine as soon as the *Chichester Special* began to break up. James and Wally clambered in, and they butted their way out across the water. The *Chichester Special* had crashed about two hundred yards away from the shore. Its mutilated silver tail was protruding from the waves; the weight of the engine and the fuel-tanks had already dragged the nose down to cockpit-level. James, sitting in the back of the speed-boat, clutching tightly on to the handrail, could see that she was filling up fast. She hadn't been designed to float, except on her pontoons. She would go down like a coffin, and Bryan would go down with her, unless they reached her first.

'There, Mr James, he's waving!' Wally shouted. 'There! Don't you see 'im! The blighter!'

Sure enough, James could see Bryan's arm waving from the cockpit. He turned to George and said, 'Hurry, damn it!'

'Doing me best, sir,' said George.

They circled the sinking seaplane, their hull slapping against the choppy waves, and then George nudged their bows up towards the cockpit. The *Chichester Special* was almost vertical, and the water had reached the windscreen. Every now and then, a wave slopped into the cockpit itself. Bryan was sitting upright; white but cheerful; and as they came closer he said, 'Bravo, you chaps.'

James balanced his way to the front of the speedboat and leaned one hand against the seaplane's fuselage. 'Bryan? Do you think you can get yourself out?'

Bryan gave him a glassy smile. 'Bit of a problem, old man. Both of my blasted feet are trapped. Rudder-pedals seemed to have twisted themselves right round the blasted ankles.'

'Wally,' said James, 'do you have any cutting gear?'

Wally stared back at him, and shook his head. 'Back at the works, Mr James, that's all. Take me an hour to get it.'

'Well, we haven't got an hour, have we?' James snapped. He seized the edge of the seaplane's windscreen, and leaned forward so that he could take a look inside. The cockpit was almost completely filled with water, and the surface was streaked with oil and glycol and blood. James cupped his hand under Bryan's chin to lift it clear of the water, and asked him, 'Can you move your feet at all?'

Bryan let out a silly gasping laugh. Although it was May, the seawater was frighteningly cold. 'Move them? Can't even feel them.'

'Well, don't you worry, old man, we'll soon have you out of there.' James turned around and said, 'George, a knife, anything.'

George reached into his trousers pocket and took out a clasp knife. He handed it to James without a word. The speedboat dipped and thudded against the side of the sinking seaplane. James said, 'I'm going to reach down, Bryan, try to pry you loose.'

Bryan nodded, and grimaced, but didn't reply. Another wave poured a pailful of water into the cockpit, and it was all he could do to keep his mouth clear.

James said, 'Steady, George! Steady as you can!' and climbed out of the speedboat on to the *Chichester Special*'s half-submerged fuselage. He was up to his waist in water, and he shouted out loud. What was worse, his weight made the seaplane angle herself even further into the water, and for a moment Bryan's face was completely submerged.

'Bryan,' James told him, 'take a deep breath. I'm going to try to get your feet free of those pedals.'

'Oh, God in heaven,' Bryan spluttered, as the *Chichester* wallowed into a trough.

James filled his lungs with air, and then plunged the upper part of his body into the cockpit, forcing his head between Bryan's chest and the instrument panel. The left horn of the joystick hit him a painful knock on the side of his forehead, but he forced it downwards, and tried to reach past Bryan's knees so that he could get hold of his feet.

It was impossible. He simply couldn't reach. His lungs began to feel as if they were collapsing inwards, and he struggled back out of the cockpit and took a harsh barking breath. Bryan had stretched his head back as far as it would go, to keep his nose and mouth clear of the water, but the next wave completely covered his head.

'James!' he choked. 'James, old chap!'

He reached out with his one free arm and clung on to James's sodden lapel. 'James!' he said. 'I can't die like this!'

James tried to answer him, but couldn't. The next thing he knew, the seawater began to pour into the rear section of the fuselage, and with a deep lurch the *Chichester Special* promptly sank beneath the surface. For one terrible split-second, James saw Bryan's face, distorted like a face in a fairground mirror, white with panic, eyes staring.

James struggled to get himself free, but Bryan was still clinging on to his jacket. James was dragged under the water in a noisy blurt of bubbles. He heard Bryan use his last breath to let out a gargled cry. But still his hand gripped James's lapel, and even when James tried to prise his fingers away one by one, he wouldn't let go.

Quickly, brutally, James sliced George's clasp-knife deep across the back of Bryan's hand, through veins and tendons, down to the bones. At once, Bryan released his grip, and James kicked himself heavily up towards the surface. He kept his eyes open all the way, and, staring downward, saw the *Chichester Special* disappearing into the greenish twilight of the Solent like a half-glimpsed fish: a quick flash of silver, and then she was gone.

James's head emerged from the waves. Wally was there, leaning over the side of the speedboat with his hand out, to catch him.

'He's gone!' James coughed. 'I couldn't save him! Couldn't!'

'Just hold hard,' said Wally. 'It wa'n't your fault; you did wotcha could.'

'Oh God,' sobbed James, 'oh God.'

Wally caught his hand, and helped him to heave himself back into the speedboat. His clothes clung to him like sodden blankets, and he was shivering uncontrollably. 'Couldn't do anything!' he wept.

Constance sat in the drawing-room dressed in black, reflected in the polished parquet as if she were the Finnish Queen of Death, on her lake of ice. James came into the room and immediately sat down in one of the chairs close by the door. He could tell by the expression on her face that she wasn't going to be easy to approach. Not directly, anyway.

It was three days now since the *Chichester Special* had crashed. James had spent most of his time at Calshot, as divers went down to locate her. Last night, shining in the light of three powerful floodlamps, she had been lifted out of the water on a crane fitted to the stern of a dredger, with Bryan still sitting in the cockpit. James hadn't stayed to watch, but it had taken Wally Field and two other mechanics an hour and a half to cut Bryan's legs free of the tangled rudder-bars. Bryan had no relatives: there was nobody to tell. They would bury him in the village graveyard on Friday morning.

James said, 'Mother?'

Constance's eyes were lowered; her fingernails traced and re-traced the carved grooves in the arm of her chair. 'I seem to be cursed, don't I?' she whispered.

'I'm sorry?'

She looked up. He had never seen her eyes like this before: watery, unfocused, almost mad. 'I said, I seem to be cursed. First your father, now Bryan. Both lost to the *Chichester Special*. Or perhaps both lost to something else.'

She paused, still staring at James in the same unhinged way. 'Perhaps they were both lost to ambition, and intolerance, and greed.'

James was embarrassed. 'I'm really sorry, Mother, I haven't got the faintest idea what you're talking about.'

'Oh, you haven't! But then what would you care, anyway! Nothing is important to you, nothing! Only yourself and your own needs!'

James stood up. 'Mother, you're very upset –'

'Upset!' she quivered. 'I loved him! We were going to be married!'

'Mother, please. This isn't going to do you any good at all.'

Tears began to trickle down Constance's cheeks. James reached forward to comfort her, but under her breath she commanded him, '*No.*'

James stayed where he was, uncertain. 'I know you were fond of him, Mother. But there's nothing that anybody can do. He's gone.'

'Gone, yes; and *why* is he gone? Because of you!'

'Mother, for goodness' sake!'

Constance rose from her chair and walked across to the connecting door that led to the back parlour. 'Mr Thompson?' she said.

Into the room came Tommy Thompson, from the *Daily Herald*,

looking too warm in a thick green sports jacket. He stood in the corner, his hat in his hand, smiling cautiously. 'Morning,' he said. 'Do you mind telling me what this is all about?' James asked his mother. 'Who is this man?'

'This is Mr Thompson from the *Daily Herald*. He came to see me this morning, when you were out. He asked me some extraordinary questions.'

James said nothing, but looked from Constance to Tommy Thompson and then back again. Constance said, 'He asked me what I knew about Jacko Gibbons. He asked me if I knew that Jacko Gibbons was suspected by the German police of having sabotaged Gerhard Brunner's seaplane last year. He asked me if I knew that Jacko Gibbons was arrested in Amsterdam, and that his defence was paid for by Lord Aeronautics, on an international money order signed by you.'

She hesitated. She was trembling. 'He asked me if I knew that Jacko Gibbons was seen in Chichester last week; and that you were seen talking to him in your office. You were also seen to give him money.'

James let out a long, patient breath. 'You're right,' he said. 'Those *were* extraordinary questions.'

'Are they *true*?' Constance demanded.

'Mother – if you're asking me whether Jacko Gibbons sabotaged Gerhard Brunner's seaplane, the answer is I don't know. I freely admit paying for his defence. He used to work for us, on the engine side. When he was arrested in Amsterdam, he wrote to us and asked us to help him, simply because we were the only people he knew who could afford to. We sent him the money out of loyalty, nothing else.'

'But you saw him last week,' said Constance. 'You gave him more money. Why?'

'One of your riggers saw you,' put in Tommy Thompson.

James said, 'This is quite preposterous! The poor fellow was broke, that's all. He came to see me to ask for his old job back. I told him that we didn't need any more engine-fitters just at the moment, but I lent him ten pounds to see him out of trouble.'

Constance turned to Tommy Thompson, but Tommy Thompson was completely unabashed. 'You seem to be forgetting about the telegram, Mr Lord.'

'Telegram?'

'The telegram that came from Mr Norman Jorritt. Or, rather, the telegram that *didn't* come from Mr Norman Jorritt. The telegram that saved your brother Richard from flying that morning. Your brother rushed off to London, yes? – because he thought Miss Elisabeth Bergner was ill – only to find out when he got to London that she was blooming, absolutely blooming, and just about to start a rehearsal.'

'I don't know anything at all about that telegram,' said James. 'Now – if you've quite finished, I want you to go. Your editor is going to be hearing from my solicitors.'

'James,' said Constance, raising her head. 'Mr Thompson is here at my invitation. I want to know the truth.'

'You see, the thing is,' Tommy Thompson added, 'that telegram wasn't sent from London at all. It was originally sent from Chichester main post office; with instructions to arrive at Calshot no later than nine-thirty. The telegraph boy was late, but as it turned out, that didn't matter, because the flight was delayed, too.'

'None of this makes any sense whatsoever,' James retorted. 'I can see what you're trying to imply, and I consider it both outrageous and criminal. I'm going to sue.'

'Well, there's one more thing,' said Tommy Thompson. 'I've been talking to Jacko Gibbons personally.'

James went to the door and opened it wide. 'Get out,' he ordered.

Tommy Thompson tugged his dog-eared notebook out of his pocket, and leafed through it with a wettened thumb. 'Mr Jacko Gibbons said that you asked him to visit you at your office, because you had a proposition to put to him with regard to the *Chichester Special*. He said you offered to pay him fifty pounds to tinker with the engine so that it wouldn't be able to fly at the kind of speeds required to win the Seraphim Trophy. He said that he was astonished at your offer, because it would put a man's life at risk, and he refused. In the end, you gave him ten pounds to keep quiet, and said you would fix the *Chichester Special* yourself.'

'He's a damned liar,' James retorted. 'Now, get out, before I throw you out.'

'James,' chipped in Constance, sharply. 'Is any of this true?'

'You obviously want to believe that it's true.'

'I just want to know what really happened.'

For the first time in a very long time, James began to lose his temper. He slammed the door so violently that the key fell out, and clattered on to the parquet floor. '*I* want to know how much the *Daily Herald* has offered to pay Jacko Gibbons to slander me.'

Tommy Thompson closed his notebook. 'We're not paying him a penny. And he's prepared to repeat everything on oath.'

James stood silent for a while, then lowered his head.

'James?' asked Constance.

'I want this man out of the house,' said James. 'I also want him to understand that if he dares to print one word of this absurd cock-and-bull story, Lord Aeronautics will sue the *Herald* from here to eternity.'

He lifted his eyes again. He looked at his mother with a bitterness that could have dissolved pearls. Then he turned and left the room, leaving the door open so that Tommy Thompson would be able to follow him.

Constance came to the library late that evening when James was working. She sat down opposite him, barely visible in the shadows in her black evening dress, except for her pale face, which hung in front of James like a dim rice-paper lantern.

'I've come to a decision,' she said.

James was checking through Wally Field's purchases of switches and wiring. 'Oh, yes?' he asked, with a deliberate lack of interest. 'And what have you decided?'

'I called John Tremlett this afternoon, after that reporter had left.'

'And what did the oleaginous John Tremlett have to say?'

'He said that the *Daily Herald* would be very unlikely to publish a story suggesting that – well, suggesting that you had anything to do with Bryan's accident.'

James kept his head lowered and twisted a pencil around and around between his fingers.

Constance said, 'He talked to Mr Ellsworthy at Gray's Inn, just to make absolutely sure. Mr Ellsworthy said it would be far too risky for them even to consider it.'

'And?' asked James.

'And that is that, as far as I'm concerned; except that a doubt remains in my own mind.'

'A doubt? About what?'

'About *you*, James. It is a terrible, terrible thing for a mother to have to say, but I cannot bring myself completely to believe you.'

James leaned back in his chair, so that all Constance could see in the lamplight were his two hands, resting on his pages of accounts. 'So,' he said, 'you seriously believe that I could have tampered with the *Chichester Special*. You realize, I suppose, that *ipso facto* you're saying that I could have been responsible for Bryan's death?'

'I cannot completely believe that you had nothing to do with it whatsoever. You were so dead set against the *Chichester Special*. And I know that you harboured very deep animosity for Bryan.'

James was silent for a very long time. Then he sat up straight again, and said, 'Well, what are we going to do now? Look at us! An aeroplane company run by an unconvicted murderer, an exiled homosexual, and a prize chump. Perhaps we ought to pack it all in, and call it a day.'

In the same quiet voice that she used to use when she was angry with him as a child, Constance said, 'I want you to go back to America for a while. Richard is quite capable of running things here. I've talked to Richard already. As you know, he's very upset. But now that the *Chichester*'s gone, you can have your money for your airline.'

'I see,' said James. 'So, it's transportation for me, too, is it? Where are you going to send Richard, if he should ever offend you? Russia?'

'James, you can have your money for your airline. Under the circumstances, I think you should take it and be grateful.'

'It's very hard to feel any gratitude when your own mother is unable to bring herself to believe you when you tell her the truth. It's very hard to feel anything but resentment and contempt. You were never much of a mother, were you, Mother, and never much of a wife, either.'

He paused, impervious to Constance's shock.

'How can you!' she trembled.

'Oh,' said James, 'I had it from the horse's mouth. Father once drank a little too much claret when we were having dinner at the Royal Aero Club. You know how claret used to affect him. He suddenly came out and said that I shouldn't have been born. When I asked him why, he said that there had always been another woman in his life, a woman who should have been his wife. "By her," he said, "I should have had just one son, and he wouldn't have looked a bit like you".'

'How can you say such a thing!' Constance retorted. 'James – you're absolutely despicable!'

'Well,' said James, 'they always say that those who are unable to tell the truth find it impossible to believe that the rest of the world isn't made up of liars, too.'

'It's quite shameful of you to take your father's name in vain.'

'It's equally shameful of you to disbelieve me.'

Constance took a deep, quivering breath. 'Very well, then, I believe you, if that's what it takes to make you behave yourself.'

'I'm still going to get my money, I presume?'

'I may be a liar,' said Constance, with chiselled sarcasm, 'but I have never once gone back on my word.'

'And I can stay in England?'

'No, James, you can't. Just for a while, I don't want to see you. I don't particularly want to think that you might drop in unexpectedly; or that I might bump into you somewhere; or that I might see your picture in the newspapers. I want you to go completely away.'

'As if I had never been born,' smiled James.

Constance didn't answer that. She was wringing her hands together, making a dry, tight sound.

James said, 'It sounds very much as if you want me to leave as soon as possible.'

Constance nodded.

'All right,' said James, 'but I won't be able to take Patricia, not straight away. She just isn't up to it.'

'I'm sure that her mother will take very good care of her. And she will always be welcome here.'

'Unlike her husband.'

Constance stood up. 'I'm not going to discuss this any more, James. My decision is absolutely final.'

As she reached the door, however, James said, 'Mother?'

'Yes?' she replied, coldly.

'There's something else, isn't there? There's more. You wouldn't usually take a reporter's word against mine.'

'Well,' said Constance, 'I suppose I can give you full marks for perspicacity. There *is* more, yes. And, like you, I got it straight from the horse's mouth.'

'Father?'

'Father's diaries. I've been reading them in chronological order, up until today. Today – because of Mr Thompson's accusations – I read his diary for last year, just before the Seraphim race.'

James said nothing, but watched her silhouetted against the doorway.

Constance said, 'He wrote in May that he would have to do something about Gerhard Brunner, he didn't know what. He was convinced, wasn't he, that Gerhard would beat him, and that he would lose the Seraphim Trophy? Of course, you'd been to Lindau in April, to watch Gerhard testing the *Lorelei*? I hadn't realized that Gerhard was flying so much faster. Your father always told *me* that of course he would win, Gerhard didn't stand an earthly.'

She turned away, so that her face was in profile, the profile that Bryan King-Moreton had worshipped so much. '"It's essential that we do something about G.B.," that's what he wrote, and he had underlined "essential" three times. On the following page, he had written "James has spoken to J. Some hope now!"'

She said, softly, 'The "J" you spoke to was Jacko Gibbons, I presume. And what your father decided was essential was the burning of the *Lorelei* so that Gerhard Brunner couldn't take away his precious trophy. Isn't that true?'

James remained silent.

'Well,' said Constance, 'it doesn't really matter now. It's all academic. Three good men have managed to lose their lives over a silver cup. It's rather pathetic, isn't it? Like burning to death, while trying to save somebody else's cat.'

James said, without emotion, 'I'll get John Tremlett to draw up the bank papers in the morning. I'll be gone by the weekend. I have one or two things to clear up first.'

Constance nodded. For some reason, she seemed reluctant to leave the room.

'One more thing, James,' she said; and her voice now was very unsteady.

'Mother?'

'What you said about your father ... about another woman. That wasn't true, was it.'

James put down his pencil. 'To be honest, Mother, I haven't the faintest idea. You know what Father's sense of humour was like.'

'Sense of humour,' Constance repeated. 'My God, James, your father had no sense of humour.'

She came across the foyer of the brand-new Dorchester Hotel, tall and elegant as ever, in a silk evening-dress of aquamarine and a white stole of Siberian fox. James approached her with both hands held out, and held her close, and kissed her perfumed, powdered cheek, soft with the softness of approaching middle-age.

'How are you, Susan?' he asked her.

She smiled up at him bright-eyed. 'Better for seeing you, after all this time.'

He lifted his eyes and looked around. 'I've never been here before. It's quite a place, isn't it?' The foyer was busy with that expensive bustle of evening dress and porters and revolving doors and people going out to the theatre or coming in for cocktails. On all sides there were bronze bowls with lavish arrangements of roses and gladioli and soft pink lights gleaming. It was all fearfully modern. *The Times* had complained that it made Park Lane look like Fifth Avenue.

James looked at his watch. 'I've booked us a table at Au Petit Coin De France. Nobody knows me there.'

'I've never even heard of it.'

'A great rendezvous for illicit lovers, so they tell me. And cheap, too. Listen – there's a taxi waiting outside. Do you have everything? We could go straight away.'

They left the Dorchester and climbed into the taxi. James said, 'Barnaby Street, if you would.'

'Barnaby Street?' asked the cabbie, without taking his cigarette out of his mouth.

'Well, it's just behind Liberty's.'

'Oh, Carnaby Street. Right-ho, guvnor.'

They sat at a small candlelit table in the corner and it was just like all those other evenings they had spent together, only this time James was married and there were questions to be asked. On all those other evenings, it had never been necessary for them to ask each other anything at all. They had accepted their affair for what it was, and enjoyed it, and never demanded anything but amusement and loyalty and truth.

Susan hadn't touched her *pâté de Strasbourg*. 'You know something,' she said, looking at James with the candle flame dancing in her eyes, 'you hurt me very much when you married Miss B-S.'

'I was bound to get married one day,' James replied.

'Well, of course. You want heirs, don't you, not to mention graces.'

'I see we're very sharp tonight.'

'You could have *told* me.' Susan insisted. 'All you needed to do was drop me a note, or pick up the telephone. What hurt so much was the fact that you didn't think to *tell* me. Who knows, I might have had the courage to divorce Rodney and marry you myself.'

James lowered his eyes. Susan reached across the red gingham tablecloth and touched his hand. 'I forgot,' she said, softly. 'I'm not really much use to you, am I, unless I'm married to Rodney? You don't want my body; you just want my inside information. The Director's missus. Mrs Leda-Hyphen-Cable.'

James said, 'I know you're hurt. But you don't have to be unfair. The fact is that Patricia was Michael's girlfriend; and Michael is the one who really loves her. I put her in the family way by accident. Well, mostly by accident. I was ashamed to tell you about it, if you want to know the truth.'

Susan laughed in disbelief. 'You've never been ashamed of anything in your life.'

'You don't think so?' James asked her, lifting his head. 'I took my brother's girlfriend to bed, made her pregnant, then married her without loving her. Now I can scarcely stand the sight of her and I don't know what to do.'

Susan drank a little champagne, and then looked steadily across the table at him, her hands steepled, her expression very calm. 'Are you going to take me to bed tonight?' she asked him.

James looked back at her, held her gaze, then looked away.

'Well, I thought not,' she said, with pain in her voice. 'That's what I've become. An old chum, that's all. A bare shoulder for you to cry on. And we swam together naked in Cuckoo Weir!'

'Droopy drawers,' James smiled, in fond memory.

Susan shook her head. 'I forbid you even to remember it. It's gone.'

'Never,' said James.

They drank more wine. A toothless man with an accordion leaned over their table and played a wheezing French tune until James gave him two bob to play on the other side of the restaurant. They had both ordered veal stew, but they ate very little of it and pushed their plates away. James lit a cigarette.

'I'm off to America at the weekend,' he said. Then he added, 'Probably for good.'

'For good? But why?' Susan was shocked.

'It's Mother. She seems to have got it into her head that I was responsible for what happened to Bryan King-Moreton. In fact she almost seems to believe that I scuppered the *Chichester Special* on purpose.'

'That's preposterous!'

'Of course it's preposterous. But I've had quite enough of Mother for the time being. And I've got the chance of going across to Florida and buying my own airline.'

'Your bloody mother,' said Susan. 'First Michael, and now you.'

'Yes,' James nodded. 'My bloody mother.'

'Is that why you wanted to see me tonight?' Susan asked him. 'To tell me that we're never going to see each other again?'

'I wanted to see you tonight because you're quite unlike any other woman I've ever known. Simply to sit and talk to you makes me remember that life is worth living.'

'Well, well, there's a compliment,' said Susan, but she couldn't stop herself from smiling.

'It's the truth,' James told her. 'And, besides, there's no reason why we shouldn't meet again, is there? Rodney takes you to America every couple of years, doesn't he?'

'Do you think you can keep a torch burning for me for two years?' Susan smiled, wryly.

James held her hand between his. 'I can keep a torch burning for you for ever and ever amen.'

Susan sat back. 'It's no use, James. It's over, isn't it? History has overtaken us at last.'

James paid the bill and then they walked arm in arm along the dark cobbles of Carnaby Street, back towards the lights of Regent Street. When they reached the corner by Liberty's, James held her tightly and kissed her, and she left one single tear on the collar of his evening-coat.

'Goodnight, madam,' James whispered.

'Goodnight, sir,' replied the Director's missus.

Darwin, 1932

She came out on deck for the first time when they were nine hours out from Ceylon, on their way towards Sumatra. Michael noticed her straight away. She stood by the open cabin doors for a moment, shielding her eyes with her hand. She wore a pale blue headscarf that flapped in the warm morning wind; and a pale blue sundress with a low waist and a square-cut neck. Plain, but not dowdy.

After a moment, she walked across to the rail, and rested her arms on it, but then immediately took them away again, because the varnish was too hot.

She walked up the promenade a little way, and then back again. A middle-aged Portuguese man in wide flappy shorts raised his hat to her, and said something, but she turned away. The Portuguese man waited beside her for a moment, and then strolled off, with his hands in his pockets.

Michael wasn't sure what it was about her that had caught his attention. She was so far away that it was difficult to tell whether she was pretty or not; although there was something about the way that her bobbed brunette hair swung when she walked, something about her narrow ankles and her long legs and the way that she carried herself that convinced him she couldn't be ugly.

He remained where he was, twenty feet above her, leaning against the rail of the first-class promenade, in his beige linen suit and his wide straw hat, watching her parade herself on the second-class promenade. He lit a cigarette. He wondered why she hadn't appeared before. She must have come out from Southampton. He hadn't seen her board at Lisbon or Port Said or Colombo, and her arms and legs were still white. Most of the English passengers, Michael included, had already lost their pallor by the time they were halfway through the Med; and by the time they had reached the southern end of the Suez Canal, and tropical kit was in order, Michael had left behind forever the pasty-faced radical in the sleeveless Fair-Isle pullover and the unpressed bags who had struggled up the ship's gangway at Southampton. He looked lean and fit and brown; he had shaved off his Hitler moustache; and a week of dinners and parties and socializing had revived his interest in having a good time.

Paul Heath and that railway compartment at Redhill seemed like nothing more than a half-forgotten nightmare, a secret box full of nasty and complicated tricks. Something to be left in the attic, along with the bald rocking-horse with the glue-scabs where its mane should have been, and the dusty cardboard boxes packed with Grandmother's neatly-folded stays.

This journey on the *Alexandria* had restored Michael's faith in himself and his upbringing. It hadn't changed his determination to be true to his own convictions; but it had led him to recognize the value of being loyal to his family; and the importance of doing his duty; and the obligation that was incumbent on every Englishman from the minute he was born to Be Of Good Heart.

Perhaps his exile hadn't yet taught him that true love can never be selfish: but he would learn.

The ocean was calm and stunningly hot. It shone like a lake of molten blue wax. The *Alexandria* passed through it at eleven knots; hardly fast enough to stir the Greek flag that hung from her stern. The days were passed in drinking gin and playing bridge and trying to sleep in sweat-tangled beds, and watching the glittering wake spread endlessly westwards behind them. Michael could already understand why India hands pined for England's cricket-pitches; oaks and green grass and Wootton Bassett.

A tall girl called Lucy Parminter came up to Michael and leaned with her back on the rail. She was on her way to join her people at K.L. Daddy was a rubber-planter, and Mummy was frightfully good at painting. Lucy had been finishing in Lausanne, but now she wanted to go back to Malaya to get married. 'Preferably to somebody who knows something about rubber.'

'Jolly warm,' said Lucy. Her freckled face was shaded by a huge straw hat, and she was sipping a crème-de-menthe frappé.

Michael smoked and nodded.

'You're not out of sorts, are you?'

Michael shook his head.

'I mean, if you're out of sorts, you shouldn't really come to the dance tonight, should you? I can always find somebody else to make up our table. Mummy used to say you can never enjoy yourself if you're out of sorts. You might as well stay at home and read a geebee.' She paused, and then she said, 'That's our family slang for "good book", of course, geebee.'

Michael stood up straight. 'I'm all right. I was just thinking.'

'Oh, yes! And what were you thinking?'

'I was thinking about class. You remember I told you all about that Socialist chap I knew, Paul Heath. He always used to say that the only people guilty of class prejudice were the workers. The workers allowed the bosses to oppress them, that's what he used to say. In fact, not only *allowed* them, but *invited* them.'

Lucy Parminter stared at Michael and said, 'Are you feeling all right? Perhaps you ought to go in.'

'Of course I'm feeling all right. I was just looking down at the second-class deck and thinking, they're the same as we are, and yet they have to stay down there, segregated. Second-class, in fact.'

Lucy Parminter turned around and frowned down at the second-class passengers as if they were so inconsequential that she found it difficult to get them into focus. 'Well,' she said, after some thought, 'you wouldn't want them up here, would you?'

'I wouldn't mind.'

'But that's what you paid for. You *paid* not to mix with them. And they paid less so that they wouldn't have to mix with you. It cuts both ways, you know, Michael. You said it yourself. The lower classes are far more prejudiced than the upper classes. Daddy says that, come the revolution, he's going to keep bottles of HP Sauce on the dining-room table, all day, in case any working-class people burst in unexpectedly.'

'What?' asked Michael. The girl in the pale blue scarf had appeared again, and was standing close to one of the lifeboats, her arms crossed over her breasts, staring out to sea.

'Michael – it's a well-known fact that all working-class people keep sauce bottles on the dining-room table all day. I don't know why, they just do. It's a kind of a symbol, I suppose. You know, like the Flying Lady on a Rolls-Royce.'

Michael turned to her irritably. Together, the heat of the sun and the clacking of Lucy Parminter's conversation were beginning to make him feel cross. 'Most working-class people don't have dining-rooms,' he told her. 'And besides, look at *her*. She doesn't look the type to be prejudiced.'

Lucy Parminter took a long time to locate the girl in the pale-blue scarf. 'Her?' she said, at last. 'What's so special about her? She looks like a fishwife.'

Michael was about to say something angry, but then he decided against it. He didn't want to tell Lucy Parminter that he had seen somebody who had caught his attention and held it; somebody he wanted to know simply because he had seen her from a distance; and who seemed to be lonely and attractive and in need of a man to look after her.

'What time is the dance?' he asked, flicking his cigarette out into the ocean.

Lucy was alert enough to realize that several cars of his train of thought had passed her by, unmarked and unnoticed; but she said, brightly, 'You're coming then? You're not all *that* dicky?'

'No,' said Michael. 'I'm not all *that* dicky.'

She was standing at the rail watching the sun drop like a blood-red fertilized egg-yolk into the sea. Only a few feet away, the Greek flag rumbled and quavered; the rising wind played Jew's-harp tunes through the wires. She still wore her pale-blue scarf and her pale-blue dress; Michael supposed that second-class passengers probably didn't have all that many changes of clothing. He walked across the deck towards her and stood a little way away with his hands in his pockets, admiring the sunset and listening to the endless churning of the ship's screws.

'Magnificent, isn't it?' he said, at last.

She didn't say anything. He suddenly realized that she hadn't noticed him; or, if she had, she thought he was talking to somebody else. He stepped closer to the rail, and turned, and smiled at her widely.

'Magnificent, isn't it?' he repeated.

'Oh, the sunset,' she said. 'Yes, it is. You never see anything like it in England.'

She had a soft, burring accent – a country accent, Wiltshire or Somerset. She turned to him, and smiled; and he saw that his first impression of her had been right. She was plump, but very pretty indeed, with wide brown eyes, amber-flecked now in the light of the setting sun, and a short straight nose, and lips that could have been made out of pink ribbons, tied in bows. She was wide-shouldered, and very large-breasted. From his vantage point on the first-class promenade, he hadn't realized how large-breasted she was, because the squarish front of her dress had concealed it. It was unfashionable, but Michael found it disturbingly attractive.

'I saw you this afternoon,' he told her. 'I was – you know, up there.' He nodded towards the first-class promenade, and then suddenly thought what a snobbish gesture that was. 'I hadn't seen you before,' he added, trying to be conciliatory. 'I mean, I noticed you straight away.'

'Well,' she said, turning back to watch the sunset, as if that were a great deal more interesting, 'I had the German measles. I was in the ship's hospital for four days. Besides that, I was seasick, too.'

'I'm sorry,' said Michael. 'Are you better now?'

'Oh, yes. Takes a lot to keep a Herridge down.'

'That's your name, Herridge?'

She nodded. 'Come from Frome, most of the Herridges.'

'Are you going all the way to Darwin?'

She smiled. 'Further than that. Barrow Creek. My husband's got a farm there. Well, we've got a farm there. Leonard went out two years ago; I'm just going to join him.'

Michael said, 'Quite an adventure. You must be looking forward to seeing him again.'

'Yes,' she replied. 'Well.'

Michael refused to let her end the conversation. He held out his hand and said, 'Michael Lord. But please call me Michael.'

She hesitated for a moment, but then she took hold of his hand, and clasped it in a peculiarly awkward way, and said, 'Violet, I'm afraid.'

'Why are you afraid?'

She shrugged, 'Violet's rather a plain name, isn't it? My Gran was called Violet.'

Michael kept hold of her hand and wouldn't let go. 'Do you know what Shakespeare said about violets, in *King John*? He said, "To gild refined gold, to paint the lily, to throw a perfume on the violet, is wasteful and ridiculous excess".'

Violet slowly extricated her hand from his. 'I'm not sure I know what that means,' she said, not upset, but bemused.

'It simply means that violets can't be improved. And I think I rather agree with that.'

Violet glanced back towards the first-class section of the ship, her brow furrowed. 'Are you allowed – being first class and all . . .?'

'Of course I'm allowed. I could travel with the stokers if I wanted to.'

'Oh,' she said. 'I just thought . . . well, I don't know.'

He stayed beside her as the sun sank and the *Alexandria* ploughed her way eastwards, towards the nothern tip of Sumatra. The stars began to come out; thousands of them, one after another, as if the streetlights of heaven were being lit. The ocean was so calm that on the horizon the larger stars were bisected by the sea. Soon it was quite dark, and almost everybody else had gone to change for dinner, but Michael and Violet stayed out on the deck together, listening to the wash-wash-wash of the screws, and the snapping of the flag.

'It's a bit frightening,' said Violet. 'You know – not having seen him for so long.'

'Couldn't you have gone out to Australia with him?' asked Michael.

'I wanted to, but I had his old Da to look after. Somebody had to. He only died this Easter. We've been writing, and that. But of course it isn't the same, you get estranged.'

Michael offered her a cigarette but she shook her head. 'Never smoked, not ever.' He lit one himself and blew smoke out into the warm darkness.

'Why did your husband want to go to Australia in the first place?'

Violet slowly shook her head. 'Don't know, really. It was always something he wanted to do, ever since he was a lad. I never believed he'd do it, until the slump; and that gave him the reason for going. He could never take the responsibility for doing what he wanted, do you know what I mean? He always had to pretend that he was being forced into it.'

Michael said, 'There's a dance tonight, in first-class. Perhaps you'd like to come.'

'They wouldn't allow me, would they?'

'If you're my guest, they'll have to allow you.'

'Oh, no,' said Violet. 'I couldn't do that. I wouldn't have the nerve. Besides, I haven't got anything to wear.'

'You must have *one* evening dress.'

She pressed her hands together. 'Well, yes, I've got *one*.'
Michael looked at his watch. 'That settles it, then. I'll meet you
outside the second-class dining-room at seven.'
He tossed his cigarette into the invisible sea.

Michael was a few minutes late, because he had stopped to knock
at Lucy Parminter's stateroom door and tell her that he wouldn't
be joining her table that evening; but in any case, *she* didn't care
(or at least she pretended she didn't) because a tall gingery Army
captain called Timothy Witherspoon had been pestering her all
afternoon to let him join what he described as 'the gay young set'.

He came down the stairs to the doors of the second-class dining-
room and Violet was already waiting for him. She was wearing a
long evening-gown of dark red taffeta, with a halter top and a
florid bow over the bust. Her hair was brushed and shiny, and
held back with two diamante clips. She carried a small silver
evening-bag that didn't match anything she was wearing.

'Violet?' he said. She turned around, but she didn't recognize
him at first in his evening-dress, white tie and tailcoat.

'Michael?'

He came forward and kissed her on both cheeks. 'You look
wonderful,' he told her.

'Oh, come on,' she said, shyly. 'It's only the dress I bought for
when we went to Taunton, to the farm ball.'

'That doesn't make it any less wonderful. Come on upstairs,
and we'll have a couple of cocktails before dinner.'

She looked up the stairway. On the riser of the top step were
painted the forbidding words, First-Class Passengers Only. 'I'm
frightened,' she said. 'I mean, it'd be different if I had a first-class
ticket.' Michael took hold of her arm. He loved the way she said
'tick-ut', in that soft Somerset voice.

'If there's any problem,' he said, 'I'll pay the difference; and
then you can travel all the way to Darwin first-class. Hob-nobbing
with the nobs. Most of whom are very un-nob-like, I have to warn
you.'

Reluctantly, she allowed him to lead her up to the first-class
promenade deck, and into the Acropolis Bar, with its pink mirrors
and its marble-effect pillars. The bar was crowded with passengers
in evening-dress; although few of them were at all fashionable.
They were mostly rubber-planters and shipping-agents and their
lady wives, returning to Singapore and Kuala Lumpur after a spell
of leave. There was one stunning woman with blonde braided hair
and a clinging silk gown in shining gold, who was surrounded by

228

six or seven attentive chaps, laughing uproariously at every tinkling remark she made. But on the whole the men wore fusty-looking evening-dress that looked as if it were too tight under the arms, and sat with their fingers laced together staring at the onions nodding in their pink gins; while the wives had fraying hair and distant, resigned expressions, and kept making isolated remarks like 'Freddie Miles should be back by Christmas,' and 'Hong Li's have stopped doing Rowntree's Cocoa, did I tell you that?'

'What would you like to drink?' Michael asked Violet, leading her up to the bar. 'Here – here's a barstool, sit yourself down.'

'I'll have a sweet sherry, please,' said Violet.

'Oh, come on, how about something more adventurous? Tonight, we're going to throw caution to the winds!'

'You do say funny things,' Violet smiled. 'I never met anybody who talked like you.'

'I'm feeling particularly cheerful, that's why,' Michael told her. 'Do you know something, I've been in prison, and I've just been released.'

'Really?' she frowned. 'What were you in for?'

'I don't mean real prison. I mean I was mentally locked up.'

'What, an asylum?' Violet began to look concerned.

Michael laughed. 'I was locked up in here, inside my own head. It can happen sometimes. You're so sure that you're right about everything, and that everybody else is wrong, that you forget to behave like a human being.'

'You seem human enough to me.'

'Well, I'm human now; but I wasn't before. That's part of the reason I'm here, on my way to Darwin.'

Violet smiled brightly. 'All right, then, if we're going to be adventurous, I'll have a champagne cocktail.'

'Good for you, I'll join you. Barman! Two champagne cocktails, if you will!'

It turned out to be one of the happiest evenings of Michael's life. He had actually forgotten what it was like to feel so exhilarated; to care about nothing but dancing and laughing. Violet was marvellous company. She talked to him so earnestly and so straightforwardly, quite unlike any of the girls he had known in London and Cambridge. She told him funny, affectionate stories about the farm on which she was brought up – about the night her father had celebrated his birthday too enthusiastically, and fallen into the pig-pen – about her mother baking and leaving the cakes on the window-sill to cool – about days when unending rain turned the farmyard into a miserable morass, and other days when the summer wind had blown across a sky the colour of cornflowers.

They had three champagne cocktails each; and then they sat down for dinner with a group of young engineers and their wives, all on their way out to Malaya to build a new road system up-country. Everybody was quite merry and laughed a lot. One of the engineers could do an impersonation of W.C. Fields. 'Were there many great men born in this town?' 'No, only babies have ever been born here.' They were served with hot consommé soup and lamb cutlets with duchess potatoes, while a Greek pianist with shiny astrakhan hair and gold teeth played a selection of un-recognizable show tunes.

Lucy Parminter came past on her way to the powder-room, and dropped Michael a sarcastic little curtsey. 'Well, well, aren't you clever,' she said. 'Fancy picking out the most attractive of all the girls in second-class.'

Michael's heartbeat quickened, but he bowed his head to her and said, 'Better than picking the least attractive girl in first-class, don't you think?'

Lucy glared at Violet, and flounced off to powder her nose, almost tripping over the carpet.

Violet looked at Michael across the table and gave him a smile that was warm and grateful.

Afterwards, they danced out on deck to the *Alexandria*'s six-piece orchestra, while the Milky Way glittered up above them, and the south-easterly wind blew softly in their hair.

Holding Violet close, Michael said, 'You've changed my whole life in one evening. How did you manage to do that?'

She smiled at him. Her eyes sparkled. 'I didn't do anything. It's you. And you've changed me, too.'

They danced into the darkness, beside the rail. They stopped dancing. Michael took Violet's face between his hands and looked at her warmly. 'You've stirred me up, Mrs Herridge.'

She whispered, 'Don't call me that. Call me Violet.'

He kissed her forehead. Her skin was very soft and slightly damp. He kissed her nose. He felt her eyelashes fluttering against his lips. Butterfly kisses.

'Let's go to my stateroom,' he said.

She nodded.

He stood behind her, and put his arms around her waist. They stared at each other in the mirror, as if they were staring at two strangers. In a way, they were. They had both discovered this even-ing a happier personality that, until now, had remained masked.

'Do you know something,' said Michael, 'I fell in love with you even before I saw your face.'

She turned her head and kissed his cheek. 'You're not in love with me, silly. You're infatuated.'

'Look at you,' he said. 'How could I *not* be in love with you?'

'I'm too fat,' she replied. 'I always have been. If you knew the diets I've tried.'

'You're not too fat, you're perfect.'

'If you think I'm perfect, you're not just infatuated. You're not in love, neither. You're cuckoo.'

He kissed the back of her neck. Her hair smelled of cigarette smoke and honeysuckle. She was wearing a white brassière and a white Veil of Youth corset, with black silk stockings. 'You're the most beautiful girl I've ever met,' he whispered, kissing her ear.

'Too fat,' she protested.

He unfastened the catch of her brassière and they both watched in the mirror as he took it off and dropped it on the bed. Her breasts were very large and heavy, but very firm. He cupped them in his hands and stroked her nipples with the tips of his fingers, until they crinkled like pink tissue paper.

She sighed, and closed her eyes, but then she opened them again, because it aroused her to watch him rolling and squeezing her nipples between his fingers. She leaned her head back on his shoulder and sighed, and he kissed her.

'Do you know what Leonard once said to me?' Violet whispered, 'He said that there isn't a woman in the world who's truly faithful.'

Michael felt the warm weight of Violet's breasts in his hands and didn't really care what Leonard had said.

Violet turned around and put her arms around Michael's waist. 'When he went to Australia, he said he wasn't going to ask me to stay true; but if I wasn't, he'd always know.'

'Do you think he really *will* know?'

'I don't know,' she said, with an unexpectedly arch smile. 'I haven't been untrue to him yet.'

Naked, Violet had a pale, Rubenesque softness about her; smooth white skin and a rounded stomach. Michael, skinny and suntanned, except for the striking white stripe where his swimming-briefs had been, knelt beside her and kissed her with all the passion that six champagne cocktails and a warm night on the Indian Ocean could stir up. He kissed her breasts, and she closed her eyes again, and moaned and murmured, and ruffled his hair with her fingers.

He kissed her between her thighs. He had never done that to a woman before. Instead of closing her legs together, however, as he was afraid she might, she opened them wider, encouraging him to kiss deeper.

He explored her with his tongue-tip. She tasted sweet and liquid, like thin honey. She grasped his arm tightly and said something that he didn't understand.

There was a brief awkward pause before they made love while Michael searched through his wallet. But Violet was patient and calm, and smiled at him while he got himself ready. Michael could glimpse their reflection in the mirror as they made love. It wasn't like strangers any more, it was actually them, Michael and Violet. Her nipples were wet from his kisses. She bit at his shoulder; a sharp painful act of union. When it was over they lay side by side in silence for a very long time, listening to the vibration of the ship's diesels. Michael's toothbrush rattled in its glass. The stateroom smelled of Violet's perfume and sex.

At last Michael sat up and kissed her. 'I'm going to have a gasper. Want a drink?'

'Only if it's champagne,' she teased him, kissing him back.

'You're getting first-class tastes already,' he remarked.

'That doesn't upset you, does it?'

'Why should it?'

'I don't know; perhaps you won't find me so interesting if I get a taste for champagne.'

Michael, naked, stood by the bureau and lit a Fribourg & Treyer cigarette. He laughed. The match tinkled in the ashtray. 'I'm not slumming, if that's what you're thinking.'

She patted the quilt. 'Come back to bed. I like to watch the smoke curling up.'

He climbed back into bed and lay next to her, blowing smoke-rings at the ceiling. Violet snuggled up close to him, her cheek against his bare chest. They stayed like that in silence for almost five minutes. It was only when a single warm tear slid down the side of his body that Michael realized she was crying.

'Ssh,' he told her. 'You haven't done anything wrong.'

'All this time,' she wept. 'I've been faithful to him all this time; and now I'm almost there, I've been and gone and betrayed him.'

'Ssh,' said Michael. And thought: you're sad, but I'm glad.

It was eleven o'clock on a hot glaring morning when they glimpsed the white lighthouse on Emery Point, outside the two-mile-wide entrance to Port Darwin. They leaned on the rail as the *Alexandria* churned her way slowly through the eddying tide rip, watching the shoreline, their hands shielding their eyes.

'Australia,' said Violet, gripping Michael's hand.

'You're not frightened, are you?' asked Michael.

She shook her head fiercely. 'Not of Australia, I'm not.'

'What about Leonard?'

'Don't ask me yet about Leonard.'

Michael put his arm around her, and kissed her. 'I think I believe in fate,' he told her. 'And I think fate's going to be very good to both of us.'

Beyond the breakers rose a low plateau, thickly forested with gum trees. Here and there, the continuity of the shoreline was broken by cliffs and small pebbly beaches, but these were darkly concealed by overgrowing banyan trees and the light feathery foliage of giant wattles, as well as glistening palms and bamboos.

Close to the shore, a pearling lugger was anchored, with greyish diving suits dancing from its mast-stays like cut-out newspaper dollies.

Michael looked to the west as the *Alexandria* sailed into the wide sparkling waters of the harbour, and set eyes for the first time on the Residency, standing on a prominent jut – the home of His Honour, the Government Resident. Turning towards the east, he saw two precipitous hills, Fort Hill and Stokes' Hill, rich with vegetation. Between them, several steamers were already moored along an L-shaped jetty, their rusty sides reflected in the bright blue bay.

Slowly, the *Alexandria* turned herself around, and was brought up to the jetty. Lines were thrown to the muscular wharfies waiting below, and accompanied by a bellowed litany of bad language, the ship was at last brought to rest.

'There's Watling!' cried Michael. 'My God, he hasn't changed a bit! Watling! Watling! Halloo Watling!'

Standing on the jetty below them was a pudgy young man with a red race and a very white shorts and socks. He was waving his hat from side to side to keep himself cool; but as soon as he caught sight of Michael he tossed it up in the air, and almost lost it under the wheels of a lorry.

'Lord!' he shouted out. 'Disembark now! Don't worry about your luggage! I'll have it all sorted out for you later!'

'And this lady's?'

'Michael, no,' said Violet, tugging at his sleeve. 'Michael – Leonard has most probably come to meet me.'

Michael stared at her. 'You don't want to say goodbye now? I thought –'

She looked back at him with agonized tenderness. 'There's no changing it, Michael, for all that we've been to each other, I'm another man's wife.'

Michael hesitated. He was close to the brink of doing something impetuous and stupid, like asking Violet to dodge her husband, if he were waiting for her, and run through the customs shed with a parasol hiding her face, and come away to live with him. But he knew from sharp experience what could happen when he tried to force his passions on to other people's hearts. He wouldn't have been exiled to Australia if he had kept his temper with Patricia. So he took a deep breath, and looked away for a while, drawing composure out of the humid tropical air, and out of the sight of Fort Hill, with its vivid green vegetation, dropping straight into the deep waters of Darwin harbour.

He turned back again. There was an expression on Violet's face that he had never seen on anybody's face before. It was a look of total loss; but also of acceptance. He could see that she had fallen in love with him.

'Well,' he said, kissing her gently, those little wisps of brunette hair that strayed from her hat. 'We were only infatuated, weren't we?'

He left her on the promenade deck and went down the hessian-carpeted gangplank with his hands in his pockets; and only looked back once. Violet was standing well away from the rail, in case Leonard was anywhere about, one hand lifted, a handkerchief pressed to her mouth.

Watling came up, his fat knees shaking, and slapped Michael on the back. 'Lord, old man! You've actually made it! Welcome to the capital of the north! Not to mention the hottest hotbed of boozers, gamblers, and licentious profligates anywhere in Australia! Damned warm, isn't it? Come along, and I'll get you through all the formalities.'

Watling put his arm around Michael, and propelled him in a chummy fashion along the jetty. He hadn't changed since the fourth form at Lancing. Still as fat, still as sweaty, still as garrulous. Watling had gone through miseries of baiting and bullying at school, but somehow he had always managed to wipe his tears and blow his nose and smile with his tormentors at his own ungainly body.

'It's a damned nuisance,' he explained, 'but everybody who arrives in Darwin has to walk half a mile along this ridiculous jetty, no matter how bloody hot it is, or how bloody wet it is! It's the L-turn in it, you see. You can't get a whole train down to the end of the jetty, where the ships lie; you can only take it carriage by carriage, which is a damned slow tantalizing business, and wangle it around on that turn-table. Still, you see, the wharfies wouldn't have it any different, because it slows up their work, and they get paid so much more. I'm not sure *I'd* have it any other way, either, because it's certainly slowed down the success of any businesses here in Darwin, and I do like it quiet.'

'I don't even know what you do,' said Michael. 'Your mother said something about banking.'

'Well, I *was* banking,' Watling told him. 'I was deputy accountant at the Tin Bank. They call it the Tin Bank because it's made of tin – or corrugated iron, actually. They also call it the Tin Bank so that you won't mistake it for the Stone Bank, which is made of stone.'

They were crossing a dusty railway yard, with overgrown tracks and sidings. On the far side of it there was a collection of huge rusting oil-tanks, a reminder of Darwin's strategic position in Australia's scheme of national defence. Watling said, 'We could go up the steps, but it's too bloody warm.'

Then he added, 'These days, well, I don't do much banking, but I do a bit of this and a bit of that.'

They left the customs shed and walked out on to the street. An enormous dusty Buick with huge headlamps was parked under the shade of an astonishingly green tamarind tree. 'That's my bus,' said Watling. 'Don't worry about your luggage. They'll send it around later.'

They climbed into the car. After he had settled himself down, Watling said, 'By the way, I don't know if you ever knew it, but my name's Clarence.'

He started up the engine, and drove off, blaring his horn at some Aborigine children playing in the road. 'I couldn't tell anybody at school, of course; they would have ragged me to death. But my people didn't do it on purpose. They thought Clarence was heroic, a hero's sort of name.'

Michael sat back and looked around him. The small city of Darwin was laid out in squares, with wide streets overshadowed by wind-rustled milkwoods and stately dark green calophyllums. In spite of the tropical humidity, however, there were few proper gardens; the ironstone bedrock was only a foot or two below the surface, and frequently outcropped. The best that anybody could do was plant crotons and other tropical plants in oil-drums and kerosene tins, painted white. The tins kept in the moisture and kept out the termites.

The rusty-coloured ironstone had been hewn out to build some of the city's statelier buildings, but most of the shops and houses were constructed of wood and corrugated-iron. 'You'll find that most people in Darwin still tend to date things before and after the '91 Cyclone,' Clarence Watling remarked. 'That was when most of the city got blown away in one night. Big-fellah wind, the Abos call it. You see that bare concrete patch where those children are playing marbles? Well, there are quite a few of those still. The owners won't rebuild, don't you know, because they're afraid the big-fellah wind might suddenly decide to play a return engagement.'

They drew up outside the Victoria Hotel, which was a handsome orangey-coloured ironstone building in the mid-Victorian style, with white architraves over its three upstairs windows. The roof, however, was corrugated iron. 'I've booked you a room here, just for now,' said Clarence. 'You would have been welcome to stay with me, out at Myilly Point, but my bungalow's rather on the tight side, I'm afraid, and I don't have the space for another bed. Besides, I'm always doing business, day and night, and you wouldn't care too much for all my to-ing and fro-ing.' He flapped his hand to and fro just to give Michael some idea of how much to-ing and fro-ing there was.

'This looks as if it will do very well,' said Michael.

'Well, then, let's go inside and have a drink,' Clarence suggested.

They walked through the stuffy lobby into the hotel lounge. The walls were hung with large dusty mirrors with gilded frames; the ceiling was alive with endlessly-turning fans. Clarence waved to the Chinese waiter, and ordered them each a gin-sling. They dragged over two cane chairs and put their feet up.

'This is the jolly old life,' Clarence told Michael, scooping macadamia nuts out of a glass dish and noisily churning them around in his mouth. 'I'll give you one word of warning, though, here and now. It's jolly easy to get too dependent on the jolly old gargle, in this climate. So keep a watchful eye on your elbow-bending. Best thing to do is to cultivate an interest: chess, or stamp-collecting, or sport. My pal Gorringe goes bird-watching. Fig-birds, wood-swallows. Packet of sandwiches and a pair of binoculars, nothing like it. There's plenty of golf and cricket in the Dry; and there's football in the Wet, providing you don't mind mud.'

He sniffed, and said, 'This, of course, is the Dry. But we'll start getting rain by the end of September. You won't recognize the jolly old place.'

'What do you do?' asked Michael, as the waiter brought their drinks. 'I mean, what interests do *you* cultivate?'

Clarence picked up his drink, and smiled broadly, and said, 'This and that. This and that. Chin-chin!'

Michael had only just raised his drink when the lounge doors swung open again and Violet stepped in, accompanied by a broad-shouldered man in a badly-creased linen suit, with semi-circles of dark sweat under the armpits. The man had a broken sun-blistered nose, and a dark crimson complexion like burned beef. His hair had been bleached blond, and was cropped so short that it stuck up at the back of his head like a cockatoo. He kept a hand-rolled cigarette permanently between his lips, so that it waggled when he spoke.

Clarence caught the look in Michael's eye, and turned noisily around in his cane chair to see what had attracted Michael's attention. 'Well, well! Wasn't that the girl who was standing next to you on the steamer?'

Violet's attention was caught by Clarence's turning around, and she saw Michael. She quickly looked away, but Michael felt that he had no alternative but to stand up. Manners, after all, were manners. Clarence stood up, too.

The broad-shouldered man stared at them as if they were off their heads. 'Here,' he said to Violet, in a whisper that could have been heard in Alice Springs, 'is *that* him? One of those two galahs over there?'

'Mrs Herridge!' said Michael, clearly.

Violet came over, bringing the man with her. The man narrowed his eyes and stared at Michael as mistrustfully as if Michael were wearing lipstick and a woman's wig.

Michael took Violet's hand. 'Mrs Herridge and I met on the boat,' he explained.

'So Vi tells me,' the man commented, with no attempt to conceal his displeasure.

Violet said, 'This is my husband, Mr Leonard Herridge, from Barrow Creek. Darling, this is Mr Michael Cord.'

'Lord,' Michael corrected her.

'I'm sorry, Lord,' said Violet. She watched with a nervous little smile as the only two men who had made love to her in the whole of her life shook hands. Leonard's grip was horny and hard and aggressive.

'Pleased to meet you,' said Michael. Leonard said nothing.

'Are you staying in Darwin long?' Clarence asked the Herridges.

'Long as it takes to get my truck fixed,' said Leonard. 'Then it's straight back to Barrow Creek, sharpish.'

'I can't say that I *know* Barrow Creek awfully well,' Clarence admitted. 'In fact, I don't know it at all.'

Leonard let out an utterly humourless guffaw. 'You wouldn't want to, mate. There's bugger-all there but sheep, sheep-dip, sand, Abos, and shit.'

'*Leonard*,' Violet protested, her Somerset accent very soft and pronounced.

Leonard grunted and grinned. 'You'll get used to it, Vi. You're not in Frome now.'

'May I buy you both a drink?' asked Michael.

Violet was obviously about to say yes, but Leonard shook his head; although he kept on grinning. 'No thanks, mate. We'll get our own. And I'd do something about that nineteen-and-sixpenny accent of yours, if I were you. We don't have upper classes in this country. That's something you're going to have to find out.'

Violet gave Michael a quick regretful glance and turned away, clutching her handbag tightly in front of her as if it were an abandoned baby. Michael was about to sit down again, and was half-bent over his chair when Leonard came up close to him, his cigarette jiggling up and down between his lips, and said in a low menacing tone, 'I don't know what kind of stuck-up ideas you've been putting into Violet's head, Mr Cord or Lord or whatever your sodding name is, but she walked off that sodding boat full to the sodding ears of what you'd been telling her. A gentleman should always walk on the outside, Leonard; a gentleman never lights one fag off of another, Leonard; a gentleman never says bog. You would have thought she was Lady Copperbottoming. All I can say to you is this. Of all the towns in the Territory, you make sodding sure that you keep yourself well out of sniffing distance of Barrow Creek. And you keep your sodding hands off of my wife.'

Michael was about to say, 'Really, my dear chap, I don't know what on earth you're talking about,' but he decided that on the whole it would be safer not to. Instead, he said something unintelligible, like 'mahumh-humh', and quickly sat down, and stared at his drink as if he were trying to melt the ice by thought-power alone. Leonard stayed where he was, threateningly close, but Michael didn't look up. He was very aware of Leonard's trouser-legs, right next to him.

Clarence caught Michael's eye, then turned to Leonard. 'I think you'd better be toddling off, old man,' he suggested. 'We don't want to have to call the manager, do we, or anything rotten like that?'

'You just sodding-well remember what I said, that's all,'

Leonard warned Michael, and marched back across the lounge to rejoin Violet, tugging his jacket tight across his shoulders.

Clarence breathed out. 'Well, well, what *have* we been up to?'

Michael, tautly, said, 'Where *is* Barrow Creek? Do you really not know it?'

'Of course I know it. It's about six hundred miles south of here, on the way to Alice Springs. Still in the Territory, of course; but not particularly easy to get to. The railway only goes as far south as Elsey Station. Your friend there obviously drove, but it must have taken him the best part of three days, and it doesn't sound as if it did his truck much good. Dust, you see, and kangaroos. Not to mention sheer bloody monotony.'

Michael focused his eyes across the room at Violet. She was sitting with her back to him, but he could see her face in one of the mirrors; like a face in a faded portrait. Up above her, the ceiling-fans turned and turned in the hot musty air, like the propellers of a forgotten air-force.

'Do you know anybody in Darwin who flies?' Michael asked Clarence.

When Michael went to the main post office the following morning, there was an old telegram message waiting for him, from Richard. It read: BKM KILLED FLYING ACCIDENT MORE LATER. He stood outside the post office and read it three or four times, watched with unwavering interest by a small Aborigine boy wearing nothing but a shirt.

Early the following week, Michael was invited to dinner with Clarence at Myilly Point. Clarence's bungalow overlooked the broad sweep of Fannie Bay, with East Point in the distance. The evening was very clear; and the sea made that warm restless noise that Michael still found exciting. They had golden-skinned chicken, cooked by Clarence's Cantonese servant, with stir-fried vegetables and rice. Now they were out on the verandah drinking brandy, and smoking cigars, and feeling unusually contented.

The sea-wind blew through the frangipani trees; the spirit-lamp hissed and flared.

'I thought you said you were pushed for space,' Michael remarked, looking around at Clarence's sprawling outhouses and corrugated-iron sheds.

'I am, yes, as far as human accommodation is concerned,' said Clarence. 'But business always takes precedence, don't you see. All of these sheds are jamful of profitable produce. That's my business, profitable produce. Bringing together those who badly want something with what they badly want. Could be tinned tomatoes; could be photographic film. Could be petrol. Could be twelve-bore shotguns, or snakeskin belts. Clarence Watling will always deliver.'

Michael swallowed a glowing mouthful of Rémy Martin. 'I thought you hadn't changed,' he said. 'You know, since school. But you have, very much.'

Clarence grunted in amusement. 'You're wrong, I haven't changed a bit. I was always a survivor, first and foremost. You had to be, if you were a fat owl like me. You had to learn to please everybody, so that they wouldn't rag you. It became something of a habit, I suppose, pleasing people. Now I do it for a living. You want it, Clarence Watling can oblige.'

Michael smiled, remembering vividly the small fat boy who had cried in the cloakrooms, hiding under the raincoats so that nobody would see him.

'For instance,' said Clarence, 'I can get you what *you* want.'

'You don't even *know* what I want,' said Michael. 'I don't even know myself.'

Clarence peered down at his expensive gold wristwatch. 'That's where you're wrong. I've got a surprise for you, in about ten minutes' time.'

'It's not a woman, is it?' Michael asked, suspiciously.

Clarence laughed out loud. 'No, it isn't! But I can get you one if you want! There's a big Irish woman who lives at the end of Cavenagh Street, Brenda the Boomer they call her. Apparently she'll do anything at all, all night, and only expect seven-and-six and a fill of tobacco.'

'Oh, pull the other one,' Michael retorted.

Just then, from the Aboriginal compound, only a quarter of a mile away, Michael heard an extraordinary breathy booming sound, like somebody blowing across the neck of a huge bottle. He sat up in his cane-backed lounger, and said, 'What on earth is that?'

'Didgeridoo,' Clarence told him, almost off-handedly. 'It's a kind of wind-instrument the blackfellows play; made from a hollow tree-branch, or a hollow bamboo. They always play it along Kahlin Beach when it's time for their sacred ceremonies. Especially the what's-it's-name. Initiation. You know, when they make young men.'

Michael remained sitting upright, listening in fascination to the mystical chorale of this North Australian night: the seductive swallowing noises of the sea and the rustling of frangipani trees, the sawing of the insects, the high-pitched squealing of a lubra, and the shouts and whoops of Aborigine children playing on the beach in the darkness. All these sounds underlaid with the deep, vibrant, endless undertones of the didgeridoo.

'I could play some dance music on the gramophone, if that Abo music gets on your nerves,' Clarence suggested. 'Personally, I'm rather taken with it.' He reached over and refilled Michael's brandy-glass. 'I mean, it's not the sort of music you hear on Worthing beach, is it?'

'Will you ever go back?' asked Michael, picking up his glass. What he really meant was: do you think that *I'll* ever go back?

Clarence shook his head. 'I'm an old tropic-bird now. I think I'd probably die, if I had to go back.'

Michael swallowed brandy and gave an involuntary shiver.

It was then that Clarence's Chinese servant Heng appeared on the verandah, followed by a tall rangy-looking man in a cotton suit and a floppy wide-brimmed hat, smoking a pipe. 'Mr Fysh here, sah,' said Heng, and Clarence at once stood up.

'Hudson,' he beamed. 'Right on time. Come and have a noggin. This is Michael Lord, just arrived last week.'

'Well, well,' said Hudson Fysh, stepping forward with a broad smile and holding out his hand. 'Good to know you, Michael. I met your Dad, once, would you believe it? That was just before we started the old Cloncurry to Charleville route. He was trying to sell me one of his Aires biplanes. Unsuccessfully, I'm sorry to say.'

Michael said, 'It's a great pleasure to meet you, sir. Qantas is quite a legend.'

Hudson Fysh stretched himself out on one of Clarence's cane chairs. 'Don't get off on the wrong foot, Michael. My name happens to be Hudson, not sir. The only time you need to call me sir is when those unappreciative bastards back in England decide to give me a knighthood. Sir Hudson Fysh of Cloncurry.'

'Hudson is the surprise I promised you,' Clarence told Michael, with satisfaction.

'I'm honoured,' said Michael. He was a little drunk.

In fact, he felt not so much honoured as unreal. When he was younger, Hudson Fysh had been one of his heroes. With his friend P.J. McGinness, Hudson had started Australia's first airline, the Queensland and Northern Territory Air Service, a seat-of-the-pants outfit that had flown between the isolated railheads at Cloncurry, Longreach and Charleville.

Almost single-handedly, Hudson had taken the terror of total loneliness out of the Australian outback; not only ferrying passengers and mail, but taking doctors out to ranches and homesteads that had once been almost unreachable. Four years ago, the Most Reverend John Flynn had contracted Hudson to fly a physician out from his clinic at Cloncurry to anywhere medical help might urgently be needed. 'A Mantle of Safety', Flynn had called it; and to be sitting out on a tropical verandah with the heroic flyer who had made it possible was, for Michael, much more intoxicating than the brandy.

Hudson scoured out his pipe with a penknife, and relit it. 'I was damned upset to hear about Herbert, you know. Herbert was one of the classics. He practically wrote the book on seaplanes.'

'I'm sorry to say that Bryan King-Moreton is dead, too,' said Michael. 'I had a telegram that he was killed in a flying accident shortly after I left England. I don't exactly know what happened yet.'

'Dear me, old Kay-Em. That *is* a blow.' Hudson puffed at his pipe for a while, and then said, 'Not known for their longevity, you know, though. Pilots.'

There was another pause, and then Clarence said, 'I didn't invite Hudson here just for the fun of it, you know. He flew all the way from Camooweal, didn't you, Hudson?'

'That's right,' Hudson agreed, relaxing back in his chair with his ankles crossed, his eyes on the stars. He seemed to Michael to be utterly imperturbable; but if half of the stories about his flying exploits in sandstorms and floods and hundred-and-thirty degree heat were to be believed, he would have to have had an utterly imperturbable nature just to keep his sanity, let alone his life.

'Hudson has an offer for you,' Clarence coaxed him. 'Go on, Hudson, tell him.'

'Yes,' said Hudson. He looked at Michael keenly, one eyebrow raised, pipe steadily puffing. 'The thing of it is, I understand that you fly quite well. You would do, of course, having Herbert as a father. But the thing of it is, I want to extend my mail and passenger services from Darwin down to the Alice. Just a small service, one pilot flying a DH 9C, twice a week maybe, and carrying a doctor whenever he's needed. Not a lot of money in it, but plenty of freedom to use your own initiative.'

Michael stared at him, with a feeling of jubilation bubbling up inside him. 'You want *me* to do it?'

'That's the general drift of it.' Puff, puff. 'That's if you *want* to do it.'

'Want to? You must be pulling my leg! Clarence, this is absolutely the most wizard thing that anybody's ever done for me!

What a friend you are! Thank you!'

'You'll have to show me how well you can really fly,' Hudson put in. 'But it you're handy enough, and if you want the job, it's yours. I flew over in a DH 50; but there's a 9C out at the aerodrome. You can take her up tomorrow.'

Clarence laughed at Michael's delight. 'What did I tell you? Didn't I know exactly what you wanted?'

Michael said, 'This calls for another drink, definitely!'

'Don't take my plane up tomorrow with a hangover,' Hudson warned him, with a grin. 'She may be a cheap old kite; but she's still fit for another few hundred thousand.' He puffed, and then he said, 'Incidentally, that was why I didn't buy an Aries from your old man. Too damned expensive.'

He smiled to himself, and then he said, 'Did I ever tell you about the time that first DH 9 of ours went down with a broken crankshaft? We had to change the engine in the desert, temperature was up to a hundred and twenty. The tools were so bloody hot we had to keep dropping them into a bucket of water to cool them off.'

Michael sat back and listened, with an involuntary smile on his face. For a young man who had come out to Australia in disgrace, there could be nothing closer to heaven than this, sitting with one of the world's most famous flyers, listening to yarns about the early days of flying in the outback, while the distant didgeridoo boomed its prehistoric song across the bay.

The next morning, Michael flew the DH 9C over Darwin harbour, looping and turning between Fort Hill and Stokes' Hill, climbing over the point, and then angling back and buzzing the Residency. He looked over the side of the cockpit and saw people hurrying out into the Residency gardens to watch him, shading their eyes. He waggled his wings in acknowledgement.

He turned again and climbed towards the sun. He let out a cheer, and rolled the biplane over. He hadn't been so happy since he was a small boy.

What had already completed his delight was that last night, after Hudson Fysh had gone, Clarence had taken him back into his bungalow and produced a well-folded map of the Northern Territory between Darwin and Alice. Without a word, Clarence had traced the route southwards.

His finger had stopped when it reached a tiny dot marked Barrow Creek.

'What did I tell you?' he had beamed. 'Clarence Watling can provide.'

Miami, 1932

Eddie Feinbacker was waiting for James when he arrived at the airfield. Although it was only seven o'clock, and the sun was just up, one of those damp blurry Florida mornings, he was holding a drink in his hand, and he was smiling broadly. His mutt Flamerino was standing beside him, in that hangdog legs-apart heads-down pose he always adopted, his tongue hanging out like a long red face-cloth.

James parked his cream-and-black Marmon convertible behind the ticketing office, and climbed out stiff-legged. He had flown one of their Stinsons back from Atlanta late last night, and he was still suffering from a stiff neck and buzzing in the ears. He walked past Eddie without bothering to stop.

'What are you celebrating *this* time?' he asked Eddie, as he went by. 'The death of Nelson?'

'James, my friend,' Eddie replied, 'the only thing I have to say to you this morning is pip-pip, and cheery-ho!'

He frowned as he followed James into the new concrete-and-whitewash terminal building, and then he said, 'Nelson? Who the hell is Nelson? You don't mean Nelson Eddy?'

James walked through to his office, and unlocked it. 'Admiral Horatio Nelson, who died one hundred and twenty-seven years ago today, at the Battle of Trafalgar.'

Eddie sat down without being invited, and hefted his boots up on to James's desk. 'Do you know something, James old boy, you amaze me, all those facts you've got salted away in that noddle of

244

yours. If you ask me, you're superhuman.'

James sat down, too, and started sorting through the flight schedules that were laid out on his desk. 'You don't have to be superhuman to read in your diary that it's Trafalgar Day. Now – did we have any mail this morning, or couldn't Clyde be bothered to bring it out on time?'

'Oh, we had some mail all right,' said Eddie, and reached into the breast pocket of his denim jacket. He produced a folded-up letter, and waved it furiously from side to side, so that it made a clattering noise. 'We had some mail all right!'

'Are you going to tell me what it was? Or do we play *Twenty Questions?*'

'It's from your very best friend,' beamed Eddie.

'I haven't got a very best friend.'

'Oh, but I think you're about to. Walter Folger Brown, at the United States Post Office.'

James was running the tip of his gold propelling-pencil down a long list of figures. 'We've got to cut down on our wages bill, you know. We can't go on paying fifteen dollars a week to those baggage-handlers at Atlanta.'

'Will you listen to me?' Eddie demanded. 'This is a letter from Walter Folger Brown *in person.*'

James didn't look up. 'What does he say? He's not complaining about our carrying private parcels again, is he?'

'Oh, no. Nothing like that. He says – and I quote – "I am reconsidering the existing award to South-Eastern Airways of the United States mail service between Miami and Atlanta." In other words, reading between the lines, he's been having *multos problemos* with Erle Pepper, all those late deliveries, all those cancelled flights, and he's seriously considering the old switcheroo to you-know-who.'

James still didn't look up, but he allowed himself a small smile. 'Eddie,' he said, 'I think you can pour me one of those, too.'

Eddie brought out another glass, and half-filled it with Haig whisky. 'Here's mud in you eye,' he said, to nobody at all, and drained his glass before James could even pick his up.

'Yes,' said James, 'and mud in yours, too. And here's to good old Enriquez, the thinking man's aero-engineer.'

'This is the big time, hunh?' grinned Eddie, so that his head looked even more like a football than ever. 'This is where we strike the mother-lode.'

'Well,' said James, 'don't let's get ahead of ourselves.'

'That's right,' said Eddie, 'don't let's count our chickens before they're hatched.'

'Why does whisky always make you talk in clichés?' James asked him.

Eddie poured himself another generous drink. 'There was a wire, too.' He was obviously making something of an effort to sound off-hand.

'Oh, yes? Who was that from?'

'That was from England. Your wife.'

James raised his eyes at last. He stared at Eddie for a moment, and then he held out his hand. Eddie passed over the wire without a word, watching James with eyes the colour of faded sky. Old pilot's eyes. James opened the wire up, and read it. Then he folded it up again, and looked up at his calendar. 'She's coming on October 24, along with our first three Aquariuses. That means she's going to be here by Monday. When was this damn thing sent? It doesn't say.'

Eddie shrugged. 'Clyde's probably had it in his back pants pocket all week. You know Clyde. No sense of urgency. Von Richthofen would've sorted out Clyde in two minutes flat.' He pretended to be the notorious Red Baron, swooping down on an unsuspecting Nieuport – presumably piloted by Carol City's dilatory postmaster. '*Neeooowwwwww, ah-ah-ah-ah-ah!*'

James said, 'Damn.'

'Why damn?' asked Eddie. 'Come on, James, count your blessings. Every cloud has a silver what's-its-name. The Post Office is asking us to tender for the mail. Next week we're going to have three new airplanes delivered, as well as your lady wife. We're turning a modest profit. What more do you want?'

James said, 'Chloe's flying down tomorrow morning. She's travelling incognito, all the way from Burbank. She's expecting to stay for a week.'

Eddie stared at James for a very long time. Then he started to grunt. Then he started to laugh. He rocked backwards and forwards in his chair, and slapped at his thighs as enthusiastically as if they were two fast-running horses. 'You big bug, you! You big bug!'

'I don't see what's so funny. I haven't seen Chloe since August.'

Eddie laughed even louder. 'That'll teach you, won't it! That'll teach you to mess with movie stars!'

'I haven't been messing with her. We're friends, that's all.'

'Closest friends *I* ever saw.'

James crumpled the wire up into a ball and tossed it at Eddie's head. It bounced off and fell neatly into the wastebasket, which made Eddie laugh all the harder. 'You big bug! You can't even throw paper at somebody without tidying up after yourself!'

James shook his head; but he couldn't stop himself from smiling. The nuisance of it was that he would have to call Chloe and ask her to cancel her trip out to Florida, despite the fact that he had already made arrangements to fly her by seaplane down to Key West to stay with the Charles B. Prendergasts, and then to take her on Pan American's $50 flight to Havana for a long weekend at the Hotel Estrada Palma.

He had been to visit Chloe in Hollywood during the summer, flying himself to California in a Ford Tri-Motor which had been one of his first acquisitions after taking over APA. But Marty Rosen had been much in evidence; and while Marty still liked James, and was still enthusiastic about cultivating a newsworthy relationship between them, he had been more interested at that particular time in Chloe finishing the principal photography of *Red, Red, Roses* with Robert Donat, which was already nine weeks behind schedule and getting more behindhand every day, mostly because of Chloe's chronic inability to remember her lines.

James had been able to take Chloe for dinner at the Beverley Hills Hotel, and had twice visited her for a salad lunch at the studio commissary, but there had been neither the time nor the opportunity for them to develop their friendship any further. Chloe had promised to come out to Florida when *Red, Red, Roses* was in the can.

In a way, James hadn't minded too much. He hadn't had time for an intense affair; or, for that matter, any kind of affair at all. He had been working eighteen hours a day, seven days a week, to reconstruct and reschedule APA so that it was an efficient, aggressively-priced, attractive alternative to South-Eastern Airways. He had borrowed thirty-five thousand dollars from the First Miami Bank and bought himself three new aeroplanes – the Ford Tri-Motor and two Fairchild FC-2W2s – and had them fitted with new seats and new red carpets. He had laid the same red carpet in APA's ticket office and waiting-rooms, and advertised APA's service as The Red Carpet Treatment to Atlanta.

He had heard in a roundabout way that Erle Pepper over at South-Eastern Airways thought he must be a lunatic, because without the mail subsidy it was almost impossible to make an airline pay. But then Erle Pepper had started running into countless technical problems with broken crankshafts, split fuel diaphragms, contaminated aviation fuel, and cracked bearings. Twice during September Erle's flight manager had called Eddie and asked if APA could carry the mail to Atlanta for them, because their own aeroplanes were temporarily out of commission. James had been only too happy to oblige. Every time they carried the mail for South-Eastern Airways they were chalking up a bonus point with Walter Folger Brown.

The office door opened and Hump Cranshaw came in: APA's new chief pilot. Hump was lean and stringy and big-nosed. He had been one of the star flyers with Gates Flying Circus before he had shrewdly foreseen the end of barnstorming and taken a job flying airliners. He was still capable of bringing a Stinson sideslipping into land with its switch cut, and rolling up to within two feet of the hangar with a dead engine.

'Morning, James, morning, Eddie,' he greeted them. 'Anybody showed up for the eight o'clock yet?'

'Not yet; but Jack Brown called up to say he was coming.'

Hump took a cigarette-butt from behind his ear, and lit it. 'Another low, slow take-off,' he remarked. Jack Brown ran the Carol City Hardware Store, and weighed well over three hundred pounds. If all the other seats were occupied, and everybody had luggage, a take-off with Jack Brown aboard usually involved scraping the palms at the far end of the airfield.

'Don't worry, Hump,' said Eddie, 'this'll cheer you up.' He passed Hump the letter from the Post Office.

James meanwhile picked up the telephone and asked the operator to place a long-distance person-to-person call for him, to Beverley Hills. Then he went outside to make sure that the Ford was all fuelled up and ready for its eight o'clock take-off to Atlanta. He walked across the dry hard-packed ground and Flamerino trotted out to join him. 'Hey, there, boy,' he whistled. He felt a satisfying sense of achievement; as he always did when a plan worked out well. He had pulled the rug out from underneath Erle Pepper's feet. Unfairly, perhaps, but running an airline was an alligator-eat-alligator business, and James was determined to make a success of APA no matter what.

He was halfway across the field when a large black Cadillac came bouncing across the grass in his direction. It pulled up between him and the Ford Tri-motor, and a short white-haired man climbed out of it and started marching towards him. 'Lord!' the man barked. 'I want a word with you!'

It was Erle Pepper himself: the tough little veteran flyer who had founded South-Eastern Airways. He had a square pugnacious face, like an Irish priest in a James Cagney picture, and fists like pork-knuckles. His grey alpaca suit was buttoned up tightly, and he wore a loud red-and-yellow necktie. He came right up to James and blocked his way, his fists on his hips, and his lower lip stuck out.

'You think you're pretty damn smart, don't you?' Erle Pepper demanded.

James said, 'Good morning. How are you?'

'I'm not in the mood for civilities, that's how I am. I know what the hell you've been up to. You've been sabotaging my airplanes, that's what you've been up to, and now you've as good as lost me the mail contract. Well – don't think I'm going to take this lying down, because I'm not.'

'I'm afraid I haven't the foggiest idea what you're talking about,' James replied.

'Don't you come that limey crap with me, you crappy limey. You've been fixing my airplanes for months and I can prove it.'

'I think if you're going to make allegations of that nature, you'd better talk to my attorneys,' James told him. 'Now, if you'll excuse me, I have a flight to make ready.'

James tried to walk around him, but Erle Pepper snatched at his sleeve. 'You listen to me, Lord, you're not going to get away with this. I'm going to have you thrown into jail for criminal damage, conspiracy, bribery, and anything else I can think of.'

James looked down at Erle Pepper's hand on his sleeve. Without raising his eyes, he said, 'I suggest you leave this airfield, and I suggest you leave now.'

'Not unless you tell me you're going to back off and stay backed off.'

'And precisely what do you mean by that?'

'I mean you're going to tell the Post Office that you're not interested in flying the mail.'

'But that would be a lie. I'm *very* interested in flying the mail.'

Erle Pepper was silent for a moment. James could feel him quivering with anger.

'Now, is that all?' James asked him.

Erle Pepper let go of James's sleeve, but didn't back away.

'It certainly isn't all. I'm going to go straight to the police, and I'm going to go to the United States Post Office, too. I'm going to tell them that you bribed Enriquez to keep my planes grounded so that you could win the airmail contract.'

'Who on earth is Enriquez?' James asked him; more coldly now.

'Enriquez happens to be my deputy chief mechanic, that's who. Or at least he *used* to be my deputy chief mechanic, before I found out who paid for his new Dodge Standard Six.'

'I think you'd better leave,' said James. He whistled to Flamerino, and said, 'Flamerino, see this gentleman off the airfield.'

Flamerino was quite incapable of doing anything of the kind, but he came trotting up to Erle Pepper with his tail sticking up like a bottle-brush and managed to look reasonably threatening in a cockeyed kind of fashion. Erle Pepper retreated a few steps, and said. 'You'd better watch your tail, Lord. I'm going to be after you now; and I'm not going to get any rest until you're behind bars, and this pissant airline of yours is folded up for good.'

'Good day, Mr Pepper,' said James, and continued his walk to the Ford airliner. He didn't turn around, even when Erle Pepper slammed the door of his Cadillac, started up his engine, and went roaring off the airfield in a high cloud of dust.

The Ford was almost ready. Fuelled up, cleaned, with fresh paper airsickness sacks and humbugs for the passengers to suck as they took off and landed. They would be carrying a small cargo of parrots today, eventually bound for the pet department of Marshall Field's, in Chicago. Hump had caustically remarked that if the parrots were any damn good, they could have found their own way there.

As James approached the terminal building on his way back, Eddie came out to meet him, still holding his whisky glass in his hand. 'Was that Erle Pepper?' he frowned.

'That was Erle Pepper,' said James.

'He didn't look too happy.'

'He wasn't. And nor am I. He's just found out about Enriquez.'

Eddie raised his eyebrows. 'Holy shit. That's bad.'

'Well, it may not be as bad as he was trying to make out. He *suspects* Enriquez, certainly, but I don't think he's got any solid proof. All we have to do is make quite sure that he doesn't get any.'

Eddie followed James into the office. 'By the way, the long-distance operator just called back. She couldn't get through to Chloe but she got through to Chloe's housekeeper. Chloe left Burbank yesterday morning, by American Airways. Apparently she finished at the studio a day early. She's expected in Miami at eleven o'clock this morning. She was hoping to surprise you.'

'Well, she's certainly managed to do that,' said James. He went into the office, picked up his drink, and swallowed it with a grimace. He couldn't worry about Chloe now. If necessary, he would move her on Monday to a friend's house; or send her back to California. What he needed to do as a first priority was contact Enriquez, and find out just how much or how little Erle Pepper had discovered about his sabotage.

The phone rang at Enriquez's house for almost a minute before it was picked up. A girl's voice said, '*Quién es?*'

'This is Mr James Lord. I want to talk to Enriquez.'

'*Enriquez es non a casa.*'

'Do you know where I can find him? This is important.'

'*No comprendo.*'

'Do you know where I can find him? Do you know where he is?'

'*No comprendo. Lo siento.*'

'Is there anybody there who speaks English?'

'*Lo siento.*'

James hung up. 'Eddie,' he said, 'call that other mechanic friend of yours; Miguel or whatever his name is. Tell him we have to talk to Enriquez urgently. Tell him you'll pay him ten dollars if he finds him by lunchtime.'

'If there's a sawbuck in it, I'll go find him myself.'

'Just do what you can. I don't want to lose this mail contract now that we've almost got it in the bag.'

At that moment, a blue pick-up truck arrived outside, and a huge man in an off-white suit like the sails of a schooner heaved himself out of the front seat.

'Hump!' called Eddie. 'Your freight's arrived!'

Chloe arrived at James's rented house at Bal Harbour shortly after twelve o'clock. James heard the taxi pull up outside, and parted the Venetian blinds to see who it was. He watched Chloe approach the house, her hips undulating busily under her tight white day dress, one hand holding her white wide-brimmed sun-hat. She was followed by the taxi-driver, who was staring at her mobile bottom as if the instructions for carrying her case were printed on each cheek in very small type.

Chloe reached the porch and rang the bell. James's housekeeper, Mrs Aguilar, came out of the kitchen with flour-dusted hands, a patterned scarf knotted around her head. James pressed a finger to his lips as she shuffled through the hallway to answer the door. She shrugged, and nodded.

'Oh hello,' gushed Chloe. 'I'm Miss Treat; Mr Lord is expecting me tomorrow. But as it turned out, I came *early*! You surely won't mind if I come in and wait for him! And if there's a shower I could use, I'd be *so-o-o* appreciative. You have no idea what it's like, flying from one side of the continent to the other. Well, it's absolutely *enfer*; and that's French for hell but I don't suppose you know that, being Cuban.'

Before Mrs Aguilar could protest, Chloe had instructed the taxi driver to carry her cases into the hall. She tipped him over-

251

generously, then called him back and actually took some of the money back out of his hand. He drove off with a furious squeal of tyres, while Chloe walked into the living-room as if she owned it, and looked around.

It was a high-ceilinged whitewashed room with a brown tiled floor and an immense arched fireplace. There were two large oil paintings of Spanish noblemen on the wall, so dark and sombre that all anybody could see of them was their olive faces. The furniture was Spanish-style, too, heavy stained oak with green and brown tapestry cushions.

'What a dreadful room!' Chloe proclaimed, walking around and around it with her high heels tapping on the tiles. 'You wouldn't want to *die* in this room, would you, let alone live in it? This must be James's taste. Or lack of it. Why do men always insist on having such *gloomy* surroundings? Look at this tapestry! Gloom from the loom!'

'I can show you to your room, if you wish,' Mrs Aguilar told Chloe, in her halting English. 'Then perhaps you can wash, too.'

'Thank God for hot water and strong men,' Chloe remarked. 'Can you imagine a world without either of them? Talk about the *essentials!*'

James had been standing silently behind the heavy tapestry drapes. As soon as he heard Chloe tip-tapping out of the room, he crept after her, on stockinged feet. He climbed the wide oak stairs, listening for a moment at the half-landing, and then he crossed the upstairs landing to the guest-room door. It was an inch ajar. Chloe was singing to herself, and (from the sound of it) undressing.

> *'I always used to dress in red*
> *The kind of girl who lost her head*
> *But now I find that I've lost you ...*
> *And so I always dress in blue ...*
> *Too-tee, too-tee, tooty-too!'*

James eased the door open a tiny crack further, so that he could see through the door-jamb into the room. He couldn't see Chloe herself, but he could see her reflection in the cheval-glass on the far side of the bed. She was pouting at herself with bright red lips like a California strawberry, and shaking her hips in the dance-routine she had learned for *Red, Red, Roses.* Her breasts jiggled underneath her white silk slip.

'Blue, blue, blue, blue,
Now I'm always dressed in blue
Blue ribbons, blue shoes
Blue pyjamas, all for you
Too-tee, woo-tee, tooty-woo!'

She tugged her slip over her head and tossed it across the room. Underneath, she was bare-breasted, no brassière. Her breasts were high and rounded with tiny little pink nipples like Japanese jellies. She danced around a little more, singing to herself in a high-pitched, breathy voice, and then she slipped out of her white silk step-ins, and kicked them across the room, too. James glimpsed blonde pubic hair: then she had danced her way, naked, into the bathroom.

'Too-tee, woo-tee, tooty-woo!'

James waited for a moment, aroused and amused. When he heard the shower running, he pushed the bedroom door wide, and stepped inside. Chloe's dress and underwear lay sprawled across the oak-posted bed. Over the high Spanish bureau, there was a sad madonna, with a tarnished halo, staring with infinite regret at Chloe's step-ins. James crossed the room, and listened at the bathroom door. He could hear Chloe singing and spluttering and gargling.

'Blllue! Blubble! Blue! Blub!'

He crept into the bathroom, and there she was, in the frosted-glass shower-stall, with her back to him, a pink soft-focus image of feminine beauty. He stood silent for a moment, watching her, tantalizing himself with the thought of opening up the shower-stall door and seeing her wet and soapy and completely naked. Chloe Treat, the most desirable motion-picture actress since Jean Harlow, all naked, and all his.

He watched with mounting stimulation as she soaped her shoulders and her upper arms. Then her hands grasped her breasts, and lathered and caressed them around and around as sensually as if she were making love to herself. She stopped singing. The steam gradually clouded the glass of the shower more and more, until James could hardly see the way her fingers fanned over her stomach, soaping it around and around in whorls of white, and at last slipped between her thighs.

She lifted her face up towards the needling water, and shook the dark mane of her wet blonde hair.

James opened the shower-stall door. Chloe let out a gargling little gasp. 'James!' she cried. Then she giggled in relief. 'James! You scared me half to death!'

'Who's been showering in *my* shower,' James demanded. 'And hasn't invited me to join her?'

'I was going to *surprise* you, you great goof! And now look what's happened, you've surprised *me!*'

'Come here, Miss C. Treat, of Beverley Hills,' James ordered her, and reached into the shower fully dressed to lift her out. She was wet and warm and very slippery, and she shrieked and kicked her legs like a disobedient child as he carried her back out of the bathroom; but when he laid her on the bedspread and kissed her she didn't struggle at all. She kissed him back, quickly and urgently, and whispered, 'James . . . I can't tell you how much I've missed you . . . I can't tell you how often I've dreamed about this.' The words could have been real, or they could have been remembered from one of her screenplays. But it didn't matter which. She said them and she meant them, and she clung to him tight, her wet body soaking his shirt.

'Thought you'd surprise me, did you,' James murmured in her ear, and laughed. 'I'll teach you to surprise me.'

His hand grasped her breast; his head bowed to kiss her nipple; and then to nip at it. She reached down and twisted open the buttons of his trousers. Then she scooped her hand inside, and clutched him tightly. He shivered with the thrill of it.

They made love with carefully-orchestrated ferocity. She clutched her legs around his back, and arched her neck back, and said things that he didn't understand. He didn't really need to; but there was a moment when she was close to her climax that he began to think that, inside her mind, she was somewhere else altogether; not thinking about anybody else, but very far away, and completely wrapped up in her own celebration of her own feelings.

Afterwards James sat up; and then stood up; and buttoned up his trousers. Chloe lay where she was, one knee raised, still naked, still damp, her chest rosy and flushed, her pubic hair twisted in little damp curls.

'You were *every* bit as virile as I knew you were going to be,' she told him. 'And who was it who said that Englishmen don't know how to *faire l'amour*?'

James unbuttoned his cuffs, and rolled up his wet sleeves. 'Some Frenchman probably. The French seem to think that they've cornered the market, when it comes to love.'

'You sound more American every time I meet you.'

'If I didn't speak the language, nobody would know what the hell I was talking about. It's worse than Germany, getting yourself understood in Florida. I went to the hairdresser the other day and asked for a short-back-and-sides and he thought I was talking about baseball.'

He leaned over the bed and kissed her, a kiss that lingered. She smiled, and touched the tip of his nose with her finger. 'Is this love,' she asked, 'or merely an expression of mutual lust? You know what Darwin said about the indelible stamp of our lowly origins.'

'As a matter of fact, I don't.'

'Well, we've all got it, brother, and it isn't the kind you stick on envelopes.'

'How about a drink?' James asked her.

'I could absorb a *verre* or two of champagne.'

'There's some Perrier-Jouët on ice, downstairs. Why don't you finish showering, and I'll bring it up.'

'I *have* finished showering,' said Chloe. She paused, and then she looked up at him. She could tell what he was thinking. 'I like the smell of it, afterwards. I like the smell of *you*. It's even more *stimulong* than Isabey.'

Later, they sat on the small white-painted verandah drinking tall glasses of champagne and looking out over the intensely blue water of Biscayne Bay. The sea-breeze made the palm-fronds dip and rustle; the afternoon sunlight danced on the waves, and the little blue herons danced on the sunlight.

Chloe had wrapped her hair in a towel-turban, and dressed herself in nothing but a pink silk bathrobe. Mrs Aguilar had stared at her balefully as she wafted through the house, leaving behind her a trail of custom-blended perfume. Mrs Aguilar had never seen a Chloe Treat movie: her sole entertainment was flamenco music on the radio.

James said, 'You and I should have met each other years ago. Or at least two years ago.'

'Your wife's in England, isn't she? So what difference does it make if you're married or not?'

James sipped his champagne, and then set it down on the table. 'That's what I have to talk to you about.'

Chloe looked at him with narrowed eyes. 'I'm not sure that I like your tone of voice.'

James lowered his head and stared at the floor. 'The point is, my love, I knew you were coming today because I tried to call you; and the reason I tried to call you was to put you off.'

'Oh, I see! Well, that's *mairvay-erx*! You drag me out of the

255

shower, make hot wet passionate love to me all over the bedspread, pour me a glass of champagne, and then tell me that I'm only here under sufferance!'

'You're not here under sufferance at all. I want you to be here more than anything else in the world. But I had a wire from England this morning. We're having three new Lord airliners delivered on Monday, and Patricia's coming with them.'

Chloe said, 'It's all off, then, you and me? Is that it? Is that what you're trying to tell me? We're not going to Key West and we're not going to Havana?'

James nodded. 'I'm really sorry. Patricia took me completely by surprise.'

'Well, at least *one* of us manages to surprise you.'

'Chloe, please don't take it badly. It's just that – well, Patricia hasn't been well. She lost a baby and now she can't have any more, and after that – I don't know. She needs somebody to take care of her.'

'How long is she planning on staying?' Chloe asked, frostily.

'I really don't know. All she said in her wire was that she was coming.'

'So *I* have to go?'

'You don't have to, necessarily,' James told her. 'You could stay with the Ortizes if you wanted to. They're very good friends; and they have a beautiful house on Biscayne Boulevard. Their own yacht, too. We could see each other practically every day.'

Chloe held out her glass for a refill. 'I hope you're joking,' she snapped at him. 'I mean, do you know who I *am*? Do you know how many men would cut their right arm off just to spend five minutes with me?'

James shook his head. 'I haven't a clue. Do you? I suppose it must be several.'

Chloe couldn't stop herself from smiling. 'James, do you know something, you're a complete rat, but I think you're wonderful. Don't ask me why. And now you've got me under your spell, you rat. God, what a rat you are!'

'What will you do?' James asked her. 'Fly back to California?'

'I suppose. Do you have a flight going out on Sunday afternoon?'

'We don't, but South-Eastern do. I think it's four o'clock, something like that. It connects directly with America's sleeper from Nashville.'

James hesitated for a moment, and then he said, 'I'm sorry,

Chloe. You don't have any idea how sorry I am. I wouldn't have had this happen for the world.'

'*C'est la vie*,' shrugged Chloe. 'I guess it's time that I was treated like an ordinary mistress; instead of some goddess or other.' She got out of her chair, and came over and sat down on his knee, and kissed him. 'Why do I like you so much? Why do I hate you so much? I think you scare me, you rat, you.'

He kissed her back. Lightly, a kiss that teased both of them. They looked closely into each other's eyes and both of them recognized an opportunist, a loner, somebody who was quite prepared to twist the rules of law and morality if it helped them to get what they wanted. The breeze stirred Chloe's curls; James kissed them; a passing motor-launch whooped and the little blue herons burst into the afternoon sky.

At six o-clock, the telephone rang. It was Eddie, more than a little unsteady. 'James? Ah! Got through at last. Kept getting myself connected to the Church of the Holy Vessel. God bless you, my son, you've got the wrong number. So of course I said – if it's the wrong number, Father – why the hell did you answer it?'

'What's up, Eddie?' asked James.

'Well, old fellow, I've earned my sawski, that's what's up. I've found Enriquez.'

'Where is he? I'll get down there right away.'

'He's down at Miami Police Headquarters, locked up. He was arrested early this afternoon on a complaint from Erle Pepper, criminal damage, something like that, and attempted homicide.'

'Attempted homicide?' James frowned.

'Fixing an airplane so that it's per-tentially dangerous to life and limb.'

James glanced towards Chloe. She was circling around the sitting-room, drinking champagne and dancing to the gramophone. 'Give me twenty minutes,' he said, and put down the phone.

James could hear Enriquez as soon as they entered the building. The big-bellied police sergeant in the tortoise-shell sunglasses waddled ahead of him, jingling his keys. 'He's been a-screaming and a-hollering that way ever since he got here. Nobody can shut him up.'

Enriquez's desperate howls echoed along the tiled corridors of the cell-block. '*La niña! La niña! Es urgente!*'

Finally they reached Enriquez's cell. Enriquez was kneeling up on his wooden bunk, banging furiously at the wall with his bare fists. There were streaks of blood on the rough plasterwork. His eyes were wild and his hair was sticking up on end and his purple-palm-patterned shirt was hanging out of his pants and black with sweat. When he saw James, he stopped screaming at once, and half-hopped on to the floor, and gripped the bars.

'Enriquez?' James asked him, hunkering down so that he could talk to him.

'Mr Lord! They locked me up!'

'Well, yes, it rather looks as if they did. But I've already called my attorneys. They're going to put up bail for you and have you let out.'

'But, Mr Lord, my child! My little girl Alicia!'

'What about her?'

'She is very bad, very sick. They called me from the hospital. I was going to the hospital when the police arrested me. Mr Lord, she could be dying, you have to get me out of here.'

James reached through the bars and clasped Enriquez's hands. 'Just hold on a minute, old chap. I'll see what I can do.' He paused, and then he said, 'You haven't been questioned yet, have you?'

'*Qué?*' asked Enriquez.

'They haven't asked you anything about what you might have been doing to Erle Pepper's airplanes?'

Enriquez shook his head. 'All they did was take my wallet and my watch and my shoelaces and lock me up.'

'All right, that's good. But don't talk to anybody – don't talk to anybody at all. My attorneys will be here soon, and they'll look after everything for you.'

'But Alicia –!'

James lifted a calming hand. 'Give me two minutes. I'll see how quickly I can get you out.'

But, downstairs, the lieutenant in charge of Enriquez's case was adamant. He sat behind his desk, thin and dry, with skinny suntanned arms and cropped grey hair, and insisted that Enriquez could not be released for any reason until bail had been properly posted.

James said, 'I sincerely hope, lieutenant, that the next judge you have to stand in front of is God.'

The lieutenant refused to be insulted. 'Even God has to obey the law, my friend.'

James stood in line for the callbox in the lobby and at last managed to get through to the hospital. He was passed from one floor to another; from reception to nurses' station and back again. At last he was connected with a ward sister.

'My name is James Lord; I'm calling about a little girl called Alicia Bocanegra.'

'Yes, sir?'

'I just wanted to know how she was.'

'Are you a relation, sir?'

'I'm calling on behalf of her father. He's had an accident. He can't get to the hospital until later.'

'Well, I'm sorry, sir, but you'll have to tell him that Alicia passed away about a half-hour ago. Her lungs collapsed.'

'She's dead?' asked James, in distress.

'I'm sorry, sir.'

He hung up the phone. Then he went to find the sergeant to take him back to the cells. The sergeant said, 'One guy asked to be released on compassionate grounds, do you know why? The tuna were running off Islamorada and he didn't want to miss them.'

Enriquez was sitting quietly on his bunk with his head lowered. James went to the bars and said, 'Enriquez?'

He told Enriquez what had happened. Enriquez listened without expression. Then at last he nodded, and sniffed.

'Are you all right?' James asked him. 'My attorneys shouldn't be long now.'

'I'm all right, Mr Lord,' said Enriquez. 'But – look now, my Alicia's gone, and I wasn't even there to hold her hand. What did she think, when her father wasn't there to hold her hand?' His eyes filled with tears.

'Wherever she is now, I'm sure she can see you,' James comforted him. 'She'll understand.'

'No,' said Enriquez bitterly. 'No.' Then, 'Erle Pepper, what did I do to him that he should have me locked up when my Alicia was dying? Did I hurt him that bad? I'll kill him, I swear it. I'll kill him.'

The police sergeant grunted and grinned. But James held Enriquez's hands through the bars and said, 'Come along, Enriquez, you're not going to kill anybody. You're not going to kill anybody.'

That evening, although she was tired, James took Chloe to a cocktail party at Henry Ruggs's, whose social credentials in Miami went almost as far back as Julia D. Tuttle. Henry Ruggs ('Boffo' to his friends) had made three hundred million dollars out of oil and natural gas, and had now retired at the age of fifty-five to fish for shark, play terrible golf, and give parties.

Six-foot-five and silver-haired, Henry clasped James by the upper arms and shook him with the kind of tidal affection that only the very rich are capable of feeling. 'James, you're a dark horse, James, and no mistake! Chloe Treat, at our party! You've made Amy's day! By golly, you've made *my* day!'

Chloe was fêted all evening; and loved it. She was wearing a sleek shining halter-neck evening gown in silver satin, so that she looked like a curvaceous fish. When she danced the rumba, weaving in and out of the huge flower-displays, everybody crowded around to applaud her, and she plucked out orchids and orange-blossom and threw them in all directions. The guests scrambled with whoops of delight to catch them, as if a flower from Chloe Treat would bring them a lifetime of luck.

Later, she and James danced quietly together on the Ruggs's private dock, while the dark water gurgled and slapped, and the sound of matronly hysteria came echoing across the lawns like champagne glasses rolling down marble steps.

'This is just the right sort of night for falling in love, don't you think?' asked James.

Chloe leaned her perfumed hair against the shoulder of his white tropical dinner-jacket. A red gardenia wilted in his lapel. 'I don't know,' she said. 'Is *any* night the right night for falling in love?'

When the party began to break up, he drove her to the Cuban district, and bought her a Suffering Bastard at the Blue Moon Club. They danced the merengue, one foot dragging. Then a huge woman in a yellow dress danced a thundering rumba on the bar.

They didn't get back to James's house at Bal Harbour until four o'clock. James was all for opening another bottle of champagne, but when he came up to the bedroom Chloe was lying face-down on the bed fast asleep, breathing through her mouth, her hair half-tangled, her silver evening dress rucked up at the back so that it revealed her bare bottom and her long bare legs. She was still wearing her silver evening slippers.

James quietly set down the ice-bucket, and tiptoed around the bed. He switched off the bedside lamp, and stood for a moment looking down at Chloe with an expression that neither she nor Patricia would ever have seen before: an expression of tenderness and enchantment.

He undressed her, and covered her up with the sheet. She murmured something, but remained deeply asleep. He drew the mosquito nets around the bed, and switched off his own lamp, and sat up in bed in the darkness for almost an hour, sipping champagne and listening to the sound of the insects and the soft breathing of the Atlantic wind through the curtains. He thought about Alicia Bocanegra, and Erle Pepper, and Enriquez. 'Such is bloody life,' he whispered to himself. He couldn't think of anything more eloquent than that. He drained his glass and settled his head down on the pillow. He could already feel tomorrow's hangover beating in his temples.

Sunday was windy and unsettled. They drove to Key Largo for lunch at the Happy Crab, where Chloe wore sinister little sunglasses all the way through the meal so that she wouldn't be recognized. The Happy Crab looked more like a flotsam museum than a restaurant, with dried-up oars and fragments of boat and fishing-nets hung up everywhere. There was a photograph on the wall of the owner standing next to a ridiculously huge marlin, 1925.

James and Chloe ordered conch chowder, for no better reason than that everybody who visits the Keys has to eat conch chowder at least once. It was similar to clam chowder except that the chopped-up pieces of conch were almost inedibly rubbery. The Saltines were stale. They drank their own champagne out of sundae glasses, with straws.

Afterwards, they stood on the beach looking out at the frisky sea, the grey sand stinging their ankles, the gulls angling silently overhead, and James put his arms around Chloe and held her tightly. 'You know how much I don't want you to go.'

'I know, *mon chèr*. But, you know, dammit, we'll manage somehow. You'll call, won't you, you rat? You'll call me and tell me how much you love me?'

There were tears on her eyelashes. They trembled in the wind.

James looked at his watch. 'We'd better start heading back to Miami. You ought to be at the airfield at least ten minutes before your flight takes off.'

They drove back towards the city in silence. There was nothing that either of them could say. James drove his Marmon out to the South-Eastern Airways building, which was a white concrete box surrounded by white-painted corrugated-iron sheds that had been hastily erected as Erle Pepper's business had boomed. A Ford Tri-motor painted in the sky-blue colours of South-Eastern Airways was already waiting on the concrete apron, and passengers' luggage was being loaded aboard.

James parked his car close to the terminal building, and then walked Chloe out to the airliner. A stewardess with a sky-blue beret and a matching cape was welcoming passengers on board.

261

Chloe's reservation had been made in the name of Shepherd. That had been her own idea – 'the Lord is my Shepherd'.

'You'll call me as soon as you're home?' James asked her. 'It doesn't matter what time of the day or night it is.'

'I'll call.'

'And give my best to Marty.'

Chloe nodded, and reached up to kiss him. 'My next picture is going to be dedicated entirely to you.'

'What's it going to be called? *The Rat of Miami?*'

She laughed. As she did so, however, James felt a hand on his shoulder. He turned around and there was Erle Pepper, in a grey fedora and a grey lightweight overcoat.

'Erle?' James said, cautiously.

'James,' replied Erle, in an even voice. Then he raised his hat to Chloe. 'Are you flying with us today, miss?'

'This is Miss Shepherd,' said James. 'She came out here to interview me for the Los Angeles newspapers. She has to be back in California by tomorrow.'

'Well, I'm sure that South-Eastern is glad to be of service,' said Erle. 'Any friend of James Lord is a friend of mine. Well, *almost* any friend. James, don't you worry, we'll take care of this young lady as if she were the finest porcelain. I'm taking this flight myself, so she can be sure of first-class treatment.'

'I hope so,' said James. He waited until Erle Pepper had climbed aboard the airliner, and then he gave Chloe a last goodbye kiss. Warm lips, the taste of Isabey. Eyelashes that fluttered against his cheek. 'Don't forget, phone!'

He stood back as the last passengers were boarded, the door was closed, and the angular all-metal 'Tin Goose' was readied for its flight to Atlanta. One by one, the three radial engines burst into life, and the airliner turned towards the runway, the grey daylight gleaming on its corrugated duralumin fuselage. James glimpsed Chloe's face at one of the windows over the starboard wing. She didn't wave. The next moment, the airliner was taxiing away, and turning to face the wind.

James stood on the apron with his hands in his pockets as the Ford took off, and droned away north-westwards, over the palm trees. In the distance, twigs of lightning flickered. He took out a cigarette, and lit it with his hand shielding his lighter from the breeze. He walked back towards his car feeling lonelier than he had ever done before, in the whole of his life.

When he returned home, the telephone was ringing. He opened

the front door quickly, and called out, 'Mrs Aguilar! Mrs Aguilar, can you answer that? *Teléfona*, Mrs Aguilar!'

It didn't sound as if Mrs Aguilar was in. She occasionally went out on Sunday afternoons to visit her sick sister in Hialeah. But the phone didn't stop ringing. James walked into the living-room and picked it up. 'Hello? Who is this?'

'Eddie,' said Eddie. 'And if I get through to that God-damned church again, I'm going to change my religion.'

'All right, Eddie, what do you want?'

'I had a call from Enriquez's sister. She's real worried. After they let him out of the pokey last night, he was acting very weird, eyes like glass, that's what she said, and threatening all kinds of black-and-blue vengeance on Erle Pepper. Anyway she hasn't seen him since, and she was calling to see if he was anywheres at APA.'

'I haven't seen him,' said James. 'My attorney called me late last night and said that he was out on five thousand dollars security, but that was the last I heard about it. I know that he was very upset about his daughter, but I wouldn't have thought he was the kind of fellow to do anything really rash.'

'I don't know,' Eddie replied. 'These Latin types can be pretty hot-headed when they're riled. His sister said that Enriquez was drinking muscadet like it was going out of style and rambling on about fixing Erle Pepper for good.'

'I shouldn't worry about it. He'll get over it, when he sobers up.'

'I guess so. Well, I *hope* so. The way his sister told it, Enriquez kept saying that next time Erle Pepper flew, he was really going to fix his wagon. You know, really going to fix him for good.'

James frowned. He suddenly thought of the Tin Goose, heading out towards Atlanta with Erle Pepper on board. And Chloe. 'What did he mean?' he asked Eddie. His lips felt as if they had been anaesthetized, ready to have his teeth pulled. 'What did he mean, fix him for good?'

Eddie sniffed. 'Don't ask me, but that's what he said. "Next time Erle Pepper goes flying anywhere," that's what he said, "I'm going to fix his wagon, and fix it for all time!"'

'Oh, Christ,' said James.

'James?' asked Eddie. 'James, you there? Can you hear me, James?'

'Yes, I hear you. Listen – Erle Pepper's flying to Atlanta tonight. He's already taken off, the four o'clock flight. But Chloe's on board that flight, too.'

There was a very long pause. Then Eddie said, 'Shit. Oh, shit, James, what the hell are we going to do?'

James, shaking, checked his watch. 'They should be nearly over Jacksonville by now. Listen – you call the South-Eastern terminal, tell them what you know. I'll try to raise Jacksonville. With any luck, they can get a radio message to the pilot, and tell him to land.'

James hung up, and then called the operator. 'Get me Jacksonville field, will you, and, please, hurry! This is an emergency!'

There was a lengthy pause. The line crackled and buzzed. Then the operator came back and said, 'I'm sorry, sir. There are heavy electric storms over northern and central Florida; all of the telephone lines are temporarily out of service.'

'How long before they're working again?'

'I'm sorry, sir, we're doing our best. It could be some time.'

James banged down the telephone, and stood for a moment grim-faced, not moving. Then he went through to the hall-table, grabbed his hat and his car-keys, and quickly left the house, slamming the door behind him. The tyres of his Marmon convertible squealed and squittered as he U-turned on the roadway and headed out towards Carol City airfield.

He drove one-handed as he lit himself a cigarette. He didn't pray. There was nothing that God or his angels could do to protect Chloe this evening. The responsibility was entirely James's. As he drove through the dull streets of Carol City, past gas-stations and petshops and fruit depots, he kept thinking over and over of Oscar Wilde's poignant words from Reading Goal: '*Yet each man kills the thing he loves . . .*'

He turned into the dusty airfield entrance, and along the concrete roadway that led to the APA terminal building. He parked directly outside the main entrance, and clambered out of the Marmon so hurriedly that he left the door open. The terminal was empty and gloomy. Without bothering to switch on the lights, James went straight to the radio room, and flicked the switches of the wireless-telephone. The dials glowed; the microphone crackled. James put on the headphones, and adjusted the tuner to the frequency used by South-Eastern Airways.

'South-Eastern Flight Nine, South-Eastern Flight Nine, can you hear me? South-Eastern Flight Nine, if you can hear me, please respond! This is APA at Carol City, please respond! Over!'

He waited for an answer, but there was nothing but distant fizzing noises. He lit another cigarette, and then tried again. 'South-Eastern Flight Nine, South-Eastern Flight Nine, please respond! This is an emergency!'

Again, there was no reply. Outside the terminal windows, the sky was beginning to darken and the wind was getting up. The palm trees on the edge of the runway were beginning to toss their arms like dancers in some primitive Caribbean ballet.

James tried for five minutes to contact South-Eastern Nine, but it was useless. He attempted instead to call Orlando, to see if they had heard from Chloe's flight as it passed on its way to Jacksonville. But again, silence. He tried South-Eastern Nine one more time, and then switched the transmitter off.

It was then that the telephone rang. It was Eddie. The lines to the north had been restored, and he had managed to get in touch with the South-Eastern Airways office at Jacksonville. Flight Nine from Miami was twenty minutes overdue, and they had failed to make radio contact with the pilot, but so far there was no 'immediate cause for alarm'.

'They said there were pretty strong headwinds; the plane could be delayed up to a half-hour. They said they weren't worried.'

James said: '*They* may not be worried, but they don't know about Enriquez. Did you tell them why you were calling?'

'Well, no, I didn't, as a matter of fact. I guessed that since they didn't have radio contact with the airplane, it didn't make much difference. Either they're going to make it to Jacksonville, or they're not.'

Rain freckled the window. James looked at his watch. 'Listen, Eddie, I'm going to see if I can borrow one of Jack Dunning's Vegas, that's about the fastest thing on the field. I'm going to follow the South-Eastern route to Jacksonville, and see if that Tin Goose has gone down anywhere. You come over to the terminal, and man the wireless for me.'

'James, you're nuts. It's storming out there, and it's even worse up north. You won't be able to see more'n two feet in front of your nose.'

'Eddie, damn it, I have to go, and I'm going! Get over here as quickly as you can!'

Eddie sighed. 'All right, old buddy. It's your funeral.'

By the time James had managed to put a call through to Jack Dunning of Speed-Air, and persuade him to lend him one of his 155-mph Lockheed Vegas, the weather had closed in completely. Rain lashed across the airfield so torrentially that it was almost laughable, as if they were on the movie set for *The Wreck of the Hesperus*. Lightning crackled wickedly beyond the treeline, and the wind tossed branches and leaves and debris across the runway in hurrying, dancing crowds.

Jack Dunning himself arrived at the airfield shortly after seven o'clock, and walked into the hangar in a dripping trenchcoat. He was a thin, rangy man with a large nose and a distinctive Tennessee accent. He walked across to his chief mechanic first of all, a bitter little man called Eggheimer, and then he came across to James, shaking his head. 'I'm real sorry, James; but there won't be any point in you taking her out in this sort of a storm.'

'I can try,' said James.

Jack Dunning continued to shake his head. 'I'm sorry. I know how you're feeling. But if you try, you're sure not trying in *my* plane.'

'What if I wait until it clears?'

'Then you're welcome to borrow it, by all means, just like I said.'

James ran his hand through his hair. Jack Dunning was quite right. There was no point at all in trying to find South-Eastern Nine in this weather, in complete darkness. He would be lucky if he managed to fly twenty miles.

He thought of Chloe. Her hair, her softness, her unique perfume. He was desperate to know if she were safe. But all he could do was nod to Fritz Eggheimer to stop fuelling the Vega, and thrust his hands into his coat pockets, and turn away to hide the distress which he knew must be showing on his face.

At dawn the next morning, when the skies had cleared, James took off from Carol City in Jack Dunning's white-painted Vega and headed north-north-east, over the eastern reaches of the Everglades. The shadow of his aeroplane was chased across the brownish swamps by the dazzling reflection of the morning sun.

Eddie had tiredly but religiously called Jacksonville once every half-hour during the night, but South-Eastern Nine had failed to arrive. A search was already being made by the police of Palm Beach and Okeechobee counties, and by two Osprey aircraft from the US Coastguard at Boca Raton.

James had borrowed flight-plans from South-Eastern Airways, so that he could trace the route of the missing airliner as accurately as possible. He flew with the map open on his left knee, tilting the Vega from time to time to get a better view of the ground below him. Most of the time, he flew as low as seventy or eighty feet.

He was exhausted, but he flew all day, landing three times at local airfields to refuel. As the shadows gradually leaned from one side of the landscape to the other, he criss-crossed the Everglades from Margate to Okaloacoochee Slough, from Andytown to Belle Glade, on the southern shore of Lake Okeechobee.

There was nothing, only miles and miles of swamp, with rivers and bends and inlets and acres and acres of dense green vegetation. At last, his neck and his knees stiffening with tiredness, Jack turned the high-winged Vega on its axis, so that the bright orange sunlight swivelled through his cockpit from left to right, and headed back to Carol City airfield. He landed in twilight, a white plane in a purple mist, and taxied slowly up to the Speed-Air hangar.

His propeller stopped, and he climbed out of the Vega and stretched his back. Joey Eggheimer was the first to reach him. He scrutinized the Vega quickly and critically, just to make sure that James hadn't scraped the paintwork or caught branches in the undercart.

'You don't find nutten?' he asked.

James shook his head.

'Vell, I gotta tell ya, I'm sorry, ' said Joey Eggheimer. 'It's – ya know – it's friggin terrible. Alvays der same, der best people gettink der vorse breaks.'

And, thought James, *each man kills the thing he loves.*

It was then that Eddie appeared, around the Vega's engine-cowling. He was wearing a plaid shirt and a flappy pair of twill pants, and sandals. 'James,' he said, 'what can I tell you? This hurts.'

'You haven't heard any more from Jacksonville?'

'Ixnay.'

'And what about Enriquez? Have you talked to him?'

'Not since yesterday.'

James smeared his face tiredly with his hands. 'I don't think there's very much more that I can do; not at the moment. They could have made a forced landing somewhere in the swamp, in which case it may take them hours – even days – to get to a telephone. Or, of course, they could have crashed.'

'They have to find them sooner or later.'

'I suppose so,' said James. 'Jack Dunning told me last night that the Everglades cover almost a million-and-a-half acres.'

'Well...' said Eddie. 'I guess there's always a *chance* that they're going to find them sooner or later.'

James picked up his bag and his maps. 'I just want to call Jacksonville one more time; then I'm going to go home and get some sleep. I'm absolutely all-in.'

But Eddie dodged sideways and blocked his way. 'You haven't forgotten what day it is?'

'It's Monday, what on earth has that got to do with anything at all?'

267

'Monday, yes, but which Monday?'

'October the twenty-fourth.'

'And what's happening on October the twenty-fourth?'

James frowned. 'Come on, Eddie, I'm really too tired for all of this.'

But Eddie laid a hand on his shoulder, and gently propelled him around the front of the Vega. And there, only two hundred yards away, in front of the APA hangars, parked neatly in line, stood three shining Lord Aquarius airliners painted in red-and-silver APA livery.

'My God,' said James. 'I totally forgot. When did they arrive?'

'Around about eleven o'clock this morning, flown straight down from Baltimore.'

'And they're all in good condition?'

'Aaaay-one.'

James began to walk towards the terminal building. He was unable to talk for a moment because one of APA's Fairchilds was taxi-ing towards the runway, its single radial engine roaring at top volume. When the Fairchild climbed away into the evening sky, however, its navigation lights flashing, he said, 'Perhaps I can use one tomorrow to search for Chloe.'

'Well, that's something else I wanted to talk to you about,' said Eddie.

'I'm sorry?'

'Look!' grinned Eddie. 'Look who it is – don't tell me you've forgotten!'

James turned towards the terminal building, and there she was, walking cautiously towards him, very thin and white in a pale-yellow dress, her hair carefully brushed and pinned back. Patricia, the same as always. Patricia, his legally wedded wife. Patricia, who could bear him no children.

She came up close and stood pale and apprehensive in front of him, her eyes flickering from side to side as she searched in his face for something that would tell her how he felt. He put down his bag.

'Hello, James,' she said, in a soft voice that sounded extraordinarily English.

'Hello, Patricia.'

He grasped her hands almost as if he needed to hold himself up, and kissed her briefly and without feeling on the lips. 'It's been a long time, hasn't it?' he told her. 'You must forgive me, I'm ah –'

'Such a long time, my darling,' said Patricia. '*And that each day is like a year, a year whose days are long.*'

For one iced, jarring moment, James could scarcely keep himself from shouting out loud; not in anger but in anguish; because those words, too, were from Oscar Wilde's poem from Reading Gaol, and when Patricia said them they sounded like a judgement. They sounded like rat-poison, being stirred into his food. They sounded like agony. They sounded like those unforgiveable words which, once spoken, could never be taken back.

'How was your –?' he managed to say. Then, after a swallow, 'trip? – over?'

Eddie picked up his bag for him. 'Steady the Buffs,' he murmured, out of the corner of his mouth.

Patricia said, 'Well, it was very long, much longer than I thought it was going to be, in any case we weren't late, I arrived this morning right on time but it *seemed* longer. I just thought it would be a nice idea if I came over with the aeroplanes. You know – so that you could have everything you wanted all at once, on one day.'

James nodded throughout this explanation, his head going up and down as if he were beating time to a church bell. He opened the terminal door so that Patricia could go ahead of him, still talking. Then he took her through to the office and she stood beside him still talking while he sorted through the day's mail and the day's receipts.

'Well, Mr Feinbacker introduced himself as soon as I arrived and told me where you were, looking for that lost airliner. He said that you airline people always stick together and help each other when something goes wrong. I think that's marvellous. I've been working for the lifeboats, with your mother; and the distressed gentlefolk; and I used to be so selfish before, always thinking of myself and what I wanted but that was one of the things that Dr Hallett told me: *stop* thinking about yourself – stop, stop, stop! – and *start* to think about other people. And adoption, too, James. We could adopt! There isn't any reason at all why we shouldn't choose ourselves a child, is there, and bring him up as our own? I mean, I'd rather we did it in England, but if you want to go on living here, then perhaps an American child would be all right.'

Patricia paused, and smiled, and then frowned. 'Isn't it *hot* here? Well, humid, anyway. Is it always like this?'

James was standing behind his desk with tomorrow's flight schedules laid out under the lamplight. His head was bowed so that neither Eddie nor Patricia could see his face. Only Eddie saw the tear that dropped on to the open file; crinkling the paper; followed by another. Only Eddie knew what strength it was taking for James to remain upright, and to carry on listening to Patricia, when he would rather have crawled under his desk and covered his head wih his hands and forgotten that the world around him had ever existed.

Chichester, 1933

The second Saturday in February was one of the coldest days for a decade. The South Downs were felted in frost all day, and even at midday the sun was nothing more than a dull orange disc on the southern horizon. It was quite possible to believe that the Earth was dying, and that they were approaching a second Ice Age.

Richard was exercising their two new Labrador puppies on the Downs at Cocking. The dogs ran figure-of-eight tracks in the frost, their tongues smoking as if they had just been boiled. Richard walked slowly and stolidly, like a man twice his age. His head was wrapped in a brown wool scarf, and he kept his hands deep in his pockets. Yesterday he had woken up in the night with a slight sore throat. Today, there was no getting away from the fact that he was in the first stages of 'flu.

He crossed a ploughed field, crunchy with ice; and he was about to climb over the stile and make his way back towards his car when a stately black Daimler drew up at the end of the lane, and a man in a black overcoat got out and started waving to him. The man was close enough to have shouted out, but instead he waved, saying nothing.

Richard hesitated, and then whistled to the puppies. 'Here, Hannibal! Here, Heracles!' The puppies had been a Christmas gift to Constance from George Woods Humphrey at Handley Page; and so Constance had loyally named them after two Handley Page airliners. Loyally, and ironically, as it turned out.

'Mr Lord?' the man said, briskly, as Richard approached. He tugged off one brown leather glove and held out his hand. 'My name's Cauthen, from the Royal Aircraft Establishment. Sorry to interrupt your walkies.'

Hannibal and Heracles jumped up and dragged their paws all over the knees of Mr Cauthen's coat. Richard snapped, 'Heel!' but they were too exuberant to take any notice.

'It's all right,' said Mr Cauthen. 'I've got a Labrador bitch of my own. I expect they can smell her.'

'I'm surprised you managed to find me,' Richard remarked. He caught hold of Hannibal's collar and clipped him on to his leash. Mr Cauthen caught Heracles for him, and pulled him over, his paws skidding reluctantly on the grass.

'Well, I went to the house first,' said Mr Cauthen. He was a pale, civil-servant type, with a little toothbrush moustache and pinched-in cheeks and a large mole on his forehead. 'I know this area. Used to fly kites here, when I was a lad.'

'What can I do to help you?' asked Richard.

'Quite a lot, really. You know the Chief Superintendent at the Royal Aircraft Establishment, don't you, A.H. Hall?'

'We've met,' said Richard. He bent down and scruffed the puppies' heads.

'Well, he certainly knows *you*,' Mr Cauthen replied. 'In fact, he's a great admirer of yours. He likes what you've been doing lately, bringing your production-lines up-to-date, initiating new research, that kind of thing. He personally thinks the Lord 'stall-flap' is rather more ingenious than the Handley Page 'auto-slot'. Wouldn't tell Sir Frederick that, of course! Ha-ha!'

'No, of course,' said Richard, with a dry throat.

Mr Cauthen said, 'There's no point in my beating about the bush. The thing is, you see, the government's beginning to get rather worried about what's been happening in Germany – what with Herr Hitler being appointed Chancellor last month. So, to cut a long story short, the Cabinet asked the Air Minister to look into the British aircraft industry in general – you know, to come up with some kind of overall report.

'The Air Minister passed the request on to the Under-Secretary; and the Under-Secretary passed it on to the Royal Aircraft Establishment; and the Chief Superintendent passed it on to me.'

Richard took out his handkerchief and blew his nose. 'And *you*, I suppose, want to pass it on to me?'

Mr Cauthen smiled, and inclined his head, as if he were trying to be coaxing. 'I didn't want to give it to anybody at de Havilland's or Handley Page's, don't you see, because, well, to put it delicately, it's a question of *attitude*.'

Although they were high up on the Sussex Downs on a perishingly cold February afternoon, without even a cow in sight, Mr Cauthen leaned closer to Richard and whispered his next few words in a cloud of vapour that was pungent with confidentiality and whisky.

'If you want to know the truth, the Chief Superintendent has considered for years that the British aviation industry is chronically behind-the-times. It's a cottage industry. Fifteen or sixteen little companies, operating in sheds. They wouldn't survive, you know – present company excepted – if the Air Ministry didn't share out contracts between them. And you know as well as I do that apart from Lord Aviation, they all rely totally on the Royal Aircraft Establishment for their research.'

Mr Cauthen held up his ungloved hand and counted off the British aviation industry's failings on his fingers. 'They haven't the management, they haven't the designers, they haven't the skilled labour. They haven't the qualified production engineers, they haven't the managers, they haven't the cost-accountants. They're amateurs; seat-of-the-pants men and backroom boys. But if we have to re-arm, which the Air Minister is beginning to think may be highly likely, then I'm afraid they're all we've got.'

Richard looked unhappy. 'If that's how the Royal Aircraft Establishment feels about it, I can see why you can't go to Sir Frederick Handley Page; or to Geoffrey de Havilland.'

'Well, of course,' said Mr Cauthen. 'They wouldn't accept a criticism like that for a moment. They'd blow their tops! They're self-made men. Practical men. Very strong personalities. As far as they're concerned, all that it takes to build an aeroplane is patriotism, ingenuity, and a little glue. But the Under-Secretary's been to Germany, to look at the Junkers' factory; and he's also been to America, to look at what they've been doing at Douglas and Lockheed.'

There was no need for Mr Cauthen to elaborate any further. Richard knew from eight frustrating months of running Lord Aviation on his own just what he was up against from the aircraft factories in Germany and America. His Lord Capricorn was one of the most advanced airliners in Britain: a twin-engined all-metal monoplane with a potential cruising-speed of a hundred and ten knots. But although it had been revolutionary when Herbert Lord has first conceived it – using all the latest American advances such as cowlings to streamline the engines and retractable landing-gear

– it was now four years late. It wouldn't be ready for its first proving flights for at least another ten months, and it was far smaller and slower than the Boeing 247 or Douglas Commercial One – both of which were expected to be flying in the early summer.

So far, Richard had received only one firm order for the Capricorn, and that was from the Air Ministry, for proving as a military transport.

'I'm not altogether sure that I agree with Mr Hall one hundred per cent,' Richard said, cautiously.

Mr Cauthen sniffed. The sun was beginning to sink, and the air was damper and colder than ever. 'You don't *have* to agree with him one hundred per cent. You don't have to agree with him at all. What you're expected to do is to approach the problem with an open mind, and report back on what you discover. I was simply stating the problem as perceived from Farnborough. How *you* assess it is up to you.'

'I'm extremely busy,' said Richard. 'I'm not at all sure that I've got the time.'

In fact, it wasn't the time that such a report would take that was worrying him: it was the effect it would have on his business relationships with the rest of the British aircraft industry. He knew without undertaking any research at all that he would have to come up with some distinctly unpopular conclusions.

The great Handley Page company, for example, were still mentally in the stick-and-string era. Their latest airliner for Imperial Airways, the HP 42, was a monstrous biplane with a fuselage as big as a Pullman car, so slow that it was frequently overtaken by express-trains on the ground. Its pilots joked about its 'built-in headwinds'.

Among the other leading firms, Richard knew that A. V. Roe were excellent managers, but bereft of any new designs; that Blackburns had some dramatic new ideas but were hopeless at putting them into production; and that Fairey Aviation were drastically lacking in skilled labour.

There was plenty of natural genius in the industry: designers like Sydney Camm at Hawkers and Reginald Mitchell at Vickers Supermarine. But in spite of their brilliance, they had very little idea how to design an aircraft that was suitable for large-scale industrial production. They were 'boys-in-the-backroom': self-educated, amateur, inspired bodgers rather than professional designers. And, if the truth were known, the majority of their most advanced ideas had been borrowed from abroad.

Quite honestly, Richard dreaded the idea of having to make an official report on all these shortcomings, despite the fact that they were all so obvious. He had no doubt at all that if he accepted Mr Cauthen's commission, every back at the Royal Aero Club and at the Hendon Air Display would be resolutely turned against him.

He looked at his watch. 'I think I'd better be getting back,' he said. 'It's going to be dark soon.'

'May I offer you a lift?' asked Mr Cauthen.

'No, thanks. My own car's just over there, beyond the hedge.'

'What will you do?' Mr Cauthen persisted. 'Will you think about it, and let me know? There's no immediate rush, of course; but I would like to have your yea or nay by the end of next week. The Ministry likes to pretend it's getting on with things, don't you know?'

'Well, I'll mull it over,' said Richard. He tugged at the puppies, and shouted, 'Here! Here, Hannibal! Here!'

The sun was almost swallowed up by the silvery evening mist. Mr Cauthen said, 'I don't want to influence you, of course, but we at the Royal Aircraft Establishment have a pretty privileged view of things – as far as the aircraft industry's concerned, in any case. We see the very latest planes from overseas, and we have a chance to compare them with the very latest designs that are being produced over here.'

'And?' asked Richard.

'And, Britain is still in the Bronze Age, as far as aircraft production is concerned. If we had to fight an air-war against Germany tomorrow, they'd overwhelm us within three days. That's our opinion, at the Royal Aircraft Establishment, and it's based on technical fact, nothing else. I personally believe if you were to take industrial capacity into account as well, the situation is rather worse.'

He looked at Richard seriously, and then said, 'This land of ours is forfeit, at the moment, Mr Lord. We are living on our reputation and on our ability to appease our enemies; nothing else. In terms of the comparative strengths of our air forces, these fields over which you are walking your dogs already belong to Germany, or to France.'

Richard had never in his life heard an Englishman say anything so heretical; particularly an Englishman who looked so mild and conventional and unassuming. To criticize the British aircraft industry (out loud, anyway) was simply not done. To question the Royal Air Force's front-line supremacy was even worse. Richard was quite shocked: but more shocked because he knew from his own experience that what Mr Cauthen was telling him was probably the truth. He said, hoarsely, confidentially, as if he were arranging a meeting with a prostitute, 'I'll give you a call. Do you have a telephone number?'

Mr Cauthen reached into his glove and slipped out a warm, bent visiting-card. 'The world is changing, Mr Lord; changing dramatically. New sciences; new industries; new politics. It's really a question of whether you wish to acknowledge the reality of those changes, or stay in your own little aeroplane factory and bury your head in the wood-shavings.'

Richard led the dogs across the darkening field, and shooed them into the back of his Austin Burnham. He drove slowly back towards the road, the suspension jostling, and saw Mr Cauthen's Daimler disappearing in the direction of Midhurst; and, presumably, Farnborough. Richard was shivering. His sinuses felt stuffed-up and his head ached; and he would have done anything for an aspirin and a large Bell's.

The puppies thrashed on the back seat. Richard looked over the chilly, misty fields and couldn't dislodge Mr Cauthen's words out of his mind: *This land of ours is forfeit. These fields over which you are walking your dogs already belong to Germany, or to France.*

His mother was at home, listening to Jack Payne's BBC Dance Orchestra on the wireless. She had been very taken with the wireless ever since the King's broadcast from Sandringham last Christmas; the very first royal message on the air. '*Through one of the marvels of science I am enabled this Christmas Day to speak to all my peoples throughout the Empire,*' the King had said, in a gruff voice. '*I speak now from my home and from my heart to you all, to men and women so cut off by the snows and deserts or the sea, that only voices out of the air can reach them.*'

Ever since then, Constance had regarded the wireless as respectable; although Minnie Hogg in *The Tatler* had noted that it was still fashionable for the upper classes to claim they never listened to 'that dreadful wireless'.

Nobody had quite decided whether it was respectable to be a 'televisor' or not, but there were fewer than fifty television owners in the whole country, so that was not yet a question of any great importance. Richard had seen the Paramount Astoria Girls dancing on television, and after the initial novelty had worn off he had found the whole thing very dull. It was certainly no substitute for live theatre.

He came into the living-room as discreetly as a guest in a

boarding-house. He had fed and kennelled the puppies. The log fire was crackling brightly and he stood in front of it for a while smiling at Constance and rubbing his hands to warm them up. Constance smiled back, but didn't answer. She was too entranced by an instrumental version of *Mad Dogs and Englishmen.*

At last, she switched off the Ekco, and said, 'Well, then! Did he find you? That man?'

'Mr Cauthen, you mean? Oh, yes. He found me all right.'

'He seemed rather a *rum* sort to me,' Constance remarked. 'Would you like some cocoa? Elsie could make you some, if you'd care.'

Richard said, 'I'd rather have a drink, actually. I think I'm coming down with the 'flu.'

'He said they'd sent him from Farnborough,' Constance remarked, as Richard walked across to the new walnut cocktail cabinet.

'That's right,' said Richard.

'Well – aren't you going to tell me why?'

'Why what?'

'Why he was sent from Farnborough on a freezing-cold Saturday afternoon to come and talk to you? Is it something to do with the Capricorn?'

Richard poured himself more Scotch than he believed he could drink: but the look and the smell of such an enormous measure were curatives in themselves. He turned to Constance, and said, 'It's to do with the Ministry, as a matter of fact. Very hush-hush.'

'It can't be so hush-hush that you can't even tell your own mother.'

'You know what they say, mothers make the best spies.'

'Oh, tosh!' said Constance. 'You're such a ridiculous boy sometimes!'

Richard looked back at her without humour. 'Yes,' he said; thinking of all those evenings when he had sat and listened with crucified patience while his mother had talked about her girlhood, her girlhood, her wonderful girlhood, and Herbert, and Bryan King-Moreton, over and over again, questioning God, questioning her friends, questioning the meaning of life. Questioning everybody and everything, except herself. *Yes,* he thought, *ridiculous.*

'They want me to look into the aircraft business,' said Richard. 'It's nothing very special.'

'*Look into?* What do they mean by *look into?*'

'Oh. This and that. Just to make sure that everybody's pulling their weight. You know the kind of thing. I think they're worried that we're not quite up to capacity.'

'Because of those ridiculous Germans, I suppose?'

'Well, because of Herr Hitler. Not that he's any threat to Britain, of course. I read in the *Telegraph* that he's quite an admirer of all things British.'

Constance nodded for a while, without speaking. Then she looked up at Richard and said brightly, 'I've got a surprise for you!'

'Surprise?' Richard didn't usually care very much for his mother's surprises.

'Do you remember the Hadleighs?'

'Yes, of course. Donald Hadleigh and I used to play cricket on the beach at Middleton, when we were little. His parents were killed on the R-101, weren't they? Why?'

'Do you remember Donald's sister?'

'I think so, yes. She was younger than him, wasn't she? What was her name, Mavis? Doris? Something like that.'

'Iris,' said Constance, with satisfaction.

Richard swallowed a large mouthful of whisky, so much that it made him cough. 'So the surprise is something to do with Iris? Am I correct?'

Constance nodded. 'Donald went off to the Sudan, as you know. He's working on the Sudanese railways, as a consultant engineer. Iris was brought up by her grandmother at Bognor. Very *happily*, from what I hear. But last month, her grandmother died.'

'Well, sorry to hear it,' said Richard, wondering what on earth that had to do with him.

Constance continued to look pleased with herself. 'The thing of it is, while you were out walking the pups, I had a telephone call from John Tremlett. It appears that Cicely Hadleigh had asked in her will that if Iris's grandmother were to die before Iris came of age we were to look after her.'

'We?'

'Herbert and I, that is. But, of course, poor Cicely couldn't have guessed what was going to happen to poor Herbert, could she?'

Richard said, quietly, 'She's coming here, then? Iris?'

'Well, that's right. On Tuesday. She's only seventeen, poor girl. But *I'm* bereft and *she's* bereft, and I really believe that we can get on frightfully well together. I'll have somebody else to worry about, won't I, apart from my silly self?'

Richard sat down by the fire. 'It won't be too much for you, will it? You haven't been feeling awfully chipper.'

'My darling Richard, I'm going to love it! While you're out all day at your beastly factory, I'll have somebody to talk to, just the way I used to talk to Patricia. Somebody to help me with my nail-varnish, somebody to run all those irritating little errands that Elsie can't do! It's going to be quite perfect!'

Richard said nothing, but stared down into his whisky, watching the distorted reflections from the fire leap up and down the rim of the glass. 'Mother,' he said, 'I think I'm going to bed.'

'You're not *annoyed*, are you, that Iris is coming to stay?'

'No, Mother, I'm not annoyed. It's nothing to do with me in any case.'

'But *do* say you're pleased! I'd hate it if you weren't to be pleased.'

Richard finished his whisky, and set down the empty glass. My God, he thought, in about five minutes I'm going to vomit.

'Yes, Mother,' he said, 'I'm pleased.'

He was woken at half-past seven on Tuesday morning by the sound of a motor-car on the shingle drive outside. He opened his eyes and peered at his alarm-clock. He should have been up at seven, but he had forgotten to wind it up. He heard a car door slam, then another, and voices. He threw back his quilt and went to his bedroom window in his green striped pyjamas, yawning and scratching the back of his scalp.

It was quite misty outside. A small Morris was parked close to the porch. His mother was out there, and so was Elsie. The Morris's driver was opening up the boot so that he could lift out a large brown suitcase. Another suitcase was already resting on the ground.

A tall slim girl was standing beside his mother. She wore a plain green overcoat with a velvet collar, and a plain green velour hat, with blonde curls bouncing out from underneath the brim. Richard leaned on the windowsill and watched her; and, as he did so, she glanced up at the house and saw him, and smiled. He jerked away from the window and hit the back of his head on the beam over the dormer.

'Bugger it!' he swore, rubbing his head. He went over to his washbasin and switched on the light. Miss Iris Hadleigh couldn't have been very impressed. He was watery-eyed, pale, unshaven, and his nose was bright red from blowing it.

Miss Iris Hadleigh, on the other hand, from what he had

glimpsed of her, was remarkably pretty, and didn't look as young as seventeen at all.

Richard was shaving when Constance came and knocked at his bedroom door. 'Richard! You'll be late for your breakfast! Iris has arrived!'

'Yes, Mother; I saw her. I'll be down in a tick.'

Iris was spreading toast when Richard came into the breakfast-room. 'Good morning!' he said cheerily, and sat down with a flourish of his napkin at his usual place, at the head of the table, where his *Daily Telegraph* was waiting for him. Elsie immediately bustled in with his bacon-and-eggs. 'Double yolks this morning,' she said, as she lifted the dish-cover. 'Any more coffee, Miss Hadleigh?'

'No, thank you,' said Iris, 'that was scrumptious.'

'Well, you're an early bird,' said Richard. 'I didn't think we were expecting you till lunchtime.'

'Mr Giddings offered to give me a lift,' Iris explained. 'The only trouble is, he has to get to the station by eight.'

'We could have sent somebody to fetch you.'

'You didn't have to.'

'I see,' said Richard, cutting the rind off his bacon, 'you prefer to be independent.'

'I hope you're not making fun of me.'

Richard looked up at her. She wasn't quite as pretty from close-up as she had appeared from his bedroom window, but she was still a very nice-looking girl. A pale freckled face, wavy blonde hair held back with an Alice-band, wide green eyes. She wore a simple low-waisted dress of plum-coloured wool, with a satin bow at the neck. She had a waifishness about her that reminded Richard of Elisabeth Bergner, but Iris was taller and louder and lacked Elisabeth's elfin grace.

Richard shook his head. 'I'm not making fun of you. I'm pleased you've come to stay. Mother's delighted.'

'You've got a cold,' Iris told him.

'A rip-snorter, I'm afraid. I always get one round about this time of year. It's this house. It's so perishing bloody cold.'

Iris laughed. 'You haven't changed, you know. You look exactly the same as you did when you used to play with Donald.'

'How do you know? You couldn't have been much older than four!'

'I remember you quite clearly. You always had your sleeves rolled up. Donald was never any good at rolling up his sleeves.'

Richard smiled, and picked up his coffee-cup. 'I don't know

whether I ought to feel flattered or not.'

'Well, I always liked you, even then. You always used to talk to me. Most of Donald's friends thought it was cissy, talking to a girl.'

Richard asked, 'Are you still at school?'

'I left last September. I wasn't very good. Besides that, Nannie was getting awfully ill.'

'So what are you going to do now?'

'I don't know. Help your mother, as much as I can. I may take a course in domestic science, in the summer.'

Richard took out his handkerchief and blew his nose. 'Wretched cold.'

'Do you want me to make you some hot lemon and cloves?'

'That sounds like a good idea. Provided you put a shot of whisky into it, too.'

'Well, I don't know about that!'

But Iris went to the kitchen and squeezed lemons, and came back after a few minutes with a steaming, aromatic glassful. She watched Richard closely as he sipped it. 'You didn't stint on the whisky, did you?' he asked her. She smiled, still watching him. He had the strangest feeling that she was doing what the Americans would call 'sizing him up'.

'You ought to be a nurse,' he told her, when he had finished his drink.

'I'm too squeamish to be a nurse. All that blood! And bedpans, too, yuck!'

'Well, you've certainly got a talent for looking after people.'

'People I like.'

Richard blew his nose again. 'I don't think I'm very likeable at the moment, with this cold.'

'Oh – that's how I can always tell whether I really like somebody or not,' said Iris. 'If they've got a cold, and I *still* think they're king; then that's a really truly empirical test.'

Richard said nothing, but wiped his mouth with his napkin. Iris smiled at him, her chin cradled in her hand, not blinking.

My God, thought Richard, *I think I'm being seduced. What on earth am I going to do now?*

Richard arrived at the Lord Aeronautics factory at half-past ten. He had stopped at the Copper Kettle in East Street to pick up a Cornish pasty for his lunch. He was unlocking his office door, his lunch in his hand, when his new sales manager Alan Waters came up to him. 'Bad news, Mr Lord, I'm sorry to say.'

'Well, that's a good way to start the day,' said Richard, in his congested voice. 'How bad, on a scale of one to ten?'

He took off his overcoat and hung it up. Then he switched on the light. It was going to be one of those gloomy short February days in which artificial lights were needed from the moment you arrived at work until the moment you left.

Alan Waters said, 'It's a ten, I'm afraid. I had a telegram from Paris this morning. Air Orient have cancelled.'

'Cancelled?' said Richard. 'You mean *completely*?'

Alan Waters nodded. 'There's talk of some sort of merger, all the French airlines getting together.'

Richard snapped, 'This is absolutely bloody outrageous! We have a signed contract! Quite apart from which, we have two specially-adapted Aquariuses out there, almost finished!'

'Yes, Mr Lord,' said Alan Waters. 'But Air Orient seem to be quite sure that they don't want to take delivery. The telegram was signed by M Truchaud himself.'

Richard sat down behind his desk. 'Damn!' he said. 'If that doesn't take the bally biscuit! Where else am I going to get rid of two fifteen-thousand-pound aeroplanes with long-range tanks and special cooling equipment for flying in the tropics?'

He was so furious that he banged his fist down on to the paper-bag holding his Cornish pasty, and smashed it. Immediately, he wished that he hadn't.

'There's something else, I'm afraid,' said Alan Waters, staring in horrified fascination at the smashed pasty-bag.

Richard looked up. 'You'd better tell me.'

'It's this,' said Alan Waters in a small voice, handing Richard a letter. His cheeks were very flushed. His tweed jacket was very green. His flannel bags were very crumpled.

Richard took the letter and opened it up. At the top, there was a letter-head of a new and unfamiliar design, but the name of the company was more than familiar. Atlantic & Pacific Airways, Miami, Florida. Executive President, James H. Lord.

Richard read,

'My dear Richard,
You will recall of course that in November last year we dis-
cussed the possibility of Lord Aeronautics supplying Atlantic &
Pacific Airways with three further Aquariuses to complete a fleet
of six.
Since that time, however, our principal competitor South-East-
ern Airways have suffered the loss of their founder and chief

281

LORDS OF THE AIR

executive, and, as a result, they have also lost the contract for carrying the United States mail between Miami and Atlanta.

South-Eastern have gone into voluntary liquidation, and we have acquired their entire air-fleet and premises at bargain prices. We have also been awarded the United States Post Office contract to carry the mails.

The airplanes which we now own will meet our carrying requirements until the anticipated availability early next year either of the new Douglas DC-1 or the Boeing 247, both of which far exceed in potential speed and capacity anything which Lord Aeronautics could hope to offer us, if at all, for six or seven years.

It is with regret therefore that I must advise you that Atlantic & Pacific Airways will not be requiring any further airplanes from Lord Aeronautics in the foreseeable future.

Personal note to follow.

Affectionately, James.'

Alan Waters gave an odd, nervous giggle. Richard folded up the letter and laid it to one side.

'Really caps it, that does, doesn't it?' said Alan Waters. 'I mean, he promised you, didn't he? *And* he's your brother! And "airplanes", intead of "aeroplanes"! He hasn't been away *that* long!'

Richard slowly rubbed his forehead with his fingertips. He wished to God that his sinuses weren't so painfully blocked. But he couldn't feel angry. Business was business, and if Lord Aeronautics couldn't produce the kind of aeroplane that the world's airlines were looking for, then he couldn't expect anybody to do him any kindnesses, not even James.

With the jingoistic influence of Bryan King-Moreton long faded out of his life, Richard could see now that James had always been right. The dazzling glory of the lone British aviator had served to do nothing but blind the aircraft industry to its own chronic deficiencies. In spite of Sir Alan Cobham flying to Australia and back; in spite of the bravery of Amy Johnson and Jim Mollison; in spite of the Schneider and the Seraphim Trophies; the plain truth was that the British aircraft industry was an antiquated shambles, his own company included.

Richard had loved his father. Even today, he missed him so much that it gave him a physical pain under his ribs to think about him. But his father had made no serious effort to bring his production methods or any of his aircraft up to date.

Even if some extraordinary miracle occurred, and the banks were to phone Richard this morning and offer to lend him three

282

million pounds, interest-free – even if twenty fully-trained aero-engineers were to come marching in through the door, accompanied by fifty non-union riggers – he still wouldn't be able to catch up with Douglas in America or Junkers in Germany for at least another six or seven years, and probably very much longer.

He felt that his father had let him down. Not by his suicide, which was stubborn enough, but by his refusal fifteen years ago to acknowledge that the war had changed the world for ever. His father and all the other fathers: the waffling businessmen and the small-minded workers. The committee-men, the procrastinators, and the backward-lookers. The men who perpetuated the hallucination of British greatness, rather than face the unpalatable truth.

Britain was economically foundering, and the British aircraft industry was foundering along with it.

Richard said, 'Perhaps you could see if you can get M Truchaud on the telephone for me. We might save the Air Orient contract, if we're lucky.'

Alan Waters saluted, and went back to the cubby-hole beside the paint-shop which was signposted 'Sales Office'. Richard stayed in his office for a while, and then went out on to the shop-floor to walk around.

The fitters stopped work to watch him. They had never seen him so silent and grim. He spoke to nobody. He walked under the wing of a shining Air Orient Aquarius, completed except for its propellers, already painted in the airline's livery, and ran his hand along its riveted fuselage.

He walked all the way around the factory. One of the foremen offered him a cigarette but he silently shook his head. Then he went back to his office and picked up his telephone. 'Operator? I want the Royal Aircraft Establishment at Farnborough. I want to speak to Mr Cauthen. That's correct, Cauthen.'

Mr Cauthen, as it turned out, was away for the day; but Richard committed himself by leaving a message. 'Tell Mr Cauthen that Mr Lord will give him all the assistance he requires; and to call back as soon as convenient.'

Constance had suffered two serious bouts of 'flu during the early part of the year; and on the following week she developed a chill and backache and took to her bed. She spent all of her time listening to the wireless and smoking and reading Herbert's old diaries; although she had now read and re-read them four times over, and had discovered nothing to confirm James's provocative claim that 'there had always been another woman' in Herbert's life.

She leafed over the pages again and again, sitting propped up with her pillows, her shoulders protected from the February draughts in a loosely-woven Shetland shawl, leaf, leaf, leaf. But there was nothing there; not even a hint. It would have been better if there had been. At least she would have been reassured that James hadn't been trying to hurt her for no reason at all, and that there *had* been a reason for Herbert's aloofness, apart from her own shortcomings as a wife.

She was searching for a single name: a name that would tell her that she hadn't been such a bad wife and such a bad mother, after all.

But there was no name, not even a pet-name; not even initials; not even an anagram.

There was, however, one paragraph that continued to puzzle her. It was the first entry that Herbert had written after returning from Lindau in 1923. Amongst all his technical and social notes, it seemed oddly lyrical, and yet it meant nothing whatsoever.

'*I feel like the swagman, caught by the billabong. Up comes the trooper, one! two! three! I wonder what he saw. I wonder what he felt like. His belly must have turned to water. God, mine would have done. To be caught, waltzing. But what a waltz!*'

That was all. Every time Constance came across it, it arrested her eye, and she read it with a frown. Herbert had just come back from Germany, and yet he had written about Australia. And what did he *mean* – 'I feel like the swagman?' What did he *mean* – 'to be caught, waltzing'? The next paragraph was all about variable-pitch propellers and wing-spans and flaps, and how well the *Lorelei* had handled in a dive.

Constance tried to keep well and cheerful. Iris was a tireless help: she came up to see her four or five times a day, either to collect her lunch-tray or to read to her. They were reading *The Good Earth*, which was all about Chinese peasants, and always sent Constance to sleep. Sometimes they played cards together, for pennies. To Constance, Iris was an angel.

February came to a bleak finish, with white skies and steady north-east winds and ice in the bird-bath. Constance's back pains grew even more severe, and by mid-March Dr Hallett was prescribing morphine. Constance began to grow confused about what she heard on the wireless, and when the Nazis won a majority in the new Reichstag elections on March 4, she rambled on about Hitler as if she knew him intimately – and if he had won the elections, why didn't he do something about pruning her pear trees?

At the end of March, the weather began to break, but Constance still felt too weak to get out of bed, even though she could see the sun shining in the garden, and the birds began to perch on the balcony-rail outside her French windows.

Sometimes Iris stood by the window and sang to her. They were always love songs. They made Constance feel embarrassed, and she never knew whether she ought to laugh or cry. Quite often, she cried, and wiped her eyes on the place-mat from under her supper-plate.

On the last day of March, Dr Hallett rang Richard at work. 'Can you meet me at the Dolphin? We ought to have a talk.'

The Lord works was almost empty. During the last two weeks of February, Richard had been forced to lay off sixteen of his fitters and three of his designers. Air Orient had refused to take delivery of the Aquariuses they had ordered: they simply couldn't pay for them. And an angry and impassioned letter to James in Florida had so far yielded no reply. Apart from contracted-out work from other aircraft companies, and a half-hearted Air Ministry commission to develop a more effective supercharger, the order books were bare.

Richard stood in the echoing factory, and said, 'It's nothing serious, is it?'

'I'll see you at half-past twelve,' Dr Hallett had assured him.

Dr Hallett ordered fatty lamb cutlets and brussels sprouts, and a bottle of red wine that dried the roof of Richard's mouth. The man and the woman at the next table were talking loudly and smoking furiously; and the smoke irritated Richard's sinuses so much that he began to cough, and couldn't stop. He seemed to have had one long continuous cold, all winter.

'It sounds as if you ought to be home in bed, too,' said Dr Hallett, cutting off a piece of white lamb fat and putting into his mouth. He chewed for a while, and then he said, 'I'll give you some linctus before you go back to work. Well – that's if you *want* to go back to work.'

'I don't think you have to pull your punches,' said Richard.

'No, well, of course I won't,' Dr Hallett replied. 'But it's very important for your mother's sake that you remain steady. She's going to be depending on you quite heavily over the next few weeks; for morale, for reassurance, for general day-to-day uplift.'

He chewed and swallowed another piece of fat, and then he

said, 'There will be times when you feel like throwing in the towel, believe me. But you'll always be able to talk to me; or to the Reverend Catesby; and I understand that young Iris Hadleigh is proving quite a help.'

Richard had done nothing more than impale a brussels sprout; but now he laid down his knife and fork and stared at Dr Hallett, and coughed.

'Prime's Paregoric & Liquorice is awfully good,' said Dr Hallett.

'Are you trying to say that my mother is dying?' asked Richard. His mouth tasted like slate.

Dr Hallett dropped his gaze sideways; then lifted it again. 'With regret, Richard, that is the long and the short of it.'

'But what's wrong with her? She's had several bouts of 'flu during the winter, and a bad backache ... But how can that be terminal?'

'You, er, remember the samples I took. Blood, tissue, and so forth. And the X-Rays that were taken at the Cottage Hospital?'

'Of course, but they were all clear, weren't they?'

'We sought a second opinion from Mr Webb-Darnley at the Royal Marsden Hospital in Surrey. Your mother has cancer of the uterus.'

Richard swallowed. When he tried to speak, his voice came out as little more than a harsh squeak. 'But surely – surely you can operate? The uterus can be removed, isn't that possible?'

'It's possible, of course, but far too late. The cancer has advanced beyond the uterus to the lymphatic system. In Mr Webb-Darnley's opinion, your mother has fewer than two months to live.'

Richard looked down at his plate. The grease in his gravy was congealing on the surface in small white discs. 'I don't think I can eat this,' he said.

Dr Hallett peered over, with his fork poised. 'In that case, you won't mind if I spear a couple of your roast potatoes, will you?'

After lunch, Richard went for a long drive, down to the sea at Selsey. He stood on the beach and watched the surf rattling through the pebbles. The sun shone so brightly on the horizon that it was impossible to look at, as if the gates of Valhalla were open, to reveal all the blinding glory of the gods. But there are no gods, thought Richard; no Wotan, no Thor, no Loki; and probably no God, either. He picked up three or four pebbles and threw them furiously out to sea.

When he got home, he went straight upstairs to see Constance, but Iris came out of her bedroom and intercepted him on the landing. She pressed her finger to her lips. 'Ssh! Don't go in now. I've just managed to get her to sleep.'

Richard hesitated, his hand on the doorknob. But then he said, 'All right. I'll look in later.'

Iris at once heard the unhappiness in Richard's voice. He seemed to have shrunk, too; or perhaps it was just because he was standing with his shoulder hunched. 'Is everything all right?' she asked him.

'Of course everything's all right.'

'But you've come home awfully early,' Iris told him.

'Have I? Well – yes, so I have. I don't know why.'

He stood with his hands down by his sides, staring in defeat at his mother's closed bedroom door. Iris, coming closer, suddenly saw that there were tears in his eyes.

'Richard! What on earth's the matter?'

He took out his handkerchief. 'It's just this – cold, that's all.'

'Richard, something's upset you . . .'

'Well,' he said, taking an unsteady breath. 'I think you'd better come downstairs. I had lunch with Dr Hallett today – at Dr Hallett's request.'

'And?'

Richard looked towards the door. 'He, um – told me what was wrong.'

They went downstairs, treading carefully so that the boards wouldn't creak. Richard opened the cocktail cabinet and poured himself a whisky. 'Sherry?' he asked Iris.

'Yes, please,' she replied, without hesitation, and sat on the rug by the fire, her legs tucked underneath her. She looked very young, in her kilt and her Fair Isle pullover, her hair tied back with a ribbon. She could have been a schoolgirl.

Richard handed her a small glass of amontillado. Then he sat down in the armchair that had once been Herbert's – 'Daddy's chair'. Of all the poignant changes that had taken place in Richard's life over the past year, none had struck him with such emotion as realizing that 'Daddy's chair' was now his. There was nobody else to sit there.

Iris turned around so that she was facing him. The firelight danced on the side of her face, and occasionally skipped in her eyes. 'Is she very badly ill?' she asked him.

'Yes,' said Richard. 'Dr Hallett says that she has cancer.'

'She's not going to die?'

Richard nodded, and kept on nodding. 'I'm sorry to say that she is. Dr Hallett has given her two months.'

Iris began to weep. Huge tears rolled out of her eyes and down her cheeks, and sparkled in the wool of her Fair Isle pullover. Richard said, 'Iris – Iris, you mustn't let yourself get too upset,' but Iris knelt on the rug in front of the fire and silently wept and wouldn't stop. 'Iris – please. There's nothing at all that we can do, except to make the rest of her life more comfortable.'

This made Iris start sobbing out loud. Richard got out of his chair, knelt down beside her, and carefully took her sherry away from her, setting it down on the hearth. Then he held her in his arms, and she clung on tightly, the hot scratchy wool of her pullover against the side of his face, a thin girl smelling of eau-de-Cologne, sobbing so wretchedly that he could feel her ribcage heave.

'Iris, please. Iris! Shush now, Iris, it's up to us to be strong.'

At last Iris lifted her head, and stared up at him, her cheeks water-marked with tears. 'Oh, Richard, how are we going to bear it?'

Richard shook his head. 'I wish I knew: but we will. We'll manage somehow, Iris, I promise you.'

Iris kissed him between the eyebrows. Then she kissed his nose, red as it was; and then his cheeks.

'Richard . . .' she whispered. 'Please help me to bear it. If Constance dies . . . I won't have anybody left, apart from you.'

She kissed him again, on the lips this time. He said, 'Mmfff, Iris –' but she wouldn't stop, he couldn't pull her away; or perhaps he didn't really want to pull her away. Her tongue-tip slid in between his lips, and explored his teeth. She kissed like a child but she certainly wasn't a child. Richard at last took hold of her wrists and pushed her gently away.

'Oh, Richard, I love you. You must have known! I loved you the very first morning, when you were so grumpy and kept making fun of me.'

'I wasn't grumpy at all!' Richard protested. Iris tried to struggle free and kiss him again, but he warded her off, and managed to get up on to his feet. She blew him a kiss instead, from the palm of her hand.

'I'm sorry,' he said, 'you simply can't love me. Well, I don't mean you *can't*, but you shouldn't. I'm nearly twenty-five. And besides, love has to be something of a two-way thing, don't you think?'

She turned towards the fire. For a long time, she said nothing at all. Richard swallowed whisky, and watched her. 'When I was little,' she said, at last, 'I used to look into the fire and see caves and tunnels, all red-hot; and imagine that was what hell was like.'

Richard said nothing.

'I saw my Nannie dying,' Iris told him. 'It was so strange. You could almost see the spirit, trying to cling on to the inside of her body until the last possible moment. *I don't want to go, I don't want to leave! I'm scared of what's going to happen next!* But then it had to let go, and her body was just a body. It was quite empty, like an empty house.'

Richard said, 'It's asking a lot . . . but I do hope that you can help me, while Mother's ill.'

Iris reached out her hand, and Richard was obliged to take it. It felt skinny and immature and a little damp. 'Oh, Richard,' she said, 'I'll help you. I promise I'll help you.'

She paused, and then she said, 'Your mother has been so kind to me. She couldn't have been kinder, even if she'd been my real mother. I'll take care of her, I promise.'

Richard cleared his throat. 'Perhaps when Mother's – well, when it's all over – perhaps we can think about some sort of guardianship arrangement.'

'I don't see why we have to do that,' said Iris.

'Well, if I'm going to continue to look after you –'

Iris squeezed his hand and frowned at him. 'Oh, you're *always* going to look after me, aren't you?'

'As far as I can, Iris, but –'

'Oh, Richard! We won't *need* any silly old guardianship arrangement! We can be married!'

May and June were months of agony. Although she was heavily drugged with morphine, Constance was unable to die quietly. As the days lengthened and the sun began to fill her room, she screamed and screamed until Richard had to press his fingers in his ears to block her out. Sometimes he felt as if she were going to scream the whole house into collapsing, as if they were all going to go mad.

At other times, she sang to the songs on the wireless, in a high, gasping voice with a death-rattle at the end of every line. 'Mad dogs and Englishmen – go out in the midday sun! The Chinese wouldn't dare to! The Russians wouldn't care to!'

Elsie and Iris did their best with Constance until midsummer's day, when she suddenly vomited blood all over her breakfast-tray. Dr Hallett came at once and said that she should be taken into the Cottage Hospital; but out of all of them Iris said firmly that she ought to stay at home.

'How long does she have left?' Iris demanded, in the hallway

289

downstairs. The hallway smelled strongly of the lavender-polish that Elsie had rubbed over everything, in an effort to conceal the smell of sickness.

Dr Hallett looked at his watch. 'Days rather than weeks, my dear; and probably hours rather than days.'

'In that case, she ought to be able to spend her last few hours in her own home, don't you think? In her own bed, looking at her own garden. You can't save her; so please don't take her away.'

Dr Hallett glanced at Richard with an obvious lack of enthusiasm. 'I suppose I could arrange for a private nurse.'

Iris took hold of Richard's arm, and begged, '*Please*, Richard; she'll be so unhappy in a hospital!'

Richard thought for a moment, and then nodded. 'All right. You understand her more than the rest of us. Can you see to that, doctor? How soon do you think we can get somebody?'

'Tomorrow, if you like,' said Dr Hallett. Upstairs, he heard Constance wailing in pain. 'I'm not at all sure that it's best – but, well, if that's what you wish, who am I to say nay?'

All through the night, Constance screamed and sang. Richard went in to see her every hour, but it was clear that she didn't recognize him. She kept calling for Herbert, and for her own mother, dead and longer dead. Iris stayed at her bedside almost all the time, giving her sips of water and pressing her forehead with a damp facecloth.

Constance was unrecognizable as the woman she had been only three months ago. Her face was garish yellow and deeply emaciated. Her eyes were as black and as protuberant as the eyes of some fetal pond-creature. Her wrists were so thin that Richard was afraid to take hold of them whenever he was called to check her pulse, in case they snapped.

At dawn on the morning of June 22, Constance became unexpectedly calm and lucid. Richard was deeply asleep on the sofa downstairs, his lower lip pushed sideways by the seat-cushion. But Iris was still there, sitting beside her, her eyes dark from stress and lack of sleep, but smiling.

'*Iris* . . .' Constance suddenly whispered. 'What a dear devoted girl you are. To sit by me, through such a terrible time.'

Iris took hold of Constance's hand, and gave it a gentle squeeze. 'Richard has been looking after you, too.'

Constance tried to focus her eyes on Iris's face. It was quite difficult, with the sunlight flooding into the room behind her. 'You quite – *care* for Richard, don't you?'

'I love him,' said Iris, simply.

Constance laid her other hand on top of Iris's hand. 'Then you shall marry him, my dear. You deserve nothing less. I shall make quite sure of it.'

She smiled and nodded and sighed; and then she abruptly looked towards the door, and said, 'Was that Herbert I saw?'

'No,' said Iris, 'that wasn't Herbert.'

'Do you know, I could have sworn –! Where *is* Herbert?'

'Herbert's out,' said Iris.

'Out? Out where? It's half-past six in the morning! Where on earth can he be?'

Iris bent forward and kissed Constance's forehead. 'He'll be back, don't worry.'

Richard came into the room shortly after eight, unshaven and frowzy. 'How is she?' he asked, stuffing his shirt-tail back into the waistband of his trousers.

'I don't really know,' said Iris. 'She's been sleeping for about an hour and a half. She doesn't seem to be feeling quite so much pain.'

Richard approached the bed and stared down at the waxen effigy which had once been his mother. 'The nurse should be here after breakfast. Then you can get some rest.'

Iris said, in a small voice. 'I can feel her slipping, you know; in the same way that my Nannie slipped. They try to cling on, but there's nothing left for them to cling on to.'

Richard laid a hand on Iris's shoulder. 'I shan't forget this, you know – what you've done for her.'

It was then that Constance opened one eye, and stared up at them like a pirate. 'Richard!' she said, quite distinctly, but with a nasty rattle at the end of the word. 'Richard – where have you been?'

'Downstairs, Mother. Asleep. How are you feeling?'

'I'm feeling very well, thank you, when everything's considered. It's not raining, is it? Is it raining? I think I shall drive into Chichester today. We must start to make some arrangements.'

'Arrangements, Mother? What for?' He dreaded that she was going to say 'funeral'.

'Why, you ridiculous boy! You always were a ridiculous boy! Your *wedding*, of course!'

Richard gave Iris a sloping smile. 'But, Mother, I'm not getting married.'

'Ah – but you *are*! You're getting married just as soon as you can, so that I can see you married before I die!'

'Mother – I'm not getting married and you're not going to die. Dr Hallett says you're getting much better all the time.'

'If Dr Hallett says that, then get rid of him, because he doesn't know what he's talking about. I'm dying and that's that. And you're getting married, and that's *that*.'

Richard let out a long, indulgent sigh. 'Mother, I haven't got anybody to marry. Running the business hasn't really left me much time for romance, now has it?'

Constance coughed, and coughed again. But then she pointed a claw-like finger at Iris. 'Her, you ridiculous boy! Iris!'

Richard stared at his mother in disbelief. 'Iris? Mother, I can't marry Iris!'

'Don't you like her?'

'Well, that's silly, of course I like her, but –'

'If you like her, you can learn to love her, because she loves you.'

'Mother, this is quite out of the question.'

Constance gripped hold of her sheet and dragged herself upward, with obvious agony. 'You listen to me, Richard. You will inherit almost everything, when I go. The house, the stocks, the capital, fifty-one per cent of the business. I changed my will in order to make it so. But let me tell you this, my lad, I want something in return. I want to go to my God knowing that you will be decently married, to a decent girl. Is that too much to ask, as one last dying wish? My God, Richard, can't you allow me to die happy?'

Richard stood by the bed, open-mouthed. The enormity of his mother's demand was almost too much for him to comprehend. He turned to Iris; but Iris was sitting by the bed smiling as sweetly as ever; unastonished, content, and obviously well-pleased with Constance's last request.

Constance subsided on to her pillow. 'Richard,' she croaked at him. 'Richard.'

'Yes, Mother?'

'Richard, let me hear you promise.'

'Mother, I –'

'*Promise!*' she screeched at him, with a vehement gargle.

He remained rigid, his arms by his sides, quivering with suppressed emotion. Then he jerked his head down as if he were saluting the dead at the Cenotaph, and said, almost inaudibly, 'I promise.'

At eleven o'clock, the nurse had still failed to arrive, and Constance had started moaning. Her moans quickly turned to screams.

Iris ran upstairs to give her an injection of morphine. Elsie stood in the kitchen peeling more potatoes than anybody could possibly eat, and muttering to herself. A marmalade cat slept on the kitchen windowsill.

Exhausted, hot, Richard eventually climbed the stairs to see how his mother was getting on. Iris was standing beside the bed looking frightened. There were spatters of blood on the front of Constance's nightdress, and stains of something dark and watery that must have been bile. Iris said, in a disconnected voice, 'I think she must be going. I'm sure of it.'

Richard went over to the bed and took hold of his mother's hand. Her pulse was thready, and she felt unnaturally cold. 'Mother?' he whispered. 'It's Richard.'

Constance opened her eyes and frowned at him. 'Just like a swagman,' she gurgled.

Richard shook his head. 'I'm sorry, Mother, I don't know what you mean.'

'Swagman,' she repeated. Then, after a very long pause, 'Sing it for me.'

'Sing what for you, Mother?'

'Once a jolly swagman. Sing it.'

Richard turned to Iris in perplexity, but all Iris could do was shrug.

'Sing it,' Constance repeated.

Richard cleared his throat. Off-key, he started to sing:

> 'Once a jolly swagman camped by a billabong,
> Under the shade of a coolibah tree,
> And he sang as he watched and waited till his billy boiled . . .'

He hesitated. Constance was clutching his sleeve, and staring at him with those black, black pond-creature eyes, a string of saliva trailing from the side of her mouth. 'Sing,' she breathed. 'Sing, damn you, you ridiculous boy!'

Richard's throat was constricted, and he could scarcely speak, let alone sing. But after a deep breath, he went on:

> 'Waltzing Matilda, waltzing Matilda, who'll come a-waltzing Matilda with me?'

He had hardly finished the chorus when Constance uttered the most terrifying of anguished screeches. Blood and spit flew out of her mouth, and she tossed her head wildly from side to side.

'Iris!' Richard shouted, in panic. 'For God's sake call Dr Hallett!'

293

'*Aaaahhhhhhhh!*' screeched Constance, beating at the air with her arms as thin as bracken-stalks, and flailing her skull-like head from one side of the pillow to the other.

Iris ran downstairs. It was all Richard could do to keep Constance pinned down to the bed. But almost as soon as Richard heard Iris dialling Dr Hallett's number, his mother stopped screaming and thrashing about, and stared up at him not with pain or hysteria but with terrible knowing. Richard felt the hair stand up on the back of his neck.

'*Mathilde*,' she said.

'Mother? Are you all right? Mother?'

'James was telling the truth, Richard. James was telling the truth! Your father did love someone else; and her name was Mathilde.'

She turned towards her bedside table, where Herbert's dog-eared diaries were stacked. Richard of course had no idea what she was looking at. 'His code,' she whispered. 'His squalid little code. And all the time, for all of those years, it was Mathilde.'

Constance smiled. But, as she smiled, a thin runnel of watery blood slid from the side of her mouth on to the pillow. She let out a low choking nose; and then no noise at all.

Richard stared at Constance. Constance sightlessly stared back. Not for the first time in his life, Richard wasn't at all sure what he was supposed to do next.

Iris came back into the room, followed by a large ruddy-faced woman in a navy-blue cape and a white starched nurse's cap.

'That's all right, Mr Lord,' the nurse boomed at him. 'I'll take charge now.'

Richard crossed his mother's arms over her bony lap. He didn't have the nerve to close her eyelids. 'There's nothing to take charge of, I'm afraid,' he said. His voice sounded oddly flat. 'She's dead.'

The nurse bustled up to the bed and frowned at Constance with obvious annoyance. 'I came all the way from Shripney, you know.'

Richard shrugged, and turned away. He simply didn't know what to say.

A month after the funeral, Richard came home from a working weekend in the West Country to find the house filled with flowers. He hung his hat on the hallstand and called, 'Elsie?' The kitchen door was open and there was a smell of roast lamb around.

He walked through to the kitchen to find it deserted: although there were saucepans on the range and plates stacked ready for lunch. He lifted the saucepan-lids and found new potatoes, fresh peas, and summer carrots. Somebody was in the middle of making fresh mint sauce, because the chopped mint was still neatly heaped on the butcher-board. The back door had been left ajar, and the warmth from the garden eddied in.

Richard stepped outside. The garden was brilliant with lobelia and flax and pink musk-mallow. He shaded his eyes, and saw a figure in a primrose-yellow pinafore bending over the flower-bed, picking poppies. He called, 'Elsie! I've just got back! Is Iris about anywhere?'

The figure turned around, and waved. It wasn't Elsie at all, but Iris herself. Richard walked across the mossy flagstones towards her. Her cheeks were pink, under her sunhat, and her eyes were bright. 'Welcome back,' she greeted him. 'Did you have a good trip?'

'Not very. I spent most of my time looking at half-finished aeroplanes. Where's Elsie?'

'I gave her the day off.'

'*You* gave her the day off? That's a little bit high-handed, don't you think?'

'Not at all. She wanted to see her cousin in Thakeham. And I can manage, just as well as she can. I always used to manage for Nannie. It's shoulder of lamb for lunch, I thought you'd be pleased.'

Richard took out his handkerchief and dabbed the perspiration from his forehead. The sky was almost cloudless, except for a thick bank of creamy-white cumulus lying low behind the trees. The swallows were flying so high that they looked like nothing more than ink-splatters from a scratchy nib. 'Well, all right, then,' said Richard. 'What about a cold glass of cider before lunch?'

Richard went to the factory after lunch. The main shop floor was very quiet, except for some paint-spraying in the far corner, where the last of the Air Orient Aquariuses was being transformed into a charter transport for the Nihon Koku Kabushiki Kaisha in Japan. Richard had been lucky to sell them at all; and as it was, he had accepted a price eight hundred and fifty pounds lower than they had cost to build.

He looked in on the drawing-office. This was the only department that was crowded and busy. In mid-June (with a supercilious note) James had sent him a report on the Boeing 247D, which was already entering service with United Airlines. Richard had realized that the 'revolutionary' Lord Capricorn was hopelessly obsolete even before its detailed drawings were complete. He had scrapped it overnight, and set his designers the task of producing an all-new twin-engined airliner, capable of carrying twelve passengers and 500 pounds of mail. It had to have every new technical refinement, from completely retractable undercarriage to controllable-pitch propellers; and it had to be fast. He called it Project Constance. As far as he was concerned, the signs of the zodiac had brought nothing but ill luck.

He talked to Wally Field; and then to Dick Mullins, his new chief designer. Then he went to his office to catch up on his correspondence and to start writing up his report for Mr Cauthen on the aircraft companies that he had looked at over the weekend. He left the factory well after seven o'clock. It was such a fine evening that he stopped at The Cricketers on the way home, and treated himself to a pint of bitter. He sat outside talking to an old local gardener about lettuces, and how to keep the slugs away by burying meat-paste jars in the soil all around them, and half-filling them with vinegar.

When Richard returned home, it was twilight, soft and smudgy, and the lamps in the house were all lit. He called 'Iris!' as he closed the front door behind him. He stood in front of the mirror on the hallstand and yawned at himself, and smoothed down his hair with his hand. 'Mad dogs and Englishmen . . .' he sang to himself, and then abruptly stopped. He could almost have believed that he had heard his mother singing along with him, up in her room.

'Iris?' he called, but there was still no answer. He peeped into the living-room, but although the lights were on, and a copy of *Punch* was sprawled open on the sofa, the room was empty. 'Iris?'

He went upstairs, crossed the landing, and opened his bedroom door. The lamps beside his bed were lit. His peacock-patterned bedspread had been folded back. Right in the middle of his bed sat Iris, her hair brushed and shiny, wearing a demure white nightdress with a broderie anglaise collar.

Richard stood in the doorway with his arms folded. 'Iris,' he smiled. 'This simply isn't on.'

'We're going to be married, though, aren't we? Your mother said so. And if we're going to be married . . .'

Richard shook his head. 'I'm sorry, what my mother said I should do and what I actually *am* going to do are two different kettles of fish.'

Iris pushed back the covers and swung her legs out of the bed. She didn't seem to be at all embarrassed or abashed. She came across and kissed him, and said, 'I love you, and you can't blame me for that; and in any case, *I* want to be married, even if you don't. Look at us! We're both lonely! All we've got is each other.'

Richard kissed her on the forehead. 'Goodnight, Iris. Don't wait up for me. I've still got some reading to do.'

'Would you like some Ovaltine?'

'No, thanks. I'll lock up. I'll see you in the morning.'

Iris left the room, singing. *'We are the Ovaltineys, happy girls and boys . . .'*

Richard unfastened his cufflinks and smiled to himself. You couldn't blame the poor girl for trying, he supposed. And she was really quite pretty, if you caught her in the right light. She'd certainly grown up a lot, since she had first arrived at Goodwood Lodge. By the time she was twenty-one, she would do any young man credit.

He went downstairs in his green silk dressing-gown and poured himself a whisky. Then he sat and read two long and tedious reports on radiator development from the Air Ministry. He wondered how ministers managed to hold meetings of such unrelieved tedium without falling asleep. Perhaps they did.

The clock in the hallway chimed half-past eleven. He yawned and shuffled his papers straight; and then he went around switching off the lights. At the bottom of the stairs, however, he hesitated, and looked up into the darkness. He was startled to find that there was a strong dark thought in his mind: a thought that refused to articulate itself, but which was deeply compulsive. *No, he thought. You're tired. You're drunk. You'll regret it in the morning.*

He slowly climbed the stairs, and paused again when he reached the landing. *She's willing, after all – she's more than willing. And if you marry her – well, she wouldn't be that bad a catch, would she? Hard-working, cheerful, always eager to please. And a good cook, too. That roast lamb she cooked for lunch was better than anything that Elsie had ever done.*

He crossed the landing and put his hand on his doorknob. He stood still for a very long time. Downstairs in the hall, the clock ticked on and on.

After all, who else have you got? he thought. *She was right, you know. All you have is her, and all she has is you.*

He let his hand drop from his doorknob. He walked along the landing until he reached Iris's room. He tugged the sash of his dressing-gown tighter, took a sharp breath, and knocked. He was almost hoping that she was already asleep, but immediately she called, 'Richard?'

He opened the door. 'Come in,' she said. 'I'll turn on the light.'

'You don't have to –' Richard said quickly, but she had stretched across and switched it on already. Her room was small, but very neat, with flowery wallpaper, and flowers in glasses of water, and a notice-board with cut-out pictures of James Stewart pinned on to it, as well as postcards from France and Switzerland.

'I – er – I just came in to say goodnight,' said Richard.

Iris said nothing, but looked up at him and smiled, and drew back her bedcover.

Richard stared at her. His chest rose and fell with his breathing. Then he loosened the sash of his dressing-gown, and stripped it off. Underneath he was wearing green pyjamas. He sat down quickly on the edge of the bed so that Iris wouldn't see that he was beginning to rise.

He kissed her. She touched his cheek with her fingertip. Her nails were bitten. She whispered, 'I knew you were going to come. I was going to stay awake all night, if I had to.'

He slipped his hand down to her bare knee; then let it run up inside her nightdress, touching thighs, hips, and at last her breasts. They were small and rounded, her breasts, and as soft as two summer clouds. She closed her eyes, and kissed him. Her breathing roared in his ear. He caressed her stomach, and then felt the crispness of her pubic hair.

She was quite difficult to penetrate. For one desperate moment, Richard wasn't at all sure that he was going to be able to force his way inside her at all. But he pushed and pushed, and gained entrace at last; rather skiddy and tight; and after that there was a short bout of jumping and jostling. He took himself out before he climaxed, because he hadn't brought a johnny with him. Most of it went on to her nightdress.

He gasped, 'I'm sorry.'

But Iris – quite peacefully – smiled at him; and then allowed her smile to spread, and her eyes to twinkle, as if she were the happiest and luckiest girl in the world. And for the life of him, he couldn't think why he couldn't quite believe it.

That year was a fine one for British aviation. In June, Jim and Amy Mollison (nee Johnson) flew east-to-west across the Atlantic in a de Havilland Dragon called *Seafarer*, although both were injured when they crash-landed in Bridgeport, Connecticut, after running out of fuel. They were photographed with President and

Mrs Roosevelt – Jim with a bandaged face, Amy with a bandaged elbow.

In the autumn, Sir Charles Kingsford Smith flew his Percival Gull from Lympne in Kent to Wyndham in Western Australia in a record time of 7 days and 4 hours and 44 minutes. A day later, an Avro Ten took off from the Great West aerodrome in Hayes, Middlesex, with a crew of three, and flew to Derby, Western Australia, in 115 hours.

But Richard, who was still assembling his report on the British aircraft industry for Mr Cauthen, was become increasingly aware of just how far behind the rest of the world Britain was lagging – particularly Germany.

On October 24, Winston Churchill warned the House of Commons that Germany was well on the way to becoming the most heavily-armed nation on earth. He harboured 'serious suspicions' that Hitler was secretly rebuilding the Luftwaffe with fast, modern monoplanes.

In contrast, most of Britain's front-line fighters were biplanes; and only two years ago the Air Staff had ordered yet another biplane, the Gloster Gladiator, which was a thoroughly dependable aircraft, but already a decade out of date.

On the first Saturday in November, Richard was married at Chichester Cathedral to Iris Hermione Hadleigh, aged 18 and one day. Elisabeth Bergner was the Matron of Honour. Norman Jorritt was the best man. It rained steadily from morning till night, and all the wedding-pictures showed were black umbrellas.

Barrow Creek, 1932

He circled Barrow Creek three times before he landed, his wheels skimming the corrugated-iron rooftops. He always did, whenever he arrived at any settlement. It brought out the storekeepers and the Bushies and the Abos, not to mention the women. It ruffled the chickens and set the dogs barking, and stampeded the horses. He hadn't earned the nickname 'Sandfly' for nothing: he was fifty times noisier and a hundred times more irritating.

He brought the DH 9C's engine right to the brink of stalling, and let her glide in for a slow, quiet, three-point landing. His shadow-plane rose to meet him, and then he was bumping over the tough spinifex and giving the throttle a last noisy rev to bring him up face-to-face with the dark stone sides of the Barrow Creek Post Office. A wedge-tailed eagle must have been following him, because it looped overhead as he climbed out of the cockpit, and then angled away.

Immediately, he was surrounded by a silent but intent crowd of whites and half-castes and Aborigines, all waiting to see what he had brought with him. He dragged out the mail-pouch, which was pitifully thin, and handed it over to Sly Barrett, the pot-bellied Barrow Creek postmaster; then he brought out the radio parts which the Bollings wanted, over at Aranda Station. He was carrying various other 'odds, sods, and impediment-i-a', as Clarence always called them. A reconditioned oil-pump for Kenneth Perry's dilapidated lorry. Aspirins and laxatives and elastic bandages for the settlement store (as well as that whirling syringe that Mrs Dobson had ordered). Mail-order catalogues from Simpkin's in Darwin; a hook-and-terret farm harness; and a book called *What A Man Of Forty-Five Ought To Know* which had already been thumbed through by every man between Darwin and Banka Banka, whether he was forty-five or not.

Michael distributed everything he could, and then carried the rest across to the post office, accompanied by the skipping Aborigine children. Sly Barrett had already opened up the mail-pouch and was thumbing through the letters with a well-licked thumb. 'See that Gordon's had another letter from the bank. They'll be closing on him soon, if he isn't careful. And Dora's heard from her sister at last. That's a bloody miracle.'

Michael unbuckled his leather flying-helmet, and wiped the sweat from his neck. It was early October, and the temperature was well up to a hundred and twenty degrees. 'Got much to go back?' he asked Sly Barrett. 'I'm pretty well loaded this trip.'

Sly pushed open the lopsided screen-door that led into the post office. 'Couple of catalogue orders, not much else. No parcels.'

'Oh, well, bring them over to the pub,' said Michael. 'I'll take them with me now.'

Sly kept the screen-door open with his foot. He was looking at Michael narrowly. His face had the texture of a withered brown mushroom-cup. 'I wouldn't hang around too long, if I were you. Not like you usually do.'

'What do you mean?'

'Mrs Violet Herridge, that's what I mean.'

'I don't know what you're talking about.'

Sly sniffed noisily. 'In that case, mate, you're just about the only bloke between here and the Alice who doesn't. It's common knowledge where the Sandfly goes when he stops off at Barrow Creek. And now Mr Herridge knows, too. So if I were you, next time I'd got anything to deliver around here, I'd drop it off by parachute, to be on the safe side.'

Sly spat across the boardwalk, into the dust. Then he stood silent, waiting to see what Michael would do next. But Michael stayed where he was, holding the hook-and-terret harness in his arms, saying nothing, and looking back at Sly just as narrowly.

'I'll bring you those letters over,' said Sly, at length.

'Bring me some cord, too,' Michael told him. 'I've got one or two bits of loose cargo I want to tie down.'

Michael walked over to the pub, a low E-shaped building constructed of brownish local stone with a corrugated-iron roof. The blue-and-white Northern Territory flag flapped listlessly on

301

the ridge. An old grizzled Aborigine sat on a disused stone oven outside, smoking a burned-down cigarette between finger and thumb. A notice outside the pub doorway said Neat Clean Dress And Civilized Behaviour At All Times. Barrow Creek was remote, but it still had standards.

There was laughter and loud conversation coming from inside the building; but as soon as Michael walked in, there was immediate silence. The atmosphere was smoky and sweaty, in spite of the tin cowling revolving on the roof. Half-a-dozen local drovers and station-hands were propping up the bar, in open-necked shirts that strained at the belly, and droopy knee-length shorts. Michael said, 'G'day,' and walked up to the bar. The men silently opened up a space to make room for him.

'How you doin', Michael?' the innkeeper asked him. Somebody sniggered, but quickly converted the snigger into a cough.

'Could be worse,' Michael replied. He looked around the pub with a curious smile. 'What's the matter with your clientele today? Two minutes' silence?'

The innkeeper had taken a bottle of India Pale Ale out of his dome-top refrigerator, and was opening it up. He was a generous, ponderous, wide-faced man, with long strands of grey hair pasted across his head to conceal his baldness. Everybody called him Dennis although his name was really Geoffrey. One day fifteen years ago he had left a thin wife and two thin children in Kingston-upon-Thames, simply walked out on them, to come to Australia and run this bar. He was unable to explain why.

Somebody piped up, 'Two minutes' silence, that's right, Michael. They always gave two minutes' silence for the dead. Or those on the verge of death.'

Michael took his beer and swigged it straight out of the bottle. Dennis offered him a cigarette, and said, 'Don't take any notice of these yattering galahs. Leonard Herridge was in here earlier. He says he's going to take out your guts and use them to mend his dingo fence.'

'Poor old Len is what you might describe as "put out",' added a bearded bespectacled drover called Roo. 'Poor old Len thinks he's been cockatoo'd.'

'Cuckolded, you dumb bastard,' somebody else chipped in.

Michael swallowed two more mouthfuls of beer and burped behind his fist and said nothing. There was nothing for him to say; and nothing that he could do, except to take Dennis's warning as seriously as it was meant. Out on the stations, a man's wife was as much his property as his sheep and his windpump and his lorry and his Abo workers. Now that Leonard Herridge had found out what had been going on between his wife and the Sandfly, he would have to take drastic and violent action – not so much because his virility had been put into question, but because his right of ownership had been compromised.

He would have been almost as vengeful if Michael had borrowed his lorry without asking.

Dennis said, mildly, 'Reckon you'd be better off putting a few hundred seat-miles between yourself and Barrow Creek; and keeping it that way, for a while. Leonard's apt to be pretty berserkish when he's riled. I've chucked him out of here more than once. He should have been a bloody bus-conductor in the middle of London, that bloke; not a farmer. All that being alone, reckon it's turned him half-barmy.'

Michael leaned over the bar so that Dennis could light his cigarette for him. 'Is Violet all right, as far as you know?'

'Can't say that I've seen her, not since the last time you were here. What was that, a month? He doesn't let her come into the Creek very often.'

'When did he find out?'

'What, about you and his missis? I dunno. I don't know who told him, neither. But it's pretty hard to keep a secret in a place like this. Reckon you were pushing your luck right from the start, 'specially going to Biddy's place.'

'There wasn't anywhere else,' Michael told him, defensively – too startled that Dennis knew where he and Violet had been meeting to deny that they had been meeting at all. If Dennis knew, almost everybody in the entire Territory must know. There were only three topics of conversation in this part of the world: when it was going to rain, who was misbehaving with whom, and when it was going to rain.

Michael hadn't planned his affair with Violet. He hadn't looked to the future at all; or considered the consequences. The very first time he had flown south from Darwin in his Qantas DH 9C (so heavily loaded with medicine and magazines and packages that he was carrying for Clarence that his wheels would scarcely come unstuck) he had known only that he wanted to see her again; and that to have had her possessively ushered away from him at the Victoria Hotel by the irascible Leonard had not been anything like a satisfactory conclusion to their affair.

That first time, Michael had daringly flown all the way out to Wurluru Station, Leonard Herridge's vast and semi-barren lease east of Barrow Creek. His pretext for visiting had been to deliver

303

a replacement set of cutter-levers which Leonard had ordered express for his Martin Standard sheep-shearing machines. He had landed close to the house: a small stone villa with a wooden verandah, shaded by gums. Violet had come hurrying out to meet him, drying her hands on her apron, almost hysterical with surprise and fear.

She had changed already. She was no longer the plump, contented girl he had met on the *Alexandria*. Her eyes were already narrowed against the demanding sunlight. Her hands were already calloused by farmwork. But they had stood in the dusty yard holding each other tight, saying nothing, for almost a minute.

Leonard and his Aborigine hands had been out looking for lost sheep far beyond the north-eastern boundary. Michael and Violet had made love in the coolness of the bedroom, on the patchwork bedspread, with the plain calico blind tapping against the windowframe. Afterwards, clasping his hand, she had said to him simply, 'I didn't believe that you would ever come to find me. I didn't dare to.'

They had seen each other four times since then – meeting each time at Biddy Cotterell's house on the outskirts of Barrow Creek. Biddy Cotterell was a widow of the First Battalion The King's Own Royal Regiment, which had been stationed in Madras in the 1920s. She hadn't been able to face the thought of life at home as a 'second-hand lady', so she had settled in the Northern Territory, in a secluded white-painted house surrounded by tropical shrubbery, occasionally letting out her back bedroom to travelling salesmen and veterinarians and whomsoever had need of a bed. She was gentle and white-haired and broadminded in the way that only well-to-do English ladies can be. She had told Michael that she had thought it 'miserable nonsense' when the Pathé Cinema in Madras had been put out of bounds to all ranks.

'We are all at liberty to love whom we wish,' she had remarked, airily, tapping her teaspoon on the side of her cup.

Michael thought about that as he finished his bottle of light ale, with Dennis watching him in the way that a boxing trainer watches a protégé fighter before his first bout, in the sure and certain knowledge that he is going to get mashed. 'Want another?' he asked, but Michael shook his head. Dennis added, 'I'd keep the empty, if I was you. Shove it in your pocket, in case you need it.'

'Good luck, mate! Hope you've got a good dentist!' one of the drovers called out, as Michael turned to leave; and his friends lifted their drinks to him, and laughed.

He stepped outside the pub into the midday heat. The old

Aborigine looked across at him with bloodshot disinterested eyes. He saw the post office door open, and Sly Barrett coming out with an armful of packages and a ball of twine. There was no sign of Leonard Herridge. Maybe he had grown tired of waiting for him, and gone home.

He crossed the dusty roadway. 'Sly!' he called. 'I'll take those straight out to the plane!' As he approached the post office, however, he glimpsed a woman coming out of the hardware store further along the street, carrying a shopping-basket. She had her back to him, but he recognized the straw hat and the cornflower-blue dress. 'Violet!' he shouted.

She began to hurry away. 'Violet!' But then she had turned the corner by the white fencing, and disappeared. Michael hesitated for a moment, and then ran after her.

He caught up with her at the end of the next street, where the few houses abruptly ended and the spinifex began. She was making her way as quickly as she could towards a small grove of dead-white ghost gums, her basket swinging as she went. He made a last effort and caught hold of her shoulder.

'Violet! It's me! What on earth's wrong?'

Violet dropped her basket. Boxes of candles and brown-paper bags full of fence-staples and blocks of yellow household-soap scattered across the grass. Violet didn't make any attempt to pick it all up; nor to speak; nor to turn around. Michael stood beside her staring at her in bewilderment. 'Violet, it's Michael!'

She remained silent, but she turned her face towards him. He said, '*Ah!*' out loud. He was so shocked that he stood open-mouthed, feeling that his entire nervous system had been disconnected.

Both of Violet's eyes were almost completely closed by huge crimson bruises. Her forehead was spotted with dark knuckle-marks; and the skin over cheekbones was lacerated. There was a sticking-plaster across the bridge of her nose; and both of her lips were split.

Although the neckline of her dress was quite modestly cut, it was obvious that she was bruised around the collarbone, and probably the breasts. Her wrists and forearms were measled with plum-coloured bruises where Leonard had gripped her while he hit her.

Her closed-up eyes looked back at him in dispassion. I have been beaten and bruised, this is my fate. I am another man's wife – tell me, what else could either of us have expected?

Michael reached out and gently took hold of her hand, but her fingers were completely unresponsive. He could have cried; but he was too angry to cry. Too shocked, and too outraged.

'I'll kill him,' he said, his voice thick with phlegm. 'Violet, I swear to God that I'll kill him!'

'No you won't,' Violet replied, in a bruised whisper. It was more of an order than a prediction.

'But look what he's done to you! Didn't you call the constable? He could have killed you!'

'Yes, but he didn't.' Violet told him – and added with the certainty of a woman who knows that she is at least as valuable to her husband as a sheep or a lorry, 'Leonard wouldn't kill me. Not Leonard.'

Michael stood looking at Violet for a moment longer; then he knelt down in the dust and picked up her shopping for her. When he stood up again, the expression in her eyes hadn't changed.

'I'd better go,' she said. 'Leonard will be wondering where I am. And if he sees me with you –'

'Violet,' Michael insisted, 'it can't end like this.'

She started to walk back towards the main street. 'It has ended like this.'

'But I love you! Don't you understand that?'

She stopped, and looked at him again. 'Do you see my face? I love you, too; but I'm not yours, and this is what happened to me because I was fanciful enough to suppose that I could be.'

'Then for God's sake leave him! Look at you! Look at what he's done to you! He's an animal!'

'I married him, Michael, for better or for worse. He told me that while he was hitting me. For better, he said, or for worse! In the sight of God.'

Michael snatched at the handle of her basket, and tried to slow her down. 'Do you honestly think that God is looking down at you now and approving of what Leonard has done to you?'

'Do you honestly think that He looked down on us when we were fornicating in Mrs Cotterell's bed and approved of that?'

'That was love, damn it! This is sheer brutality! The man ought to be locked up in jail!'

Michael hop-skip-jumped and managed to get in front of her, and stop her. He laid his hands on her shoulders and looked intently into her eyes. 'Violet, I have an aeroplane here. You could set down that basket of shopping right this minute and fly with me back to Darwin. There's plenty of room, if I leave my cargo behind. Violet, listen – it's as simple as walking around to the post office and getting into the aeroplane and leaving. No more Wurluru, no more Leonard, no more beatings.'

Gradually, very gradually, Violet lowered her head. She didn't weep. Whatever Leonard had done to her, it had put her beyond weeping. 'Do you know what Wurluru was named after?' she whispered. 'Wurluru was named after Halley's Comet, when it appeared in 1910. Wurluru is what the Pitjantjatjara people call comets. It means the terrible giant hunter in the sky who lives alone and carries many spears.'

She attempted a swollen smile. 'I always think of Leonard when I think of Wurluru. He lives alone, but I live with him. That's my life.'

She paused, and then she said, 'I'm sorry, Michael. I didn't mean to cause you any pain.'

Michael could have shaken her. 'Don't you understand what you're doing? Has he really beaten so much out of you? We could go – now – and you could escape – and we could live in Darwin and never have to worry about Leonard ever again!'

Violet looked up; but at that moment Michael heard two or three scratchy steps in the dust behind him. He didn't turn around, but he could feel the sudden drop in temperature on his back as somebody stood between him and the sun.

Then a voice said, with chilling venom, 'Get your hands off of my wife, you bastard.'

Michael lowered his hands. Violet glanced at him fearfully; and then at Leonard. Leonard was standing only four feet away from Michael, in a red flannel shirt and a droopy hat. He was unshaven, glistening with sweat, and he smelled of beer.

'Well, well,' said Michael. 'If it isn't the hero who beats up innocent women.'

'You,' said Leonard. 'I'm full of you. From the moment my wife stepped off that bloody ship, I've had nothing but you, you, bloody you!'

Michael stepped back a little. Leonard was advancing on him, his hands by his sides, but with an expression of grinding fury on his face that could have cut through rock.

There was no further conversation. Nothing was going to deter Leonard from hitting Michael very hard; and there was nothing Michael could do or say to stop him. He could run away, of course, but somehow that didn't seem to be the most practical answer; and quite apart from that, his legs didn't seem to want to.

Leonard grunted, and swung at him. Michael dodged back. Leonard swung at him again, and again Michael dodged. Then – just when he was thinking that he was getting rather good at this – Leonard hit him with a fast, unseen left on the side of the chin –

a blow that knocked him sideways into the dust, jarring his shoulder.

Michael sat up, his ears ringing. His jaw felt as if it had been shifted three inches to the right. He touched it, tentatively; and then Leonard punched him hard on the side of the head, and Michael found his cheek pressed against the ground and his mouth full of grit. He had never seen such a concentrated close-up of the ground before. It occurred to him that somebody ought to make a scientific study of the ground from this position. It would give everybody a totally different view of the world we live in.

Leonard walked silently around him, and then kicked him in the hip, and then the ribs, with his steel-capped working boots. Michael felt two stabs of unbelievable pain – pain so intense that he wouldn't have believed it was possible. He coughed, and then he vomited. Nothing much – he rarely ate breakfast before he flew. But it flooded his nose with harsh acrid fluid, and almost choked him.

He thought he heard Violet crying out, then Leonard's gruff voice.

'Haven't you done *enough*, Lennie?'

'Enough? You tell me what's enough! Bloke gets caught shagging another bloke's wife – bloke wants gelding.'

Michael tried to turn over on the ground. The sun glared in his eyes, so that all he could see of Leonard was a threatening silhouette in a wide hat. He reached down to the wide pocket of his flying-jacket, and discovered that his empty beer-bottle was still there, unbroken. Leonard wasn't even looking at him, he was shaking Violet by the arm and saying, 'Talking to *me* about good taste – look at the state of this drongo. At least you could have picked yourself a man.'

Michael clawed himself up – knelt on one knee – almost lost his balance. Leonard turned back to frown at him, then to laugh. 'Want some more, do you, darling?' But then Michael gripped the beer-bottle by the neck and smashed it hard against a stone, and Leonard's laugh died away. He took three or four sideways steps, forcing Michael to follow him around on one knee, and his face was hard and grim and there was nothing forgiving there at all.

'You break a bottle at me, you bastard, you'd better know what you're doing.'

'Michael! Don't!' Violet cried out. 'Michael, he'll kill you!'

'You bastard,' Leonard breathed. Michael, dizzy, held the broken bottle well out in front of him. It suddenly occurred to him that if he was going to have any chance of winning this fight, he was going to have to cut Leonard very badly, perhaps kill him. Trying to protect himself, he had raised the stakes dangerously high – higher than he could cope with.

Leonard ducked and feinted, and jumped in towards him. Michael slashed wildly at the air. Leonard lunged at him again. This time Michael flicked the bottle up, and snagged Leonard's sleeve. Leonard kicked at his wrist, and then kicked at his chest. Michael felt as if his entire ribcage had exploded. He dropped backwards, screeching for breath – too bruised and too winded even to see that Leonard was bending over casually now and picking up his broken bottle.

Violet screamed, 'Leonard!'

Michael tried to roll away, but Leonard grabbed hold of his right arm and yanked it painfully behind his back, pressing Michael face-down into the dust. 'You're pathetic, do you know that?' Leonard panted. 'You're nothing but a piece of dingo-shit.'

He forced his knee into the small of Michael's back. 'Oh God, get off!' Michael begged him; but that only encouraged him to dig his knee in even harder.

With three sharp tugs, Leonard pulled down Michael's twill trousers at the back, exposing his bottom to the sun. Then he leaned forward so that his mouth was close to Michael's ear, and hissed at him, 'You know what I ought to do, I ought to cut you where you deserve, you bastard. I ought to make you sing soprano for the rest of your life.' He pricked Michael's cheek with the edge of the broken beer-bottle, and Michael felt blood slide down to his chin.

'For God's sake,' said Michael. 'For God's sake, I'll go – I'll go away – you'll never see me again.'

Violet stood watching with her face like a swollen Aborigine mask, slitted eyes and hideously pouting mouth, her hands slightly raised as if she were warming them in front of an imaginary fire.

Leonard twisted Michael's arm even harder. Then he reached back with the beer-bottle, and cut without hesitation into the white flesh of Michael's buttocks. The brown curved glass flashed in the sunlight. It was sharper than a surgical scalpel. Leonard cut deep, a ten-inch cross on each cheek, slicing audibly through skin and fat. Blood welled up immediately from each gaping cross, and ran down the sides of Michael's thighs.

Leonard stood up, and tossed the bottle into the bushes. 'We're done now, you and me,' he said, in a voice that was remarkably changed – quieter, more English, without any of the grating threats. Michael turned his head to see Leonard take hold of Violet

by the arm and lead her away. They stopped on the street corner –
then Violet came back to pick up her shopping-basket.

'Michael – I'll get somebody to help you,' she whispered, in a
panic. 'Just hold on, please!'

Michael lay where he was without moving. He could feel the
blood dripping down in between his legs. He could feel the sun
beginning to dry some of it around the edges of his wounds; but
for some reason the sun felt quite cold, and he began to shiver. He
wasn't sure whether he was dreaming or not – but one thought
remained in his mind, floating up and down on the chilly waves of
encroaching unconsciousness. *I'm going to take Violet away from
that maniac if it's the last thing I ever do.*

He was still lying in the dust when Sly Barrett and Dennis came
around the corner. 'Bloody hell,' said Sly.

Dennis heaved himself down on one knee, and gently lifted
Michael's face in his hand. His hand smelt strongly of beer.
'Michael?' he asked. 'Michael? Are you still with us.'

'Bloody marked his arse,' Sly commented, in prurient wonder.
'Never saw an arse marked like that before.'

'Stop talking bollocks and help me carry him down to the pub,'
Dennis told him.

Michael was distantly aware of being carried face down between
the two men. The ground bobbed up and down in front of his
eyes, and his blood dripped on to the dust. 'You wouldn't think a
skinny runt like this would weigh so bloody much, would you?'
Sly Barrett remarked.

They laid him on a camp-bed in a darkened room. They pressed
wet towels against his buttocks to stop the bleeding. A large
bristle-chinned face leaned close to him and said, 'Don't worry,
mate. They're calling the doctor from Cloncurry. You'll be all
right. Won't be able to sit down for a bit; but you'll live.'

Michael stayed with Clarence at Myilly Point for almost six weeks,
convalescing. With all the elbow-digging humour of an Old
Lansonian (O.L.s. as they were generally known), Clarence had
found the whole business of Michael's injuries to be thoroughly
amusing, and made daily jokes about 'the seat of all your problems', and 'you really ought to get to the bottom of all this'.

Michael, with seventy-eight stitches in his buttocks, spent most
of October and November lying on his stomach on Clarence's
verandah, sweating in the seasonal humidity and reading out-of-
date copies of the *London Mercury*. He felt desperately homesick.
Clarence thought he was 'going troppo', but the simple truth was

that he was desperately lonely. Violet had been a friend to look forward to; as well as a lover. Clarence was too busy and too self-contained to be a friend to anyone.

The grass had started in mid-September. Now the Wet was imminent. Thunderstorms banged in the distance, way out across the harbour, with occasional tantalizing flickers of lightning. It was like living next to argumentative neighbours. But until December the oppressive humidity continued, and Darwin itself was given a 'go-by' by most of the equatorial storms.

One night, in the second week of December, Michael was woken up at two o'clock in the morning by the screaming of a north-west wind, clashing the shutters and setting the tin roofs rumbling. A full-scale monsoon wind was blowing down from near the equator. Thunder rolled and detonated in a way that he had never heard it before. Lightning crackled and flared like blazing trees.

He eased himself stiffly out of his cot, and hobbled out on to the verandah. He stood clutching the rail and watching the lightning sizzle, his hair blown up on end by the howling nor'-wester, exhilarated, full of agony and vengeance.

'Leonard!' he screamed, and he didn't care who heard him. 'Leonard! I'm going to kill you!'

Then the rain came sheeting down, misty swathes of it, drowning the garden and spouting off the rooftops of Clarence's storehouses. Michael walked straight-legged down the verandah steps, and stood in the rain in his nightshirt, his arms wide apart, crucified by vengeance, electrified by nature, water pouring off the end of his nose as if he were a gargoyle and plastering his hair flat.

'Leonard, you bastard! I'm going to kill you!' he screamed.

He had woken Clarence. Clarence was never woken by storms; but he could be disturbed by human cries. Still, Clarence had opened his eyes with a smile. Now he was watching Michael through the sitting-room window, wrapped in nothing but a large white bath-towel, his face possessive but placid. He saw Michael drop to his knees in the cascading mud that, until recently, had been a dry path down to the beach. He felt tired but pleased. He found passion very entertaining, he revelled in eccentricity. He lived his life here in Darwin in ways that Michael hadn't even guessed at. He lit a cigarette and remained by the window for almost a quarter of an hour, humming ' . . . *get his clothes and help him pack: If your kisses can't hold the man you love, Then your tears won't bring him back.*'

*

It was still raining two days later when Michael said, 'I need one or two bombs.'

Clarence was sitting at his rolltop desk, writing long lists of figures. He carried on writing for a while; but then he took off his reading-glasses and eased himself around in his chair and said, '*Bombs?*'

Michael tossed aside his magazine. He looked quite serious. 'Yes,' he said. 'Bombs. I've decided what I'm going to do.'

'You're going to declare war on Japan.'

'Not quite. I'm going to declare war on Leonard Herridge.'

Clarence thought about that for a while, and then sighed, and went back to his accounts. But Michael came over and leaned on the top of his desk and said, 'Clarence, I'm serious. I'm going to bomb Wurluru Station, and rescue Violet.'

'I seriously hope you're *not* serious. And I'm serious.'

'Just two, Clarence, you can get them. Two one-hundred-and-twenty-five-pounders.'

Clarence puffed his cheeks out. 'What on earth makes you think that *I* can get them?'

'Because you can get anything.'

'Oh, don't talk such nonsense. Bombs?'

Michael grinned. 'Perhaps those people who sell you all that raw opium – perhaps they can get you some bombs.'

Clarence looked up at him with eyes as small as pinpricks in a home-made camera. 'Raw opium? I hope you're joking.'

Michael stood up and walked across to Clarence with his hands in the pockets of his khaki shorts. 'Come on, Watters. I'm not completely stupid. You were so trick keen to fix me up with Hudson Fysh, there had to be something in it for you.'

'You bloody well opened the packages,' said Clarence, accusingly.

'Yes,' said Michael, 'I bloody well did. First trip. I didn't even know what the rotten stuff was, until I showed some of it to Dr McLeish at Cloncurry.'

'I hope you weren't daft enough to tell him where you got it.'

'Well – you would have been arrested by now, if I had, wouldn't you? I decided to keep mum about it, just in case I ever needed anything that you weren't particularly prepared to give me.'

'Like bombs?' asked Clarence testily.

'That's right. Like bombs.'

Clarence heaved himself out of his chair and waddled over to the window. The rain was blowing straight into Fannie Bay from the Arafura Sea, beating down the banyans in Clarence's garden and sluicing across the verandah. Clarence coughed, and then he shrugged in resignation. 'It's a bit thick, blackmailing an old school pal, don't you think? But if it's bombs you want, then I suppose it's bombs you'd better have.'

Michael said, 'I don't think blackmailing an old school pal is any worse than tricking an equally old school pal into carrying illicit opium for you, do you?'

Clarence took hold of Michael's arm. 'It's a pretty good wheeze, you know. Most of the opium used to be smuggled out of Singapore and then directly westwards to Europe on cargo-ships. But the jolly old European customs were wise to that, and any Oriental ship that docked in London or Rotterdam or where-have-you was pretty thoroughly searched. Still is.'

He gave a small smile of personal pride. 'It was my idea to have the opium brought from Singapore to Darwin, and then taken southwards by lorry to the Alice. From the Alice, it's taken on the train to Adelaide, and shipped to Europe from there, all bundled up in bales of wool.'

'How on earth did *you* get involved in all this?' asked Michael. 'Watters of the Lower Landing, last in cross-country, last in maths, most-whacked pupil of 1924?'

'It was when I was working at the Tin Bank. I did some accounts for a Chinese chap on Cavenagh Street. Well, nothing unusual about that – most of the businesses in Darwin are run by Asiatics these days. Practically all of the white businesses have closed down. There are only eight hundred whites here now; most of whom you've met. But there are nearly fifteen hundred Chinese and Aboriginals.'

Clarence coughed again, and then he said, 'This Chinese chap introduced me to another Chinese chap from Singapore; and *he* was grumbling that the Belgian customs in Antwerp had confiscated a shipment of opium of his worth thousands of pounds. That's when I had the idea. Now I've got a small, well-organized little export business, and it makes more rhino per man-hour than any other business you could think of.

'Almost all of the opium is brought into Darwin by Trepangers. You've probably seen their praus out in the harbour. They're Macassans, from Sulawesi. They've been coming down to Darwin every year quite literally for centuries – even before Australia was discovered by the Dutch. They fish for trepang, which is what they call sea-slugs. Very highly prized, in China and Singapore, our friend the sea-slug. They make a soup out of it which is supposed to drive you bonkers with sexual desire.'

'I don't think I need any of that,' said Michael.

'I wasn't offering you any,' retorted Clarence. 'You wouldn't be able to afford it, anyway.'

Michael said, 'So I was recruited to speed up the traffic between here and the Alice?'

Clarence nodded. 'You've done wonders, I must tell you. Business has never been so brisk.'

'I don't suppose Hudson Fysh knows what's going on?'

'Good Lord, no. Scarcely anybody knows. You, me, a chap called Lim Kim, and my runner in Adelaide, who goes by the unlikely name of Jeffrey Purselady.'

Michael looked at Clarence for a very long time in silence. Then he said, 'What about these bombs?'

Clarence pulled a face. 'Well . . . I can't make any promises. I'll have to go to Chinatown first thing in the morning. You can come with me if you want to. In fact, you'd better. You know what you want, better than I do.'

He stood in the middle of the room, without changing his expression. Then he added, 'You're not thinking of doing away with him, are you?'

Michael shook his head. 'Believe me, I'd like to. No – all I want to do is to create a diversion, and give him the fright of his life.'

'Well, just so long as you don't do away with him. It wouldn't do to have the constabulary looking into it, would it?'

The following morning, the rain had stopped and the north-westerly wind had fallen to a steady breeze. Clarence was out early, in a kimono and sandals, picking paw-paws from the trees in his garden. He had been lucky with the weather: if it hadn't been storming during the evening, the chances were that the flying-foxes would have raided the fruit, since most of it was nearly ripe. Two paw-paw trees had been blown down by the wind – their trunks eaten away to the frailest shells by white ants.

'Breakfast,' Clarence remarked, as Michael came out on to the verandah. 'Then we're off to Chinatown.'

They drove through the grey, humid streets as far as the huge banyan tree known to local wits as The Tree of Knowledge, since it was here that Darwin's amateur politicians gathered in the evenings to smoke and 'talk agin the Government'. Clarence parked not far away, and then led Michael along the street, past the clustered shop verandahs and the closed-up restaurants and the shabby houses of Chinatown. Halfway along Cavenagh Street, Clarence looked quickly around to see if there were any Territory police in sight: then stepped into a long alleyway between two corrugated-iron buildings, and up a flight of rickety wooden steps. A young Chinese boy was sitting at the top of the steps, showing off the pink socks which happened to be the local fashion, and placidly smoking a cigarette.

'Yes, Mr Clarence?' he asked, without looking up. His skin was as smooth and pale as ivory, with scrimshaw eyes.

'I'm looking for Chue Yingfa,' said Clarence.

'You want a game of Pak-a-Pu?'

Clarence shook his head briskly, so that his cheeks wobbled. 'I want to talk.'

'Very well,' the boy replied, and sighed, as if he were granting Clarence an enormous favour. He got up from the steps and led the way into the house. Michael and Clarence followed him along a narrow smoky corridor, and into an office stacked high with tea-chests. Although it was daytime, the blind was drawn tight, and a thirtyish Chinese man in shirtsleeves was working at his desk under the light of an electric lamp without a shade. On the wall was a calendar for 1931 depicting Tian Dan recovering the Qi Territory in the Warring States Period, around 200 BC. On the desk was a Dutch Shell ashtray, in which a cigarette smouldered.

The Chinese looked up as Clarence and Michael came in. 'Ah, my old friend Clarence,' he said, without much in the way of obvious pleasure. He stood up and held out his hand.

'Top of the morning, Chue Yingfa,' said Clarence. 'This is my friend Michael Lord. You've probably heard of him: he's been flying down to the Alice for Hudson Fysh.'

'Well, well, good to know you,' replied Chue Yingfa, in a strong Australian accent. Like many local Chinese, he had been educated at the Darwin State School, as well as the Chinese school. 'Michael Lord, is it? Been here long?'

'Six months,' said Michael.

'Sorry to see you're palling with mongrels,' Chue Yingfa remarked. 'How about a Scotch?'

'Bit early for me, thanks,' Michael told him, guardedly.

'Chue Yingfa, you really are an obnoxious bastard,' Clarence declared, sitting down heavily in the only spare chair in the room. 'Especially since you still owe me two consignments of perfume.'

'What was wrong with that Oriental Lily?'

'What was right with it, you mean? Show me a lady who likes to dab sheep-dip behind her ears, and I'll show you an eager customer for Oriental Lily! My God, Michael, you should have smelled the stuff! The two and seventy stinks of Cairo weren't in it!'

315

Chue Yingfa picked up his cigarette and sucked on it. 'You want something, though? You've come to see me this morning because you want something.'

'I wouldn't come to see you otherwise, now would I?' Clarence beamed. 'My friend here requires a little something in the way of ordnance.'

Chue Yingfa glanced at Michael, still sucking at his cigarette. 'What do you want? An automatic? A rifle, maybe? If you can wait two or three days, I can get you a Thompson sub-machine gun, 1928 model, with six fifty-round drums. It all costs money, of course.'

Clarence continued to beam. 'My friend here has slightly more spectacular tastes than that. He's looking for bombs.'

'Bombs? What kind of bombs?' Chue Yingfa demanded, his accent betraying a very Chinese bark.

'The kind of bombs you drop from an aeroplane,' Michael explained. 'Nothing too big – perhaps a couple of one-hundred-and-twenty-five-pounders.'

Chue Yingfa stared at Michael in silence for a moment, then he burst out laughing. 'You come and ask me for *bombs*! Where the bloody hell am I going to get *bombs*?'

'Your friends in Shanghai should be able to help you,' Clarence suggested.

But Chue Yingfa barked again, and said, 'Oh, no! I'm not asking them for bombs! Hah! It's enough of a risk asking them for Army surplus penknives!'

'Yingfa,' said Clarence, in a soft but threatening voice. 'Do you remember those cases of whisky you were supposed to deliver to Mr Stretton?'

A.V. Stretton was the Inspector of the Territory's Mounted Police. Certain cases of malt whisky that had been directed to him from London had somehow disappeared while passing through Chue Yingfa's warehouses. Since then, guests *chez Chue* had been regularly and openly plied with the Macallan, in large measures.

All the same, Chue Yingfa emphatically waved his hand from side to side, as if he were wiping a window. 'Anything, Clarence. Anything! A gun, a Rolls-Royce, a woman, whatever you want! But not bombs; don't ask it of me.'

Clarence took out an orange-stick and began to clean dirt out from under his nails, his tongue stuck out in concentration. He wasn't going to say anything else, but on the other hand it was clear that he wasn't going to leave, either, not without satisfaction. Michael found the threatening force of his presence quite remarkable. He supposed it was something he had acquired after years of being bullied at school.

Chue Yingfa took out a cigarette and fussily lit it. Then he said, 'Maybe Wang De can help you.'

'Wang De?' asked Michael. 'Who's Wang De?'

Clarence smiled in satisfaction. 'Wang De is our local firecracker-maker. Very loud noises a speciality. Are you coming with us, Yingfa, to act as interpreter? I know that Wang De doesn't speak much English.'

Chue Yingfa nodded. 'You're a white Devil, Clarence. I always said you were.'

Late the following week, against a north-west wind that was blowing almost gale force, Michael took off from Darwin aerodrome in his Qantas DH 9C. The headwind was so strong that he was hoisted into the air like a kite, pitching and yawing, his engines screaming against the storm in a desperate effort to keep flying forward.

He was carrying no medicines, no mail and no parcels; he wasn't carrying any of Clarence's opium, either. He had paid for the fuel that would take him down to Barrow Creek out of his own money. He had, however, borrowed the aeroplane without official permission from Hudson Fysh. There was no chance at all that Hudson would have approved of a Qantas aeroplane going off on a bombing mission – however high-minded the reasons for it may have been.

Once he had turned tail to the wind, his flight south-eastwards was fast and bumpy and exhilarating, with the DH 9C occasionally flying at over a hundred miles an hour. Michael steered along the railway-line as far as Elsey Station, and then carried on by compass-bearing. He was glad that he was making this trip in the Wet. In the Dry, when the wind was as boisterous as this, the dust would blow up from the west in blinding storms called Bedouries. The only way to fly through Bedouries was to stick your head out of the cockpit and look backwards, to see if you had passed over anything familiar.

He stopped for the night at Banka Banka, at the Hubbards' farmhouse, and all night the wind screamed at the windows. In the morning, however, it was calmer, and he took off just as the sun was rising behind the gum trees, carrying a flask of hot tea and a goat's-cheese sandwich that Mrs Hubbard had made for him.

It was almost noon when he turned the biplane eastwards at

Barrow Creek, and flew out towards Wurluru Station. His heart began to beat so violently that he imagined he could hear it over the throbbing of the engine. The shadow of his aeroplane crossed over gullies and gum-groves, scattering kangaroos and sending up bursts of pink-and-grey galahs.

At one point, he flew over a strange city of termite nests, tall spires and misshapen pinnacles. He was flying very low now, lower than sixty feet, so that he wouldn't be seen by anyone at Wurluru until he was almost overhead. He checked the two wires that ran into the cockpit from each lower wing. When he tugged those wires, they were supposed to release a catch and drop his bombs.

He didn't have an awful lot of confidence in Wang De's weaponry. In a pungent shed on the outskirts of Chinatown, this white-haired whiskery firecracker-maker had packed two sections of iron drainpipe with wet guncotton, and then sealed each end by hammering a circular brass plug into it. He had wired rudimentary fins to the tail-end of these makeshift devices; and inserted a mercury-fulminate detonator in the nose. He had spent almost ten minutes warning Michael in Cantonese that it was essential to keep the guncotton damp until the last possible moment, otherwise he would see heaven much sooner than he expected.

Michael's biplane roared over the last ridge, and suddenly he was up over Wurluru Station, startling a small flock of sheep so that they flowed away to the side of their pen like cream on a tilted plate. Then he was thundering right over the corrugated-iron rooftop, his starboard wing almost touching the tall wireless aerial, before banking and climbing and coming around for another pass.

This 'dummy-run' was crucial. Just as he had always flown low over the communities he had visited on his mail-carrying trips, in order to bring everybody out in the open, he needed to find out whether Violet was at home – and equally importantly, whether Leonard was there, too.

He buzzed the farmhouse, climbed over the barn, and angled the DH 9C to clear a tall grove of gum trees. He turned around in his cockpit so that he could see what was happening in the farmyard. There were three Aborigine boys out there already, shading their eyes as they watched him circle around. Then – as he was gaining height for another pass – he saw Violet come running out, in a bright pink dress.

He yelled '*Violet!*', even though she wouldn't be able to hear him, and waved his arm. Violet waved in return, and he could see that she was shouting. That meant that Leonard was away some-where – either in town, or out riding the perimeter fences. Michael throttled back the biplane, lowered the flaps, and brought her down on the flat dusty field next to the sheep-pen. At least, the field had appeared to be flat from the air. As he touched down, Michael discovered that it was so bumpy that it rattled his teeth and gave him a real moment of fear that the undercarriage might collapse. He didn't feel particularly happy about shaking up Wang De's bombs, either.

He had hardly swung his leg out of the cockpit than Violet was running towards him, holding up her skirts to keep them out of the dust. 'Michael! Michael!'

She reached the plane and he held her tightly in his arms. Her hair was tied back and her hands were covered in flour. 'Oh God, Michael, I thought that I was never going to see you, never again! Oh, Michael!'

Violet's shoulders shook with emotion. Michael kissed her forehead, and then her cheeks, and then her lips. 'Violet, I've come to take you away. Do you understand me? I've come to take you back to Darwin with me.'

Violet stared at him, her eyelashes spiky with tears. 'What about Leonard?' She still bore a splotch of red on the side of her jaw, from Leonard's beating, and there were fresh bruises on her wrists and around her elbows.

'I'm not taking Leonard,' Michael replied, trying to relieve her agony and her fearfulness by being funny.

'But he'll come looking. And I can't leave him here. He hasn't got anybody.'

'Violet, he beats you. He hates you. He's completely mad.'

Violet twisted around. 'You'd better leave, Michael. He didn't go far – only down to the creek to look for one of his ewes. He's bound to have heard your aeroplane.'

'Violet,' said Michael. 'Listen to me, Violet. I love you. I want to take care of you. Do you know what they've got in Darwin? Lights, dancing, parties, people. They've got a Chinese market where you can buy cotton and silk to make dresses. They've got a cinema. Do you know what I saw last week? *I Am A Fugitive From A Chain Gang*, with Paul Muni. It's still on. If you come with me now, we could see it together.'

Violet hesitated for a moment. One of the Aborigine boys was running in the direction of the creek, waving both his arms. 'Leonard's coming,' said Violet. 'Oh my God, he's going to be so angry.'

'Violet, come with me!' Michael insisted. 'Violet, I love you! I love you! I love you! Doesn't that mean anything to you at all?'

Violet suddenly made up her mind. Her eyes switched like a floodlight from hesitant to fierce. 'My jewellery, that's all I need. Give me just one minute!'

'Well, hurry,' Michael told her. 'I'll start up the engine, and have the plane ready for take-off.'

Violet snatched his hand, kissed him, and then went running back towards the farmhouse. Michael climbed up into the De Havilland's cockpit, switched on, and started up the engine. It turned over four or five times before it abruptly burst into life, sending up clouds of dust and chaff. Michael taxied it around so that it was facing the wind, and then waited tensely for Violet to reappear.

Supposing she changes her mind, he thought. *Supposing she doesn't want to come with me after all? What the hell am I going to do?*

But then – like the figures for Sunshine and Rain both appearing at the same time out of the doors of a weather-house – Violet came hurrying out of the farmhouse, clutching her jewellery-box, and Leonard came over the ridge, carrying his rifle.

Michael lifted himself up in his seat. 'Violet! He's coming! For God's sake, hurry!'

Violet couldn't see Leonard, because the stables blocked her view. She ran a little way, then she slowed down, obviously out of breath. Michael waved at her frantically. 'Violet! Hurry! It's Leonard!'

Violet waved back at him, and continued to walk.

Leonard had caught sight of Violet now, and had broken into a dog-trot. He was still too far away for Michael to be able to see his face; but Michael could imagine those grim burned-beef features as clearly as if they were pressed right up close. Violet hadn't yet turned around to see Leonard jogging towards her. She was smiling, her jewellery-case clutched to her chest.

Michael thought, *That's it, there's only one thing for it. If she can't get here in time, I'm going to have go and get her.*

He revved up the biplane's engine, and swung it around, taxiing in a semi-circle all the way past the sheep-pen. His starboard wingtip caught on the fence, and part of the fabric was torn, but he kept on going, steering the DH 9C towards the house, on a course that would take him in between Leonard and Violet.

Violet couldn't understand what he was doing; and when she saw him coming close she slowed down even more, and then stopped. Michael yelled at her, '*Leonard! It's Leonard!*' and only then did she look over her shoulder to see her grim-faced husband running towards her – even faster now that he understood what Michael was trying to do.

Michael taxied the biplane as fast as he dared. He couldn't see the bombs under the wings, but he could picture them joggling dangerously at every rut and furrow. It was quite possible that the guncotton had dried out by now, in which case the main charge of the bombs would be just as volatile as their detonators.

Something whizzed like a wasp and smacked into the side of Michael's cockpit. He couldn't understand what it was at first. He thought a wire must have snapped. But then he looked towards Leonard and saw his rifle to his shoulder, and a puff of blue-grey smoke rolling away, and he realized that Leonard was shooting at him. Not just shooting, but aiming to kill.

Violet saw what was happening at the same time, and now she picked up her skirts and began to run towards Michael in earnest. Another bullet sang close to Michael's head, and hit the leather rim of the cockpit. It ricocheted off with a melancholy moan. Michael ducked, although it was far too late.

With a fresh surge of the throttle, he brought the biplane around so that Violet could run up close to the cockpit.

'On to the wing!' he shouted at her, slowing down almost to a standstill. 'On to the wing!'

She clambered up on to the wing and pushed her jewellery-box at him as urgently as if it were a baby. He shoved it down beside him, and then took hold of her hand. 'Climb into the rear cockpit!' he told her, and while she was still trying to tuck her skirts up between her thighs and swing herself bare-legged into the open cockpit, he gunned the engine and swerved the biplane around and headed away from the farmhouse in a twin trail of billowing dust.

Leonard fired twice more. One bullet sang harmlessly between the wings. The second penetrated the fuselage and lodged itself into a spar. Then the DH 9C was bouncing out over the flat field, gaining speed, turning its shining propeller toward the wind. Michael lifted the wheels just as Violet managed to scramble into the cockpit, and he lifted the biplane's nose so that it climbed into the sun at almost forty-five degrees.

At two hundred feet, Michael banked and turned and flattened out, and looked back towards Wurluru Station. Leonard was standing in the yard with his rifle slanted over his shoulder, watching them. Michael glanced back at Violet. She was flushed and weeping; but he smiled at her and blew her a kiss.

'You've escaped! Your new life starts here! And this is something that's going to guarantee that Leonard stays well away!'

He swooped the biplane towards the farmhouse. Leonard
stepped back a few paces, obviously unsure of what Michael was
trying to do. But as Michael saw the corrugated-iron rooftop right
ahead of him, he yanked at the wires that were supposed to release
the two bombs.

They roared over the house. Michael heard a sharp *donk!* as
one of the missiles penetrated the roof, and as he turned and
climbed, he saw for a split-second the triangular hole that it had
made in the corrugated iron. Then there was a deafening explosion,
and the farmhouse burst apart. Windows shattered, stonework
burst apart, and the iron roof was flung high into the air like a
twisted pterodactyl. As Michael circled the station yet again, a
cloud of grey smoke billowed out of the shattered building, and
fragments of timber and angle-iron came raining noisily down all
over the yard. Leonard had been blown over on to his back, and
now he was sitting up and staring at the debris in stupefaction.

Violet screamed, with horror and joy. But Michael was shouting
at her, 'There were two! There were two! Did you see where the
other one went?'

'The other what?' she shouted back.

'The other bomb! There were two bombs! They were hanging
underneath the wings! I didn't see where the other one went!'

Violet craned her neck and looked around, but there was no
sign of the second bomb anywhere around; not even a depression
in the ground where it might have landed and failed to go off.

'Oh, well, it probably landed in the scrub,' said Michael, although Violet couldn't hear him. He checked his fuel gauge. He
was going to have to get going if he wanted to refuel at Banka
Banka. He lifted the DH 9C's nose, and gradually started to gain
height, heading north-north-west, in the direction of Banka
Banka, Tennants Creek, and Darwin.

When he was up to five hundred feet, and the plane was droning
steadily over the scrub, he turned around to Violet and smiled at
her. 'Happy?' he shouted. She enthusiastically nodded yes.

They flew for almost an hour-an-a-half under clouds that hung
over their heads like dirty white bathtowels. Michael was growing
anxious about the fuel. The needle was almost trembling on
Empty; and he knew from experience that when a DH 9C told
you it was empty, it was empty. They were still a dozen miles from
Tennants Creek, where Michael had planned on refuelling, and

the last thing that he fancied right at this moment was a twelve-mile hike across the bush. If he was very miserly, however, he might be able to eke out the last few drops of aviation fuel just enough to get them to the Hubbards'. Once or twice the engine stuttered, and Michael recognized that as a sure sign that the tank was getting chronically low.

Almost at the same time, however, the scattered buildings of Tennants Creek came into view, on the grainy horizion. 'Tennants Creek!' he shouted at Violet.

'What?'

'That's where we're going to land! Tennants Creek!'

Michael concentrated on bringing the biplane down slowly and carefully. His altimeter gradually wound itself down from five hundred to two hundred and fifty, then to one hundred and fifty. 'Are you all right?' he asked Violet. 'If you feel pressure on your ears, just swallow, as if you're eating something.'

Violet was silent for a while, swallowing presumably; but then she tapped Michael on the shoulder and said, 'What's that?'

'What's what?'

'That!' she said, pointing under the port wing. But from where Michael was sitting, it was impossible to see what she was pointing at. 'What does it look like?' he shouted at her. 'What shape is it?'

'It's like a drainpipe! It's got little wings on it, though! It's swinging backwards and forwards underneath the wing! It looks as if it's caught up in something; some wire or something.'

Michael thought: *Oh no! It's the bloody bomb! It must have got itself caught up in its release-wires!* He checked his watch. *It'll be well dried-out by now. If it hits the ground with any force when we land, this aeroplane is going to be matchwood, and Violet and I are going to be shredded like roo meat after the eagles have been at it.*

'I'm going to try something!' Michael shouted. 'I want you to fasten your safety-belt, and hold on tight!'

Once Violet had assured him that she was well strapped-in, Michael took the biplane immediately into a steep nose-dive. The brownish ground bulged up to meet them like rising bread. Then – when they were only seventy-five feet from crashing directly into the scrub – Michael simultaneously pulled back the stick and yanked at the bomb's release-wire. He climbed and turned as fast as he could to get clear of any explosion; but by the time he had circled around again, it was obvious that there wasn't going to be any explosion.

Violet peered under the wing. 'It's still there!' she called. 'It looks as if it's even more tangled up than it was before!'

323

Damn and double-damn, thought Michael. *If this thing goes off now, and blows us to Kingdom Come, that'll be the most devastating example of poetic justice I've ever come across; and the only trouble is, I won't be here to appreciate it.*

But at the same time that he was chattering to himself in Tom Merry platitudes, he was experiencing a deep intestinal churning, like violent peristalsis, which had been set in motion by the sheer dread of dying.

'I'm going to try something else!' he yelled to Violet. 'Were you ever taught to fly?'

'What?' she screamed at him, against the slipstream.

'I said – did anyone ever teach you to fly?'

'No" she shouted. 'Why? You're all right, aren't you? Leonard didn't hit you?'

'I'm absolutely A-One, and Leonard's the rottenest shot I've ever seen. But that drainpipe swinging underneath the wing is one of my bombs – and if I don't get rid of it before we land – it'll probably kill us. You saw what it did to your farmhouse!'

'What are you going to do?' Violet screeched at him.

'I'm going to go out on to the wing, and reach down, and cut the release-wires, so that the bomb drops off.'

'You're going to walk out on to the wing? You can't!'

'I have to, it's the only way.'

'But when you're out on the wing, who's going to be flying the pl –?'

'There's nothing to it,' Michael assured her. 'The only difficult bits are taking off and landing.'

'Michael, I can't! I just can't!'

Michael turned his head around. 'You must! It's easy! All you have to do is take hold of the stick and keep the plane straight and level. If the plane starts to dive, pull the stick back a little way. If it starts to climb, push it forward. Keep your feet on the rudder bar to hold the plane straight; and that's all you have to do.'

Violet stared at him wildly. But, all the same, they both knew that if she had mended fences and dug irrigation ditches and combed out tangled sheep-fleeces for Leonard, she was going to have to fly this aeroplane for Michael. Aeroplanes were Michael's life. If she couldn't cope with them, she might just as well ask him to turn around and fly her back to Barrow Creek.

'All right, now, take over!' Michael shouted, and before she had realized that she was in charge, he had climbed right out of his cockpit and on to the wing. The biplane nosedived with an awful sawing noise and Violet screamed. But Michael gripped the edge of his cockpit and leaned towards her and bellowed, 'Keep the stick back! Hold her level! That's all you have to do!'

Violet drew the joystick sharply back, and the biplane tilted its nose up and began to climb. *'Forward!'* Michael shouted at her. *'Forward!'*

She pushed the joystick forward and the aeroplane nosedived again. Anybody watching from the ground would have thought that she was flying stunts.

'All right now, steady!' Michael told her, as she managed to level the aeroplane out. 'And keep her as steady as you can! I have to get right out between the struts and cut that bomb's release-catch.'

Violet nodded dumbly. That was all she could do. She knew that she was grinning like an ass but that was the tension. There was nothing at all she could do about it. If she stopped grinning she would lose her concentration and if she lost her concentration the aeroplane would go diving into the ground.

Michael, out on the wing, stepped forward, clinging on to the wires and the struts. The wind buffeted past his ears. He looked down, and the tawny ground seemed to be moving beneath him like a dry, glaring ocean. He never felt vertigo when he was sitting in the cockpit, but out here on the wing he was seized by an unrelenting fear of falling, and his muscles felt as rigid and clenched-up as those of a tiny baby, hoisted up too high in his father's arms.

The wing lifted and dropped beneath his feet, and the engine droned loudly. He turned back to Violet and shouted at her, *'Steady! For God's sake!'*

Violet's face was a colourless mask. Michael attempted to give her a reassuring smile, but it came out like a maniacal leer. He felt like Quasimodo, out on the wing, all hunched over and snuffling with fear. He shuffled his way forward to the wing's leading edge. 'Oh God, our help in ages past,' he muttered to himself; and gradually knelt, clutching on to the leading strut with irrational tightness.

The DH 9C angled and swayed. The more that Violet tried to keep it level, the more it wanted to slide away from her. She felt as if she were trying to stir a Christmas pudding in a mixing-bowl that was bobbing around in a sinkful of water.

Not only did the aeroplane refuse to behave itself, but the ground wouldn't behave itself, either. It kept swelling up to meet her, or shrinking away, or tilting off at ridiculous angles. She glanced out at the wing and saw Michael crouching right over the front of it, and she prayed to her mother's memory that he would hurry up.

Michael was now bent right forward over the leading edge of the wing, so that he could see the mechanisms which Wang De had rigged up for him for releasing the bomb. It had been improvised out of the latch for a garden-gate, and should have dropped the bomb quite easily when the wire was tugged from the cockpit. But the wire had somehow looped itself around the bomb's makeshift fins; and even though the catch had worked, the bomb was now swinging and dangling like a trout on the end of a line.

Michael gripped the strut with his left hand and reached down to his trouser-pocket with his right. He tugged out his pliers, and then eased himself down so that he was lying on the wing. The plane yawed again, but he forced himself not to look back at Violet. If she made a fatal mistake, he wouldn't be able to do anything about it, anyway, so he might as well get on with the job in hand.

He crooked his arm around the leading edge of the wing, and tried to snip at the wire with his pliers. The first time, he missed. The second time, he snicked the side of the wire, but didn't manage to cut it through. As he was stretching his arm out for a third try, the biplane's engine suddenly started to cough, and surge, and cough again, and Michael knew for certain that they were almost out of fuel. Over the rushing of the slipstream, he could vaguely hear Violet screaming at him, '*Michael! Michael! Argle-argle-are!*' but even though he couldn't make out the words he knew damn well what she was screaming and he was far more concerned with getting rid of the bomb.

He thought of his father, summoning him into the library after a poor term's report at Lancing. 'The trouble with you, Michael, is that you *can* do it. You can do almost anything. But you have to give of yourself. You have to throw that last one per cent of effort into achieving what you want, when anybody else might have given up.'

The biplane's engine coughed again; then burped; then stopped. The sudden quietness was extraordinary. Only the wind, sailing past them. Only the wires, whistling in cheeky chorus. Only Violet, screeching at him, 'Michael! the engine's conked out! What am I going to do-oo-oo!'

Michael had a sudden and terrible recollection of crashing through that pantechnicon in Cambridge. Furniture, bruises, and blood.

'Steer!' he shouted. They were losing height with embarrassing rapidity. 'You've got plenty of forward speed! *Steer!* Just the way I told you!'

With that hair-raising minor-key whistling in his ear, that sound of a powerless and falling aeroplane, Michael made a deliberate effort to block their predicament out of his mind. He was not clinging to the wing of a helpless aircraft two hundred feet above the bush, and there was no chance at all that they were going to be blown up by Wang De's bomb or (if not) smashed to death by hitting the ground at ninety miles an hour. He was simply carrying out a small technical repair that any apprentice could have done in less than a minute, without even sweating about it.

He crawl-shuffle-crawled just a few inches nearer the leading edge of the wing. Then he bent himself forward, right under the wing, gripping the forward strut with knuckles so white that even Violet could see them, from the cockpit. The wire had snaggled itself up into a cat's-cradle. Michael snipped at two or three loops of wire, and the bomb suddenly dropped six or seven inches, but remained twirling on yet another loop.

The DH 9C was now gliding just sixty feet above the ground. Michael was aware of rocky outcroppings and spinifex grass, not too far below his head. A big red kangaroo was bounding across the landscape, right on the edge of his upside-down vision.

'Oh, God!' he shouted, at nobody at all, and stretched forward with his pliers one last time. He caught the wire, missed it, then caught it again. He snipped.

Thirty feet above the ground, the bomb suddenly dropped. Michael, grasping the wing to stop himself from falling, saw the bomb tumble away behind them. There was a deafening bang, which startled the bounding kangaroo so much that it changed direction in mid-hop and went streaking off at express speed through the spinifex.

Now – grunting with effort – Michael lifted himself up on to his knees, and balanced his way back to the cockpit. He heaved himself back inside, knocking his head painfully on the top of his seat. 'Damn it,' he muttered. But then he was wriggling himself back into his seat, and taking hold of the controls, and immediately he was able to bring the biplane's nose up again, turning it into the wind to gain maximum lift. The DH 9C glided silently and gently down towards the ground. They bumped once, twice, then they were bouncing up and down like novice horse-riders across clumps of tufted grass. At last, the DH 9C came to a standstill.

Michael climbed out. The only sound was the wind, blowing

327

unsteadily through the grass. Over towards the north-west, the sky was darkening dramatically, and it looked as if they were in for a storm. Tennants Creek was a good half-hour's walk, and that only if his legs would stop trembling. Violet climbed out, too, the wind ruffling her dress, and stood beside him. She brushed her hair back with her hand.

'I think you've just qualified for an honorary pilot's licence,' said Michael. He took her in his arms, and kissed her forehead. She smelled of lavender, and warm woman.

'I think you've just qualified for a medal,' she replied.

He reached into the top pocket of his flying-jacket and took out a packet of Senior Service. 'As long as I've qualified for you.'

They lit cigarettes, and they stood side by side, smiling but not saying anything, neither of them wanting time to continue, neither of them wanting anything else but to stay close, and to relish this first real moment of being together, and being safe.

'I reckon Leonard's spitting tintacks,' said Violet, in a very Aussie accent; and then burst out laughing.

England, 1936

The two detectives were waiting for James as he came through the customs hall at Croydon Airport. Although it was a warmish May day, both of them were wearing fawn trenchcoats and brown trilby hats – as if they were afraid that, if they wore ordinary summer suits, people somehow wouldn't believe that they were real detectives.

'Mr James Lord?' asked the shorter of the two, stepping forward and producing his warrant card.

'Yes?' said James.

'Detective-Inspector Willis of West Sussex police, sir. Sorry to – well, you know. Something rather serious has come up.'

'It's nothing to do with my family?' asked James.

'No, sir, nothing like that. But I'm afraid we're going to have to ask you to come with us.'

'Well, is it important?' James demanded, testily. 'I've just arrived this minute from America. My brother will be here to take me home. Can't this at least keep until tomorrow, or the next day? I'm thoroughly bushed.'

'You're *bushed*, sir?' asked Detective-Inspector Willis, in perplexity.

'Exhausted,' James explained. 'I've been two days on the *Hindenburg*, Lakehurst to Friedrichshafen, and four hours on a Heracles. Friedrichshafen, Paris, and now here.'

'I'm sorry, Mr Lord, but a very serious allegation has been made against you.'

Over the Tannoy, Imperial Airways were announcing the departure of their Heracles HP-45 flight to Paris. James said loudly, 'You'd better tell me what this is all about.'

'Manslaughter, sir, I'm sorry to say.'

'Manslaughter? There must be some mistake.'

Detective-Inspector Willis rummaged in the depths of his trenchcoat and produced a handful of elastic bands, a half-eaten bar of Palm Toffee, and a notebook. 'Sorry, sir. No mistake. The suggestion is that on the night of March 16, 1932, you did jointly with one John Philip Gibbons tamper with the seaplane known as the *Chichester Special* with the intention of compromising its airworthiness, thereby causing as a direct result the death by drowning of one Bryan King-Moreton.'

James set down his suitcase. 'Are you arresting me?' he asked, incredulously.

'Not exactly, sir, not exactly *arresting* you. But we are asking you to assist us in our inquiries.'

'And if I refuse?'

'Then, sir, we *will* arrest you. But just at the moment I hope that won't be necessary.'

Just then, Richard appeared, pushing his way through the crowds who were waiting for the arrival of the afternoon flight from Bombay. He came straight up to James and picked up his suitcase for him. 'James! Jolly good to see you! What a suntan! I was hanging around for you outside.'

'I've been detained,' said James, coldly.

'I'm sorry?' asked Richard. He was wearing a creased linen boating-jacket, and his hair was sticking up at the back like a duck's tail.

329

'These gentlemen here are detectives from West Sussex Constabulary. They seem to think that I had something to do with sabotaging the *Chichester Special*.'

'Oh,' said Richard, uncomfortably. The two detectives lifted their matching brown trilbies, and gave him matching nods of acknowledgement smiles. 'I didn't think they were going to be quite so quick off the mark.'

'You *know* about this?' James demanded.

'Well, I'm afraid so. Detective-Inspector Willis came round last Friday.'

'But it's ridiculous!' James protested. 'What possible evidence can they have?'

Detective-Inspector Willis interrupted, 'It's rather public here, sir. Do you mind if we continue this conversation at police headquarters?'

'I think I have a right to know what evidence you have,' James retorted. He felt tired and angry, and he would have done anything for a long Scotch-and-soda.

Detective-Inspector Willis consulted his notebook once more. 'It's first-hand evidence, sir, from Mr Gibbons. He says that you and he entered the Lord Aeronautics factory at three o'clock a.m. on the morning before the *Chichester Special*'s last proving flight, and that he assisted you to make modifications to the engine and control wires which would in certain aeronautical situations have rendered the aircraft unmanageable, even by a skilled pilot like Mr King-Moreton.'

'This is complete fantasy,' James protested. 'Why on earth should I have done anything like that? Quite apart from the sheer absurdity of destroying an aircraft in which I had a considerable financial interest, I didn't even know that Mr King-Moreton would be flying that day. My brother Richard was supposed to be taking her up. You're surely not trying to suggest that I would have done anything to harm *him*?'

Detective-Inspector Willis tucked his notebook back into his raincoat pocket. 'Mr Gibbons said that the modifications wouldn't have rendered the aircraft dangerous, sir. Just slow, that's what he said, and difficult to handle. But they were subtle, that was the way he put it, subtle; the sort of modifications that they would have had to strip the whole aeroplane down to discover.'

'And why has Mr Gibbons suddenly decided after all this time to make such preposterous claims against me?' James demanded.

'Well, sir, it isn't entirely due to his sense of public duty, I must admit. He was arrested last month for robbing a post office in

Balham. His explanation was that he was suffering from headaches.'

'*What?*' said James. 'What the devil do Jacko Gibbons's headaches have to do with me?'

Detective-Inspector Willis smiled another policemanly smile. 'Well may you ask, Mr Lord! According to Mr Gibbons, his headaches started after he helped you to sabotage the *Chichester Special*. That's what he said, anyway. He didn't realize, you see, that somebody was actually going to get killed, and he wouldn't have agreed to help you if he'd known what was going to happen. After the crash, he was too frightened to own up straight away, which I suppose is understandable. But Mr King-Moreton's death preyed on his mind, as it were, causing blinding headaches from time to time and causing complete lapses of memory.'

'Ham-knees-ia,' put in the other detective, with matching triumph. Detective-Inspector Willis quashed him with a sideways look.

'You don't believe any of this nonsense?' James asked.

'We did take it with a pinch of salt to begin with, sir,' said Detective-Inspector Willis. 'But when we made further routine enquiries into the matter, we discovered that a reporter from the *Daily Herald* newspaper had sent a file on the matter to Scotland Yard only a week after the crash. No police action had been considered advisable at the time. But certain allegations were made which corroborated Mr Gibbons's story, at least in part.'

James said, 'I think I'd better see my solicitor.'

'Well, sir, we do have some questions to ask.'

'You can ask as many questions as you wish, but I'm not going to answer them. Richard – will you call John Tremlett and tell him what's happened. And tell him to get in touch with Derek Ellsworthy, too.'

Richard looked extremely distressed. 'Well, yes. Righty-ho. What shall I say?'

'Tell them I've been bushwhacked by two flatfoots.'

Richard frowned, and blinked, and turned around on one heel, and looked desperate.

James was already sitting up in bed with his breakfast tray in front of him when Richard came in with the *Daily Telegraph*. Richard was wearing a maroon wool dressing-gown and the same abashed expression that James remembered from his boyhood, when he had stolen some of his mother's steel curlers to make into model aeroplane fuselages.

Richard said, 'They've made rather a song-and-dance about it, I'm afraid.'

James cut the top off his boiled egg. It was perfect – yolk runny and white just set. Iris might be less than entrancing to look at, but she was obviously an excellent housekeeper. James dipped his toast in the yolk and began to eat, watching Richard as he did so.

'It's here on page five,' said Richard.

'Read it to me,' James told him.

'Well, the headline says "Mr James Lord Is Charged With The Manslaughter of Mr King-Moreton, Allegations Made That He Sabotaged The *Chichester Special.*" I'm afraid they've even printed a photograph of you. That old one they took at Bosham.'

James took the newspaper and scrutinized it while he ate. It was a long story, almost half a column. It ended, 'Mr Lord was released at nine o'clock last night on bail in his own recognizance of twelve thousand pounds. He will appear before Chichester Magistrates next Thursday.'

Richard said, 'It's been absolute bedlam. We've had to take the phone off the hook.'

'I'm sorry to have caused you so much trouble,' said James.

'Well, what are brothers for? I just hope that everything turns out all right.'

'Is there any reason why it shouldn't?'

'Of course not, no,' said Richard. 'I didn't mean that.'

'But you're still not sure? I mean, you're still harbouring a sneaking suspicion that I might actually have done it?'

Richard's cheeks coloured. 'It's not that at all. It's just that it's such a worry. You do hear of juries coming to the wrong decision, don't you? You know – miscarriages of justice. And you have to admit that all this Jacko Gibbons business is pretty queer.'

'Pretty queer is it? In what way, precisely?'

Richard tried to laugh. 'For goodness' sake, James, you've only been back five minutes and you're picking a quarrel already.'

'I simply want to know what it is about Jacko Gibbons that you consider to be pretty queer,' James insisted.

Richard shrugged, and smiled, and then said, 'The telegraph message, if you want to know. I've always been puzzled by that telegraph message. I mean, I could never work out for the life of me who sent it.'

'Jacko Gibbons says he sent it, on my instruction.'

'Well, yes. And that's what's queer.'

'Do you believe him?' James asked, sipping lemon tea.

'Your word against his, do you mean?'

332

'No, not my word against his. *His* word, plain and simple. Do you believe him?'

Richard's face went through an extraordinary display of emotions, like a pack of Tarot cards being shuffled. 'That's not exactly a fair question, old man. It was queer, that's all. Norman didn't send me that telegram; and Elisabeth certainly didn't. So who else could it have been?'

'Some theatrical chap?' James suggested. 'Some flame of Elisabeth's, who wanted you to look like a clot?'

'You know jolly well that Elisabeth and I are only chums.'

'Well, perhaps you are. But the way you used to moon on about her, you could forgive anybody for thinking you were madly in love.'

'James, I'm married now.'

James put down his teacup and helped himself to another piece of toast. 'You know what Shaw said. Marriage combines the maximum of temptation with the maximum of opportunity.'

'That still doesn't answer the question of who sent the telegraph,' Richard retorted, trying hard not to sound offended.

James nodded in mocking assent. 'Nor, indeed, the question of who sabotaged the *Chichester Special*, if anybody did.'

'The *Chichester Special* was in tip-top shape. Bryan said so himself, the first time he took it up. Absolutely tip-top. It wouldn't have crashed without a reason.'

'It could have been pilot error, couldn't it? And *there's* a possible suspect for you,' said James.

'Bryan? But Bryan was killed!'

'Perhaps Bryan didn't mean to be killed. Perhaps Bryan simply wanted to fly the *Special* instead of you. He was always a glory-seeker, like Father.'

Richard repeatedly ran his hand through his hair, trying to tidy it. 'You really think that Bryan could have sent that telegraph? And that the *Special* could have crashed by accident?'

'You don't honestly think that *I* sabotaged it, do you?' James asked him, with intent eyes and a small curved smile like a fish-hook.

Richard said, 'You must admit, James, that you *did* have a motive. You were always dead set against the *Chichester Special*. And Jacko *did* say you hired him to sabotage it.'

'Well,' said James, noisily dropping the *Telegraph* on to the floor. 'You're entitled to your own opinion, I suppose. And to hell with family loyalty.'

'I'm sorry,' said Richard. 'This is all very harrowing. I'm the very last person who wants to see it all dug up again. As far as I'm concerned, what's done is done; and no amount of huffing and puffing is going to bring Bryan back up out of his grave, and marching back home like a hero.'

'My dear Richard, what a generous spirit you are,' James replied. 'For four years, you can seriously entertain the idea that I sabotaged the *Chichester Special* and killed poor B.K-M, but in spite of that you're prepared to say that it's all water under the bridge, let bygones be bygones, kiss and make up.'

'James! For God's sake! You're being prosecuted for manslaughter!'

'By whom?' James shouted back. 'By the Crown, or by you?'

Richard stood with his fists clenched, quivering. From downstairs, they heard Iris's voice calling, 'Dickie? Is everything all right?'

'Tell her that everything's all right, Dickie,' said James.

Richard took a deep breath; and then he called, 'Fine, dear, thank you!'

James smiled. 'You'd better run along. Oh – and while you're at it, you can take my breakfast tray. And you can tell Iris that her boiled egg was perfect.'

Richard said nothing, but picked up the tray, folded its legs, and carried it out.

James lay back on his pillows for a while with a serious face. Then he wiped his mouth with his napkin, swung his legs out of bed, and went to the wardrobe to find his clothes.

Susan was in the garden when he arrived, tying up her *celastrus orbiculatus*, which had been blown adrift from the vine pergola during last week's strong summer winds. She was wearing a wide-brimmed summer hat of pale yellow, with an indigo ribbon around it, and a summer dress of indigo cotton, with a sleeveless pinafore of pale yellow broderie anglaise.

James had parked his borrowed Armstrong Siddeley in the lane at the side of the house, and entered the grounds through the small back gate. He was now approaching the vine pergola through the kitchen-garden, along the brick path, between neat rows of early lettuce and wigwams of breeze-rustled beans. The white summer clouds were reflected in the lean-to roof of the greenhouse, like an endless newsreel of passing English days.

James stood for a moment in the archway of the kitchen garden wall, and took out his cigarette case. He thought that he had never seen Susan looking so beautiful; so much like what she was. A lady of culture and poise and sophistication; a lady who could tie up a staff vine with the same dexterity with which she made love to her lovers.

He hadn't realized how much he would miss her. At the same time, however, he hadn't realized just how short a time his exile in America would seem once he set eyes on her again. All those years in Miami shrank away; because here she was, a little older, but no less beautiful.

He glanced up to see where the sun was. Then he tilted his cigarette-case in the palm of his hand so that a bright reflection shone against Susan's cheek. She turned at once, and shielded her eyes against the dazzling light, and called short-temperedly, 'Who's that?'

James tucked the cigarette case back into his pocket and walked towards her, smiling.

She dropped her twine and her pruning-shears into her trug and said, 'Good God, it's a ghost.'

He came up and took hold of both of her hands. 'Hallo, Susan. No ghost. Real flesh and blood.'

He kissed her cheek. She tugged off her gardening-gloves, and reached up and touched his face, and kissed him back, on the lips this time. James glanced around and said, 'No staff within snooping distance, I hope, I hope?'

'I don't give a damn if there are. James, you look even more wonderful than I could have imagined! And you sound so American!'

'Only to you limeys. The Americans think I sound like Leslie Howard.'

'Oh, my darling,' she said, and kissed him again, clasping his face in her hands.

'I was expecting you to look me up in Miami,' he told her.

She took off her hat, brushed back her hair with her hand. Her eyes were sparkling with the pleasure of seeing him. 'I didn't forget you!' she said. 'We were in New York about this time last year; then Washington. I asked Rodney if I might have some time to myself. I thought perhaps that I could sneak away on a plane or a train and come to see you! But dear Rodney said it wouldn't look right if he had to attend any of his dinners or functions on his own. Talk about *ennui*, my dear! We seemed to spend all of our time watching aeroplanes fly round and round; or peering at aeroplanes on the ground; or talking about aeroplanes to fat, fat Americans who never stopped smiling and never *once* tried to put a hand on my bottom. What a country! USA must stand for Un-Squeezed Arses.'

James laughed. 'You don't change, do you? I must admit they're a beastly moral lot, the Americans. But you could have telephoned me, surely?'

Susan looked away. 'I didn't want to. I missed you, to be perfectly frank; and telephoning would only have made me feel even more low about you than I did already.'

'I see, flesh and blood or nothing.'

'Don't worry about the blood, the flesh will do.'

James took her arm and they strolled across the roller-striped lawns towards the house. It was a huge grey-painted mansion in mid-Victorian Gothic, with tall elms around it, which were always harshly clamorous with rooks. In the distance, a gardener was puttering up and down with a lawnmower, but otherwise the house seemed to be deserted.

'Come in and have a drink,' said Susan. 'I could mix you something American, like a Sidecar.'

'A Scotch will do. *Whisky escocés.*'

She went to the scullery to put away her gardening things, and then she took James through to the drawing-room. It was long and airy, all the windows were open so that the lace curtains billowed. There was elegant antique furniture upholstered in pale peach *moiré* satin and huge porcelain bowls overflowing with flowers. She went to the cocktail cabinet and poured drinks for them both.

They clinked glasses. '*Salud!*' said James.

'Welcome home,' Susan replied.

They sat on the sofa by the open window. 'I've been reading about you in *The Times*,' Susan remarked.

'Well, yes, I expect you have. You should have read the *Mirror*. Airline Tycoon Charged With Killing His Mother's Fiancé.'

'I'm not going to ask you if it's true,' said Susan.

'I don't mind if you do. Mother could never quite believe that I'd had nothing to do with it. That was the reason I had to go off to America. Well, I wanted to go, but it did rather hasten the process. And Richard still frowns at me as if he expects to see horns growing out of the top of my head.'

Susan raised an eyebrow. 'Good to hear that the Lords haven't lost their unfailing capacity for mistrusting each other. The Borgias of Chichester.'

James took out his cigarette case and offered Susan a cigarette. 'They're American, I'm afraid. Very moral. Neither drugged nor poisoned.'

Susan said, 'There isn't any danger of your going to prison, is there?'

'Of course not. I've talked to my solicitor already. He says the prosecution evidence depends entirely on circumstantial evidence – apart, that is, from the gospel according to my alleged co-conspirator.'

'He's lying, surely?'

James blew smoke into the breeze. 'That's up to the jury to decide, isn't it?'

Susan reached down and gently stroked the suntanned skin on the back of his hand. 'When I read that article in the paper, I thought, well, James is quite *capable* of doing such a thing. Not many people would believe it of him; but I know him better than most. I know, for instance, that he loves success more than he could ever love any woman. That's probably what makes him so attractive.'

She looked at James closely. James looked back at her, unblinking.

'If you did it,' she said, in a voice like rubbed velvet, 'I'm sure that you had your reasons. If you didn't, well, then, I'm glad.'

James was silent for quite a long time. Then at last he said, 'I should have married you, shouldn't I?'

Susan shook her head. 'I'm too old for you now, my darling. I always was. But now you've missed the best of me. For me, from now on, it's the long slow decline into autumn.'

'I suppose you know I don't love Patricia.'

'Why should you? No man is obliged to love his wife. In fact many men prefer not to. Rodney doesn't love me, I'm quite sure of that. And these days, I think I prefer it that way, too. Living with somebody you love can be very tiresome indeed, especially at my age. Rodney moved into the end bedroom about two years ago and I've never slept so blissfully in my whole life.'

James crushed out his cigarette, and shrugged, and smiled. 'You should be warned when you're at school, you know, that life is very short, and that if you choose the wrong partner it may be too late to pick another. They should tell you when you're seventeen that if you blink, when you open your eyes you'll be getting on for forty.'

Susan leaned across the sofa and kissed him. 'Don't be sad. We met each other and loved each other, and that's more than most people can say.'

They motored out to Chislehampton, to a small pub called the

Ducks & Drakes. In the low-ceilinged bar, they sat on an oak settle and ate Gloucester cheese and fresh home-baked bread and James drank a pint of Oxfordshire bitter.

'Warm beer at last,' he said. 'I lie awake in Miami and dream of warm beer.'

'Are you going to eat your pickled onions?' asked Susan.

'Why?'

'Because if *you're* not going to, then *I'm* not going to.'

James lifted his towards the oak-beamed ceiling. 'There's a room upstairs.'

'Yes?'

'There's a card on the bar that says it's vacant, 7s 6d the night, including breakfast.'

Susan stared at James for a moment, expressionless, and then reached down and opened her handbag. 'I'm not sure that I've *got* 7s 6d. Can you lend it to me?'

There are days which are perfect when they happen and which retain their perfection in the memory for ever. This day for James was one of them. In the warm upstairs room of the Ducks & Drakes, with the tiny leaded window open so that the afternoon sunlight could shine on the bed, he and Susan made love.

She lifted her indigo cotton dress like a huge convolvulus, or a parachute. It was soft and smelled of the rose-garden and of her. James took off her slip, and gently released the catch of her brassière, and she rested one hand on his shoulder to balance herself as she stepped out of her silk camisole knickers.

Her breasts were soft and white and nippled pink; her skin glowed pale. As James made love to her, he could feel the warmth of the sun on the backs of his legs; he could hear the doves warbling and scratching in the thatched roof just above their heads; he was conscious of the murmuring and the laughing in the bar down below.

Afterwards, lying close together on the high carved bed, they slept for almost an hour. The sun crept across the room and shone on the oak panelling, so that it glowed crimson. A bee droned in through the window and then droned out again. But far away, across the fields, came the sound of an aeroplane, summoning them back to reality.

James's case came up at West Sussex Assizes in the last week of September; a grey Tuesday morning with an unseasonable wind blowing from the south-west. James appeared in the family

Daimler with his silk Mr Ellsworthy, his junior barrister Mr Edward Pollock, and his solicitor Mr John Tremlett. He wore a light grey overcoat with a black velvet collar, and a black Homburg hat. As soon as he stepped out of the car he was surrounded by shouting press photographers; and the police had great sport jostling them all back. 'Come on now, chum! Where do you think you are? The Windmill effing theatre?'

James took his place in the stand looking edgy and tired. The past three months had worn him out. Quite apart from having to prepare for his appearance in court, he had been obliged to run APA at second-hand by trans-Atlantic telephone and telegraph. And – to cap it all – Richard had still not been able to give him a firm delivery date for the four modified Capricorns that he had wanted to fly his short-haul routes between Tampa and Orlando and the Florida Keys – which were the whole reason he had come back to England in the first place.

Richard had argued that the modified aeroplanes were more than adequate, and that James's specifications were too demanding. 'You'll never *need* to take off within five hundred feet – not unless you're thinking of using your sitting-room carpet as a runway.' James had smoked and marched up and down the room and retorted that Richard was just as slipshod a planemaker as all the other companies he was supposed to be checking up on. 'It's what the customer wants, Richard – not what you think you might just be bothered to give him.' Iris meanwhile came and went, came and went, cooking and ironing and polishing the silver and arranging flowers and organizing teas for the cathedral restoration fund.

It had not been a happy summer. The only joy, the only escape, had been Susan. James had seen her whenever possible. They had lunched in Oxford; they had gone to the theatre together in London; they had tried the Dorchester's bedrooms as well as its lobby. They had both realized that this was probably going to be their very last Fling, and that once James's trial came up it would all be over, one way or another – either prison for James, or back to Florida. But somehow that sense of finality had lent their hours together a sweetness that could never have been matched by an affair with a future.

Patricia had written a plaintive little letter, asking whether she ought to come over from America to England to keep James company during the trial, but James had wired back simply 'No need'.

The ushers called, 'All rise!' and Mr Justice Lombard-Andrews appeared, a huge man of twenty-one stone with an explosively florid face and robes that seemed to be gathered around him in uncontrollable folds, like a Leonardo study of heavenly drapery.

Mr Ellsworthy QC turned his toucan-like profile and gave James the most economical of reassuring smiles, but James took no comfort from it. He had been smiled at reassuringly by lawyers before.

Mr Nigel Stuart QC was prosecuting: a short, compact man with brilliantined chestnut hair and a red neck and a tendency to bark.

It took most of a tedious first day for the jury to be sworn in and for Mr Stuart to outline the prosecution's case. James returned to Goodwood Lodge that night feeling withdrawn and exhausted.

The house felt draughty. James wondered if he were coming down with a cold. Iris had cooked oxtail stew, the only dish of hers that James positively disliked. He couldn't have eaten any of it even if he had been hungry. Richard came home at half-past eight and he was tired, too, and argumentative. The modifications to the Capricorn's engine cowlings were giving him one production difficulty after another, and two of his best engineers had been seriously hurt yesterday evening in a motorcycle accident.

To add to these problems, Mr Cauthen had telephoned Richard yet again, the third time this week. Mr Cauthen seemed worried. He was pressing Richard to come up with some comprehensive ideas for restructuring the British aircraft industry. 'We should be ready, you see, in case we have to face The Unthinkable.'

Richard had found this request unexpectedly depressing. Mr Cauthen might call it The Unthinkable, but from what Richard had been reading in the papers throughout the summer, war with Germany had been becoming more and more Thinkable by the minute.

In July, civil war had broken out in Spain, and both Hitler and Mussolini had immediately sent troops and aircraft in support of General Franco's fascists. In August, the Olympic Games had been held in Berlin, and the world had been thrilled and frightened by the barbaric pageantry of Hitler's Thousand-Year Reich. The flags, the parades, the marching bands, the glittering fireworks. And this month, September, at Nuremburg, the Nazis were holding a party rally of thousands of the faithful; a huge political and military spectacle that was still going on.

It seemed to Richard that a good many British politicians who should have known better were quite bedazzled by Germany's new Man of Destiny, and by what he had achieved for Germany in four years of power – a new national spirit, a new national effort, a population lifted from its knees. Either that, or they were desperately afraid of him, and preferred not to speculate what he might do next.

The signs of war, however, were already in the air; and they were there for everybody to see – except, of course, if they preferred not to look up. Richard had already been able to study the prototypes of some of the new German warplanes, the Junkers and the Dorniers and the Messerschmitts. In the spring, his friends at the Heinkel factory had taken him up for a trial flight over Hamburg in a Heinkel 111 twin-engined bomber of the type that Hitler had sent to Spain. The Heinkel 111 was based on an old airliner design, but in Richard's opinion it was ten years ahead of anything the Royal Air Force could put into the air. That was why he painstakingly continued to write his unpopular reports for Mr Cauthen. It was his duty to Britain, and his duty to his family, too. For when Germany was building squadron after squadron of such fast and powerful aeroplanes, how could anybody still believe that they had no interest at all in using them?

James said, after dinner, as Richard sat by the fire listening to the wireless, 'You're glum.'

'Yes,' said Richard. 'You don't mind if I listen to the news, do you?'

'More about Spain, I shouldn't wonder.'

'Yes, that's right, more about Spain. Not that you lot over in America have very much to worry yourselves about.'

James poured himself a glass of whisky. 'Not until somebody invents a bomber capable of flying three thousand miles and back, without refuelling.'

'Well, you can make a joke of it,' snapped Richard.

James sat down on the arm of the chair. 'Believe me, Richard, I'm not making a joke of it. Lord Aeronautics should be working on one right now. Then you can send it over whenever you feel a fit of pique to drop bricks on my house.'

'What on earth are you talking about? I'm trying to listen to the news!'

'I'll tell you precisely what I'm talking about. I'm up in front of West Sussex Assizes charged with manslaughter, and from the way things went today, I'm beginning to wonder if I'm going to get away with it.'

'Oh, nonsense,' Richard retorted.

'Oh, nonsense, is it?' James flared back. 'You certainly wouldn't think it was nonsense if you were me. You haven't done anything to help me at all. You haven't even shown the slightest interest. You couldn't even tear yourself away from your blessed factory for five minutes to see how I was getting along.'

'Well, that was no fault of mine! I was struggling all day with those blasted specifications of yours!'

'If you're finding them that much of a struggle, perhaps I've given the job to the wrong company,' James suggested.

Richard looked up, and James was quite unsettled by how old his brother appeared. Richard said, 'We certainly don't need any favours, if that's what you're trying to imply. We have plenty of British work on our order books, thank you, without begging for crumbs from the other side of the Atlantic.'

James was about to say something sarcastic in reply; but decided against it. He was too tired; and Richard was obviously too irritable. He waited for a moment without speaking, listening to the rest of the news. Deep concern was being expressed for the health of Reynoldstown, the horse who had won this year's Grand National, because he was refusing his feed. There was a shortage of mild ale in London's public houses.

Just like the English, thought James. All they care about is beer and racing. Richard didn't even look up when he left the room.

Iris came out of her dressing-room just as James crossed the landing on his way to bed. 'You're off early,' she said, although she looked ready for bed herself. She was wearing a thick red dressing-gown and slippers, and her hair was tied up in a pink turban.

'Well, I have to be up at six tomorrow,' James told her. 'And it's no good trying to face one's accusers on nothing but a couple of hours' sleep.'

Iris touched his arm. 'I didn't hear you and Richard arguing, did I?'

'Of course not, why?'

'It's just that – well – you have to make allowances for him.'

James frowned at her. 'Is everything all right? He's not ill, is he?'

'It's nothing like that. It's just that – these days – he seems to take the problems of the whole world on to his shoulders. He worries about Spain; he worries about Hitler. He worries about the business. He seems to think that it's all his fault if it rains when the forecast said sunny. And there's nothing that I can do to make him understand that he's not personally responsible for everything and everybody.'

James looked thoughtful. 'Perhaps he needs a holiday. He has been running the business pretty well single-handed.'

'I don't know whether it's that,' said Iris.

She sounded as if she had something else to say; and James waited for her to say it. Downstairs they heard Richard switching off the wireless and closing the doors in preparation for coming up to bed.

'If I give you something –' Iris said, quickly, '– if I let you have a look at it – will you promise me faithfully that you won't tell Richard – I mean, you won't tell Richard that I've let you look at it.'

Bemused, James smiled and said, 'All right. It depends what it is.'

'No, *promise* me. You must. Don't tell him that you've seen it – please – but *do* try and have a word with him about it.'

'All right, then, I promise.'

'Wait there,' said Iris. She tiptoed back across the landing, and into the bedroom that used to be Constance's. She returned almost straight away with a large manila envelope, which obviously contained a book of some kind.

'Have a look at it, and then give it back to me as soon as you can. But don't let Richard see that you've got it, whatever you do.'

James took the envelope and saluted. 'Your wish is my command.'

'Please,' begged Iris. 'Don't joke.'

When James returned to his room, and slid out the contents of the envelope, he realized immediately why Iris didn't think that this was funny. It was indeed a book – a large ledger with a marbled cover and red leather corners. But there were no accounts inside, only newspaper and magazine cuttings.

There must have been hundreds of them, page after page, all carefully cut out and pasted into the book in date order, with neat captions printed in Richard's handwriting. There were also one or two snapshots, and some letters; and one page was devoted to a dinner menu from Monseigneur in Jermyn Street and a spray of pressed freesias.

There were poems, too. Some of them were copied from Keats and Browning, but one or two of them looked as if Richard had written them himself.

To Elisabeth . . . your open eyes contain my dreams . . . your wistful smile enchains my heart . . .

343

James closed the book with an extraordinary feeling of sadness and sympathy, not only for Richard but for Iris. What a shock it must have been for *her*, to come across this book which was devoted to the point of obsession with another woman. James flicked through to the last page and saw that it contained a photograph from the *Tatler* which was dated last week. *Miss Elisabeth Bergner and friends at the Trianon for the opening night of Firework Follies.*

He returned the book to its envelope, and then went to his bedroom door and opened it a little. Richard was still downstairs, he could hear him calling in the cats. He crossed the landing and rapped at Iris's dressing-room door. Iris answered it at once, as if she had been waiting with her ear pressed against it.

'Well?' she whispered.

'I wouldn't worry about it one bit,' James told her.

'But it seems so *peculiar*. And, if he loves me, why does he do it?'

James said, 'Believe me, Iris, it's nothing more than a schoolboy daydream. He always adored Elisabeth; she's very pretty, you know, and just the sort of woman who appeals to his sense of – well, I don't quite know *what* you'd call it. His sense of wanting to *look after* people. She's *petite*, don't you see. Rather elfin. But this is only a daydream. It doesn't mean for a moment that he doesn't love you. That's what you're worried about, isn't it? But it doesn't mean that at all. I mean – if you were potty about Robert Taylor, and cut out every picture of him you ever found – that wouldn't mean that you felt any different about Richard, would it?'

Iris clasped the envelope to her breast. She lowered her eyes. 'I don't know what I feel about Richard, sometimes. Just at the moment, he's off in a world of his own.'

'Well, give him time,' James reassured her. 'He'll snap out of it.'

'But would you have a word with him – you know, about this Elisabeth Bergner?'

James puffed out his cheeks. 'I'll *try*, Iris. Bit ticklish, but I'll try.'

'Please,' Iris appealed.

'All right,' said James, and smiled, and kissed her goodnight on the forehead. Afterwards, he wished he hadn't, because she had already smeared her face with Pond's Cold Cream.

During a long and rainy afternoon, Dr Jacob Lelew, the head of the Structures Department at the Royal Aircraft Establishment, sat in the witness box and gave a dry-voiced dissertation on the stresses and strains to which aircraft components were subject during high-speed flight. He explained that, in his opinion, it was quite conceivable that the damage which had been discovered in the engine and tail structure of the salvaged *Chichester Special* had been caused 'not by the hand of man, but by the fearful wrenching of God's own elements'.

Nonetheless, he admitted, when he was questioned by Mr Stuart, '. . . it was indeed remarkable that an aeroplane which had been designed by so reputable a British aircraft company as Lord Aeronautics should have failed so spectacularly and so completely.'

The jury, judging by the way they stiffened their backs and lifted their chins, were left in no doubt that all British aeroplanes and this British aeroplane in particular were of such faultless manufacture that only sabotage could pluck them out of the sky.

Cross-examining, Mr Ellsworthy asked Dr Lelew how *he* would go about sabotaging an aeroplane so that it was likely to crash in flight.

'It would never occur to me to perpetrate such a dastardly act,' Dr Lelew exclaimed, in horror.

'My dear Dr Lelew,' smiled Mr Ellsworthy, 'I am not asking whether you would personally undertake such an act of sabotage. I am asking what you – as an expert in matters aeronautical – would consider to be the most efficacious method of bringing down an aeroplane in flight.'

'Mr Ellsworthy, I would appreciate it if you would say what you mean,' grumbled Mr Justice Lombard-Andrews.

'I apologize to your lordship for any unwitting circumlocution,' replied Mr Ellsworthy, tartly.

Dr Lelew said, 'It was a bungled effort, no doubt about it.'

'I beg your pardon?' asked Mr Ellsworthy.

'The sabotage, a bungled effort.'

'But it appeared to be effective, if indeed it was sabotage.'

'Well, yes,' replied Dr Lelew. 'But the aeroplane could have been brought down far more effectively by simply re-adjusting the control-wires; and there would have been no evidence afterwards of any tampering.'

Mr Ellsworthy lowered his beaky nose and looked thoughtful. 'You are telling me, then, Dr Lelew, that the mischief wrought upon this aeroplane, if mischief it were, was not the work of a man with any aeronautical expertise?'

'That is my opinion, yes.'

'Yet my client here is considered by some to be one of the leading aeronautical figures in the world – not only a successful businessman but a trained pilot and a skilled mechanic.'

'Well, yes.' Dr Lelew admitted.

At once, however, Mr Stuart rose to his feet, and asked Dr Lelew, 'Is it conceivable that an expert saboteur – fearing that his evil handiwork might be discovered upon later examination – might have damaged the aeroplane in such a way as to give the *impression* that he was an amateur?'

Mr Ellsworthy stood up again at once. 'That question, your lordship, would appear to be outside this witness's expert competence.'

Dr Lelew sneezed twice, and whipped a huge white handkerchief out of his sleeve as if to show the court that he was expert at *something*, at least. Mr Stuart bowed his head and sat down. James slowly massaged his aching forehead with his fingertips.

Jacko Gibbons was brought in front of the court first thing the following morning. He was wearing a cheap brown suit and without hair-tonic his hair looked thick and gingery and oddly springy, as if he had tried to make his own wig out of coconut doormats.

He was asked by Mr Stuart to recount the conversation that had taken place between himself and Mr James Lord on the occasion when he had visited the Lord Aeronautics factory.

'Mr Lord said he would give me a pony if I adjusted the *Chichester Special*'s engine so that it flew too slow to win the Seraphim Trophy.'

'And what did you perceive to be the reason why Mr Lord asked you to make this adjustment?'

'I didn't perceive nothing. He told me straight out. He said he didn't want the *Chichester Special* to win. He said it was a waste of time and money, and he didn't want no more truck with it.'

'I see. And what was your response?'

'I told him to stick his head in a bucket.'

'You didn't want to make yourself this, ah, pony?'

Mr Justice Lombard-Andrews leaned heavily forward on his bench and asked, 'Didn't it strike you as unusual that Mr Lord should have offered you a horse for your services?'

Mr Stuart bowed his head. 'May it please your lordship, pony is a low term for the sum of fifty pounds; just as monkey is a low term for five hundred pounds.'

Mr Justice Lombard-Andrews slapped his open hand on to his

notes. 'How many times must I repeat that I demand clarity of expression in my court! Ponies, monkeys! Are we discussing manslaughter or livestock?'

'I apologize, your lordship. Mr Gibbons – may I ask you kindly not to use the vernacular?'

'Why, is the chain busted again?' asked Jacko, with sudden cheerfulness.

The questioning continued. Jacko said that when he had refused to tamper with the *Chichester Special*, James had given him ten pounds to keep him quiet. Jacko had taken this money 'very reluctant, sir, very reluctant indeed', and in the small hours of Saturday morning, plagued by his conscience, he had returned to the Lord Aeronautics works to push the money back through the office door, with a note to James saying that he could never accept it.

'Well – you could have knocked me down with a feather when I found the door was open and the lights was still on. I went inside and there was Mr Lord, messing around with the *Chichester Special*. I asked him what he was doing and he said what do you think. I said I didn't want nothing to do with it, but he said it was too late now, I was trespassing in his factory in the middle of the night, and he could call the Old Bill and have me banged up as soon as look at you. He said if I didn't help him then it was curtains for me. So I helped him, just a bit, but I didn't do nothing dangerous; I wouldn't. I didn't do nothing that would have jeopardized life and limb.'

'You were prepared to regulate the *Chichester Special*'s engine to the extent that it would be rendered too slow to qualify for the Seraphim Trophy, but you were not prepared to adjust the controls or control-surfaces in any way which might have led to an accident in the air?'

Jacko sniffed earnestly. 'You've got to draw the line somewhere, as the monkey said when it peed across the carpet.'

Mr Justice Lombard-Andrews leaned forward again and growled, 'Will the witness refrain from turning this court into a menagerie of colloquialisms?'

The case was adjourned until the following Monday morning. It rained all weekend: that steady cold persistent rain that makes the English believe that it will never stop raining and that it will never again be warm. James drove to Brighton on Saturday to buy himself a hat that he didn't need. He spent a miserable afternoon walking around the Lanes with his hands in his raincoat pockets. Then he stood defiantly on the front, while the grey sea crashed by the ton on to the shingle, and he felt for a few exhilarating moments like Captain Ahab, on the bridge of the *Pequod*.

On Sunday, Iris roasted a leg of lamb, with roasted potatoes and broccoli, and spotted dick to follow; and James spent the whole afternoon drinking musty claret and listening to the wireless and watching the rain make fairy eggcups in the puddles outside.

Richard was scarcely around to be spoken to. He spent most of Saturday at the factory – 'doing the figures' was how he described it – and for two hours on Sunday afternoon he talked on the telephone to one of his designers, still trying to satisfy James's demands for a better engine cowling. James heard him shouting, 'Well, that won't bloody well work, either, will it? Use your head!'

After tea, Richard went out, and didn't return until late in the evening, slamming the front door so furiously that the long-case clock in the hall chimed twenty-past nine. It was clearly not the evening to raise the subject of Elisabeth Bergner.

The following morning, at nine o'clock sharp, Mr Justice Lombard-Andrews began to hear the evidence of a counter clerk at Chichester's main post office, who said that the telegraph message about Elisabeth Bergner being ill had been written at the counter by a gentleman – yes, she was *quite* positive it was a gentleman – just after lunch on the day before the *Chichester Special*'s fatal crash.

'Would she know the gentleman again, if she happened to see him?'

'Oh yes, sir. Never forget a face.'

'Was the gentleman here in court today?'

She thought so.

Would she point him out?

He was the accused, Mr James Lord.

Was she quite certain?

'There couldn't be *two* gentlemen who looked like that, could there?'

In James's opinion, Mr Ellsworthy's cross-examination was disappointingly muted and muddled. 'Out of all those scores of people you serve in a day, you are trying to convince us that you can accurately recall just one?'

'Well, sir, yes sir. Well, sir, I believe so, sir.'

Mr Ellsworthy said that there were no further questions, and sat, the toucan collapsing into its nest. James stared at him but he didn't once look around. There was already a subtle feeling in the court that the counter clerk's evidence had set the seal of authenticity on Jacko Gibbons's story, and that James had no coherent answer to it. Some of the spectators in the public gallery began to feel dry-mouthed in anticipation of a guilty verdict; and there was murmuring.

'Stop that murmuring,' commanded Mr Justice Lombard-Andrews, without looking up from his notepad. The murmuring stopped.

At that point, very much on cue, one of John Tremlett's clerks came into the court. His back was hunched in an effort to make himself less conspicuous, as if he had arrived late at the cinema. His face was scarlet with acne and embarrassment.

John Tremlett listened gravely to the message that the clerk whispered into his ear. He flinched from time to time, because of aspirates or spit; but when the clerk had finished, John Tremlett laid a hand on the lad's arm in a theatrical gesture of appreciation. Then he beckoned to Mr Ellsworthy, and whispered in turn in his ear, and Mr Ellsworthy flinched, too, but began to nod, and to smile.

At last, Mr Ellsworthy rose to his feet. 'Begging your lordship's indulgence, the defence wishes to introduce one further witness.'

Mr Stuart bounded to his feet. 'I must object, my lord. We have had no prior notice of any further witnesses.'

Mr Justice Lombard-Andrews moved his face from side to side on its plinth of chins, looking first at Mr Stuart and then at Mr Ellsworthy.

'Mr Ellsworthy – do you regard this witness's testimony to be pertinent and relevant?'

'Oh, yes, my lord,' beamed Mr Ellsworthy. 'She can cast considerable new light on the whereabouts of the accused on the night when he was supposed to be sabotaging the *Chichester Special*.'

'Indeed?' the judge inquired. '*She?* You must remember that the sabotage was alleged to have occurred at three o'clock in the morning.'

Mr Justice Lombard-Andrews was playing to the gallery. There was a sharp intake of breath from the public, like the sea drawing back over the shingle; and for no reason at all, a man who looked like a greengrocer cried out, 'Shame!'

'Call your witness, then,' Mr Justice Lombard-Andrews agreed.

Mr Ellsworthy beckoned the usher, and the usher cried out, 'Lady Susan Sheffield! Lady Susan Sheffield!'

Instantly, there was uproar. Four reporters scrambled out of the press box, their shoes kicking the panelling; there were screams of excitement from the public; and James stood up and shouted at

Mr Ellsworthy, 'No! Do you hear me? I won't have it! Ellsworthy, what the hell is going on?'

Mr Justice Lombard-Andrews knocked his gavel and bellowed at everybody to keep quiet, this was a court of law. Of course he adored every minute of it. This would mean a whole column in *The Times* tomorrow; as well as days of fond attention from the tabloids. Pictures, perhaps; and a profile in *Nash's*.

At last the court settled down, although there was still an undertone of feverish excitement. From the side doors, Susan appeared, in a dramatic pale-blue silk dress with a huge bow on the front, and an enormous pale-blue hat. Her face was white; her lipstick startlingly red. She entered the witness-box without looking at James at all.

When she had taken the oath, Mr Ellsworthy stood up, and coughed, and bowed his head to her. 'Lady Sheffield, I am given to understand that you can enlighten this court as to the whereabouts of Mr James Lord in the early hours of the morning before the fatal crash of the *Chichester Special*?'

Tension in the court was almost at breaking-point. Even Mr Justice Lombard-Andrews was sitting with his thick lips drooping open. A woman in the public gallery was clenching her fists in anticipation of what she was going to be able to tell her knitting-circle, and uttering a strange high-pitched sound that was almost beyond the range of the human ear.

Susan said in her softest voice, 'I can, yes.'

Mr Ellsworthy smiled indulgently. 'Please take your time, Lady Sheffield. There is no need for you to upset yourself.'

'I'm not upset,' Susan told him.

'Good,' replied Mr Ellsworthy. 'Then perhaps you can tell us what information you have on the matter.'

Susan hesitated for a moment, and then said, 'Mr Lord was with me.'

'At three o'clock in the morning?' Mr Justice Lombard-Andrews inquired.

'No, your lordship. At three o'clock in the morning he had just left. He wanted to drive back to Chichester so that he could see his brother Richard flying the *Chichester Special*.'

There was a moan of scandalized delight from the public gallery. Mr Justice Lombard-Andrews lifted one finger in warning. 'Any further moaning, and I shall hear this witness's evidence *in camera*.'

Mr Ellsworthy said, 'Where exactly *were* you both?'

'At my home in Oxfordshire, Great Milton, seven miles from Oxford itself.'

'So even at that time of the morning, when the roads would have been completely free from other traffic, Mr Lord would still have been able to return to Chichester before, say, half-past five?'

'I would think so, yes.'

Mr Ellsworthy drew back his robes and propped his hands on his hips. 'Were there any other witnesses to Mr Lord's presence at your home?'

'No, sir. None that I am aware of.'

'Was not Sir Rodney at home?'

'No, sir, he was in Ripon, at a conference.'

'So you and Mr Lord were completely alone together?'

'Yes, sir.'

James had covered his face with his hands. He couldn't believe what he was hearing. He felt like roaring at the top of his voice that it was all lies; that Susan was perjuring herself for the sake of saving him from jail. But at the same time, the voice of reason within him argued that whether the jury believed her story or not, all the world now knew that they had been lovers, and nothing could alter that. She had offered him her honour as a sacrifice, and he would be committing a crime worse than manslaughter if he refused to accept it.

In a voice as calm and as cool as bisque porcelain, Susan said, 'James Lord and I are lovers, your lordship, and have been for many years. I am not ashamed of it; but I would have been eternally ashamed if I had allowed him to go to prison for an offence which he could not possibly have committed, simply to protect my reputation.'

Mr Justice Lombard-Andrews beamed at Susan and said, 'Greater love hath no woman than to lay down her reputation for a friend.'

Mr Stuart rose to his feet and asked Susan if she knew the penalties for telling lies on oath.

'Divine retribution,' she replied. 'As well as a jail sentence.'

'I put it to you, Lady Sheffield, that you are lying now, to protect your lover.'

'If I were lying, I would have been foolish indeed not to invent a lie that did not compromise my reputation.'

'Well, quite,' said Mr Justice Lombard-Andrews, mostly to himself.

'Begging your lordship's pardon,' said Mr Stuart, 'but whether or not the jury cares to believe Lady Sheffield's account of Mr Lord's whereabouts in preference to that of Mr Gibbons, there still remains the matter of the telegraph message.'

351

Mr Justice Lombard-Andrews was entranced by Susan; and very short with Mr Stuart. 'That, Mr Stuart, proves only that Mr Lord sent a misleading telegraph message, which is not in itself a criminal offence. Evidence, Mr Stuart! Evidence! You cannot erect a lean-to without a wall to lean it against.'

It was all over in half an hour. Mr Justice Lombard-Andrews directed the jury that if they harboured the slightest doubt about James's whereabouts on the night in question – 'was he warming Lady Sheffield's bed, or was he tinkering with his brother's aeroplane?' – they should find him not guilty. They did so, within six minutes of retiring.

James came out of the court feeling shell-shocked. He was hoping that Susan would still be there, but John Tremlett told him that she had left immediately after giving her evidence. Standing at the bottom of the courtroom steps, however, was Richard, looking tired and drawn. Ignoring the reporters and the photographers who jostled around him, James came down and took hold of Richard's hand.

'Congratulations,' said Richard.

James nodded, looking his brother straight in the eyes. 'Yes,' he said.

They climbed into the Daimler, and John Tremlett closed the door for them.

'I don't suppose Sir Rodney's going to be very pleased,' Richard remarked, as they were driven away.

'I don't suppose Patricia's going to be very pleased, either,' said James. 'I'm going to have some explaining to do when I get back to Miami.'

'You're going straight away?'

'I'll catch the first ship.'

'What are you going to tell her?'

'Who, Patricia? Oh, something or other. I'll probably tell her that we were nothing more than good friends.'

'Do you think she'll believe you?'

'I'm sure she'll try.'

They drove in silence for a time. Then James said, 'Poor Susan.'

'She did it of her own free will,' remarked Richard.

'Perhaps.'

Richard was boyishly enthusiastic. 'You have to admit that it's quite something when a woman loves you as much as that.'

James shook his head. 'I don't think she did it because she loves me. I think she did it to spite the Director. I only hope that she

352

can live with the consequences. One moment of high drama can cost you a lifetime of bitter regret.'

'Well,' shrugged Richard.

James took out his cigarette-case. 'Talking of high drama,' he said, 'how are you and Elisabeth getting along?'

Richard accepted a cigarette, and said, 'You can hardly call it "getting along". I scarcely see her. She's a star these days.'

'And how are you and Iris getting along?'

'That's an odd question. You've seen for yourself.'

'I know. I've seen you rub along from day to day. But do you love her?'

Richard flushed. 'Of course I love her. You're really being pretty damned personal, aren't you? What's this all about?'

James lit his cigarette. 'I don't know. Facing reality, I suppose. It seems like the day for it.'

'Facing reality? What on earth do you mean?'

'Take my advice,' said James. 'Give Iris a child.'

'James,' Richard protested, 'I do believe this court case has affected your brain!'

'Give her a child,' said James. 'It's about time the Lord family had some sons and heirs. And it's about time you started looking forward instead of back.'

Richard didn't know what to say. He stared at James as if he had momentarily forgotten what you had to do to keep on living from one minute to the next.

James clasped his arm, and gently shook it. 'I promised Iris I wouldn't tell you, so don't blame her. But there's a book you keep hidden at home.'

'You have absolutely no right – !' Richard exploded, but James raised his hand to silence him.

'Take it out to the garden,' said James. 'Burn it, along with all the rest of the dead flowers. Forget about Elisabeth. Learn to live with the wife you've got.'

'You're a fine one to talk,' Richard retorted. There were tears glistening in his eyes. Rage, and grief, and embarrassment.

'Well, yes,' smiled James. 'I *am* a fine one to talk. I've had the experience, you see.'

He called Susan all evening and all the next day, but there was no reply. At last he managed to get in touch with her friend Gillian Longbotham, who said that Susan might just possibly have gone to the Sheffields' cottage in Whinnyfold, in Scotland.

It took him four hours to get through. The line was crackly and

353

distant. Susan sounded as if she were speaking to him from ten years ago.

'You shouldn't have done it!' he shouted, eyes squeezed shut with concentration, one finger stuck in his ear.

'I wanted to!'

'But you could have been sent to prison. I didn't want you to take that risk for me!'

'It was my own decision. I'm a grown woman, James. I can do what I like.'

'Well, I'm never going to forgive you. I hope you realize that.'

'I love you, too, my darling, and I always will. At least I can grow old gracefully now. At least I've made one Grand Gesture!'

'I should have married you!'

'Too late! Born at the wrong time!'

'I could kill my parents, if they weren't already dead!'

The line crackled even more loudly. James could hear nothing at all for a while; then all he caught was '. . . ever, my . . .' and something that sounded like 'frying pans'.

He lost her. The operator tried to reconnect him, but couldn't. 'It is awfully far away, sir, and the Scottish operators don't exactly understand English. They'd rather put the phone down on you than try to translate.'

James sat in the library while it grew dark. He didn't switch on the lamps. 'Frying pans,' he thought. What an odd way for it all to end.

By Friday lunchtime, James was ready to leave. Richard was going to drive him down to Southampton to catch the *Queen Mary*. Since they were going through the centre of Chichester in any case, Richard had also offered to call at the post office to send off a package of blueprints to the Patents Office in Chancery Lane. 'Not that much of what we're doing these days is worth patenting,' he complained.

James waited for him while he queued at the counter. 'Have you thought about a child yet?' he asked.

'I'm mulling it over,' Richard told him, testily.

'It's a good idea, you know,' said James. 'It'll give you something else to worry about, apart from meeting my absurdly demanding specifications for engine cowlings, and pining over waiflike Jewish actresses who won't marry you.'

It was five minutes before it was Richard's turn at the counter. He placed the package on the scales; but, as he did so, the girl

354

behind the grille said, 'Hallo, Mr Lord! How are you, then? I'm ever so glad you got off!'

Richard stared at her. 'I –' he began. Then he turned to James, and for once James couldn't understand the expression on his face at all. Alarm? Guilt? Confusion?

'Isn't that Lady Sheffield a beauty!' the girl chattered. 'And to think she did all that for you! I read in the paper that Lord Sheffield was going to divorce her. That would be a shame, wouldn't it? I mean it was real true love, wasn't it?'

Richard managed to say, 'It wasn't me, you know, it was –'

James said, 'It's all right, Dickie old boy. Obviously a case of mistaken identity.'

'Yes,' said Richard, uneasily, and turned back to the counter girl. 'You see – we're brothers.'

The girl frowned at them. 'Oh, yes. So you are! And seeing you side by side, you don't look at all alike, do you?'

As they walked back to the car, Richard suddenly said, 'I say – you're not thinking it was me, are you? You don't think I sent that telegraph, to myself?'

'Why should I think that?' asked James.

'Well . . .' said Richard, and stopped, and looked at James as if he were suffering from a headache. 'I just didn't want you to think that, that's all.'

James raised an eyebrow. 'Come on,' he said, 'we've got a ship to catch.'

Darwin, 1937

Michael was vigorously brushing his teeth over the kitchen sink when Violet came in with the morning post. 'There's a letter from home,' she told him. 'The postmark says Chichester, Sussex.'

Michael spat out foam and bent his head under the single stand-up faucet so that he could take a drink. He came over to Violet wiping his hands on a fraying hand-towel. He was naked to the waist, thin-chested, with his yellow braces dangling over his faded khaki pants, like a recently-fired catapult.

'It's from Tremlett,' he said, taking the letter and turning it over to look at the return address on the back. 'Wonder what the bloody hell *he* wants.'

'There's one from the bank, too,' said Violet.

'Open it and see what it says.'

Violet sat down in one of their two armchairs, which was top-heavy and brown with varnished arms. Michael always thought that it looked like an elderly kangaroo, with a sagging pouch. Violet was eight and a half months pregnant with their first child. She was enormous, and carrying the child very low. Her stomach looked as if it might drop out from under her housecoat at any moment and rumble across the floor. Her hair had grown: there was even the faintest hint of a moustache on her upper lip. But to Michael she had never looked more beautiful; nor more desirable; even in her plain printed housecoat and her scarf knotted into a turban.

Violet said, 'It's from Mr Harris, at the bank. He says he can't lend you the money to buy your own aeroplane unless you can give him a better idea of how much extra you might be earning.'

Michael didn't hear her. He was holding John Tremlett's letter in a hand that wouldn't keep still.

'Michael?' asked Violet. 'Michael – what does it say?'

Michael finished reading the letter and then slowly shook his head.

'The exile is over,' he told her.

'I don't understand.'

'It's the family solicitor, John Tremlett. He's written to say that five years is up; and that I won't get any problems from the police or the Burne-Stanleys if I decide to return to England. In fact – if I want to go back and work for Lord Aeronautics, Richard might even be generous enough to re-assign me my share of the family trust.'

Violet stared at him. 'You're not going to go?'

Michael handed her the letter. 'We're talking about a lot of money, Violet. Let's face facts, a third share of the Lord family trust is slightly more substantial than £8 7s 11½d in the Farmers & Stockbreeder's Bank.'

'But England, Michael . . . it's so stuffy and petty. And I hope you haven't forgotten why they sent you here in the first place?'

Michael picked up the letter from the bank. It was ironic that the two letters should have arrived on the same day, two weeks before their first child was expected. He had scarcely enough money to clothe it, let alone buy Violet a decent present. The bank manager wasn't being unhelpful: he was simply looking for some kind of reassurance that he wouldn't be lending Michael three hundred and fifty pounds for a second-hand Bristol Tourer without some way of getting his money back. Reasonable, Michael supposed; but he wouldn't know how long it would take him to repay the loan until he actually started to pull in the work.

He had been thinking of starting his own air service ever since Violet had fallen for the baby. He still enjoyed working for Hudson Fysh; and he still made a few bob on the side by carrying ask-no-questions cargoes for Clarence. But if he was going to be blessed with his own son and heir, he wanted something to pass on to him, and he couldn't think of an inheritance that would be more exciting or more worthwhile than an independent air service.

He had been to talk to the bank manager (best suit, shiny brown shoes, only to be drenched by a monsoon downpour two streets away from the bank). He had discussed the idea with Clarence (who was all in favour, provided Michael kept on running his little errands for him). And he knew that he would pick up a lot of business from his old Qantas customers – most of whom welcomed the Sandfly more enthusiastically than their visiting relatives, especially since the Sandfly brought letters, and magazines, and spare valves for their wireless receivers, and tins of chocolate.

But on one hand, here was Mr Harris the bank manager asking Michael for evidence that he would be able to make money; and on the other hand here was John Tremlett offering him back his social position and his rightfully-inherited fortune.

Michael went across to the clothes-horse and picked up his freshly ironed blue shirt. He buttoned it up, looping his braces over his shoulders. Violet was watching him all the time, her hands cradling her stomach, her eyes uncertain.

'Supposing you talk to Mr Harris again?' she asked him.

'What difference would that make? We'd still have only £8 11s 7½d in the bank, as well as a debt of three hundred and fifty pounds, plus interest.'

'Do you *have* to go back to inherit your money?'

'I don't have to; but it's all up to Richard, isn't it? He's the executor, and the chairman of the company – and I can't really see him agreeing to give me a third share of Lord Aeronautics if I don't even work there. Richard's always been fair, don't you know. The quality of mercy isn't in it. A fair day's work for a fair day's inheritance. I can just imagine him explaining to me why he can't *possibly* let me have any money unless I actually *contribute*. Very fair chap, Richard; very reasonable; and as weak as water.'

Violet said, 'Michael – I really don't want us to go back to England.'

'Oh, come on, England's not all that bad.'

'But we're Australians now. We're not English any more. Going back to England – well, I'd rather just *remember* what it was like. I'd rather just think about the nice parts. You know, the fields, and the cows, and going to church in the summer. I don't really want us to go back there.'

Michael looked around their apartment. They had rented it for 13s 0d a month from a friend of Clarence's, a Portuguese called Simões who wore old but beautifully-tailored sharkskin suits and open-toed sandals and habitually chewed betel-nut. Right at the muddier end of Cavenagh Street, the apartment was sandwiched between Ah Yum's perpetually hissing and clattering and arguing laundry, and the empty offices of an English solicitor who had drunk himself into grand insanity, and on whose door still flapped and twirled the faded message 'Gone To Lunch'.

The apartment consisted of a single back bedroom, furnished with a heavy brown colonial bed and a blighted dressing-table mirror; a small distressed kitchen with chipped enamel worktops; and a slightly larger but equally distressed sitting-room with a dado of tongue-and-groove, painted mustard-yellow, which surrounded them when they sat in their shabby little chairs almost like a stockade, and nightmarish green-and-yellow wallpaper, which rose above the dado like the leprous and mouldering tropical jungle from which the stockade had been erected to protect them.

Michael and Violet had been saving for a year now for an apartment that was less damp and cramped, but Michael's informal divorce settlement with Leonard had set them back three months' earnings. Leonard had insisted on two hundred and sixty pounds for a new tin roof, to replace the roof that Michael had bombed – otherwise, he had warned, 'I'll give you trouble with a capital T, I'll charge you with bombing and battery, you see if I don't, and I won't let Violet go, neither.'

In the evenings, after supper, Michael quite often talked to Violet about his jolly life at Cambridge and Goodwood Lodge, about those sparkling days of parties and dancing and driving sports cars and flying for fun. But as the years had passed – five years of living in Darwin through Wets and Drys and screaming typhoons; five years of dealing with Chinese who thought he was pink like a sugar-mouse and clumsy like an elephant, and Aborigines who thought he was half-magic and pointed bones at him, and Bushies who regarded him either as a saint and a saviour or a silly arse; five years of flying out week after week to hard-bitten sheep stations across the hard-baked desert; wind, sunshine, grit, and kerosene – that sparkle had begun to dwindle in his memory, and now it seemed as fleeting and as far as the last windblown ashes of a burned photograph, and he could scarcely believe that any of that life had ever really happened. As the sparkle had dwindled, so too had his own capacity for fun. He adored Violet, yes, but he rarely laughed.

He had read a book by D. H. Lawrence called *Kangaroo*, and Lawrence had written about, 'the indifference – the fern-dark indifference of this remote golden Australia. Not to care – from the bottom of one's soul, not to care.' And he had closed the book then and read no more, clapped it shut in mid-paragraph, because he had recognized that indifference in himself. Anything, good God, to get his sensitivity back. Anything to live that sparkling life again. And money wouldn't hurt, either.

359

He looked up at the clock. 'I have to go,' he told Violet. 'I'm expected down at Willeroo by lunchtime.'

Violet said, 'Do you want to take your flask?'

He leaned forward and took hold of her shoulders and kissed her. 'I'll be all right. I'll probably land at the Johnson Station for some breakfast.'

'Then you watch out for Mrs Johnson, that's all. Especially if her old man's away.'

'You think I'm the Don Juan of the outback, don't you?'

'I think you're a good-looking chap in an aeroplane, that's what I think. That darling young man in the flying DH 9.'

Michael picked up both letters; the letter from the bank and the letter from John Tremlett. He held one up in each hand as if he were weighing them, one against the other. Then he folded them together and tucked them into the kitchen drawer, next to the bills.

'You know, Michael,' said Violet, as he laced up his boots, crouched on the kitchen linoleum like a runner. 'All I want is you, and your baby. I don't need your money. Especially if it means going back to England.'

'Going back to England may be the only way.'

'Michael – no amount of money is worth your self-respect.'

Michael stood up, and went to the door, and glanced around the apartment. If this is self-respect, he thought, give me the money any day. But he said nothing more to Violet. He didn't want to upset her while he was away for the day.

They stood in the street together. Although the sky towards the north-west was cloudless and clear, a strong ocean wind was getting up.

She gave him a last kiss. 'Be careful,' she told him, and watched him walk away, holding his unborn baby in her arms and feeling its urgent, impatient kicks.

He took off from Fannie Bay shortly after nine o'clock, into a hot gale that picked his DH 9C right off the muddy airfield and lifted him up two hundred feet before he could breathe. The engine droned and grumbled as he turned south-south-eastwards, but he was soon gaining height over the outskirts of Darwin, and heading steadily inland. He lifted his goggles and looked westwards. He always enjoyed the view as he flew southwards from Darwin, no matter what the weather was like. Today, the banyans along the coastal cliffs were waving their leaves in a frenzied dance, and surf broke into the beaches in explosive white surges.

DARWIN, 1937

The wind died as Michael's shadow flew south along the gleaming railway line, and by the time he passed Rum Jungle the weather was breezy but the worst of the storm was well behind him. He held the stick between his knees and opened a packet of fruit pastilles. His wireless set wasn't working (short-circuit again, probably) and he was looking forward to a dull trip of perfect peace.

He wondered as he sucked his pastille how he was going to persuade Violet to come back to England with him. There wasn't any question about his own desire to go. Yet he thought it vaguely odd he hadn't been counting off the years for himself; and that it had taken John Tremlett to remind him that his banishment was now over. Perhaps he had adapted to life in Australia's northern capital more than he knew.

But he could still dream about Cambridge; about the gardens of Clare College; and punting in the sunshine under Etheridge's wooden bridge over the Cam, with pretty girls in short dresses. He could still dream about London, and dancing at the Trianon.

He landed at the Johnson Station at half-past eleven, circling over the tall gums and the white-painted fences at the eastern side of the farm so that he could land well into the wind. The ground was tussocky but quite level here. An experienced bush pilot got to know his sheep stations as well as he knew his airfields. The first time Michael had landed here, his undercart had disappeared into a huge hole, and his plane had dropped flat on its belly, splintering his propeller like a smashed-out cigar.

Mrs Johnson was waving to him from the house as he blipped the biplane across the field and then parked her with her tail to the north-west in case the wind suddenly got up and tipped her over.

He jumped down from the cockpit, and walked around the chicken-pen, stretching himself as he tugged off his gloves and unbuttoned his coat. 'Good day, Mrs Johnson! Thought I'd treat myself to some of your chicken fruit, poached would be nice.'

Mrs Johnson was a big blonde woman, more like a Swede than the Dorset woman she had originally been: pale-eyed, pale-skinned, big-breasted, and always smelling of frying. She was wiping her red hands on her apron and her face was bright with excitement.

'They thought you'd land here for a bite of tucker!' she told him. 'They thought you would and thank goodness you did!'

'Who did?' asked Michael, tilting his head sideways as he tugged off his flying helmet.

'Cloncurry, of course, the Flying Doctor. They've had an SOS call from Jim Robinson out at Banka Banka; his wife's been in labour all night, and he's scared as hell he's going to lose the both of them, baby and Nora too.'

'Oh, God,' said Michael, slapping his helmet tiredly against his thigh. 'Isn't there anybody nearer?'

Mrs Johnson clamped her arm around Michael's shoulder and almost frogmarched him back to his plane. 'You're the one, Michael. And I wouldn't trust anybody else, neither. You look lively, but take care, too. Nora's my next-best friend.'

Michael swung the biplane's propeller and started the engine just as Johnson came jolting towards them from the west in his old rust-coloured Austin van. Mr Johnson came hurrying over, his blue overalls rippled by the draft from the propeller, and clasped Michael's hand. 'Good on you, Sandfly, thank God you turned up. You come back for your breakfast any time you feel like it.'

Michael climbed back into the cockpit and gave the Johnsons a quick salute. Mr Johnson cupped one hand against his mouth; and with his other hand pointed to the west. 'Just watch yourself! There's a fair old wind getting up. You'll be running into a dust storm, less you're careful.'

'Thanks for bugger all!' Michael shouted back, cheerfully, and wheeled the DH 9C back to face the wind. Mr Johnson was right. He could hear the grit whispering against his windshield already; and the western horizon had taken on that familiar murky beige appearance that was a signal for any pilot who knew what he was doing to stay on the ground. It was a Bedourie, one of those overwhelming dust clouds stirred up during the Dry by hot gusts of wind. The heavier particles of dust would gradually sink, obscuring the western horizon completely. And if a pilot had the sun in his eyes, he would be virtually blind.

As he turned the biplane over the Johnson Station, and headed south-south-east again, Michael calculated that at top speed he could probably outrun the worst of the storm. He knew the topography of the area just about as well as he knew the fungoid outbursts on the wallpaper in his apartment; every billabong and every bukkulla, at least that's what Hudson used to tease him. A bukkulla was a tall black stump.

He tried his wireless a few times, although he knew that it was hopeless. He had been having trouble with it for weeks, crackling and fading and popping. He should have taken it to the little Chinaman two doors down to have it fixed.

He sang a silly song that Leslie Henson had recorded. 'If you have toothache or paralysis . . . if you want to know where Aunt Alice is . . . tell the doc!'

He flew steadily on towards Danka Banka. Now the wind was turbulent enough to make the DH 9C lift and drop in a way that made him glad that he hadn't eaten any of Mrs Johnson's poached eggs. Dust began to sizzle and lash against the fuselage, and stream through the wires with a high-pitched hissing sound that he could hear over the roaring and burping of the engine.

He turned around in his cockpit and looked behind him. The western sky had disappeared. In its place was a blur of dust, over a thousand feet high, and stretching from one side of the world to the other. A huge, rising, impenetrable Bedourie; and it had caught up with him.

He kept his course steady by his compass, and gradually took the DH 9C down to five hundred feet. It was almost suicidally dangerous, flying so low, but at least he might have a chance of picking out a landmark or two, and keeping himself on course. At a higher altitude, there was nothing but blindness, nothing but dust.

Losing his way wouldn't have mattered so much, on any other trip. Early in last year's Dry, he had flown around in a dust-storm for four hours, and discovered when he emerged from it that he was more than a hundred miles away from where he wanted to go. But today the Robinsons were depending on him, and one careless mistake in navigation could mean that Jim Robinson woke up tomorrow as a childless widower.

The hot wind gusted even more forcefully. The biplane dipped and dived through the dust. For one nerve-tightening moment, Michael completely lost his sense of balance, and he didn't know whether he was flying upside-down or the right way up. He glanced at his artificial horizon and saw that he was angled at forty-five degrees.

He could hardly see anything at all now, even on the ground. He saw a rush of dark shapes fleeing through the dust, and when he tilted his starboard wing a little to try and make out what they were, he realized that they were kangaroos, big reds, running for shelter. A wrinkled hill reared up in front of him, then another, then another, and he took the biplane sharply upwards. The dust blew against the back of his neck and streamed off the top of his flying-helmet like the heroic plume of a knight-in-armour.

He was beginning to feel distinctly un-heroic, however. His

engine was running audibly off-tune, and he hadn't recognized those last hills at all. With great care, straining his eyes, he took the DH 9C down to five hundred feet again, then to four, trying to pick out some creek or outcropping that might look familiar. He flew over a deep, twisted gully, like the pursed lips of a very old man. He lifted the biplane's nose again, to gain some height. The risk of colliding with the ground was now so great that he found himself leaning forward and staring so hard that his back ached. He had to admit to himself now that he was utterly lost; and that he had no idea how to find out where he was.

For the first time in his flying career, he felt a vacuum in his stomach which was real panic. He had felt fear before – clinging to the wing of his last DH 9C, trying to free his home-made bomb; and the second before he had crashed the Cambridge Aero Club's pride and joy right through the sides of the furniture van – but *that* fear had been deliciously hair-raising, the kind of fear you could brag about afterwards.

Flying blind through this Bedourie inspired a very different kind of fear, a fear that was nauseating, and persistent, a fear of failure and hopelessness, and helplessness, too. And all he could do was to grind on and on through the dust, taking himself further and further away from the woman and child who desperately needed him.

He flew for almost another hour. During the whole of that time, he saw nothing but dust. His eyes were streaming, even though he was wearing goggles, and his tongue was coated with grit. He found it mildly amazing that the biplane's engine kept going. The air-intake was probably clogged up, and the fine dust that rose into the upper atmosphere during a Bedourie had a way of getting into every joint and bearing and gasket.

He checked his watch. It was well past two o'clock now. He could be anywhere at all, and his fuel indicator was already beginning to creep down past the quarter-mark. He decided cautiously to lose a little height, to see if any friendly landmarks were miraculously waiting for him to spot them. Or, failing that, if there was anywhere smooth enough for him to land, and wait till the dust-storm had died down.

Easing the stick forward, almost standing up in his cockpit so that he could see directly in front and below, surrounded on all sides by fuming dust, he took the biplane down to three hundred feet. He crossed a broken rock face, and a wide sheltered river-bed. He didn't recognize them at all. But, as he began to climb back up to a safer altitude, he glimpsed a dark squarish shape off to his left. He turned, and banked towards it, and almost at once he realized that it was a truck, parked well into the lee of the rock face for shelter. As he passed overhead, the truck door opened and a man climbed out and waved.

He lifted the DH 9C back into the dust again, turning his head so that he wouldn't lose sight of the truck. If it vanished into the storm, he might never find it again. He wheeled around the river-bed, trying to make out if there were any severe cracks or potholes in it, but it looked smooth enough for a landing. Dry, and crusted with salt, and sprinkled with a few small pebbles, but better than some of the fields which had been prepared for him by well-meaning Bushies who expected him to land for a postal delivery, or wireless parts.

'Oh well, bugger it, here goes,' he whispered to himself, and lowered the biplane's flaps.

Slanting the aircraft diagonally to the wind, he brought it down as slow and as low as he could. He was almost touching the ground when he saw that the salt crust which had seemed faultlessly smooth from the air was deeply rutted and ridged, like a petrified beach, and that the few small pebbles weren't pebbles at all but respectably-proportioned boulders. But by then he was six feet off the ground and it was too late.

The aeroplane touched, skidded, jumped, and the next thing Michael knew the starboard wheel had struck a ridge in the salt-bed. There was a sharp crack, as loud as a pistol-shot, and the DH 9C collapsed on to its belly on the ground and slid helplessly sideways until it was brought to a halt up against a rock-slide.

Michael released his seat-belt and scrambled out of the cockpit as quickly as he could, in case of fire. But the biplane didn't burn. It just lay on its belly looking sad and broken, its wings a confusion of splintered struts and fraying wires.

The truck-driver came hurrying over. He was a short, bow-legged man with big ears and a face that looked as if it had been pickled in beetroot-juice. He held out his hand and gave Michael a firm welcoming shake.

'Bit of a duff landing,' he remarked.

'Yes,' Michael agreed. He still felt winded and shocked.

'Come and have a shot of tea. I've just brewed up. Anything to get rid of the taste of this dust, aye? My mouth feels like a lizard's arsehole.'

Michael followed him back to the truck. Up above their heads, the dust clouds came billowing off the rock-face, and sifting down to the river-bed with a sound like a cloak dragging across a concrete floor.

'My name's Ken Bryce,' the man declared. 'But you can call me Brycey, if you like. Everybody else does.'

'Michael Lord,' said Michael.

'Oh, you're a Pom,' grinned Brycey. 'You're sure it's Michael Lord, and not Lord Michael? I mean I do like to know if I'm having the aristocracy to tea.'

Brycey opened up the truck. He had brewed up tea on a small spirit-burner on the floor of the passenger side, and he reached into the back behind the seats to bring out two brown enamel mugs. 'Hope you don't mind condensed milk, your lordship.'

Michael said, 'You don't have a wireless, I suppose?'

Brycey shook his head.

Michael tugged his hand through his dusty hair. 'I was trying to fly to the Robinson place at Banka Banka. Mrs Robinson's having a baby, and I was supposed to take her to Cloncurry. Then, of course, this damned dust-storm got up.'

'Well, you didn't do bad, did you?' said Brycey.

'What do you mean? I'm totally lost, and I've just written my bloody aeroplane off.'

'You're not lost, mate. You're about a mile from the Robinsons' south-east boundary. Here, come on, grab hold of that tea and I'll drive you there.'

Michael took hold of the scalding mug. Holding it in both hands he looked up at the dust clouds for a second, and thought to himself, *thank you, God, somebody's looking after me today.* But at the same time he still had to help Mrs Robinson somehow, and he had no aeroplane to take her over to the Flying Doctor head-quarters.

The journey to the Robinson house was short, violent, blind, and noisy. It involved almost continuous swearing and gear-clashing from Brycey, and most of Michael's tea being slopped and jolted on to his trousers. But Brycey knew where he was going, and got there, too. He drew up outside the Robinsons' back door with his mudguards juddering, and pooped the truck's horn three or four times.

Jim Robinson came out almost at once. He was thin-faced, with deep-set eyes, and a cropped lopsided haircut that had obviously been done by his wife. He looked exhausted.

'Brycey, what are you doing here?'

'I brought your Flying Doctor, that's what.'

Michael said, 'No aeroplane, I'm afraid. I crashed in the storm. It was only a stroke of luck that I came across Brycey.'

'You mean you can't fly her out?'

'I'll call up Cloncurry and get them to send another aircraft as soon as they can. But meanwhile, we're just going to have to make the best of it. Is your wife still in labour?'

'Oh, God,' said Jim Robinson, biting his lip. He was obviously close to breaking-point.

Michael took hold of his arm. 'Listen,' he said, 'I've got my bag with my medical stuff. I've had a course in first aid, and all the rudiments. Let's just see what we can do.'

Jim Robinson took out his handkerchief and wiped his eyes. Not far away, the windpump whirred wildly in the storm, making a flurried pattern in the airborne dust. 'All right,' he agreed at last. 'All right, you go ahead.'

Nora Robinson was lying in semi-darkness, her face the colour of the wax that drips from communion candles, her eyes glittering with pain and fatigue. Her knees were lifted under the brown cotton bedspread; her thin hands clasped the sheets with terrified tightness – as if she believed that her only slim chance of survival was to hang on to them, hang on, and not let go.

The bedroom was papered with small brown flowers. It smelled of blood and perspiration and amniotic fluid. Up above the wooden bedhead, there was a small brown painting of pilgrims praying in a field.

Michael sat down on the edge of the bed and laid his first-aid bag on the floor.

'Doctor?' whispered Nora.

Michael shook his head. 'I'm not a doctor, Mrs Robinson. But I have come to help you.'

She stared at him in resignation, as if that was all the good fortune she could ever have expected, to be dying, and for her baby to be dying, and for Michael not to be a doctor.

Michael swallowed dust, and tried to smile. 'Let's have a look at you, shall we?' he said, trying at least to *sound* like a doctor.

He opened his bag and took out the old red-rubber stethoscope that Clarence had found for him. He lifted Nora's chilled, sweat-soaked nightdress, and felt the wax-white dome of her stomach with his hand. He could feel the baby's limbs; he thought he could feel its head. But unlike his own baby, inside Violet's stomach, there was no movement. The baby wasn't kicking.

He pressed the stethoscope against Nora's side, and listened. Nothing, but the rushing of blood in his own eardrums.

Nora said, 'It's dead, isn't it?'

Michael gave her a quick smile, and lowered her nightdress. 'I can hear *something*,' he lied. 'Are you still having contractions?'

'Now and then, but they're very weak, and I'm so tired I just can't push any more.'

'Well, we'll just have to see what we can do.'

Michael stood up. Jim was waiting in the doorway, his arms folded. Michael beckoned him through to the living-room.

'The baby's a goner, isn't it?' asked Jim.

Michael nodded. 'I'm sorry. I think it is. It's not moving, and I can't hear any heart-beat.'

'Can you save Nora?'

'I don't know. You don't have any books on childbirth, do you?'

Jim went across to the small oak bookshelf that stood next to the wireless receiver. There was a Bible, a Sheep Farmers' Almanac, a copy of *The Railway Children* and a thin green book called *Maternity Without Suffering*.

He gave it to Michael with a shrug. 'It's Nora's. I've never read it myself.'

With shaking hands, Michael turned to the chapter marked 'The Birth'. He read: '*A few steady bearing-down pains will soon bring the little stranger, and at the same time great happiness and rest to the patient, for are not all the bugbears she had conjured up a myth, and she a blessed mother?*'

The only treatment for difficult labour that he could find was 'a glass of hot milk, or malted milk if the patient prefers it'.

'I think we'd better call Cloncurry,' he said. 'Can you get them on the wireless?'

'It's not working, I've tried. It must be the storm.'

Michael turned back towards the bedroom. As he did so, Nora let out a hideous scream. She screamed and screamed and screamed again, and Michael and Jim almost collided with each other in the bedroom doorway.

Nora was clutching the bars of the bed, her head thrown back, her neck bulging. Her stomach was hard as a drumskin. Without hesitation, Michael dragged back the bedspread. Nora's vagina was stretched wide, and the dark furrows of the baby's hair had appeared.

'It's coming!' said Michael. 'For God's sake, Jim, get hold of her head and push her chin down to her chest. Tell her to push. Push, Nora, push! And tell her you love her!'

Nora held her breath and pushed until her face was purple.

Then she dragged in another breath with a long, high, quivering shriek. Then pushed again.

Gradually the baby's face appeared, tiny and slimy and mystical, eyes closed tight, its cheeks blue with oxygen starvation. Nora pushed twice more, and Michael took hold of a worn-out red-and-white tea-towel, and tenderly lifted the little body out. Nora gasped, and wept, but Jim held her close and shushed her and mumbled his thanks to God that she was still alive.

They wrapped the baby in one of the sheets that Nora had sewn for its cradle, and took it out to the shed where the Robinsons usually smoked their beef and chickens.

'I'll call the doctor as soon as this storm's died down,' said Jim. Michael nodded, and wiped his mouth with the back of his hand, and then his eyes. Dust could always make you cry.

'We were going to call it Gerald,' said Jim. He brushed the dust from his hands. 'Or, you know, Geraldine, since it was a girl.'

'Well, nice names,' said Michael.

Jim clasped his shoulder. 'You did what you could, mate. I won't forget you for it. There's plenty of blokes wouldn't even've bothered to come.'

Michael said, 'You don't have a beer, do you? Even a warm one would do.'

He was flown back to Darwin two days later by Hudson Fysh himself, in a DH 50. Hudson was feeling talkative, so Michael let him get on with it. It was a fine warm day as they landed, and Violet was waiting for him at the airfield. He recognized her white cloche hat from the air.

'I was so worried about you!' she said, hugging him as close as she could. 'I couldn't believe it when they told me you'd crashed!'

Michael grinned. 'I'm afraid that was embarrassing, rather than fatal.'

They walked along the wide white streets under the shade of the milkwood trees. Violet took hold of his arm. 'I've been thinking you know, about England.'

'Oh, yes?' said Michael. 'And what were you thinking about England?'

Violet looked pleased with herself. 'I was thinking, at least you'd be safe, at least you wouldn't be flying all the time – and we *would*, after all, be wealthy.'

Michael kissed her cheek. 'I've been thinking about it, too.'

'And?'

'And, what can I say? Sometimes you can find that the job you're doing is more important than what you get paid for it.'

Violet frowned under the shadow of her hat. 'I don't understand. You mean you've changed your mind?'

'I suppose you could say that, yes.'

She half-laughed. 'Well, I really don't understand you at all!'

Michael squeezed her hand, and smiled at her, but didn't explain, not yet anyway. This wasn't the time to be talking about children who had died without even opening their eyes; or the deep silent feeling that had grown within him that all across the Northern Territory, every night, under that fern-dark sky, there were lonely and isolated people who needed him to stay.

London, 1939

Richard was spending the weekend with the Jorritts, in St John's Wood, and he had woken up late. Sunday mornings at the Jorritts were always haggard and monochromatic occasions, a direct result of the number of bottles of claret that were consumed by the Jorritts over Saturday evening dinner. Saturday evenings at the Jorritts were always memorable. Wit and fun and wireless music and rolled-back carpets for dancing. Sunday mornings by direct contrast were like silent films of famous railway crashes in very slow motion.

Iris had been invited, too, but Iris was appalled by Norman Jorritt, and had invented a chill. Richard had piously suggested that he should stay at home and nurse her; but she had Elsie to look after her, and in any case she was tired of Richard fretting about business and money and what was going to happen if war broke out.

Richard went downstairs and found Norman in the kitchen with his sister Twilla. Norman's hair was sticking up and he was wear-

370

ing a scarlet-and-purple bathrobe that looked like a hangover in its own right. He was moistening his lips with the tip of his tongue, over and over again, and blinking.

Twilla, who didn't look at all like Norman, was already dressed in a mustard twin-set and a black pleated skirt. She wore odd earrings, one pearl, one plain, and she was concentrating with controlled nausea on smoking a Woodbine, even to the extent of squinting at it with both eyes as she sucked in the smoke.

Richard tightened the belt of his bathrobe because there was a lady present, but Twilla didn't even turn round. 'Is that coffee?' he inquired, trying to be bright.

Norman cleared his throat, but still sounded phlegmy. 'I sincerely hope so. If it's horseshit, it's going straight back to Twinings.'

Twilla edgily blew smoke. 'Don't be coarse, Norm. Not on a Sunday.' She didn't make it clear if she objected to his language because it was the Sabbath or because she had a hangover.

Richard, embarrassed, found himself a cup. 'The Prime Minister's coming on in a minute, isn't he?' he asked. He poured out coffee and sniffed it with pretended relish. It was the Viennese fig variety, which he hated.

Norman nodded, his head going up and down, up and down, in resigned agreement.

'I suppose really we ought to listen,' Richard suggested.

'Listen to what?' demanded Norman. 'To more wishy-washy . . . washy-wishy . . . I don't know ' He licked his lips again, and sniffed. 'I told – who was it? – well, I told *somebody* important. I know who it was! It was the King! That's who it was – when he came to see *The Round Table* at the Criterion. Or was it *The Square Chair* at the Prince of Wales? Well, something like that. But I told him – right to his face – Your Majesty, that's what I said, and *bowed* of course, very *low*, because all kings expect to be called "Your Majesty" and bowed low to. It couldn't have been *Chu-Chin-Chow*, could it? No. But I warned him not to trust Herr Hitler. And that was years ago. It speaks for itself, I said. And I beckoned him forward and I whispered in the majestic lughole, *"Any man with a head the shape of a turnip is not to be trusted."* '

Twilla ignored him, and said to Richard, 'If you detest that coffee as much as I do, I'll make you some fresh.' She crushed out her cigarette in the sink, flushed it away with a burst of cold water, and turned to Norman and said, 'Figs! You're obsessed with them. Oh, and prunes too. Norm is nothing but a large intestine with a mouth at one end and a penny-whistle at the other.'

Norman threw out his arms. 'You see how she speaks to me! And when she was a baby she called me Naw-naw.'

'I didn't, I called you Mun-mun.'

'Good God!' Norman shouted, in spite of his headache. 'No wonder they never ask women to write history. Can you imagine it? The Mun-mun Conquests!'

'Well that's a bloody sight better than the Naw-naw Conquests,' Twilla retaliated.

Richard glanced up at the kitchen clock. 'It's almost quarter-past,' he put in.

Norman stared at him in bewilderment. 'Yes,' he said. 'You're right.'

'Well,' said Richard, shuffling his slippers and trying to be jocular. 'The Prime Minister's on.'

Norman waited. Then he blinked and said, 'Is that the end of the sentence? The Prime Minister's on –?'

'The wireless,' said Richard.

'Ah,' said Norman. 'The wireless. The why-er-liss, as they call it in Wales. Or the wahless, as they call it in St John's Wood.'

Twilla said, 'You know where it is, Dickie, I should switch it on now, if I were you. It takes about a minute to warm up.'

Richard went through to the sitting-room. The dark-blue velvet curtains were still drawn, and the room smelled of wine and stale cigar smoke. He went across to the large walnut cabinet, and switched on the brown Bakelite knob. The lights behind the dial began to glow, and he tuned in to the BBC. Last night they had been listening to dance music on Luxembourg.

The kitchen clock must have been slow, for the faint crisp voice that came from the speaker was already that of the Prime Minister, Neville Chamberlain.

'. . . at 10 Downing Street. This morning the British Ambassador in Berlin handed the German government a final note, stating that unless we heard from them by eleven o'clock that they were prepared at once to withdraw their troops from Poland . . .'

Norman had appeared in the sitting-room doorway. 'Great incandescent excrescences,' he complained, 'he's not still rabbiting on about that, is he?'

'Sh!' said Richard, and it wasn't a request, but an order.

'. . . no such undertaking has been received, and that consequently this country is at war with Germany.'

Norman was silent for a very long time. Twilla, standing behind him, hadn't heard properly, but looked as though she didn't like to ask what had happened.

372

LONDON, 1939

'It's not war?' she managed to say. 'I mean, not actual war.' Norman nodded. 'War,' he declared. 'Real, actual war.' He paused, and then he added, 'Real, authentic, genuine, certified, fully-guaranteed, actual *war*.'

Richard switched off the wireless. He looked at Norman but said nothing. Then he walked decisively to the far end of the room, drew back the curtains, and slid up the sash window. The sweet familiar smells of an early-autumn Sunday in London came breezing in through the house. Richard leaned on the windowsill and looked up at the pale blue sky, and the high white clouds.

'There you are,' said Norman, 'what a man! War's been going for only a minute-and-a-half, and already he's out spotting German parachutists. How can we lose, with men like Dickie on our side?'

'Pipe down, Norm,' said Twilla.

Norman sniffed. 'This calls for a drink. A drink, a drink, champagne I think! How about you, Dickie? Can you tear yourself away from your ARP duties long enough to refresh the jaded gob? You should wear a tin hat when you do that, you know. I wouldn't put it past those Nazi bastards to try to land on your head.'

Five-and-a-half minutes later, three things happened almost at once. Norman popped the cork of a bottle of Perrier-Jouët, the telephone started ringing, and London's air-raid sirens began to wail. Outside the window, a policeman in a steel helmet came pedalling along the street on a bicycle, blowing a whistle. A cardboard notice was tied around his neck warning 'Take Cover'.

'Shut that window and get your bonce in!' he shouted at Richard. Richard, red-faced, did as he was told.

Twilla said, 'My God, what are we going to do? They're going to bomb us!'

'Get dressed quickly,' Richard told Norman. 'Then we'll go down to the cellar.'

The phone stopped ringing. Norman said, desperately, 'What do we need to get dressed for? You don't have to be wearing anything special to be bombed, do you?'

'What if they knock half the house down, and you're left standing in the middle of St John's Avenue wearing nothing at all but that dog's-dinner of a dressing-gown?'

Norman frowned down at his lapels. 'Hmph,' he said, 'I thought you rather liked it.'

Richard said, 'Come on,' and for one of the first times in his life found himself missing Iris very keenly.

373

They heard people screaming outside. A woman came running along the pavement, pushing a pram. Norman for once looked grave. 'Take the champagne, old man,' he told Richard. 'I'm beginning to think this may be serious.'

Darwin, 1939

M ichael heard about the declaration of war quite casually, as if it were a football result. Clarence had called him over to the bungalow to pick up some packages that he was supposed to fly down to the Alice on Monday morning. When Michael arrived outside the picket fence in his borrowed Morris van, Clarence was already standing on the porch. He was looking pink in the face, and wearing a huge pair of khaki twill shorts that looked as if he might have borrowed them from Sydney Greenstreet.

'Evening, Clarence,' said Michael, slamming the van door and setting off a nearby treeful of shrieking galahs.

'Evening, old man. Care for a whisky?'

Michael shook his head. 'No thanks, Watters. I want to do some work on the kite tonight; the timing's been off.'

'That's always the trouble with working for yourself,' Clarence declared. 'You can never switch off the light on your desk and leave it all behind you.'

He led Michael around the side of the bungalow, past the white-painted tubs of brightly-coloured crotons. 'Mind you,' he remarked, 'this is your chance to get rich.'

'What is?' asked Michael. 'This stuff I'm carrying tomorrow? What is it, opium paste or T'ang Dynasty jade?'

'The *war*, I'm talking about, you duffer,' said Clarence.

Michael made a face. 'If there *is* a war. Chamberlain will probably manage to pull some last-minute trick out of the hat.'

Clarence turned around. 'What do you mean *if*? There's no if about it, old man.'

'What do you mean?'

'It was on the wireless, only about five minutes ago. The Germans won't pull their chaps out of Poland, so Britain has declared war. It's official.'

Michael stared at him. 'Good God. Do you know, I never thought they'd do it.'

Clarence led the way up the steps of the verandah, and then eased himself down into his basketwork sun-chair. 'Bound to happen, when you think about it. It's in their blood, the Hun, pillaging and rampaging and all the rest of it. They're only two steps removed from Goths and Visigoths, aren't they? God alone knows why we let them re-arm.'

Michael slowly sat down. 'I think I will have that drink, thank you.'

'Splendid,' said Clarence. 'It's Glenmorangie, if you like Glenmorangie.'

'Anything, as long as it's strong.'

He returned to their house near the harbour to find Violet waiting for him in the garden, under the banyan tree, holding Elizabeth in her arms. He climbed out of the van and looked at her, and she looked back at him. There was a dark cloud-bank overhead, but the last of the sun gilded them, so they looked like ordinary people raised to a kind of sainthood.

'You've heard, then?' said Michael.

Violet nodded.

'I'll see if I can send a telegram to Richard tomorrow morning, just to make sure that everything's all right at home.'

Violet caught hold of his sleeve. 'You won't go back, will you?'

Michael smiled, and kissed her, and then kissed Elizabeth, who pushed her small hand against his cheek. 'I thought about it,' he told her. 'You know – joining the RAF, something like that. But then I thought about something else, too.'

Instead of going inside, he took her for a walk along the L-shaped jetty at which they had first disembarked when they arrived in Australia. The sun glittered on the grey-green sea, and there was a strong aroma of oil and fish and tropical mustiness. Violet held Elizabeth's hand tightly to stop her from running too near the edge.

It was then that Michael told Violet all about Nora Robinson's baby. Violet listened in silence, but when he was finished she took hold of his hand and gave it a single, simple squeeze. 'Why didn't you tell me before? I always wondered what made you change your mind about going back to England.'

'There was nothing to tell, really,' said Michael. 'I walked out of the house one day as an English immigrant; and I came home two days later as an Australian. I was naturalized, if you like. Not by law, you see, but by being needed.'

'I love you,' said Violet, and that was all she had to say.

Miami, 1941

Early on Sunday evening, James took Diamond for a walk along the beach, throwing his walking-cane into the surf for the collie to retrieve. It had been a chaotic week, and he needed to unwind. Atlantic and Pacific Airways had opened three new gates at their main terminal building, and at the same time started up a nightly through-service to Washington and Newark. Because of the growing political crisis with Japan – with Government officials and military personnel to-ing and fro-ing around the country like ants in a worried anthill – every flight had been overbooked, and on Friday evening James had been obliged to borrow two extra aircraft from Eastern Airlines.

Business was better than ever, but for James and his staff of thirty pilots and seventy-six hostesses and forty mechanics that meant long hours and interrupted sleep and unrelenting stress.

Those first faltering days out at Carol City with Eddie Feinbacker's Stinsons seemed to James as if they had happened a lifetime ago.

James had grown heavier in the last five years. He was suntanned and reasonably fit, but there were criss-cross lines around his eyes, and one side of his hair was streaked with grey. Patricia called his grey hair his 'distinguished service discolouration'. She herself had dyed her hair brunette, because a good-looking young lawyer at a party at Coral Gables had told her she looked like Hedy Lamarr. At first, James had found her new hair colour intensely irritating. Every time he glimpsed her out of the corner of his eye, he thought that there was a strange woman walking around the house. But he was too busy to be irritated for long. He was now the owner and executive president of the largest airline in the south-eastern states of America, and the fourth largest airline in the world.

He stood on the shoreline with his shoes tied around his neck, allowing the incoming surf to soak the bottoms of his rolled-up ducks. He didn't know what he would have done without the ocean. He always walked along here when he felt tired or tense or disappointed with life, and he always came back restored. The ocean was his 'other woman'.

In five years, James had remained faithful – not so much to Patricia, but to two sentimental memories. Susan Sheffield, who had been divorced and remarried and now lived in Scotland, and Chloe Treat. Of course, Chloe hadn't been particularly easy to forget. Every now and then, one of the mass-circulation magazines would run front-page pictures of her, and splash a story like *What Really Happened to Chloe Treat?* or *Chloe Treat Speaks To Me From Beyond The Grave* or *I Saw Chloe Treat In Rio Bordello*. They always ran the same picture, too, of Chloe pouting her lips in a pretended kiss, her hair curled, wearing the sheer embroidered dress she had worn that day when James had first danced with her, on board the Dornier Do-X.

He thought of her now, as he turned around and walked back along the beach towards his new eleven-bedroom house facing out towards the Atlantic. He hummed to himself,

> '*I always used to dress in red*
> *The kind of girl who lost her head*
> *But now I find that I've lost you . . .*
> *And so I always dress in blue . . .*
> *Too-tee, too-tee, tooty-too!*'

Diamond ran on ahead, barking and jumping at the seagulls. 'Mairvay-erx,' James said to himself, softly. The sea washed in behind him and filled up his bare footprints. Within a few minutes, the house came into view. It had a high white wall with white urns on top, and twenty or thirty tall palm trees blowing around it. It had been designed for James by Richard Neutra, whom James had flown over from California. It was rectangular and white, with very modern windows and sliding doors and rectangular loggias. Patricia called it 'the hospital'. James didn't mind her calling it that, because in a way it was. A hospital for the healing of damaged memories, and for the gradual convalescence from guilt.

To James, one of the greatest surprises of growing older was not that he had changed but that he had remained so much the same. He was conscious of developing middle-aged habits, and of repeating himself a little too often; and he was also conscious that his readiness to take dangerous risks had become blunted. But when he drove each morning past the shining ranks of APA airliners marshalled outside his terminal building at Miami International Airport, he still felt an extraordinary sense of disbelief that this all belonged to him. Ten DC-3s, the very latest in luxury airliners from Douglas; four DC-2s; four DC-1s; and a fleet of three Martin M-130 flying-boats to fly first-class passengers down to the Caribbean – 'Blue Wing Tours' these were called.

James had believed since boyhood that the future of flying lay in transporting as many people as possible as quickly as possible and for as low a fare as possible; but his father had always expressed so little regard for his beliefs that, even today, he found it difficult to accept that he had actually been right.

Sometimes James felt that he had inherited nothing of any value from his father except the unswerving conviction that – for a Lord – success was its own justification, no matter what that success had cost. It was a conviction that had been instilled in Herbert and many of his contemporaries by their middle-class Edwardian parents, and in England it was still held worthy. But when James thought of Susan; and Chloe; and Gerhard Brunner; he wasn't at all sure that this conviction was a legacy at all, but a curse of almost medieval dreadfulness.

He threw his walking-cane one last time for Diamond to fetch. It tumbled end-over-end in the afternoon sunshine, Diamond sprinting after it. Before Diamond had brought it back, however, he caught sight of Patricia and Eddie standing outside the gate, waving to him.

At first he thought that they had simply come out for a stroll along the beach, but then he realized that their waving was urgent. He quickened his pace, and Diamond, confused by his lack of interest in taking his cane back, came running along beside him.

He reached the house. Eddie looked serious. Patricia was almost in tears.

'What's happened?' James asked them.

Patricia clung on to him. 'It's going to happen here now – not just in Europe! Oh, James! It's terrible!'

'What's going to happen here now? What are you talking about?'

'They just announced it on the radio,' Eddie told him. 'Those bastard Japanese have bombed Pearl Harbor.'

'Good God,' said James. He was quite stunned. 'So they've done it! Good God! Was there very much damage?'

'They didn't say nothing on the news. Well, not much, excepting the Japs came right out of the blue. Couple of battleships damaged, that's what they said.'

James put his arm tightly around Patricia's shoulder. 'You're quite sure it wasn't another one of those Orson Welles stunts?'

Eddie shook his head. 'That's what I thought at first, but no. This is the real McCoy.' He paused for a moment, looking miserable. 'I never thought, twice in the same God-damned lifetime. I never thought that.'

Patricia said, 'I'd better send a telegram to Mummy and Daddy, just to let them know that we're safe. And you'd better send one to Richard.'

'I don't think we have to worry too much about that,' said James. 'Your father and mother must have a sufficient grasp of geography to realize that Pearl Harbor is a good six thousand miles away.'

'But supposing they invade?' asked Patricia.

James took his arm from around her shoulders and looked at his watch. 'At this particular moment, darling, I don't think there's very much likelihood of that. Besides, that doesn't concern me. What *does* concern me is what's going to happen to Atlantic and Pacific Airways.'

'What do you mean?'

'It's obvious, isn't it? If we're going to go to war with Japan, the government is going to be looking for all the air-transportation it can get. This is the opportunity we've been looking for – government contracts to guarantee profit on every flight – and a chance to cut through the usual regulations and extend our routes. You mark my words – the very next call we get from Washington is going to be from the Secretary of the Army.'

He began to walk smartly towards the beach-gate that led into their garden from the rear. 'Patricia!' he called back, over his shoulder. 'Get hold of Diamond, will you! And see if you can't get in touch with Mr and Mrs Ramirez, and cancel dinner.'

Eddie tried hard to keep up with him. 'What are you going to do?'

'What do you think I'm going to do? I'm going to offer my services to the government before anybody else does. Atlantic and Pacific Airways is going to be available to fly government officials and military personnel all over the United States, day and night.'

'We're not allowed to fly all over the United States,' Eddie protested.

'Not yet we're not,' James agreed.

James pushed his way through the wrought-iron gate into the formal modern garden, where fountains played out of abstract sculptures, and palms grew in white concrete planters. Outside the wide rectangular windows of the sunroom, beside the severely rectangular swimming-pool, a young blonde-haired girl of five years old was being towelled dry by her Cuban nursemaid.

James left Eddie for a moment and went down to the edge of the pool, and ruffled the little girl's damp curls. She looked up at him, squinting against the sun. 'Daddy, I can nearly swim now.'

James smiled. 'Is that true?' He turned to the nursemaid and said, 'Is that true, Esmeralda? She can swim?'

Esmeralda tittered, and shook her head. 'You don't swim, you bad girl! Why you tell Daddy you swim? No, Mr Lord, she don't swim. She splish-splash, like Diamond. She don't sink, but she don't swim.'

James knelt down beside the little girl, and said, 'You've got to learn to swim properly, you know, Helen, if you live by the sea.'

The little girl hid her face with her hands. Esmeralda said, 'Helen! You don't hide!' But James stood up again, and told her, 'Don't worry. Just as long as she isn't afraid of the water.'

He went inside the house, to his large white-painted study, dominated by a huge polished-oak desk and a muted, severe painting of aeroplane construction by Charles Sheeler. Eddie followed him, saying, 'That Helen of yours, she looks like a picture, don't she?'

James said nothing, but sat down at his desk and took out his black telephone book. Adopting Helen had been his idea, but for some reason he always found himself disinclined to discuss her with anybody else. Perhaps he felt that he had adopted her for the wrong reasons: not because he loved her, but because he had urgently needed to find some way of keeping Patricia occupied. Not just occupied, but happy, too; and out of his God-damned hair, as Eddie would have put it. With Helen taking up most of her days, Patricia had less time to resent the fact that James's affection for her was formal and ritualistic, rather than spontaneous.

After the scandal of the *Chichester Special* sabotage trial, James had managed to persuade Patricia that Susan had been 'wildly exaggerating', but their marriage had taken a nasty knock from which it had never quite recovered.

'Who're you calling?' Eddie asked him, parking his right buttock on the side of James's desk.

'To start off with, I'm calling Neal Billings, at the War Department. I'm going to tell him that APA is immediately available for military transportation, anywhere in the continental United States, if he can help to push through the authorization. That's the first step.'

'And what's the second step?'

'The second step is, we get hold of our lobbying friends on Capitol Hill, and start putting pressure on the House Appropriations Committee, to see if we can't get permission to extend our operating area outside the US and the Caribbean. All part of the wartime effort, and all that.'

'You're way ahead of me,' said Eddie.

James found the telephone number he was looking for. 'Do you want to pour me a drink?' he asked Eddie. Then – while Eddie was unstoppering and sniffing decanters in his search for the bourbon – he looked up and said, 'I'm an Englishman, Eddie, and I'm a businessman. You know how long I've been trying to get the authority to fly the Atlantic. Miami, Azores, Lisbon, London. Now that the British have let Pan American in, why not us?'

Eddie looked wary. 'Pan American ain't going to like it one bit. Juan Trippe's going to blow his fusebox.'

'Of course. But now's the time. This war with Japan could be the making of us, Eddie. We could break Pan American's monopoly on international flying-boat flights; we could start flying routes all over America. And if we can get enough guaranteed income from the government, we can build up our fleet, too.'

Eddie handed him a whisky. 'You're expecting a whole lot out of this war, ain't you?'

'What do you want me to do? Sit on my hands and watch United and TWA take all of the cake?'

'What's this cake? We're supposed to be fighting for freedom and honour, aren't we? Not cake.'

James lifted his drink. 'A toast to freedom and honour. Freedom and honour for ever! But just remember – we can't keep an airline running on freedom and honour alone. We need money, Eddie. We're desperately short of investment capital. And if there's any going, I want it.'

He sipped his whisky, and then he said, 'If we're smart, Eddie, you and I, we could come out of this conflict with the greatest airline ever seen, anywhere.'

'And if we're not smart? If we're just dumb and ordinary and patriotic?'

James snapped the telephone book shut. 'There is nothing patriotic about being dumb and ordinary. And there is nothing *un*patriotic about expanding your business by catering for critical wartime needs. This war's all about business in any case – Japan trying to corner the Pacific for its so-called Greater East Asia Co-Prosperity Sphere – the US resisting it.'

'Well, I'm sure glad that *you* understand it,' said Eddie, gloomily. 'I thought it was something to do with the Yellow Peril, something like that.'

James stood up. 'Eddie,' he said, 'when I first met you, you were fast asleep in an out-of-date airplane you couldn't afford. Now you're one of the wealthiest men in Miami.'

'Maybe I don't need to get any richer,' said Eddie, in a guarded voice. 'Well – not by making a buck out of my country's woes, anyway.'

James pretended to think seriously about that, and then nodded. 'All right, Eddie. If that's the way you feel about it, I quite understand. I'll buy you out, for whatever you feel is fair, and then you won't have your country's woes on your conscience any longer.'

But Eddie slowly shook his head. 'Oh, no. Not on your life. I'm holding on to my stake. If you're going to do what I *think* you're going to do, then I want my share of it.'

James picked up the telephone, waited for a moment, and then asked the operator to put him through to Washington. 'What can I say?' he asked Eddie, as he waited. 'A principle is a principle, but a dollar is a dollar.'

Eddie said, 'I'll drink to that, I suppose.'

They sat in silence for a while. James remarked, 'Sounds like the lines are all busy. Not surprising, I suppose.'

'How long do you think it's going to last?' Eddie asked James.

James made a face. 'Who knows? They thought that the war in Europe would be over in six months, didn't they? Why don't you turn on the radio, perhaps there's some more news.'

'There ain't nothing but,' said Eddie, but he turned on the large Zenith radio all the same.

Just then, the telephone operator said, '*Hold on, please, sir, I'm connecting you now.*'

The office door opened and Helen came running in, wearing a

MIAMI, 1941

pink-and-white candy-striped beach dress. She climbed up on to James's knee, and said 'Can I talk, too?'

'Not this time, darling,' said James. 'This time it's serious.'

But he kept his arm around her while he said, 'Neal? Is that you? Neal – this is James Lord! Yes – fine, how are you? Well, I'm devastated, naturally. Absolutely devastated. But we can't be too surprised, can we – all things considered? Listen, Neal, I was wondering if you could do me something by way of a small favour –?'

All the time he was talking, he was stroking the baby curls at the back of Helen's neck; but what he didn't see was that Patricia was standing in the open doorway, her arms down by her sides, watching him with a sadness that was almost musical.

When Patricia opened her eyes the following morning, she found that James had already gone. His pillow was striped by the sunlight that penetrated the white Venetian blinds. It still bore the impression of his head. She reached over and smoothed it out, so that it looked as if nobody had been there at all.

She stretched, and lay for a while staring at the ceiling. She still felt tired, even though she had taken a sleeping-pill before going to bed, and had slept soundly all night. No dreams. Well, none that she could remember, anyway.

She could hear Helen playing outside in the yard, pushing her baby-carriage up and down the paving-stones and talking to her dollies. She smiled. She loved Helen more than she could ever explain. It was Helen who had restored her sanity: Helen who had made up for almost everything. Two weeks after bringing Helen home from the hospital, Patricia had looked at herself in the mirror one afternoon and realized that she was Patricia again, not the anxious babbling woman that her miscarriage had turned her into. Ever since then, she had become steadily calmer and more fulfilled. Her beauty had returned to her like a soft veil being drawn over a flower.

Her friends had noticed. Esmeralda had noticed. Only James had failed to notice; or, if he had, he had failed to remark on it.

She wondered when she had stopped loving James. Perhaps that had happened at the same time that her sanity had returned to her. Perhaps it had been when she had first heard about Lady Susan Sheffield – although in an odd way she had found that exciting as well as distressing. She doubted if she would ever leave him. He was always courteous to her; he never raised his voice; he gave her anything she wanted. She had three mink coats hanging in her wardrobe, which she never wore, and a brand-new Lincoln convertible coupé in the garage, which she never drove. Her dresses were made for her by Anna Miller and her hats by John-Frederics. They went to all the parties and all the dinners and everybody told her with italics and double exclamation-points how lucky she was to have such a *dish* of a husband!

But, she didn't love him. And he, she knew, didn't love her. Although the strange thing was – and this always intrigued her about him – he always seemed to give her the impression of being *in* love.

She had thought at first that he might have another mistress, another Susan, somewhere in Miami. But after three or four years of living with him, she realized that he was far too busy with his airline to keep another woman, and that he was rarely missing for long enough. No unexplained absences. No telephone calls that turned out to be wrong numbers if *she* picked them up.

He was in love with somebody, she was sure of that – but with whom, she simply couldn't understand.

He still (infrequently) made love to her; and that was when she felt most intensely that James's heart was somewhere else. But she couldn't challenge him. What could she say? He never whispered other women's names when he was asleep. He never carried other women's photographs in his wallet.

Yet after their lovemaking he always looked at her as if he wished that she were somebody else.

'*Buenos días señora!*' said Nina, brightly, bringing in her breakfast tray and setting it over the bed. Fresh orange juice, tea, and hot blueberry muffins. A trembling pink-and-white orchid in a slender Lalique vase. A copy of the *Miami Herald* with the huge black headline DAY OF INFAMY.

'Did Mr Lord leave me a message?' asked Patricia, deliberately turning the newspaper face down.

'He had to fly to Washington, *señora*. He said he was going to be away until Friday. Something to do with Pearl Harbor.'

Patricia nodded. 'I see. He didn't mention dinner at the Tulleys tonight?'

'He said to go without him, if you wished. Or not, whichever you prefer.'

'Well, that was big of him, wasn't it?'

Nina shrugged. Her big round Cuban face was always expressionless. James had once remarked that the quality of British servants had started to deteriorate when their employers allowed them to show their feelings. 'No demonstrations of emotion of any kind are necessary for the carrying-in of a coal-scuttle.'

As usual, Patricia hadn't known whether to take him seriously or not.

She finished her breakfast; then she got up and put on her bright blue bathing-costume and went for a swim. Helen pushed her baby-carriage close to the pool and watched her. 'Daddy said he was going to bring me back another dolly.'

'Oh, yes? Daddy spoils you.'

'He said he was going to bring me back a dolly with golden hair and a drawdrobe.'

'You mean a wardrobe.'

Helen solemnly repeated, 'Drawdrobe.'

Patricia swam up and down the pool six or seven times, but in spite of the sheltering wall around the garden, the wind from the ocean was a little too chilly for her, so she called Nina to bring her robe. Then she went in to dress.

While she was brushing out her hair for her, Nina said, 'You want me to call Mrs Tulley, *señora*, and tell her you cancel?'

Patricia looked at herself in the mirror. A slim and pretty woman of twenty-eight, with a small splash of freckles across the bridge of her nose, and her faded blue eyes faded still further by the Florida sunshine. A woman who now should be going through the best years of her life; a woman who deserved to be loved.

'*Who is she?*' she whispered to her reflection. '*Who is she?*'

'I tell her you sick, yes?' asked Nina.

'Yes,' said Patricia. 'Tell her I'm sick.' But then she saw herself saying it, and called out, 'No! Don't tell her I'm sick. Tell her I'm coming. Tell her that James had to go to Washington; but if she doesn't mind – if I'm not going to make it thirteen or anything – I'll come on my own.'

'You go?' asked Nina, in surprise, but still expressionless.

'Is there anything wrong? Don't you think I ought to?'

'You *never* go out on your own, *señora*. Not without the *señor*. Always you keep at home.'

'I think I'm going mouldy with over-keeping,' Patricia retorted, feeling pleased with herself for remembering her *Don Quixote* from school. As Nina finished brushing out her hair, however, she remembered another line from the same book: 'A broken leg and an honest woman are best at home.'

She laughed at herself for being so serious and literary. Nina fussed with her hair, tugging it too hard. 'I suppose you wear your black dress, *señora*.'

'Then you suppose wrong. I'm going to wear the red. Not the dull red, the *very* red. The one with the bow at the front.'

'*Si, señora,*' Nina replied, and for the very first time ever Patricia saw a gleam of disapproval in her eyes.

Because of Pearl Harbor, the Tulleys' party was much more subdued than usual. The enormity of what had happened early yesterday afternoon was gradually beginning to sink in, and the news that had come from Hawaii during the day had been unrelievedly depressing. In 110 minutes, the Japanese had sunk or damaged eight major battleships and three light cruisers, destroyed 188 aeroplanes on the ground ('*On the ground!*' the President had raged) and killed 2,400 American servicemen.

Just ten hours later, the Japanese had caught eighteen Flying Fortress bombers and more than fifty P-40 fighters refuelling on the runway at Luzon, in the Philippines, and destroyed almost all of them. The military slang-word 'snafu' was already being heard in American living-rooms – 'situation normal, all fucked up'.

Mrs Tulley had thought of cancelling at first, but the story had got around that the President and Mrs Roosevelt had carried on regardless yesterday evening, and entertained the journalist Ed Murrow and his wife for dinner. 'We all have to eat,' Mrs Roosevelt had told him.

The Tulleys were Republicans, but this was a national crisis, and so for once they were prepared to make an exception and follow the President's example. Apart from that, they had already spent two thousand dollars on flowers and catering.

The Tulleys owned a big pink house overlooking Biscayne Bay. Mr Tulley spent most of his time in New York, making his fortune as president of the Tulley Publishing Corporation, but every December he came down south for the Florida sunshine. His dinner-parties were unusually eclectic. He invited bankers, poets, admirals, ballet-dancers, anybody who interested him.

Patricia arrived late, a few minutes after eight o'clock. Most of the guests were already in the hall, drinking cocktails. The men had bunched together in serious councils of war, hands in pockets, cigars well alight, while the women drifted from one side of the room to the other, uncertain of what to say. It seemed fatuous to talk about hairdressing and nail-varnish, considering what had happened at Pearl Harbor, and yet very few of the women could think of anything to say about the war except that it was 'dreadful'. For the first time since she had been living in Miami, Patricia saw the women conversationally disenfranchised.

Ida Tulley came streaming up to her in a satin gown with black-and-white checkers on it that made her look like the prototype for a new board-game. 'Patricia! I'm so delighted you could come! No use mope-mope-moping alone at home, that's what I always say. And I'm afraid we wives are going to find ourselves *increas ingly* abandoned, now there's a war on. We're just going to have to get used to going out on our owny-owny-ownsome!'

'I suppose we're going to have to do our bit,' Patricia agreed. 'I think I'll be rather relieved, in a way. All my friends at home are driving ambulances and serving out soup in the bomb-shelters and things like that. I've been feeling rather cowardly, over here.'

Ida Tulley took her arm. She had a marvellously eroded face, like the Painted Desert of Arizona seen from the air. 'You're a dear girl! Didn't I always say that? A dear, dear girl. And I'm so glad you've come. Emmet was dying to talk to James; and now he can talk to you.'

'Emmet?' asked Patricia. Even after eight years, American names still took her by surprise. She had laughed, once, when a serious young man had been introduced to her as Kermit; not realizing that President Teddy Roosevelt had christened his favourite son Kermit, and that this Kermit had been named in his honour.

'Emmet works for the *Washington Examiner*,' Ida Tulley explained. 'That's one of George's papers. He's very good-looking, may I add!'

Patricia didn't wholly agree with her; because she had already caught sight of a man who had to be Emmet across the hall – a man who *must* have been Emmet, because every other man in the room was either too old or too ugly, or else she knew them already.

The Man Who Had To Be Emmet was six feet three inches tall, with the body of a college football-player and one of those huge handsome American faces that was more like a pasture than a face. Placid, and broad, and tanned to the colour of ripe wheat. Almost at the same time that Patricia realized he Had To Be Emmet, he turned and looked towards her and knew that she Had To Be Patricia. He smiled a little 'hi, there!' smile; and then returned with stagey seriousness to the conversation in which he was currently involved.

Ida Tulley steered Patricia forward, breaking into the circle of conversation. 'Everybody! This is Patricia Lord! Well, you've all flown APA – if anybody doesn't know Patricia by now, they ought to! Patricia's husband James is the president of APA, and it's a darn shame that he can't join us tonight, but what with the Japanese . . . I never liked Japanese food, did you? All that squid and *raw* fish!! And I think anyway it's time we taught them a darn good lesson! But Patricia's here on her ownsome tonight, and why don't you gentlemen make her feel at home?'

The Man Who Had To Be Emmet stepped forward and said, 'Mrs Lord? I'm real pleased to make your acquaintance. My name's Emmet Bell.'

'Mrs Tulley tells me you work for the *Washington Examiner*,' said Patricia.

'That's right. The financial pages.'

'I'm afraid I only read the fashion pages and the funnies.'

'"Tillie the Toiler", I'll bet,' said Emmet – and when Patricia smiled, 'Will Mac ever get his girl, we ask ourselves?'

Patricia said, 'You wanted to talk to my husband. Was it about anything special?'

'Nothing that can't keep. I've been writing a big background article on all of the major airways. I wanted to ask him about his early days at Atlantic and Pacific – how he managed to get the mail contract from South-Eastern, that kind of stuff.'

'I'm sure he'll be only too pleased to talk to you when he gets back from Washington.'

Emmet suggested, 'How about a cocktail? No – you don't look like a cocktail lady. You look like a champagne lady.'

'What's the difference?'

'If I told you, you'd think I was making cheap flattering remarks.'

Patricia laughed. 'I don't mind being flattered, even cheaply.'

Emmet beckoned to the waiter. 'Bring this lady a glass of champagne, would you please? And I'll have another old-fashioned.' Then he turned back to Patricia and said, 'Champagne ladies always have a smile in their eyes. That's the way you can tell.'

'And cocktail ladies don't?'

'Cocktail ladies have eyes like gimlets, sizing you up, weighing the odds, looking for what they can get.'

'What about men who drink old-fashioneds?'

Emmet grinned. 'The drink describes the man. Old-fashioned.'

There were over sixty guests for dinner. They sat at a long Cuban mahogany table facing each other over sheaves of white lilies and sparkling candelabra. The cutlery was gold-plated silver; the glasses were hand-cut Waterford crystal; the pink-and-white Royal

Doulton plates were heavily gilded and decorated with the Tulley crest.

Mr Tulley stood up like a tired puffin, and knocked his knife-handle on the table for silence. 'Dear friends,' he said, in his elliptic Illinois accent, 'we stand in the shadow of tragic and terrible events. For all we know, the world in which we grew up will be swept away, never to return. I just want to say that we place ourselves tonight in the hands of the Lord, and ask that he protects us in the dark times to come.'

He paused, and then he added, 'I ask you all to stand in silence for one minute, in honour of our dead at Pearl Harbor.'

They rose from their chairs; and as they stood in silence, Patricia began to realize for the first time that Japan's attack on Pearl Harbor had changed all of their lives for ever. The old values had been put to the test, and found to be perilously wanting. From now on, they would have to forge new values, both political and personal. This one minute's silence had silenced a whole generation – Father Charles E. Coughlin on the radio, calling the President 'anti-God'; Clark Gable saying 'Frankly, my dear, I don't give a damn'; E. H. Crump, the Boss of Memphis, declaring that 'you should never put a sponge on the end of a hammer if you want to drive a nail'; W. C. Fields telling Mae West that she was 'a banquet for the eyes'.

She glanced over at Emmet, who was standing with his head bowed and his hands clasped behind his back, and she allowed herself to think that he was attractive. It was a heresy, this thought; her very first heresy in eight uncertain years, and it alarmed her. Not just by its unexpectedness, but by its allure.

He's attractive, she thought. *He's really attractive. And the worst thing is, I'm looking at him and thinking how attractive he is, and all the time I'm married to somebody else.*

The minute's silence was over. Everybody drew back their chairs to sit down. In that instant, Emmet lifted his head and looked across at Patricia and Patricia knew that what she was thinking was written quite explicitly on her face. Emmet kept his eyes on her for a moment, and then sat down. Patricia felt breathless, as if the candles had burned all the oxygen out of the room. She looked at Emmet's hands and even his hands were attractive, tanned and broad with well-trimmed nails.

'Do you know something,' Emmet remarked, unfolding his napkin, 'you don't seem to me to be anything like the wife of an airline tycoon. You're quiet, you're gentle. Do you paint, or play a musical instrument? That's the type you seem like to me.'

'I used to play the violin, when I was at school,' said Patricia. 'I used to *adore* the violin. I still do. But my father pomised to buy me a pony if I gave it up. He said if he wanted to hear a noise like that, he'd go out and strangle a pig.'

Emmet raised his glass. 'I'll bet your father had a tin ear.'

The waiters brought round stuffed Union League clams and chilled crawfish tails with Louisiana chili-pepper sauce. This was followed by wild duck with peanut stuffing; carpetbag steaks stuffed with oysters; and strawberries with sherry cream. The guests were served with California wines, both white and red. Mr Tulley had a good stock of French wines – 'but who the hell knows when we're ever going to get any more'.

After dinner, there was dancing in the hall to the Ted Mullet Five. Patricia danced once with Emmet and once with Mr Tulley, and then decided to leave.

'You won't have one more dance?' Emmet asked her, as she put on her white mink wrap.

'It wouldn't be right.'

'Then may I see you home?'

'It's all right. My chauffeur's waiting.'

'I sure would have liked to talk to you some more.'

Patricia took his hand. 'I know you would. And I would have liked to talk to you. But I'm a married woman; and married women have to think of appearances.'

'How about lunch tomorrow? Somewhere discreet, where you won't have to worry about appearances.'

'Emmet, I'd love to, but –'

He thrust his hands into his pockets and looked down at the floor. 'Okay. I understand. That's another thing about champagne ladies. They're always spoken for. It's a well-known characteristic.'

Emmet walked her to the door. Her chauffeur started up the limousine, and drove it up to the steps. Emmet said, 'I'll call your husband when he gets back from Washington. Maybe I'll see you again then.'

'Maybe.'

Patricia turned around in her seat as Fidel drove away from the Tulley's house and headed south. Through the tinted glass of the limousine's opera-window she saw Emmet standing on the steps watching her go. He lifted one hand briefly in a wave, even though he couldn't have known that she was looking at him. She sat back in her seat, holding on to the braided silk strap, and her expression was unusually grave.

Fidel said, 'Is everything okay, Mrs Lord?'
'Oh, yes,' Patricia replied. 'Everything's dandy.'

She was sitting in her dressing-room combing out her hair when
the doorbell rang. She looked at the clock by the bedside. Nearly
midnight. She had given Nina the night off, and Esmeralda was
already asleep, so she got up and went to the bedroom window to
find out who it was. At first she couldn't see anybody at all; but
then a figure in a tuxedo stepped two or three paces back down
the path and waved to her.

She opened the window. 'Emmet? What are you doing here?'

He lifted a violin up to his chin, and played the opening bars of
Oh, For The Wings Of A Dove. Sweetly, tremulously, sadly.

'You said you adored the violin. I couldn't let you go to bed
without playing you a lullaby.'

She laughed in delight. 'You're quite mad! No – don't play any
more, you'll wake Helen up.'

'You don't want an encore?'

'I'd adore an encore, but not in the front yard, at midnight.'

'You've broken my heart,' said Emmet.

'Don't be silly. You've had too many old-fashioneds.'

Emmet lifted up both arms in mock-despair. 'If that's the way
you feel, I shall have to go.'

'You're not too squiffy to drive?'

'Oh, don't you worry about me. Driving into Biscayne Bay isn't
the worst way to end your life. To lie at peace amid the tuna.'

'Emmet, listen, I'm serious,' said Patricia. 'Come in and have a
cup of coffee before you go. I wouldn't want you to be stopped
for drunken driving.'

Emmet played a high, keening note on his violin. 'Very well,
then, I accept. A cup of coffee from the champagne lady. What
better way to end the night's relevries. I mean revelies. Well, you
know what I mean.'

Patricia put on her square-shouldered yellow-silk dressing-gown
and went downstairs to open the door. Emmet was leaning against
the pillar at the side of the porch, beaming. He stepped inside,
clicked his heels, and bowed his head. 'Mrs Lord, you have saved
me from myself.'

'Just be as quiet as you can,' Patricia cautioned him. 'Helen can
never get back to sleep if you wake her up.'

She led the way through to the kitchen, and put on the kettle. It
was a wide, modern kitchen, decorated in green and cream, with
windows overlooking the beach to the south, so that it was almost

always sunny. Emmet perched himself on a bar-stool and laid his violin on the counter. 'You don't happen to have anything stronger than coffee? I think I need to get drunk again, before this hangover gets any worse.'

'Coffee,' Patricia told him, sharply.

'Coffee and a shot?'

'Coffee and nothing, unless you want a cookie.'

Emmet shook his head violently. 'Dinner at the Tulleys is the gastronomic equivalent of a .45 bullet. It's guaranteed to stop a man dead in his tracks.'

'You weren't forced to clear your plate.'

'Oh, but I was. It's in my character, you see. When I have an appetite, I won't stop until it's completely and utterly satisfied.'

Patricia spooned out arabica coffee into the jug. She knew what Emmet was saying to her. If it had come from another man, she might well have been offended by such a suggestive remark. But Emmet was so lighthearted that she found it flattering. She poured hot water on the coffee and stood with her back to him while it brewed. She knew he was looking at her. She enjoyed the feeling of it.

'Do you know something?' he asked her. 'The backs of your ankles are just perfect. Whenever I meet a woman who has perfect backs to her ankles . . . that's when I know that I'm in the presence of class.'

She turned round and looked at him intently. 'You're not really drunk, are you? You're only pretending.'

A broad smile crept across his face. 'You're a very clever lady. How did you guess?'

'I don't know. Complimenting the backs of a woman's ankles isn't the kind of thing that drunk people do.'

'They don't? I'll have to remember that. What part of a woman *do* drunk people compliment?'

Patricia opened the cupboard and took down two breakfast-cups. 'Where did you get the violin?' she asked him, to change the subject.

'The violin? Oh, it belongs to young Laura Tulley. I'm supposed to bring it back tomorrow morning on pain of death.'

'You play it very well.'

'I used to. I'm pretty rusty these days. I was first violin in the high school orchestra. My father taught me. He was a professional musician. He used to play background music for movies. You remember that Deanna Durbin picture about the orchestra of unemployed musicians? He was in that.'

'What made you want to be a journalist, instead of a musician?'

392

Emmet blew on his coffee to cool it down. 'Actually, I wanted to be a private detective. I tried it for a while, but I didn't make any money at it. It's not as much fun as you think, hanging around outside motel windows, trying to catch people in bed together. I found somebody's lost dog, about ten minutes too late. A tractor-trailer had driven over it, and it was just like a large sheet of paper with a picture of a dog on it.'

Patricia laughed. 'That sounds terrible.'

Emmet shrugged. 'Financial journalism isn't too bad. It can be quite exciting, especially if you dig up some dirty dealing on the stock market; or find out that some well-known reputable corporation is up to its neck in corruption.'

'I hope you're not writing a story like that about James.'

'I hope he hasn't done anything to warrant it,' Emmet replied. His voice was a little sharper than Patricia would have liked.

'Of course not,' she said. 'He's the chairman of the Miami Chamber of Commerce.'

'Back in the days of Prohibition, the chairman of the Phoenix Chamber of Commerce used to be a bootlegger.'

'Well, James certainly isn't a bootlegger.'

Emmet laughed, and put down his coffee cup. Almost as quickly as he had laughed, however, he turned serious, and he looked at Patricia in a way that no man had looked at her for a very long time. He said, quietly, 'I don't think there's very much point in my lying to you. I came round tonight because I find you very, very attractive.'

Patricia was silent for a moment. Then she said, 'I know.'

'I guess it was pretty stupid of me,' Emmet went on. 'After all, you're a married woman with a young daughter . . . and you're probably twenty times better-off than I am. But there are times when your heart gets the better of your head, and you don't stop to think what's stupid and what isn't. I wanted to see you again, and so I borrowed Laura's violin and came on over.'

Patricia kept turning her coffee-spoon over and over and over. At last, she said, 'Are you sober enough to drive?'

Emmet nodded.

'You'd better go then. Do you have very far?'

'Only about a half-mile. I'm staying at the Regency.'

Patricia said, 'Don't misunderstand me, Emmet. I'm not angry. I'm not throwing you out. You've been a marvellous escort, and I've enjoyed your company. But there are some things in one's life that one can find it possible to do; and there are things that one simply can't.'

Emmet stood up. 'Your father's a Member of Parliament, isn't he?'

Patricia nodded. Emmet seemed to be standing awfully close to her. She could smell his cologne and the fragrance of cigar-smoke on his tuxedo.

'You know what they say about politics being the art of the possible.'

'I didn't inherit my father's political instincts, I'm afraid,' smiled Patricia.

Emmet held out his hand. 'In that case, I'd better be a good fellow and say *buenos noces*.'

He leaned forward and kissed her on the cheek. He was about to kiss her on the other cheek when she turned her face full towards him and kissed his lips.

Afterwards, when she thought about that moment, she couldn't understand what it was that had made her do it. Perhaps she had known all evening that they would fall for each other. Perhaps both of them had known it, right from the moment they had met. But once she had kissed him, a feeling surged up inside her that made her head feel as if it were resonating like a church-bell, deaf, blind, speechless, helpless, numb.

They kissed for what seemed like hours. When at last their lips parted, Patricia stared directly into Emmet's eyes, saying nothing at all.

Emmet said, 'Do I still have to go?' It was a question but it didn't really sound like one.

Patricia shook her head.

Naked, he had extraordinary beauty. His muscles were well-developed, but smooth. His chest was broad and hairless, his hips narrow. His buttocks were rounded but very firm. He had legs that moved like an anatomical diagram of leverage and power.

But he was more than just an athlete; more than just another man's body. He held her and touched her and made her shiver, and whispered words in her ear that made her wonder if she were drunk or mad. When he ran the tip of his tongue around her nipples she gasped as if he were burning her. When at last he slid himself inside her, she cried out loud, not caring who heard, almost *wanting* them to hear, so that they would know how excited she was, how demanding, how shameless.

She closed her eyes tightly. Emmet, Emmet, Emmet! If only James knew what she was doing! If only Ida Tulley knew! She felt for one instant as if her entire being were being compressed into a single fist. Then she was convulsing and crying and hurling her head from side to side, her teeth clenched with ecstasy.

She opened her eyes. She was still shaking. Emmet lay close beside her, the hair under his arm making a fan against the lamplight. He wasn't smiling but he didn't need to. She reached out and touched his lips with her fingertips.

'Nothing like that has ever happened to me before,' she told him, truthfully.

'I knew you were a champagne lady,' he told her. They were both out of breath.

She clasped her hands between her thighs, partly out of modesty, partly out of possessiveness. 'Some things are very much more precious than champagne.'

He lifted his eyes for a moment to look at the bedside clock. 'One-fifteen,' he told her. 'Only an hour and twenty-three minutes since I rang your doorbell.'

'Is that a record?' she teased him.

He kissed her forehead, and then her eyes, and then her lips. 'Perhaps I can start calling you Patricia now, instead of Mrs Lord.'

'You're too familiar.'

'But I love you.'

'You can't possibly.'

He kissed her again. 'I don't think you can claim to be much of an expert on what's possible.' He kissed her again, and again. '*Anything's* possible.'

'I think . . . I'd like a glass of champagne,' said Patricia, stretching herself luxuriously out on the bed. 'There's some Moët in the icebox.'

'All of a sudden I'm the butler?'

She touched his cheek, and kissed him. 'No, you're not the butler. The butler gets paid. You have to do everything for free.'

'That means I'm a slave.'

'Yes,' said Patricia. 'I've always wanted a slave. Especially a sulky, good-looking slave like you.'

Emmet got up, and picked up his pants. 'What happens if I run into the nanny?' he asked.

'Tell her you came to varnish the floors.'

'At a quarter after one in the morning?'

'Don't worry, Esmeralda will believe anything.'

Emmet went downstairs to the kitchen to find the champagne. Patricia lay back on her pillow, feeling extraordinary – as if by taking Emmet into her bed she had metamorphosed into somebody else altogether. She held her hands in front of her face, just to make sure that she was Patricia. But her hands could have been anybody's. The only sure identification was her wedding-band. She slipped it off, and turned over towards the lamp so that she could read the words that were inscribed inside it. *To P For Ever J.*

Emmet came back, carrying the bottle of champagne and two tall glasses. He stopped in the doorway and said, 'What are you looking at?'

Patricia woke up just before dawn and reached across the bed. The sheet was wrinkled but there was nobody there. For an instant, she thought that she must have imagined making love to Emmet, but then she opened her eyes and knew that it had been real. A feeling of catastrophic dread came over her, and she sat bolt upright and whispered, '*Emmet? Emmet, where are you? Emmet?*'

There was no reply. Perhaps he had decided to get up in the middle of the night and quietly leave. She switched on her bedside lamp and climbed out of bed. She was still naked, so she picked her yellow dressing-gown up from the floor and draped it over her shoulders. '*Emmet? Are you there?*'

She went out on to the galleried landing. There was a light on downstairs. Perhaps Emmet had gone down to the kitchen to make himself a cup of coffee. Patricia tied her sash around her waist and tiptoed barefoot down to the hall. On the wall hung an oil-painting of James, standing next to a Ford Tri-motor with a self-satisfied look on his face. My God, she thought, he wouldn't be looking so smug if he knew what his wife had been up to last night.

Surprisingly, the kitchen was in darkness. The light was coming from under the library door. Patricia frowned, and hesitated. Perhaps James had come back during the night. Perhaps Emmet had heard him coming, and escaped. She went to the library door, and called, 'James?'

Immediately, she heard a rustling sound, and the bang of a desk-drawer closing. She snatched open the door, and there was Emmet, fully-dressed, standing behind James's desk with papers and books strewn all over it. He stared at her rigidly, but didn't speak.

'Emmet?' she asked him. 'Emmet, what are you doing?'

He raised both hands in a gesture of surrender. 'I'm sorry. This isn't exactly what it looks like.'

Patricia came forward and stared at all the papers on James's desk. 'You've been going through his things!'

'Yes, I have. I admit it. I thought you were asleep. It just seemed like a chance that was worth taking.'

'But *why*? What are you looking for? And do you mean to say that you took me to bed and made love to me and all the time you weren't interested in me at all? Do you mean to say that you seduced me so that you could get into the house and burgle us?'

Emmet came around the desk, trying to be conciliatory, but Patricia spat at him, 'Don't touch me! Don't you dare!'

'Patricia, listen – I don't want you to get the wrong idea about this.'

'Then what, pray, is the right idea? I've always been faithful to James – always. Last night was the very first time I've even allowed another man to kiss me, let alone –' she gasped for breath, and smeared the tears away from her eyes with the back of her hand. 'Because I believed you!' she shouted at him. 'Because I thought you meant it! Because I was stupid enough to think that you really did find me attractive!'

'Patricia, please, listen,' said Emmet.

'Listen to what? More words of love? More sweet nothings?'

'I meant them, for God's sake!'

'Then what are you doing here, going through James's papers?'

Emmet tried to come closer again, but Patricia stayed back. 'Listen,' Emmet told her, 'just give me two minutes to explain what I'm doing, and why, and what I feel about you, and then if you're still not satisfied you can call the police and have me taken in.'

'How can I call the police? What am I going to tell them? That my lover of one night's standing has broken into my husband's desk, and tried to steal his papers? I can imagine what *that* would look like on the front page of the *Miami Herald*, can't you?'

'Patricia, give me a break.'

'A break? Why should I? Why shouldn't I just – throw you out on your ear?'

'Well, you could,' said Emmet. 'But you're going to hear about this sooner or later, from somebody, and it might be better if you heard it from me.'

He picked up one of James's old business diaries, for 1933. 'This is what I was looking for, and there's enough in here to confirm what I suspected all along. In the early days of Atlantic and Pacific Airways, when James and Eddie Feinbacker were right on the brink of bankruptcy, James bribed one of South-Eastern Airway's mechanics to sabotage South-Eastern's airplanes.'

'What?' Patricia demanded. 'Why on earth should James have done a thing like that?'

'Simple. There was only one government mail contract for the south-eastern states, and South-Eastern had it. Without it, APA couldn't have survived. So James made sure that South-Eastern lost it.'

Patricia said, coldly, 'I suppose you've got some proof of all this?'

Emmet ran his hand through his hair. 'I'm afraid I do. I've been corresponding with several journalists in England, who have been helping me out with background on Lord Aeronautics. One of those journalists is writing propaganda for the War Office now; but back in the early thirties he used to work for the *Daily Herald.* Tommy Thompson, that was his name. Kind of a left-wing character, but I guess that was partly why he had it in for your husband.'

'I do seem to remember James talking about somebody called Thompson,' said Patricia, her voice fainter.

Emmet said, 'Well, it's not surprising, judging from what Thompson found out about him. You remember when James was tried for sabotaging the *Chichester Special?*'

'Of course,' Patricia retorted, flushing. 'But he was found not guilty.'

'Well, he may not have been guilty on *that* particular occasion,' Emmet agreed. 'But the same guy who claimed that James had offered him money to fix the *Chichester Special* – Jack Gibbons, that was his name – this same guy swore that James had paid him money the previous year to go to Germany and sabotage a racing seaplane belonging to Gerhard Brunner, who was a famous German aviator.'

'But *why?*'

'Again, it's simple,' said Emmet. 'Herbert Lord was supposed to be racing against Gerhard Brunner for the Seraphim seaplane trophy, but both he and James were pretty sure that they couldn't win it. You probably know by now that the Lords don't care too much for losing.'

'But did Tommy Thompson have proof of this?' asked Patricia.

'Well, there's proof and proof. He received a letter from Jacko Gibbons, when Gibbons was serving a two-year sentence for robbery. He sent me a copy of it. Apparently Gerhard Brunner was so distraught by the loss of his plane that he committed suicide.'

Patricia sat down. 'Whatever you say, I can't believe that James could be capable of anything like that. And if Tommy Thompson knew all about it, why didn't he print something in his newspaper, or go to the police?'

Emmet said, 'That's what I mean by proof and proof. Tommy Thompson couldn't give his newspaper the kind of cast-iron evidence they needed to publish the story without risking a ruinous libel action. Quite apart from the fact that the Lords had friends in high places. Including your father.'

Patricia said nothing, but reached out and touched the papers on James's desk as if they carried some secret message of reassurance in Braille.

Emmet continued, 'Tommy Thompson still believes that James might have been responsible for sabotaging the *Chichester Special*, too.'

'But James was innocent; the court found him innocent.'

'Solely on the uncorroborated testimony of Lady Sheffield; which Thompson has always considered to be highly suspect.'

'You mean he wasn't with her at all that night?'

'Nobody else saw him in Oxfordshire, only Lady Sheffield.'

'So what are you looking for now?' Patricia asked.

'I'm looking for solid evidence that your husband was paying a man called Enriquez Bocanegra to sabotage airliners at South-Eastern Airways. And, here, in this diary, I've certainly found two references to somebody called Enriquez, and a reminder to buy this man Enriquez a Dodge Standard Six.'

'Is any of this going to do anybody any good?' Patricia wanted to know. 'It all happened so long ago – and nobody was hurt by it, after all.'

'That's where you're wrong,' said Emmet, soberly. 'In fact, that's why I'm down here in Florida this weekend. Four days ago, an alligator hunter was out in his pirogue not too far from Devil's Garden at the edge of the Okaloacoochee Slough. The keel of his pirogue knocked against an underwater obstruction, which he eventually discovered was the tail-fin of a crashed airliner, lying in twenty feet of water. The airliner was brought up by police and accident investigators on Saturday afternoon.'

'I haven't heard about it on the news.'

'Not so far – but you're just about to. The *Washington Examiner* got a beat on it from one of the accident investigators from Ford. The police have been keeping it quiet because they didn't want the press trampling all over the place. So we did a deal. We're going to keep the story under wraps until tomorrow morning, in exchange for exclusive pictures. The police'll have finished examining the aircraft by then, and contacting the next of kin.'

'Next of kin? There were people on board?'

'Oh, sure. The crew, and seven passengers, although there isn't too much of them left. The police believe that one of the passengers is Erle Pepper, the founder and president of South-Eastern Airways, who went missing eight years ago, on a flight from Miami to Florida. Not only that – another passenger has been tentatively identified as Chloe Treat, the movie actress. They found her rings, you know, and her pocketbook. Mind you, they've been down there for over eight years, lying in warm water that's full of fish. It's been pretty hard to make any positive identifications.'

'You're trying to suggest that James had something to do with this, too?'

'I don't know for sure. But Enriquez Bocanegra certainly did. The accident investigators found out straight away that part of the tail section was blown away – maybe a small bomb in the luggage compartment.'

'But is there any proof that James was involved?'

Emmet said, 'No, to be honest, there isn't. Only hearsay and rumour, and men offering to badmouth your husband for money.'

'So what are you doing here, if there isn't any proof?'

'Well, Patricia,' Emmet told her, 'I'm trying to find some proof. Journalists aren't like lawyers, you know. I'm not assuming that James is innocent until he's been incontestably proven guilty. In fact, quite the opposite – I'm assuming that he's guilty until he's incontestably proven innocent. Even *then* we'll often keep on after them, if we don't happen to like their face.'

'And you don't happen to like James's face, is that it?'

Emmet closed the 1933 diary and dropped it back on the desk. 'I'm really sorry you found out. Everything that I said to you in bed tonight was true. When you walked into the Tulleys' yesterday evening, I couldn't believe my eyes, and I couldn't believe my luck.'

'And I don't believe *you*, you arrogant hog,' she told him. 'You just get all of your things together, your dinner-jacket and your tie and your pathetic violin, and get out of my house and never come back.'

Emmet hesitated for a moment, his head bowed over James's desk. 'All right, Patricia. But I still want to talk to your husband about this airplane wreck.'

'That's entirely up to him; although I strongly suspect that he won't want to have anything to do with it.'

'He already has a very great deal to do with it. That airliner crashed on the very Sunday before you first came to Miami. You've heard me say that Miss Chloe Treat the movie actress was probably on board. Well . . . if it *is* her, she was travelling under an assumed name, and her ticket was paid for by Atlantic and Pacific Airways. What's more, she was travelling under the assumed name of Shepherd.'

'Shepherd?' frowned Patricia. 'I –?'

'The Lord is my shepherd,' Emmet interrupted her. 'I shall not want. He maketh me to lie down in green pastures.'

Patricia was silent, thinking, for a very long time. Then she looked back at Emmet and said, 'But if what you're suggesting has any truth in it, any truth at all – why should James want to have the airliner sabotaged?'

'I don't know,' Emmet admitted. 'That's why I wanted to talk to him face-to-face.'

'Supposing I were to ask you for James's sake – for our daughter's sake – for *my* sake – not to take this matter any further?'

'Patricia, there's nothing I can do. Sooner or later, *somebody's* going to start asking why the leading movie actress of 1933 was travelling incognito from Miami to Atlanta on a ticket paid for by James Lord. Come on, the disappearance of Chloe Treat ranks with Bigfoot and the Marie Celeste and Amelia Earhart.'

'Then I suppose you'd better just go,' said Patricia.

Emmet looked down at the desk.

'It's all right,' Patricia told him. 'I'll tidy it up.'

'Listen,' said Emmet, 'about last night –'

'I'll just have to live with it, won't I?' Patricia replied. 'What's done is done. I rather wish I hadn't found it so exciting, that's all. My life's been rather short on excitement.'

'There's a war on the way. I guess that should be more than exciting enough for all of us.'

Patricia came around the desk and took hold of his hand and kissed him. 'Once I was almost mad, you know,' she told him. 'Then I adopted Helen and learned not to be mad. Now I think I've learned to behave like an adult. I've taken a long time growing up, but it does, you know, when you're living with a man like James.'

Emmet was about to give her one last kiss when they heard a terrible shrieking in the hallway. '*Señora! Señora! Señora, where are you? The baby! The baby has fallen in the pool!*'

*

401

Clutched with stark terror, Patricia had opened the library door and was running through the kitchen even before Esmeralda had stopped screaming. The back door was open and she jumped down the steps on bare feet and across the flagstones and there in the grey light of morning Helen was floating face-down in the middle of the swimming-pool, her dolly floating face-up, smiling, right beside her.

'*Helen!*' she cried, and plunged waist-deep into the water. But Emmet had already dived past her, hitting the surface with a tremendous splash.

Panicking, breathless, Patricia tried to wade towards the centre of the pool, then swim. But her sodden dressing-gown dragged her down, and Emmet was already kicking his way towards the side, his arm around Helen's neck. He lifted her little body up so that Esmeralda could lay her down on the concrete, and then he heaved himself out of the water and knelt beside her.

Shivering, distraught, Patricia struggled out of the pool again and ran to join him.

'Is she dead?' she asked, in a voice as transparent as glass.

Emmet had tilted Helen's head back to clear her nose and throat. Now he was kneeling astride her, and systematically pressing on her chest to push the water out of her lungs. Helen's face was grey from lack of oxygen, and her eyes were closed.

'Oh God,' wept Patricia. 'Oh God, oh God, is she dead?'

Emmet said to Esmeralda, 'Call the ambulance. *Ambulancia!* and make it quick! Then bring me some warm blankets.'

He kept pressing on Helen's chest. Patricia couldn't do anything at all but watch the tiny blonde curls at the back of Helen's neck drying in the morning wind. She was wearing her pyjamas with Minnie Mouse pictures on them, and the silver bracelet that James had bought for her the last time he had gone away.

She must have been woken up by Patricia going downstairs to the library, and decided to get up and take her dolly for a morning swim.

She passed us by, thought Patricia, in total agony. *She passed the library door – where my one-night lover and I were arguing; and I didn't even know.* Her guilt and shame almost suffocated her.

Emmet kept pressing. Helen didn't stir. Her little fingers opened out as if she were letting go of a favourite toy. Patricia bent forward so that her forehead was touching the concrete and she felt that her heart would stop out of sheer misery.

'Esmeralda!' called Emmet. 'Esmeralda, where are those blankets?'

Patricia slowly unbent herself. 'I'll get them,' she whispered. Then, 'She's dead, isn't she? You might as well stop.'

Emmet ignored her, but pushed and pushed. Then he leaned forward and pressed his ear against Helen's chest.

'I'll get the . . . blankets,' Patricia repeated, and unsteadily stood up.

It was then that Helen coughed, and abruptly regurgitated water. She coughed again, and spluttered, and took a deep, gargling breath. Emmet lifted his head and said, 'She's okay; her heart's beating okay. She couldn't have been floating out there for too long.'

Patricia dropped to her knees. Helen coughed once more, and then opened her eyes, pink and watery from the chlorine. 'Mommy . . .' she whispered, thickly.

Patricia wanted to pick her up and hug her but Emmet gently restrained her. 'I have to get her on her side. You know – just to make sure that her windpipe's clear.'

Esmeralda came hurrying out with blankets, her slippers slapping on the poolside. 'The hospital man, he say they come pronto. Is the baby okay?'

Emmet wrapped Helen in a big Spanish blanket and lifted her up. 'She's okay,' he replied. 'Let's get her inside, and wait for the ambulance.'

Esmeralda covered Patricia with a blanket, and together they went into the house. They left behind Helen's doll, still smiling, bobbing up and down on the gradually-settling surface of the pool.

Eddie called James, and James flew back from Washington immediately. He piloted the DC-2 airliner himself, arriving just before lunchtime after a flight that had broken unofficial commercial airspeed records. Fidel met him at the airport and drove him straight to the Flagler Memorial Hospital.

Patricia was still there, sitting on her own in the waiting-room, unable to read *McCall's* or *Time* or *Reader's Digest*. Two hours ago, Dr Braunschweig had given Helen a mild sedative to help her get over the shock of what had happened. When she was awake and alert again, he wanted to put her through a comprehensive series of tests to make sure that the lack of oxygen hadn't impaired her mental capacity in any way.

James came straight into the waiting-room and took Patricia in his arms and held her uncomfortably tight. 'Are you all right?' he asked her. 'I could hardly believe it when Eddie told me what had happened. How's Helen?'

'She's sleeping at the moment. Dr Braunschweig thinks she's probably going to be fine.'

'Probably? What does that mean?'

'James, there's always a risk of brain damage when your oxygen supply is cut off. That's what Dr Braunschweig said. But he's very optimistic.'

'Where is he? I want to talk to him. I want to see Helen, too.'

Patricia took hold of his hand. 'James, just for a moment, sit down. It's no use being angry. Everybody's doing everything they can.'

James, testily, sat down. In spite of the sign saying 'No Smoking', he took out a cigarette and lit it. 'How did she get into the pool in the first place, that's what I'd like to know.'

'She woke up early. It looks as if she was taking her dolly for a swim. She's found out how to open the lock on the garden door, and nobody knew.'

James blew out smoke. 'She could be dead, do you know that? She could be laying in a coffin now, instead of a bed.'

'James, dear, don't think that hasn't been going around and around in my mind, too. I've been torturing myself.'

James shrugged, and then said, 'I'm sorry. It was such a shock, that's all. Thank God you managed to pull her out.'

'Yes,' said Patricia.

They returned to the hospital just before nightfall, when the sky over Miami looked as if God had been stirring boysenberry jelly into it, and the bays and inlets and canals were all secretive mirrors. As soon as they arrived, Dr Braunschweig took them straight through to see Helen. She was sitting up in bed, white-faced but cheerful, and surrounded by flowers, orange gladioli and yellow lilies.

'Daddy, you came back!'

James sat down on the side of the bed and kissed her. 'When daughters fall into swimming-pools and nearly manage to drown themselves, Daddies are always around.'

'It wasn't you who saved me, though.'

'No, I couldn't save you. I was all the way away in Washington, talking to some Army people about the war. But if I'd been there, I would have saved you.'

'How are you feeling, precious?' asked Patricia, anxious to change the subject.

'I have a headache, and my nose is sore, and my chest is all bruised – '

'That was the artificial respiration,' Patricia interrupted, quickly. She mimed Emmet's pumping pressure on Helen's chest, so that James would know what she meant.

'Well, don't you worry,' said James, squeezing Helen's hand. 'All those aches and pains will soon go away. Tomorrow I'll come back and bring you that new dolly I promised you, the one with the wardrobe.'

'Didn't you buy it yet?' Helen asked, in disappointment.

James shook his head, and laughed. 'I haven't had time. But I promise to get it for you tomorrow. I'll bring you some books, too, and some candies.'

He stood up, and kissed her again. 'Give Mummy a kiss too. She was the one who saved you.'

Patricia bent over the bed, thinking to herself, please, Helen, don't say anything; please – not yet. But she heard the childish words come marching out like rows of little tin soldiers who didn't know what havoc they were going to cause.

'But Mommy didn't save me. A man saved me.'

'A man?' James asked Patrica. 'What man? Eddie told me *you* saved her. *You* told me you saved her.'

Patricia kissed Helen and then stood up, opening the clasp of her pocketbook and then closing it again. 'Well, it doesn't really matter *who* saved you, does it, darling, as long as you were saved.'

'It matters to me,' said James.

Patricia turned and looked him full in the face. 'In that case, we'd better continue this conversation outside, don't you think?'

The swamps were still chilly and white with mist when the Hendry County deputy steered the motor-punt in between the oaks, and brought them at last to a scrubby low-lying island, distinguished only by a dilapidated jetty and a small hut with a green moss roof and a Charley Noble chimneystack.

The morning was surprisingly chilly, and James was glad that he had brought his overcoat. Emmet had been obliged to borrow a blanket from the boatman.

The deputy laconically powered the punt up to the jetty, and threw the mooring-rope around it. 'This is it, folks,' he announced. James said to Emmet with a coldness as cold as the morning, 'After you.'

They were taken through the bushes to a small clearing, where the bodies of the Tri-motor's passengers had been laid out neatly

405

under tarpaulins. Not far away, the airliner itself, a wingless fuselage, had been propped up on trestles, so that it could be closely examined by police and newsmen and officials from Ford and South-Eastern Airways.

A young medical examiner with a bald head and spectacles was eating a cheese sandwich and filling in the last details about the dead on a clipboard. James marched directly up to him and said, 'Where's Chloe Treat?'

The medical examiner, with his mouth full, glanced at the deputy for authorization, but the deputy nodded okay. 'Over there,' he said. 'Third one along, third row.'

Followed by Emmet and the Hendry County deputy, James walked over to the rows of tarpaulins, and lifted up the third sheet in the third row without any hesitation at all. He looked for a long moment at the grey mummified face that protruded from the tattered dress; the hanks of mud-grey hair; then he let the sheet fall back again.

Emmet stood and stared at him. He didn't have to ask him any questions.

'It's her,' said James. He began to walk away.

'But how do you know?' Emmet demanded, trying to catch up with him.

'It's her, damn it!' James shouted at him, his eyes filled with tears. 'It's her!'

The medical examiner had swallowed his mouthful, and approached James with his clipboard under his arm. 'The nose of the airplane sank under the mud . . . you know, because of the weight of the engines. The pilot and the co-pilot and the two passengers sitting in the front seats were sort of preserved, if you can understand what I mean.'

James said, 'Can I have the body flown back to Miami?'

The deputy took out his notebook and thumbed through it. 'I'm sorry, Mr Lord. There's a prior claim from next-of-kin.'

James nodded. 'Very well. Let's go.' He took out his handkerchief and blew his nose.

Emmet followed close behind him as he walked back to the jetty. 'I'm only going to ask you one question, Mr Lord,' he said. 'Did you have anything to do with this'

James stopped and looked at him with reddened eyes. 'I've got two things to say to you, my friend,' and for the first time in a long time he sounded very English. 'The first, don't make allegations you can't substantiate. The second, is leave my wife alone, because she belongs to me.'

Emmet coloured, and drew his blanket more tightly around his shoulders. 'I, uh –'

James said, 'I don't expect any explanations, thank you. I know exactly what happened. And take that blanket off, you look like a squaw.'

He turned away; but then he hesitated, and turned back again. 'And by the way,' he added, 'thank you for saving my daughter's life.'

Emmet had to knock five or six times at the doorway of the second-floor apartment on Ojus Street before they heard him over the rumba music on the radio. All the time he was watched solemnly by a small boy wearing nothing but a T-shirt, and a puppy with the permanent shivers.

At last the door was opened and a fat woman in her headscarf appeared. 'I don't need nothing,' she told him. 'No brush, no Bible, no innacycalopedia.'

'I'm not a salesman,' Emmet smiled. 'I'm a reporter, from the *Washington Examiner*.'

The woman eyed him suspiciously. 'What you want?'

'I'm looking for a man called Enriquez Bocanegra. I was told that he lives here.'

'I am Mrs Bocanegra.'

'His wife?'

'His mother.'

Emmet had already guessed that she was Enriquez's mother, but years of on-the-job experience had taught him that, with women, it was always better to take a shot at the younger option first. He smiled, and shrugged, and said, 'Well, I wouldn't have said so.'

The woman was unimpressed. 'What you want?'

'I was wondering if you knew where Enriquez was?'

'Sure I know where Enriquez is.'

'The thing is,' said Emmet, 'I'd really like to talk to him.'

'You can't do that.'

'I only want to ask him a couple of questions. I can pay – you know, maybe ten dollars.'

The woman shook her head. 'Not possible.'

'Well, could you at least give him my card, and ask him to call me?'

'Not possible.'

'I'm straight about the ten dollars,' said Emmet. He opened his wallet and took out five. 'Here, look – give him this – and I'll pay him the rest when he calls.'

'Enriquez no call, mister. Enriquez was airplane engineer, at Pearl Harbor.'

'You mean –?'

The woman looked past Emmet's shoulder at nothing in particular, far away. 'My son Enriquez is dead, mister, God rest his soul.'

Emmet replaced his hat. 'I see. Well, I really am truly sorry. Please forgive me for disturbing you.'

The woman nodded and closed the door.

Emmet walked down to the street. Down on the sidewalk, he looked back at the shabby apartment building and frowned. It seemed hard to believe that a mother would be playing loud rumba music only a few days after her son had been killed. Still – maybe that was a way of keeping herself from thinking about it. Kind of a rumba therapy.

He climbed into his rental car and started up the engine. He didn't see the face that was watching him from the Bocanegra's apartment. He didn't see the curtain fall back.

He pulled away from the curb just as Eddie Feinbacker appeared on the street, one hand thrust into the pocket of his baggy trousers, the other shading his eyes against the December sun, just to make sure that Emmet had gone for good.

The following morning, the *Miami Herald* headlined the discovery of Chloe Treat's body in Okaloacoochee Slough, and carried the same familiar picture of her in her Dornier dress. The newspaper remained unopened beside James's breakfast plate.

'I have to go back to Washington tomorrow,' James told Patricia, forking up his eggs Benedict.

Patricia wasn't eating ànything. She looked at him over her coffee cup. 'Do you know when you're going to be back?' she asked him.

He made a face. 'It depends. It seems as if two-thirds of American industry is lobbying the Army and the Navy, looking for war contracts. It may be a week.'

He finished the remainder of his breakfast in silence. Then he stood up, tugged his cuffs straight, and came across to give Patricia a goodbye kiss.

'I thought you might like dinner at the Pelican tonight,' he told her.

She stared at him for a long, extended moment. Then she nodded, and said, 'Yes, I'd like that.'

He glanced at the folded newspaper next to his plate. Habitually, he took it with him to the office. This time, he left it where it was, still unopened, still unread.

Fidel was waiting for him outside the door.

London, 1943

Richard left Iris at the Ritz and walked to Whitehall. Around lunchtime, it had looked as if the fog might be clearing; but the temperature had dropped sharply at around two o'clock, and now Piccadilly was almost invisible.

This was the first time in almost a year that he had brought Iris with him. Although there had been two Luftwaffe raids in January – in retaliation for the British and American bombing of Berlin – it seemed at last as if the worst of the blitz were over.

Richard was looking tired; and for the past six months, Iris had been complaining that he was working too hard. But Lord Aeronautics had been building Lancaster bombers at a record rate of one-and-a-half every week, and Richard was determined to keep up his quota. Vickers, with a workforce of more than 14,000, was producing only nine aircraft a week.

He was tired, but the war had brought him the investment capital he had badly needed to bring Lord Aeronautics up-to-date. The factory at Chichester had been extended during 1942 until it was almost twice its pre-war size; and he had re-opened the research facility at Haywards Heath.

Now that the tide of the war seemed as if it was beginning to turn, Richard was already making plans for what aeroplanes he would be building when it was all over. A four-engined airliner was already on the drawing-boards, the Lord Sagittarius.

He walked along Pall Mall. Most of the cast-iron railings had disappeared from the elegant facades, supposedly to make muni-

409

tions, but more importantly to show working-class Londoners that the wealthy were having to make sacrifices, too. He passed the Ladies Carlton Club, where the swimming-pool had been drained and converted into a giant pig-sty. A little further on a building was missing and a hoarding erected to cover the gap. The hoarding was plastered with posters exhorting householders to SAVE COAL! and reminding 'Every Woman Not Doing Vital Work' that she was 'needed NOW!'

He was one of the few men walking through the fog who was not in uniform. But in his homburg hat and his severe black overcoat he looked exactly what he was: a man of seriousness and duty.

Mr Cauthen met him in his high-ceilinged office overlooking the Cenotaph. A small shovelful of nutty slack was pouring out cold yellow smoke in the fireplace. Mr Cauthen didn't seem to have aged at all since Richard had first met him on the Downs at Cocking. The enclosed administrative atmosphere of the civil service seemed to have preserved him, like amber.

'I suppose you'd like a cup of tea?' Mr Cauthen asked him.

'No, thank you, I've just had lunch.'

'Ah, lunch,' said Mr Cauthen. 'Do you know something, now that they've introduced this five-shilling limit for a restaurant meal, I can scarcely be bothered to go out and have lunch.'

'Well, I spent £1 17s 6d and nobody seemed to object.'

'Well, they wouldn't, would they? They wouldn't. And, after all, you are one of Britian's élite, so to speak. One of the warriors of industry.'

Richard lit a cigarette. 'I suppose you've read my report.'

Mr Cauthen nodded. 'I have, yes. I have read it in considerable detail, and with considerable anguish. It has been circulated all around the Ministy of Aircraft Production. In fact, Sir Roy Fedden will probably wish to discuss it with you himself.'

Richard said, 'What was the Minister's reaction?'

'We, ah – haven't quite got as far as showing it to the Minister. It's going to be rather touchy, don't you see? Particularly when it comes to making recommendations and changes to the industry itself, along the lines you suggest.'

He gave Richard a smile as tight as a tourniquet, and then said, 'The name of Richard Lord is not one which is guaranteed to evoke cheers of gladness at Vickers-Armstrong or Fairey Aviation or A.V. Roe. Even Sir Charles Bruce-Gardner calls you the Fifth Horseman of the Apocalypse.'

Richard had already heard that nickname. Sir Charles had first called him that after his 1937 report on the defects of the British aircraft industry. He found it distressing, but it hadn't deterred him. Since he had first been given the unwelcome task of assessing the shortcomings of his fellow aircraft manufacturers, his mild concern had gradually developed into crusading fervour.

More than one aircraft constructor would cross the street if they saw him coming; and last year he had failed to receive an invitation to the Society of British Aircraft Constructors' annual dinner.

Mr Cauthen said, 'I've already had some telephone calls which virtually amount to threats.'

'From whom? Or is that classified?'

'From the senior management of some of the firms you have criticized; and also from the trade unions. The senior management are deeply offended because you have questioned their refusal to delegate and their poor production planning. The trade unions are even more deeply offended because you have called them restrictive, slack, and ill-disciplined.'

'It's true,' Richard replied. 'And it's not just my personal opinion. The facts bear me out.'

Mr Cauthen nodded. 'I know. And I am quite prepared to forward your report to the Minister unchanged. But you and I have been friends for quite a while now, haven't we, and I do wish to warn you that you will bring nothing down on your head with this report as it stands but resentment and hatred.'

He paused, and then he said, 'You have a wife; and a young son. I'm not saying that they would come to any physical harm, but you know as well as I do that Britain is not the cheerful patriotic place that the BBC is pretending it to be.'

'Did any specific person make any specific threat against Iris and Thomas?' Richard demanded. 'If they did, I wish to know who they are and what they said.'

Mr Cauthen coughed. 'Let me put it this way. An anonymous spokesman from the Sheet-Metal Unions made it abundantly clear to me with a number of arcane expletives that any attempt to suggest that any sheet-metal work of any kind was semi-skilled, and could equally well be carried out by women, could result in "nasty trouble at home" for whoever had suggested it.'

Richard leaned forward and crushed out his cigarette. 'No mention of what he meant by "nasty trouble"?'

Mr Cauthen shook his head.

Richard, at last, stood up. 'I suppose I ought to thank you for warning me,' he said. 'I must say, though, I'm not terribly surprised. You would have thought the people in this country would be bending their backs to win the war against Germany, wouldn't you? Instead they seem to be putting most of their efforts into the bitterest class-conflict you could possibly imagine. There's no doubt that war has brought out the worst in us.'

Mr Cauthen said, 'I'm wondering whether you ought to reconsider that bit in your report about the Spitfire. After all, the Spitfire is a little bit more than just an aeroplane. It's a national symbol. The Few, and all that.'

'I simply told the truth,' Richard retorted. 'It takes over thirteen thousand man-hours to build one Spitfire, which is nearly two-and-a-half times longer than it takes for Jerry to build one Messerschmitt. If it makes you feel any better about it, I suppose you could delete my remark that the Spitfire would never be commercially saleable in peacetime because it would be far too expensive: but I would rather the Minister were aware of it.'

'Yes,' said Mr Cauthen, unhappily.

'What about the strikes?' Richard demanded. 'Or do we want to delude ourselves that they didn't happen, either? We've had eight serious strikes in the aircraft industry in four months – over pay, over piece rates, over canteen facilities, over the use of non-union labour. And this is at a time of total war!'

'Yes,' said Mr Cauthen, keeping his eyes on his blotter.

Richard said, with a slight wavering of anger in his voice, 'The British aircraft industry is in a more chaotic state now than it was before the war; and, by God, it was bad enough then. They keep asking for more labour and more machine-tools; but if the existing workforce did their stuff – if the management weren't so incompetent and the workers weren't so bloody slack – they could literally double their production without the need for any more men.'

Mr Cauthen stood up. 'Well, Richard,' he sighed. 'If that's the way you see it . . . that's the way the story will have to be told.'

'You don't sound very enthusiastic,' said Richard.

'Oh, I'm enthusiastic all right,' Mr Cauthen told him, taking his elbow and steering him towards the door. 'It's just that we've reached something of a turning-point, don't you know; and all that anybody wants to hear these days is good news. *This Happy Breed* and all that kind of thing. Those who bear messages of doom and despondency tend not to be popular. And one does have to think of one's career once the war is over, doesn't one?'

Richard put on his hat. 'Let me tell you something, Cecil. One has to win the bloody war first.'

*

LONDON, 1943

Iris was unusually quiet during the drive back to Chichester. Although the government had severely rationed petrol for pleasure motoring, Richard's supply as an aircraft manufacturer was almost completely unrestricted. He enjoyed driving now the roads were so empty. He had once driven all the way from Horsham to Pulborough at 100 miles an hour.

'You haven't told me what you bought,' he said, as they drove through the blacked-out streets of Wimbledon.

Iris shrugged. 'There was a dress I quite liked, but I didn't have enough points. I bought a cardigan instead.'

'You're not upset about something, are you?'

'Not really.'

'Come on, Iris, you can't pull the wool over my eyes. I know when you're upset.'

Iris looked out into the darkness. 'It's just that I can remember Daddy and Mummy taking me up to London when I was little. We had ice-cream at the Trocadero. It all seemed so wonderful then. So bright and exciting! And yet I looked at it today, and it was all so drab and bombed-out, and I wondered if Thomas will ever be able to see it like it was.'

Richard drove in silence. Then he said, 'Nothing will ever be like it was.'

'But they'll rebuild it, won't they? The bits that were bombed?'

'I'm not talking about buildings,' said Richard.

Thomas was already in bed when they got home. Elsie had given him a boiled egg for supper, with toast soldiers and a mug of Bovril. While Iris went to change, Richard went along to Thomas's bedroom and quietly opened the door. The light from the landing fell in a triangle across his bedspread. Richard could see a small arm in green-striped pyjamas, a mop of fair hair, and a hot plump cheek.

He tiptoed into the room and straightened Thomas's quilt; then kissed him on the cheek. Thomas would be five in February. He was ten months younger than James's adopted daughter Helen. It was curious, Richard thought, that having children had brought him and James back together again. They hadn't seen each other for years, but they wrote to each other quite regularly now, and exchanged snapshots. This is us, paddling at Middleton with our trousers rolled up. This is Thomas, trying to walk. This is Iris pushing Thomas in his pushchair the day before war was declared.

Richard stood beside Thomas's bed for two or three minutes,

simply watching him sleep. He was surprised how much Daddy-like he felt these days. As soon as you had a child, you realized that your chin was prickly and your collars were starchy and your waistcoats were very tweedy and smelled of tobacco. Without you knowing how it had happened, the goblins had crept up on you in the night and turned you into your own father. Although his mother's face still haunted him in the mirror.

He heard the telephone ringing, so he left Thomas's bedroom and closed the door. Elsie had set out a supper of cold mutton and pickles in the dining-room, and she had put her coat on ready to leave. She came to the bottom of the stairs and said, 'It's for you, Mr Richard.'

'Oh, say that I've gone to bed, would you?'

Elsie disappeared, but she came back almost immediately and called up the stairs, 'Mr Richard! It's Wally Field! He says it's urgent!'

Richard was unfastening his collar-studs. 'Oh, very well, I'll take it in the dressing-room.' He picked up the receiver, and said, 'Wally? It's almost midnight. I've had a damned long day in London.'

'Better get over 'ere right away, Mr Richard. The factory's on fire.'

Richard went cold. 'How bad is it? Is anybody hurt?'

'No, nobody's 'urt,' said Wally, 'but it's well alight, the 'ole place.'

'You've called the brigade?'

'They got 'ere just about five minutes ago.'

'Hold on, then,' said Richard, 'I'm coming straight over.'

He opened up his chest-of-drawers and took out a thick guernsey pullover. Iris was unpinning her curls at the dressing-table. 'Richard? Richard, darling, what's wrong?'

'The factory's on fire. I have to go there right away.'

He ran quickly downstairs, collecting his overcoat from the hall-stand. Iris stood at the top of the stairs and called, 'Richard! For goodness' sake be careful!'

'Don't worry!' he told her. 'I'll telephone you as soon as I can.'

'Richard, I love you!'

He hesitated, with the front door half-open. Then he said, 'Make sure you lock the door after me, and put on the chain. Don't answer it for anybody except me.'

'Richard?'

'Please, Iris, just do what I tell you!'

He was thankful he hadn't put the Austin away. He wiped the

cold condensation off the windscreen with his glove, then started up the engine and drove off towards Chichester.

The blaze could be seen five miles away, a lurid bonfire flickering behind the silhouetted spire of Chichester Cathedral. Richard knew before he was halfway there that the damage was going to be disastrous; and when at last he reached the Lord Aeronautics factory and parked on the grass bank opposite, he had completely lost the urge to hurry. Why rush to your own funeral?, he thought wrly; although his heart was sore with the sense of loss.

He walked up to the gates of the yard and stood staring at the flames. Four Dennis fire-tenders were trying to cope with the blaze, but at the moment it was ravenously out of control. The main workshops were roaring like a blast-furnace, the bare ribs of their roofs exposed, and curds of thick brown smoke were pouring out of the paint-shop and the offices. Through the glare of the flames, Richard could just about make out the skeletons of three unfinished Lancaster bombers.

Wally Field saw him standing at the gate, and negotiated his way across the snaking fire-hoses. ''Fraid it's a bloody write-off, Mr Richard,' he said, by way of a greeting. 'Nobody hurt, though, thank Gawd, excepting they can't find the cat.'

Richard said, 'Hallo, Wally. Thanks for calling me out.'

Wally sniffed, and wiped his nose with the back of his knitted glove. 'Well, don't mention it. But there ain't much that anybody can do about it, is there? One of them firemen said you might as well piss into Mount Etna.'

'Does anybody know what caused it?'

'Not so far. Could have been anything. Fag-end, left in a rubbish-bin. Short circuit in the wiring. Sabotage, even, there's a possibility.'

'Not an incendiary?'

'Well, not from the air, no. Nobody heard nothing going over, and the Old Bill's already rung up the Raff at Tangmere and they said there weren't no Jerry raiders tonight.'

At that moment, with a soft threatening roar and a terrible creaking of broken glass, the paint workshop flared up. Richard watched it dully, his hands in his pockets. Years and years of expertise and planning were being reduced to ashes in front of his eyes. Hundreds of volumes of research notes; thousands of design drawings; every single technical notation that he and his father had ever jotted down, every single bright idea, every single file and photograph and film; everything was gone. Three Lancaster bombers, too – although it wasn't these three Lancasters that mattered so much as all the Lancasters they might have built if they had been able to carry on full production.

Richard could feel the heat drying the moisture on his eyeballs. He didn't shed any tears, although he almost wished that he could. It was as if Lord Aeronautics had never existed.

Detective-Inspector Frank Warren came over to talk to Richard. He had broken veins all over his cheeks and eyebrows like a bramble-thicket. He had retired in 1938, but he had volunteered to go back into the Sussex Constabulary when war had broken out. Richard knew him for a pompous old busybody.

'Hallo, then, Richard,' he said, extending his hand. 'I don't know what to say about this, I really don't. Quite a blow for the war effort, wouldn't you say?'

'Do you have any idea how it might have happened?'

Frank Warren puffed out his cheeks. 'Doubt if we'll ever know, to tell you the God's honest truth. German saboteur, most likely. I'm having a check made of all the local hotels and boarding-houses, just in case they can remember somebody suspicious.'

'You mean somebody with a thick German accent and a suitcase marked, *Vorsicht! Bomben!*'

Frank Warren pouted in annoyance. 'I wouldn't have said this is really the time to make humorous remarks, Richard, would you?'

'Well, I'm sorry,' said Richard. 'But I really can't think what else to do.'

The fire burned all night. When dawn began to wash the streets of Chichester with milky-grey light, Richard could see at last the remains of his family's kingdom. He walked with his hands in his coat-pockets across a factory-floor black and crunchy with ash, while tired firemen hosed down skeletal timbers and roof-supports, and chopped down the precariously-sagging roof of the paint-shop.

Frank Warren followed him, occasionally bending over to pick up a piece of glass, or a stud, or a spanner that had been turned rainbow-coloured by the heat.

'What do you think you're going to do now?' Frank asked him.

'I don't know,' Richard told him. 'I really don't know.'

'It just goes to show how vulnerable we are to Jerry saboteurs, doesn't it?' Frank remarked.

Richard said nothing; but Frank was alerted to something in the quality of his silence, and suddenly frowned. 'I mean – you don't doubt that it *was* Jerries, do you? Jerries, or fifth columnists?'

'I'm not sure,' Richard told him. 'It really depends what you mean by fifth columnists.'

He began to walk back through the smouldering factory. Frank Warren hesitated, and then came after him in a kind of panic.

'You think it was fifth columnists, then? Or *sort of* fifth columnists?'

'Frank,' said Richard, tiredly, 'I think you're right. I think you're going to find this case impossible to solve. But one day, you'll look back on it, and you'll *know* who did it, as sure as eggs are eggs.'

'I don't understand you,' Frank told him, quivering. 'If you suspect someone of doing it, tell me, and I can have them in for questioning at least.'

'Frank,' said Richard, 'you can't bring in three-quarters of the entire nation for questioning. It just isn't practical. There does come a time, you know, when so many people commit a crime that it isn't a crime any longer.'

Frank Warren coughed; then turned away and coughed harder. Then he looked back at Richard with an expression in his eyes like an imbecile who suddenly suspects that somebody has stolen something from him; but knows with impotent ferocity that he will never be able to remember what.

'It's being so cheerful as keeps me going,' said Richard, quoting Mona Lott, the dismal charlady from *ITMA*.

'Bloody hell,' said Frank Warren.

Richard went home stunned and filthy like a coal-miner at the end of a double shift. Iris ran him a hot bath, and he put on his pyjamas and crept into bed and slept. He dreamed vividly, of fire and fog; and of his father, too. He dreamed that his father was sitting astride an equestrian statue in Trafalgar Square, barricaded by sandbags, sufficiently alive to smile, but irrevocably dead.

At half-past eleven, however, he was woken up by Heracles barking in the garden. He eased himself out of bed, and dressed with an unaccustomed sense of luxury in a big worn-out Fairisle jumper and brown corduroy trousers. Iris met him at the bottom of the stairs.

'You could have slept longer,' she said.

He smiled, and kissed her; and he was conscious as he kissed her that he actually enjoyed kissing her; for her softness, for her reassurance, for the smell of her perfume. 'I don't want to sleep,' he told her. 'I want to go out for a drive.'

417

They drove eastwards on the coast road towards Brighton; past deserted beaches and concrete tank-traps and barbed-wire and shore-batteries. Then they turned inland, over the Downs. It was a bitter, clear January day; and in the shadowy hollows around Devil's Dyke, the grass remained rimed in frost. The English Channel, in the distance, looked as white and glutinous as semolina. There were anti-aircraft batteries and observation posts all around them, manned by miserable-looking men in khaki greatcoats. Nobody challenged them or asked them where they were going, puttering over the Downs in their Austin Burnham.

They had lunch at a country pub called The Crabtree, in a gloomy cream-painted room with bevelled glass windows. They ate big doorstep sandwiches with home-made cheese and home-made chutney, and pickled onions. Thomas had a Cornish pasty, and ate it all, even though it was filled with nothing more than a Woolton recipe of potato, swede, cauliflower, and carrots. Richard watched him with quiet affection as he ate, and couldn't help smiling at the way the sun shone scarlet through his ears.

Iris had grown plainer in the years since she and Richard had been married. Well, perhaps not plainer but less well-defined. She was a good cook and a doting mother; but somehow her hair had grown duller and her eyes had grown less interested, and she had never managed to elevate herself above the role of obliging housekeeper. Perhaps she was unable to. Perhaps she didn't want to. Today, however, now that he was unexpectedly free of Lord Aeronautics, Richard supposed that he might grow to know her better, and to like her more.

In the pub, he sat drinking King & Barnes beer, and smoking a cigarette, and talking to Iris quite sentimentally, almost as if he loved her. He thought to himself: I'm probably hysterical with exhaustion, or drunk.

She said, lightly, 'We're not ruined, are we?'

Richard shook his head. 'Of course not. The whole business was very well insured. We're not as wealthy as we were. We lost an awful lot of valuable paperwork last night – you know, designs and things like that. Things you couldn't really insure, because you couldn't put a price on them. But – we still have our goodwill – and our designers – and our engineers –'

They drove home over the Downs as it was growing dark. Iris began to sing. '*Horsey, horsey, don't you stop, just let your feet go clippety clop. Your tail goes swish and the wheels go round, giddyup, we're homeward bound.*'

Thomas joined in. Richard remained silent. They drove past

Sompting, at the foot of the Downs, with its dark medieval church like a cowled nun. They drove through Worthing, six miles of tired Edwardian suburbs and gelid sea. At last, as they came close to Chichester, Richard sang too, '*Horsey, horsey, don't you stop, just let your feet go clippety clop!*'

In later years, in the 1950s, when Richard thought about that day, he would remember it as one of the happiest days of his life, although he would never quite know why.

Darwin, 1943

T hey were still eating lunch when the telephone rang. Michael wiped his mouth with his napkin and pushed back his chair, but Violet said, 'It's all right, I'll go.'

Michael returned to his corned-beef pie. Violet walked across the sunlit kitchen and picked up the telephone. 'Hallo? Mrs Lord speaking.'

'It's Clarence,' she told Michael. 'Clarence, he's having his lunch at the moment. Yes, all right, then. Fine. I'll tell him.'

She came back to the table and sat down. 'Clarence says could you go over to Myilly this afternoon.'

Michael nodded, with his mouth full. 'I was thinking of going over there anyway.'

'Can you take Willy with you?'

'I'll take them both, if you like. They can play on the beach.'

'Well, just you keep your eye on them, that's all.'

Michael finished his glass of beer, and took his plate and his glass over to the sink. Outside the kitchen window, there was a small back yard with a broken fence, and a view of the docks. Today there were two American destroyers in the harbour, as well as a British minesweeper.

Willy came running into the kitchen from upstairs. He was four-

and-a-half now, and Michael called him 'my monkey'. He was curly-headed and snub-nosed and endlessly mischievous. Elizabeth had grown up to be much more serious and sedate. As far as Michael was concerned, both of them looked exactly like their mother.

Michael took his cotton jacket down from the hook on the back of the kitchen door while Violet started the washing-up. They lived an extraordinarily quiet life these days. It wasn't the kind of life that Michael would ever have imagined himself living. They had very little money, even though Violet was working as a typist for the Royal Australian Navy, and Michael was flying almost every day. On the day after Pearl Harbor, he had volunteered for the Navy himself, as a pilot, but because of his age, and because so many outback stations depended on him for supplies and medical help, the draft officers had kept him on the reserve list. Every Wednesday, though, he gave navigation lessons to novice Navy pilots; and occasionally the Navy asked him to ferry supplies to Brisbane or Adelaide.

Violet called Elizabeth and wiped Willy's face with a wet flannel. 'You two behave yourselves on the beach. And don't go into the water unless Daddy's there.'

Michael kissed her, and said, 'I won't be more than an hour.'

'Well, don't let Clarence get you on the whisky, that's all.'

'I won't.'

Elizabeth said, 'Can we take Pongo?'

Pongo was the family's pet mongrel. Michael had found him straying around the docks one day and had christened him Pongo because he ponged.

Violet came down the narrow carpetless stairs to the front door. 'I wish you'd stop doing things for Clarence,' she said to Michael.

Michael kissed her again. She always amused him when she was anxious; her West Country accent started to come out broad and strong.

'Vi – if it hadn't been for Clarence, I never would have got started. You know that. I never could have rescued you from Leonard, either.'

'You probably would have done a whole lot better. Everybody knows that Clarence is a black-marketeer.'

'Black-marketeer,' Michael mocked her. 'He runs a tatty little import business, that's all.'

'Mary Crouch says he's a black-marketeer. And if his business is all that little, and all that tatty, how can he afford such an expensive car?'

'I'll see you later,' Michael told her. 'And don't worry about Clarence. I know he's fat, and I know you don't like him, but he's really quite harmless.'

Michael ushered the children through the back yard, past the big banyan tree which also did duty as a gatepost, and out to the street, where his fourth-hand Plymouth station-wagon was parked. Pongo jumped in the back, his tail lashing against the windows; the children squeaked and squawked to see who was going to sit next to Daddy.

'You always sit next to Daddy!'

'Yes but you sat next to him last time!'

Michael drove out to Myilly Point, whistling as he drove. The children sang, 'Run rabbit, run rabbit, run, run, run!'

'I'll tell you what we'll do, we'll go and see Uncle Clarence, and then we'll go to Mr Mariti's and buy ice-creams.'

They were approaching the seashore when Willy said, 'Look, Daddy! Aeroplanes!'

Michael didn't bother to look at first. Aircraft were flying in and out of Darwin day and night, mostly B-25s from the American Fifth Air Force, on their way to north-western New Guinea. But then he ducked his head so that he could see through the windscreen. Almost at once, he jammed on the Plymouth's brakes, and the station-wagon rattled to a halt by the side of the road.

'Out!' Michael shouted at the children. 'Out of the car!'

White-faced with fright, Willy and Elizabeth scrambled out of the door. 'This way!' Michael shouted, and together they ran into the bushes by the side of the road. Michael lay flat on his stomach in a small depression carpeted with dry banyan leaves, and made the children lie close to him, with their heads well down.

The aircraft were almost immediately overhead, and their engines made a deep grinding, groaning noise. It was difficult to see through the branches how many there were, but Michael guessed at least a dozen. Already, the ack-ack battery over by the point had started firing at them – sharp punching noises, accompanied by echoes from the opposite side of the bay.

Michael had recognized the aircraft instantly. He had seen them in newsreels and Navy training films. They were Mitsubishi 'Bettys' – twin-engined Japanese bombers.

He and the children lay in the undergrowth as the bombers passed over Darwin. They couldn't see anything, but they could hear the eerie whistling of bombs falling, and the sporadic *crump-crump-crump* of anti-aircraft fire, and then a whole deafening series of deeper and louder explosions.

After a short while, the bombers came back overhead. The anti-aircraft fire kept up, although to Michael it sounded very haphazard. There were two or three more sharp whistles, followed by more explosions – so close that Michael felt their concussion slamming through the earth. One bomb must have fallen in the bay, because when Michael looked up again there was a tall fountain of white spray hanging in the air.

They waited until the sound of the Bettys' engines had completely dwindled away. Then Michael stood up, and brushed down his clothes, and led the children back on to the road again.

'Those were Japs, weren't they, Daddy?' asked Elizabeth.

'Yes, my darling, they were. Listen – we'd better go straight back home and make sure that Mummy didn't get too frightened.'

'I hope they didn't drop a bomb on our house,' said Willy, making nonsense of Michael's pretence.

Michael drove the Plymouth as fast as it would go, which wasn't much more than forty miles an hour. A smudge of black smoke was hanging over Darwin like an evil genie let out of a bottle. Fires were burning over by the docks, and Michael could hear alarm bells ringing.

He turned the corner, and to his relief their house was intact. In fact, no bombs seem to have been dropped in that part of the city at all, although everybody was hanging out of their windows, and some people were cycling towards the docks to see what had happened.

Michael told the children to wait in the car while he went upstairs. Violet was in the kitchen, her washing-up mop dripping unnoticed on to the lino, staring out of the window at the smoke billowing out of Bundy's wool warehouse.

'Violet? Are you all right?'

She turned and stared at him, pale and shocked. 'They were bombers!' she whispered.

Michael held her close, and stroked her forehead. 'It's all right now. We're all safe, and they're gone. We waited until we couldn't even hear them any more.'

'They dropped bombs on us!'

Michael kissed her, and then went over to the telephone. 'I just want to call Clarence and tell him I won't be coming.'

He dialled Clarence's number, but all he could get was a crackling sound. 'I'd better run over there,' he told Violet. 'You know what Clarence is like when you let him down.'

'I'll be all right,' said Violet. 'It was just such a shock, that's all.

422

And it was so *loud*, I didn't have any idea. I practically jumped out of my skin.'

He could see what had happened at Myilly Point from half-a-mile away. A small crowd of neighbours and Aborigines had already gathered around the bungalow, and were picking through the wreckage like farm-labourers pulling turnips. There was no fire. There wasn't even any smoke. Clarence's bungalow had simply been blown flat, right down to the carpets. There were chairs and tables in the garden, and a sofa on the beach. A large bamboo blind had been blown up into the top of a palm tree.

Michael parked the station wagon and told Elizabeth and Willy to wait where they were. 'What's happened to Uncle Clarence's house?' asked Willy.

'It's been bombed, silly-billy-Willy,' Elizabeth retorted.

Michael walked through the rubble and the crumpled cor-rugated-iron until he reached what was left of Clarence's ver-andah. He recognized Clarence's next-door neighbour Phil Cogley, who was standing in the middle of what had once been the hallway, his hands on his hips, puffing his pipe.

'Never seen anything like it,' Phil remarked. 'One second it was there; the next it was gone.'

'Where's Clarence?' asked Michael. 'Is Clarence all right?'

Phil stared at him as if he had said something totally absurd. Then he nodded his head towards the flattened kitchen.

Clarence was lying under a pair of bloodstained tapestry cur-tains. Michael recognized his podgy knees, protruding from the lower hem.

'I wouldn't look if I were you,' said Phil, puffing away at his pipe. 'It must have been the what-d'you-call-it, the blast. A bloody great glass paperweight went right through his head like a can-nonball.'

Michael didn't know what to do. 'I was supposed to be seeing him this afternoon,' he said. 'Five minutes earlier, and I would have been here.'

'Well,' said Phil, quite unnecessarily, 'damn lucky for you that you weren't.'

Michael took two steps away from Clarence's body. 'I went to school with him, you know. He was always getting the whack.'

Phil said, 'How about a drink? Have you got the kids with you? Come on over to the house. Peggy would love to see the kids.'

Michael still couldn't take his eyes off Clarence's knees. 'He held the school record for getting the whack.'

'Poor bugger,' said Phil, philosophically. 'Mind you, there used to be funny goings-on in this house. Lot of Chinks and niggers, coming and going. and some bloody funny music, too. Opera, you know. I've always said that anyone who likes opera is going to come to a bad end.'

'What on earth made you say a thing like that?' asked Michael, still shocked, but suddenly irritated by Phil's stupidity.

Phil took out his pipe and pointed at Clarence's body with the stem. 'There's the proof. There's the proof. Chap liked opera, and the bloody Japs came and dropped a bomb on him. You can't come to a worse end than that.'

Chichester, 1946

It had already begun to snow when Richard arrived at the factory that morning; thick feathery snow like burst-open pillows. He came into the prefabricated offices stamping his feet and banging his gloves together, and somebody shouted out, 'Shut that bloody door! Oh – sorry, Mr Lord. Didn't realize it was you.'

Richard closed the door behind him and pushed the home-made draft excluder along the bottom of it, although that scarcely made any difference. There were two upright paraffin stoves, one at each end of the building, and yet the draftsmen and designers still sat at their drawing-boards in their overcoats, and kept a glove on the hand they weren't using to draw.

After the fire of 1943, it had taken Richard nearly two years and most of his financial reserves to get the factory back into full production. The first Lancasters that Richard had been able to build had been rolled out of the prefabricated assembly-shops only six months before VE Day.

Nobody had ever been arrested for burning the factory down,

although Richard strongly suspected that Frank Warren had eventually found out who was responsible. A shop steward, probably, or a local Labour Party activist.

Richard was only too aware how touchy the unions had been during the war years about the sacrifices they were making for the common good. The bosses were supposed to be grateful even before the war was won, and at the slightest sign that they weren't, the workers would down tools and walk out, regardless of the Essential Work Order.

In his regular reports to Mr Cauthen, Richard had noted that in the same year as the Lord Aeronautics fire, 1943, aircraft workers at a score of other factories in England had taken strike action for the pettiest of provocations. One strike had been called after complaints about canteen facilities; another because one over-enthusiastic sheet-metal cutter was working too quickly and making 7s 9d an hour instead of the union-agreed rate of 4s 6d; yet another because shop stewards had been refused permission to collect money for the Red Army during working-hours.

Richard guessed that somebody in the government had directed that Frank Warren should turn a blind eye, and bring no charges against the arsonist, for fear that the Amalgamated Engineering Union would cry 'victimization!' and go on strike for the duration of the war, no matter who won it.

Richard hung up his hat and walked the length of the hut to talk to David Bright, his chief engineer. David was thirty-one years old, a former De Havilland man, and boyishly enthusiastic about everything that he was doing. His cheeks always looked as if they had been freshly scrubbed, and his nose as if it had been recently blown. Richard had brought him in last year to work on designs for a new advanced airliner, the Lord 101.

They had lost Wally Field in November, 1944. Wally had gone to visit his mother in New Cross, in east London, and on the way he had popped into Woolworth's to buy her a set of table-mats. While he was there, the store had taken a direct hit from a V-2 rocket, killing a hundred and sixty people outright, and injuring two hundred. That was the bombing in which an eye-witness saw a baby's arm, still wearing the pink knitted sleeve of its matinée jacket, falling out of the sky. Wally Field had been killed instantly, next to the sweet counter.

David Bright, however, had never been intended as a substitute for Wally Field. Richard had been trying to cajole him to come over to Lord Aviation (as it was now called) for almost six months before Wally was killed.

It was David's unique experience with jets that Richard had been after.

De Havilland's was the only company which had built a jet engine and designed a jet plane – a fighter called the Vampire – and David Bright had been closely involved in both projects right from the very beginning. 'Bright by name and bright by nature,' Sir Geoffrey de Havilland had described him; but Richard had offered David twice as much money to come and work at Chichester.

Like Sir Geoffrey de Havilland, Richard had been convinced since the beginning of the war that jets were the next great step forward. As early as 1944, when the new Lord factory was still being erected on the ashes of the old one, and Richard was using the library at Goodwood Lodge as an office, he had collected together a small team of aero-engine and airframe engineers, and set them to work throwing out new ideas for a medium-sized jet airliner.

That morning in January, Richard leaned over David's drawing-board rubbing his hands, and glanced over some of his tracings. 'Any difficulties with that turbine housing?' he asked.

David dropped his pencil on to the drawing-board and sat back. 'It should work very well. Theoretically, anyway.'

'Well,' said Richard, 'it's beginning to look like a very fine aeroplane.'

This grand generalization didn't go unnoticed. David knew Richard for a detail man, not a visionary. He never said things like 'very fine aeroplane' unless he had reservations about it.

'You don't sound very sure about that,' he remarked.

Richard tugged off his gloves because he was having difficulty turning the pages of the tracings. 'No, no, of course I'm sure. It's just that my old friend Mr Cauthen gave me a call this morning. He's working at the Ministry of Supply these days.'

'And?'

'It's difficult to say for certain. But it looks very much as if the Ministry will ask De Havilland's to build the first pure jet airliner, rather than us. It's partly the old boy network, and partly the fact that they're much bigger than we are, and more geared up to it.'

'I suppose one has to admit that Ronnie Bishop's the very best,' said David, referring to De Havilland's chief designer. They had all been expecting that the Ministry would look to De Havilland's or Bristol's, rather than somebody smaller; but there was no hiding his disappointment.

Richard made a moue. 'You know the figures,' he said. 'It's

going to cost at least four million to get us to the prototype stage, and without the government to back us up, and some firm orders from BOAC, we just won't be able to do it.'

'Well, then,' said David. 'That appears to be that, doesn't it? And I always got the impression that Mr Cauthen was your pal.'

'A pal is somebody who tells you the truth, no matter how unpalatable it is,' Richard replied. 'That's the only thing you can say for Mr Cauthen: that he tells the truth, and that he expects to be *told* the truth. Chaps like that are rather a rarity in England, and especially in the civil service.'

David shook out a Gold Flake cigarette and tapped the end of it on his drawing-board. 'I'm surprised he's survived for so long.'

'Well, he has the other great British quality. Or failing, depending which way you look at it. He's an inspired bodger. He can always make the best out of a disastrous situation.'

David lit his cigarette and sat back in his chair for quite a long time looking at his drawings for the Lord 101's engine nacelles. If the Ministry of Supply didn't give them the backing they needed, these drawings would be no more useful than the architectural plans for some elaborate imaginary city. 'I get the feeling you're trying to tell me something,' he said, at last.

Richard said, 'You're right. I've been thinking this over for a day or two now, and I think I've come up with the answer. Actually, to be quite fair about it, it was *Iris* who came up with the answer. She was making a rabbit casserole the other day. Well, that's not particularly relevant, but she always seems to come up with inspired ideas when she's cooking. I told her that we probably wouldn't be able to afford to develop the 101, and she said, "It's a pity you can't put a jet engine in a Capricorn." '

David looked up at him warily. 'It *is* a pity, yes. But she's right, you can't. A jet consumes too much fuel to operate economically at lower than thirty thousand feet. And you couldn't fly a Capricorn at that altitude, even if it *did* have jet engines. The structure wouldn't stand it. The cabin would have to be pressurized, to begin with. Eight-and-a-quarter pounds per square inch, which is five pounds per square inch greater than it is outside. The whole aeroplane would burst like a bomb.'

Richard nodded in enthusiastic agreement. 'You're absolutely right, David. But Iris *did* set me thinking. If we can't afford to develop a pure jet airliner, why don't we go halfway, and develop a turboprop airliner. A scaled-up Capricorn with propellers driven not by pistons but by jet-engine turbines. De Havilland's won't be able to bring out a prototype jet for two or three years at the very least; and they certainly won't have much chance of an airworthiness certificate much before 1951 or 1952. That leaves us plenty of time to go on the market with a fast, reliable, proven design.'

'I suppose you're aware that Vickers are working on something similar.'

Richard said, 'Of course; but we can do better. We can produce better quality, and better craftsmanship, and better after-sales service. Every airline knows that. Look at the Capricorn.'

David folded down the sheet of heavy black cartridge paper which protected his drawings when he wasn't working on them. 'Obviously,' he said, 'I'm going to have to.' He crushed out his cigarette, and then he added, 'I must say, I didn't think I was coming here to work on stopgaps.'

Richard laid a hand on his shoulder. Richard wasn't usually very good at being reassuring. 'You'll get your jet, David. If we can bring out a good turboprop airliner, and bring it out quickly, there's every chance that we can make enough money with it to develop a pure jet airliner later on. De Havilland's may be the first; but we'll be better. After all, we can benefit from their mistakes.'

'Supposing they don't make any.'

'David,' said Richard, with one of his very Richard-like smiles, '*everybody* makes mistakes.'

Richard himself made a mistake, only ten days later. He was lunching at Overton's in St James's Street with Sir Kenneth Wells from British European Airways. It was another bitterly cold day, and the menu was restricted to beef stew and grilled cod, because of shortages. Sir Kenneth was being boring about payloads when a striking-looking middle-aged woman walked into the cocktail bar and stood with her purse clasped under her arm, her eyes flicking from one side of the restaurant to the other as if she were expecting to see somebody there.

Richard didn't recognize her at first in her wide-shouldered dark mink coat and her mink-trimmed Genghis Khan turban, but when she stepped nearer to one of the pink-shaded wall-lights he suddenly realized who it was.

'Sir Kenneth,' he said, wiping his mouth with his napkin. 'Do excuse me for just one moment. There's a lady there I haven't seen for donkey's years.'

Sir Kenneth, who had been trying to explain that it wasn't worth carrying fewer than forty passengers anywhere by air, was startled, and said, 'What?' and turned around in his chair to see who had attracted Richard's attention.

'Great heavens,' he exclaimed. 'That's – that's – what's her name? Dear me, it's right on the very tip of my tongue. The titled lady who –'

At the same time that he remembered who she was, he also remembered what she had done, and he cleared his throat with a sound like an aero-engine bursting into life, and said, 'Fathead' – presumably though not certainly to himself.

Richard pushed back his chair and went down the length of the restaurant to greet her. 'Susan!' he said; and when she obviously didn't recognize him, he inclined his head to one side and widened his eyes, and said, 'It's me! Don't you remember?'

Very slowly, very theatrically, she lifted her fingertips to her lips. 'My . . . *God*,' she said. 'It's Dickie Lord. But you've put on so much – well, you're – I don't know, Dickie, you must have been eating too much jam roly-poly.'

'I'm only twelve-and-a-half stone,' Richard protested. Susan lifted her veil and he kissed her, once on each cheek, mwuh, mwuh, very de Gaulle. Then she took hold of his hand with her cold black-leather glove and squeezed it.

'I must say you look absolutely ravishing,' Richard declared.

'I should do, I've been dieting since 1936. Have you ever tried laver bread spread with sunflower butter?'

'I can't say that I have.'

'Well, don't,' said Susan, 'it's positively revolting.' She glanced over each of his shoulders, and then turned around and looked back towards the door. 'You haven't seen Terence Collins, have you? He's supposed to be meeting me here.'

'I'm afraid I wouldn't know what Terence Collins looked like even if I bumped straight into him.'

'Well, he's tall, my dear; broad-shouldered, with brown wavy hair; and one of those mouths that looks as if he might be going to sneer at you at any minute.'

Richard said, 'Even if I *had* seen him, and even if I *had* known who he was, I'm not at all sure that I would tell you.'

Susan raised one eyebrow. 'You're almost as bad as your brother. By the way, how *is* James? Has he honoured our miserable freezing-cold half-starving country with his celestial presence lately?'

Richard shook his head. 'He hasn't been back to England since –well, you know, the trial and everything.'

'That was all a very long time ago,' said Susan, in a voice which revealed quite unequivocally that she found it just as painful as if it had happened yesterday.

'I'm sorry,' said Richard, 'I didn't meant to –'

Susan gave him a quick, dismissive, unforgiving smile. It was meant to make him feel worse, and it did.

'I'm having lunch with Sir Kenneth Wells,' said Richard. 'Won't you join us until your friend turns up?'

'Sir Kenneth Wells?' Susan replied, peering myopically into the smoky, clamorous restaurant. 'I think I'd rather not, thank you. The Director always used to say that the only compliment you could pay Sir Kenneth Wells was that everything he said was good for the roses. That was one of the six times when I actually agreed with him.'

Richard suddenly said, 'Why don't you meet me for a drink this evening – I mean, you know, if you haven't any plans – and tell me what the other five were.'

'The other five what?' she queried.

'The other five times you agreed with Sir Rodney.'

'Oh,' she said. Then she laughed. 'What a peculiar invitation! Well, yes, all right, if you must. I do like to indulge myself in morbid monologues about what might have been. But look at your face! You're just as surprised that you asked me as I am!'

'Where are you staying?' asked Richard. 'Listen – I must get back to Sir Kenneth. He's finished his pudding and I've barely started mine.'

'I'm staying with the Ollenshaws, number fifty-five Duke Street St James's. Pick me up at seven.'

'You're on,' said Richard – even though he hadn't yet thought how on earth he was going to tell Iris that he wouldn't be home tonight for dinner with the Scotts, and those other people from the bell-ringing society whose names he could never remember but who always wore algae-green knitted windcheaters, both of them, husband and wife, which had inspired him to christen them the Pondworthys.

At the moment, just as he was kissing Susan again, a very tall young man came into the restaurant, wearing a long overcoat of oatmeal tweed which smelled of cold and fog and pipe-smoke. He had short waves of chestnut-brown hair, a broken nose, and pale blue eyes; and if his accent when he spoke hadn't been quite so BBC, and his name hadn't been Terence, Richard would have considered him to be blessed by God with everything that a forty-year-old woman with healthy appetites could possibly want in a younger man. Athleticism – asymmetry – beauty damaged by war or sport or public-school boxing – innocence – and eagerness.

'Dickie, my dear, this is Terence Collins,' said Susan. 'Terry, my darling, this is Mr Richard Lord, of Lord aeroplanes, who should have been ennobled years ago, or at least given a season ticket to the Royal Enclosure at Ascot.'

Richard and Terence shook hands. Terence said, 'I've heard an awful lot about you, sir. It's a pleasure to meet you.'

'Well, you too,' Richard replied, glancing anxiously back to his table, where Sir Kenneth had finished his pudding and was impatiently drumming his fingers.

'Terence used to fly Lancasters for 57 Squadron,' said Susan. 'Now he's got a job with the Ministry of Supply.'

'Flying a desk,' grinned Terence, a little sheepishly. 'Not quite the same thing.'

'But you're good at it, my darling,' Susan told him, squeezing his hand. 'And, one day, you're going to be right at the top of the ladder.'

'I wish you luck, then,' said Richard. 'I really must get back to Sir Kenneth.'

Susan said, 'Don't forget, seven.'

'I won't forget,' Richard assured her.

When he returned to his table, Sir Kenneth was ready to leave. 'Look, old man, I really can't stay; meeting with the Minister at three; but let me have your specifications and then we'll talk some more.'

He looked across the restaurant as Susan and Terence were seated by the head-waiter. 'Lovely woman, you know, in spite of everything. What did you say your new aeroplane was going to be called?'

'It's Lord 102 just at the moment,' said Richard. 'But we'll probably call it the Sagittarius.'

Sir Kenneth finished his coffee and pushed his cup away. 'Not particularly auspicious for me, I'm afraid. My wife's a Sagittarius.' Then, with a fierce shout of amusement, 'Ha! Ha!'

He took her for cocktails at the Dorchester, because she said she had happy memories of the Dorchester, and then they went to a small Italian restaurant that Richard liked, in Greek Street.

She was smartly dressed in a black-and-white polka-dot cocktail dress, and her conversation was bright enough, but after about an hour of talking to her Richard began to feel uneasy. There was something about her that was slightly unhinged. She smoked incessantly – so much, in fact, that the people at the next table asked to be moved away. And she kept coming back to the same topics of conversation again and again and again.

'Your brother James, of course – now there's an interesting man. When you first meet him, you can never quite catch his eye. No matter which way you approach him, he always seems to be looking at something or somebody else. Then, when you first get to know him, you think – behind all this mystery, the man is dull! He's nothing but a salesman!'

Richard tried to look interested, but the very last thing in the world he wanted to talk about was James. 'How's . . .?' he asked, referring to her second husband Vicent Blas Perera, the Argentinian polo-player.

'Oh, Vicky,' said Susan dismissively. 'Do you know, I always judge a man by what he can teach me. That is the measure of a true man.'

Richard finished his lasagne and tidily arranged his spoon-and-fork side by side on his plate. 'And what did – Vicky – teach you?'

'*Oid, mortales, el grito sagrado Libertad*,' she sang, banging the tablecloth. She laughed at Richard's bewilderment. 'The Argentinian national anthem.'

'I hope that isn't all,' said Richard, surprising himself with the sophistication of his own comment.

'Almost all,' said Susan. 'Do you know something, James has such eyes! And why are you being so stingy with that Chianti?'

Richard said, 'Are you down in London for long?'

'Oh, I don't know. I came down to cheer myself up; but look at it! Nothing but bomb sites and whining Socialists. Hitler has a lot to answer for, you know. He should either have not attempted to fight Britain at all; or, if he really *had* to fight us, he should at least have had the decency to win. As it was, he fought us, and lost, and that's given us the worst of both worlds. Short of divorcing Lady Docker, there is hardly anything that you can do that is more expensive than winning a war.'

'What about Terence?' asked Richard, trying to change the subject.

'Terence, well, Terence! I'm pleased you mentioned Terence! Do you like him? He's very – I don't know – *Pan-like*, if you can understand what I mean. I can imagine him trotting on cloven hoofs to tootle his flootle by the river, all that kind of thing.'

'I thought he was rather ordinary, to tell you the truth,' said Richard. 'Pleasant, but ordinary.'

He thought for a moment that Susan would be cross. But she took out a cigarette and twisted it into a very long holder, and said, 'You're right, of course. He is very ordinary.'

'I'm surprised you go out with him. You're not at all ordinary.' Susan laughed, and for the first time that evening she sounded pleasant and unaffected. 'No, Dickie, I'm not, am I? I should have married one of you Lord brothers when I had the chance! James even asked me to marry him once. Can you imagine it? But of course I told him I was over the hill.'

'Nonsense,' said Richard, feeling quite racy. 'You're a very attractive woman.'

Susan stared at him. 'You're right, of course. I am. But you are also a very attractive man. Do you know, I never really looked at you before, but you are much more attractive than James. Your face is far more interesting. Far more Saxon, but far more interesting.'

Richard lifted the Chianti bottle. 'Will you have some more wine?'

Susan hesitated, and then smiled, and raised her glass. 'Why not?'

It was almost midnight by the time Richard managed to get her back to the Ollenshaw's flat in Duke Street. 'Come on in for a nightcap,' Susan insisted, as the taxi drove noisily away. 'Peter and Jonquil have gone down to Cornwall for two days. Jonquil's father has hepatitis. It almost serves him right for calling his daughter Jonquil. Mind you, her brother's called Hereward.'

'I really shouldn't,' said Richard. 'I have to get back to Chichester first thing tomorrow morning.'

'One brandy killeth no man,' said Susan, taking hold of his arm.

'I really shouldn't,' Richard repeated.

'Thou shouldest and thou willest,' Susan told him; and lurched slightly, so that he had to catch her. Without any warning at all, she put her arms around his neck, right there in the street, and kissed him.

It wasn't much of a kiss; wet and erratic; but it had all the arousing effect of something forbidden. Richard took hold of Susan's wrists and gently lowered her arms, but the kiss had changed it all. The kiss had made it impossible for him to say no.

'A small one, only,' he insisted.

'I'm sorry,' asked Susan. 'A small what?'

'Brandy.'

'Ah,' she said, and opened up her black patent handbag so that she could find her keys. Further along the street, another returning reveller tripped over a whole row of empty milk-bottles.

*

433

The flat was high-ceilinged, drab, and decorated in a style which might have been called 'sumptuous' in 1934. Peter and Jonquil were obviously a very conservative pair, their chairs and sofas were huge and rounded and beige, with fringes, and their sitting-room was an obstacle course of reproduction magazine-racks and nests of tables and beige pouffettes. The wall on either side of the beige tiled fireplace was hung with horse-brasses.

They did, however, have a Marconi television, which Jonquil's father had bought for them in 1938 to watch the Coronation of George VI. The top of it was clustered with tarnished gymkhana cups, and a pair of African ivory bangles.

'Brandy, my dear,' said Susan, bringing over two balloon-glasses that looked as if they held almost half-a-bottle between them. 'Why don't you light the fire? I'm just going to powder my nose.'

Richard took his brandy, and looked up at her, and said, 'Cheers.'

'Cheers,' said Susan, and clinked glasses. 'Thank you for making my evening.'

While Susan went through to the bedroom, Richard got down on his knees in front of the hearth and lit the gas fire. It popped loudly, and then lit, and it wasn't long before the fireclay was beginning to glow scarlet. He took off his jacket and hung it over the back of the armchair.

He didn't quite know what he was doing here, drinking brandy at midnight in a strange London flat with a woman of startling reputation, his own brother's former mistress; but it seemed exciting and reassuring at the same time. The shabby comfort of the surroundings put him in mind of uncles and aunts, and well-meaning friends of his mother's; and yet there was something about the cognac and the lateness of the hour and the fact that he was playing truant from Iris that gave it a taste of the *risqué*.

'Have you been flying lately?' Susan called from the bedroom. 'You used to fly a lot, didn't you?'

'I took up a Catalina flying-boat about two weeks ago, on the Solent,' replied Richard. 'That was quite marvellous. I'd buy one for myself, just for the fun of it, if my money wasn't all tied up in the Sagittarius. I'd paint it white, and fly to the South of France for the weekend, and anchor in the harbour at Cannes.'

'I never knew you were such a romantic!' said Susan.

'You never knew me at all!' Richard called back.

The bedroom door opened. Susan reappeared. 'Perhaps it's time for us to rectify that,' she suggested; and this time her voice was soft and exaggeratedly suggestive, a film star's voice, with a timbre like silk stockings whispering darkly over warm skin.

She stepped forward, into the light from the fringed parchment-effect lampshade. She was wearing a silk robe, the very palest pink, with wide padded shoulders and wide lapels, drawn tightly at the waist with a wide silk sash. Her bare legs slid through the front of the dressing-gown as if cream had been poured down the front of it.

'There,' she said, coming close to the hearth and picking up her cognac. 'I've done what they do in the movies. I've slipped into something more comfortable.'

Richard's cheeks felt hot. He got up off his knees, and backed his bottom into one of the armchairs. 'Well . . .' he said, and lifted his glass.

'Chin-chin,' smiled Susan.

Richard sipped a little brandy, and then said, 'I suppose really I ought to be going. I don't want to keep you up.'

Susan at once knelt down beside him and propped her elbow on his knee and pouted at him. He couldn't believe that she was behaving like this. He couldn't believe, either, when the front of her robe opened a little, that he could glimpse freckled cleavage and no nightdress or negligée. That meant that underneath this thin silk covering she was –

'You can't possibly go,' she told him. 'You haven't drunk your drink.'

'Susan –'

'Dickie?' She smiled, and then touched the tip of his nose with her finger. 'You don't mind if I call you Dickie? I've never asked you. Some people hate their names being shortened. I hate it when people call me Sue, or Suzie, or Suzie-Q.'

'Well, I prefer Richard, but if you *want* to call me Dickie . . .'

'What I want, my dear, is utterly irrelevant. It's what *you* want that's important. Tell me, Dickie –' and here she snuggled up to him even closer '– what do *you* want?'

Richard swallowed more brandy, and shivered. 'Susan, I really have to go.'

'Stay,' she told him. 'You know that I want you to stay. You know that *you* want to stay. For once in your life, Dickie, just for once, do what you *want*, and not what you feel you *ought* to do. Life isn't *all* duty.'

Richard took a deep, wild breath. 'Susan, this is quite impossible. I'm a married man.'

'Well, that's all right, I'm a married woman!'

435

'Susan –' and here he tried to stand up, but Susan caught hold of his trouser-leg, and he stumbled, half-hopped, and spilled his cognac all over the shoulder of her robe.

'Oh, my God, look, I'm most fearfully sorry –'

He took out his handkerchief, and dabbed at her shoulder, but she reached up and clasped his hand. 'Don't,' she said, and there was such a wealth of fleshly implication in that one word that Richard shivered as deeply as he had shivered when he had drunk his cognac.

'It has to be dry-cleaned; otherwise it'll stain.'

Richard said nothing. He could see with extraordinary clarity what was going to happen next, whether he wanted it to happen or not. He felt as if he had become nothing more than an actor in the story of his own life; and not a very good one, at that. Somehow he had forfeited any say in his own destiny; and become an unwilling victim of his own weaknesses.'You must let me pay for it,' he said, following the screenplay to the word. And each word brought the inevitable one step closer.

It wasn't just his inability to prise himself loose from Susan's grip on his trousers, and to put on his jacket, and go. It was everything he did or had ever done. His cowardice in marrying Iris because his mother had insisted on it. His feeble agreement to give Iris a child simply because James had thought it would be a good way for him to get over his infatuation for Elisabeth Bergner. His acquiescence when John Tremlett had recommended that Michael should be sent no share of the family funds. His clerk-like fact-gathering for Mr Cauthen.

He had tried to think of his life as something of a sacrifice; a private crusade; a daily martyrdom; an unsung pageant of unpopular duty, bravely borne, as they said in the obituary columns about illnesses.

Instead he saw it now for what it was: thirty-nine years of blind funk, in all its ignoble manifestations.

Susan smiled: a smile that began in the very centre of her mouth and then spread across her lips like red ink filling a curved crevice in a desk.

'You'll pay for it, Dickie,' she whispered.

She tugged loose the sash. She opened up the lapels. Richard saw bare breasts; a lean middle-aged figure; dark pubic hair; slender thighs. He stared at her and she stared back. The gas fire hissed and flared.

'First installment,' she said, and reached up to kiss him.

'What about Terence?' he found himself asking, with her lips

436

already pressed against his. That, at least, was a departure from the script; and it was quite hard to say the name 'Terence' in the middle of a kiss.

Susan didn't stop smiling. 'Terence is just a *lagniappe*,' she said. 'You my darling, are a meal.'

He didn't know whether they had made love skilfully or clumsily. They did it on the floor to begin with, on the rug in front of the fire; but somehow their rhythms didn't seem to synchronize and the floor was too hard and the gas fire began to scorch Richard's right buttock.

He was excited by the thought that he was making love to another woman apart from Iris. She, Iris, would be sleeping now, with her scarf tied tightly over her hair, and her face white as a wall with make-up. But Susan was almost *too* unfamiliar, and after ten strenuous minutes he began to die away, and bend, and eventually curl up.

'I'm sorry,' he said. 'Too much brandy, I expect.'

'Too much guilt, I expect,' smiled Susan, sitting up cross-legged on the carpet, and leaning forward to kiss him. 'Let's go to bed; you can relax in bed. Floors get a bit uncompromising on the back at my age.'

'I'd really better go.'

'At half-past one in the morning? Where are you going to go? And you haven't finished fucking me yet.'

Richard was shocked. He had never heard a woman say that before. He felt as if he had suddenly dropped three hundred feet in an air-pocket.

Susan took hold of his hand. 'Do you know something,' she said, 'you still have a wonderful innocence about you. That's rare, in a man, especially these days, after the war. That's one of the things I like about Terence, his innocence. Most men you meet are so jaded and cynical. But you – you're still like a boy.'

Richard didn't know whether he ought to take that as a compliment or not; but he followed her meekly through to the bedroom, where a wide country-brass bed was waiting, with a heavy patchwork quilt.

'Come on,' Susan urged him. 'You're getting all goose-pimply, and your balls have gone small.'

He was awakened a few minutes after four o'clock by the sound of rustling. He opened his eyes, and at first he couldn't think where he was, but then he heard the sound of early-morning traffic in the street outside, and he remembered.

There was another rustle; then a sound like somebody walking across the room. He reached across the bed, but Susan was still there, warm and naked and fast asleep. He was about to shake her shoulder and wake her up when the quilt was lifted up and somebody heavy climbed into the bed, right behind him.

Richard was so horrified that he swallowed saliva and almost choked. But then a hairy arm was wrapped around his waist, and two thick hairy thighs were pressed up against his bottom, and a muscular hand groped at his chest.

The hand groped, hesitated, and groped again, and then slapped Richard two or three times on the breastbone. Richard, wide-eyed, felt Susan stir, but he couldn't find the breath or the words to cry out.

There was a moment of total disbelief, when all three people in the bed lay rigid. Then the heavy body bounced violently up into sitting position, so that Richard was tumbled straight into Susan's back, banging his chin on her shoulder-blade, and the bedside lamp was switched on.

'*Madre mia!*' the newcomer roared; and even though Richard had never met him before, he knew that this must be Vicent Blas Perera – Vicky, the Argentinian polo-player, Susan's second husband. He had black Astrakhan hair and black near-together eyes and his chest and his arms were thick with greying fur. He was glaring at Richard with the hysterical rage of an Argentinian polo-player who had not only found another man in bed with his wife, but had made the mistake of trying to caress him, too.

'Ah!' shouted Vicent. He clenched his fists and pummelled the mattress. 'Ah! Ah! Ah!' He was clearly too angry even to articulate.

Susan touched Richard's arm. She was extraordinarily calm. 'I know it's still a little early, Dickie darling, but I think it might be an idea if you – well, you know, went off and had breakfast somewhere.'

'I will *kill* you!' screamed Vicent.

Richard eased himself out of the bed, and circled around towards the door, covering himself with his cupped hands. He needn't have worried. Vicent seemed far angrier with Susan than he was with him.

'I will *kill* you!' he repeated. 'Ah! Ah! Ah-ah-ah-ah-ah!'

Richard hesitated in the doorway, but Susan waved him away. 'Go on, Dickie, don't worry about me. I'll be quite all right. It's just a tantrum, isn't it, Vicky darling?'

'I will trottle your neck!' Vicent screeched.

'Vicky, really – it had to happen sooner or later,' Susan soothed him. 'You have your women, it's only fair for me to have some men.' She paused, and then she said, 'Do you know something, I've only just thought. Vicky and Dickie! The two men in my life.'

But Vicent stood up, his hairy chest heaving, and stabbed a stubby finger at Susan in rage. 'I am no longer in your life, and you are no longer in mine! It's all finish, this marriage! This time, it's all finish!'

'But, Vicky, you're a Catholic,' said Susan. 'You swore to the Holy Mother that you'd never divorce me, ever.'

Vicent turned around and glared at Richard, who was balancing on one foot in the sitting-room as he tried to force his leg into his inside-out trousers. 'For this, I give up my principles! God will understand!'

'Well, he might, I suppose,' said Susan.

'You!' Vicent bellowed at Richard. 'You expect to be named, co-respondent! I will teach you to cuckold me, you chicken! Look at you! Chicken! You even have legs like a chicken!'

Richard thrust his tie in his jacket pocket, and hurried out of the flat without saying a word, almost knocking over a magazine-rack stuffed with copies of *Horse & Hound*. After he had slammed the front door, however, he knelt down and opened the letter-flap and shouted, 'I'd rather look like a chicken than a gorilla, any day!'

But he went home on the train that morning feeling trapped and ridiculous, and grievously embarrassed about what had happened.

On the telephone, Susan was quite level about it. 'Vicky says we can have a quiet divorce or a loud divorce.'

Richard was standing in the drawing-office in his overcoat. Outside the window, the snow was still falling, although it was thin and wet and it wasn't settling. 'I'd rather it were quiet, if it's all the same to you.'

'He says he wants your admission of adultery, and an out-of-court settlement of five thousand pounds, and everything will be done discreetly and quickly.'

Richard whistled. 'Five thousand pounds! That's a bit steep!'

'He says he needs the money to cover his legal costs, as well as a new polo pony. He says a pony is not a substitute for a wife, but it will do for the time being.'

'And what if I say no?'

'Well, then, the divorce will be loud. And if I know anything about Vicky, that means very loud.'

'Doesn't he care about you? What about your reputation?'

Susan let out a humourless laugh. 'My dear Dickie, I haven't *got* a reputation. I gave up my reputation to save your brother.'

'All the same, five thousand pounds . . .'

'Oh, I expect you can manage it one way or another,' said Susan. 'You don't want Iris to find out about it, after all. The dutiful Iris.'

Richard frowned. David Bright saw him frowning, and asked, 'Everything okay?'

'Yes, yes,' said Richard. Then, to Susan, 'What will *you* be doing? I mean, once it all goes through?'

'Marrying Terence, of course. What do you think?'

Richard rubbed his forehead with the heel of his hand. 'You framed me. That's what they say in the gangster films, isn't it? You set me up.'

'All right,' said Susan, 'I admit it. But it wasn't planned; I mean not in advance. It came to me during dinner, if you must know, when I was eating my *tagliatelle*.'

'But why? Why couldn't you have done it with Terence? He's the man you want to marry, after all.'

'Oh, lots of reasons,' Susan told him. 'One – poor Terence hasn't got any money, and I knew that Vicky would want some kind of financial settlement out of it. Well, wounded South American virility, all that kind of thing, quite apart from the fact that Vicky's perpetually broke. Two – Terence has only just started at the Ministry, and there are two thousand other demobbed airmen who would take his job like a shot, if there was any question that he wasn't quite the right sort of chap. And the right sort of chap doesn't go around getting himself named in divorces.'

'My God,' said Richard.

Susan laughed. 'You're paying the price for your brother's freedom. I gave up my reputation for James Lord; now you can give up something for me.'

'But five thousand pounds . . .'

'Don't you think my reputation was worth five thousand pounds? That court case ruined my life! Now I'm doing my best to put it back together again.'

'But you gave evidence of your own free will,' Richard protested.

'Yes, I did. But then you went to bed with me of your own free will. Nobody forced you, all you had to do was say no.'

'But if I'd known what was going to happen –' Richard interrupted.

'My dear Dickie, if *I'd* known what was going to happen when I stepped up in that witness-box, I wouldn't have done it, either. But there we are. Perhaps we're both victims of Mr James Lord. Perhaps we're both less wary than we ought to be. It's a hard life, Dickie, a very hard life. But you were good, that second time. You were lovely.'

Richard couldn't think of a single thing to say. He put down the phone, and stared at David as if he didn't know who he was.

'You look as if you could do with a cup of tea,' said David.

At the end of April, with firm orders from BEA for two aircraft, and provisional orders for four more, Richard and David and their small team of designers and aero-engineers began work on the Sagittarius turboprop airliner.

The Sagittarius would be almost exactly what Iris had suggested – a scaled-up and strengthened version of the Capricorn, powered by four jet engines, each of them using its turbines to drive a propeller. Even David's most sober estimates suggested that the airliner would be able to fly fifty passengers a distance of fifteen hundred miles at a speed of three hundred and fifty miles an hour.

'It has to be two things,' Richard told David one dazzling April morning. 'It has to be good, but most of all it has to be first. I've seen some drawings from Vickers, and their new turboprop airliner looks like a certain winner. That's unless the Sagittarius pips them at the post.'

David swallowed a mouthful of cold tea. 'It'll be tight; but I'm sure we'll do it.'

'Well, I'm going to make certain of it,' said Richard. 'I talked to the banks yesterday afternoon. They've agreed to stump up another three hundred thousand pounds so that we can build two prototypes simultaneously instead of just one.'

'*Two?*' asked David. 'Why on earth do we need two? And both at once?'

'Ah,' said Richard, pleased with himself. 'The idea is that while the first prototype is here at the factory, being tested for stress and handling and metal-fatigue and all that kind of thing, the second prototype can already be flying around the world selling for us. We'll save ourselves six or seven months.'

'That's a bit tricky, isn't it?' said David. 'What if we find there's something seriously wrong?'

'Do *you* think there's anything seriously wrong? Or any chance of it? We're using a tried-and-tested airframe design, coupled with engines we've developed ourselves. There are bound to be minor modifications; but all we have to do is cable details out to the second prototype, wherever it is, and have the necessary adjustments made on the spot.'

David raised both eyebrows. 'It's a hell of a risk.'

'This whole business is a hell of a risk.'

David thought for a moment, looking over his drawings for the Sagittarius's elevators. Then he nodded, and shrugged, and said, 'Perhaps you've got something.'

'You know I've got something,' grinned Richard.

'Oh, yes,' David agreed. 'More bareface bloody nerve than I've ever seen before. And where did you get *that* from?'

Miami, 1948

The helicopter came clattering over the roof of James's office and hovered for a moment over the concrete apron just below his window, before gently settling itself down, its rotors shining in the mid-morning sunlight.

James was on the telephone to Seattle, trying to talk to the vice-president in charge of sales at Boeing. The line was echoey and indistinct enough as it was, without some idiot landing a helicopter right outside. James said, 'Hello? Hello?' and then, 'Damn it, I can't hear you, I'll call you later.'

He put down the phone and went to the window. He was just in time to see the helicopter pilot climb out of the cockpit and start walking towards the Atlantic and Pacific Airways building. 'Damned idiot,' he said, out loud. But then, just before he disappeared beneath the canopy below, the pilot took off his flying helmet, and James saw by his dark braided hair that he wasn't a he at all, but a she.

He buzzed his secretary. 'Pearl – can you find out for me who that helicopter belongs to? Yes – the helicopter that just landed right outside. Well, yes, I want it moved. That apron belongs to us and nobody is authorized to land anything on it, particularly a helicopter. And can you book me another call to Boeing. I couldn't hear a damn thing the last time.'

He put on his sunglasses so that he could see the helicopter more clearly. It was a Sikorsky R-4B two-seater, painted lipstick red. He couldn't make out the registration numbers on the tailboom. 'Damn women flyers,' he said to himself. 'They fly worse than they drive.'

His intercom buzzed. 'Mr Lord?'

James picked up his telephone. 'Thanks, Pearl. Is that my call to London?'

'No, sir. There's somebody out here to see you.'

James slowly replaced the telephone receiver. 'I don't have any appointments this morning, do I?'

'No, sir. This young lady doesn't have an appointment. She says she just dropped in on the off-chance.'

'Well, tell her to leave her number and we'll get in touch.'

'Sir?'

'Yes, Pearl, what is it?'

'She's the young lady the helicopter belongs to.'

James frowned. He hesitated for a moment, and then he leaned over the intercom and said, 'Send her in.'

The door opened almost immediately; and into James's spacious red-carpeted office stepped a girl wearing a white cotton flying overall, and carrying a flying-helmet in her hand. She stood in the doorway for a moment, as if she were waiting for James to tell her to come in.

'Miss Emily Browne, sir,' said Pearl.

James sat on the edge of his desk. 'Miss Browne,' he said. 'Do you happen to make a habit of landing your helicopter whenever and wherever it pleases you?'

Emily Browne came across to the window and looked out at her aircraft. Then she turned to James and flashed him a winning smile. 'You don't really mind, do you?'

'Oh, not at all,' said James. 'I was only trying to make a telephone call to England, on a half-a-million-dollar business deal. You and your helicopter were quite welcome. How about flying it over to my house tonight, when I'm asleep, and landing it in my garden? I'd enjoy that.'

'You're upset,' said Emily. 'I didn't mean to upset you.'

James folded his arms and looked at her. He was going to say something really dismissive and sarcastic, but then he realized that he didn't want to. Emily Browne – whoever she was – was stunningly pretty. She was a small girl, not much taller than five-feet-four in her flying boots. Her eyes were wide and dark, with slightly lazy-looking eyelids. Her mouth looked as if she were just about to whisper something disturbingly suggestive. Even under her overall, James could see that she was very full-breasted.

It was not only her prettiness that attracted him, though. There was some quality about her – some indefinable look – that James found completely irresistible. If somebody had ever asked him to imagine his perfect woman, she would have looked like a twin of Emily Browne.

Neither James nor Emily spoke for almost a minute. During that minute, their eyes challenged each other, searched for clues to each other's character. At last, James walked around his desk, and opened up the silver cigarette-box that Eddie Feinbacker had given him when he retired to Key West.

'I don't smoke,' said Emily, even before James had offered her a cigarette.

James took one out himself, and lit it. 'You didn't just come here to interrupt my telephone call, did you, or to tell me that you don't smoke?'

Emily shook her head. 'No,' she said. 'I didn't. As a matter of fact, I came to ask you for money.'

'I see,' said James, and sat down. 'Money for what, precisely?'

'Money to fly. Flying's becoming real expensive these days.'

'Well, helicopters are pretty heavy on juice. Perhaps you should take up gliding instead. Where did you get that one?'

'It used to belong to the 6th Aircraft Repair Unit. My mother bought it for me.'

'Your *mother* bought it for you? You must have quite an unusual mother.'

'She is. She's *very* unusual.'

James waved smoke away with his hand. 'And if you'll forgive my saying so, lady helicopter pilots are pretty unusual, too.'

Emily smiled at him. He heard himself saying, '*And* unusually pretty, too.'

'Does that mean you'll help me?' she asked him.

'Steady on!' James grinned. 'You're not exactly the bashful type, are you?'

'I don't come from a very bashful family.'

Aroused, interested, James looked at Emily even more keenly.

He couldn't think why he was allowing her to talk to him like this; but then he couldn't think why she *wanted* to talk to him like this. He had an oblique, edge-of-the-consciousness feeling that they weren't talking about money or flying or families at all, but about something else altogether.

'You need money to run your helicopter then, is that it?' he asked her.

'Oh, no. I run the helicopter out of my allowance. I need money to fly round the world.'

'You want to fly round the world?' James forced a laugh that turned into a cough. But this time Emily wasn't smiling. She stayed where she was, by the window, the sun shining in her braids so that James could see streaks of Titian and blonde in them; very pretty and totally serious.

'I've always wanted to fly round the world,' she repeated. 'You know, like Amelia Earhart, or Wiley Post.'

'Well, you know what happened to *them*,' said James, more soberly now.

'Of course I do. But that's what makes it all the more exciting.'

James sat and smoked and thought for a while, without once taking his eyes off her. Then he said, 'How much flying experience do you have?'

'Five years. I'm twenty-four this year; I've been flying since I was nineteen.'

'What made you want to take it up?'

'I think it's in the blood. My father was an aircraft-designer.'

'Oh, yes? Who did he work for?'

'Allan Loughead for a while, then Douglas.'

James blew out smoke. 'Browne? That was his name?'

'Gerry Browne. You probably never met him.'

'No,' said James. 'I can't say that I did. But he must have been pretty successful, to keep you in airplanes and helicopters. Is he still alive?'

Emily shook her head. 'He died before the war. My mother's still alive, though. She's in a nursing-home in Sarasota. We used to live in Pittsburgh right up until the time I was seventeen, but we moved south when my mother contracted TB.'

'What airplanes have you flown?' asked James.

'Apart from Piper Cubs and PT-19s – Vegas, mainly. But I've flown an Electra, like Amelia Earhart; and the longest flight I ever did was in a DC-1 – Pittsburgh to San Francisco and back again.'

'That's your only experience of long-distance flying?'

445

'I flew solo from Sarasota to Toronto. That was in September last year.'

James sucked in his breath. 'Flying around the world – that's going to be something quite different.'

'I know,' she told him, but her eyes brightened like lamps with darkly-tinted glass. 'I know it is. But I've been practising night-flying and blind landings and flying out over the ocean. I've been up in a hurricane. And there's something else, too.'

'Tell me,' said James.

Emily leaned forward on James's desk with a smile of such sensuality and determination that it made the back of his neck prickle. 'I've got the *nerve* to do it, that's what.'

James held her gaze for one silent moment. Then he sat back in his high-backed leather chair, and nodded in his superior airline-president way, and said, 'All right. I'm interested. Why don't you tell me all about it over lunch. What do you think about soft-shelled crab?'

'I think they're just like men,' she said.

James gave another awkward laugh. 'Is that because they taste good, or because their shells are soft?'

Emily didn't answer that, but unfastened the top button of her flying overalls.

James went back home that night and sat silent over dinner.

'Aren't you hungry, dear?' asked Patricia, from the other end of the candlelit dining-table.

James picked up his fork and reluctantly twisted tagliatelle around the tines. 'I'm sorry. I don't seem to have much of an appetite.'

'You're not sickening for one of your colds, are you?'

James poured himself another glass of cold Chablis. 'I've got a lot on my mind, that's all. Pan Am are still doing their darnedest to keep us from flying to Europe. Not only that, our Constellations are five months behind schedule. We'll be lucky to get delivery by Christmas. And – I don't know – seat-miles were down last quarter by four per cent. We don't seem to be challenging Eastern the way we used to.'

'Well, I think APA is getting rather dowdy, to tell you the truth,' Patricia said, helping herself to another spoonful of Parmesan cheese.

James looked up. '*Dowdy?* What the hell do you mean by *dowdy?*'

'Well, don't you think it's time you changed those awful red carpets, and redecorated your aircraft? Your terminal could do with some redesigning, too. All those dark oak counters and dreadful wooden seats. I always get the feeling when I fly by APA that I'm back on Southern Railways.'

'I suppose you want the place to look like Buck Rogers in the twenty-first century.'

'It would be a jolly sight better than James Lord ten years behind the times.'

'Patricia,' said James, testily, 'you simply don't understand. We're trying to present our customers with the idea of a solid, dependable airline. Dependable, that's the whole key to it. We service Florida. More than forty per cent of our passengers are over retirement age, and people of that age want to feel reassured when they fly. They don't want to sit in an airplane and feel as if they're just about to take off for Mars. The want to feel *safe*.'

'Well, I think you're going about it the wrong way,' said Patricia. 'You're being too *English*. Americans aren't frightened by things that are modern and new. In fact, they find them reassuring.'

'And since when have you been an expert on what Americans are reassured by?'

Patricia said, 'James, my darling, I've been living here for nearly thirteen years. I don't sit in an ivory tower at Miami Municipal Airport all day, like you do. I shop and meet friends and watch television and read newspapers. And, believe me, if you want APA to do better, you're going to have to think of a really exciting gimmick.'

'Gimmick, for God's sake,' James breathed, pushing away his pasta.

But that night, he lay in bed unable to sleep, thinking of Emily Browne.

She had stepped out of her flying overalls right there and then, in the middle of his office. Underneath she had been wearing an expensive striped pink-and-white New Look dress, with pink-piped lapels and a tightly-belted waist. James hadn't failed to glimpse her slim calves and her perfectly-seamed stockings. 'My sandals are in the helicopter,' she said; and so James had sent Pearl out to fetch them.

He had taken her for lunch at the Corale, overlooking the indigo waters and the shatteringly white yachts of Biscayne Bay. He had ordered shrimp and soft-shelled crabs and mango salad, with Moët & Chandon *non-cuvée* champagne. Emily had been appreciative

447

but not wildly impressed. She was obviously wealthy enough to be able to eat like this whenever she felt like it, and apart from that she was far more interested in flying than she was in food.

She had talked very little about her family; but she had talked quickly and breathlessly and knowledgeably about flying. She flew almost every day. If she didn't fly, she became tetchy and bad-tempered. She had wanted to race, like Jackie Cochran, who had beaten all the other male competitors in the Bendix contest, but her mother had forbidden it. 'Mother's absolutely convinced that I'm going to kill myself. She's always saying, "Don't you dare die before I do."' She adored large multi-engined aeroplanes. 'I should have flown Flying Fortresses. Jackie Cochran used to ferry them across the Atlantic during the war. Can you imagine doing a loop-de-loop in a Flying Fortress?'

She had leaned close to James and told him, 'I have absolutely dozens of press cuttings. If you want to, I'll send you my scrapbook. The *Sarasota Herald* called me "Florida's Airborne Angel". Isn't that cute?'

She had teased and flirted and played games with James all the way through lunch. He had said very little; there really hadn't been the need for him to say very much. He could tell that she was quite determined; and from the way she talked about flying he was beginning to believe that she was probably good enough.

Between the mangoes and the cream chiffon, she had said, quite simply, 'The whole thing is, I'm looking for a sponsor. A really serious sponsor. I want to fit out a twin-engined airliner so that I can fly to London, Paris, Rome, Cairo, Delhi, Singapore, Darwin, and so on, across the Pacific and back to Florida.'

'Why?' James had asked her.

'I want to do it because I want to do it,' Emily had replied.

'That's exactly what Amelia Earhart said.'

'Amelia Earhart also said that women must try to do things, as men have tried.'

'And you believe that, too?'

'Don't you?' Emily had challenged him.

Now he was lying in bed, sleepless, thinking about her. It was a very difficult thing for him to have to face – especially since he had reconciled himself to living with Patricia and Helen for the rest of his life – but he was almost completely sure that he had fallen in love with her. Well, not love exactly. And not irrevocably, not yet. He was supposed to be flying up to Sarasota sometime next week to watch her putting a Vega through its paces. He could always call her and cry off. But he knew that he wouldn't. He knew that in spite of all the pain and all the complications he was risking, he would see her again, and do his damnedest to make love to her. Somebody at the *Sarasota Herald* knew what he was writing about: she was Florida's Airborne Angel, and no mistake about that.

And if she flew around the world in a plane sponsored by APA – why then, wouldn't that be just the gimmick that Patricia had been talking about? And wouldn't it give him every credible excuse to spend as much time with Emily as he wanted?

He thought: I'm too tired. I'm fantasizing. He turned in the dimness of the room and looked at Patricia lying asleep on the white embroidered pillow.

He couldn't deny it. There was something about Emily which wrenched him deeply. Some nuance in her expression which suspended all discretion and critical judgement. It didn't make any kind of rational sense, but he felt that he had already been in love with her before he met her.

He thought of her face, laughing at him over the lunch-table. He thought of her hand, lying on the tablecloth; thin-wristed, with pink-varnished nails. It was dawn before he fell asleep; and even then, when Patricia touched his shoulder to wake him up for work, he thought for one impulsive second that it was Emily Browne.

It was Richard's letter which finally convinced him to put up the money for Emily's flight. It arrived three days later, on Saturday morning, a large manilla envelope printed with the flying-swan logo of Richard's new Lord Aviation Holdings Ltd, and addressed in Richard's own handwriting. James took it out on to the verandah, where he was having a late breakfast of coffee and brioche rolls and apricot marmalade. The yuccas were rustling in the soft Atlantic breeze. Helen was swimming up and down the pool with the easy splashless strokes of a perfect swimmer. James tore open the envelope.

Inside, there was a long handwritten letter, as well as drawings, blueprints, colour photographs, and pages and pages of specifications.

'Dear James . . . as you know I have rarely asked you for anything in the way of a favour . . . but Lord Aviation is teetering on the brink . . . and right at the moment there is nobody else to whom I can turn.

'We have invested more than one and a half million in developing the Sagittarius, but so far we have had only two firm orders . . . it

449

has been necessary for me to give my personal guarantee to both banks, and to put up Goodwood Lodge and the factory itself as security. The first prototype is ready, and the second is almost completed. Our first turboprop airliner! But as you probably know Vickers have been working very much along the same lines . . .

'In many respects, the Sagittarius is superior to the Vickers project – it carries four more passengers and it cruises at least thirty miles an hour faster . . . but the fact is that the industry hasn't yet forgiven me for my work for Mr Cauthen before and during the war. There has been a considerable whispering campaign against the Sagittarius, suggesting that it has serious structural defects . . . which of course are utterly without foundation . . .

'I know that you have been looking to Douglas and Boeing for a new short-haul airliner . . . but I can offer you the Sagittarius at a price that neither company can match . . . A firm order from APA for three or four aircraft would see us through the next half-year . . . and encourage other airlines to give the Sagittarius more serious consideration. . . .'

James skimmed through the rest of the specifications, and then thoughtfully sat back. If the Sagittarius was as good as these figures suggested – and if Richard was prepared to sell it at a knock-down price – he would be doing himself a serious disservice if he didn't at least try one out.

And perhaps the most profitable way of trying one out would be to lend it to Emily Browne, so that she could fly around the world in it. A newsworthy gimmick for APA; and proof to the British airline industry that the Sagittarius was reliable and sound, and a far better airliner than the Vickers jet.

He picked up the white telephone on the breakfast table. 'Operator? I want to book an international call to London, England. Yes, that's right. Yes, I know what time it is in England.'

Helen climbed out of the pool, and came up the garden, drying her hair with a bright yellow towel. 'Dad? You've let your coffee go cold. Do you want me to call Nina to get you some more?'

James shook his head. 'I just have a couple of calls to make. I'll be coming in soon. Maybe you'd like to go to lunch at Nestor's today? Hamburgers, shakes? All those things that turn slim young girls into wobbling mounds of human jelly?'

Helen laughed, and kissed him.

He called Emily's number in Sarasota. Usually, he had a terrible head for telephone numbers, but this one seemed to have embossed itself indelibly on the front of his brain. The phone rang and rang for a long time before anybody answered.

'Hello? Who's this?' demanded a suspicious Cuban voice.

'My name's James Lord. Is Miss Browne around anywhere?'

'Miss Browne? No, not today, Miss Browne is flying today. You know flying? Weee-owwww, up in the sky.'

'Yes, I know. Can you tell her I called? Mr James Lord.'

'Mr Jem Sludd, yes.'

'Mr James Lord. *Lord*, have you got it? As in Lord thy God is a jealous God. And tell her this – tell her I've found her an airplane. Tell her the flight can go ahead.'

'Yes.'

'You've got that?'

'Yes.'

'You're sure?'

The Cuban voice suddenly, magically, changed. 'James? This is Emily. Well, I know, but I always do that, in case it's somebody I don't want to talk to. But is it really true? Is it really, really true? You've found me a plane?'

James couldn't help laughing. 'You're nuttier than I thought you were. But, yes – I've found you a plane. At least, I'm ninety-nine per cent certain I've found you a plane.'

'Oh my God, you're wonderful. What is it? Is it second-hand?'

'It's brand-new. It hasn't even been put into production yet. A twin-engined turboprop, capable of flying three thousand miles non-stop, provided we fit it with additional fuel-tanks. My brother Richard designed it.'

'How soon can we get it?'

'Well, I'm not too sure about that yet. But I'm going to telephone him this afternoon. I'll let you know as soon as everything's fixed up.'

'You're still coming up to Sarasota next week?'

'Of course I'm coming up to Sarasota next week. You don't think I'd miss an opportunity to see Florida's Airborne Angel actually airborne, do you?'

'Oh, James, you've made me so excited.'

'Well,' said James, choosing his words carefully, 'one good turn deserves another.'

It was a warm, windy day on the Gulf when Emily took James up in a borrowed Vega. James was relaxed in white shirtsleeves and light grey slacks. Emily wore a pale yellow silk blouse and flappy white silk trousers. Her hair was combed into two long schoolgirl braids, tied with yellow ribbons. James couldn't keep his eyes away from her.

They took off north-westwards into the wind, lifting up from the dusty airfield at Bee Ridge and climbing sharply over Sarasota Bay. Emily flew with the understated skill of somebody who has been born to fly; turning the Vega due westwards over Longboat Key and heading out over the Gulf. Below them, the sea was blinding.

'Watch this,' said Emily, and took the Vega through a barrel-roll, and then again, and then again. Then – before James could get his breath back – she lifted the nose up almost vertically, and looped one long slow loop after another.

The sun spun around them; the sea appeared over their heads. Then the windshield was filled with nothing but sky. 'Oh shit,' said James, under his breath.

James had an aviator's stomach, but after fifteen minutes of white-knuckle aerobatics, he tapped Emily on the shoulder and pointed to the ground.

'You haven't had enough?' she laughed. 'I'm just warming up!'

'I think I'm sufficiently impressed!' James told her. 'In fact, you've nearly impressed my breakfast out of me!'

She brought the Vega down for a neat, pretty, three-point landing. She taxied it over to the brown-painted shed of Bee Ridge Air Rental, where a laconic man in a bear-hunting hat and slack suspenders was waiting for her.

'Thanks, Freddie,' she told him. James – although he wasn't sure about the etiquette of it – handed him a ten-dollar bill. Freddie accepted it without comment and tucked it under his ear-flap.

Emily drove them back to Sarasota in her new Pontiac Silver Streak convertible. James smoked a cigarette and watched her as she drove. 'My brother called yesterday,' he told her. 'I think I've managed to persaude him to lend you the Sagittarius. He can't release it until he's completed the second prototype, but he's promised to have that finished by the end of June.'

'That's marvellous. I've already talked to my navigator, and he can't believe his luck. You'll be able to meet him in a couple of weeks' time. He used to fly for Pan Am, but they fired him because he drank.'

She glanced across at James's expression, and laughed. 'Oh, he doesn't drink now! I cured him! I took him up for an aerobatic flight when he had a hangover, and he hasn't touched a drop since. Mind you, we had to wash the cockpit out with carbolic.'

She pulled up outside a neat split-level house overlooking the bay. One side of the sloping garden was planted with orange trees, already heavy with fruit. The house itself was draped in flaming red bougainvillaea. A Mexican gardener was watering the dusty soil.

'Would you like some lunch?' Emily asked him.

James looked at his watch. 'I'm sorry, I really have to get back to Miami. I have a meeting with the municipal aviation people at four-thirty.'

'But it's all ready. I made it myself.'

'You can cook, as well as fly?'

Emily climbed out of the car and propped her elbows on the top of the door and coquettishly wrinkled her nose at him. 'Come on, you can call those tedious old municipal aviation people and tell them you've come down with *delirium tremens*.'

James shrugged. 'How can I refuse an offer like that?'

Emily set the lunch table on the balcony overlooking the small back garden. While she busied herself in the kitchen, James wandered around with a glass of dry white wine, admiring the house. It was cool, white-painted, with sanded wooden floors. In the living-room, there were two bookshelves filled tightly with books on aviation and aero-engineering. On the wall there was a small collection of framed photographs of Emily at various air meets. In one, she was holding up a large silver cup.

Another photograph caught James's attention, too. It was standing on a small side-table in a silver frame. A strikingly beautiful woman in an evening-gown, sitting on a verandah somewhere. James picked it up, and called, 'Is this your mother?'

Emily, wearing an apron, came to the kitchen door. 'Yes,' she said, 'that's my mother. That photograph was taken in 1922.'

'You're very alike.'

'I don't think so. I think I look more like my father.'

She went back into the kitchen. James wandered around a little more, and then came in to join her. 'Your father must have done rather well. It's odd that I've never heard of him. I thought I knew every good aircraft designer worth knowing.'

She was taking a seafood quiche out of the icebox. 'Well,' she said, 'he was always a very private sort of a man. Look – it's ready now, why don't you bring out the wine?'

They sat on the verandah and ate quiche and fruit and cheese, and threw broken-up bits of breadstick to the birds.

'I hope you realize that you've made my wildest dream come true,' said Emily.

'Not yet,' James cautioned her. 'First of all, you have to fly twenty-five thousand miles around the world.'

'But you've found an airplane for me.'

James shrugged. 'I think you probably deserve it – for sheer brass-necked bravado, if nothing else. I'm going to call Richard later today, and see how soon he can fly it over. I might even be able to persuade him to fit the extra fuel-tanks at the factory.'

He sipped a little more wine, and then he said, 'What made you pick on me?'

She glanced away. 'I don't know what you mean.'

'Well, you could just as easily have gone to Juan Trippe at Pan Am. He would have jumped at the chance to sponsor you.'

Emily didn't answer. James propped his elbows on the table, and said, 'Of all the airlines in the world, you had to pick on mine.'

'My mother suggested it.' Emily seemed unexpectedly cool. James felt as if a small cloud had passed over the face of the sun.

'Your mother? What does your mother know about airlines?'

'Hardly anything, I don't suppose. But she knows an awful lot about an awful lot of things.'

'Such as?'

Emily held out her glass. God, thought James, you're a beautiful girl. She said, 'Will you pour me some more wine, please? I feel like getting tiddly.'

After lunch, they went inside the house, and Emily showed James her press cuttings. She played Schumann on the gramophone, a dreamy little piano piece called *Curiose Geschichte*. She sat on the arm of her white-upholstered armchair staring out of the window towards the sea, and James felt that, momentarily, he had lost her.

At four o'clock he said, 'I have to go. I have a dinner tonight.'

She turned and smiled. 'I hope you enjoyed your lunch.'

She collected her car keys while he waited by the door. He opened it for her, but then, before she could go through, he closed it again. She looked up at him. There was no question in her eyes, no surprise. In an odd way, he found that more difficult to cope with.

'I, ah –'

She waited, and said nothing.

'I, ah, think you're very attractive.'

'Thank you,' she replied. 'I think you're very attractive, too.'

He didn't know what to say next. He took hold of her elbow,

and leaned forward to kiss her. She deflected her face ever so slightly, so that his lips grazed her cheek instead of her lips.

'I'm behaving like a schoolboy,' he said.

'No, you're not. You're just being honest.'

'Honest?'

'Yes, you think I'm attractive and you're showing me just how attractive you think I am. That's better than pretending, don't you think?'

James stared at her. 'I'm not at all sure what I think.'

She took hold of his arm. 'Come on,' she said, 'I'll drive you to the airfield. You'll call me, won't you, if your brother has any news about the plane?'

'Yes,' said James. 'I'll call you.'

On July 9, the second prototype Lord Sagittarius 002 arrived at Miami Municipal Airport on the back of a long tractor-trailer, wingless and shrouded in tarpaulins. It had been shipped from Southampton to New York, and driven by road down to Florida. Emily flew her helicopter over from Sarasota to see it, and she and James stood side by side with a shared feeling of excitement and achievement as the airliner was backed slowly into the APA maintenance hangar.

Emily's navigator Roger Boone arrived later in the afternoon. He was a thin, long-legged mid-Westerner with a head as big as a horse; married, with twin sons. Emily liked him and trusted him; and after an initial twinge of jealousy at the closeness of their professional rapport, James had grown to like him and trust him too. You hardly ever saw Roger without his maps and his Coke bottle. 'Just so long as I keep on drinking Coke, I don't feel thirsty for the other stuff.'

There were no press here today. Both James and Emily had decided to wait for the day when the Sagittarius was ready to fly. Richard had put the airliner through eight weeks of flight tests; and had then fitted it out at Haywards Heath with four supplementary fuel tanks which raised its capacity from two hundred and fifty gallons to one thousand, two hundred and fifty, and gave it a possible range of four thousand miles without refuelling.

Roger had already plotted Emily's route – landing at all the major capitals along the way. *Time* magazine had called the flight 'A Capital Jaunt Around The World'.

'Well, Roger,' said James, as the hangar doors rumbled shut. 'There it is. Your one-way ticket around the Earth.'

Roger approached the shrouded airliner with obvious respect. 'What are we going to call this baby?' he wanted to know.

'Oh yes,' said Emily. 'She has to have a name; and we have to break a bottle of champagne over her nose.'

James stayed where he was, his hands in his pockets. 'Let's just call her the Angel, shall we? That seems suitable.'

Emily smiled. 'James, you're being provocative again.'

'I'm never going to stop being provocative,' said James. 'It's my nature.'

'Yes,' said Emily. Then she said, 'I thought you were stuffy, you know, that first day I met you. A real stuffed shirt. But you're not, are you?'

James didn't answer. Roger – who was used to Emily's banter – was examining the Sagittarius's undercart.

Emily came up to James and said, 'I'll bet money you're just like your father.'

'My father's dead.'

'I know. But I'll bet money you're just like him.'

James said, 'My father was arrogant, brave, intolerant, badly-educated, and attractive to women.'

'There you are, then,' Emily told him. 'I win.'

James gave her a tight, closed-mouth smile for a moment, and then laughed. 'I may be all of those things, but I'm not like my father. There are all kinds of ways of being arrogant; all kinds of ways of being brave.'

He looked at her, still smiling, and then he said, 'All kinds of ways of being attractive to women, too.'

Roger came over, swigging Coke. 'Do you think we'll be able to have her ready for the end of August?'

James nodded. 'You can have all the mechanics you want and all the money you want. Richard's done the most difficult parts of the conversion, back at the factory. He called me last night and told me that he was sending over new landing-gear doors, too. And apparently Marconi have improved the radar for you.'

'This is going to be the flight to end all flights,' said Roger, appreciatively.

And Emily took hold of James's hand and said, 'You've been marvellous. I don't really know how to thank you.'

James kissed her cheek. 'You'll think of something.'

By the second week in August, the Sagittarius airliner called *Angel* was ready for her flight round the world. She had been painted bright orange (in case, like Amelia Earhart's *Electra*, she went down at sea). On her fin she bore the insignia of Atlantic and Pacific Airways, and all along the fuselage were painted the words Lord Aviation, Chichester, England.

James's staff had assisted Roger to prepare full navigational maps of every leg of the 29,360-mile journey, and had arranged with BOAC for high-grade fuel to be available at every stop – as well as providing emergency fuel dumps in the Saudi Arabian desert, in India, Australia, and Howland Island in the Pacific.

APA's caterers supplied canned and pre-packed meals; as well as plenty of Beech Nut tomato-juice and dried fruit.

On Monday, August 23, the Sagittarius was rolled out shining and fuelled-up at Miami airport, to the cheers of four thousand enthusiastic spectators. The press had gone 'Emily Browne crazy'. There were front page stories in newspapers coast to coast, with headlines like THE NEW AE and BON VOYAGE, ANGEL! Emily had been interviewed by more than forty magazines, and appeared on *Movietone News* and even the *Texaco Star Theater*.

James and Emily and Roger posed for official photographs in front of the Sagittarius's nosewheel. The sun was brilliant; the clouds were as puffy as lambs.

'This is it, then,' said James. 'It only seems like yesterday that you were landing your helicopter outside my window and interrupting my phone-call.'

'The credit's all yours, James,' Emily told him. 'All I did was to pick the right man to ask.'

'I thought coming to me was your mother's idea.'

'It was. But then I think I deserve some credit for doing what she suggested, for about the first time in my life.'

'Here's a suggestion: take care.'

Emily kissed him. James glanced up and saw that Patricia was watching him from the flower-decorated podium where she was standing next to the Governor of Florida and his portly honour the Mayor of Miami. There was a look in her eyes that he didn't much care for.

Roger and Emily climbed aboard the Sagittarius, waving and posing for pictures on the steps. Then the door was closed, and Emily went into the cockpit to start up the engines. James stepped back as the turboprops burst into life, and Emily built up the revs to a healthy high-pitched whine.

She taxied the airliner out to the end of the runway. Then she turned, and built up the power until the engines were screaming and the crowds pressed their hands over their ears. With its huge

457

load of fuel, the Sagittarius weighed well over twenty tons, and Emily would need every ounce of power to lift her off the runway.

At last, she released the brakes, and the crowd cheered again as the Sagittarius roared off along the airstrip, its orange outlines distorted by the heat-shimmer rising up from the concrete, and rose into the clear morning sky. Within minutes, the airliner had dwindled out of sight.

James went around to shake hands with his engineers and his navigation staff; and then shook hands with the state governor.

'I just want you to know that our hearts are with you,' the governor told him. 'That little lady of yours is the pride of Miami.'

After the celebrations were over, James and Patricia walked back to their new white Cadillac convertible. James had given Fidel a few days off, and so he was driving himself. He opened the door for Patricia and then climbed behind the wheel.

'Well,' he said, as he started up the engine, 'all she needs now is luck.'

'She has everything else, hasn't she?' said Patricia.

James was backing the car out of the parking-lot. 'What's that supposed to mean?'

'She has looks, youth, wit, intelligence, and she can fly like an angel.'

'And?'

'And I haven't, that's all.'

'*Patricia*,' James protested, although he protested just a little too much, 'you're not jealous, are you?'

'Do I have anything to be jealous about?'

'Of course you don't. You're my wife.'

Patricia was silent for a while, but she was obviously fuming. 'Ever since the day you met her, you haven't talked about anything or anyone else. It's been Emily Browne, Emily Browne, Emily Browne. I suppose she reminds you of Lady Susan Sheffield, or Chloe Treat.'

'Don't you mention Chloe Treat to me!' James shouted, suddenly angry. 'I had to identify Chloe Treat's dead body!'

'And I'm not supposed to be upset that you were *capable* of identifying her dead body?'

James took a deep breath. They had stopped at a red traffic signal on NW 17th Street, and the family in the next car were staring at them with unremitting interest, father and mother and two children, all of them wearing spectacles.

When the signal changed to green, he said, 'As a matter of fact, she doesn't remind me of Susan at all. And Chloe's long dead, isn't she, so you don't have anything to fear from *her*.'

'Do I have anything to fear from Emily Browne?'

James shook his head. 'I'm not even going to dignify that question with an answer.'

'That's because you *can't* answer.'

'Of course I can answer. I just don't think you have a right to ask me, that's all.'

Patricia leaned across the front seat of the car and stared at him close. 'You're in love with her, aren't you?'

James said nothing. The muscles in his cheeks tensed, and he clenched his teeth tightly together to stop himself from saying something which he knew he would always regret.

'Are you in love with her?' Patricia asked him, more gently this time.

James looked at her, but still said nothing. It was then that both of them knew for certain that he was.

Late the following afternoon, when the sun was beginning to etch its way into the palm trees around the airport, and the last DC-3 for Puerto Rico was taxiing out to the main runway, James picked up the telephone and called Patricia at home.

'Patricia? It's me. Listen, I'm not coming home tonight.'

Silence.

'As a matter of fact, darling, I'm taking a short trip.'

Again, silence.

'Patricia? Did you hear what I said?'

'Yes, James, I heard what you said. How long are you going to be away?'

'Well, the thing is, I think I've been missing an opportunity with this round-the-world flight.'

'What opportunity?'

'It's really a question of selling Atlantic and Pacific Airways in Europe. I really think I ought to go to London and see what I can do to set up some meetings with the civil aviation people. You know – to coincide with Emily's trip. I mean, Richard's taking full advantage to promote the Sagittarius. It seems like a senseless waste of good publicity if I don't do the same.'

Short silence. Then, 'When are you going?'

'I'm already booked on tonight's Pan Am flight from New York.'

'Don't you need any clothes?'

459

'I'll send Pearl around to pick up a bag. I don't need much. A suit, a couple of shirts. A couple of changes of underwear.'

'Will you be going for long?' asked Patricia. Her voice betrayed nothing at all.

'A week, two at the most.'

'Be careful, then,' said Patricia, and put the phone down.

James sat with the receiver in his hand, wondering if he ought to call back and tell her he loved her. But then Pearl came in and said sharply, 'Mr Lord? If you want me to go fetch your suitcase, you'd better let me go right away. You don't want to miss your flight to New York.'

'No,' said James. Then, 'No,' and hung up the phone.

London, 1948

Sagittarius KHALL appeared in Richard's binoculars as a bright orange speck, high above the Berkshire hills. He called to Iris, 'I can see her! Just over there! That's right! Just over the village!'

Iris was sitting in the Daimler eating sandwiches. She had insisted on making three packets of sandwiches before they left home that morning, one for each of them. She and Richard had argued about it. Richard had wanted to go to a pub, but Iris didn't like pubs. 'Pubs,' she said, 'smell.'

Thomas hadn't wanted to come at all, and he had whined all the way there. Thomas hated dressing up in his best clothes and he hated having his hair brushed and he hated aeroplanes and he hated grown-ups. Richard had put his foot down. This flight was historic, he said. This flight was going to make the name of Lord rank with Wellington and Baden-Powell and Churchill.

The Sagittarius droned low over the village of Hazeley as she made her approach to Blackbushe aerodrome. The afternoon was warm and fresh: one of those days when Richard would quote to himself, 'Fair stands the wind for France', and the horse-chestnut trees would surge and rustle, and cloud-shadows would sail deliriously across the Downs.

David Bright came up to Richard rubbing his hands in glee. 'She's made it! What a cracker! And listen to those engines!'

'Sweet as a nut,' said Richard, remembering Wally Field.

'Good crowd, too,' said David, continuing to chafe his hands. At least a thousand people had come to see the American angel in the British-built aeroplane. Her radio-call sign KHALL had already been made famous by Arthur Askey, who had sung a song on *Band Waggon* with a chorus that went, '*Call the angel called KHALL,* kay-aitch and that's all. If you're far too fat and your wings are too small, if you want to fly but you're afraid to fall; call the angel called KHALL.'

The dazzling orange Sagittarius flew overhead with that distinctive turboprop whistle, while the crowd waved their hats and cheered in excitement. Richard stood with his hands on his hips, watching in admiration as the airliner turned and banked, and then settled down at the far end of the runway for a slow, beautifully-controlled landing.

'Gosh,' said David, 'she can certainly fly, can't she! That was a better landing than Ginger's.'

'I think I can safely say that I'm proud of us,' Richard replied. 'This time, we're going to make our fortune, you mark my words.'

The Sagittarius came slowly up to the apron. The engines died, and the propellers slowed and stopped. At once, the crowd began to run forward, and in spite of the efforts of a dozen cheerful policemen, they soon surrounded the airliner completely. Richard was lost amongst running boys who wanted to touch the aeroplane, and hurrying women who wanted to get a close look at Emily Browne.

The door of the airliner was opened, and Roger was first to appear. He raised his hands in a triumphant wave, and called out, 'Hallo England! How're you doing?'

The maintenance crew were having difficulty pushing the steps through the crowd. 'You want me to fly from here to the ground?' Roger joked, and everybody laughed good-naturedly.

At last, Roger was able to step down. He waved again, and was applauded and cheered and slapped on the back. But then Emily appeared in the aircraft doorway, and the huge *hurray!* that went up was deafening. She had already changed out of her flying clothes into an elegant white calf-length summer dress, and she was carrying a white straw hat with black feathers on it. She smiled and waved and blew kisses, and the men whistled and the women cheered. The press photogaphers shouldered each other out of the way to take pictures of her as she came down the steps, still waving, and still blowing kisses.

'Well, *well*!' exclaimed David Bright. 'What a corker!'

Richard was silent, but waited for Emily at the foot of the steps with his arms by his sides, unmoving, as if none of this were real, and he was nothing but an extra in a play. Emily came down and held out her hand and smiled at him. 'Mr Lord? Mr *Richard* Lord? I have a message from your brother James. He says, good show.'

She leaned forward from the last step and kissed him on both cheeks. There was a furious clattering of camera shutters; and spent flashbulbs were being ground underfoot everywhere.

'Welcome to England,' said Richard. 'That's a beautiful dress.'

'Why thank you,' smiled Emily. 'I was thinking of coming out in my slacks; but then I thought about Jean Patten and she used to fix *engines* in a white silk dress, and I thought Emily, my dear, style is all.' She giggled.

The newspaper reporters were shouting at her now. 'How was your flight, Miss Browne?' 'Are you confident you're going to make it around the world?' 'How does the aeroplane handle?' 'Do you wear that dress when you fly?'

Richard protectively put his arm around her. 'Let me get you through to my car. We have rooms booked for you in London; and there's a dinner tonight at the Connaught.'

'Should I bring my luggage?'

'Don't you worry about that, my secretary will take care of your bags.'

'What about my navigator, should I bring him too?'

Richard suddenly realised that in his enthusiasm to push a way for Emily through the crowd, he had forgotten Roger.

'I'm sorry, Mr Boone. Do follow!'

Roger shook his head and grinned. 'It's all right. I'm used to it. You know what they say, if you want to make your name as a famous flyer, never go up with animals, old ladies, or pretty girls. They always steal your thunder.'

They made their way at last to Richard's limousine, and Emily climbed into the back with Iris, who was neatly folding up her sandwich-paper.

'Emily, this is my wife Iris. Iris, my dear, this is Emily Browne.'

Iris shook Emily's hand. 'Well done,' she said, rather snappily. 'You must be very proud of yourself.'

Emily looked warmly across at Richard, who had eased himself into one of the jump-seats. 'I think your husband's airplane deserves most of the credit, Mrs Lord. She's easily the most well-balanced aircraft I've ever flown.'

David Bright appeared with Thomas, struggling their way through the crowd. They climbed in, too, and Thomas whined, 'Somebody stepped on the back of my sandal.'

'This is Miss Emily Browne, Thomas,' said Richard.

'Hullo,' Thomas sulked.

'Thomas, will you please shake Miss Browne's hand and congratulate her on flying across the Atlantic?'

Thomas gave Emily's hand a quick, desultory shake, and muttered, ''Gratulations.'

Iris said nothing but, 'Shall we go now? I have to go to Rayne's to buy some green shoes to go with my dress.'

'Oh, I have green shoes, if you want to borrow them,' said Emily. The car was driving off now, bumping slowly over the grass, followed closely by the cheering crowd. 'What size do you take?'

'Eights,' said Iris.

'I take five and a half,' said Emily. 'What is that in English sizes, Richard?'

'Fours,' Richard told her.

There was an expression on Iris's face which Richard hadn't seen for a very long time. He frowned. What he didn't yet realize was that Iris had immediately recognized Emily as *one of those girls*. One of those particularly flirtatious self-confident girls to whom Richard was invariably and irresistibly attracted. To Iris, he was like a poor dumb horse trotting towards an open gate to graze on the grass in the next field, forgetting that he was pulling a fully-laden dray behind him. She had seen him looking at those girls before, at dinner-parties and dances, and even if he hadn't ever been unfaithful to her, not legally unfaithful, he had committed adultery dozens of times in his imagination.

Thomas said, as they drove towards London, 'I feel sick.'

'Can't you wait until we get there?' asked Richard.

Thomas shook his head. He looked pale and glassy-eyed, and he was perspiring.

Richard knocked on the glass partition. Jeremy the chauffeur drew the Daimler in to the side of the road. Richard took Thomas into the bushes, where he noisily vomited half-chewed sandwiches all over a blackberry bush. Then Richard had to take him walking up and down the road, until his stomach was settled.

Absolutely bloody tip-top, thought Richard. A beautiful girl aviator flies the airliner that's my pride and joy across the Atlantic, and all my wife can do is sulk about her big feet and all my son can do is puke in the bushes.

Eventually, he climbed back into the car. 'Those stupid bloody sandwiches,' he said.

Iris retorted, 'He would have been worse if he hadn't had anything to eat at all.'

Richard said nothing. He didn't want a family squabble in front of Emily and Roger. But as they started off towards London again, he caught Emily looking at him in a way that made the insides of his wrists tingle.

As they drove through the suburbs of Sunbury and Hanworth, row after row of semi-detached houses with sunray-patterned gates, he caught her looking at him again. He smiled. She smiled back. He felt disturbed. He glanced quickly at Iris and Roger to see if either of them had noticed; but Roger was looking out of the window and Iris was searching through her handbag as if she suspected it contained a time-bomb.

Richard looked at Emily directly, holding her eyes with his.

'I was telling Thomas this morning, this is quite an historic occasion,' he remarked.

'Yes,' said Emily, 'I do believe it is.'

Richard was about to leave his London office the following morning when the telephone rang. 'Miss Browne for you,' his telephonist told him.

He took off his brown pork-pie hat and laid it on top of his blotter. 'Emily? Good morning! I'm just on my way down to Blackbushe.'

'I want to thank you for a wonderful reception last night,' said Emily.

'You're not too hung over, I hope? All that champagne.'

'Nothing that two cups of strong black coffee couldn't deal with.'

'Has David Bright called you?'

'Yes. He said the plane is all fuelled up and raring to go. Roger's there, too. He reckons that we should leave for Paris right on schedule.'

'I'll be rather sorry to see you go.'

'I'll be rather sorry to leave.'

Richard rubbed the back of his neck. Outside in the Aldwych, buses roared past, taxies honked, and fine golden dust floated through the air like bright but dwindling memories.

'We could have lunch,' Richard suggested. 'That is – if you want to eat before you go.'

'I'd love to. Just tell me where.'

'Well, we don't want to be too far away from Blackbushe, do we? There's a hotel in Camberley which does rather good steak-and-kidney pies.'

'I don't think I've ever eaten a steak-and-kidney pie.'

'Well, you must, it's the national dish. I'll pick you up in – what shall we say? – just under an hour. We'll drive down to Camberley together.'

'I'll look forward to it.'

The steak-and-kidney pie wasn't as good as he remembered it. In fact, it was dreadful. The meat was gristly and the crust was burned on one side, and it was served up with woody swede and potatoes which had been boiled without salt. They sat at a table in a gloomy corner of the room, next to a dessert trolley that featured cold jam roly-poly and cold bread-and-butter pudding. The old man at the table next to them smoked all through the meal and coughed as if he were terminally ill.

'I'm sorry,' said Richard. 'The last time I came here, the food was quite good. Or perhaps it wasn't.'

'I don't mind,' Emily smiled, sipping her tea. 'I wasn't hungry anyway.'

'You wouldn't like anything stronger to drink?'

'No, thank you. I'm flying, remember. I have to have a clear head.'

Richard paid for the meal and left only a threepenny bit for the grumpy waitress. Outside in the car park, as he searched through his pockets for his car keys, he said, 'I was thinking, you know, that it might be a good idea if I followed on.'

'I'm sorry?' Emily asked him.

'Well, the British trade people in Paris are having a reception tonight, aren't they, and there's going to be some sort of publicity do every time you land. I was thinking it might be a good idea if I sort of trailed along behind you and helped out with the press and the business side of things. You know, personally, instead of leaving it to the usual trade people.'

Emily slanted her hand over her eyes to keep out the sunshine. 'You don't have to ask my permission. If you want to come along, come along. I can't stop you.'

'I know that. That wasn't what I meant. What I meant was, would you mind? I don't want you to feel that my trailing along behind will – *diminish* what you're doing in any way. And I won't be going any further than Darwin, I shouldn't expect. My younger brother lives there. It's about time I paid him a visit.'

'You seem to have all kinds of reasons for coming along,' Emily smiled at him. 'Why don't you come?'

Richard at that moment very much wanted to say to Emily that visiting Michael and publicizing the Sagittarius were not really the reasons behind his suggestion to 'trail along'. But he wasn't yet capable of putting the real reasons into words; or even of admitting to himself that her sudden appearance in his life, piloting the airliner in which all his future hopes were invested, had tugged one rug out from under his feet after another.

He had watched her last night at the Connaught, bare-shouldered in an iris-blue satin evening dress, laughing and dancing. And damn it, she knew everything about aeroplanes, too! She was the kind of girl a chap could only dream about. He thought about Elisabeth; and remembered his scrapbook burning, page by curling page.

And there had been something there, surely, in the way she had looked back at him across the room; some suggestion that she found him attractive, too. After all, her life depended on the aeroplane which he had designed and built, and if it wasn't for the Lord Sagittarius, she wouldn't have been able to fulfil her life's ambition.

That was the way Richard liked to think of it, anyway.

'We'd better get down to the aerodrome,' he told her. 'You don't want to be late for your own flight.'

'How will you follow me?' asked Emily, as they drove out of Camberley.

'Oh – we've got two or three Capricorns ready to fly. They're not as fast as the Sagittarius by any means, but I'll take two of my test-pilots and we should be able to keep up just by flying in shifts. I can navigate the plane myself, if I can make a copy of Roger's charts.'

'Richard – it sounds like a very arduous thing to do, just on the spur of the moment.'

'I like to do things on the spur of the moment,' said Richard, although usually he didn't. 'In any case, I should have thought of it before, shouldn't I? There's nothing like the personal touch when you're selling aeroplanes.'

'You'll need to pack a tuxedo, and lots of clean evening-shirts.'

'Yes,' said Richard, with a small smile. 'I suppose I will.'

*

But there was a surprise waiting for them at Blackbushe. The Sagittarius had completed her fuelling, her technical overhaul, and her ground-checks, and was ready to go. Standing under the wing, however, in a very American-looking summer suit and a Panama hat, his hands in his pockets, was James.

Richard climbed out of the car and stared at his brother in astonishment. 'James!' James took off his hat and said, 'Hello, Richard. Good to see you.' He sounded more like James Stewart than ever.

Richard came up to him without a word and the brothers embraced. Then Richard stepped back and exclaimed, 'What do they say in America? You look swell!'

'Well, life in Miami is a little less austere than it is here. And here's Emily. Hello, Emily, my love. Congratulations on crossing the pond!'

He put his arm around Emily's waist and kissed her on the lips. Richard watched this with an unexpected feeling of – what? It couldn't be jealousy. Or perhaps it could.

'What brought you over to England?' asked Richard. He couldn't get over how suntanned and well-fed and prosperous James looked, and the yards of material in his suit! It was like two suits sewn into one! In England, you only saw suits like that on the cinema-screen. Richard suddenly felt very sweaty and old-fashioned in his navy-blue barathea blazer and his grey flannel bags. Even his shoes were pre-war.

James kept his arm around Emily's waist and smiled. 'I thought I'd do a bit of carpetbagging. It seemed like rather a waste, sending Emily all the way around the world without promoting Atlantic and Pacific Airways up to the hilt. I've already had one meeting with the civil aviation people this morning; and this afternoon I'm going to be seeing International Aeradio and BOAC.'

Richard said, 'It really is terrific to see you. I'm sorry if I'm rather taken aback. Goodness me – if I'd known you were coming –'

'You'd have baked a cake? Oh, come on Richard, it's good to see you, too. You've done marvels with Lord since the war. Why don't we have dinner tonight? I was thinking of flying over to Paris tomorrow morning to talk about landing rights at Le Bourget.'

Richard buttoned and unbuttoned his blazer. 'Well, actually, I'd love to. But I've already planned to fly over to Paris this evening. I thought I might – well, what do you call it, you Americans? – tag along – perhaps as far as Darwin.'

'Richard suddenly felt madly impetuous, didn't you Richard?' said Emily. 'I think that steak-and-kidney pie was just about the last straw. Anybody would want to emigrate from a country that served up steak-and-kidney pies like that.'

James gave Emily a quick sideways glance and then looked back at Richard. 'Are you sure it's such a good idea, your following along behind?'

'Why shouldn't it be? *You've* done it.'

'Well, I don't know,' said James, 'it just seems to make the flight look so darned *commercial*, if the airplane's manufacturer is chasing around the world after it, trying to sell it to anybody who's interested.'

'James,' Richard retorted, 'that's the way aeroplanes are sold. Or at least, that's the way they *should* be sold. You can't have scruples about being commercial when you're in business. That's half the problem with this country. The workers don't like to work and the managers think it's *infra dignitatem* to get their hands dirty. Selling aeroplanes is no different from selling fruit-and-veg from a barrow. You always said so yourself. And you can't sell very much fruit-and-veg if you're too élitist to stand behind the barrow and shout rock-hard tomatoes.'

'I agree!' said Emily, with mock-stoutness.

James was thoughtful for a moment. Roger was coming across the grass in his flying-gear, with his Coca-Cola bottle and his flight-plan. 'Afternoon, people, are we almost ready for the off?'

'I think so,' said Richard. 'I've decided to fly along behind for some of the way, to help with the sales side.'

'Suits me,' Roger told him. 'I was never any good at selling anything.'

'Well, Richard,' said James, in a tight voice, 'it does seem rather nonsensical if both of us follow the *Angel* at different times in separate aircraft, doesn't it? Why don't we both fly to Paris tonight? Then I can buy you dinner at Le Crillon. Eddie Feinbacker was always talking about Le Crillon.'

David Bright was calling Richard from the other side of the aircraft. Richard said, 'Just a minute, James. Do excuse me, Emily,' and went over to see what the matter was. Immediately, James turned to Emily and snapped, 'What the hell's all this?'

'What do you mean, what the hell's all this? What the hell's all what?' Emily retorted.

'I mean, what the hell's going on between you and my brother?'

'Nothing at all is going on between me and your brother. Come to that, nothing at all is going on between me and *you*.'

'How the hell can you let him follow you like some kind of wet-

468

nosed dog all the way to Australia?'

'For gosh sakes, I can't stop him. I'm not his mother. And, besides, I think it's quite a good idea. And double besides, *you're* following me like some kind of wet-nosed dog, too.'

James took a deep, steadying breath. 'Listen to me, Emily, what do you think it's going to look like if your heroic two-man flight all the way round the world has a sales-team shuffling along behind it, rattling their begging cups?'

'Maybe the rest of the world will think that Britain's aircraft manufacturers have at last come to their senses,' Emily replied.

'Oh, God Almighty, I can tell you've been talking to Richard,' said James.

Emily held out her hand. James wouldn't take it at first, but she grasped his fingers and squeezed them, and smiled.

'James, you don't own me. I'm very fond of you, but you don't own me.'

James looked away, out across the aerodrome. A De Havilland Dragon Rapide was landing on the far side of the field. Its silver fuselage flashed like a trout in a trout-pool. 'Well,' he said, 'we'll have to see, won't we?'

'James,' Emily repeated.

James looked at his watch. 'Let's just get on with it, shall we? I'll see you tonight, in Paris.'

Roger swigged more Coke, and said, 'Are we ready at last?' and burped.

James was dressed for dinner and about to leave his suite at Le Crillon Hotel that evening when there was a single knock at the door. 'Come on in!' he called, straightening his white tie in front of the gilt-framed mirror. He had been expecting room-service with a bottle of whisky and a bucket of ice.

The door remained closed, and the knock was repeated. Tugging his starched white cuffs, James strode impatiently across the room and opened up.

It wasn't room-service at all. It was a mealy-faced middle-aged man in a crumpled grey suit, with a rolled-up newspaper in his pocket. 'Mr Lord?' he said. 'I was wondering if you could spare me a minute.'

'Well, what is it?' James demanded, consulting his wristwatch. 'I'm due downstairs in five minutes.'

'I don't expect you remember me, do you?' the man asked, with a peculiarly self-satisfied smile.

'You're absolutely right, I *don't* remember you.'

The man leaned forward so that he could peer into the suite. 'Very nice, isn't it?' he remarked. 'They've done a wonderful job of redecoration.'

'Well, I'm sorry,' said James, 'I'm really very pushed for time.'

'Tommy Thompson,' the man declared, holding out a hand with closely-bitten nails. 'Late of the *Daily Herald*, late of the War Office; now with the *Daily Mirror*.'

James stared at him hard for a second, and then said, 'Get out.'

Tommy Thompson smiled even more widely and made no move to comply. 'I didn't hear that you were coming to England until it was too late. Just missed you at Blackbushe, by ten minutes! So I caught the flight from Croydon. Paid for it out of my own pocket.'

'I'm afraid you've wasted your money,' said James, patting his pockets to make sure that he had remembered his cigarette-case and his lighter. 'You've been nothing but an unpleasant nuisance to me and my family ever since my father died, and I have nothing whatever to say to you. Not now, nor ever. Goodnight.'

Tommy Thompson took out a box of Woodbines and shook out one that was half-smoked. He tucked it between his pursed lips and rummaged around in his pockets for a box of matches. 'You Lords were always a bee in my bonnet,' he remarked, his cigarette waggling. 'A *bête noir*. I don't know why, particularly. There are scads of other capitalist families, just as off-colour as yours. Perhaps it was the way you Lords always felt you had to cheat to make sure of your glory. Couldn't trust to fair play and good old-fashioned bravery, could you? You didn't care who you hurt, did you, as long as you got your applause? You didn't even care if somebody got killed; or if you made their life such a misery that they wanted to die.'

James presented himself at the doorway. 'You'll excuse me, Mr Thompson. I have to leave now.'

'They've found Enriquez Bocanegra,' said Tommy Thompson.

'I beg your pardon?'

'They've found Enriquez Bocanegra. Well, I always thought they would. He's still living in Miami. More to the point, he's still alive. Surprise, surprise, he didn't get killed at Pearl Harbor after all. Even more to the point, he's prepared in return for suitable bunce to say what happened all those years ago to South-Eastern Flight Nine, and who paid him to tinker with South-Eastern's airliners, and who paid him to go to Tucson for most of the war, and lie doggo.'

James stayed where he was, one hand grasping the door-handle, stony-faced.

Tommy Thompson lit his nip-end with a flaring match, and blew smoke out of the side of his mouth. 'More than likely, *you're* going to say that this is slander,' Tommy Thompson remarked. '*You're* going to ask me, where's your evidence, Mr Thompson, where's your per-oof? Well, the per-oof is on the way, from a man called Emmet Bell who never forgot you any more than I've ever forgotten you. A sworn statement from Enriquez Bocanegra himself, not to mention twenty pages of corroborating evidence from other South-Eastern mechanics and two private detectives and an airline accident investigator from Washington.

'And *this* time, Mr Lord, there won't be any Lady Susan Sheffield to give you an alibi.'

James said, in a dark voice, 'You'd better leave this hotel at once, Thompson, or I'll call the management and have you thrown out on your ear.'

'Oh, don't worry,' said Tommy Thompson. 'I was leaving anyway. I couldn't possibly afford to stay in a place like this.'

'You'd better understand that if you attempt to print one word about me, you'll be hearing from my solicitors.'

Tommy Thompson shook his head. 'We don't intend to *print* it, Mr Lord. We intend to pass it to the State's Attorney in Florida. As far as Emmet Bell and I are concerned, Mr Lord, this isn't just a question of news, this is a question of *justice*.'

He smiled, and then he added, 'I think my only regret is that poor old Jacko Gibbons won't be around to see you get what you deserve. He really *was* killed, poor sod. Jumped out of a landing-craft at Arromanches, on D-Day, straight into seven feet of water. Fifty other blokes promptly jumped on top of him. At least he deserved his glory, not that he got very much.

'Oh – and I suppose my other regret is that nobody will ever be able to prove that you and that saintly father of yours drove Gerhard Brunner to top himself.'

James didn't hesitate. With his white-gloved fist he punched Tommy Thompson hard and straight on the bridge of the nose. There was a sharp snap like a chicken-breast breaking, and blood sprayed everywhere, spots and squiggles all across the new pale-grey wallpaper, and on James's immaculate shirtfront.

Tommy Thompson collapsed on to his knees on the carpet, holding his nose in shock. James slammed the door of his suite and walked straight past him, without a word, expressionless, furious, and ran down three flights of stairs as fast and as angry as Rhett Butler running down the stairs of Tara.

The ballroom downstairs was already crowded. Chandeliers glittered, press cameras flashed, conversation rose like an amplified BBC recording of swarming bees. Richard was waiting on the far side of the room with Emily and Roger and the British Ambassador. 'My God,' said Richard, 'what's happened to you?'

James looked down at his bloodied glove. 'Nothing. Just making a point, that's all.'

Emily lifted her eyebrows. 'Some point,' she remarked.

James took hold of her hand and squeezed it. 'Everything's fine,' he reassured her, although already he felt that a long-locked door had opened up, just an inch, and that whatever he did, he would never be able to close it again.

Darwin, 1948

Michael arrived late at the airfield, and he was pushed by the crowd against the corrugated-iron fencing next to the Qantas hangar, so far away from the runway that there was no hope of him being able to reach it. He jumped up and down a couple of times, trying to see if he could see anybody he knew, but the airfield was packed solid with two thousand brown wide-brimmed hats and two thousand sun-reddened necks, and every hat and every neck looked exactly the same.

The afternoon was sultry and suffocating. The rains had arrived about a week earlier this year, and the sky was dark and overcast. Out across the Arafura Sea, lightning was crackling, and Michael could hear the distant battering of thunder.

Emily's flight had been fast and uneventful. From Rome she had flown to Istanbul; and then to Cairo, Karachi, Bombay, Rangoon, and Singapore. She was nearly half-a-day ahead of schedule, and the Sagittarius was flying, in her own words, 'like milk and honey'. But in spite of its speed and smoothness and lack of drama (apart from a split fuel diaphragm at Cairo, and a burst tyre on the runway at Karachi), her trip was arousing an almost hysterical enthusiasm in the press, and an extraordinary swelling of public delight.

It was almost as if – instead of a con-trail – Emily's *Angel* was spinning out behind her a long white ribbon, which was tying the world together again after all the hostility and bitterness of war. There was a feeling, too, that the amateur pioneering spirit of pre-war days was combining with modern technology to promise everybody a brighter and more prosperous future.

And, of course, the girl who was offering this promise was young and beautiful and self-confident, a perfect example of the new woman who had proved herself during the war-years to be the equal to any man.

In India, cinema audiences had stood up in their seats and cheered when newsreel pictures of the *Angel* appeared. When the *Angel* arrived in Bombay, the crowds had been so huge that the aerodrome had been closed down for three days because of the number of people camping on the runway. By the time Emily arrived in Singapore, she was being written about in the newspapers almost as if she were a deity. The *Straits Times* called her 'A Goddess For Our Age'.

The *Angel*'s imminent arrival in Darwin had brought farmers and settlers in from as far away as Cloncurry and Alice Springs. In Sydney, where the *Angel* was expected to arrive two days later, a huge civic reception was being prepared.

James had warned that Emily's glory would be diminished by the Lord Capricorn following on doggedly behind – the 'Camp Follower' he had christened it – but in fact hardly anybody had noticed it, or cared; and along the way Richard had managed to win provisional orders for ten new aircraft. James had found the flight interminably boring, and had wished several times that he had never volunteered to come along. He had been smoking too much, and sleeping too much, and he was generally bad-tempered and unapproachable.

As the *Angel* was making its approach to Darwin, James and Richard were still three hundred and fifty miles behind them, droning through bumpy weather over the eastern tip of Timor.

Long before Michael was able to see it, the crowd in the middle of the airfield set up a cheer. The orange airliner had suddenly appeared out of the clouds, like the hand of God in a medieval stage-play, and was making a fast, direct approach over Darwin Harbour. Jumping up again, Michael glimpsed it whistling down to land; then all he could see was an orange tail-fin and the jostling backs of the crowd.

Somebody let off Chinese firecrackers. One man, on his own, sang *God Save The King*. 'Long live our no-oh-oh-bull King!'

Only after darkness had fallen and most of the crowd drifted off home was Michael able to push his way through to the Qantas office where Emily was being officially welcomed. The room was hot and crowded, but he found her close to an open window, enjoying the evening breeze on her face. She was wearing a black-and-white polka-dot dress, and she looked chic but very pale. Oddly, she was on her own. The press had all finished their drinks and gone off to write up their stories about her; and the petty government officials and their lady wives were too shy to come up and talk to her. Roger Boone was lying sprawled in a chair close by, his head back, his legs stretched out, his eyes tightly shut.

'Miss Browne?' said Michael. 'I'm Michael Lord.'

Emily gave him a weary smile and held out her black-gloved hand. 'So you're the third musketeer,' she said. 'And do please call me Emily.'

'I've had a radio message from James and Richard in the Capricorn. They should be here in a little over two hours. The weather's not helping.'

'Well, we had a little trouble ourselves,' Emily told him. 'We ran into some terrible turbulence, and Roger knocked his knee on his navigating table. He's had it strapped up, but it still looks pretty swollen.'

'Did they tell you what the arrangements were?' asked Michael. 'You've been booked into the Mandorah Beach hotel, that's where they're having a dinner for you, tomorrow night.'

'Between you and me, if I have to attend another official dinner, I'll scream out loud,' said Emily. 'These official dinners are about ten times more gruelling than the flying.'

Michael looked around. The office was noisy and smoky, and people who weren't used to drinking champagne were beginning to slap each other on the back and laugh too raucously. 'Did you see that bloody Abo match the other day? They didn't have football jerseys, so the home team painted their chests with distemper. Then it started to rain, of course, and all the bloody distemper washed off, and they spent the rest of the game asking each other, "Which side belong you? Which side belong you?"'

Michael said, 'I'm sorry. I think everybody's rather over-excited.

We don't very often get celebrities here in Darwin.'
Emily brushed back her hair. 'Do you *think*,' she said, in a
conspiratorial murmur, 'do you think that you could get us out of
here? I'm just about ready to drop on my feet.'

'You want to go straight to your hotel?'

'I want to go somewhere completely quiet and completely private, where nobody cares who we are. My eyes are aching and
my ears are drumming and my whole body seems to think that
it's still flying across the Arafura Sea.'

'Well,' said Michael, rather doubtfully, 'you could always come
home with me. It's not very posh, I'm afraid. James and Richard
are the well-heeled ones. I'm the one who sold his mother's cow
for a handful of beans.'

Emily laughed. 'I don't want anything posh. I want an ordinary
meal and an ordinary bed and a long and very ordinary sleep.'

Michael smiled at her. There were dark circles around her eyes,
but those did nothing to detract from her prettiness. In fact, they
gave her an extra vulnerability which brought out all of his pro-
tective instincts. He decided that he liked her very much. 'Is your
friend asleep?' he asked her, nodding towards Roger, whose mouth
had now fallen open.

'If he is, we'll carry him,' said Emily.

'We can't carry him,' Michael objected.

A few minutes later, while the party and the laughter still went
on, Emily and Michael abruptly appeared at the side door of the
Qantas building, carrying Roger between them – Michael clutching
him under his arms, and Emily holding his ankles.

'My car's just outside the gates,' Michael whispered.

'Why are you whispering?' asked Emily, hoisting up Roger's
left ankle to stop it from falling further down.

'I don't want to wake him up,' Michael told her.

'But if you could wake him up, we wouldn't have to carry him.'

Perhaps it was the champagne; perhaps it was the tiredness and
the strain. But Emily dropped Roger's feet to the ground and
collapsed on to her knees in helpless laughter. Michael tried to
stop Roger from falling; but when Emily lay on her back on the
ground in her $300 Mainbocher dress and laughed so much that
she was almost choking, Michael started laughing too, and Roger
fell on his side on to the ground. That finished off both of them.
Michael walked around in circles, weeping with laughter, while
Emily was reduced to thin high breathless screams.

Roger stayed where he was, not even snoring; exhausted beyond
any kind of waking.

Michael knelt down and helped Emily up. 'Oh, God,' she gasped. 'Oh, God, poor Roger.'

But it was then that her laughter turned without any warning at all into tears; and she clung to Michael as if she would drown if she let him go, and that was how her reception in Darwin ended, kneeling on the ground, in the shadow of the Qantas building, under the Southern stars, crying for tiredness.

An hour before dawn, with the distant thunder still rumbling over the sea, Michael eased himself out of bed, leaving Violet clutching her pillow as she always did, and padded barefoot to the sitting-room.

Emily was asleep on the sofa, under a draped mosquito-net. The Atkinsons downstairs had gladly taken Roger in, feeding him faggots and gravy and canned peas, and lending him a pair of huge pyjamas, and tucking him up in bed like a small boy.

Michael stood watching Emily sleep. Her sheet was tangled and one of her breasts was bare. There was just enough light in the room to bring out the pinkness of her nipple. Michael did nothing but watch, and think.

He went back to the kitchen and poured himself a glass of water. In the half-darkness, he could see the cranes at the docks, and the mooring-lights of the ships at anchor. Every few seconds, the lighthouse flashed at Emery Point.

He felt disturbed; as if the wind had changed; as if his life had changed. He felt as if the ground had suddenly dropped away in front of him, as if his next step would take him into emptiness, and darkness.

He finished his water, rinsed the glass, and laid it on the draining-board. He glanced back at the sitting-room door. Then he went back to the bedroom and climbed into bed. Violet held her pillow tightly, and said, 'Leonard?'

James and Richard came around early the next morning. Violet showed them up the stairs, fussily rubbing her hands together. Violet told Willy and Elizabeth to shake hands with their uncles, which they did, and then retreated to a corner, next to a small triangular table with blown-glass animals on it, where they stared and said nothing, but from which they couldn't be shooed away.

'You've put on weight,' Michael told James.

James gave him a peculiar wincing smile, like Robert Newton. He didn't appreciate comments about his weight, particularly in front of Emily. Apart from that, he had been expecting to meet

Emily at the Mandorah Beach Hotel last night. He wouldn't be able to follow her very much further – the Capricorn wasn't equipped or prepared for a flight across the Pacific, and neither was he. He had hoped somehow to be able to give her a convincing demonstration that he loved her. Or, at least, that he cared for her deeply. To find her here, in his younger brother's tatty flat on the wrong side of Darwin – not only well-rested and well-fed but demonstratively happy – was like being obliged to eat a small but very unpleasant fruit.

'Well, I can't say you guys look exactly overjoyed to see each other,' Emily said cheerfully, reaching up to tie a scarf around her hair. 'Where are the hugs? Where are the tears? Where are the reminiscences?'

Richard came forward and took hold of Michael's hand, then held him close. 'You're looking tremendously well,' he said. 'It's really rather awkward, isn't it, after all this time?' He looked towards Willy and Elizabeth. 'They're jolly nice children, Michael, they really are – and Violet, well, she's a very lovely lady, and you're a lucky chap.'

'Where's Roger?' asked James.

'He stayed with the people downstairs,' Michael told him. 'He'll be up in a minute.'

'Won't you have a cup of tea?' Violet suggested. 'Or, sit down, at least.'

James said, 'That's very nice of you, Violet, but we really have to get back to Mandorah Beach. They're giving us lunch at twelve; and then we have business meetings with Qantas. You're coming along to the gala reception tonight, I hope, at the Residency?'

'Well, I –' said Violet.

'Good,' said James. 'How about you, Emily, are you ready? Michael – why don't you go downstairs and see if Roger's managed to gird his loins.'

Michael was about to say *go downstairs yourself*, but then they heard footsteps on the stairs and Roger appeared. Richard glanced at James but made no comment. Roger looked terrible. His eyes were puffy and his face was blotched and he was limping so badly he had to hold on to the door-jamb for support.

Only Emily had the nerve to say what every one of them was thinking. 'Roger, you've been drinking.'

Roger lifted a conciliatory hand. 'It's all right. Everything's under control. My knee hurt during the night, that's all. Bill Atkinson gave me a couple of glasses of whisky just to ease off the pain.'

'A couple of glasses?' Emily demanded. 'More like the whole damn bottle.'

Roger shook his head. Willy and Elizabeth watched him in wonder. 'Emily, it was half a bottle, no more.'

Emily stood up, and reached for her bag. 'We'd better go,' she said, angrily. 'Otherwise I'm going to say something to Roger in front of the children that isn't fit for children's ears.'

Roger said, 'Jesus. Isn't it always the same?'

Emily turned to Violet and clasped her hand. 'Thank you for looking after me, both of you. I won't forget you.'

She kissed Michael on both cheeks. Violet, in spite of herself, looked away. Then, followed closely by James, less closely by Richard, and then Roger, she clattered down the bare wooden stairs and out into the yard.

Violet stood where she was, long after the screen door had banged.

'Are you all right?' Michael asked her.

'I don't know. Are you?'

He shrugged, and made a face. 'As far as I know. Is there any reason why I shouldn't be?'

She said, 'Those were your two older brothers, they haven't seen you for fifteen years. Fifteen years! And what did they do? They rushed in, said two words to you, wouldn't have a cup of tea, and rushed out again.'

'Violet,' said Michael, 'it isn't easy getting to know somebody again after fifteen years. You have to give it some time.'

Violet folded her arms over her apron. 'It's nothing to do with time. It's that girl. It's that Emily Browne. Your two brothers are like dogs on heat.'

'Violet – please, the kids.'

'It's true, though, isn't it?' Violet challenged him. 'You could see it for yourself.'

'Yes, well, probably. She is a very pretty girl.'

'As long as you don't start making a fool of yourself, the same as your brothers.'

'Me?' said Michael. And at the same time, he thought with chilling vividness of Emily lying under the mosquito-net, in the opalescent light of early morning, cheeks pale, lashes closed, one full breast bare, dreaming of flying.

The radio call came from the Alice just before lunchtime the following day. It was laconic, concise, and contained only one swear word. Emily had made an unscheduled landing because the *Angel* had lost hydraulic pressure in the rudder controls. The local mechanic had managed to patch it up, but in the meantime Roger had found himself a pub, and had drunk over three-quarters of a bottle of whisky. He was now lying in the bunk at the back of the aircraft, singing and weeping. Without a navigator, Emily was unable to continue.

James put down the phone at the Mandorah Beach Hotel; took out his handkerchief, and wiped the sweat from his neck as if he had been gardening.

'What's wrong?' asked Richard, who was sitting at the table in his shirtsleeves, working out fuel-consumption figures. Up until now, the Sagittarius had been disconcertingly heavy on aviation spirit.

James said, 'Emily had to put down at Alice Springs for a minor repair.'

'Well? Is it going to take long to fix?'

'It's fixed, don't worry. But so is Roger. While they were working on the plane, he went out and got himself pie-eyed.'

Richard sat back. 'Damn it. That's bad news. They've got a civic reception waiting for them in Sydney.'

'It's not just the civic reception, Richard. It's the whole damned flight. I can't trust Roger to navigate Emily across the Pacific. And *you* can't trust him to navigate your aeroplane.'

Richard put down his pencil. He sniffed, and thought, and then he said, 'In that case, we're going to have to find a reliable substitute, and quickly. Perhaps the best suggestion is that I navigate the Sagittarius myself.'

James said, 'No.'

Richard looked up. 'Come on, James, I know that aeroplane better than I know my own face in the mirror.'

'I said, no,' James told him. 'I'll do it myself.'

'James, for goodness' sake be sensible.'

'I am being sensible. I fly my own airliners; I can fly the Sagittarius. And I put up the money for this venture, after all.'

'I put up the bloody aeroplane,' said Richard, with unusual vehemence.

James came across the room and stood over Richard with his fists planted on his hips. 'Richard – *no*. The answer is no.'

Richard held his stare for a short moment, then lowered his eyes. 'It's Emily, isn't it? You don't want me to spend all that time with Emily.'

'It's nothing of the kind. This flight was my idea, my investment, and if anybody's going to take care of it, I am!'

'Oh, don't talk rot,' Richard retorted. 'Emily's turned you inside-out and upside-down. You flew all the way from Miami, just to make sure that you could keep an eye on her. You talk about nothing else. Have you heard yourself lately? You talk about nothing else! You're obsessed!'

'Then why the hell did you want to follow her, too?' James yelled at him.

Richard stood up, and faced his brother in a way that he had never faced him before. 'Because she's just about everything that I could wish for, and I don't mind admitting it!'

He paused, breathing stertorously, his face red. Then he sat down, and picked up his pencil. 'There,' he said, 'I've said it. And what a bloody fool I am. God, James, I haven't imagined for one moment that she'd give me a second look. But I'm infatuated with her, and that's that.'

James went to the cigarette-box and took out a cigarette. 'I'll take the Capricorn down to Alice Springs,' he said. 'I'll arrange for somebody to fly it back.'

There was a long silence. Richard sat staring sightlessly at his fuel figures.

'Richard,' said James. 'I'm sorry. She's a wonderful girl. There's something about her that defies description. She's attracted me, and she's attracted you, no doubt about it, and at least you've been man enough to admit it.'

Richard turned his head away and looked at the opposite wall. It was rough-plastered, with an out-of-fit reproduction of Whistler's mother hanging on it. God, he thought, mothers and fathers and sons and daughters. They tumble through life like a bucketful of live rats being emptied down a well. Clawing and scratching and screaming and fighting, and then it's all over.

'Go on,' he said, because he was Richard. '*You* have her.'

Late that evening, Richard was lying back on the double-bed with his shoes on, drinking Scotch, when the telephone rang. He tried to scoop up the receiver, but he missed and knocked the whole instrument on the floor. 'Bloody – Australian telephones –' he grumbled.

He heard a shrunken voice calling, 'Hello? Hello? Richard? Richard, can you hear me?' so he heaved himself up into a sitting position and made a grunting ape-like swing to pick the telephone up.

'Hallo?' he said. 'Hallo?'

'Richard? Are you all right? This is Michael. You sound as if you're drunk.'

'No, no,' Richard protested. 'Merely – celebrating. All failures, whatever their ilk, deserve to be celebrated.'

'Richard, listen –'

'I'm listening, I'm listening.'

'Richard, for God's sake. I've just had a message through from London. It was passed to me by Qantas. Do you have somebody on your staff called David Bright?'

'Of course,' Richard replied. 'He's my sheef – *chief* engineer. Good chap, too. Never gets downhearted. Never lets life get him down.'

'Richard – he's been testing your first prototype, Sagittarius 001.'

'That's right, that's absolutely right.'

Michael was growing panicky. 'Richard, will you bloody well listen to what I'm saying? He's been testing the tail section in the pressure-tank. He says he went to inspect it this morning and it's cracked.'

'Cracked?' said Richard, sitting up straighter. 'What's cracked?'

'The whole bloody tail section, as far as I can make out. Fundamental structural defect, that's what he says. Something to do with the tail-section undulating up and down during flight, because of the way in which you stretched the original Capricorn fuselage. He says bring the *Angel* down at once and don't attempt to take off again until he's made further tests.'

Richard was abruptly sober. 'Does he say how long it took for this to happen? How many hours of simulated flight?'

'Four hundred and fifteen.'

'Jesus Christ, the *Angel* has done at least five hundred.'

'We've tried to get in touch with her already,' said Michael. 'The trouble is, there's a hell of a dust-storm just blown up, and we can't make any kind of contact.'

'Well, you don't have to worry,' said Richard. 'She's made an unscheduled landing at Alice Springs. No – nothing wrong with the plane. Her navigator has come down with boozer's elbow.'

'Is James there?'

'No, he left earlier on. He must have got to Alice Springs by now. Since Miss Browne's navigator can no longer be relied upon to see one Southern Cross instead of two, James has gone galloping off to the rescue. He's going to navigate the plane himself, for the rest of the flight. At least, that's what he *thought* he was going to do. Now there's a question about the tail section, we're going to have to cancel.'

Michael said, 'We can't get through to the Alice, either. There's no chance that James would take off before this storm has blown out, is there?'

'Don't ask me. Am I my brother's keeper?'

'Well, is he likely to?' Michael demanded.

'Yes,' Richard retorted. 'I expect he bloody well is. The flight's behind schedule already, and as far as *he's* concerned, the most important aspect of this flight is getting around the world on time. He's advertising an airline, after all.'

'Bugger it,' said Michael. 'I'd better get down there, and make sure he stays on the ground.'

'How can you fly, if it's dark, and there's a dust-storm blowing?' Richard asked him.

Michael gave him a dry laugh. 'You're a Pom-and-a-half, aren't you? You can't, technically speaking, but you do. And anyway, I've done it before. You develop what you might call a technique. That is, you close your eyes and pray hard.'

'Well, all I can say is, Michael, for God's sake be careful. And try to get through to me as soon as you can. If James takes that Sagittarius up and it crashes – well, even supposing he gets out of it unscathed –'

'Don't worry,' Michael assured him. 'They don't call me the Sandfly for nothing.'

Michael took off from Darwin Airport in his elderly Lockheed Vega just after nine o'clock. It was warm and windy here on the coast, but there was no dust in the air. The lights of the city were sprinkled in the darkness beneath him. All along the northern shoreline, the surf showed up like ghosts rushing in towards the beaches with their white robes trailing behind them.

He gained height quickly, and set his course. Darwin dwindled into the distance behind him, until its lights were indistinguishable from the stars, and ahead of him lay nothing but the widespread bushland of the Northern Territory, and the stormy night. He opened up the flask that Violet had given him, clenching it between his knees, and poured himself a cup of hot sweet tea. Later on, he would take a couple of benzedrine tablets to keep himself awake.

The engine droned on and on, repeating the same drumming rhythm again and again, and the slipstream whistled against the struts; and he was completely alone.

Ghirralangbone, ghirralangbone, ghirralangbone, the engine repeated. It was an Aborigine word that Michael had heard soon after he had started flying for Hudson Fysh. It meant, the place where stars fell.

As he passed the halfway mark on his way to the Alice, the Vega began to be buffeted by westerly gusts. Soon, he heard the sizzle of dust against his cockpit canopy; and the few stars that had glittered through the cloud cover completely vanished. It was blindingly dark, and he was flying deep into a Bedourie, but he trusted his compass and his altimeter and his artificial horizon, and most of all he trusted in the luck of Michael Lord, who had flown through furniture-vans and lived to tell the tale.

He thought about Violet as he flew. Dear, sweet, dedicated Violet. She had never shown herself to be anything else than a woman of frankness and sincerity and simple tastes; and he knew very well that he loved her for it. A woman like Emily Browne could make your hair stand on end. She could make you dream exquisite and sentimental dreams. But Emily Browne was looking for something, a woman on her way from A to Z, or as far as she could get, and somebody like Michael would only get to see her in profile as she passed.

A hot, bleak gust of dusty wind almost blew him off course. He checked his compass and his altimeter, and his artificial horizon, too. Once he was satisfied that he was still heading directly towards the Alice, he tried his wireless again; but all he heard was a rushing noise.

He flew on, whistling for a while. Selections from *La Traviata*, off-key, between overcrowded teeth. He wondered if James would get anywhere with Emily. He was frightened of James. Well – not so much frightened as thrown off balance. He had always been kind, as far as he was able. He had always been moved by the desperation of other people. He found it very hard to understand James's unswerving need to have whatever he wanted.

The wind began to worsen. Torrents of grit lashed against the Vega's fuselage. The aeroplane ducked and dived and lifted its nose; and the engine began to sing a different song. *Gerringong, gerringong, gerringong*, an unbalanced noise with a metallic ring to it, as if a bearing was loose. *Gerringong*, in Aborigine dialect, meant fear.

Michael switched on the wireless, and called Mayday from one side of the waveband to the other. But the rushing sound was absolute; and he was quite alone.

'Bugger it,' he said, 'I got to Nora Robinson, didn't I?'

James and Emily were still sitting at the airfield at Alice Springs when Michael's Vega flew overhead at less than four hundred feet. They didn't see it; but they heard it; and Emily got up at once and went to the window.

'That was a plane. Somebody's flying out there. Maybe they're trying to land.'

James tossed his cigarette-butt on to the floor and stepped on it. Then he came to join her at the window. Because of the dust, visibility was down to seventy-five feet, and they could only distinguish the runway as far as the fourth runway light.

Emily looked tired. There were mauvish circles under her eyes. But to James she was still irresistible, especially in that starched white flying-suit, which emphasized the slimness of her waist. He reached across and touched her hair; but she brushed him away.

'If *they're* flying why can't we?' she wanted to know.

Slim Gifford, the Qantas man at Alice Springs, came sauntering up with his hands in the pockets of his creased khaki shorts and a cigarette stuck to his top lip. 'Believe me, lady, whoever that was, he'd rather be down here. Most likely he flew right over us, and didn't even realize we were here.'

James made a drama of looking at his watch. 'We've wasted a day already. Surely this storm can't be too much of a problem – especially since we'd be running with it.'

'You can go if you want to,' shrugged Slim. 'But I wouldn't; and I've been flying through Bedouries for thirty years, in planes a lot less appetizing than yours. Turboprop, isn't it? What happens if you get sand in the turbines? You'll drop like a flaming stone.'

Without warning, they heard the Vega pass over again, then climb, then turn, then disappear.

'He's found us,' said Emily, excited. 'Come on, let's go outside and help him down.'

She opened the door of the bare concrete waiting-room. Outside, the wind was gusting and wuffling; thick with dust; and James had to shield his eyes with his hand. He hesitated for a moment, but Emily was ahead of him, as always, her white flying-suit already disappearing into the murk, and he didn't want to be left behind.

'Wait!' he called her.

Slim said, 'Watch out he doesn't come in too low and chop your flaming head off. Seen that happen. Bits of bonce everywhere.'

They heard the Vega before they saw it. Then, waggling its wings, it appeared out of the cloudy dankness, searching for the runway, although both James and Emily could see at once that it was still too high. It dropped, throttled back, almost stalled, and then burst into life again, and roared up into a climb, so that it could try for another approach.

'My God,' said James.

'What's the matter?' Emily shouted back.

'I'm sure that's Michael!'

'Michael *who*?' frowned Emily, against the wind.

'My brother Michael. I'm sure that's his plane!'

'Well, what's he doing here? He wouldn't come out for a joyride, surely, not in this storm?'

Slim Gifford came out of the building behind them, his hands cupped around his eyes. 'That's the Sandfly! I'd know that kite anywhere!'

Michael had already told James about his nickname. James brushed dust out of his hair, and said, tautly, 'Yes; I think you're right.'

They waited in the billowing darkness for what seemed like twenty minutes, but which was probably nearer two. Emily came close to James, and took his arm, and said, 'Please God, keep him safe. He's the very nicest one out of all of you.'

James looked at her; and after a while she looked back. 'Niceness isn't everything,' she said. 'On the other hand, neither is arrogance.'

There was no time for James to reply. At that moment, without warning, the Vega reappeared out of the dust, much lower this time.

'Come on, Sandfly, you can do it!' Slim shouted out, smacking his fist into the palm of his hand.

'My goodness,' said James. 'I do believe he's managed it.'

'Bravo!' shouted out Emily, and clapped.

The Vega's wheels were almost on the runway. Michael was already pulling back the throttle. In the dusty prune-coloured darkness, the silver aeroplane looked like a visiting spaceship from another world.

James was already turning away when the Vega's engine suddenly screamed and its nose plunged towards the runway. James said, 'What –?' and looked back in time to see the Vega cartwheeling nose-over-wingtip, a silver crucifix, with pieces flying out of it in all directions.

'My God,' said Emily. 'The Sagittarius.'

The Sagittarius had been parked at the very end of the runway; and covered with tarpaulins to protect it from the dust-storm. But it looked as if nothing could prevent the tumbling Vega from hitting it sideways-on, at fifty or sixty miles an hour.

The Vega was unstoppable. It was like a relentless medieval instrument of divine justice. The cross of holy retribution. It tumbled wing over tail, nose over wheel, and collided with the orange-painted Sagittarius just behind the starboard wing.

James remembered that instant for years to come: that instant when the Vega bounced and jolted to a standstill, and the cockpit door swung downwards. In that one instant, he believed that Michael was safe.

He said, 'God, thank God.' Perhaps he didn't even say it aloud.

But then the Vega exploded, with a bang that made James's eardrums sing. A ball of yellow flame rolled voluptuously up into the dust, and was swallowed up.

'Michael!' shouted James; and began to walk towards the blazing aeroplane, one foot after the other; and with every step he was praying to God that this hadn't happened at all, that he was still asleep in Darwin; that he was still asleep in Miami; that he had never grown up.

There was another deafening explosion, and fiery pieces of the Vega's fuselage came dropping out of the dust-clouds.

Emily was silent, and fell on to the runway on her knees.

'The *Angel*,' James called out, to nobody in particular. 'We have to get the *Angel* away.'

But it was already too late. The *Angel*'s starboard engine nacelle was fiercely alight. In a matter of seconds, the fully fuelled-up Sagittarius was burning from nose-to-tail like a Viking funeral ship. James and Emily could do nothing at all but watch it, their faces reddened by the heat.

The wing tanks exploded; then the fuselage tanks – over a thousand gallons of high-grade aviation spirit. Huge billows of roaring flame rolled up in the dust-clouds; dragon's breath; one after the other. There was yet another explosion, and the Sagittarius broke her back and collapsed on to the sand.

James stayed where he was until the wreckage was nothing more than embers, like an abandoned Aborigine campfire. He didn't even notice when Emily walked away.

He found the letter the next morning, beside his bed. He held the envelope up to the light, and there was something heavy inside it, something like a coin. He sat up, and tried to focus on the handwriting on the front of it. Outside the window of his plain whitewashed room, the galahs were laughing, and the broad sun was coming up.

He tore open the envelope with his thumb.

Inside, there was a letter, in a rounded, feminine hand. It said, *'You will know by this token who I am. My mother gave it to me, because it was given to my mother by my father, and it was my mother's idea to return it to you. I give it back to you now with grief and sadness.*

'Perhaps both my mother and I were looking for revenge. Wounded pride is the most frightening of all emotions. Perhaps, on the other hand, we were looking only to be remembered. But, whatever it was, I should have known that it would end in tragedy. Sadly – it is only now, after Michael's death – that I truly believe that the sins of yesterday should be forgotten and forgiven, and that the book of past mistakes should be closed.

'You will have realized by now that I am not Emily Browne but Emily Brunner; and that Gerry Browne was not Gerry Browne but Gerhard Brunner, and not my father after all. Your father Herbert Lord was my father, too. We are brother and sister, you and I.

'Not long after Gerhard Brunner killed himself, my mother emigrated to America, and took me with her; but she never told your father that he had conceived not only three sons, by Constance, but a daughter as well.

'After what has happened; after my mischief; I cannot think of seeing you again. But at the very end of all this, I bear you no ill-will, and I hope one day you will be able to find it in your heart to forgive me. I will always love you and Richard, and hold Michael's memory dear. Forgive me, please, for everything.'

The letter was signed, *'Your loving sister.'* And, when he tipped it out of the envelope with shaking hands, James recognized the Oswald Boelcke medal that he had given to his father when he was nine years old.

In a grey-painted room in the Palms Nursing Home in Sarasota, Florida, a white-faced woman lay in bed quietly dying. Her daughter sat by her bedside, holding her hand.

'We are frogs,' the woman whispered. 'We are frogs who jump a little further.'

'Mother?' her daughter frowned.

'Frogs,' the woman repeated. 'No matter how high, no matter how far, we always have to come to earth.'